ACROSS THE BRIDGE

ACROSS THE BRIDGE

Elizabeth James

To order additional copies of this book, contact:
Xlibris Corporation
1-888-795-4274
www.Xlibris.com
Orders@Xlibris.com
25219

CONTENTS

ACKNOWLEDGMENTS

T he valuable assistance provided by the following individuals is gratefully acknowledged: Mr. Roger C. Norris, Deputy Librarian of the Dean and Chapter Library, Durham, and Mr. Brian A. Harrison, Yeoman Warder and the Honorary Archivist at the Tower of London, who were extremely helpful in their responses to inquiries.

The author's gratitude also goes out to the staff of the British Library for allowing entry and examination of some of the old texts.

The author is also indebted to the local Writer's Group. The meetings that were held twice per month have been fruitful, productive, and fun. For these interactions, the author is grateful and thankful to the members of this group.

And last, but by no means least, the author is also indebted to the following authors and their respective texts for providing valuable background information. These are listed in chronological order by year of publication so that no preference is shown for any text above the others. The texts are the following:

Joseph T. Shipley, ed., *Dictionary of Early English*, Philosophical Library Inc., New York, NY, USA, 1955.

Robert E. Diamond, *Old English Grammar and Reader*, Wayne State University Press, Detroit, MI, USA, 1970.

Christopher Brooke, *The Structure of Medieval Society*, Thames and Hudson, London, UK, 1971.

Michael Packe, Edited by L. C. B. Seaman, *King Edward III*, Routledge & Kegan Paul Ltd., London, UK, 1983.

Barbara W. Tuchman, *A Distant Mirror: The Calamitous 14th Century*, Ballantine Books, New York, USA, 1987.

David Edge and John Miles Paddock, *Arms & Armor of the Medieval Knight: An Illustrated History of Weaponry in the Middle Ages*, Crescent Books, New York, NY, USA, 1988.

Douglas Pocock and Roger Norris, *A History of County Durham*, Phillimore
& Co. Ltd., Chichester, Sussex, UK, 1990.

Scott L. Waugh, *England in the Reign of Edward III,* Cambridge University
Press, Cambridge, UK, 1991.

J.A. Burrow and Thorlac Turville-Petre, *A Book of Middle English,* Blackwell
Publishers, Oxford, UK, 1992.

FOREWORD

T his is a work of fiction. It is a sequel to *Bridges of Time* (First Books, 2001) and the locale of this story is the village of Bridgeford (chart 1), a fictitious village in the county of Durham, and the medieval city of Durham (chart 2). Frequent reference is made to the lineage of Edward III, King of England (1327-1377). To help the reader understand the relationship of some of the characters in the story, an outline of Edward's lineage is included (chart 3).

The story is structured within an accurate historical context, but with the exception of some of the historical characters and several specific historical events, all of the characters and the events described herein are imaginary.

Modern place-names are used instead of the more confusing, older names. The language used throughout the text is English even though it must be recognized that in the historical time in which the story is set, an archaic type of the English language not yet fully evolved to the modern-day form would have been spoken. Other than the occasional word, no attempt is made here to represent the various English dialects as the characters in this story may have spoken them.

Chart 1: The location of the village of Bridgeford.

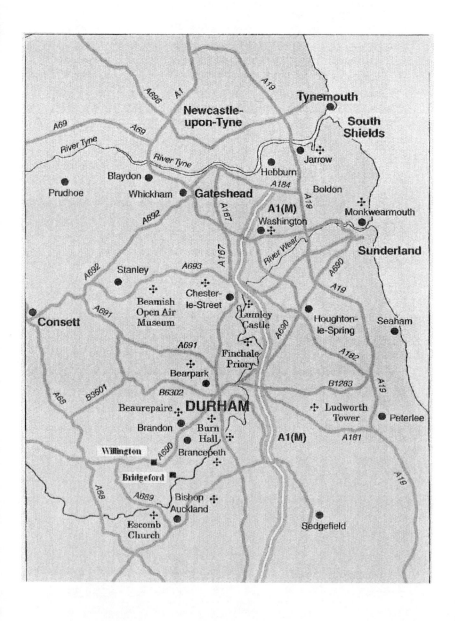

Chart 2: The medieval city of Durham.

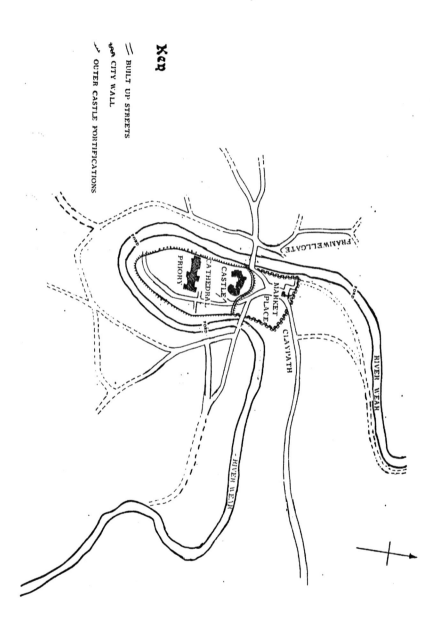

Chart 3: The lineage of Edward III, King of England
(1327-1377) that is relevant to the story.

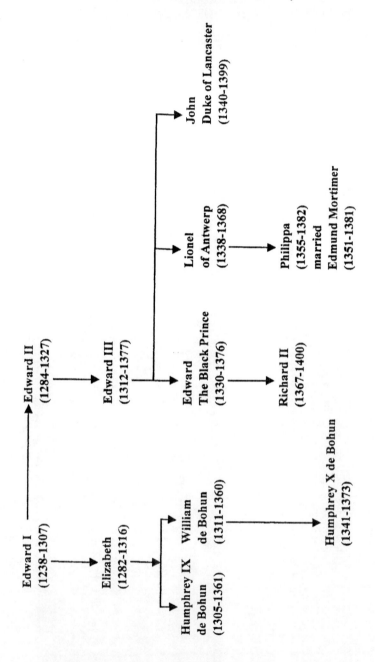

PART I

MODERN TIMES

CHAPTER 1

The city of Durham lies 265 five miles north of London and 125 miles south of Edinburgh. The village of Bridgeford, much less spectacular and much less well known than the city of Durham, lies about one mile south of the A690 and almost five miles or so to the southwest of the city of Durham, between the villages of Brandon and Willington. A side road from the A690, which did not even warrant a highway number, leads to Bridgeford. The only other major interruption on that short stretch of road between Brandon and Willington was the small settlement of Brancepeth and its old castle.

The villagers referred the road between Bridgeford and the A690 as the Bridgeford Road. After a slight downhill slope, or uphill slope depending upon the direction of the traveler, the Bridgeford Road joined another road at the south end of the village. It was the same route as that taken by an old coach road that wound its way from Durham to Willington. The fairly level pitch of this road as it followed the course of the river made it much easier for the horses than the undulating ups and downs of the current highway.

There is no official name for the Bridgeford Road on any maps, and in fact, most maps did not even recognize the road as being worthy of inclusion. A faint, almost unmarked, line on the ordinance survey map of the area is all that attests to the existence of this umbilical pathway that connected the village to the outside world.

A surrounding curtain of trees maintains the privacy that the villagers enjoy. To find this settlement, it is helpful to be told of its whereabouts and it is also possible to enter the village by making a wrong turn off the A690 on to Bridgeford Road.

The village is not exceptional, even quite ordinary. The spoken language is, of course, English, although to an outsider this might be hard to believe. A dialect that contains many words that had their origins in a

Germanic-Saxon language is the means of communication and a few words from the Old Norse language are also included. To anyone other than those born and raised in the area, the general daily speech of the villagers is difficult to understand.

At a point, almost half a mile from the A690 highway, Bridgeford Road becomes Bridgeford High Street on its north-south track before it turns sharply west and becomes Willington Road. The village blossoms forth at the point where Bridgeford Road becomes the High Street. The fields that are separated by hedgerows and stone walls give way to clean and colorful houses. But the thick growth of trees in the area is sufficient to mask all of the houses from the curious onlooker on the A690. Even in winter, when most trees are devoid of their summer foliage, the thickness of the tree growths makes it difficult to detect any houses to the south.

As with all villages, High Street is the heart and soul of Bridgeford and is the focus of all life and social and business activity. The women of the village meet there as they go about their daily shopping. The houses, some built of very old gray stones and others of an old gray brick, are as colorful as the villagers.

The clean and sanitary appearance of the village is preserved by the fresh whitewash and paint that are applied every two years to the exteriors of the two-story houses. The different colors of the doors and window frames present a sense of gaiety to the visitor. What also makes the village picturesque, and so typically English, is the proliferation of flower gardens. The terraced houses on the main street do not have the space for the luxury of a front garden but cultivated flower boxes make up the lack of front garden space.

The houses that do not lie on the main street are also a sight to behold with their manicured lush green lawns and flower gardens. A wide variety of flowers are always in evidence whether they are in the earth of the garden or in the earth of a flower box. The three seasons—spring, summer, and autumn—provide splendid color to the village.

The High Street boasts several businesses on both sides of the roadway. A post office, a butcher's shop, a fish shop, a bakery, a newsagent, and tobacconist's shop, a grocery that also serves as a greengrocery, and an ice cream shop are the highlights of Bridgeford's business life.

Knitting is an honorable pastime for the women of Bridgeford. There is a Knitting Circle, with its informal membership, that meets every Wednesday morning at ten in the church hall. Coffee, tea, biscuits, and scones with butter are provided on a rota system. Any place where a weary female can sit for tea and conversation will see the immediate appearance of cutting, thrusting, parrying, and clicking sounds of knitting needles. The men will not, under any circumstances, visit the Knitting Circle. There is always the risk of being pierced, if not by a flashing needle, then certainly by a biting tongue.

The knitting does not end at lunchtime on Wednesday but continues throughout the week at home. The "circle" provides an outlet for discussing the week's events that are missed in the chemist's shop or in the coffee shop. The arrival of any stranger will give the "circle" more than enough conversation for several days or months, depending, as always, upon the circumstances.

The educational needs of the village are served by a small school to the west of High Street and at the south end of the park with direct access on to Willington Road. Children, from age five to age ten, are taught by one teacher in this one-roomer, after which they attend school in Willington. These older children walk to the A690, and a bus picks them up at eight in the morning, every school day, and deposits them at that same point a few minutes after four fifteen in the afternoon.

A major surprise of Bridgeford was the presence of a swimming pool. It was built in 1952 through a generous, but anonymous, donation to commemorate the coronation of Queen Elizabeth and is called, without surprise, the "Queen Elizabeth Swimming Pool." Although there are grave doubts the queen, or any member of her family, will ever have the time to call in and swim there, the villagers are prepared. A private dressing room had been set aside and is maintained in spotless condition for just such an occasion. In 1960, a roof was built over the pool, again through the generosity of an anonymous donor, with all of the other amenities that go with an indoor pool such as lockers and showers. Within a week of the completion of the roof, the building had been renamed the "Queen Elizabeth Royal Swimming Pool" with all of the accompanying pomp and circumstance.

Bridgeford does not have a railway station, and for that matter, anyone can't ever remember that there has been one, even though the first public railway in the world ran between Stockton and Darlington less than fifteen miles from the village back in 1825. Since then, no one had thought so much as to lay a track to Bridgeford or, for that matter, from Bridgeford. Even in the heyday of horse-drawn vehicles, most people preferred to travel by "shank's pony," as they were wont to call travel on foot.

Just as the railway, even in the golden age of steam, bypassed the village, so has the bus service. There is no local bus service, so any villager who wishes to travel has to walk to the A690 to take the bus for the two- or three-minute ride west to Willington or for the ten minute ride further west to Crook. When feeling more adventurous, a villager or two might take the bus in the other direction for the near twenty-minute ride to Durham or other sundry points east.

There is also a police station. The police station has the familiar blue light over the door with the word Police prominent below the light to remove any doubts regarding the nature of business conducted there and also to announce that law and order is firmly established in Bridgeford. In most villages, the police station is a comparatively new building as evidenced by the red brick appearance. But not so in Bridgeford. This building boasts a history. Formerly, a house belonging to a merchant of a previous century, and not necessarily the nineteenth century, the police station has almost the same appearance as any other building in the village.

This bastion of law and order is situated at the head of High Street. At that point, the main street turns directly west and meanders, along with the river, through the countryside, and eventually brings the traveler to Willington. To any first-time visitor to the village, the main street looks as though it is a dead end with the police station presiding over all of the affairs of Bridgeford at the head of the street.

There is one public house in the village and to balance the presence of the police station and pub, the Church of the Holy Trinity, Church of England, serves the spiritual needs of the villagers. As with all small villages, the ever-dominant steeple of the church is the focal point of the village, but because of the coverage afforded by the heavy growths of trees, the steeple is not visible from the A690.

The church lies a little to the west of the village, and the church land abuts on to the western boundaries of the school property and is less than one hundred yards north of the river. The stone church, with its exquisite stained glass windows that cast hues of the primary colors (red, blue, and green) on to the interior on sunny days, is one of the sites of the village, and having been built almost six hundred years before the present day. The services and activities of the church were amply presided over by William Charles Kirkby, BA, MA, DPhil, who was simply referred to as "Vicar" by his parishioners or "Charlie" by those close enough to him to call him a friend.

The cenotaph, where the villagers remember their dead from two world wars every year, stands to the west of the church. On the eleventh hour of the eleventh day of the eleventh month, every year, the last post, blown by none other than Lennie Farmer on his old military bugle, is heard throughout Bridgeford. All activities cease and the village only comes back to life after two minutes of utter and complete silence. An outside service at the cenotaph commences thirty minutes before the eleventh hour of the nearest Sunday, and again, Lennie Farmer brings all village life to a halt at precisely eleven in the morning of that day. Even the ever-present chirping of birds that have not yet migrated south for the winter also ceases, as if by command from a higher authority. The 149 men and women of Bridgeford who have died in the service of their country during the wars are given the utmost respect.

To the immediate west of the cenotaph sits the local park that contains a football and a cricket field. Teams from other villages are hosted during the respective seasons. The game times always coincide with the opening hours of the Duke, and so Lennie, with his permit for the sale of alcoholic beverages for consumption "on or off the premises" and the field being obviously "off the premises" fits very well into the provisions of his permit. After the game, be it football or cricket, the team would enjoy the hot water showers of the Club House, and then as if by some magical effect, manage to arrive at the Duke somewhat inebriated, but not from victory or defeat, and certainly not from tea.

The village is almost a closed community, with only a few of the residents working outside of the village, in nearby Willington or, heaven forbid, as far away as Durham City. This is a veritable "Brigadoon" where few strangers venture.

*   *   *

Bosford Grange, or the Grange as the locals call it, is connected to Bridgeford by a bridge just to the west of the village. Most days, the solitary figures of several villagers can be seen walking westward on Willington Road as they go to work in the morning, making their way to the Grange.

The Bosford Library, located in the Grange, has a collection of books and manuscripts that is one of the most impressive private collections in England. Perhaps even in Europe. The manuscript collection is priceless. Access to the contents of the library is rarely granted, and even then, books and manuscripts can only be examined under strict supervision.

Finally, what is not known to any of the locals is that Sir Ranulf de Boise is the forefather of the Bosford family.

For services rendered to King Edward III, Sir Ranulf was given a considerable piece of land, the palatinate of Durham, where the Lord Bishop had more power than anyone, with the exception of the king. Sir Ranulf is also, through the marriage of his daughter to Oswald's nephew, an ancestor of James Simpson, the main character in this story.

Oswald, another prominent character in this story, was a soldier of King Edward III, who rose from the ranks to become commander of the king's guards. Oswald died tragically leading a convoy of wagons containing gold coin from London to the northern city of his birth, Durham. But Oswald was no ordinary soldier. His ability to read and write stems from his boyhood in the city of Durham where he helped the monks at the priory, now known as Durham Cathedral. Oswald has a deep interest in books and documents that are the source of his learning and his activities as a surgeon.

*   *   *

CHAPTER 2

I t was the start of a new day. A Friday in late January. And as always, whenever a hectic travel schedule did not interfere with his exercise plans, James Simpson was out in the fresh morning air.

The long winter night was giving way to a gray dawn that was beginning to make its presence felt as the darkness faded into the frosty sunrise of a January morning. The silence of the still morning air hung as if a curtain shrouded the countryside. As dawn spread her gray-tipped sharp-edged fingers into the sky, a single bright planet hung brightly in the grayness, as though heralding the day ahead.

As he jogged through the dim light, his breath formed silver clouds before him. Thoughts sped through his mind making him wonder about the events of the past months when autumn had sped toward the Christmas season. A time when he had almost—but he preferred not to think of that gloomy condition known as death!

The last months of the past year had been, to say the least, interesting, and now, as the old year had given birth to a new year, there was the promise of spring only a few short months away. A few short months, that is, depending upon the weather. But this day, even though it was still January, albeit late January, the promise of the new seasons hung in the air. At this time of the morning, the air was cool, but it could be much worse so why complain. The English and their weather!

The leaves that had fallen in the autumn months formed a crisp carpet under his feet where the frost had frozen them to Mother Earth, back to the earth from whence they had originated. His feet made noises as he walked through the barren trees. But other than the sound of his footfalls, there was silence—utter and complete silence.

Now and again, the bare branches of the trees brushed his shoulders but he was prepared for their chastising lashes. He never ran along the side of the road. Not only did the traffic fumes counter any fresh air that he inhaled, but running on the narrow English lanes and roads that were home to many speeding vehicles could be a hazard to one's health! Especially when a dawn mist could wrap him in a soft gray cocoon . . .

A heavy sweater beneath the sweat suit jacket made sure that the early-morning chill would not cut to the bone. There was a small patch that had been sewn on to the left breast of the jacket. A patch that he treasured above all of the many things he owned. It was the symbol of an achievement of which he had been proud. The *color* had been awarded to him many years before when, as a schoolboy, he had played soccer for the North of England U17 Boys. The single word *soccer* was a quiet testimony to his past activities in that sport. Soccer had not been his calling and now he could pass through the highways and byways of England with little recognition except for those avid readers who might recognize him from one of the rare photographs that might appear on the dust cover of a book.

As a writer, James Simpson required thinking time, and for this reason he enjoyed the sacred golden silence of the early-morning hours before villages, towns, and cities awakened to the coming day. As well as organizing his thoughts, he knew that the early-morning exercise sessions stimulated his brain and brought out new ideas and helped organize his thoughts for the day ahead.

His personal belief was that a first-rate physical condition would ensure a clear mind and his athletic build attested to his determination. His persistence was his strength, almost to a fault. Salads, fruit, and fresh fish were the mainstay of his diet.

As his cottage became visible through the dim light, he smiled to himself as he saw smoke from the fireplace curl upward through the still air. His mind started to focus on the day.

The exercise would be followed by a shower, breakfast, and the remainder of the morning would be spent in the development of ideas for his latest manuscript. Afternoons were devoted to research into the historical back-up for the ideas. There might even be the opportunity to prepare a manuscript for presentation at a scientific meeting.

*   *   *

James had spent the autumn and winter months of the past year in a situation that might be called strange, very strange indeed. Almost unbelievable. But believable by whom? As the thoughts tumbled through his mind, he knew the events of the last four months were the good stuff of which novels were made. But for such events to occur in real life. Especially his life . . .

He had made contact with a man from the past. From the late fourteenth century to be precise! A man who had served in the army of Edward III. And who, it seemed, had died more than six hundred years before in a freakish accident at a spot only a short walk from where James lived. Even on what was now James's property.

But *Oswald Dunelmensis*, Oswald of Durham, was not any ordinary man. He may have even been an enigma for his time. He was a soldier who did not live like other soldiers. Soldiers often lived worse than animals. They rarely bathed and were riddled with body lice. They ate roots and berries when their food stores ran out. Dirt and disease, as well as death, were their constant companions.

Oswald was different. He could read, write, and was educated in the arts and sciences of his era. He believed in cleanliness and that disease resulted from dirt. He had medical skills that may have even been advanced for his time. And who knows with what mental powers this man had been endowed. There had been evidence, perhaps imagined by James or perhaps real, that Oswald had played a role in diminishing the aftermath of an accident that almost took James's life. But most of all, and this was what James found really fascinating; Oswald seemed to be a relative of a time long past. Perhaps not a direct forefather since the man had died after his son and wife.

As the finale to their meetings, James had also seen Oswald's wife and son, both of whom had died in 1348 during the outbreak of the plague that had swept through Western Europe.

The happenings were now contained in a new novel that he had written since that day in mid-December when he had last had contact with the man. And James had a sense that what he had written contained many elements of truth, as if the thoughts that flashed into his brain as he sat at his computer had been placed there deliberately.

There had been no more contacts with Oswald since that morning, when he had read the last rites over the place of Oswald's death. Nor did James expect any contact. But what puzzled him now were Oswald's final words, as they stood there in the stillness of a December morning:

"I will not forget you, James Simpson. We have crossed the bridges of time. We will cross the bridges and we will meet again. Enjoy your world that you may one day see mine. Until that day when we meet again . . ."

His voice had trailed away and the shadows had faded and the only sound was the thought that had entered James's mind. A quotation from the Roman poet Catallus:

"*Soles occidere et rederre possunt*" (Suns that set are able to come back again).

James had returned to his cottage and from that morning the words had flowed from his fingers on to the computer monitor screen. He had filled in a well-researched background to the story using the notes that he had made on loose pieces of paper and those engraved on the hard drive of the computer as well as those imprinted in his mind.

His thoughts had become final as the Christmas season arrived and departed, and now his publisher was in a state of extreme excitement about this new novel that would "certainly do at least as well if not much, much better than any of your previous works, James."

These cautious words, James knew, were the prelude to a bestseller!

Such were the current thoughts of James Simpson, formerly a scientist of world renown and now the author of historical fiction. His books were sold worldwide and were eagerly sought as soon as they appeared on the shelves of bookstores.

*   *   *

As he approached his cottage, his senses told him that something was wrong. Very, very wrong. Every sense in his body told him that something was out of place. The feeling that he was being watched had been with him for the last few days.

He had spent Christmas Day with his friend Kathryn, a real estate agent from a Durham City company with a one-person branch in Willington.

James and Kathryn had invited the Reverend Kirkby and his wife Sylvia for a late-afternoon dinner.

Charlie's standard mode of dress was the typical gray tweed suit with a black shirt and white clerical collar. Sylvia, who had a BA in medieval history and had not quite finished her PhD when she left the university to marry Charlie and accompany him to his first parochial assignment, was less formal in her attire, preferring to wear a variety of the latest styles.

Charlie had dispensed with the Christmas services at the church by late morning. Almost the whole village had turned out for Christmas communion and the church had burst forth with the sound of singing that would have not been out of place in one of the larger cathedrals where the choir was next-to-professional singers. Such was the vocal talent of the people of Bridgeford.

Kathryn had accompanied James to the church sensing that he was ill at ease. As they had walked the distance from his cottage to the church, arm in arm, she had resisted the temptation to hug him, thinking about the time they had spent together, getting to know each other, and how she enjoyed those weekends when he was not traveling. This was a long weekend, with Christmas Day being a Monday and a Boxing Day holiday to follow the next day. She wanted the holiday to be so relaxing. She did not know how much the accident had taken out of him, but she did know that James was tired.

She had broached the subject very carefully. After all, James was the love of her life. She had not been able to express her feelings to him, being cautious and not wishing to jeopardize their very close friendship. Her thoughts were a momentary distraction as she recalled that Black Saturday some years ago when she received the news that her husband, the only other man that she had ever loved, had been killed in the collapse of a football stadium. And now, she had learned to love again.

"James, my dear."

He looked at her with a mixture of emotions. Sorrow and an emotion that she could not place. The darkness of his eyes would not let her penetrate his thoughts.

"Kath, me bonnie lass," at the sound of his lapse into the Northern dialect, she relaxed, "there's nowt wrong," he said as if reading her mind. He continued, "I've been having some strange sensations this last week. Thoughts of being followed, and I'm not able to explain it!"

She breathed slowly, wondering if the blow to his head that he has suffered in the car accident was starting to manifest itself after several weeks.

"And it's not the bang on the head."

His assertive comment worried her. She wondered if he really was reading her mind. She preferred not to give away any private thoughts!

The rest of the day had passed quietly. James feeling his normal self. Charlie and Sylvia had joined them by the midafternoon. The two men had it all planned. They tended to cooking the goose, making sure that it did not rest too much in the large discharge of fat, and that the herbs added during the basting were just in the right amount. Then they cooked the vegetables, and last but not least, the plum pudding.

During a visit to the vicarage the previous week, James had suggested to Charlie that they cook an old-fashioned Christmas dinner. Charlie had almost leapt out of his chair at the suggestion and had heartily agreed that they keep it a secret from the two ladies, who, no doubt, expected to slave away in the kitchen over a hot stove on Christmas Day!

Even Kathryn had been surprised when James had not thought about shopping for the usual dinner items the previous Saturday when they had been in Durham. And equally surprised, all the way to church, when James had made no mention of the list of items for dinner.

None other than Nonky Wood, owner of the local service station, and Jackie Hall, the butcher, had been involved and seen to the arrangements.

The service station was obvious from the large Esso sign. Norman Wood, known as Nonky since his schooldays, catered to the needs of the limited number of Bridgeford motorists. His son, Alan, was co-owner of the business. Both made extra money from their skills as bricklayers, plumbers, electricians, and joiners or carpenters, as those in trade of woodsmiths are often called.

Jackie Hall, florid-faced, owned the butcher's shop and he was adept at lending ear and tongue to the daily news. In fact, he revamped any news older than half a day, often with a much different perspective, when the occasion arose.

Nonky and Jackie had conspired with Charlie and James and had delivered the ready-to-cook food to the cottage during James and Kathryn's walk. The surprise had been complete when fresh flowers for Sylvia and Kathryn had been delivered plus an open house that was to follow dinner.

Guests started to arrive a few minutes after six o'clock and continued to drop in for a *wee drop* of whiskey, what else, until almost ten. During this time it had given James and Charlie great comfort to see Kathryn and Sylvia laughing with the villagers, thoroughly enjoying themselves.

It was during this time that Kathryn sensed that there was something amiss with James.

He had gone out to get wood to renew the stock for the fire. The silence of the evening and the lightly falling snow oozed a serenity that was difficult, if not impossible, to imitate. As he placed the four logs onto his left arm, he sensed a presence. Almost at the very spot where he had one of his early sightings of Oswald. Dressed in his soldier's uniform of the late fourteenth century, he had been an imposing figure.

But this time it was different. The soft lines of the shadow were not those of a husky well-made man. They were softer, almost blending in with the shimmering lines from the lighted window in the background. Much softer lines, as if . . . And a soft voice, as though he was being called.

As Joan of Arc heard voices and was called, so it was with James. But by whom? Or was it the sound of the gentle breeze whistling through the eaves of the cottage?

He shook his head and the shadows disappeared, but he could feel the early sensations of a migraine pass through his brain. Then, as suddenly as it had started, the discomfort stopped. He leaned against the woodpile for a moment or so to recover his senses, smiled to himself, wondering if he had not had too much wine with the Christmas goose, and walked back into the cottage.

James did not bother to mention this to his guests, although Charlie, as perceptive as ever, noticed the change in James's expression as he reentered the room and he was determined that the matter would be the subject of discussion at a later time.

Charlie refilled his pipe, staring at James, and knowing that something was out of place. His nimble fingers pressed the tobacco into the bowl as the thought was whispered within James's hearing:

"James my boy, you and I need to have a little chat! There is something in your manner that bothers me! And I have made a discovery that might be of interest to you. Very interesting indeed . . ."

Charlie settled himself to recall the story for James, but they were both recalled to the festivities.

"Later, James. Later."

Charlie's raised eyebrows made James even more curious. He knew that Charlie often talked in riddles but this seemed as if it might be important. But what?

*   *   *

Thus James started the Christmas and New Year celebrations, pleasantly in the company of Kathryn, Charlie, and Sylvia, and many of the other villagers who happened to be passing by. They were always welcome in James's cottage. Knowing this, they had no wish to impose, but at Christmas . . .

Nonky Wood, Jackie Hall, Joe Dobson, the fishmonger, and Bob Fenwick, the local medical doctor who always enjoyed tending to the welfare of his patients personally, and sundry others made several visits and returned to their respective homes somewhat the less able.

As the need arose, James shuttled them home in the Jaguar that purred its way through the High Street thanks to Nonky's capable care. Each visit was a new experience in the art of appreciating the fine single malt whiskeys that James had brought in for the occasion. He always had at least one malt whiskey on hand to offer visitors; this was the festive season!

The malt whiskeys of the Western Isles of Scotland, the highlands, and the lowlands were all available. They had matured in their respective casks for twelve or fourteen years and their character had remained unaltered in the bottle. In this village, there were the experts. The conversation had focused on the relative merits of Cragganmore and Dalwhinnie malt whiskeys. Both from Speyside with subtle differences.

*   *   *

And so it was on New Year's Eve at the vicarage. Charlie and Sylvia always threw open their home to the whole village, as James had done for the first time at Christmas. The village experts appeared again, this time with a different collection of malt whiskeys but of equally alluring taste to those chosen by James. The laughter without drunkenness continued, as the evening became night and the gathering looked forward with anticipation to the New Year.

As midnight and the start of the New Year approached, James realized that, for some reason, Charlie was trying to attract his attention. Perhaps to talk over some point of history, as was frequently the case. James saw that Sylvia and Kathryn were engaged in a lively discussion about . . . but he would not presume to even hazard a guess. He knew better than to attempt to second-guess both of these ladies!

Charlie decided that it was time to have the heads-together session with James that had not yet materialized. But it was not to be.

The sound of the door chimes announced the arrival of the local constabulary—Sergeant John Anderson and Constable Bryan Jones.

"What's goin' on 'ere, then?" was Anderson's good-natured entry into the vicarage.

"Looks like a wild party in progress, Sarge," Jones responded smiling.

"Aye, lad. Let's join in."

Thus was attention diverted from Charlie's proposed heads together with James.

"Ah well, there's always another time and Charlie's sure to engineer a meeting," had been James's thought as he and Kathryn left the vicarage early in the first morning of the New Year. The start of a new week and a new year.

As he had helped Kathryn into the Jaguar, her features had shimmered in the crisp moonlight almost changing her countenance and making James wonder . . .

"Come on, James. Open the door, please, it's cold out here."

The engine had roared to life and threw heat into the interior of the car within moments of starting.

"Penny for them, James."

"It's nothing, Kath, me bonnie lass. Just a random thought or two."

"Oh, cheeky thing. Having a little dream, are we?"

Had James been able to see the gleam in her eye, he would have known her thoughts, and he would have seen the impish smile on her face. But this strange feeling had occurred twice in one week, with no obvious explanation.

"James! Anything wrong?"

"No, Kath. I'm fine. How about a nice cup of tea when we get to your place?"

"Anything you want, James dear . . ."

She had that twinkle in her eye but his serious expression told her not to go any further with comments in a lighter vein. James's mood was not one of levity at this time. His furrowed brow and quiet demeanor told her that he would talk when the time came. She smiled gently at him and the car continued on its route to her home.

*   *   *

And so as these thoughts had passed through his mind, James brought himself back into the present. He had decided that there was some very necessary research to be done in the Dean and Chapter Library. This library had descended in direct historical continuity from the library of the Benedictine house at Durham that had been founded in the twelfth century. The manuscripts that it contained had survived from its earliest beginnings and served as a valuable reference source for James.

James's work for the four previous days had required the kind of detail that could only be obtained by meticulous research. He had been partially successful and a cup of coffee in the cafeteria was warranted. A time to collect his thoughts and glance through his notes.

As he swirled the coffee in the heavy cup, James smiled at the memory of Christmas and New Year. And now on this late-January Friday, he felt that he was not alone. He was very uneasy.

It was the very same feeling that had been with him before. Late last year, in fact, from late summer until three weeks before Christmas, but he thought that it would be over, without any recurrence. But there had been that occasion on Christmas Day. Then the sensation in the early hours of New Year's Day. And now, the sensations again. As if . . . But that was absurd! Had he not performed all of the necessary rites?

The cafeteria, located in the undercroft of the cathedral at Durham, was a favorite place to relax. He had spent an hour in the Dean and Chapter Library, alone and without the usual guardians of the valuable antiquarian books. Courtesy of his old school friend, Tommy Smith. Now, the Very

Reverend William Thomas Smith, dean of the cathedral at Durham or more correctly dean of the Priory Church of Christ and Blessed Mary the Virgin.

He shifted in his chair and looked around the cafeteria, but there was little to see. It was a time of the day when few people chose to drink tea or coffee.

He had been in the library alone but thought that he heard the sounds of soft-shoes on the wooden floors.

Not being content with any status quo, he had searched row after row between the book-lined shelves. But there was no one. So he had settled down to work. The arrival of the staff had brought new life and new sounds to the rows of books. Inanimate objects to some, but alive with the marks of previous owners, shouting their messages from the old paper and vellum. A treasury of life in past ages.

He had hoped to have a conversation, and coffee, with Alice. Alice Campbell that is. A young woman who had recently obtained her PhD in medieval history and who had made the Dean and Chapter Library the focal point of her emerging career. But she was out on a fact-finding trip to the British Library in London and was not expected back "for a day or so." Pity. She would have been so helpful. Knowing the contents of the library like she did, Alice would have been able to put her hands on the right texts without so much as a second thought. And even if the desired texts were not available, she could have recommended the texts that James should consult in the British Library. But it was not to be.

So James sat thoughtfully in the cafeteria. His eyes wandered to an older couple, three tables away, sipping coffee and engaged in quiet conversation with each other. He could hear the faint sounds of their southern accent. He wondered if they were on vacation but realized that they were months away from the summer vacation season, preferring the quietness of the off-season to the hustle and bustle of the usual frantic summer holiday madness. Summer was that time of the year when everyone, even those not on vacation, rushed around as if they were lemmings about to leap over the cliff edge and hurl themselves to the other world.

The woman behind the counter smiled as he looked around. James guessed that she was probably a little older then he, a quiet testimony from her graying hair, and very smartly dressed.

She looked at him curiously.

James was distracted from her gaze by the sound of her two assistants having their cup of coffee in the back room. Their animated chatter, and words that hurled themselves at his ears, indicated that they were comparing notes about the trials and tribulations of another night with their respective boyfriends, the night before.

He smiled as he heard snippets of the conversation.

"Geroff ah said. Dinna dee ut here!" (Get off I said. Don't do it here!)

James continued to sip his coffee. He looked out of the door but could not see anyone in the walkway between the undercroft and the treasury. The exhibits of long-dead churchmen and monarchs were of little interest to anyone at this time of the day. As he looked back to the counter, he saw the woman still smiling. A few moments later, a voice penetrated his thoughts.

"Excuse me."

James felt as though he had performed one of those impossible actions that involved leaving the chair and touching his hands to the eleven-foot ceiling. He turned to see the woman from the counter standing at his left side. The two vacationers ceased their chatter and were now looking across at him, wondering if there was something amiss.

"Oh, I am sorry to surprise you, dear. But you are Mr. Simpson, the writer?"

He smiled, more in relief than being recognized.

"Yes ma'am."

"I've heard you were living around here. Nancy, my relief supervisor, said she'd seen you."

James recalled the younger, tall, dark-haired woman who greeted him at the counter on many occasions as he'd picked up his morning or afternoon coffee.

"I've read all of your books. In fact, I have one here. Would you autograph it for me? I'm sorry it's only paperback."

"I would be glad to sign it."

She turned and walked quickly back to the counter and took the book from her bag that lay on a shelf under the cash register. She was back in moments and handed the book to James. A new unopened paperback. He must have looked at it quizzically and she anticipated his question.

"Just been keeping it new, hoping that you would come in."

James smiled, putting her at ease.

"Not to worry . . .," he looked at the name tag on her left breast pocket as he was about to sign the inside front cover.

"To Vera with my best regards?"

"To Arthur," she added by way of explanation, "my husband. He's read all of your books too."

James smiled and signed the page and gave the book back to her with a smile.

"I do have another question that I'd like to ask. If you don't mind?"

"Sure, Vera. Fire away. Sit down, bonnie lass."

"*Oooh, ah canna.*"

"Oooh, I cannot. Not while I'm working. But your accent," she paused as if trying to carefully choose her next words. Instead, her thoughts came out directly translated into words.

"You're one of us!" she said.

James laughed at the surprised look on her face. He felt accepted as a "lad o' the North" again.

"Most authors have their pictures on the back cover of books, why don't you?"

James was about to reply when he saw the light go on in her eyes. And then she answered herself.

"So that you can get around without too many curious people. Oooh, I am sorry, Mr. Simpson!"

"Don't worry, Vera. It really is a pleasure to meet people like you. It's the crowds that I don't . . ."

"Say no more, Mr. Simpson," she cut off his answer, "I'll keep quiet."

"Appreciate it, Vera. If anyone wants to find out who I am, let them figure it out . . . just as you did."

James invited her to sit down for a few minutes, which she accepted, after looking around furtively as though she feared being caught in this moment of relaxation, and they chatted enjoyably before James got up to leave. As he bade her "goodbye, see you again," she smiled and thanked him for his kindness, again apologizing for her interruption of his coffee break.

"Not to worry, Vera. Anytime. And really, it was a pleasure."

She beamed a smile that lit up her face, and the spring in her step was very obvious as she took his cup and saucer back to the counter.

James left the undercroft, walked through the cloisters, crossed through the west end of the building close by the front, and exited through the main door. His Jaguar sat in the parking spot where he had left it more than two hours before as he arrived at the Palace Green, the open area that lay between the sturdy castle and elegant cathedral, both showing many remnants of their eleventh-century Norman beginnings.

James switched on the powerful motor, smiled in response to the attendant's cheery "morning, sir" which sounded more like "mornan sor" as the words in the dialect of the North filled the air between them. The powerful engine in the Jaguar had now brought the heating system to full temperature as the car glided out of the site of the original city of Durham having almost steered itself through Owengate, turning left on to Saddler Street, and after several more maneuvers, he reached the A690 that would take him home to Bridgeford.

He allowed his mind to wander as the car sped past the leafless hedgerows. James had almost forgotten about his trip to London. His ideas for the manuscript were starting to come together and his planned visit to a symposium in London was very opportune. Perhaps he would visit the British Library, perhaps a prowl around some of the other sites that he might use as background for his book. Yes, the trip to London was timely.

He knew that at sometime during the next two days, if not that evening, Kath would stop by to say "hello" and have tea. He would spend Sunday afternoon packing and preparing for his journey to London the next day.

His attendance at the symposium, conference, or by whatever name it was known this time, had been eagerly sought and he had reluctantly agreed to the not-so-timely but very courteous invitation. But now, as the thought recurred in his mind, the visit was very timely and he could feel the pull of London away from the winter of the North.

And there were always the scientific aspects of his life that could be tendered. But who knows? It might, after all, help him keep up to date with the various aspects of coal technology. His chosen scientific field was petroleum, but it always helped to have other knowledge at hand in order to construct realistic energy scenarios.

Suddenly, the cottage appeared in front of him. After the inevitable, but always welcome, cup of tea, he sorted and packed his clothes for the three-day conference. He would return home on Friday, and as he packed, he uttered a silent prayer of thanks for the convenience of same-day laundry service that allowed him to travel light.

Although he had plenty to occupy him, his mind was not at ease. The thought that he was continually being watched bothered him, and he did not have any answer to dispel his worries.

*   *   *

CHAPTER 3

The weekend did not quite pass as he had anticipated. The two days of planned work had an extremely pleasant and welcome interruption.

On Saturday evening, Kathryn appeared at the cottage, as if knowing that he needed the companionship. The double rap of the knocker on the wooden door caught James's attention. He responded and there she stood. His sharp intake of breath registered his surprise. Kathryn raised an eyebrow.

"James. Surely you are not surprised?"

"No, Kath. Of course not. You always seem to know when I need a little company. Not reading my mind, I hope?"

"Not at all, James. Wouldn't want you to be too embarrassed!"

She stepped into the warmth, shedding her sheepskin coat to reveal a Black Watch kilt; a white shirt and knee-high polished boots completed her outfit. Kathryn's brightness filled the cottage and made James's evening so much more pleasant.

Even though they talked about his suspicion of being watched, he felt at ease in her presence. The conversation continued without interruption. The music from the stereo filtered through the air. Light rock tunes, James's favorites. When they had finished, the player immediately changed to the sound of Bach. A contrast perhaps, but nonetheless relaxing. And so the music and the conversation continued.

James felt as if a weight had been lifted from his shoulders. Kathryn was a good conversationalist. Meaningful. Able to fit the mood of the moment. A woman of quality, distinction, and bearing. Almost turning his mind to something more permanent.

In the midst of a late-evening cup of tea, the silence of the moment was broken by the shrill blast of the telephone. James picked up the receiver and spoke into it in a non-committal tone. A simple "hello."

"James? It's Alice. I hear you were looking for me."

"Alice!"

He turned to look at Kathryn with a smile. She busied herself pouring another cup of tea. And then preparing the water in the kitchen for a fresh pot.

"Nice of you to call. Where are you?"

"London. But enough of the niceties of the evening. How can I help?"

James related his needs and the results of his search in the Dean and Chapter Library earlier in the day.

"Ah, James then you need . . .," she paused as she realized that he was busy, "by the way I hope I did not disturb you. Can I hear noises in the background?"

"Not to worry, Alice. Go on."

"If it's Kathryn, please offer my apologies."

Alice continued the conversation and mentioned the British Library. James interrupted.

"The British! I'll be in London on Monday afternoon."

"Well, I return to Durham on Monday but I'd like to talk with you. There are more findings here as I do my research."

"I hope to return on Thursday," James proceeded to inform her, "but by the time I get back here, Friday would be the best day to meet."

"Where are you staying? The Cumberland?"

"Correct," he said.

James remembered the words of Sidney Greenstreet as he responded to a Bogart comment in the Maltese Falcon: "Mathematically precise, my dear Rick," but decided against paraphrasing the expression.

"Good. I'll call you when my schedule is confirmed and then we can set up a meeting time at my office."

"Fine. But?"

"I know what you require and I'll have a list of material for you to consult."

James took a deep breath.

"Great. When I can see it?"

"At my office. I should have it all organized and coordinated into a story by then."

"Fantastic!"

"Say 'hello' to Kathryn for me."

James hung up, and turning, almost walked into Kathryn as she carried the pot of fresh tea from the kitchen.

"Tea, James?"

"How do you always know what I want? Reading my mind?"

Kathryn smiled secretively. Then she asked, "How is Alice doing?"

"She's putting a list together for me that will help my thought process."

After the tea they talked for a while before Kathryn left for her home a short drive away. He spoke again of his apprehensions about being watched. She listened sympathetically and tried to offer advice, but as she admitted and as much as she tried to offer words of comfort, it was difficult to imagine since she was not the person being watched.

After she left, James decided to work on the manuscript, but his thoughts were not clear. It was a jumble of different emotions and images that defied interpretation. And the minor headache that had plagued him all day was not about to ease. A time to rest. But it was a restless night.

*   *   *

James dreamed. In his dream there was a constant darkness. He could hear strange sounds. Not the sounds of man. Sounds that were uncontrolled. As if made by animals. He could hear the soft sounds approaching. Surrounded by the darkness of night. The faint clicking of . . . teeth? And then he sensed the movement near to him.

James fought to become aware of his surroundings and he did not realize for some time where he was. Then it sank in. There was only this suspended sphere of self-awareness beyond which he could discern certain dim essentials of the earth.

He heard himself speaking in the Saxon language as consciousness started to return. The words were clear and their meaning was obvious. They were words of warning.

*   *   *

He finally awoke to the darkness that persists in a winter morning. Startled and drenched with the sweat that accompanies the fear of the unknown. He sat up in bed and listened. He could hear the clicking sounds of hailstones as they hit the window.

He showered.

The remainder of Sunday passed as he planned. Working. The ideas flowed from his mind into the memory banks of the computer. But by midmorning, he was ready to put his foot through the screen as retribution for the computer's know-it-all behavior, advising him by sounds of spelling errors and keyboard errors, but he thought better of it. Disabling the computer sound program was far more economical! So, the work progressed throughout the weekend.

As was his custom, he liked to parcel his time into neat whole-hour bundles, a habit he'd carried over from school where the bells demarcating the hours also signaled a shift of mental gears. So it was with his writing. Neat parcels of time to develop an idea and reduce it to word on a page. And now and again, he took a break for tea and time to read the Sunday *Telegraph.*

The Sunday newspaper, which he hardly bothered to read because of his total envelopment in the work, was full of the usual stories. All bad. Very few of the stories were really newsy. There were political actions going on all over the world. Yet the headlines screamed for mercy and justice. A juvenile offender who had been convicted of a crime and who is now on his third conviction for a similar offense. But the do-gooders wanted him paroled. His mother was quoted as saying, "He's a good lad." His father added something about "just boyish pranks." Everyone seemed to forget about the victim and her rights. A twelve-year-old girl who had been walking home now would have nightmarish memories for the rest of her life . . .

James made a mental note to use the newspaper either to light the fire the next day or to wrap some garbage in it and throw it out. He did the former.

And then it was Sunday night. His carefully laid plans for packing were completed. As he contemplated the small suitcase, the computer case, and his briefcase, he was pleased with himself. He wondered about the journey to London when it came to him, a voice, as if carried on the wind.

Not a voice that he recognized. Almost completely unknown. And yet, there was something about the voice. Soft. Haunting. As a whisper in the wind can be haunting. He heard his name being called. And then it was gone.

He went to the door and switched on the outside lights. He could see no one through the adjacent window. The tree branches waved back to him as they danced in the wind. But there was no one!

A quick refreshing shower helped clear his mind, but he could not forget the voice. The sense that he was being watched made him apprehensive. Then he smiled. If anyone wished to watch him in the shower, good luck! Especially since there was no window that would help the peeping Tom!

The rest of the night passed slowly and sleep did not come easily. He was troubled again. Kathryn's presence earlier in the day had helped him move his fears to the back of his mind. But the voice had brought fear and wonderment back to the fore. As he sat, drinking tea and working on his computer, he could not help but know that some happening was close. As if by some sixth sense, he was slowly becoming aware of some strange feelings.

And then it was five o'clock. At this time of the year not even the gray tint of dawn was present. After a shower and a quick breakfast and a last-minute check of his baggage, it was suddenly time to leave for the drive to the Durham City railway station.

The blustery wind swept in from the north and made the railway station a veritable agony. He remembered a previous occasion when he had dreamt that he was standing on the platform awaiting the train to London and he had seen people of another time standing across the line on the opposite side. This had been one of his introductions to the world of Oswald, without knowing that Oswald's original home had been within a few yards of his present position.

He looked across the line. A young woman stood waiting for the next train to Newcastle; otherwise there were no signs of life on the platform. He looked with a concentration that focused his whole mind. There was nothing.

The northbound train from London, due a few minutes before his train, arrived at the station blocking out his view of the opposite platform and the woman. The snorting sounds that would have been evident if it had been a steam train were replaced by the more powerful sounds of the diesel locomotive. The northbound train eased out of the station as James's London-bound train arrived at the platform.

He had not bothered to reserve a seat in the first-class "G" compartment, as he knew that there would be ample space. He was right, there was only one other passenger who barely acknowledged his presence as he sat in a forward-facing seat of the four-seater giving himself the room to spread out and work at the table between the seats. Two minutes later, at 9:48 a.m., the train departed and as the engine left the station, he booted up the notebook computer and retrieved the file that he had been working on earlier that morning.

James spent the time working at organizing the sections of the manuscript. The hypnotic rhythm of the train against the lines helped him cast his mind back and allowed the alchemist to come to life as James's fingers tapped away at the keyboard. James would nourish his existence until the alchemist's character was fully developed.

This was a story that he must write. It had started as an idea almost two years before. But he had spent all of the previous summer in an attempt to give the alchemist's character the depth that he felt was necessary for his story. Nothing worse than a shallow, characterless, dull scientist! And now it was happening. The story had started to unfold before Christmas and James felt that he now had the character of the alchemist so well defined that the story might even start to write itself. He could not help but smile to himself as another thought crossed his mind.

"Better not make him Nobel Prize material!"

"Come to think of it," he mused, "he would be out of date by five centuries!"

The man of whom he wrote was a late-fourteenth—and early-fifteenth-century character. The time that was so interesting to James because it was that time when science and medicine were becoming realistic again in Western Europe, after a lapse of over one thousand years during which time Europe had been in the scientific and technical dark ages. There had been those few sturdy souls who had refused to accept the shackles of the doctrines of successive churchmen. These were the men who had tried against all odds to rejuvenate science and medicine.

The powerful laptop computer had become his constant companion on his many travels. Entering his notes and thoughts had become a substitute for talking.

As the train left Darlington Station, he felt eyes upon him. He looked up quickly from the computer and smiled at a woman staring at him. She looked away nervously, thinking that he was staring at her, blushed, and attempted to disguise her attributes by sucking in her stomach. This action did not help at all and it only served to draw James's attention to her, perhaps even making matters worse, or better as the case may be!

James smiled, making her blush even more, as the fleeting thought of two soccer balls sped through his mind. Perhaps he would use this in a future novel. He returned to his reading and editing. The interlude had passed!

From then on, he barely noticed the stops at York, Doncaster, and Peterborough. Nor did he notice the seven additional passengers who joined him and his original companion in the carriage. He did remember declining the attendant's invitation to lunch in the dining car. There was a man needing his attention, his life to be developed, and his adventures to be described!

The remainder of the train ride to London was uneventful.

And then the powerful engine started to slow as it drew into the King's Cross Railway Station. The train arrived at six minutes after one o'clock. Four minutes early!

"Ah, the big city once again."

The sensations were strong. His head began to pound as the thoughts danced in his brain. And then he knew what was happening. It was Oswald's thoughts that were with him. Oswald's last words shot into his mind:

"We will cross the bridges and we will meet again. Enjoy your world that you may one day see mine. Until that day when we meet again . . ."

James knew not why but he sensed that he was closer to Oswald now than he ever had been, but suddenly he felt alone again. The thoughts abated, as if they had never been with him. He shook his head as if to clear his mind, but he was really ensuring that a doozer of a headache would not follow.

He carefully packed away his computer, made sure he had not left anything behind, and dismounted from the train at Platform 7. Only a few short yards away from the very spot where the remains of Boudicca lay buried.

As always, he looked along the platform. His eyes were drawn to the spot where he believed that her remains lay, uncovered and undisturbed over the centuries. This powerful queen of the Iceni who had been able to withstand the military might of Rome two thousand years ago deserved to rest in peace. The thoughts of her were strong in his mind as he imagined the quiet conversations of her followers as they buried her in a place where the Romans would not be able to defile her body as they had defiled in life the bodies of Boudicca, her daughters, and the bodies of countless other women. The queen's loyal court would not allow this to happen in death. Boudicca had rested in this place for almost two thousand years. The discovery of what were purported to be Boudicca's remains had caused a stir in historical circles, but British Rail had no intention of excavating a portion of one of its main rail terminals. Boudicca's remains would stay at rest for some time to come. As he walked to the exit, he glanced once again along the platform, as though paying tribute to the presence of the great queen. He looked in the direction of where he sensed her remains to be and gave a nod of respect.

A taxi ride to the hotel, a relaxing shower, dinner, and he would be ready for a good night's sleep.

*   *   *

The hotel room was comfortable. It was not, as is very often the case, dominated by the double bed. A dining area and a sitting area were added to the size and comfort of the room. But more important there was a work area where he could sit at a desk and work on his computer. The whole room was tastefully furnished to complement this home away from home.

The hotel had been one of the most luxurious in the city and a multimillion-pound face-lift had retained that splendor and maintained the hotel as one of the premier hotels in London. In fact, parts of the renovation program were still under way, to the discomfort of some of the guests. There had been some doubts about the ability of the hotel to retain its former glory. Like Tara in *Gone with the Wind*. The war had ended and the grand old estate had lost the battle.

But not so this hotel. The renovation had breathed a new life into the aging structure and the temporary inconvenience was nothing to many of the guests. And now, it was the host hotel for a major international conference. Glory had indeed returned to this bastion of eloquence!

* * *

The next morning, James arose at five o'clock. He entered the bathroom and prepared to shave. As he looked in the mirror, a shiver ran down his back. He was conscious of a shadow in the doorway but in a flash it was gone. He suddenly felt cold. He had to fight to bring his mind back to the subject matter of the meeting. He even had to decide if he should attend but he was one of the featured speakers; he had to be there.

His mind needed the change of focus.

James looked, rather stared, out of the window to the alley below. Lost in thought. Wondering. What would his alchemist have seen looking from a window? Certainly not six floors up. But perhaps on to a similar back lane. Stacked with garbage and human waste that had been thrown from windows of a second floor.

He could hear the distant noises. Unidentifiable in the confusion of sound. There were the metallic sounds of men loading a truck; chattering, in a fashion, to anyone ready to listen. The sounds of human voices from the hallway behind him, almost as if from another world. The noises floated to his ears as if struggling on the heavy, almost solid, air.

And then he heard it. The sound. Someone breathing. Whispering. Powerful. But calling his name. He turned quickly, almost in shock. Then he saw her, or at least he saw her outline. The smooth curves that were not hidden but accentuated by the shadows. He sensed her words, "James, my husband and I have a need of you. Please help us."

The words lingered in the air.

* * *

The shrill blast of the telephone interrupted the thought as the shadows took on the more familiar shapes of the room. She had disappeared . . .

"Hello."

"James. Good to hear your voice."

"Who is this? Alice!" James exclaimed as he recognized Alice's voice.

"James, are you all right? Your voice . . ."

"Aye, Alice. I'm fine. Just woken up and still groggy."

She was surprised that he even admitted to sleeping, but thought better of commenting. More to her style, Alice got straight to the point

"Are we still on for later this week?"

"Sure. Just as we arranged. Looks like Friday is a good day for me. I'll return to Durham on Thursday morning. Get my stuff cleared up and see you Friday morning."

"Fantastic! Do I have a story for you!" Her girlish enthusiasm showed clearly that she enjoyed her work. "Just checking, James. This is something that will really interest you!"

"Do tell!"

"Not on your life, James. This is a face-to-face conversation."

"Hope it's worth it! Where are you?"

"At my hotel. Just leaving for the station. Got to get back to my office to check my files. Some very important findings!"

"I'll meet you as planned. Your office. Friday. Tenish?"

"In time for coffee.

"See you then, Alice."

"À dix heures, monsieur. At ten o'clock."

"Oui, mademoiselle."

Both lapsed into French naturally. James thought of Alice's research work. Did she really have a story to tell? Hopefully by the end of the week he would know the answer to his questions.

* * *

Registration for the meeting began at nine in the hallway outside of the banquet room, which was also serving as the meeting room. The organizers appeared as if they were trying to accomplish all of the details in this hour before the speakers commenced their presentations. The usual fussing and rushing around the conference by organizers who seemed, or at least pretended, to be busy with the one thousand and one details that still remained unattended.

James arrived early so that he would miss the usual rush of registrants that was bound to happen at ten minutes before nine. He had preregistered by mail and all that he needed to do was pick up his packet, discover the contents, decide what he really needed, and ignore the remainder.

Why was he here? Had it not been for the very convincing invitation to be a keynote speaker and the overall caliber of the conference, he would have refused immediately.

James was a scientist and his strong interest in fossil fuels was still evident by his requested presence at the meeting. The conference chairman had called him some weeks ago to discuss the framework that he was using to build the conference theme. Thus, James had put on his scientific hat and written his presentation accordingly.

A group of three people had also had similar thoughts and were chatting quietly, packets tucked under their arms. Two women sat behind the registration desks, obvious employees of the association responsible for calling the meeting. They smiled at James's approach. He retuned the three smiles, picked up his registration package, and decided to help himself to coffee from the heated urn. He retired to a nearby couch. This action seemed to serve as the impetus for the other early birds to also have coffee. Two decided to join him either to remove preconference jitters or to be sociable. James thought that it was probably the former since within moments he had spotted the collection of slides in the young woman's briefcase and her young male companion seemed to share her nerves.

"First time?"

She looked surprised.

"First presentation?"

"How did you know?" Then she added, "Shows that much, does it?"

James smiled at her response.

"It will show every time. Later on, you learn to handle it but you never get used to it!"

"Your accent? But you're not American?"

"No, ma'am. I was born on this side, but I've lived in Canada and the United States for many years. Now I'm back here, in Durham."

"Oh, please forgive me. I'm Dr. Shirley Johnson, from the Coal Board."

James did not say anything and stifled the inward smile at the use of her title. So English and not really out of place. She was telling him by the use of her title that she had worked for it and wanted others to recognize her abilities. She turned toward her companion.

"This is my colleague, Dr. Tony Burgess."

James shook their hands in turn and responded with his name. Then the penny dropped. Or, he wondered, had it dropped some time ago and was this a meeting of convenience. He doubted it as her eyes opened wide.

"You're Dr. James Simpson. The author?"

Tony's lips parted slightly, perhaps in surprise, but he did not say anything.

"Aye, lass. I am that! See, I do speak English."

They laughed at his lapse into words that were a combination of the Durham and Lancashire dialects.

This seemed to break the tension and they talked about the future of coal research in England, with some reference to his author activities. But James was very loath to fill in the details of his life to complete strangers. They would need to do that for themselves. They chatted about the apparent resurgence of coal as the number one fuel for the Western world. During this time, their eyes wandered over and beyond his shoulders, as if searching for someone else.

"Sorry, Dr. Simpson. But we have to keep a lookout for our boss. Oh, there he is. Please excuse us. Good to meet you. We'll see you later, I expect. Come on, Tony."

*   *   *

Suddenly it was approaching nine o'clock. Time to start. James had already entered the room that was equipped with approximately two hundred seats. After a quick mental count, he shook his head. No way would they fill up all of the chairs!

Fifteen minutes later, he mentally retracted his words. The room was packed.

The chairman of the organizing committee stood at the podium and introduced the theme of the conference and then proceeded to announce the first speaker "who I am sure that most of you know and will give us an injection of reality into the various energy scenarios. Please welcome Dr. James Simpson."

James got up from his seat and walked to the raised podium. He reached the podium just as the chairman finished his introduction using the brief résumé that James had provided.

The audience listened intently to his words, laughed at the injection of some of his humor, and then it was over to an applause that was much more than polite. His call for energy dependence from foreign sources was met with thunderous approval. He offered to answer questions during the break and resumed his seat in the front row.

The ten-thirty break came and he was besieged by members of the audience and one very familiar face.

"Dick, you old son of a gun, what are you doing here?"

Dick Jordan, the CNN correspondent that James had known for some years and who had interviewed James several times when they were both living in the United States, greeted him. Dick had reappeared in Bridgeford several months ago. He shook James's hand warmly.

"James, you know I like to get your good-looking face on camera. So, coffee and a few minutes of your time later, James?"

"Sure, Dick. Let me just answer a few questions."

"Till then, James."

James answered questions put to him by fellow scientists, going beyond the time of the signal that the session was about to restart. A few reporters from the newspapers were evident from their badges. James had no fear of the press and all in all, he was able to field all of the questions to everyone's satisfaction.

Then he and Dick Jordan talked for some time with some minor interruptions until lunchtime. The topics involved the conference theme, the events that had shocked Bridgeford in the last few months of the previous year where James and Dick had renewed their friendship again, to the latest novel. The latter item, Dick promised to keep under his hat until a more appropriate time.

James knew that it was Dick's reporting of the Bridgeford events that had ensured that justice would be served, and it had started. Mrs. Bosford had been charged with murder, and as a result of the ensuing publicity, had suffered a massive stroke resulting in her death.

Even though his mother was involved, Henry Bosford paid his respects to James and thanked him for seeing that justice was done. And he bore

James no ill will as a result of his mother's death. But that was another story, and Dick had urged James to write a nonfictional account of those events. James continued to decline the suggestion and told Dick that he felt satisfied with the novel and he would leave it at that. It was time for Bridgeford to sink from the front pages of the daily newspapers and return to anonymity. Dick sighed and agreed. This story would not be milked any further!

They parted as the lunch break became obvious from the attendees leaving the meeting room. James could not avoid the lunch; he had been informed that he would be sitting at the head table and the absence of the kick-off speaker would be considered impolite in England and definitely uncool elsewhere!

Two o'clock. The time for the afternoon session to start was upon him. A heavy lunch was not James's personal choice and he knew that afternoon session would be difficult, perhaps tiresome. And it was.

The first speaker was quite logical and entertaining but it was the second speaker who brought on a new experience in pain. He droned on and on and on! James lost his focus on the words as the man began the sixth slide of his presentation. How many more to go? One more slide would be too many!

And so the first day of the conference came to an end. James toyed with the idea of missing the reception but, for the same reason that he attended the luncheon, decided that his presence was required. He did not wish to disappoint the conference chairman, who seemed a decent fellow.

The reception that evening was, as he had correctly anticipated, one of those "glass of sherry in the hand and be polite to everyone" affairs. The usual collection of dark-suited men, and a few women still trying to break into what had remained a predominantly man's world.

And now, there they all stood in little groups. Standing in awe of one member of the group who was on his or her soapbox, pontificating, and solving all of the world's problems. The pseudo-polite conversation over a glass of sherry, or even beer for those who wished to appear normal, was very evident.

James wondered about how many such meetings took place in any given year. At least enough to keep the boondogglers fully employed! And then, if they had not done so already, they would form a club to present each other with awards. Awards that none of them deserved. He could almost guarantee who would be the award recipients for the first five to ten years.

As the first day drew to a close, James was ready to return to his room and have a restful evening. Perhaps he would take time away from work and watch a movie on television?

*   *   *

CHAPTER 4

I t was three o'clock in the morning and James awoke with a shiver. The room was cool because he had opened the window before retiring to bed. He still had his warm robe pulled about his body as he moved to the window to close out the coolness of the early-morning air. He called the night porter and requested a pot of tea and toast.

"Very good, sir. I will have it to your room in ten minutes."

James thanked the man and, true to his promise, he arrived ten minutes later with the tea and toast. The porter placed the tray on the table, everything in the correct place, and thanked him profusely, but with dignity, for the lavish tip. He withdrew with the advice that "if sir would be so kind as to place the tray outside the door, it would be collected before five o'clock in the morning."

As he drank the tea and ate the hot-buttered toast, James thought about the words that the woman had spoken to him in his dream, "My husband and I have need of you. Please help us." The words remained clear in his mind. It was not like other dreams where he started to forget the events soon after waking up. These words were clear. But, other than her call for help, there was nothing. Not even a clue. Only the foreboding that the dream might have some meaning about an event that would occur.

Warmed after his tea and toast, he was able to sleep until dawn. And so the conference passed into the second day.

After the usual breakfast of cereal and fruit, he forced himself to the conference and the first speaker, who looked as though he would have trouble coming up with a timely answer for the old "what's two and two?" question. The time passed and minutes seemed like hours. Two hours later, with other speakers, of a similar caliber to the first presenting equally insipid stories, a whole week seemed to have passed!

James could only nod perfunctorily. He had an uneasy feeling. The general feeling that accompanies the onset of a bout of influenza. Muttering expletives to himself at the thought of an attack of the "flu," he tried to concentrate on the speaker. But this was not to be. He knew that he had to leave the room. The feeling of running a high temperature coupled with the near suffocating atmosphere was too much for him.

He stood up silently and quietly left the room. No one appeared to notice. The fresh, cooler air in the hallway helped a little, but it was not enough to dispel his discomfort. He walked quickly to the lobby and took the elevator to his room where he removed his overcoat from the closet and then returned to the lobby. He needed to get away from the crowd and the stifling atmosphere of the hotel.

The hotel lobby was busy. But the smartly dressed men and women hurried by on their business barely giving him a glance, most not being aware of his existence. He felt the need to sit down. Or fall down. The comfortable chair in the shaded corner of the lobby was ideal. And then he knew what was wrong. A bloody migraine.

James had suffered migraines in the past, but he had learned the art of self-control during his sojourn in northern Japan almost two decades before. The technique enabled him to handle a migraine by dismissing it from his mind and from his conscious thoughts. They stopped after a few minutes. Even the threat of a migraine was no problem, as long as he recognized the symptoms.

All he needed was a few minutes' concentration. It was his usual custom to cease his activity and sit in a comfortable position while he focused his mind on a distant object, at the same time thinking of a pleasant event. His heart rate would drop to about fifty-five beats per minute and disgorge the tiny blood vessels in his brain of their pulsating fluid. James knew instinctively that this one was going to be one hell of a doozer that could not be dismissed lightly. The splinters of pain were already shooting through his head and the flashes of light before his eyes were starting to affect his vision.

A clock in the lobby chimed fifteen minutes past the hour. If only he could concentrate for fifteen minutes, he would be all right!

Ten minutes later, as the effect took hold, he had the sudden urge to visit the tower. He did not know what driving force has brought this about, but he left the hotel and hailed a taxi. Perhaps a somewhat more expensive way than the tube to reach the Tower of London, but efficient and less bothersome when he needed to be alone. He sat silently in the taxi, allowing his mind to relax.

At Tower Hill he got out, gave the driver a handsome tip, and received a very hearty "*ta, myte*" in the very recognizable cockney accent that could be translated as "thanks, friend."

The coolness of the air was bracing as James walked away from the taxi and he drew in a sharp breath as the cold air met his lungs. He walked the short distance to the gates that had just opened, paid the entry fee, and walked into the historical site. The Tower Green offered seats, wooden benches where the visitor might rest to soak up the atmosphere. He needed to think and he remembered Will Shakespeare's words, "*Perchance to dream.*"

The moist breeze from the river came up to meet him and a general feeling of well-being traveled through his body. He leaned against the wall to watch the groundsmen cleaning refuse from the lawn that filled the area between the low wall where he stood and the tower walls that had once housed a very large moat.

And then it happened.

He could feel his mind reeling as other sensations entered his consciousness. The sounds became different. Horses snorting at their objection to the bridles. The clang of metal against metal, as though a thousand blacksmiths were plying their trade. The guttural sounds of men as they made their opinions known in another language. And suddenly, he knew where he was.

*   *   *

The odors of the city assailed his senses and the noise from the tower yard as men went about their work rang in his ears. He could hear the sounds of horses, and there was water.

The sensation of her hand on his arm made his whole body tingle. He was showing her for the first time where he spent most of his days when he was in London.

She was not tall enough to reach his shoulder so she leaned her head against his upper arm as they walked through the gate. The acknowledgement of their presence by the guards brought a whisper of surprise to her lips.

"They seem to know you."

"Aye, lass. So they should. I see them every day."

He smiled at the two men. The faintest crease in the corners of their eyes and the slight incline of their heads showed a sign of respect for him.

"Hold on to my arm and walk on the straw. It is spread for the ladies lest they soil their gowns in the mud."

He stopped, turned, and looked directly into her eyes. Her eyes sparkled as she looked back at him. Smiling. The signs of love and affection bridging the gap between them.

A tall man looked at them from a stairway that was raised above the base of the tower yard. He was going into the central building, often called the White Tower. He stopped and looked directly at them, then smiled and nodded his head in acknowledgement of their presence.

Her eyes opened wide. Mouth agape. The words could only come with difficulty. Almost stuttering. The tall man had actually smiled.

"But . . . but . . . that was . . . ?"

"Aye, lass. So it was. That was our king. Edward. Also called Plantagenet. And the third one to bear that name since the time of William of Normandy."

Then he thought that he could hear a guard shouting. At him? His mind started to swim and he knew that the transition was starting. He could feel the gentle pressure on his arm.

* * *

"Sir! Sir!"

James was conscious of his arm being shaken. And yet he was still at the entrance to the tower yard, leaning against the wall. But the voice was different. He felt the hand on his arm. Firm but gentle.

He shook himself back into the present and took deep breaths to clear his head. For a moment the vision appeared so clear that he felt it had been real and he knew that he had been there.

"Sir! Are you all right?"

"Aye. I'm fine."

He felt the coolness of the January air. James knew that it had happened again. He dreamed about being in the past. A continuation of the dreams that he had been having since last year. It was as if his mind was flitting back and forth through time. He could not get used to it. But he had learned to handle it. But now his memories were much clearer. He could now recall most of his dreams.

Then he added to the attendant, "I'm a writer. Just deep in thought about my current book. In order to bring the characters to life, I need to close my eyes and focus on them. It helps."

The attendant nodded in agreement. But the puzzled look in his eyes indicated that perhaps he was not convinced.

James thanked him and continued his tour of the tower. Looking. Thinking. Searching. He thought about what it might have been like to live there, or at least to live close by . . .

And so the remainder of the morning passed in the tower. In thought. In pleasure. There were not many visitors and so he had most of the yard to himself. He walked, making notes and even commenting on his own ideas. Midafternoon galloped toward him when he realized that the breakfast was wearing a little thin. Time for a light tea.

James was pleased with the material that he had collected, but the thoughts that had come to him through his dream were becoming a reality. He could even feel the sensations of being in the past. For the moment he could not think of the time or the place.

It would come back to him.

He shook his head, somewhat tentatively, not wanting to encourage a reoccurrence of his headache. He suddenly felt much better. He paused before taking the small battery-operated tape recorder from his briefcase and started to speak quietly into it, lest he lose the thoughts still in his mind.

He left the tower and, after walking a short distance, he noticed a restaurant named very appropriately after the beefeaters who patrolled the tower grounds. As he entered the restaurant, the warmth enclosed him. He looked around at the almost empty dining room, and turning suddenly, he almost knocked over the hostess who had silently approached from the rear. Her smile and quip, "It was almost a pleasure," brought a throaty laugh from James. He requested a quiet table, somewhat shadowed because of his "flu-type headache," which he had explained to the hostess. Sandwiches, a salad, and a pot of tea were just what he needed.

James left the restaurant almost one hour later feeling much refreshed. He decided then and there that he needed to spend more time at the

British Library. He was thorough in his search for material. When he arrived, he used his reader's pass to get the documents from the shelves. The more he found from the old documents, the more the story started to gel in his mind. Page after page of penciled comments started to fill his notebook. By then it was late in the afternoon and the reading room was ready to close. He would need more time, but at a later date. He thanked the attendant who arrived to pick up and return to its rightful place the last manuscript that he had studied and he left for the hotel.

He arrived back at the hotel feeling much better than he had for some time. The lobby was filled with a variety of visitors, not the least of which were those spilling out of the room from the meeting. He shouldered his way, politely, through the throng of bodies in an attempt to move toward the elevator. And surprisingly, in the midst of all of the noise, he heard the familiar voice.

"Jimmy, my boy. What brings you to this den of iniquity?"

Even before he turned toward the sound, he knew that it was the voice of his classmate, Tommy Smith. More formally known as "The Very Reverend William Thomas Smith, Dean of the Priory Church of Christ and Blessed Mary the Virgin" or known somewhat less formally as "The Dean of Durham Cathedral."

James found his friend, fully garbed with his clerical collar, amidst the noisy multitude and gave him a very warm handshake. Somewhat surprising since they had only seen each other two weeks prior to the current meeting when James had attended the evensong service in the cathedral. But it was a handshake of relief. Relief at seeing a friend. And hearing a familiar voice.

"Dinner tonight, Jimmy? Or are you playing scientist again?"

"Yes, to the first question. No, to the second question, Tommy."

"Greta," Smith referred to his wife, "will be with me. She has been visiting our daughter Alison and should arrive back here at any time. In fact," he glanced at his watch, "her train should have arrived at Paddington minutes ago. So she'll not be long now. Remember? Alison is—"

"At Oxford."

James finished Smith's sentence and added, "Doing a PhD. In church history I believe. I assume that Greta—"

"Is up to date on the events in Bridgeford? Yes she is. And really wants to meet you as my old school friend. The author business is of some little consequence!"

A smile creased the edges of Smith's mouth and eyes as he made light of his friend's worldwide reputation.

"Thanks, Tommy. I really needed to hear the latter statement!"

"Must keep your feet on the ground and head out of the clouds, Jimmy!"

Some members of the crowd had turned to see the two men in the midst of a very animated conversation. Shrugged their shoulders and returned to, for the most part, the pseudo-scientific mumbo jumbo that was so common at these meetings. James and Tommy took no further notice of the mass of bodies.

"Tommy. There must be some luck to your being here . . ."

"It is said that I do have access to a higher authority . . ."

"Really!"

"Sorry, Jimmy. Ecclesiastical humor, you know. Is there something particular on your mind?" Smith asked.

"Aye, Tommy."

"Problems?"

"I'm not sure, Tommy. Let me talk and think out loud at dinner. If Greta—"

"Won't mind at all, Jimmy. At seven then? Here? They do a nice bit of lamb or roast beef and Yorkshires . . ."

"I'm convinced! And please, one question at a time. Yes and yes. Gives us a little over an hour to wash up."

One hour later, James walked from the elevator to see Tommy and his wife waiting in the now almost empty lobby. Smiles, and introductions since James had not formally met Greta Smith, were again exchanged as James looked around.

"Everything all right, Jimmy?"

"Sure, Tommy. Just wondering where the scientific types are."

"A busload just left for a show in the West End."

"Good! The restaurant will be less crowded than I had thought." James gestured toward the restaurant. "Shall we?"

"Fine, Jimmy. Had a nice bit of lamb here last time. And Jimmy my boy, dinner is on me. I'll see to the reservations." James opened his mouth in an animated imitation of a guppy.

"No argument, Jimmy." There was a finality in Smith's words. "This is my treat."

Greta smiled. "He's very determined, you know."

They were seated by a friendly maitre d' in the restaurant located away from the lobby and the main entrance to the hotel. Smith had, as promised, made the reservations and they were led to a well-lit table.

The conversation that transpired was animated as Smith told his wife more details of James's exploits on the soccer fields of Europe and fame as a writer, much to James's embarrassment. And then from out of the blue, as he was wont to do, Smith changed the topic of conversation. Right in the middle of dessert!

"All right, James. Out with it. What's troubling you?"

"And I'm not sure myself what it is. But I do believe that there's something afoot, sorry for the Holmesian slip, but . . ." James shook his head unable to complete the sentence.

"Well, Jimmy, how about starting at the beginning."

James looked at Greta, the question written into his face, but she sensed his worry and answered immediately.

"Don't worry about me, James. I'm as up to date as Tom. Please do go on."

"We'll there's something about the incidents last year that I have not told Tommy . . ."

James took a deep breath, feeling lost for words and knowing that as his thoughts became firm there was no doubt in his mind that Oswald's last promise might be on the verge of coming true!

James allowed himself to dream as he related the moments to Tommy and Greta Smith when he had last seen Oswald, his wife Margaret, and their young son.

It had been a crisp December morning, one of those mornings where the bright sunlight was still not enough to warm the earth, as she lay desolate waiting for the spring. That morning, the thought had suddenly burst force from the recesses of his mind that there was one last task that he needed to perform. As if someone's life depended upon it. And for his peace of mind.

*   *   *

That December morning, more than one month ago, he had walked purposefully from his cottage to an area close by, on the bank of the River Wear. He had taken with him pieces of wood, at the time not knowing why, but it had become obvious, as he has tied them with the string and fashioned a simple crucifix. He had taken his own crucifix from his pocket and the *Liber Usualis*. This version of the prayer book, all in Latin, had been produced by the Society of Saint John the Evangelist and edited by the Benedictines. He had found the book in a used bookstore in Denver when he had lived in the Rocky Mountain region of the United States.

He had forced the wooden cross into the earth close to one of the trees where he stood with the book and crucifix in his hands and he began to recite, in Latin, the order of burial. The night was beginning to transform into day as he quietly uttered the words that are necessary for peaceful eternal life. As the first rays of the sun were starting to bring strong light to the clearing, James started with the words to bless the grave.

"*Deus, cujus miseratione* . . ." (God, whose compassion . . .)

He had felt the tears welling up in his eyes as he thought of this man Oswald. A soldier who was loyal to his king. A man who had saved his life. And a man to whom James felt a closeness. Perhaps even a kinship.

Then he had gone on to recite the masses for man deceased, for the anniversary of a death, and for the absolution. James's upbringing in a predominantly Roman Catholic mining village made the change to the Latin order of service easy for him. The words came back to him and he lapsed into the chants, silently, and reverently.

"*Inclina Domine aurem tuam et exaudi me* . . ." (Bend your ear, O Lord, and hear me . . .)

As he had continued the words of each prayer, he frequently crossed himself, finishing each action by kissing the nail on the thumb of his right hand, in the medieval style. As the sky became lighter, the shadows fluttered and formed before his eyes. The forms had taken human shape. There were three human shadows that took shape. The man he had lately started to call Oswald, in his medieval battle dress as James had seen him before, holding the great two-headed axe across his right shoulder and his left hand resting on the hilt of his long sword, the point gently penetrating the hard, frozen earth.

There was also a woman and a young child. A boy. She had her left arm entwined in Oswald's arm, and the young boy stood on Oswald's left side, his left hand clutching the belt that held a pouch and dagger. There was love and joy in their eyes. The woman was looking at Oswald, and the boy was leaning forward to look at the woman. They all turned to look at James. And that was when Oswald spoke. Physically! And not by the usual mental communication that he had used over the past weeks.

"James Simpson, you who know the language of my father and his father before him, you who know the language of my king, and the language of the church, we can now talk."

The words flowed easily from his tongue, a mixture of words from the languages that would become English. James recognized the Latin, the Norman French, words that sounded as though they were English, but above all he recognized the lilting dialect of the North, and he was able to understand what was being said to him. But how would he reply? The combination of words had been difficult for James to formulate.

James replied in Latin, the best Latin that he could conjure up at the moment.

"*Lingua ecclesiae scio* . . ." (I know the language of the church . . .)

James paused as the man smiled then he continued using Latin.

"But it is many years since I spoke that language. It would honor me if you would speak in the Saxon tongue of your father and of his fathers."

"*Nis naenig swa snotor* . . ." (There is no one so wise . . .)

Oswald lapsed easily into the Saxon language.

"Who can speak the language of his fathers. It is I who will be honored, James Simpson. You have the same first name as my father and as my son," Oswald's head nodded to the young boy, "and the son of my sister Elizabeth from whose line you are descended."

James now recalled that he had breathed deeply as Oswald stated his lineage with a certainty that did not allow any questions. Oswald heard the surprised intake of James's breath.

"Yes. I realize that I may have surprised you, perhaps even shocked you. But I cannot deny what is to be." And then he continued, "You have united me with my wife and son after the terrible sickness that caused us to spend so many years apart."

As the man, woman, and child had looked at each other, James had known instinctively that Oswald was referring to the plague—he knew not which outbreak but he was sure that it may have been one of the summer outbreaks that occurred after the introduction of the plague to Britain from Europe in the late 1340s.

James stood motionless. The words came to him clearly. He was not imagining what he heard. For the first time, James was able to observe the breathtaking beauty of Oswald's wife, Margaret. The thought had sped through his mind and to his surprise, Oswald had looked directly at him and continued.

"She is beautiful, is she not, James? And I thank you for that. Be aware of your woman, James Simpson. She is also very worthy and beautiful."

Oswald's blue eyes twinkled as he looked into James's eyes, as though he knew James's innermost feelings. Feelings that James had not yet identified.

"We thank you for bringing us together again. You are a man of honor, James Simpson. You would have been worthy to stand in battle for my king. We are two of a kind, you and I. We left the villages of our birth to journey to lands that were unknown to us. But we returned to our homeland."

Oswald paused and looked again at his wife and son.

"And you almost died in your machine, James Simpson."

James had cast his mind back to that night of the accident when his Jaguar had decided to leave the slippery, rain-soaked road.

"But," Oswald continued, "it was decreed that you live. By whom I know not. But we can only imagine by someone greater than all men."

All four stood in the heavy silence as James remembered his closeness with death. And then he knew that it was Oswald who had saved him, as he lay in the wreck of the automobile, his eyes closing and his senses fading. He felt a warmth as Oswald's mind probed his own mind, comforting him, assuring him, telling him that there was no cause to worry.

Oswald continued.

"I will not forget you, James Simpson."

"Nor will I forget you, Oswald."

"We have crossed the bridges of time. We will cross these bridges again. And you and I will meet again, James Simpson."

Oswald read James's puzzled look.

"When? I can tell you not. Now, I pass to the other side to be with my wife and son. Enjoy your world that you may one day see mine. Until that day when we meet again and we will be close comrades once more, I will be watching over you, James Simpson. As I have watched over others of my time."

As James looked at Oswald, the woman and child smiled at him. He had become aware of a new sensation of well-being and the thought expressing the words "thank you" passed through his mind. First, in a woman's voice and then in a child's voice. Both voices of the North.

He thought his eyes were playing tricks, but again he felt the reassurance and the warmth of Oswald's strong presence. Then he realized that it was over. The shadows fluttered and began to fade and he was alone once more. A quotation from the Roman poet Catallus floated once more through James's mind as the shadows dissipated.

"*Soles occidere et redere possunt*" (Suns that set are able to come back again).

James knew what had happened over the past months. He had tears in his eyes for the man, Oswald, who had lain in the sinkhole for the centuries waiting patiently to be reunited with his wife and son. All of those years had been protecting the treasure of his king.

James looked up at the blue sky. This was a good day. He smiled thinking about Oswald, about his last words, wondering . . .

*   *   *

James looked across the table to Tommy and his wife. Both were silent. Greta, her mouth open, astonished. Smith his elbows resting on the table, upright, and the fingers of his hands interlocked with his chin cradles on the fingers. Greta recovered her composure and dabbed her eyes with a lace handkerchief. She sniffed.

"James, what a beautiful story. Such a lovely story. A love story. What a man, this Oswald. Is he really a relative?"

Tommy put his hand on top of her arm.

"Jimmy. Coffee?"

Smith nodded to an unseen person and a waiter appeared from nowhere. A pot of hot fresh coffee in his hand.

"On second thoughts, I will have a brandy to go with the coffee. How about you, my dear? James?"

"Sherry for me, please." Greta added, her usual smile lighting up the room as she looked in the direction of the waiter. James took the cue and added, without a smile,

"Aye. Brandy please."

The waiter left to fulfill the order.

"James, I don't know what to say!"

"Then don't say anything, dear."

"It sounds amazing, almost unbelievable, doesn't it, Tommy?"

The waiter arrived with the drinks, placing them carefully in front of the respective recipients.

"Jimmy, being a person of the religious persuasion, I have looked a little into the supernatural," Smith paused apologetically. "Sorry, Jimmy, I should have said 'into the concept of life after death.'"

"No, you are right, Tommy. It is macabre. But I know that it happened. I have thought of nothing else for the past month. I've not even told Kathryn."

"How is the dear girl?"

"Very well."

"Now James, what about Charlie Kirkby?" Smith asked then continued, "He's a man of the cloth in the old-fashioned sense, very educated, anything of interest in the historical sense and Charlie will delve into it. Sylvia also. Although their specialty is somewhat different."

Tommy looked at the ceiling, deep in thought, took a sip of his brandy, and then as though the warm fumes had stimulated his brain.

"If I remember correctly, Charlie had some evidence at one time of strange happenings in the area."

Tommy thought again as James and Greta sipped their drinks.

"Do you remember the movie *Brigadoon* where a village in the Scottish highlands goes to sleep each night and each night lasts one hundred years?"

"Aye, Tommy, but what has that got to do with my situation?"

Greta also stared at her husband, wondering where he was leading them and why bring dear old Charlie Kirkby and his wife into this.

"Well, it seems that not too long ago, Charlie was inspecting the headstones at the back of the cemetery, the oldest part so he told me . . ."

"Yes. I know it. The headstones go back to the fourteenth century."

"Well . . . according to Charlie those stones have hardly aged at all, considering the weather and all in these parts . . ."

"Thomas? Are you suggesting something magical?"

"No, my dear. But it's one of James's words that struck me, let's see now. You said that he used the words 'as I have watched over others of my time' and it just seems a little strange that . . ."

Greta broke into her husband's thoughts. "Isn't that a little far-fetched, dear?"

"Possibly, my dear, but let me add something else. Charlie gave himself a task. He decided to test the qualities of the stones by rubbing dirt into them, without desecrating the burial places of the dead of course."

Another sip of brandy.

"The very next day, the stones were as clean as they had been before meeting with the dirt! Charlie, thinking a prankster was in the area or since there had been a rain shower that night, decided to repeat the venture the next night. This time he remained at his post in the cemetery, Sylvia being out of town," he added the last words by way of explanation for Charlie's behavior.

"I don't think Sylvia would agree with such a hair-brained scheme."

Smith looked at his wife, smiled, and continued as if she had not spoken.

"There was no rain and Charlie stayed awake all night, a little cold, but again the same result. And my dear," Smith looked at Greta as if to emphasize his point. "Sylvia has since confirmed the cleanliness and longevity of the stones."

Smith smiled in triumph and finished his brandy. He finished the still-warm coffee in one gulp and turned to motion to the waiter for refills all round.

"But Tommy, how do you account for the fact that neither Charlie nor Sylvia thought to mention this to me when I discussed some of my adventures with them?"

"I might suggest that if you talked with them now and gave them the same detail that you've given us, it might jog their memories."

"Point well taken, Tommy."

James turned to Smith's wife.

"Greta. What do you think?"

"Well, James, coming from an author of fiction, who knows? I do not believe that anyone could think this out as a work of fiction. I believe that what you've told us really did happen. In which case," she took a very deep breath before continuing, "you have relayed some very interesting happenings to us, but for this man to cross time, it just seems so strange!"

"Rare would be a better word, my dear. But who knows when there is a purpose." Smith paused and then the idea came to him. "That's it, Jimmy," he exclaimed. "If what he said is true and destined to happen, he will attempt to meet with you again. At that time, I suggest that you try and find out his purpose."

Smith looked thoughtful for a moment, as if thinking out his next words.

"To everything there is a season and a time to every purpose under heaven."

"Pardon?"

"In Ecclesiastes, Chapter 3:1, 17, we read, *For there is a time for every purpose and for every work.*"

"I can appreciate the biblical quotes, Tommy, but do you really think there is something in what he said?

"I do, James. But let's recap. From what you've told us, here is a man who dies before his time. Even though, I might add, he seems to have had a full and productive life. Nevertheless, there have been frustrations in his life. The early death of his wife and son. The plague. An extremely loyal man who was, through a freak accident, prevented from carrying out his last mission. A man who, by any stretch of the imagination, was a rare bird for his time . . ."

"A man, James," Greta added as Smith sipped his coffee, "who could read and write and who seemed to know many, if not all, of medicinal practices of the time. A seemingly very intelligent person, James. And a very strong-willed man. Maybe even a little too strong-willed. It may even be this strong will that led him to the situation where you met him, James."

"You may be correct, Greta, but I'm still in a daze over the whole incident. The question that occurs over and over again is, why me?"

"That you may never be able to answer, James."

Greta frowned as she appeared to attempt to answer her own question.

"The only clue that we have, Jimmy, is that it does appear that you are related to Oswald. Distantly. There certainly seemed to be no doubt in his mind!"

"And," James offered, "I did talk over, without going into detail, the idea of genetic inheritance with Phillip Spiller at Dryburn."

"The young resident?"

"Aye, Tommy."

"Seems a bright lad."

"He is. He did give me some insights into inheritance through generations, as if the DNA code planned it that way!"

"Well, James, it seems to me that the next step is to follow Tom's recommendation and discuss the details with Charlie and Sylvia. They may be able to offer something."

"Aye. I'll do that, Greta."

James allowed the words to trail off as he became engrossed in his thoughts. Thoughts of Oswald. Thoughts of the well-preserved headstones of the older graves. Thoughts of watching out for unusual events.

"Well, Jimmy. What say we call it a night?"

"Sure, Tommy. Greta, it was a pleasure. And it sure was helpful to talk this out for once. And I will confer with Charlie and Sylvia."

They finished the coffee, declined more drinks from the waiter after which Smith signed the bill to his room. As they stood up from the table, James shook hands with Smith. Knowing that they'd be in contact within a day or so of having returned to Durham. He leaned over to Greta and kissed her on the cheek and she reciprocated with the gentle pressure of her hand on his arm.

James stepped from the elevator, leaving the Smiths to go to the eighth floor. As he walked along the hallway to his room, the frown became deeper and deeper. If what Smith had said was true, there must be a reason. He felt as though he was in for a night without much sleep.

*   *   *

That night, James heard the voice again. Gentle, whispering, requiring his presence. Where? James knew not. He was confused. And then sleep caught up with him. He was surprised when he awoke the next morning at five thirty, refreshed.

He had his material and he was going home.

*   *   *

CHAPTER 5

J ames sat in the restaurant waiting for his breakfast. His mind was still in a turmoil. The conversation with Tommy and Greta Smith at dinner had opened up thought after thought. The dam had burst and his mind was flooded with thoughts about Oswald. About himself. His role, if any, in Oswald's world. He was confused.

He was being drawn back to the tower. There was something about the magnetic effect of the tower that he did not understand. But he would find out.

His breakfast arrived, delivered by a smiling waitress. He looked at the breakfast and wondered about calorific intake. When he had finished eating, he sipped his coffee amid the general chatter and sound of utensils, signed the chit, left a generous tip, and went to his room to collect his belongings and prepare for the day ahead.

He was determined that he had to discover the whereabouts of his dreams. He felt that he was back in medieval England. Was it merely one of those flukes of nature where old memories see the places of previous lives? He could not offer himself any answers to these questions or any explanation.

His preparations were soon completed. The early train to Durham was his goal, with the enticing odor of fried bacon and the other tasty delights of an English breakfast.

He was anxious to see Charlie and Sylvia. The latest developments made it imperative that they talk again, in detail and in confidence.

He arrived at King's Cross Railway Station early. He would rather be a lot early than a little late!

James was a people watcher and would always be. This allowed him to add realism of everyday life to his stories. People rushing around, trying to get from here to there in the quickest possible time.

It was possible to compare an English main line railway station with any one of several American airports that he remembered so well. The dark suits, carry-on bags, briefcases, baggage wheels, smartly attired businesswomen wearing dresses or two-piece business suits of more sober tones, the continuous sounds of the luggage carts as they moved an assortment of bags and boxes around the station, the telephone banks in perpetual use, and the cell phones seemingly molding a hand to an ear; if only Alexander Graham Bell had known what a can of worms he was opening! Train crews, their bags full of schedules, rules of the line, and other sundry items and regulations, moved to sleeping behemoths.

Yes, this was comparable to any major airport, be it London's Heathrow or Gatwick's Airport, Chicago's O'Hare, Atlanta's Hartfield, New York's John F. Kennedy and La Guardia, Boston's Logan Airport. He had seen them all, and they were busy at any time of the day and often at night. What could be busier than Denver's Airport during a snowstorm when air traffic was prohibited from landing and taking off and several thousand passengers had to use the concourses as campgrounds?

The sounds of different languages as though the Tower of Babel existed once more on earth, even with the different dialects and accents of the English-born natives.

And there were also London's finest! Navy-suited policemen, austere guardians of law and order, serious, with little tendency to smile, walked steadily, often monotonously through the crowds, always vigilant.

*   *   *

The train started to move slowly away from the station. Picking up speed. The movements of the people remaining on the platform and waiting for another train became rapid and jerky. The early days of filmmaking shot through his mind. And then the train emerged from the cover of the station into the dull grayness of the morning.

Breakfast was announced on the public address system as James made his way to the dining car. He recognized the white-coated steward from several previous journeys and greetings were exchanged.

Having already had breakfast at the hotel, he purchased a strong cup of coffee, made with hot milk. He carried it back to the seat; the fragrances from the eggs, bacon, sausage, fried bread remaining in his thoughts. These same fragrances made other passengers decide that breakfast was not such a bad idea after all. Once seated, a silent prayer that his careful eating habits would not be forsaken, James sipped at the coffee.

He settled into his seat, but it was a restless journey. His mind aflame with thoughts and ideas. The stops at Doncaster, York, and Darlington were uneventful. He looked out of the window, almost with unseeing eyes barely conscious of the busy world at each of the stations.

The visions had returned. He knew not why. But they seemed to be so much more intense than they had been and he saw everything clearly. But he could find no reason for his current state of mind. He knew that he was being called. But why?

And then at 10:39 the train pulled into Durham, exactly on time and some three hours and nine minutes after it had left London. James dismounted from the train amidst the scurrying of other passengers to board. Business travelers to Newcastle and points north, perhaps to Edinburgh.

The Jaguar sat just where he had left it four days previously. The powerful engine fired immediately giving life to the car. Within moments, or at least it seemed that way, he had moved beyond the outskirts of the city and was following the well-contoured lines of the A690 to his home.

*   *   *

When he arrived at the cottage, there were two items that he needed to attend to almost immediately. First, a phone call to Alice. She was not in her office, but he was assured that she would call him back as soon as she returned.

The second was a call to Charlie Kirkby, remembering Tommy Smith's suggestion.

"James, my boy. Welcome back. You must have received my message that I left on your recorder."

James had not even checked the messages in his haste to make the two calls. Charlie noticed James's pause and continued.

"Well, have I got an interesting story for you? Sylvia is just bubbling to tell you the news and get it off her chest. How about dinner tonight?"

"Well, Charlie, I'm all ears, so can you . . . ?" James's words trailed off leaving the question hanging within the electrons of the telephone line.

"More than my life's worth, James, old son. Sylvia will have my head if I so much as breathe a word. It really is something for your ears."

James felt tired and the last thing he needed was another late night. But this seemed important to Charlie.

"Sure Charlie. What time?"

"Sixish."

James knew what this meant. Please arrive at 6:00 p.m. and after a glass of sherry, dinner would be served before seven o'clock.

"Sounds great, Charlie. But please give me a hint."

"Mustn't spoil Sylvia's surprise, James, but I do have permission from my dearly beloved that it concerns the situation that you were going through late last year. Appears to involve your man, Oswald."

James's sharp intake of breath told Charlie that he now had James's full attention.

"Heck of a clue, Charlie. I'm not sure I can hold on till six."

"Patience, James. Besides, as I have indicated, I'm under oath to Sylvia not to breathe another word before you show up here. See you at six."

"Six it is, Charlie."

James placed the receiver into the cradle, suddenly remembering that the message light was flashing. Three messages.

There was a welcome back message from Kathryn informing him that she had a client visiting on Friday morning. To complete her message, she added that she would see him at Charlie's later in the evening. He thought of Sylvia playing matchmaker again. If only she knew!

The second message was from Charlie and had nothing further to offer than a request to call as soon as possible. James shook his head at the timing of the two calls. Something definitely was going on! Alice Campbell had also called with more news about other documents that she had found.

"Strange thing, James," Alice had said in her message, "They all seem to point to the fact that our man lived for quite a while. Perhaps well into the fifteenth century. Must have been quite an old codger when he finally died. Please call as soon as you get back."

There and then, James made a promise to himself that the next time, he would listen to his telephone messages before he made calls.

The tone signaled the termination of the message as James laid the receiver back into its cradle. He made a note on the pad near to the telephone and his mind returned to the focus of his thoughts. Charlie's phone call.

Then he worked on the latest manuscript to incorporate the tape recordings of his day at the tower.

Darkness had settled on the countryside when he stepped into the shower, wondering what Charlie and Sylvia had in mind for the conversation this evening. They had been full of surprises and information in the past.

Why not now?

*   *   *

Instead of dressing immediately after the shower, James wrapped himself in his full-length hooded robe, poured himself a generous helping of Talisker, a smoky single malt whiskey, and sat in front of the fire.

As if to stimulate his thoughts, he moved his toes around in the thick warm bedroom slippers. His thoughts went first to the meeting in London and then to his experience at the tower, but his mind forced him into areas of mental darkness.

The flickering flames from the fire caused the shadows to dance before his eyes. And suddenly, he was very tired. He put the whiskey glass onto the table, switched off the light, and lay back to relax, fearing that a migraine was imminent. He was about to swallow two aspirin tablets as a precaution but decided against it. He remembered putting the small bottle of tablets into the pocket of his robe. He would try his other technique to remove the migraine, the self-hypnosis technique that he had learned some years before when migraines had occurred with alarming frequency.

He focused his eyes on the mantle above the fireplace, allowing pleasant thoughts to percolate though his mind. After a few minutes, he sensed that he was in control as his fingertips traced the decrease in his pulse rate and the slow beat of his heart as it approached fifty beats per minute from the usual eighty. Once more, the technique worked.

A smile spread across his face. He would not have a migraine this time. He would rest, his mind in tune with the shadows from the flickering flames. Knowing that he would return to full consciousness soon.

However, there was something else, an awakening.

And then, nothing. Only darkness.

*   *   *

When the darkness began to clear, his senses told him that not all was as it should be. During the periods of self-hypnosis, he had never before lost consciousness.

The fire still caused the shadows to dance around the cottage and a quick check of the time told him that only a few moments have passed. It was not yet five o'clock. He still had ample time to dress before he left to have dinner with Charlie and Sylvia. He was not sure if Kathryn would call for him or meet him at the vicarage.

The benefits of using only one vehicle were well pursued by Kathryn and by himself on occasion, as it gave an opportunity for both to leave together. A few moments alone before bidding each other "good night" were always welcome.

And then it happened!

His eyes were drawn back to a shadowy figure. The image shimmered in the firelight, wavered, as a blur before his eyes, then it materialized. It was a woman. She seemed to glow and her eyes were staring, almost vacant. The woman looked directly into his eyes and smiled. He was uncertain for a moment but then he recognized her.

"Margaret? Good Lord. It's you!"

"Aye, James. You are the one I seek. Not having the power of my husband, it took time. But I knew you were here. I searched for your thoughts."

She smiled and reached for his hand, taking it in hers. He could feel her warmth as the tingling sensation of her touch took over his whole body.

"I searched for your thoughts. And then you came to me."

The self-hypnosis to deflect the migraine! The sense that the procedure was different this time. That had been the sensation that he had felt! He was about to say something but her words cut him short.

"Aye, James. And I do apologize for the discomfort in your head."

"She's reading my mind!"

Margaret smiled again.

"Yes, I can read your mind but I chose only those thoughts that are of interest to me. There are those thoughts that need to remain private!"

James breathed a sigh of relief.

"I can also sense some of your feelings and emotions. That is how I searched for you."

He felt her pull him to his feet, but there was no effort involved. It was as if she was bidding him to rise by using her thoughts.

"I see that you are appropriately clothed. I hope that you will not be too cold."

"Why do you ask? Where are we . . . ?" James's words trailed off as he became unable to finish his question.

"My husband and I have need of you, James. A short journey."

James shrugged and returned to the bedroom where he took off the robe, put on his sweat suit, and put the robe back on. Margaret waited for him and firmly took his hand. It was as if he could sense the beat of her heart and her blood pulsed through his veins.

"Come, James. We have been waiting for you and I have searched for you these past days. I have seen the Priory Church of Christ and Blessed Mary the Virgin as you know it and it has changed greatly from the time of my husband and I," she paused as if she was looking at the city all around her and then she continued, "if this be your Durham, it surprises me since it is much changed from the Durham that my husband and I knew. Now, let me show you our Durham, a part of our world that my husband did promise to show you."

James stood next to her, holding her hand, unmoving. He felt that he should try to move, but the lead weights that anchored his legs to the ground would not respond to his attempts.

She took several steps away from the fireplace, still holding his hand and the leaden weights left his feet. Her dress rustled as she walked ahead of him, turning to smile, gently, as if to reassure him that no harm would come to him. Her fragrance was that of flowers in the spring. Fresh and pleasing to the senses.

The room and its contents disappeared in a silent mist. The lithe figure that he had seen only once but that he felt he knew so well led him through the mist, to the gray light at the other side.

But it was not to be so easy. He felt that he was being buffeted by mighty winds. Abruptly the present was gone and felt as if he was floating near the ceiling of the room. Then, there was pain. Or perhaps it was discomfort. As if every strand of his very being, the material that those of a medicinal persuasion call DNA, the molecular building blocks that dictate the physical and mental make-up of life forms was being stretched to the limit. About to snap. But deeper within him changes were occurring within components that there were smaller than the smallest components of the living cell, smaller even than the intertwined strands of DNA, within the individual molecules, and within the spinning orbits of the atoms themselves. And just as soon as it began, it ceased.

*   *   *

He appeared in the street, as if by magic, in a sudden brief, shimmering burst of light. And yet his coming went unnoticed by the occupants of the street. As he looked around, the sights and sounds assailed his senses. The filth was everywhere.

But his arrival was not unnoticed. The large brown rat foraging in the dark corners on the outside of the houses sensed his presence. It had eaten little that day, only a nibble here and there from the garbage piles that had not offered much in the way of sustenance. Hunger made the animal bold.

It approached him as he stood, thinking, wondering where he was, as he supported himself against the wall of the house. Hovel might have been a more correct description. Where was she? Why had she left him alone in this strange, vile-smelling place?

The rat, emboldened by his lack of motion, approached him, wondering what he was and why he had suddenly appeared where there had been no sign of life before. It sniffed the air, sensing a lively meal.

It was then that she appeared. From where, he knew not. But Margaret was with him again. She reached out, barely touching the rat. The rat hissed once, teeth snapping, before it leapt into the air and then its loose, limp body fell to the earth, dead.

James was suddenly shocked out of his soporific stupor. This was not the dream of his efforts to relieve himself of his migraine. Good God! This was real. He was almost attacked by a bloody great rat!

Margaret turned and smiled as if to reassure him again and to answer the question forming in his mind. Margaret, the wife of Oswald, spoke. Oswald, soldier of King Edward III of England, was her husband and James was back in the England of the fourteenth century.

"My Oswald is tending the ailing son of a friend. He suffers from fever and we fear that he will not recover."

She continued to lead James by the hand. Her pace quickened as they approached a house. Nothing that James could recognize as a house of his time. The building stood shoulder-to-shoulder with its Siamese twin neighbors in a dim, narrow, unlit street. The foul odor of garbage was almost overpowering. James wanted to gag but he was able to control himself sufficiently, not wishing to cause embarrassment to himself.

As they entered the house, James could not help but feel the thrill of the unknown as well as the cold sweat of apprehension as he followed Margaret. She was greeted by a group of stiff, middle-aged people dressed in somber colors of gray and dark brown, and a brittle thin little man with a face like a hatchet and a faint wispy beard across his upper lip and chin . . .

An involuntary cough escaped from James's lips. It would have gone unnoticed, except for the stares of the occupants. Their eyes opened wide, not at Margaret but at the man with her. James Simpson was not what they expected. His robe, passable by Margaret, might be acceptable to some but was not recognizable as the clothing of the day. These people of the late fourteenth century would never understand!

James sensed Oswald's presence before he turned. He had been leaning over a bed, more correctly a bundle of straw, his attention focused on the occupant. And James heard the familiar, guttural tones that he remembered from not so long ago.

"Ah, James. I bid you welcome. We have at last found you. My dear Margaret has been searching for you. Did I not tell you that we would meet again?"

James was about to fill the air with numerous questions when Oswald answered.

"She now has the powers that I have. She can contact you when she wishes, although her first attempts have taken a somewhat longer time than we thought. She is now my protector!"

"Oswald, my friend. Why . . . ?"

Eyes opened even further. The four words that James uttered were not spoken in the English of a man of the time.

"Did I not tell you at our last meeting that I would show you my world. This is it. This is the Durham that I know. This is the Durham of your dreams. But," Oswald looked at the young man lying on the straw pallet, "he has the fever that I cannot control. When I was summoned here, I believed that I might save him but now . . . I fear that it is the fever of death."

James looked at the youth. He was pale, febrile, and looked close to death. He was dressed in a heavy woolen nightshirt that was soaked with sweat. His eyes appeared almost sightless and the shiny moisture glazed his features. Without thinking, he took the small bottle from his pocket. Two tablets, grandsons of what had used to be known, in the twentieth century, as aspirin tablets but now available under a variety of other trade names.

"Here," James proffered eight tablets in his hand. "Give him two of these now with a drink of water that has been boiled recently."

"Thank you, James. We do have such water already available at my request."

Oswald cradled the young man's head under his arm and helped him swallow the tablets with a mouthful of water.

"He will need two more of these tablets. Every," James hesitated not sure of his next words, "four hours."

"Do not worry, James, I understand."

Oswald whispered something unintelligible to the other occupants of the room. They nodded, understanding, but never letting their eyes leave James. His strange clothes. His even stranger speech. His appearance with Margaret. Obviously someone who was known to Oswald and his wife. But such a strange man. And now offering two small white candy pieces to their dying son and brother. But Oswald followed his command without a word of protest. This same Oswald who, with his wife Margaret, would appear when he was needed. Always when disease or death was imminent.

Oswald took James by the arm and moved him away from the sick youth.

"My friend, there is little we can do here now. Perhaps we should leave and return in the morning. The family has their instructions from me and they will follow them to the letter."

James now had the chance to survey his friend for the first time since he had arrived. The blond hair was gathered at the back of his neck. The surcoat was very white and clean, as though he had not changed since James had first seen Oswald in his visions not long ago. And Margaret, just as James had seen her on that December morning, still beautiful to the eye.

"James, my friend, did I not tell you that I would show you my world? It is as though my meeting you was just the beginning. It seems that we," he looked at Margaret, "have been released from a prison. Death no longer holds us. I can, with my lovely wife, command my body and spirit to move over great distances at will. I have spent my time since I left you healing the sick. It is a good feeling, James, much like when I helped heal some of my men after the great battle near Poitiers. But there are some things that I cannot explain. I have seen different visions in my travels. Visions of machines that are strange to me."

Oswald paused.

"Margaret accompanies me in my journeys, it is as though it has been decreed that we will never be separated again. For that I gave thanks to our Lord."

James was about to ask a question when it was answered without effort by Oswald.

"Yes, you may ask about our son, also called James. He is well. A little too young to travel with us. He remains in the care of my parents."

The young boy had been very evident when he had seen Oswald and Margaret fade into the mists along the banks of the River Wear, a short distance from his cottage at the edge of Bridgeford.

"It is some time since we first met and we have much to discuss. Come, we will walk together."

Oswald turned to his wife. No words were spoken, but James sensed that he was asking Margaret to remain at the house.

*   *   *

Oswald and James stepped from the house into the cold street. Oswald had given James a heavy cloak that had been hanging near to the door. James was unsure where to start his questions and was about to begin when a man stepped from the shadows, menacingly, knowing that he had partners-in-crime lurking in the shadows to assist him if needed.

The man stared at James who looked back at him. A dirty, unshaven, foul-smelling wretch who made James wonder if evolution was still at work and had much ground to cover between this fourteenth-century man and a man of the twentieth century. Then James noticed the foot-long blade, as if it was an extension to the man's arm, reaching toward him.

Without uttering a word, Oswald stepped up to the man, knocking the blade to one side as he did so, and drew his sharp dagger across the exposed throat. There was a slight hissing sound, the man stared in disbelief, clutched his hands to the open, blood-spouting wound.

As the man stared at Oswald and James in startled disbelief, he realized that his life was over. He attempted to look to the shadows for help, but his companions of the night forsook their dying companion and melted even further into the shadows.

The man's last breath escaped as he fell to his knees and the fixed mask of death descended upon his features.

Oswald took James by the arm and led him toward the river where the cooler air might help him recover from the shock. James could only sense Oswald's voice in his ear; calming, reassuring him that all was well. Telling him that in this violent world even a man of medicine had to protect himself against the vagabonds and cutpurses who roamed the city streets.

James shook his head as Oswald cautioned, "James my friend, if you are to accompany me on these journeys, you must learn that I live in a violent and less protected world. You have the machines that kill. We have no option but to look a man in the eye as we take his life." Oswald continued,

"I do have need of you. There is about to happen a very strange event where I need your assistance. The outcome will decide the fate of England."

Somewhere in James's mind a thought sent electrical impulses to the rest of his brain. Warning him of the outcome of changing history.

"Quick, James. I have need of you now."

Oswald took his arm and they ran to the bank of the river. A man had been dragged from the river and looked to be near death.

James bent over the victim who lay face down on the footpath and James wondered if the man had drowned or died from contact with the polluted river.

James reacted as if electrified. He turned the man's face to one side, knelt beside the prone form, and checked the man's chest. He detected barely perceptible breathing. In the meantime, like moths drawn to a flame, human forms had appeared from the darkness.

There was a sharp gasp of anguish from the bystanders, unsure of James's actions, but still willing to watch. Wondering who would be custodian of the body and the clothes, especially the shoes, when death was announced. In the meantime, they would be concerned, and self-serving. Ready to pounce at the thought of a body no longer needing clothes. But James's actions had thwarted their plans.

James continued his actions in spite of the comments that came to his ears, his mind focused on the man lying before him. He straddled the victim's legs and pressed into the abdomen with a quick upward thrust. And then it happened.

Water and the meager contents of the man's stomach—his last meal had not been too nourishing from what James saw—poured from his mouth onto the earth. Then the man coughed and moved. A few more minutes and he was sitting up, coughing, spluttering, and alive much to the astonishment of the onlookers.

Oswald took James by the arm to lead him away, having decided that this was as good a time as any to depart from the scene of what would later be embellished around the hearths to be a miracle, or sorcery, perhaps a little of both but to James's detriment. The news of his accomplishment would travel on the wings of rumor and rather than being able to go unobtrusively on his business, he would be the source of wonderment and awe. Perhaps even persecution!

Oswald led James farther along the riverbank, toward what looked, in the night shadows, to be a fort. Of course, James thought, the Castle of Durham.

"James, you have seen part of my violent world. But there are gentler parts to it. And as I have told you, I have need of you here. And I hope that you will give me your help."

"Aye, Oswald. You have no need to ask."

"Good, then let me explain to you over a warm drink what I believe will happen and why I have need of you."

*   *   *

CHAPTER 6

He must have visibly jumped. The sound of the banging on the door was loud. Too loud to be made by a hand. He ran to the door almost tripping over the folds of his robe. And there she stood. Log in hand, ready to strike again.

"Kath, what are you doing?"

"I've been knocking for three minutes and I was worried that you . . ." She did not finish her sentence as James smiled and took the log from her hand. He laid it on the ground and guided her through the door into the warmth.

"Sorry, Kath. I fell asleep. Strange dream."

"Are you all right? Thought I'd call in and we'd go the vicarage together."

James stared back at her. Unblinking. Fixing her in space with his dark brown eyes.

"Aye, lass. I'm fine."

He cleared the fog from his brain as he helped her out of her coat. His first thoughts, as he tried to focus his eyes, were "She's wearing a see-through blouse and miniskirt!"

Kathryn was actually wearing a slim hunter plaid skirt with its red, white, navy, and yellow stripes laid onto a dark green background. Her gray V-necked jacket covered a black silk blouse.

He shook himself out of the dream world.

"What time is it?"

"Twenty-five minutes after the hour."

"Which hour?"

She blinked. Wondering. Then deciding that he must be a little groggy after his deep sleep.

"Twenty minutes after five. Are you sure that you're all right?"

"Aye, bonnie lass. I'm fine."

"I am worried about you, James. I hope it's nothing to do with the accident?"

She referred to the accident before Christmas in which he had suffered what was initially thought to be a severe head injury but which had, miraculously, healed.

"Sure. I'm OK, Kath. Just getting over a migraine."

"We . . ."

James's select thoughts intruded and became words.

"I know. We are due at the vicarage at six."

"How about a cup of tea?"

"Sure, Kath. Sounds great. You make the tea. I'll get ready."

"Need any help?"

Her humor was returning and he playfully pulled her to him and kissed her.

"No need to bother yourself, Mrs. Stainsby. I'll manage fine. Thank you. This time, anyway!"

James smiled as the color rushed to her cheeks and the effects of the deep sleep began to wear off. But the visions that remained with him could not be shaken. As he dressed in the bedroom, he could not forget the dream. He even wondered why he was wearing his sweat suit under the robe. The thoughts came back to him. All were so real. Almost too real. Margaret. The house. Oswald. The youth lying on the straw pallet. Then the idea struck him and the thought thundered through his head. Quickly James plunged his hand into the pocket of his bathrobe and took out the small bottle. A quick count of the contents would . . .

"Damn!"

"Really, James."

Kathryn had entered the bedroom carrying a steaming cup of tea.

"Sorry, lass, but . . ."

There were several tablets less than he remembered earlier in the afternoon when he had first decided that aspirin might ward off the migraine. But he had not taken any. But he had given some of the tablets to . . . He paused trying to collect his thoughts. And then he remembered that he had given the tablets to Oswald for the young man on the straw bed.

"But surely, the dream . . ."

"Here you go, James. A nice hot cup of tea."

Kathryn placed the tea on the dressing table in front of him.

"I also took the liberty of bringing you a few biscuits. You might feel the slightest bit hungry. And knowing that a glass of sherry or two may be the order of the evening before we eat."

"Great idea. Thanks."

"If you need anything else . . ."

The words were left hanging in the air as she departed. A few minutes later he turned to the tea and the biscuits that were welcome refreshment.

He left the bedroom. Ready to escort Kathryn to dinner. And wondering what he could relate to Charlie and Sylvia that was believable. He answered his own question.

"Nothing."

*   *   *

Charlie and Sylvia welcomed James and Kathryn warmly with beaming smiles on their faces. Sylvia had the inevitable look of matchmaker on her face. Pleased that James and Kathryn had arrived together.

The conversation from the inevitable glass of sherry to the coffee after dessert was the usual friendly chatter. Charlie and Sylvia showed more than a passing interest in James's new manuscript, although James was loathe to pass on too much of the plot. He had an author's superstition that talking about the plot before the book was complete would bring bad luck.

Finally, after dinner as Kathryn and Sylvia busied themselves clearing the table, having refused help from James and Charlie knowing that any such help would be minimal, they left the two men drinking their coffee in the study. It was at this moment that James decided to get to the point.

"OK, Charlie. What is the big story that you wanted to share with me? You never did follow up on the story that you had for me at the Christmas party. Then there was your brief telephone message earlier today . . ."

"Got your interest, I'd say."

"You bet!"

"First my story."

Charlie did not omit any of the details. He included his inspection of the headstones in the oldest part of the cemetery. The fact that they had hardly aged at all and when he had tested the qualities of the stones by rubbing dirt into them on several occasions the stones were as clean as they had been before meeting with the dirt!

Finally he was finished. James sat silently. Even though James had now heard the story from Tommy Smith in London, he still wondered about its meaning. Charlie did suggest that they take a look at the headstones at some later time when the weather improved and the remaining snow cleared.

"Might even find some carved letters if we do a rubbing?"

Charlie referred to the placement of paper on the stones and rubbing with a piece of charcoal that might help emphasize any carved letters that were too faint to read. James agreed. Then he asked Charlie to go on with the further news.

"Well, its Sylvia's story," Charlie added, "not mine."

The door opened and Kathryn entered the room with Sylvia just two steps behind.

"Timing's perfect, m'dear," Charlie said. "James is most anxious to hear your story."

The sound of wood crackling on the fire was the only sound in the room. The ladies helped themselves to coffee, cream, and sugar from the silver service on the sideboard. James was ready to scream as both ladies took the time to sit correctly in the two remaining comfortable chairs.

James sipped his coffee and waited impatiently. He sensed that Charlie was not the melodramatic type to build him up for no reason. The thought rushed through his mind, "Patience, Jimmy, me old lad."

Sylvia placed her cup and saucer on to the nearby side table and looked directly at James. Charlie played with his pipe and managed to light it at the first packing. A notable achievement.

"James . . ."

Sylvia's voice finally split the thick silence, like a hot knife sliding through butter. Every eye in the room was now focused on her.

"A few days ago I decided to give the church a good going over, with the cleaning ladies."

She referred to the ladies of Bridgeford who made sure that the church received a weekly clean.

"Well, there was the usual chatter and news. Some of the ladies were after all the members of the Knitting Circle who saw everything, heard everything, and talked about everything." She continued after the brief pause.

"But to cut a long story short, I may have found something of interest to you," she said. She sipped her coffee as if renewing her energy for the remainder of the story.

"As I was cleaning out a difficult to reach spot behind the altar, I noticed a strong breeze in my face. A little too strong when one considers that the rear of the altar is sheltered. There is sufficient space to squeeze behind the altar and I am not sure why our ladies have not noticed the breeze before."

The ubiquitous grandfather clock that seems to be present in every vicarage study decided to suddenly chime seven thirty. Kathryn's attention was so focused on Sylvia's words that she appeared to rise three feet out of her chair without the benefit of moving her legs.

Charlie looked at the clock with some annoyance, fiddled with his pipe mumbling about a useless timepiece that had seen its day. James continued to stare at Sylvia in anticipation of her next words, sensing that he was about to hear something of extreme importance.

"Well, not wishing anything of interest to be heard on the winds of the air," she said referring to the members of the Knitting Circle, "I decided to investigate later. Charlie was in Durham for the afternoon so there was my opportunity."

"Steady on, m'dear, I'm not that much of a . . ." Charlie interrupted but did not finish his sentence as James and Kathryn looked at Charlie, willing him to be silent.

"Well I decided to imitate your hero, James," in response to his puzzled frown she added, "you know, Sherlock Holmes."

James nodded in agreement, wondering when they had ever discussed the famous detective.

"Wondering what Mr. Holmes would do, I went back to the scene and found out the direction of the breeze using the old lighted match trick."

Charlie interrupted again. "I nearly fell out of my chair when she told me. Could have been a gas leak. Scared the wits out of me, it did."

James smiled at Charlie's outburst. He was correct for there were many pipes underground that were a mystery, even to the energy companies, and who knows when one might rupture.

"Well anyway, it turned out that there's a double-headstone-size block behind the altar and . . ." Sylvia did not finish her thought but looked at her husband, "your turn Charles."

"Well, after inspecting Sylvia's find, we decided that the stone might be moved. It took almost an hour of scraping the cement with a fine blade," Charlie added as an afterthought, "ruined two of Sylvia's steak knives. After a while I finally got the stone to move."

Being the archetypical raconteur, Charlie had to fill his pipe again, much to Sylvia's feigned annoyance. James looked up at the ceiling, mentally thanking an invisible being for this stroke of luck and asking for more patience!

"Well, to cut a long story short, the entry led to what I believe was a crypt at some time in the past . . ." Charlie turned in his chair and stared straight at James as if to emphasize his next statement. "And would you believe it, James, the place appears to have been used as a library or accounting room. There are papers, and I think, shelves that appear to line the walls from floor to ceiling!"

"Sometimes, Charles annoys me." Sylvia looked at her husband. "I told him not to go down the stairs. But he had the bull by the horns and would not listen . . ." She left her sentence unfinished as an unspoken warning to Charlie.

"Couldn't resist it, m'dear. Spirit of adventure and all that."

"But to go venture into an unknown that is no better than a hole in the ground!"

Kathryn looked at James and murmured, "Reminds me of someone I know," as she recalled James's account of his descent into a hole with a rope around his waist and Billy Walker as his only safeguard. She left the comment unfinished but gave James a look that would have stopped a charging bull in its tracks. Kathryn was well versed in the art of looks and James knew it!

James's brain was galvanized into action. He recalled that Alice Campbell had guessed that the soldier-scribe might have been a prolific writer.

"Penny for them, James."

"Just some wild thoughts, Sylvia. Alice Campbell and I have come across some interesting writings by a man whom we believe may have been a soldier as well as a scribe . . ."

"I remember, you did mention it to us."

"Aye, and I was wondering . . . Although the writings could be any age from the fourteenth century to now. I am hoping—Charlie, did you . . . ?"

"It just so happens that I did take a small piece of material."

Charlie offered the material to James. It was a piece of vellum with some marks that were difficult to identify. Possibly writing.

James held it up so that the lamp on the table next to his chair gave extra light from behind the piece of vellum. The marks were faint but there was nothing identifiable. The letters, if that is what they were, would hold their secret for many more centuries.

James remembered Alice's comment about the soldier-scribe liking to doodle as if testing his quill pen, and he was hoping that there would be recognizable writing.

"Nothing that I could make out, James."

James nodded his agreement.

"Although," Charlie continued, "Sylvia does believe that the vellum is no later than fifteenth century. So it could be older material, perhaps fourteenth century, that has been scraped clean for reuse."

James helped himself to more coffee, the last cup having disappeared down his throat in the excitement of the moment.

"Let me summarize, Charlie. You've found a cryptlike underground storage area that you did not know existed."

Charlie nodded as he puffed the smoke into the nether regions of the room.

"If memory serves me correctly," he said "an older church usually had a crypt only if it was to be used for burial of members of a family. Especially the family that owned the land."

"Then what you're telling me, Sylvia, is this might be the burial crypt of the Bosford family?"

"But they obviously know nothing of this crypt, James," Sylvia responded. "There has been no mention of it in any of the records that I have seen."

"Then Sylvia, me bonnie lass," Sylvia and Charlie smiled at James's use of the dialect, "it might go even further back. A piece of fifteenth, possible fourteenth, century vellum is an interesting find."

James sat back in the chair as a silence descended upon the room. Hours seemed to pass in the silence of the next two minutes. And then the peace was shattered as James leaned forward to Sylvia and the words burst forth.

"De Boise. Ranulf de Boise. He was the lord of the manor. Alice Campbell has some evidence of such a character."

Sylvia looked at James puzzled.

"There is very little history about this place. The major works seem to be within the Bosford Library . . . as if there was an attempt . . .," Sylvia's eyes lit up as she continued James's thought, "to maintain secrecy about Sir de Boise and his family, the goings-on or whatever!"

Then came the smile of recall and recollection from her training.

"Of course. He was the mystery man who suddenly appeared as the founder of the Bosford family and their estate. Little is known of him. A virtual unknown man who was given land in the palatinate of Durham!"

She placed her forefinger on her lips, allowing the thoughts to solidify.

"Sylvia, my dear . . ."

But she would not allow Charlie to interrupt her thoughts. The light in her eyes came on again as her ideas crystallized.

"Must have done his king a whale of a service! And I would guess that he may have been a confidant of Edward to receive such a gift since most gifts to relative unknowns were an acre or two here and there but nothing so splendid as the estate seems to be, or may have been in days gone by. And in a palatinate!"

She pursed her lips. Charlie looked at her, proud, and trying to encourage her thought process. Kathryn and James had their eyes transfixed on Sylvia.

"Ah, yes! There also appears to have been another man who was close to de Boise and to the king."

"John, Duke of Lancaster?"

"Possibly, Kathryn." James said. "But somehow, we may be looking at someone else, a third party not of the royal family."

The vision he had of a woman on his arm in the yard of the tower and the tall man who raised his arm in their direction! James recognized Edward and he believed he knew the identity of the other man. Oswald! James was on tenterhooks. He fidgeted in the chair. Kathryn knew what he was about to suggest, which made her nervous. She spoke with feeling.

"It's too late tonight. And I assume that the entry has been closed?" Charlie and Sylvia both nodded in the affirmative.

"Then I suggest, to put James's mind at rest, we take a look at the first possible opportunity."

After some back and forward discussion, they looked at each other and Charlie concluded the negotiations with "Saturday it is. Tenish? Here?" All were agreed.

James smiled at Kathryn as Charlie opened the cabinet and took out a bottle of Glenkinchie. A single malt from the lowlands of Scotland that was soft, restrained, and had a touch of sweetness. One of the few that Sylvia would touch and he was sure that Kathryn would enjoy.

"A wee dram of this will put hair on your chest . . ."

Kathryn and Sylvia laughed at Charlie's response. James laughed so hard that he almost fell out of the chair. The tension was leaving his body. The feeling of well-being took over.

Finally it was time to leave. James and Kathryn bid their goodbyes to Charlie and Sylvia. James took Kathryn to the cottage to pick up her Range Rover and watched her as she drove off.

Soon he was sitting in front of the rejuvenated fire, a cup of hot milk on the table next to the chair as the flames found their newfound life from the fresh wood that he had placed in the grate as soon as he entered the cottage.

He could hear the rich tones of Oswald's voice, the soft silkiness of Margaret's laughter. And he knew that he was not dreaming. He had experienced their presence. As they had experienced his.

It had been real. His mind started to wander again and then he was seeing things other than the furnishing in his room.

*   *   *

The knife was honed to razor sharpness. And it was clean. The extract of the poppy had done its work and the man lay quiet on the table. His attention was focused on the task at hand.

The physician washed the area of skin around the wound with a solution of vinegar, knowing that it would sting. But the man only smiled. He opened up the wound and started to remove the broken knife blade. It was deeply embedded in the muscle of the man's thigh, next to the bone, but accessible. The blade had broken on impact and had folded itself under the skin and lay at an acute angle to the large leg bone. Were it not removed the man would surely die from infection from the dirty blade. Any slight movement would cause the loss of too much blood.

The physician's eyes did not wander from his task as he carefully cut through the layers of flesh to find the offending piece of metal. But his mind was active. Thinking of why he was here. In this place.

The knowledge of human anatomy was scanty indeed. How else would it be possible to probe the body for a piece of metal and remove it to save a life? Despite the doctrines of Mother Church, there was the need to cure men of wounds without allowing them to die.

Successive monarchs and their bishops were very concerned about the spread of knowledge among the lower classes. The use of medical techniques was threatening to prolong the active life of people and spread knowledge away from the crown, the church, and the royal physicians who might otherwise be known as superstitious quacks. Control would be lost with this spread of knowledge and the shackles of fear and ignorance would be loosened.

But he continued on with his work. Cutting. Cleaning. Swabbing and sewing until the bleeding was stopped, the wound was clean, and closed. He washed the blood from the man's leg with warm water and again with vinegar.

The man, in spite of being in pain, raised himself on to his left elbow and looked straight into the eyes of the physician.

"I know not who you are. Yet you have a look of someone who was close to me but is no longer of this world."

The man looked at the physician through squinting eyes. Trying to focus on his face. Then he continued.

"But I do know that I still have a leg that will be useful to me and not whither and die like the limbs of so many of my comrades."

The man's breathing was labored and there was tiredness in his voice as he spoke through tight lips. The effects of the poppy extract were wearing off. The man had been lying under the care of the physician for one hour. He was coherent once again. The authority started to return to his voice.

"But I believe that you are a good man. Not one to be afraid of the superstitions of the priests. I thank you. Go now and protect yourself. I sense the soldiers of the prince bishop approaching. Probably instigated by those idiots who call themselves medical men. I would not trust them with a dead cat, let alone with a live man!"

The man smiled weakly and watched the physician as he washed his implements in hot water, wrapped each one carefully in a piece of goatskin, and placed them in his satchel. He then washed his own hands before he opened up a smaller pocket of the satchel.

"Why is it that you cleanse everything if you are to use it again under similar conditions of blood and dirt."

It was the physician's turn.

"Sire, I can only tell you that dirt in a wound causes it to fester and the limb to turn black. And then you will lose the leg and your life. Because it is clean," the physician indicated the vinegar-soaked cloth, "you will feel some discomfort because of my crude methods of cleaning the wound. But rather some discomfort than the pain of losing the leg and then death."

"Your tongue is strange, of the North I suspect, and not unlike that of my friend, but begone, Physician. I must get word to the king of your deeds before those idiots of medicine color his mind. Before you leave, Physician, your name?"

The physician smiled again. He did not answer the man's question. Preferring to continue as though the question had not been asked.

"I will leave this extract of tree bark, which is called Witch Hazel, to apply to the wound lest it begin to fester. You should not walk on that limb for one week, or at least until I see you again. I need your word that you will follow my instruc—," he cut the word short knowing that a person of this man's position did not take instructions from a physician and added, "advice."

The physician decided that he should not give instructions to the man. It would be most unusual to do so and he could not predict the consequences of such actions.

"You have it, Physician! Now, who are you?"

The physician picked up the satchel and prepared to leave. He looked around at the man before he opened the door to the winter coolness.

"You shall know me when I return. I shall find you and make sure that your wound heals. I will see to it that you recover, Sir Ranulf de Boise."

The man looked puzzled that the physician should know his name.

"Begone if you must, Physician." Then he added in a much softer tone. "And I thank you for saving my leg."

The physician smiled, bowed slightly with a nod of the head and then he was gone as the soldiers of the prince bishop burst through the front door. They made a move toward the back of the house but de Boise stopped them with a motion of his hand.

"You will find no one there. Return me to my home and thence you have my leave to return to your bishop."

And so it was done.

*   *   *

His head ached as segments of the dream shot through his brain, scorching and searing their way from back to front.

James raised himself from the chair where he had fallen asleep, but a few moments ago. The fire was still cheery and alive in the grate. But the odor? Then it came to him. Vinegar! His hands reeked of the smell. He looked at them, noticing the red coloration under his fingernails. Blood!

As he stood in the shower cleansing the vinegar and the blood from his hands and fingernails, James recalled all of his last sensations. It was not a dream. Nor could he call it a vision. It had been so real. And was real. He had the proof. Just as he had the proof of the number of aspirin tablets left in his pocket.

James's last thought as he lay in bed was that there must be a reason for the transposition of his body and mind into a bygone era. Six centuries before the present time!

He heard the soft silky and gentle voice reassuring him that all was well. He was needed and they would come to call him again.

Soon.

*   *   *

CHAPTER 7

James walked into Alice's office promptly at ten. She was standing looking at books on the shelves. Hearing the sound of the tap on the door followed by the door opening, she turned and greeted him with a smile.

"Good morning, James."

"Morning, Alice. Coffee? Or do you wish to talk first. I am very keen to hear your story."

"Coffee and let's talk at the same time."

"Where?" He looked directly at her and saw the word forming.

"Crypt?"

"Can I leave my briefcase here?

"Of course, James. It will be safe in my office. Anything of value in it?

"No, just notes. Shall we?"

He held the office door open for Alice and once outside of the library, they walked the short distance, passing through a corner of the cloisters, to the crypt where they were soon greeted by the aroma of fresh coffee. Upon entering the Crypt Coffee Shop, James saw Vera alone behind the counter. He smiled.

"Morning, Vera."

"Good morning Mr . . . . Ooops, I'm sorry, Dr. Simpson."

James smiled. Obviously Vera had been making inquiries about his title, he looked back at her. "It's OK, Vera. I won't break if you call me James."

Vera then turned to Alice with a smile and a cheery, "Good morning to you, Dr. Campbell."

They ordered the coffee. Vera informed them that the scones were fresh out of the oven. James raised his eyebrows as he asked.

"Scone, Alice?"

Alice nodded and he ordered two scones to go with their coffee. He followed Alice to a table that was in a corner and set aside from the other tables. They both sipped the hot liquid while munching on the fresh buttered scones.

James decided not to push Alice for the information. He allowed some time to pass for her to come back down from the emotional high that had been forced on her by a week or so in London. He knew that she would be going over her findings and organizing the thoughts in her mind. The trait of any self-respecting researcher. She put her cup onto the saucer and allowed her fingers to trace the edge of the rim. Playfully. But her eyes told James that she was still deep in thought.

James sat silently. No words passed between them for several moments. He excused himself, obtained two cups of fresh coffee, and sat down. He knew that she was ready to talk and nodded his head indicating that he was ready to listen.

"You have my attention, Alice."

"The purpose of this meeting is to get you acquainted with the latest developments in my research."

She sipped the fresh coffee. Then a furrow appeared in her brow as she continued to think out the approach to her findings.

"Well, James, as you would say, let me give you the bottom line first."

"I'm all ears."

"When we first met, can you recall that I showed you several manuscripts that had been written by an unknown fourteenth-century scribe?"

"Aye." But there was no need for James to recall this at all. The manuscripts had been on his mind since that first day that Alice had shown them to him.

"Well, here's the punch line. This scribe, as you will also recall, has cropped up again as author of some more writings that I've located."

James sucked air through his teeth. There was no doubt in his mind that the scribe was Oswald. But he did not want to betray his thoughts. He feigned surprise and curiosity.

"So?"

"Strangely enough, these writings are a little different. I am certain that they are the writings of the same scribe but the contents are much more of a medical nature. A lot less of a diary than his series of manuscripts. And James, believe it or not, some of his writings are among the uncataloged works in the storage vaults of the British Library. Just found them last week. I have also found a reference to such a man as our scribe in another document that I'm working on and attempting to place in time. The document I am researching is a page that contains some of Geoffrey Chaucer's scribbling. Until I identify the handwriting, the author remains a mystery but, whoever it is, he or she seems to know our scribe."

She took another sip of coffee. She was almost breathless.

James said nothing. He did not even touch his coffee.

"James, I had believed that this man died in the late 1360s, perhaps 1370."

James knew exactly when.

"December 11, 1369, to be precise. A Monday, I believe. Old calendar, of course," he thought to himself. But he did not dare speak the truth, as he knew it. That would really take some explaining, and Alice was not ready for it yet.

"So Alice," James asked, "you have found that the man died and there were more writings. Probably by someone else with a similar background?"

Her eyes were fixed as though she was recalling the pages that she had seen and worked on in the British Library. Her focus was intense. James knew the signs and waited for Alice to continue.

"The writings I have located are in the Dean and Chapter Library and in the British Library." She waited for a moment for her words to take effect then she continued. "The pages that I examined last week are written in the hand, or perhaps I should say, by the hand of our soldier-scribe-medic. But James and I consider this to be significant in terms of our dating of this man's death, these just-discovered documents were written in the 1420s, at least fifty years after we had thought that our soldier-scribe had died."

James closed his eyes for a moment to fix in his mind what Alice had just told him. He could feel his heart pounding as he tried not to show any emotion. The blood was pounding in his head and he could sense his old injury, the injury to his head that had almost killed him last year. And then he felt as though a cool hand had been laid on his forehead. He felt, rather than imagined, the smooth touch of a woman's hand and he knew that

Margaret was close by, in his thoughts. As if to comfort him, he heard Margaret's gentle words as they passed across through his mind, "Do not worry, James. All is well."

Alice's voice snapped James's attention back to the present. She noticed the furrow in his brow.

"James, are you all right?"

"Yes, Alice. Just a passing thought or two."

He heard Margaret's whispered laugh, "Oh, James, you are so like my Oswald," and then her presence was gone. Alice's voice was steady and resolute as she continued to talk to him across the table.

"Well, James, do you remember that I can pick out scribes from their handwriting like the old Morse code operators could pick out each other from the tapping of the keys?"

"Yes. But . . ." James was about to ask a question and his eyes narrowed and his mind was in turmoil as Alice's comments registered. The thoughts flooded back to James's mind. Especially the comments about "seeing my world" which James had not taken to be a promise but now started to appear more so. The latest attempts at contact! Were these attempts by Oswald to reach him across the centuries? "Oswald. Alive beyond his time? There must be some mistake!" And then he responded to Alice.

"Yes, I do remember."

Alice had noticed his puzzled expression.

"James! What is it? You seem distracted."

"Sorry, Alice, just another passing thought. Got a little sidetracked with my own mental meanderings."

Had he looked into her eyes, he would have realized that she did not accept his explanation. There was something going on "out there" and it made him nervous indeed!

James could not understand the idea of Oswald living beyond his time. He knew that Oswald had died on that fateful December day in 1369 in a sinkhole that was located just a short distance from his cottage. He knew that Oswald had visited him. He had seen Margaret and heard her voice. But accepting that Oswald, who had died, was still living was not acceptable to his scientific mind. All that had passed before and up to this point had been dreams or his imagination. Or had it? To his limited knowledge, on the basis of a very brief and dangerous visit into the sinkhole, there were no skeletal remains in the dark depths. And now, Alice's findings brought turmoil into his mind. He stroked his forehead with his right hand, as if in deep contemplation of Alice's words, and then he asked her to continue.

"James, some of the things I'll tell you are repetitive, but I do need to give you the story as I have discovered the various parts, and in the correct order."

He nodded, knowing that it would be far from repetitive and very organized.

"You know that I have the ability to identify the scribe and date documents almost within five years of when they were written!" She continued. "Well, the scribe that I identified from records in Durham always fascinated me. He was not a monk, the usual background of many scribes, but from his writings I always assumed that he was a soldier with some medical background. In fact, as you know I have tended to refer to him as a soldier-scribe-medic because of the contents of his writings. He describes wounds from the viewpoint of a soldier as well as a healer. Unusual, don't you think?"

At the sign of her raised eyebrows, James nodded to show that he was in agreement. Alice was on a roll.

"Such a man must have been an enigma. A soldier who could read, write, and also act as a medic when needed. I found this to be a challenge, since one does not often come across such men throughout history. An issue that is definitely worth researching!"

Alice took a sip of the almost depleted coffee as James decided to speak.

"So let me recap to this point. One. You discovered a scribe. His writings, the pages that you saw in Durham, indicate an interesting, perhaps unusual is the better word, background. Two. We have assumed that he died in the late 1360s or early 1370s. Or at least he seems to have disappeared. But why did we assume that he died? We do not know the answer."

"James. I must answer. And you cannot have known this."

James paused, toyed with his coffee cup, and looked at her, indicating that she should take up the conversation.

"There is a letter in the Documents Section of the British Library that has an apparent connection to this matter. A certain Ranulf de Boise who resided in the area during the late fourteenth century and who may be a forerunner of the Bosford family wrote a letter to King Edward, the Third that is, informing Edward of the death of his most trusted commander."

James groaned inwardly. He knew most of this from his own experiences with Oswald's visitations and hoped that he would not have to go through the thoughts and experiences again.

"The man died in an accident. Apparently after days of heavy rain, the River Wear, somewhere close by where you live, turned a little awkward and our soldier-scribe-medic was drowned. Or lost. Perhaps in a cave-in of some sort. The document indicates that, if I can recall the words of the incorrect Latin grammar, *humus habeit*, that is, the *earth has him*. So I am assuming that it may not have been a drowning."

Alice was determined to tell all.

"I knew nothing of de Boise until late last week, just before I called you. And I did not even connect him with you-know-who. It was almost as if by accident that the thought came to me."

Alice paused again. Sipped the last of her coffee.

"You remember the scribe's sign, Saint Cuthbert's cross in a large circle" James nodded.

"De Boise made reference to this in a document to King Edward and I was able to put two and two together."

"And you came up with our soldier-scribe-medic?"

Alice nodded in agreement.

"Well done, Alice." James appeared to think for a moment before he continued. "So our man was well placed in the circles of the notables. But where does this lead us?"

James was curious. How far had she been able to go in her deductions. He was hungry for the information.

"But there is more, James."

"Go on, bonnie lass."

"I looked for more references to him. And I even found more of his writings, some contemporary with those in Durham, others from a somewhat earlier time frame. Apparently he was writing shortly after the

Battle of Poitiers, that is, after September 18, 1356, and continued to do so for many years afterward, until his death or so-called death. At least that is what I thought."

She paused for effect. James remained silent, not wishing to spoil her moment.

"Even considered writing another thesis. This man was becoming more fascinating by the minute."

"And you found more of his work?"

"Certainly did. The writing by the same hand with the same scribe's mark, Cuthbert's cross in a ring."

"Good for you, Alice. So what's next?"

"What's next as you put it may rock your socks. In the later writings, please note, James, I said later, he is more medically inclined and he refers to the king."

James sensed that her punch line was about to hit him in the face.

"The king that he refers to takes three forms. The first is Edward. Obviously, Edward III. King of England from 1327 until 1377. The victor of Crécy and Poitiers and the king at the time when our soldier-scribe-medic lived. But then the story takes a twist and we have a problem.

"The second king that he mentions is Richard, *Ricardus, secundus nomini*, Richard, the second of that name. But there is more. He also mentions another king, *Henricus, quartus nomini*, Henry, the fourth of that name. Our scribe also makes reference to knowing about the marriage of John of Lancaster to Katherine Swynford. That happened in 1394! Now we seem to be talking of time periods several decades after the soldier-scribe's apparent death. There is even a suggestion in some of the writings of a baby king! The only one that I know of was Henry VI, baby son of Henry V, who became king upon the death of his father on September 1, 1422, at the ripe old age of nine months!"

"And you're certain of this, Alice?"

"I'd bet my . . . well . . . whatever . . . on it. That is our man. That very same man who appears to have fought at Poitiers, perhaps Crécy also, and who disappeared for some years in the late 1360s, who we assumed had died in an accident somewhere in the vicinity of Bridgeford and perhaps quite close to your home."

"This must be quite a man."

"Of course, James, me bonnie lad," she said, imitating his expression as she sipped more of her coffee, "quite a man."

She thought for a moment, her lips exploring the rim of the cup.

"Do you realize that if he had disappeared for three decades or so, and then reappeared in the early fourteen hundreds and having possibly fought at Poitiers, perhaps Crécy also, he would be about seventy, assuming that he was born . . ."

"In 1330!" James finished her thought.

"James! How did you know?"

"Just a wag."

"A wag?"

"A wild arsed guess. Intuitive, if you will. Writer's intuition!"

"Sometimes, James, you never cease to surprise me. How did you know that I had estimated the same time, give or take a year or so, for his birth?"

"Oh, just . . ." James did not complete his response but Alice did.

"I know, a wag."

"Aye."

"But anyway, James, do you see my point?"

He nodded and finished his coffee as she continued.

"For a man to live in that time until he was seventy was possible but unusual. What makes it more interesting is that there is no sign of aging in his writing. The steadiness of his hand is remarkable, and it is as though he had a vision of the future. He speaks of medicines that cure fevers. And believe it or not, medicines in tablet form. As well as medicines that are uncharacteristic of his time, medicines that are made from different chemicals and not from herbs. Of course he does not call them *chemicals*; he uses the Latin words *remedia quimica*, which is an early way of saying *chemical remedies*."

Alice frowned as she attempted to put her thoughts together. James took the opportunity to add a thought of his own.

"He may have taken a colloquial version of the Arabic words *Al Khimiya* that means chemistry. *Quimica* is not too much of a stretch of the imagination to change Arabic into Latin, and the words do convey the thought of medicines."

Alice added, "But it is clear that he is not talking about herbs or herb extracts."

She noted the look of surprise on James's face and mistook it for disbelief.

"Perhaps I'm being too literal here, but how would you, James, translate *salix remedium?*"

James looked suitably blank and shook his head in answer to her question.

"Remedial salix or aspirin!" Alice exclaimed as she answered her own question.

"Come on, Alice, do you really think that he used aspirin tablets? In his day and age?"

"Of course I really think that. I did some research this past week and I know that our friend Hippocrates, a fifth-century BC Greek for whom the Hippocratic oath is named, wrote about a bitter powder extracted from willow bark that could ease aches and pains and reduce fevers. The active extract of the bark, called *salicin*, after the Latin name for the white willow, *Salix alba*. And so," she continued, "why would our soldier-scribe-medic, I will add the last word to his description, not know of aspirin?"

"You may have a point, Alice." James responded in agreement with her logic knowing the truth behind Oswald's use of aspirin.

"James, I know that there are holes in my conclusions but my instincts are strong."

"Never mind, follow your instincts."

Her findings were a surprise to him. Even he had not expected her to discover any part of Oswald's background. Other than what she had gleaned from her readings of his manuscripts in Durham. And her conclusions that he appeared to have lived beyond 1369 were a surprise, although shock would be a better word!

He needed to think. She was not available for lunch. But rather than wait until next week, he offered to return to her office in the early afternoon. She agreed. He made the decision quickly. He took his briefcase and left her office.

*   *   *

Instead of a sit-down lunch, James ate a sandwich quickly in the Crypt cafeteria and retired to the cloisters to think. He had found in the past that the cloister area that surrounded the central lawn with its statue of Saint Cuthbert was an ideal place to relax and cast his mind over their conversation and update his notes. As he sat in silence, collecting his thoughts, alternately making notes and staring at the statue of Saint Cuthbert, the words formed in his mind.

"Alice, me bonnie lass, you may have strayed into the territory of the mind that you and I know nothing about." James continued his thought, "This may be one very large can of worms that you have opened!"

His mind focused on Oswald and his apparent life after death. Assuming that death, as James knew it, had occurred. Had not Oswald talked with him and mentioned the day of his death? Of course, James remembered that conversation. So, something else was afoot. The thought passed through James's mind, "Oswald, my friend, what are you doing to me?" and was immediately answered by the words passing through his mind, "You will find out soon, James."

The characteristic sounds of Oswald's voice filled James's ears as if to answer his question. The words were so close that James imagined that Oswald was standing next to him. Had he half-turned on the seat, James would have seen the dark hazy shadow against the wall that swirled and disappeared as the sounds of the footsteps of other visitors to the cathedral could be heard approaching.

James sat still and closed his eyes. He wondered about his mind and his sanity. Had he really recovered from the accident before Christmas that caused a massive head trauma and that had, mysteriously, healed itself overnight while he was in the hospital? He could find no answers. His eyes felt heavy and he drifted into sleep, with a look of peace on his face.

Passersby were not surprised at the man sitting on the seat catching a few moments' rest before facing the workload of the afternoon. Was this not the purpose for which the cloisters were built all of those centuries ago?

James awoke ten minutes later refreshed and feeling much better. Oswald's words had brought tranquility. He felt relaxed and there was a calmness within that he had not felt for many years.

*   *   *

When James returned to Alice's office, she was in a state of highly agitated excitement. Unusual for her and James knew instinctively that she must have discovered more information.

"James, as we were talking this morning, I remembered a collection of papers so high," she indicated an imaginary pile three feet high using her hand above the desk, "that I needed to examine. Hence my urgent need to spend an hour or so alone while you were having lunch."

James did not offer to tell Alice that he had taken a small lunch and sat in the cloisters for an hour, and he was not ready to tell her anything about Oswald. He needed her unbiased opinions on the matter and did not wish to cloud or bias her judgment in any way.

"And I've found more of the same. Nothing really new but confirming what I've already deduced. Something else, though, a reference to an item I believe I've seen in a document in the Dean and Chapter Library."

James could see the light in her eyes. And he knew that Alice was excited at the prospects that lay before her.

"With this new pile of material, I'm just starting here. Another hour or so studying my notes and then sorting out the pile over the weekend."

"Alice, if you need any help, I am available"

"No thanks, James. I need to handle this on my own. No offense to you and no disrespect to your abilities. I just need the time alone," Alice added by way of explanation, "to form my own opinions. Then I can offer them to you."

James nodded to show he was in agreement. He also needed a break and was anxious to get back to his notebook computer and the manuscript.

"Good luck, Alice. Let's talk on Monday or whenever you are ready."

"Thanks. And James,"

"Aye?"

"Thank you for listening to my ramblings."

James retrieved his briefcase and they said their goodbyes. After he had turned away and was closing her office door, he muttered, "Ramblings indeed!" Alice was as close as anyone could be, himself excepted, to knowing about Oswald's life. Could Oswald have lived beyond his apparent death? How did this tie in with his previous sensations of hearing voices and seeing shadows that formed from the darkness. He thought of his previous private comment.

"A can of worms. A very large can of worms!"

*　　*　　*

The journey back to his cottage seemed to take longer than usual in the Friday afternoon traffic.

"Steady on, Jimmy, me lad." James needed to focus on his driving, thinking that he did not need to be in another accident. "Might not be so lucky this time."

Once in his driveway, he switched off the powerful engine. He gathered his belongings and walked into the warmth of the cottage. The temperature was well above the background temperature that he maintained during periods of his absence. The fire was well stocked and lovely. James looked around, wondering, tensing, ready to meet the intruder. And then she appeared.

"Tea, James?"

"Kathryn, there are times," he gave her a hug and kissed her lovingly, "when it is so nice to see you. I thought that someone . . ." Without finishing his sentence, he looked around as if searching for something. "Where is your vehicle?"

"James, you are crushing my," Kathryn paused for effect, "scones."

The twinkle in her eye left no doubt about the double meaning. But she did wave the baker's packet at him that she was carrying to the table to where the plates and cups were set. As Kathryn placed the scones on to a plate, James took off his overcoat, set down briefcase, and then she continued.

"Nonky Wood is doing a quick oil change for me. Have it ready in an hour. He dropped me off here and took it to his garage." Then she frowned. "You thought that I was someone else? And who might that be, may I ask?"

He saw the playful but almost guarded look in her eyes and decided not to follow up any further.

"I just was not sure." He smiled. "But seeing you is like seeing a vision."

"James, you do say the most wonderful things!"

"OK, tea?"

"Aye, lad."

They smiled at each other, playtime was over. Her tone took a serious turn as she asked the question.

"Now, what have you been up to, James, me old lad?"

Between sips of tea and mouthfuls of scones, James told Kathryn about the visit to the Dean and Chapter Library, Alice's findings, and the implications of her comments. He consulted the notes that he carried in his briefcase to refresh his memory.

As they cleared up the remnants of the refreshments, Kathryn conveyed to James that she was very uncertain what all of this could mean. At that point of the conversation, they heard the sounds of the Range Rover in the drive. James stepped out of the door and invited Nonky in for tea. Nonky declined because of another job that was awaiting his attention. Kathryn announced that she did have to visit her office in Willington and would see him tomorrow, on the way to the visit to the vicarage and hence to investigate Charlie's discovery in the church.

She kissed James on the cheek and went to the vehicle. Nonky surrendered the driver's seat to Kathryn and they were soon disappearing down the lane in the direction of Bridgeford.

James was alone. Wondering what to do next. Why not a change? His new novel would occupy his time for the next hour or so. He set up the computer and started to enter information and more of the text. He had already described the alchemist and was now at the stage where he was allowing the character of the man to take over. The events came naturally as he kept in mind the simple questions.

"If you lived at that time, Jimmy, me boy, how would you handle the situation without modern knowledge? What would your instincts make you do?"

And so the manuscript grew. As the night wore on, tiredness began to impose itself on his eyes and weary body.

After a refreshing shower, he lay on the bed to think about the story but Morpheus, the god of sleep, decided to take over and his heavy eyelids closed.

And James started to dream once more.

*   *   *

CHAPTER 8

James dreamed that he was alone. The images were vividly expressed in his mind. He was in a city. It was night and he was cloaked by the darkness.

As he walked through the almost deserted streets, he could hear scuffling sounds in the alleys. Once he heard a muffled curse and then a groan as though someone unknown was breathing his last. The groans continued, getting weaker and weaker. But he was not sure of the origin of the sounds.

He wondered that it might not be safe to walk alone in the suffocating darkness. He was sure of the continuous dripping rain which soaked him to the skin as he trudged along the muddy, filth-strewn streets to . . . where? He knew not. Perhaps his home. The rain fell from the dark skies and poured off the rooftops without remorse, as though some unseen rain god took pleasure at his discomfort.

The aching cold seemed to creep into every muscle and bone of his body. After a time, he sensed warmth, as if a fire burned brightly somewhere near and he moved closer to find the hungry tongues of warmth.

Everything was still dark. There was no light from the heavens and he was alone in a mysterious place. Then the darkness cleared burst and he found that he was wearing clothes of a style that was unknown to him. A light shone ahead from a window of a house. He shivered and moved toward it, and the warmth.

He could see the dim outline of the castle and the cathedral on the hill, realizing that there would always be activity and the lamps that offered light to the soldiers and night workers would spread their faint glow to the heavens above.

His satchel was slung over his shoulder as he moved quickly and silently through the darkness. He could sense the instruments in his satchel, each one individually wrapped in soft cloth, and moving in time with his step. He had further work to do. His walk brought him to the northern gate. The soldiers looked at him carefully, recognized the physician, and waved him into the *intra moenia*, the space between the outer and inner walls of the castle-cathedral fortifications. From there he walked until he passed through another gate, where he nodded to the soldiers, who allowed him to enter the inner bailey. From the gate, he walked toward the central stone building—the keep that was the last line of defense against invaders who might have been so fortunate to get this far. His instincts told him that such an event would never happen and that the castle and cathedral of Durham would remain unconquered for the rest of time.

In the last remnants of his dream, he remembered that he was the physician who had been called to attend an emergency.

*   *   *

And then he suddenly awakened to the dawn of a new day. It took James a few minutes to realize where he was and the time of day. And which day? He had to squeeze his eyes shut as he realized that he was in his cottage and in his own bedroom.

It was Saturday. The early-morning light was not full of any form of benevolent promise. Rather, the promise of snow. The dull gray clouds threatened to deposit their cargo at any moment. The first Saturday in February. Of course it would snow!

His dream of the night before remained a dim memory. It had ended just as soon as it had begun. And there had been no apparent indication of the meaning or reason for the dream. A physician going about his business . . .

After the usual morning exercises followed by a shower and breakfast, James had entered his thoughts, as best as he could remember them, into his computer. Knowing that they would be useful at some future time.

The light tap on the door brought him back to the present.

He had heard the sounds of the vehicle moving into his driveway. The door opened and Kathryn entered. Smiling. Cheeks red with the cold.

"James. Busy again, but what else is new!"

He stood up and moved to help her remove the heavy sheepskin coat. His eyes wandered up and down her well-fitted slacks. Creased to perfection and fitted to perfection. She turned and saw his eyes taking in all of the details!

"James, please be a dear and pop your eyes back into their sockets!"

He did. Slowly.

"Could not resist the view of your rump."

"James, I am not a horse!"

He decided to change the course of the conversation.

"Cup o' tea, lass?"

"Aye, lad."

He was surprised, but smiled at her lapse into the Northern vernacular, instead of the usual "yes, please." But her voice had that pleasant ring to it that took away some of the rough edges of the dialect.

They sat with the mugs of tea cradled in their hands, and Kathryn looked straight into James's eyes.

"OK, old lad."

James fixed her with an icy stare. He remembered the use of the aging word from yesterday.

"Ah touched a nerve, did I, James? Well other than your bristling at the use of one word, you have something on your mind. Don't deny it! I can tell from your expression. Come on out with it."

She took another sip of tea.

"Well, Kath, you sense that I do need to talk. So, here goes."

James related the general content of his dreams but decided against going into the fine detail. Kathryn took a deep breath at the end of his story. Sipped her tea for a few moments and shook her head slowly.

"James . . ."

"Well, you got the name right anyway."

"Shush, James, it would be too easy to suggest that you have a vivid imagination," Kathryn fidgeted and ran her fingers along the creases of her slacks. She paused in her thoughts. It was as if he could see the brain activity through her eyes. And then she spoke.

"It seems to me that there must be a connection between you and this man Oswald. Some connection that appears to be much closer and much more necessary than him being a mere forefather."

She tapped her long fingernail on the side of the mug, thoughtfully, and shook her head.

"Let's have some more tea while we think about it some more," James suggested.

James poured the boiling water on to the leaves and as they stood together in the kitchen.

"James, what do you think of these dreams?"

"I've no idea, Kath. It seems that there is a need for me. If what I am supposedly hearing is true. I now know how Joan of Arc felt when she heard her voices."

They sipped the tea standing, without moving, staring out of the window as the snow started. Each new flake seemed to know where it was going and wound its way to the earth. The cold ground welcomed the snow as more and more flakes settled to form a white blanket.

James looked at his watch.

"Are you ready to go to see Charlie and Sylvia?"

"Yes, James. And please . . ."

"I know."

"No heroics. After all . . ." She allowed her words to trail into the air.

"I'm an old guy!"

They both laughed and James helped her into her coat before getting his own coat from the closet.

"Your car or mine?"

"Let's take mine, James. It will still be warm."

*   *   *

The vicarage door opened to flood the steps with warmth from the interior of the house. Charlie, grinning, pipe in mouth, welcomed them.

"Kathryn, James, do come in."

Charlie grinned. He closed the door after them as they made their way into the lounge.

"Good to see both of you," Sylvia exclaimed when she saw them. "Put your coats on the chair over there and we'll have a quick cup of tea before we get to the serious business of the morning."

Sylvia had the tea ready and proffered a teaspoon of brandy over the first cup as an additional guard against the chill. They could not refuse knowing the coolness of the empty church and assuming that the crypt would be even colder.

As they sat down, Charlie was still fiddling with his pipe and in that by-the-way manner of the English clergy wondered out loud if James was all right. He did, after all, look a little tired!

"Had another dream last night, Charlie."

James blurted out the words and surprised his three companions.

"Oh, Really!" Charlie looked up from his pipe as he spoke.

James sipped his tea and felt the brandy-stimulated liquid flow down his throat. He collected his thoughts as the others waited in anticipation.

"Yes, another vision. And I know that I was there. If I was not watching the surgery, then I may have actually been performing it. Primitive surgery. But seemingly effective surgery."

"James," Charlie paused as he filled his pipe and looked intently into the cured vegetation in the bowl. "Sylvia has given this a lot of thought since you first brought these experiences to our attention."

The tobacco refused to ignite, much to Charlie's disapproval. He looked across the room at his wife.

"Why don't you go on, my dear? You'd do it better than I. Tendency to ramble and all that."

Sylvia placed her cup on the table by the side of her chair and took on a more serious look as she formulated her words carefully.

"It seems to me that you are not the first person to have the sensation of a contact with the past. I'll call it contact for the time being as that is the only thing I can think of for now. It also seems to me that you may have some relationship to this man, Oswald."

Kathryn smiled at James, her eyes said, "See. I told you so."

"In fact," Sylvia continued, "I seem to recall reading an article in my monthly history journal where the author wondered about genetic connections with the past. Not just the usual family tree kind of stuff. Much more than that. A strong mental connection that allowed the modern person to transport himself or herself," she smiled at Kathryn, "back into the past."

Sylvia sipped her tea as she looked at her audience. No one moved. James knew that she was on the right track. Had not Dr. Spiller hinted at some form of genetic inheritance during a conversation last year?

"Sorry to interrupt, Sylvia, but are you," Kathryn asked, "suggesting that because of James's past, there remains within him a tie to the man Oswald?"

"I believe that I do, my dear. All very hypothetical you know. But it might fill in some of the gaps and give James some reason for what is happening."

Silence filled the room. James knew that they were close. He had recently started to feel the ties of kinship to Oswald. The ties were those that he might feel to a brother but he had not been able to identify the feelings before.

"Well ladies," Charlie looked directly at Sylvia and Kathryn, "and gentleman, shall we set about the business at hand? Our entry into and examination of the crypt!"

"I'll help you with the cups, Sylvia."

The tea utensils were cleared very quickly; James's and Kathryn's coats were taken from the chair where they had been carefully laid. Charlie reached into the closet adjacent to the door and pulled out warm coats for him and Sylvia and they made their way along the short walkway to the church. No words were spoken. Each member of the quartet was immersed in private thoughts. Wondering about James's link to the past and wondering what they would find in the unexplored crypt.

Unexplored, that is, except for Charlie's brief incursion. And the thoughts that the crypt might offer some evidence for the existence of an unknown man. A man who seemed to have profound influence on the present. And a man from the past who seemed determined to contact James.

*   *   *

The old church was a testament to the strength and architecture of its day. It had withstood the storms and environmental hazards of the centuries well. The square tower dominated the west side and the entrance was only a few yards to the right of the tower. The solid oak door, which now was locked continually in case of vandalism, had weathered the centuries and on opening brought the parishioners into a delightfully well-preserved interior. The pews gleamed from the constant polishing and care that had been given them over many years. The overhead arched wooden beams contrasted well with the off-white walls. A single rectangular window dominated the wall above the altar. It showed the Resurrected Christ and the morning sun brought a rainbow of color into the east side of the church. The original stone altar was still very beautiful and the carvings of saints gone by were amazingly preserved.

The space behind the altar was not obvious unless one looked carefully. Charlie led them through the narrow access that opened out into a larger area approximately twelve feet square. And then they saw it, the entrance to the crypt. Now, it was so obvious to them that they were surprised that no one had ventured into the area and made a record of it.

A ladder lay on the floor at the wall. Charlie smiled.

"Brought it here earlier. Knew that we would need it," he said as if to explain its presence in the church.

The large four-inch-thick flat stone, approximately the size of a double headstone, sat on top of four eight-inch-thick concrete lintels as though it had been a base for a statue at some time in the past. James and Charlie knelt and put their combined efforts into moving the stone and gradually they were able to set the stone aside. James wondered how Charlie had been able to move it his own.

The cool air rushed at them through the blackness of a four-foot square opening. Charlie looked very pleased with himself, his mouth creased in a wry smile as much to say, "See, I told you so!" And for the first time they heard the soft voices as a reminder that the two ladies were standing nearby.

"Moment of truth, James."

"Aye, Kath."

"Do be careful, Charles my dear."

Charlie looked at his wife, smiled, and moved to where the ladder lay on the floor. Kathryn and Sylvia proffered the flashlights, shining them into the cavernous hole in the floor. They were able to see steps that began some four feet below the entrance. Seeing this Sylvia and Kathryn both muttered in unison.

"Oh dear. Not quite dressed for this."

Sylvia, like Kathryn, also was wearing dress slacks, being well fitted and not amenable to clambering in and out of a four-foot drop. Kathryn gave James one of those don't-you-dare looks as he rolled his eyes and gazed at her as he had earlier that morning. He started to smile and Sylvia interrupted his thoughts, much to Kathryn's relief.

"Charles, why did you not warn us of this?" Sylvia's gentle admonishment brought a shallow smile from Charlie.

"Sorry, m'dear. Slip of the mind."

There and then, before the conversation became more involved, James decided on a different course of action.

"Charlie, no need for the ladder. I suggest that a stepladder will suffice for the ladies. If," he added with tongue in check "they wish to accompany us?"

The looks in two pairs of eyes told James that he had better not think otherwise. They were going into the crypt, despite any protestations of masculinity versus femininity from the two men.

"The stairs seem to continue to the base of the crypt," James observed out loud. "Let's take the flashlights with us and have . . ." His words trailed into silence as she wondered about a light for the crypt.

"The large storm light, m'dear!"

"Do not do anything without us," came the sharp command as Sylvia turned on her heel to retrieve the storm lantern that had been put into the nearby vesting room. At about the same time, Charlie returned with the stepladder that had been stored in the garden shed.

The lights in place, Charlie and James lowered themselves to the first level, looking around cautiously as the beams from their flashlights uncovered the floor of the crypt. There was a gentle breeze that seemed to have maintained a dryness in the air that they did not expect. The odor of dust assailed their nostrils. And James sneezed loudly. Sylvia and Kathryn called out wondering what was happening but were reassured by Charlie that nothing was amiss.

"Seems to me, Charlie, old lad, that the ladies would be much happier down here. Especially with Sylvia's background."

"And Kathryn's intuition, eh, James!" Charlie finished the thought.

The two women heartily agreed. James climbed the steps and helped both ladies on to the top landing area. Sylvia announced that she had locked the church door lest they be disturbed.

The two men led the way slowly but surely down the steps, with the ladies carrying one of the lanterns to help them see their way. The flame in the storm lantern flickered gently, tantalizing, offering an eerie glow to the entryway. The beams from the flashlights cut through the darkness and banished the shadows from their presence.

As they found their footing at the bottom of the stairs, Kathryn looked around unsure of the shadows in the darkness, suddenly exclaiming:

"The smell! It seems like . . .," Kathryn said

"Books? Old books!" James finished her thought.

And then the beam from Charlie's flashlight pierced the darkness and brought the shelves into focus. There were no stone sarcophagi or burial tombs that one usually finds in a crypt. Instead, and much to James's surprise, there were shelves! The shelves were constructed from rough-hewn wood that straddled gray stones. Stones large enough to have been a part of the walls of a castle or a fortified manor. As the flashlight beam traversed the space they saw it. Simultaneously. They inhaled in surprise and wonderment.

The sword stood alone in the corner. Just a few feet away from the base of the steps. James moved toward it and let forth a low whistle of surprise. The weight was not what he expected.

"Not much of an arm needed to wield this thing!"

They examined the sword in detail. The hilt was bound with leather thongs. Dry. Cracked in many places. And hard to the touch. The blade, a little less than thirty-six inches long, as James estimated using the eighteen-inch elbow to fingertip distance, was pitted in several places but in generally good condition.

"Sylvia, m'dear. Interesting item here for you to examine."

Charlie passed the sword, hilt first, to Sylvia, who only needed seconds to examine it in the light of the lantern and flashlights before she had an identification.

"Soldier's sword. Nothing fancy. But very functional. Very functional indeed. A killing weapon. Nothing dressy about it. Blade, next to hilt, has some marks on it that identify it as being manufactured at the Tower of London, that is. Late fourteenth century. Perhaps 1360s. Single-handed weapon. Not meant for two-handed swinging. Would have a four feet, or even longer, blade. More for cut and thrust stuff. Very useful for fighting in close quarters. Appears to have good balance. Center of gravity is only a few inches from the hilt. A nice weapon."

"Well done, m'girl." Sylvia was amazing at times.

Kathryn continued to look at James. Her eyes telling him to be careful. James and Charlie looked at each other and read each other's individual thoughts. The books and manuscripts, many of which were in the form of scrolls that lay packed on the shelves. They were now the focus of their attention. They turned instinctively to look at Sylvia, who moved forward cautiously to the shelves. James used his flashlight to examine the nooks and crannies of the crypt whilst Charlie used his to help Sylvia make her way to the shelves. A glance from Sylvia told her that she was looking at centuries-old books and documents combined with centuries-old dust, piled high enough to be dangerous.

James looked around and smiled; he felt the gentle touch of Kathryn's fingers on his arm as she sensed that they had made perhaps the find of the century. No one spoke. Sylvia took the flashlight from Charlie as she focused on a different part of the crypt. Books and documents were everywhere. The crude table that consisted of carved four-foot lintels placed onto stones came into view, this would have been used frequently she mused.

Charlie could only mutter to himself "Goodness gracious me" over and over again. It must have been similar to the scene when Howard Carter first poked his head into the tomb of Tutankhamen and saw the riches concealed for centuries.

"There is something very strange about this room," Sylvia exclaimed. All eyes were focused on her as she continued. "Here we have a very large room that essentially has the same width as the church but is only about two-thirds as long and we have supposed it to be the crypt. It has pillars and arches that have been built into the walls for support as we have two central pillars and arches to support the altar and the nave of the church above. But there are no signs of any burials. No coffins in alcoves. But there are alcoves in the walls, which are filled with shelves, as well as other nooks and crannies that give extra space. Seems to have been built for a different purpose."

"Where are you going with this thought, my dear?" Charlie asked.

"Well, Charles," Sylvia responded as James and Kathryn remained silent, "from earliest Christian times there has been a cherished church tradition of burying the dead in crypts. This is not the case. In fact," then suddenly the thought came to Sylvia that this was not a crypt, "there is nothing that will ever convince me that it is a crypt or that it was even built with that purpose in mind!"

In the dim light, they could see from Sylvia's face that her thought process was working overtime and then she smiled.

"Of course! Silly me. Why did I not think of that earlier? This is not a crypt," she concluded, "it is a storage archive! Just look at the items on the shelves!"

James's eyes lit up at the thought of an archive of old books and documents. He knew that he would be happy here. For several more minutes no one spoke. As they allowed their eyes to feast on the shelves. Here were literary treasures that had been hidden for centuries. Lying in vellum piles and stacked in the old manner. The books lay on their sides, piled neatly one on top of the other. More writing material than many past civilizations with their clay tablets and cuneiform *styli* had ever imagined! This was not the library of Ashurbanipal at Nineveh. This was not the library at Alexandria. This was the library of some past knight of the realm that had been hidden for centuries and was now open to the four inquiring minds.

And this archive contained hundreds, if not a thousand or more, books and documents, many bound in the form of books. The dates told them that the books were collected at a time, the late fourteenth century, when a knight might boast if he possessed two books, a bible and a Book of Hours. Yet here was a repository of such a size that would have astounded many of the monastic librarians of the time.

And then Charlie spoke, shattering the silence with his soft tones.

"Need time to think, m'dear. I'll have a pipe outside and let my mind wander."

"I see the light in James and Sylvia's eyes," Kathryn announced, "so I'll go with you and we can find more illuminating power!"

"Charles, you're a dear," Sylvia smiled at her husband. James helped Kathryn negotiate the steps and the stepladder and then he quickly became involved in the matter at hand. Old books and documents.

James's senses told him that he would find something that would offer some explanation of his visions. Looking at Sylvia, her face softened in the shadows, as the years appeared to have dropped away, he took off his jacket and smiled as he placed his flashlight on a nearby stone that even looked as if it might have been used as a seat.

James followed Sylvia's lead and stood back as she gently lifted a large volume from the top of a pile. Folio size, with a leather-bound, studded-oak board, and each page a delight as the vellum of centuries past lit up before their eyes. The hand-drawn pictures embellished every page of text. The gold inlay had withstood the ages to now delight two people from the twentieth century.

They lost themselves in the book for almost thirty minutes. They found that the carefully placed gothic lettering was hypnotic, and they continued to admire the scribe's calligraphic art. They became conscious of something different in the text, not the usual Latin words that adorned such pages. Sylvia had quietly identified the book as being of the late fourteenth century, and she had added with some degree of confidence that the materials used for the book, and the ink used by the scribe, were of the same era.

"Late fourteenth century, James. Even go so far as to state 1350s and/or 1360s. Of that I'm certain!"

It was the writing that caught their attention. The text was in an old form of English. At a time when the English language was not even born, so historians had told everyone. Let alone being written down.

"Sylvia. This is a medical text."

And then they heard the sounds. It was the voices of Charlie and Kathryn that brought them back to the present.

"James, dear. If you would be so kind, I will need a bit of a hand to get out of this crypt."

James wondered why Sylvia wished to leave.

As she turned away from her search to move to the steps, a package caught her eye. Alone on an out jut of stone that was in the form of an internal buttress about four feet high. There were several such structures spaced at regular intervals within the crypt and were placed strategically to support the walls against the pressure of the earth.

Then she spoke excitedly, "Wait!"

She retrieved the package. Examined it carefully and started the unwrapping process. The vellum wrapping was not the quality of writing vellum but more of the coarse protective type that might be used as waterproofing. It was wrapped around a breviary. As she opened the wrapping, her fingers moved nervously over what she knew to be a fine piece of work. She was surprised at the lack of dust on the vellum. Almost as though the package had just been placed there recently!

The breviary was not a large book as the dimensions of many of the Bibles of the fourteenth century. It was almost eight inches long by four inches wide and two inches thick. The original back and front boards had been covered with white pigskin that had been lightly stained to emphasize rosette-shaped patterns in triangular fields. As she opened the brass clasp, he could see that many of the pages were decorated with painted initials. And there were woodcut pictures, some painted, throughout the text, depicting the various activities of the saints.

Sylvia almost became lost in the book as she turned page after page. James looked over her shoulder and saw the fineness of the work—the careful writing and the graphic lettering at the beginning of each chapter.

"We're back!" Charlie's voice broke into their concentration.

Sylvia looked at James, who nodded in agreement with her unspoken thought that she should take the breviary and vellum wrapping with her.

James helped Sylvia out of the crypt. They walked to the pews at the front of the altar. Charlie and Kathryn were waiting. An old miner's lantern lay on the front pew. Charlie then helped up the miner's lamp in the direction of Sylvia and James, holding it proudly at arm's length, pointing out the brass base and top and the number 12 on the top section. The glass that protected the flame in the chamber was spotless.

"Belonged to my father," Charlie said proudly, "and still puts out a good light. Spent some time cleaning it, and do you know . . ."

The three listeners smiled and Charlie, who realized that he was wandering off into one of his famous monologues, cut himself short. He put the lanterns on the stone floor and rubbed his hands expectantly.

"Well, let's not stand here talking all of the time. What have you got," Charlie asked looking at the package in Sylvia's hands.

They sat in the front pew focused on the package in Sylvia's hand. Noticing this, James made the announcement.

"Charlie, Kath, me bonnie lass, do we have a story for you! Sylvia, fire away."

Sylvia gave Kathryn and Charlie a summary of what they had seen in the crypt. Her eyes had caught much of the detail of the documents, even though there had only been time for a glance at many of them. James was surprised at the intimate aspects of many of the documents that Sylvia could recall. And her final words stunned them all.

"It is my belief that we have discovered a repository of medieval documents. Perhaps the original owner intended it to be a crypt but I have reason to believe, speaking off the cuff and without further investigation, that it was not designed as a crypt as you and I know it, Charles. It is more like an archive or a library or a room that is almost equivalent to a modern-day office, if there was such a thing. And this breviary," she passed the book around for all to see, "is a direct line to our friend Oswald."

The stunned silence allowed Sylvia to take a sip of tea and nibble at one of the cookies they had brought. She was deep in thought her brows furrowed.

James continued Sylvia's thoughts.

"In the front. The words. *Oswaldo amico meo*. To Oswald, my friend. Plus the words that were written on the final page. *Requiescas in pace, Oswaldus Dunelmensis*. May you rest in peace. Oswald of Durham."

Sylvia looked at the words.

"In two different writing styles. The first as though it was a gift and the later hand as though . . ."

"It was a note in remembrance," James added.

And then the idea hit.

"There is a name that we have seen reference to before on several of the documents down there, a fellow by the name of Ranulf de Boise, who appears to have been the prime depositor, if not the owner, of the material. The rest-in-peace hand is in his style. Need to investigate further of course. Also some documents with the sign that you have told us about James. You know. Cuthbert's cross in the circle."

"Oswald's sign! Any dates that you could see?"

"Nothing, James. But, you know, a glance here and there is not sufficient . . ."

"Aye."

Sylvia spoke again.

"But I have one thought that does not ring true and I cannot get it out of my mind." She paused before continuing. "As far as we know, no one has been down here for a long time. The dust on the steps is undisturbed except for our footprints," Sylvia looked at the two men to answer her question, "Charles, James?"

"Sure" came the response from James as he and Charlie stood up and made a sudden departure to the entrance to the crypt and returned two minutes later.

"You are right, Sylvia, only four sets of footprints that Charlie and I can discern. Please go on with your thought."

"So, as far as we know, there has been no entry into the crypt from this vantage point. And yet the vellum covering on the breviary was not at all dusty. At least not what one would expect after centuries of being down here, especially when one considers the dust all around the place! Almost as though the package had been deposited yesterday!"

They all wondered at this piece of conjecture but no one could offer any comment. The lack of dust on the wrapping was singularly strange. And then it was Kathryn who could not contain herself any longer as she gave vent to her thoughts.

"It seems to me that we are on to something, something big. One must wonder how many people of that period kept a repository of documents. Outside of the church, of course."

All eyes turned to Kathryn, who blushed in the pale light at being the sudden focal point of three pairs of eyes.

James broke the silence. Gently. Almost in a whisper. "Go on, Kath. Follow your thought." He reached over and touched her hand.

She smiled at him and continued.

"Well, it seems to me that our friend de Boise is much more prominent a person than history would have us believe. In fact, there appears to be no mention of him in the material that James and I have studied. So," she looked into the eyes of the other three, "I have to believe that there was a reason for his existence. His name seems to pop up on many occasions when we think we are getting closer to Oswald. It seems to me that these two were together quite often. Perhaps working together. You might even wonder if they were not up to something."

"But what could that be?" Charlie asked.

"Oh it could be anything, Charles, we must consider all possibilities. It is a little strange that we have, on several occasions come across Ranulf's name. He did own this land and the original house must have been quite a fortification."

"Indeed, Kathryn. I have been prowling around a little this last week or so and it seems to me that there was also a defensive perimeter wall associated with the manor house. I am assuming that the building stood on a slight rise. But my main clue came from the unevenness of the surface as though a thick wall had been constructed there. From what I could determine, the wall must have surrounded the house on all sides, from the river in the north and approximately the same distance from the house to the south, east, and west. It is now surrounded by trees so little reason for anyone to prowl in that area. Took me an hour or so to trace the pattern of the walls."

Charlie smiled in triumph at the impact of his news as James let out a low whistle. Sylvia cut into James's thoughts, knowing by instinct that Ranulf de Boise was no mere bystander in history.

But the piece of the puzzle that now needed their attention was the relationship between Ranulf de Boise and Oswald.

*   *   *

CHAPTER 9

T he silence was as thick as the proverbial London fog of Holmesian times. They were engrossed with their individual thoughts about de Boise and Oswald. How were they connected? Finally Sylvia broke the silence in a voice that was clear and seemed to fill the volume of the church.

"This fellow, Ranulf de Boise, must have been quite a person—a man of consequence and in a position of some authority. Perhaps even a relative of King Edward. And yet he is not mentioned in any of the history books. His sole claim to existence seems to be in these documents . . . but to return to my original thought. Owning a manor house is one thing. But to have such a fortification that is not documented in the literature of the time," Sylvia paused as she looked in the downward direction of the crypt.

"He would," she continued, "have needed to have the king's permission to construct such a fortification. Edward was at war with our Scottish cousins almost continually," she let her words trail away in thought and then added, "but there must be more to it."

Sylvia again stimulated the conversation by asking the obvious question. "Why would anyone build such a fortification out here when there was Durham so close? It seems so completely out of the character of the times. Extra manpower would be needed. Extra money. An army would have had little trouble taking the place or even by-passing the place without fear of an attack from the rear."

Then Kathryn added, "Would the king have any reason for such an act?"

Sylvia responded "Don't think so, Kathryn, unless . . ."

But it was James who provided a partial answer. Perhaps even a near complete answer.

"Would it have to be the king?"

There was a pensive moment. Then Kathryn spoke again.

"John of Lancaster! Father and grandfather of kings. The real power behind Edward in his aging years. James?" Kathryn looked directly at James as she answered her own question. "And regent when his nephew Richard II first ascended to the throne. The novel that you have just completed focuses on Lancaster's tendency to be a plotter and planner. Could it be that your research and writer's imagination have come close to the truth?"

"Not sure, Kath. Where does fact cease and fictitious dreaming take over?"

The silence descended on them again. Heavy and unmoving. Charlie stood up, stretched, and made the deep pronouncement.

"It seems to me that we are starting to go around in circles. There is, obviously, something to the whole business. But at the moment, we do not know. I suggest that we retire to a warmer place."

He raised his eyebrows, pursed his lips, and puffed out his cheeks, as if daring anyone to disagree with his words. Charlie also added another even more pertinent thought.

"Time is getting on. And some of our parishioners will be coming in to prepare the church for the services tomorrow."

James had lost track not only of the time of day, but he had also lost track of the days and suddenly realized that it was Saturday. It seemed like a long month since the previous Monday! He helped Charlie to replace the stone and realizing that they did not need the ladder, carried it back to the garden shed lest its presence in the church make some of the parishioners a little more than curious. The stepladder was left in its position beneath the stone cover. It would be needed again.

The words had not been spoken, but it was in the minds of all four that their discovery should remain a secret.

Their thoughts were individual and focused on the same point. The repository! The archive! The workplace or office! An unusual and significant discovery. A repository in a cathedral, priory, monastery, or a nunnery was to be expected. These were the centers of learning and each institution or prayer and learning had a scriptorium as well as a library. But to make a discovery such as this was completely unanticipated and, for now, unnerving.

Seated in the lounge in front of a rekindled fire, they discussed the ramifications of their find. Charlie reminded them that the crypt, being on church property, fell under his jurisdiction. At the correct time, when they could discern the nature of the contents of the crypt, would it be proper to inform the rightful persons, that being the bishop of Durham and the dean, Tommy Smith. Until such time as they needed for investigation, the crypt should remain, for the time being, their private curiosity.

And Charlie put into words what they were all thinking.

"A busy day coming up tomorrow. Not possible to do any more investigating. Let's get together again Monday morning. Tenish? Here? You can manage this, Kathryn?"

"Wouldn't miss it for the world. I do have some property to check for a potential buyer. But there may be other property close by that I need to look over . . ."

She allowed her words to fade into the silence as all nodded in agreement with Charlie's proposal. Charlie finished the thought.

"Well . . . Now, that's settled. Lunch, anyone?"

"Last thing." James spoke. "Could I borrow the breviary? There is something about it that puzzles me and I'd like to do a quick check of an item or two."

"Of course, James. Say no more." Sylvia said as she handed him the breviary and the vellum. James rewrapped it in the vellum. His fingers tingling with emotion as he did so. He was surprised at the softness of the vellum.

James sat silently through the lunch. He sensed that what they had found this morning was just another piece of the puzzle to add to the mystery of his contact to the past. The cold fingers of time tickled his spine as he shivered in the warm room.

*   *   *

James and Kathryn returned to his cottage. First things first, after removing the heavy outer winter clothing, was to put on the kettle for tea.

As the water heated, they talked about their morning activities. The indication that the crypt might have been a memorial to Oswald, perhaps an archive for books and even for Oswald's notes that had come into the possession of Ranulf de Boise. Their thoughts were interrupted by the noise of the kettle whistling to indicate that the water was boiling and ready to pour onto the leaves in the teapot.

As they sat and sipped the hot liquid, their minds were running back and forth wildly from the present to the fourteenth century. In their own individual thoughts, they were trying to make some sense of their findings. Suddenly, James spoke. Kathryn was visibly startled as James's voice intruded into her quiet thoughts.

"Sorry, me bonnie lass. Just had a thought."

"Kath," James was very pensive and deliberate in his speech as though he took moments to think before each word was spoken. "I believe that what we have found is a true archive."

She listened intently as James related Alice's findings and thoughts about Oswald. He added his own suggestions and thoughts to Alice's findings. Then there was silence; he had finished his story.

Kathryn looked at him. Open-mouthed. Speechless. And then finally she found her tongue and the ability to speak.

"You are trying to tell me that Oswald, that same Oswald who died in the sink hole out back of your property, and into which you foolishly descended," she would never let him forget that event, "lived beyond death as another person?"

James paused unable to answer. He looked out of the window. The sky had darkened; snow had begun to fall and was increasing in its intensity. It seemed like an ominous moment in time. Finally James answered her question.

"Yes, I believe that he continued to live," he paused and added, "as Oswald. As strange as it may seem."

"But, James, how?"

"That I cannot tell you, Kath. There is something about my dreams that tells me that what we believed, his death in that sinkhole, did not turn out to be the case. But I cannot tell you how or why. My dreams tell me that something happened that required his presence on this earth. I just have that feeling. My scientific instincts tell me that it is wrong. But my mind is telling me something different."

He picked up the breviary from the table and carefully unrolled it from its vellum packaging.

"And now we have this," he brandished the book before her "another thing that cannot be explained. There is a note in the front as though it was a gift to Oswald. From a Brother Thomas. And a note is written in the back, as if in remembrance of Oswald. Perhaps written by Ranulf de Boise"

She could see that the constant buzz of information in his brain was playing havoc with his senses.

"Sit, James. We both need time to think."

As he sat next to her, Kathryn leaned over and kissed him lightly on the cheek and ran her fingers through his hair.

"Kath?"

"Do shut up, James. Give yourself a moment and stop being a fidget."

She guided his head to her shoulder as she put her arm around him. He felt relaxed as his head rested against her, still holding the breviary in his hand. He could feel his senses giving in to her command. The flames of the fire flickered with warmth. His head felt heavy and he allowed her shoulder to take the full weight as he nestled against her. He could smell the scent of the fresh flowers in the perfume that she had used. Suddenly he was asleep. A gentle sleep.

And then . . .

"James. James."

He could feel her gentle hand against his head. He was conscious of a feeling of calmness and well-being. The hand was on his brow. Soothing. Cool.

"James!"

Her voice sounded more urgent. He forced himself into consciousness. First noticing that the fire was low.

He looked around and shivered. Kathryn felt the shiver and moved him gently to bring the fire back to life. As she bent over to attend to the fire, she heard him mumble.

"Magnificent!"

"Don't you dare comment on my . . ." She allowed the unspoken word to trail off into the air.

"Why not? It is!"

He was awake! She continued with the fire, brought it to its brightness again, added wood, and sat down.

"Now tell me, James, who was this woman you were talking with in your dreams."

"I was only asleep for a few moments. So, what are you talking about?"

"No such thing, James. Take stock of your surroundings. The fire has lost its glow. How long do you think that takes?"

He did not answer.

"One hour. You were in dreamland. Talking with a woman who, I know, was definitely not me!"

"Jealous, Kath?"

"Knock it off," his favorite Americanism was thrown back at him, "James, be serious!"

"Yes, ma'am."

She glared at him. Stood up, put her hands on her hips, and looked directly into his eyes.

"Sit down, bonnie lass. We need to talk."

He needed to put things right. His words were tender and soft.

"No, Kathryn. Do not think for one moment," he took her hand and felt its warmth. "Kathryn, I have never thought of anyone in the way that I think about you. If there is to be one woman in my life, you are that woman."

"But, James," Kathryn sniffed as she spoke.

"It was Margaret." The light went on in Kathryn's eyes.

"Oswald's wife?"

"Yes, my dear."

"You are dreaming of a dead woman? Well, that makes me feel a whole lot better, especially when you have your head on my shoulder!"

He could hear the sarcasm in her voice and decided to put a stop to it.

"Kathryn, please shut up and listen."

She opened her mouth in surprise. But maintained a dignified silence.

"Margaret has been appearing to me for this past two weeks. First, as a voice. Then, as a shadow. And finally, in human form. It seems that Oswald has a message for me. I have even seen him. And if my dreams and my mind are not playing tricks on me, I have even seen Oswald and helped him to heal people."

"All in your dreams?"

"Unfortunately not, my love."

She leaned over and kissed his cheek. Her threatened tears of sorrow were now turning to tears of joy.

"And by the way, they both think that you are a fine woman," Kathryn smiled in surprise at his words before he added, "and Oswald thinks that you have a magnificent rump."

"He does not think any such thing!"

Sorry, Kath, just had to put those words in to make sure that you were listening. But seriously, both Oswald and Margaret have commented that you are a fine woman."

She smiled, and then, "Good lord!"

"What's up?"

"Do you mean that he can see me?" And then the form of her question became more serious, "Even when I'm in the shower?"

"I've never asked him. But I doubt that he would intrude into a lady's privacy. And besides, I've never had that concern about Margaret seeing me!"

"But all men are show-offs. Strutting around and showing . . ." She did not finish her sentence but added, "Well, women are different!"

"Kathryn, does it really matter? There are more important things to think about than Oswald seeing you naked in the shower!"

"I suppose."

"So what. Show yourself off. You have magnificent . . ." He was not allowed to say the next word as Kathryn exclaimed.

"James! Really!"

"All right, Kathryn. I'll ask him in my next dream. I am worried, though. What if I am being taken back to Oswald's time? Everything is so real."

James related to her the episode of the aspirin tablets. Her questions were searching and surprised him in their detail. He even brought his notes to his computer screen and allowed her to sit and read everything. He left Kathryn at the computer screen, spectacles perched firmly on her nose, and went into the kitchen to make another pot of tea to replace the cold tea that had been made more than one hour ago and had not been consumed. He could only hear her silence but he could imagine the expression on her face as sentence after sentence, line after line of electronic words revealed to her the innermost thoughts of his dreams.

As he walked into the lounge with the tea tray, she was sitting in front of the computer. Looking off into nowhere. A faraway look in her eyes.

"Kathryn, are you all right?"

She shook her head gently back to the present, from wherever she had been.

"James, my dear, I do not know what to say."

"Then say nothing. Just think about it and we can decide our next steps. But first?" he asked as he lifted the teapot.

"Tea? Biscuits?"

"No thanks. Just the tea. Still full from lunch."

She looked at the computer screen. "Save the files?"

"Yes."

Then she moved away from the computer to sit on the floor next to him in front of the fire. Kathryn had much going on in her mind.

"It certainly is a mystery," she said, "But you have the two instances where in one case you have a mystery about the aspirin tablets that you put into the pocket of your bathrobe and the other is much more surprising."

"Aye."

"And your dream," she continued, "but let me call it a vision, that you had last night in which you were involved in a surgical procedure. Seemingly, very effective surgery insofar as the patient did not die, that you know of. You wake up with the odor of vinegar on your hands and the suggestion of blood under your fingernails!"

The silence hung like a heavy curtain across the room. James and Kathryn were lost in their own individual thoughts. James fingered the breviary and started to turn the page. And then the thought hit him.

"Kath, we need to go back to the crypt. Right now!"

"Let's go then. But wait!"

In this moment of indecision, James decided that to call ahead would be the most courteous thing to do. Charlie had mentioned something about preparing for the Sunday services and having parishioners around the church.

Sylvia answered the telephone after one ring.

"Sorry, James, Charles is out," was her response to his question. Then she added, "The matters with the parishioners took only a few moments and the church is empty. Come over whenever you wish."

James muttered, "Fifteen minutes, Sylvia, and thank you."

Kathryn stood up and looked down at her clothes.

"You know, James, I am not quite dressed for this type of activity and I intend to keep up with you this time."

"Say no more, Kath!"

James disappeared and reappeared almost immediately with a sweat suit in his hands. Not his running suit but a cleaner, neater one that he had worn only a few times.

Kathryn looked at it, wrinkled her nose wondering about the style, and went to the bathroom to change. She appeared wearing the suit.

"It is a little large but it works."

Kathryn looked at him and felt that it was good that he seemed to be relaxing.

"Now that you mention it . . ." James disappeared and reappeared two minutes later wearing his sweat suit. "Now we are both ready, come what may."

A few minutes later they arrived at the vicarage and were ringing the doorbell. Sylvia appeared, also ready for a fresh venture into the crypt. Seeing the look on their faces, she responded, "You did not think that I would be happy to stay here with all those books and other items down there?"

They all smiled. All had one purpose in mind.

Sylvia had made a thermos of tea and away they went to the church. James started to move the heavy stone cover, but it would not move. Then he discovered that placing his hands into predetermined places made it much easier, as though the original designer had intended the use of minimal effort, to anyone who knew of the crypt. He began to understand how Charlie had been able to move the stone, perhaps without realizing he had followed the designer's intent. Within moments the crypt was once again exposed and open for entry.

This time it was easier to descend the steps into the crypt. The two ladies were wearing appropriate clothing and more comfortable shoes. Sylvia immediately began to examine the section that had caught her attention earlier in the day. James and Kathryn could hear her sharp intakes of breath as she opened up one treasure after another. And then silence as Sylvia became immersed in one particular book, a family tree of Ranulf de

Boise indicating the death of Ranulf's parents during the early years of his life and also showing King Edward as Ranulf's guardian.

"This is a first," she muttered out loud, catching the attention of James and Kathryn. "It shows the relationship of Ranulf to King Edward! Now I am starting to understand the connection between the two and why this place was fortified. I'll bet that Ranulf was Edward's most trusted Northern watchdog and protector against intrusions by the Scots!"

James and Kathryn were delighted at his finding. It seemed to be the first building block of the story. They left Sylvia to her search and decided to investigate further the contents of the crypt.

Looking at the walls, James's senses told him that something was amiss. The wall on one side of the crypt seems to be shorter than its opposite companion. And then he found a crevice that was hidden in the shadows that contained shelf after shelf of books and document collections. He whispered Kathryn's name to get her attention without disturbing Sylvia. Kathryn's eyes opened wide when she saw the storehouse of knowledge.

As James and Kathryn carefully removed one book after another from the shelves and skimmed through the pages they saw that each one was a vellum-bound collection of handwritten notes, medical notes with some drawings of wounds, as well as handwritten commentaries about battles and military strategies. And all were in the same handwriting and same mixture of Latin, Saxon, and blossoming English that James had seen before. The same handwriting that James recognized. The penmanship of *Oswaldus Dunelmensis!*

James was looking through one of the notebooks when he heard her calling his name, softly and gently, as if in a whisper. Thinking it was Kathryn, he made no formal acknowledgement other than a muttered "Be with you in a moment, my dear." Then he heard his name called again. He drew in a sharp breath as more words came to him. More clearly than before.

"James, I rejoice that I have found you again. I have searched further this time than I have ever searched before. For reasons that are unknown to me, I had to concentrate even more this time. I never thought to seek you here, in this place that is familiar to me. But please, I must have your attention."

James sensed the breathlessness of her voice. His thoughts went out to Kathryn, wondering what she was doing and wondering if she could see him.

"Ah, James, I see that your thoughts are with your woman. Forgive me but I do need to speak to you and my time here is limited."

James breathed evenly and started to relax.

Her words continued in soft gentle whispers as her shadow then her human form shimmered before him. He smiled at the thought of her beauty, preserved over the centuries and now for him to see. Her voice came back to him, gentle and sweet as he had heard before, out of the shimmering mist before him. He heard her gentle laughter.

"I see that you are willing to help us. You and my Oswald are very much alike. I grow tired and I must leave you now, James."

He saw the twinkle in her eyes.

"Go to your woman. Tell her about us. I must go. My Oswald needs me. Do not worry. We will find you. Soon."

Her form returned to a shadow that swirled like a mist and as though a light breeze had been let loose in the corner of the crypt. She was gone before he could ask her why it was so urgent that they had a need of his presence. He could only wait for . . .

"James? Are you all right?"

His attention was turned to the voice. She stood in the shadow and he wondered if Margaret had returned. Then he realized that it was Kathryn who stood there, a light behind her from one of the flashlights that she had laid on the ledge emphasized her shape but had hidden her face. It was the cup of tea in her hands that gave her away and forced James's mind back into the present. He looked across the crypt and saw Sylvia so immersed in her latest find that an earthquake might not have disturbed her.

"Kath, what was I doing as you approached?"

Kathryn was taken aback by this question and she knew immediately that something was amiss.

"James," Kathryn answered, "don't tell me . . .," but he cut off her unfinished question and said, "Aye, Kath. Did you see any movement in the corner?" He indicated the corner with a nod of his head.

"No."

"She was here!"

"Who? Oswald's wife?"

"Aye."

"Did she say anything?"

"Yes. They have need of me."

"Oh, James, I'm frightened!"

Even in the dim light of the crypt, he could see the fear in her expression.

"Kath, I don't think that Oswald would lead me into danger. And she asked me to tell you about them."

"But what does he want? This figure from the past. Where is he leading you? And why?"

"I cannot answer your questions."

"Are you two all right back there? I can hear a lot of whispering."

"Yes, Sylvia. All is well. Kathryn and I have found a hoard of handwritten notes bound in vellum that might be of interest."

"Well, I'm up to my eyes in good stuff over here. So that will have to wait. I suggest that we take one or two pieces each for further study without trudging back down here every time we think of something."

"Excellent idea, Sylvia. We've been down here almost an hour. How about another five minutes?"

"I did not realize . . . Good idea, James. Charles will be returning soon and wonder where I am. Let's do that."

Kathryn, with supreme effort, shook the worried look from her face and put on the best smile that she could.

"We need to talk, James."

"Anything you say, my dear," he whispered, kissing her on the cheek. An action that did not go unnoticed by Sylvia, who smiled at them.

Within two minutes they were ready to leave the crypt. James helped the ladies out on to the church floor and then turned and moved the large stone back into its place.

They sat once again in the front pew and had tea from the thermos. Each one wanting to talk at the same time.

"What did you take, Sylvia?" James asked as he nodded his head in the direction of the large volume that Sylvia had brought out of the crypt and placed onto the pew.

"As near as I can tell, it is a family history of Ranulf de Boise as well as a diary of some of his activities. And you, James?"

"This," he said, brandishing the volume toward Sylvia, "is a diary of Oswald's actions during the 1360s. It seems to end sometime around 1368 or early 1369. So I thought I might as well get some detail abut the man."

The tea seemed to have helped Kathryn to quell some of her worries, but he knew from the look in her eyes that she was not about to forget the conversation in the crypt.

Sylvia noticed that Kathryn looked preoccupied and was about to comment when she thought better of it. She would have a word with Charles who, she knew, would have a quiet word with James. That would help put things right.

Sylvia had it all worked out. She just did not know the cause of Kathryn's mood.

*   *   *

CHAPTER 10

K athryn was silent for the few minutes that it took to return to the
cottage. James did not even try to intrude into her thoughts. He
drove the purring Jaguar through the snow that now covered the road to
his home and forged new tracks in his driveway. As they entered the cottage,
Kathryn finally had to give way to the tears that had collected. As he closed
the door, she leaned against him. A low moan escaped.

"James, what are we going to do? I am so frightened. This whole
business of your dreams. The continuous request that Oswald needs you.
Where will it end?"

He stroked her hair as he felt the convulsions shake her body. The
tears were flowing freely down her cheeks. He offered his handkerchief
and she took it gladly.

"Kath, how about—" he started the question knowing that Kathryn
would answer.

"A cup of tea? That would be very welcome, James. But contrary to
your thoughts, a cup of tea does not cure everything!"

James smiled inwardly at the recollection of all those hot, sugary cups
of tea that had been given to his footballer colleagues after a major injury.
The hot, sweet liquid had stopped them going into shock after a broken
limb. Giving the ambulance time to arrive . . .

He released her from his arms and went into the kitchen to perform
the necessary actions for the all-healing beverage.

He could hear Kathryn bringing life back to the fire.

"No need to do that, Kath, I'll see to it."

"It's done, James. Just see to the tea please."

"Yes, my love."

"Second time today that you have used that word, James."

He could hear the pleasure in her voice. "Well, it is true. Is it not?"

He heard the sound of her movement before he realized that she was standing behind him. Her arms attempting to encircle his waist.

"You know, James, you are such a charmer when you wish to be!"

He smiled. "Tea, my dear?"

"Yes, let's concentrate on the matter at hand. I am so worried about where this might lead us."

"Us? No way, Kathryn. If there is any danger, you will not be a part of it!"

"So you admit that there might be danger?" she asked immediately.

He could have bitten his tongue.

"I will not have you exposed to any possible—" he stopped but there was only one word that he could use.

"Danger!" Kathryn spoke the word for him. "But," she added, "You will have need of me so I can act on the home front for you."

James poured the tea. Then Kathryn spoke.

"I need to change out of these dusty clothes. Would you mind if I showered?"

"Of course not. Go ahead," James answered.

While Kathryn was occupied, he picked up the collection of notes that he had brought from the crypt and opened it to the first page. A new sensation took over his body. He sensed that Oswald was close. And as he lifted his head from the collection, the sensation from Oswald's presence was strong. He turned but there was no one there. A shadow had hardened almost into human form, and he heard the lilting voice that he knew to be the voice of Oswald. He was being called again.

"James, my Margaret has told you that I have need of you. I must have your attention."

James sensed the seriousness of Oswald's voice. He listened.

"Thank you, James. I now know of your willingness to help."

Oswald's figure shimmered before him. James smiled at the thought of this former soldier of King Edward III, reaching out over the centuries. His voice came back to James as gentle as before, but as if he was smiling within the shimmering mist. Oswald's shadow moved and swirled and then he was gone, before James could ask him why it was so urgent that they had a need of his presence. He could only wait for . . .

"James? My dear, are you all right?"

His attention was turned to the voice. She stood in the shadow and he wondered; then he realized that Kathryn stood in the doorway, a light behind her and hiding her face, but illuminating other aspects of her form. James forced his mind back into the present.

"Aye. I'm fine. Just letting some thoughts go through my mind."

Kathryn had changed back to her normal very dressy day-clothes, having shunned the now dusty sweat suit. So she mistook his double-edged words to mean thoughts about the documents that he had placed onto the floor. She sat on the floor with him. He decided to keep his brief conversation with Oswald to himself for the moment.

James briefly talked about the pages that he had looked through and then he asked Kathryn questions that he knew would tax her knowledge and draw some facts from the recesses of her mind. She accepted the challenge and they talked. They talked about his dreams, about the crypt, about history, and about books.

And before they realized the time, it was seven o'clock. Their minds were still very active. Then Kathryn made a suggestion; she insisted that he sit still and she would make dinner. He responded immediately.

"Go to it, me bonnie wee lass," with the usual "I never say 'no' to a lady, especially . . ."

"One so forward?"

"One so beautiful!"

She raised herself from the floor, noticing his wandering eyes as he watched her every move.

She made her way to the kitchen and soon he could here the sounds of food being prepared. Minutes passed and she appeared with a tray of fruit, cheese, bread, and white wine. German wine, his favorite. The collection of documents was forgotten as they munched, chewed, drank, talked, and renewed the fire to keep the chill from the room. It was as though they had both forgotten the mystery that surrounded them. A warm feeling enveloped them as the night wore on. The subjects that they discussed ranged from James's latest manuscript about the alchemist to the history of the city of Durham. Kathryn offered some suggestions about the life of the alchemist that James gleefully accepted.

Looking at her watch, Kathryn realized that she needed to leave, since she had to be up and about early the next day to take care of several items. James was worried about the snow but it had stopped soon after their return from the vicarage. Kathryn assured him that all would be well.

"I'll be back tomorrow morning. Nine thirty?"

"Aye, lass. I need to re-examine some of these manuscripts and I want to talk out loud about my ideas. There was one date in particular that you have noted as around 1410 but I think the date might be closer to 1370."

"See you then."

"I'll have the teapot on and ready for you."

She laughed at his mischievous smile and playfully slapped his shoulder.

"Night, James." She kissed his cheek. "Tomorrow, nine thirty."

She paused at the door of the Range Rover and playfully blew a kiss from her fingertips then opened the door and settled herself into the vehicle. Moments later disappeared in a blaze of red tail lights.

James was glad to step back into the warmth in the cottage. He sat in front of the fire and wondered why Oswald would need him, and either from the warmth or tiredness he fell asleep envisioning Oswald as he had seen him on that day last December. He could see Oswald clearly as though he was in the room and he heard his words once more.

"I will not forget you, James Simpson."

"Nor I, Oswald."

"We have crossed the bridges of time. We will cross these bridges again. And you and I will meet again, James Simpson."

Oswald had read James's puzzled look.

"When? I can tell you not. Now I pass to the other side to be with my wife and son. Enjoy your world that you may one day see mine. Until that day when we meet again and we will be close comrades once more, I will be watching over you, James Simpson. As I have watched over others of my time."

He felt the reassurance and the warmth of Oswald's presence. The shadows fluttered and began to fade and he was alone once more.

*   *   *

James slept the sleep of a child. Deep and unmoving. He awoke at six o'clock feeling refreshed and ready for the day ahead. He even whistled in the shower until he heard the sound of a movement outside of the bathroom. He opened the shower door so that the frosted glass did not hinder his vision and then the bathroom door opened. Slightly at first and then there was Kathryn's smiling face. Not a hair out of place and dressed immaculately in a black skirt and white blouse. She smiled sweetly as she placed a freshly made cup of tea on to the counter.

"Good grief! Kath!"

"My goodness, James. Don't you look clean!"

"What . . . ?"

"Couldn't sleep. And I had an idea or two so I thought that an earlier visit than we had planned and breakfast would be rather nice. So, continue with your shower, James. I promise not to peep. Or stare. Of course, the thought never crossed my mind but now that I mention it . . . it may not be such a bad idea!"

"Begone, woman!"

Kathryn withdrew from the bathroom leaving James thinking that his plans for a long hot soak in the shower had just been canceled. Minutes later he arrived in the kitchen and kissed Kathryn on the proffered cheek. Her hands were enclosed in kitchen gloves as she prepared the scrambled eggs.

"Morning, Kathryn, again."

"Ah, James, you do look so clean and neat!"

"Thank you, Kathryn. I'll plan my next visit to your house for the time that you are showering."

"Promises! Promises!"

Kathryn smiled sweetly sensing and said, "Let's have breakfast."

She took him by the hand and led him to the table. James looked at the food—scrambled eggs, bacon, buttered toast, marmalade, and the pot of coffee—as a change to the ubiquitous pot of tea.

"Ah, a well-balanced low-calorie repast. Let's dive in. I'm hungry."

"Well, James, you need a good meal now and again. Fish and salad will only go so far, as long as you are a penguin or a rabbit."

"Point taken, Kath. Let's be at it."

"James, really! At breakfast time too!"

They talked about the events so far. But, moreover, they talked about the possible meaning and consequences of his dreams. James made sure that Kathryn understood that Oswald continually offered assurances that James would not be in harm's way. She was not convinced. He reached over and held her hand.

"Don't worry, Kathryn my dear. You are such a treasure and a dear person to care for me so much. It has been a long time since I've had anyone care for me as you do. I sense that all will be well and I also sense that Oswald will not lead me into danger."

He stood up, pushed his chair back from the table, and offered his hand to help her to her feet. "A big hug?"

She leaned her head on his chest as he held her. Her anxiety was subsiding and she continued with breakfast. It was a few minutes before she spoke.

"Speaking of Oswald, are we going to look at the collection of papers, his diary so to speak, that you brought home."

"Sure, Kath, if you would like?"

"Of course I would like! Why do you think I got rid of my other tasks and I am here so early?"

"And I thought that it was my natural charm and good looks!"

"Do eat your breakfast, James."

It was then that he heard Oswald's soft voice.

"Ah, James. Your beautiful woman has the same behavior of my Margaret. Always trying to keep me on the correct side of the road. I see that you also love your woman for being herself, as well as for her beauty."

James was surprised at Oswald's perception, but he dared not even show that he heard the voice. His thought gave him away.

"Don't worry, James. She does not sense me, at least for the moment until I am ready. But you do love her, don't you?"

"Of course." James was surprised with his own quick mental soundless admission. Then there was silence.

All of this time, Kathryn had been chatting to James and he had not heard a word. He had better pay attention.

"James, you have not heard a word that I have said."

"Of course I have, Kath."

"All right, James. You wash the dishes and I'll start on the notes."

He must have looked like the proverbial guppy. Mouth open. Speechless.

"What I did say, was that when we," she emphasized the plural pronoun, "have washed the breakfast dishes we will examine the collection of notes. For simplicity, let's just call it *Oswald's Diary*, until we know otherwise. If you will read them, because of your fluency in the necessary languages of Latin and Saxon or Old English, I will help."

"By the way, where were you when I was talking?"

James did not know how to respond, but Kathryn read the look in his eyes.

"I have an idea, but let's not get into that now." She knew!

All was ready. James collected the items from his desk and began to spread the sheets of vellum out as best as he could on to the nearby table.

"Good idea, me bonnie lad."

They settled themselves on chairs next to each other; James opened the collection and found that the individual vellum pages had been strung between vellum-covered wooden end-boards. As he had already noted, it was not a printed book having originated almost one hundred years before the advent of the moveable-type printing press in the west.

It was a collection of what had been loose vellum pages and the writing varied from faded brown to almost black letters, as though the ink had varied in composition with the efforts by the scribe. Other than that, the handwriting was clear, not miniscule, and without the many abbreviations that allowed a lot of information to be collected on one page. Oswald had, obviously, access to a plentiful supply of vellum but he had written his works on both sides.

"Overall the writing is clear so I can probably read most of this today."

"So, James, should we unstring it first for ease of handling?"

The ties were simple, as one might use without bothering about the intricacies of binding, merely to make sure that the pages stayed together and in the correct order. After several minutes, mostly through Kathryn's persistence, the collection was untied and the pages ready for examination. James got up, went to his desk, and returned with a blue pencil of the type often used by draftsmen for marking pages when they did not want the marks to show on camera-ready copies of their work. James passed each page in turn to Kathryn and she marked the top right hand corner with a number so that after thirty minutes' careful work they had a pile of consecutively numbered pages. The table that they were using suddenly seemed pitifully small and inadequate. Kathryn looked at James, quizzically. He thought for a moment and then the idea hit him. He quickly put on a warm sweat suit jacket and asked Kathryn to be ready and hold the door open when he needed it.

She waited and two minutes later he arrived with two table trestles and two eight-foot-by-twelve-inch boards.

"James, you are a wealth of ideas. Where did you get those?"

"Back end of the garage, and they are dry."

He set up the makeshift table that now occupied most of the lounge and then decided to move it into his office, close to his desk where they had more space to walk around the table as they worked.

"A moment, James!"

Kathryn disappeared into the bedroom. He heard the sound of a cupboard door opening and closing, and then she reappeared with a clean bedsheet that she folded and placed onto the planks to use as a tablecloth. She secured the cloth to the wooden planks with thumbtacks, taken from James's desk, so that it would not slip off. All was ready.

"Now James, the pages will be protected as best as we can."

"Good lass."

They laid them out in numerical order, knowing that the side of the vellum that was face down also contained writing and that they should not miss this in their work. James's eyes followed line after line of the multilanguage writing. He surmised that the writer, Oswald, had written the page-by-page account of his life at different times.

"OK, Kath, these pages were written as one would compile a diary, just as you suspected. As near as I can tell from a few minutes' reading is that the diary starts just after the Battle of Poitiers in 1356 and goes on until at least his death."

"Until at least his death?"

"Yes, Kath. The last pages seem to have been written in the latter part of the fourteenth century. At least at first glance. I need to spend time on a careful translation. So are you up to an all-day session?"

"Of course, James. How do we start?"

"I thought that we should put all of my comments on to tape. If you would manage the tape recorder and make sure that my words are recorded and also take notes that would be a great help. Save me a lot of work!"

James frowned as if in deep thought, and suddenly, as if a light had been switched on, he added, "Wait. I have a speech recognition program on my computer that will save us the time of transcribing the notes when we are finished. Just need to get your voice recognized by the computer."

"Got you. That is a great idea, James."

"Sometimes I am so clever I amaze myself."

He went to the desk and took his pocket-sized tape recorder from the bottom drawer. But he had one more thing to do before starting the task at hand.

"Kathryn, my sweet," she beamed at his use of the endearment, "I need to have old Phredd here go through some preliminary steps at recognizing your voice."

"Of course, my dear. But, Phredd?"

"Pictographic high resolution electronic data device. My computer."

"Silly me! Why would I not think of that? Then again, only the mind of an errant scientist could devise such an acronym! As you say, James, a mind is a terrible thing!"

They progressed through the several easy steps of voice recognition. Kathryn was surprised when the computer responded to the set-up that her voice was "new voice. Do you wish to have the voice stored?" The task was duly completed and the computer told them that her voice was now acceptable and was the second programmed voice in the system. Kathryn made a comment about having a computer "talk back like that" and that it might surprise him one day. They were ready to start.

"As I make the rough translation, I will keep my voice low. You speak directly into the tape recorder. If you have any questions, switch off the recorder and we can get the detail that you need. Save us from confusing old Phredd—"

"With a lot of unnecessary words."

"Right, me bonnie wee lass. Ready?"

"Rock on, dude!"

"Where on earth did you hear that?"

"Too much rock on my car radio, James, as I travel around the area. Got to stay awake, you know. Go on, dear. Don't dawdle."

James started to read and translate the documents. Kathryn changed the tapes as necessary and finally, six hours and four pots of tea later, the task was completed. They went into the lounge, rejuvenated the fire where they both sat back on the couch, close to exhaustion.

"James, my dear, that was a monumental session. How are you feeling?" She reached over and touched his hand.

Without thinking he responded using the Saxon English that he had been reading and simultaneously translating during the session.

"Þæt is æðele stenč. . ."

He shook his head, blinked, as though trying to focus and then he realized what he had been doing.

"Sorry, Kath. Don't know what happened. The words seemed to come naturally to me."

"I do apologize. Must have got carried away in the activities of the afternoon." Then he added, "We are well into the afternoon so how about a walk in the fresh air?"

"Sounds delightful. And I think that it will help you to clear your head."

They donned warm coats and a few minutes later were walking arm in arm into the wooded area behind his cottage.

"This path leads in the direction of the sink hole, doesn't it?" Kathryn asked.

"Yes, Kath. We'll not go too near but I just feel that I need to be here to clear my mind and help me think."

She could hear the difference in tone in his voice and knew, instinctively, that there must be a reason.

"Well, James, my dear, I also have something that we need to think about."

They stopped as she took the pocket-sized tape recorder from her coat and switched on the last tape, about halfway through.

The voice came across clear and understandable. In Saxon English. But what surprised James was that it was not his voice.

"Recognize the voice, bonnie lad?"

James could not speak at first. When he found his tongue. He stuttered before the words emerged.

"Of course, it's Oswald!"

"As you progressed through the diary your voice took on more of this tone than at the beginning. Now you hear your Saxon English in the background, before you translated into modern English, I realized that something was going on. But I did not wish to interrupt so I let you carry on with your work and thoughts. And here we are."

They walked in silence back to the cottage. James made sure that the fire was alive and very few words were spoken. The revelation of the tape recorder had taken James by surprise. Kathryn did not know what to say and James was lost in his thoughts. Finally, she broke the silence.

"So, James, it seems like your Oswald is becoming, through you, a real person. This might help you get beyond the Joan of Arc feeling that you are hearing voices. I know that you have dreamed of him and that you believe that you have visited Oswald, but this transposition of his voice into you is something new to both of us. It makes me feel a little less apprehensive but I still worry about your going back in time."

"Kath, my dear, I do not know what my next steps should be."

"But don't sit here and brood. Leave this stuff and come into the kitchen with me and we'll put the kettle on."

The tea was duly made and they sat on the couch in front of the fire where they talked about the latest event, the transposition of Oswald's voice into James's speech, that was on their minds.

"Since," Kathryn exclaimed, "we have this situation occurring in which it appears that you did not realize anything about your voice change, it seems that you may not have realized what you were saying."

James thought a moment, and then he responded. "You are right. The last hour or so of my translation is not something that I can remember too well. So, Kath?"

"You were talking about dates that go beyond 1369. You were talking about dates in the early fifteenth century. And you talked as though you were there!"

James groaned inwardly. His private fears were now coming to the fore and that Alice Campbell's suspicions might be well founded. He could see from Kathryn's expression that her worries were real.

They had just opened another window into the past and they did not know where it would lead.

*   *   *

CHAPTER 11

Kathryn helped James clear away the few remaining dishes from the tea and other food and then she left for her home. As he watched the Range Rover disappear along the road, he felt an overwhelming sense of tiredness. The pounding in his head was now continuous and sharp. He could feel the beginning of a migraine. He had suspected that it was about to commence just before Kathryn left. And he had been correct.

He sat in front of the fire and allowed his eyes to focus on a corner where the wall joined the ceiling. He then started to imagine a pleasant event. In his mind, he and Kathryn were walking through the wooded area near to his cottage. The snow was falling gently and the silence was intense. Not a sound of any animal or bird. Only the pleasant quietness.

James could feel his breathing becoming steady and he knew from experience that his pulse rate would be reduced. After twenty minutes the migraine had disappeared completely. He allowed himself to slowly gather his thoughts and refocus his eyes on his surroundings and then all was well. And now he needed a glass of water. Such mental exercises often left him feeling dehydrated.

A shower and get ready for bed. Yes! That's what he would do.

The shower was refreshing but his mind now awake, he decided to look at Oswald's diary once more. The neat handwriting shone from the vellum pages. How would he handle this with Kathryn? And with Charlie and Sylvia. They knew part of the story but not the complete story. He knew the date of Oswald's death and other facts that he had not even broached during earlier conversations. He knew that the visitations to the past and hearing the voices of Oswald and Margaret had come to him particularly when his mind was open and receptive.

He ran to the telephone and made the quick call to Kathryn. Hoping that it was not too late. Her answering machine offered his only option. James started to record the message, when the sleepy voice came on to the line.

"James, what on earth are you doing? Do you know what time it is? Is everything all right?"

"Kathryn . . . I need to see you. I have a lot of explaining to do. I need to talk."

Kathryn could sense the urgency in his voice. And the unspoken cry for help. She was now fully awake.

"Give me thirty minutes and I'll be right there."

"Kath . . .," he attempted to formulate the words but they would not pass through the dryness of his mouth.

"Don't say anything, James." There was a pause, each not knowing what to say. Kathryn broke the silence.

"James, be a dear and put the kettle on."

Before thirty minutes had passed, the light tap on the door signaled to James that she had arrived, as promised. He had been making himself busy in the kitchen and had not heard the Range Rover as it has glided into the driveway, the light snow fluttering in the headlight beams.

James opened the door. Bright, fresh, rosy-cheeked, not a hair out of place, only a few stray snowflakes on the shoulders of her long winter coat, Kathryn breezed into the cottage. James helped her with her coat.

"Good grief, Kath!"

"Good morning to you too, James. Nice to see you!"

James kissed her on the cheek.

"Sorry, Kath. Thank you for coming."

As she took off her boots, his eyes were focused on her long dressing gown and filmy nightdress underneath. She took her slippers from the bag that she had been carrying.

"You said that you needed to see me and your tone of voice told me that it was urgent. Just enough time to run a comb through my hair!"

James looked at the immaculate coiffure. He could not think by any stretch of the imagination that the mere running of a comb through her hair would . . .

"Well, James my dear, are you going to stare at my night attire?" She mistook the direction of his look, "Or shall we have tea?"

"I was looking at your hair and not staring at your night attire, I was looking at what running a comb through your hair can do, but now that you mention it. Your night attire—"

"James!"

"Yes, dear. Tea."

He disappeared into the kitchen, and a few moments later, reappeared carrying a tray. Kathryn, not being able to resist the challenge, had made sure that the fire was throwing out sufficient warmth. James almost dropped the tray.

"Kathryn! Do you not realize the dangers of being that close to the fire in your night clothes?"

"James, dear, do pour the tea!"

As they sat on the couch and sipped the hot liquid, Kathryn sensed the tension in James's demeanor. She decided to bide her time and let him introduced the topic that had brought her driving to his cottage in the early hours of the morning on a cold snowy winter night. But she could not resist some conversation.

"James, do you realize that we are sitting here in our night clothes looking like a monk and a nun. Your dark robe with the hood and my dark robe, we could be . . ." He appeared to search for the word but James spoke first.

"Benedictines?"

"Yes, I suppose we could."

"There is a reason that I am dressed this way. In addition to the warmth of the robe," Kathryn opened her mouth to speak but James continued, "and I will get to it as soon as I can."

She sensed the strain in his voice and made no effort to finishing her sentence. She leaned over and kissed his cheek.

"I am not sure how to tell you this, but I suppose straight out and to the point is the best way."

He took a deep breath and took her hand in his. He turned to face her and looked straight into her eyes.

"Kathryn, my dear, there are some things that I have not told you. Perhaps I have not even been straightforward and as honest as I should."

He could feel the increased tension in her hand and could see the soft look in her eyes meeting his gaze. Curious. Wondering what was coming next.

"James, I am not sure what you mean."

He reached over and kissed her lightly on the forehead.

"I need to give you the complete story of Oswald and my thoughts about, or ventures into, the past. And a revelation that has come to me that caused me to telephone you. Hence, the reason for my call at this early hour."

She sat with her feet curled underneath her at one side of the couch, and then he began. He covered all of the details, even to the point of consulting his computer files and notes to make sure that he missed nothing from his story. Every small detail was included. The fire had to be replenished twice, but these were only minor interruptions in his monologue. Kathryn listened intently and made no interruptions. His story took almost two hours.

The room was suddenly silent except for the crackling of the fire. Kathryn remained silent as she got up from the couch and went into the kitchen. James could hear the sounds of tea being made. As he entered the kitchen, she looked directly at him and he could see the lines of thought across her brow. The silence was broken.

"So, James, to summarize, you know the exact date of Oswald's death . . ."

"December 11, 1369," he said to emphasize her statement, but Kathryn continued her summary as though James had not spoken.

"You also know details of his life, and you feel that you may even be living a part of his life when you are transported back through time. And you also say that you believe that you have visited Oswald in the past in a time frame after he had died."

The last sentence was not a question. It was a statement. James was surprised but pleased at Kathryn's lack of emotion as she analyzed his story. She recited the summary in a monotone and without question. As though it was an already foregone conclusion.

They returned to the couch and sat once more in front of the fire. Cups of hot tea in their hands. Both deep in thought. She looked at James.

"Yes, I know what you are thinking, Kath. The next step? Well that is why you are here."

Kathryn raised her eyebrows in question as she picked up her cup to take another sip of tea.

"I have, for some reason, been passing over a very important point that just came to me earlier, hence the reason for my telephone call. That is," James paused for a reaction from Kathryn, but seeing none he continued. "As near as I can recall," he said, "I am transported back into the past at a time when I am fully relaxed. As though my mind is open and has no resistance to such thoughts."

Kathryn nodded. "Go on, James, I'm listening."

"There have been various times when I thought that a migraine might be coming on. As you know I have a procedure for averting such an event." Kathryn nodded again. "I use a form of self-hypnosis that I learned some years before when migraines had occurred with alarming frequency. In that technique, I focus my eyes on a distant object in the room and allow pleasant thoughts to invade my mind. After a few minutes, there is a decrease in my pulse rate and my heartbeat slows from the usual eighty beats per minute to about fifty beats per minute. It generally takes fifteen to twenty minutes to slip back to return to full consciousness. Migraine free!"

The shadows from the flickering flames cast a soft light on Kathryn's face. He could see the light in her eyes.

"And James my ever-experimenting scientist, you want to try to do that now? With me here?"

"How did you know?"

"James, my dear, it was a calculated guess!"

"And?"

"I am worried, James. But if it will help, I will do it for you."

James reached over, took her free hand in his, and lightly kissed her fingers.

"Of course it will help, Kath," he said gently, "I have to try!"

Kathryn put down the teacup and resumed the clinical and analytical demeanor that she had taken when she had analyzed his story.

"James, you need to tell me the how, why, where, when, and who so that I am aware of what is happening."

"How? I think that you already know. I will attempt self-hypnosis in your presence and you can monitor my body signs. Why? I have to, Kath. There is no other way to know whether or not . . ."

"You are sane and experiencing these forays into the past," Kathryn interrupted, "or whether you are dreaming?"

James took her words as meaning that she agreed with his innermost thoughts. And he continued to respond to her questions.

"Where? Here, with you, as I said, monitoring my physical signs. Vital signs, I think that the medics call them. When? Right now, or at least as soon as I can get myself prepared. Who? Me. To see if I can contact Oswald or Margaret rather than wait for either of them to contact me!"

Kathryn took a deep breath as she realized that James was serious.

"All right, Kath?"

"*Arl reet*, Jimmy me boy."

Not a time for levity but she sensed that she needed to break the ice by slipping into the Northern vernacular and repeating James's words to show her agreement. The tense look that had shrouded his face softened and he smiled.

"You are such a treasure, me bonnie lass. What would I do without you?"

She smiled back at him, feeling that he needed a break after the intense session that they had just been through.

"What's next?" she asked.

"Well, let's clear away the teacups and I'll show you."

Moments later, James sank to the floor and stretched out on his back. He motioned for Kathryn to join him on the floor, but in a comfortable sitting position with her back to the couch for support. She adjusted herself to sit cross-legged.

"What's next?" she asked again.

James explained that he needed her to monitor his pulse rate and heartbeat, especially the latter if she could. She nodded in agreement and exposed the watch that had been covered by the sleeve of her robe. And then the light went on in her eyes.

"James, your robe!" she exclaimed. "It could be mistaken for a medieval outer garment. It has the style and texture of that era. Now I see the reason for your comment earlier about why you were dressed that way. In addition to the warmth of the robe you wished to dress for your part! You knew that we would be . . ."

She stopped talking as James smiled from his supine position. And then she smiled gently to show that she was in agreement with his foresight.

"James, there are times . . ." She left the threat unspoken. "All right. Next step?"

He explained the procedure and added that if she felt the need to speak it should be only in low quiet tones. She agreed but promised to allow his journey to take its natural course. It was still dark outside and the night sky was not yet ready to convert to the gray of early morning. They would have at least two hours before another day started to make its presence felt. The chances of being disturbed were minimal.

James began his procedure and within minutes Kathryn was monitoring a pulse and heartbeat in the midfifties per minute. He knew that she was with him and would remain by his side. His senses dimmed but he was conscious of her. And then, darkness and a sense that he was no longer lying on the floor. There was something else. James sensed an awakening. The *corpus callosum* of his brain—that bundle of fibers that links the brain's two hemispheres, its function to regulate, pattern, and cross-index the flow of all conscious and unconscious thought—now brought him to another consciousness. Kathryn was no longer there. He was walking.

Alone.

*   *   *

The deserted dark street was not a friendly place. It was cold. Cold enough to be winter, but he was unsure of the season. He turned from the street into an open area that followed the slow-moving river that was dreary and somber in the light of the well-placed lamps. A thin fog had started to creep shoreward along the water's surface. He stopped as he felt the hand on his arm.

"James, you have come on your own! Without our help."

The deep voice of Oswald relieved the tension that James felt at being accosted in such a dark lonely place.

"It is as well that you have come," Oswald took James by the arm. "Come let us retire to a warmer place where we can talk.

Oswald led James through a series of dark streets. James could hear the distant noises in the menacing shadows, diffused and not readily identifiable. The mumbled sounds of human voices, almost as if from another world. The noises floated to his ears as if struggling on the cold night sluggish air.

And then he saw it. The light. A halo around a window covering. The house was built into the side of a hill. The solid stones must have been taken from elsewhere. And suddenly he was walking through the doorway and into a brightly lit room.

The woman was tending to a pot on the fire and pouring steaming liquid from a ladle into a cup.

"Ah, James. My Oswald sensed that you were present. He was uncertain, but he did find you. Here, warm yourself with this pottage." She placed the cup on the table and gave James a kiss on the cheek. As a sister might give a brother. "Now warm yourself lest you freeze. We cannot let you go back to your Kathryn as a sick man!"

James raised his eyebrows, much to Oswald and Margaret's amusement. Margaret continued.

"Yes, James. We are aware of your Kathryn."

Oswald placed his sword on the bench by the wall and sat next to James at the table as Margaret provided a similar bowl of hot vegetable pottage for his warmth.

Then she joined them at the table with a bowl of the hot food. They sipped the pottage from their bowls until the warmth spread through their bodies. Oswald broke the silence.

"Now, James, to business." Oswald paused for effect. "We have need of your help. Although along what lines we cannot tell. It is early in the game!"

James nodded in agreement. "Then, Oswald, tell me what you need."

"We know," Oswald nodded in Margaret's direction and she nodded in agreement, "that there is a game afoot to cause great changes in the way of life in this England. I speak not of a mere murder but a change that could bring about a civil war that would be so devastating that it would change this country forever."

James felt bound to ask "Who?"

"All that we know is it bears a relationship to the death of Sir William de Bohun. He was the cousin of the king, both having the same grandfather, Edward I."

James nodded, having heard of the powerful de Bohun family. "Beyond that, we are not certain of the next step that will lead us along the path to anarchy."

"What do you seek from me?"

"We are not sure, James. All we know is that there is danger about. Our," he looked at Margaret again, "senses tell us that we must be watchful."

"I will do what I can, Oswald."

Margaret smiled and touched his arm. The pressure on his arm continued and he heard the voice, "James, James," but it was not Margaret that spoke. He could feel the gentle pressure of a hand on his arm.

*   *   *

"James, James."

The voice came to James through a cloud. A cloud with a silver lining as he recognized Kathryn's voice. He focused his eyes on Kathryn's face as she leaned over him, still lying on the floor, to help him regain consciousness. He could feel the cold moistness of the facecloth against his brow. His eyes began to focus and then he was back to his normal self, a smile on his face.

Kathryn helped him to get up from the floor and on to the couch. The fire was still resplendent and threw out continuous warmth.

"Tea or a cool drink? You looked to be sweating during your sleep."

"It was the hot pottage."

"What on earth are you talking about, James?"

"The hot pottage. The broth. That Margaret gave me!"

"Come with me. I am not leaving you alone." Kathryn led the way into the kitchen.

"You know why men always allow ladies to go first?"

"James, behave yourself. You have been asleep for twenty minutes and then you tell me you were made to sweat because you drank hot broth?"

Kathryn brandished a can of ginger ale. James nodded in agreement. She took another one for herself, closed the fridge door, and they made their way back to the couch and the fire.

"Now, James. You are telling me that you had hot broth for a meal. You called it pottage."

"Same thing."

"Let me recap for you," Kathryn said. "You went through the procedure that induced self-hypnoses and then promptly fell into a deep sleep. After about ten minutes you started to sweat and then as I tried to wake you, I distinctly heard the words 'I will do what I can, Oswald.' Please explain, James."

James told every detail of his adventure to Kathryn who listened to every word without interruption. Then she spoke.

"First, you look remarkably well for someone who had been awake most of the night. Second, I am tired. Third, you have added another twist to this series of interesting events. Fourth, are you sure of what you are telling me?"

"Absolutely, my dear."

"Oh, James, I am so tired that I do not know what to think."

"Then, what would you like to do?"

"I would like to sleep. It will be dawn in two hours or so. And I am not driving home in this," Kathryn looked in the direction of the window but could not see anything from the drawn curtains, "weather."

"I am not at all tired. And I must get all of the events of the last few hours into my computer while the thoughts are fresh in my mind. So I will work. My bed is yours for as long as you need it. When you awake I will have breakfast ready. But . . ."

"What about my clothes? I remembered to bring an overnight bag with me."

Tired as she was, the light suddenly went on in Kathryn's eyes.

"Good Lord! They are in the Range Rover. And they will be as cold as . . ."

"Iced buns!" said James, referring to small loaves of currant bread with icing on the top but always looking for a play on words in the form of an innuendo or a pun.

"Not funny, James."

"No worries, my love. I'll get them for you."

"I'll spread them out in the bedroom so they will be warm when you awake."

Kathryn sat on the couch and James put on his coat and boots, then struggled through the cold snow and retrieved the overnight bag from the vehicle. He entered the cottage in triumph, brandishing the bag to Kathryn, who was fast asleep on the couch.

He lifted her gently into his arms and carried her into the bedroom. Within moments, he had placed her under the covers and left to work on his computer.

* * *

The next three hours passed quickly. James worked on the computer then he dozed for a few minutes on the couch and was making tea when he heard movements from the bedroom. Kathryn's appearance at the kitchen door took him by surprise.

"Morning, Kath. Sleep well?"

"Who put me into bed last night? And who laid out all of my clothes on the chair?"

"And I'm fine too, Kath. Nice of you to ask."

James turned from the teapot and looked at her standing with her back to the light from the hallway.

"James, sometimes I . . ." No more words could be said and they both dissolved in laughter.

"Go get your robe, bonnie lass, a little cool in some parts of the cottage. What would you like for breakfast?"

"Cereal and hot milk, please. After I shower."

James retrieved the morning paper. The paperboy had thoughtfully placed the paper on a pile of covered logs that was well above the snow line. James thought that another good tip for the boy was in order.

The news was the same as always, with some very poor reporting of the real facts. Well, the newspaper would help light the kindling when the fire had to be started again.

And then Kathryn appeared. Showered. As always, she had not a hair out of place. He looked at her.

"You look lovely, my dear."

This brought a smile to her face. She moved to him and held him for a moment, as if for reassurance.

"Breakfast, James?"

"Right. Here, Kath."

The milk was heated and ready for the cereal. James had the same and then he departed for the shower suggesting that Kathryn use the computer to review the notes that he had written during the night.

Soon he emerged from the shower and dressed to find Kathryn engrossed in reading his notes on the computer.

"James," Kathryn looked at him over the top of her reading glasses, "when I put all of these notes into context, I see a pattern emerging. Oswald is taking you from point to point in chronological order. As though he knows . . ."

The telephone cut off Kathryn's thoughts and made them both jump at the sudden sound.

"Hello."

"James, good morning." James recognized Charlie's voice immediately. "Sorry to have missed you during your last visit. Sylvia tells me you have made one or two nice discoveries. Wondered if you and your good lady would like coffee? Tenish? Here? Not much of a business day. Snow is playing the devil with the traffic. Kathryn might need to be picked up. Would you or should I?

"Yes, Charlie, coffee at about ten. And no need to worry about Kathryn. She is here now. We also have some thoughts to pass on to you and Sylvia."

"Ten it is. See you then, James."

James related the substance of the call to Kathryn. And he also added the part about hearing cooing sounds in the background and the reason for the sounds.

*   *   *

CHAPTER 12

Breakfast was over and the dishes washed and retuned to their respective shelves. They sat on the couch, each with the ubiquitous cup of tea on the nearby table. As if they were at peace with the world. But both of their minds were active. No words were spoken as each pursued individual thoughts. And then, James sensed that Kathryn was about to speak.

"Now, James," her brow furrowed in curiosity, "why are you smiling?"

He decided not to tell her that she was being predictable. "Just smiling at your beauty!"

"Thank you, James, but do be serious!" But he did see the faint traces of pleasure as the corners of her mouth almost moved into a smile. "Now as I was saying, before I was interrupted, what do we tell Charlie and Sylvia?"

Kathryn continued without waiting for, or expecting an answer to, her rhetorical question.

"How much detail should we tell them? You have had many visitations, but unfortunately I cannot confirm any of them. They are yours alone. But I can and will give you all the support that you need. The diary. Your voice change. James, my dear, I hope that Charlie and Sylvia—"

"Do not think that I am a wee bit nuts. Because of my accident last year?"

"But do we have to go into all of that? We have more than enough to hold their interest when we disclose what we found out about the diary. Speaking of which, we have to take it with us."

"Yes," he agreed. "Charlie and Sylvia need to see it."

James got up and wrapped the collection of pages into the protective vellum covering and placed the package into his briefcase. As he sat down he turned so that he could face Kathryn.

"Sooner or later, Kath, I feel that we will have to take Charlie and Sylvia into our confidence."

"Then, James, dear boy, let's play it by ear."

"Of course!" James smiled. "OK, it is decided. Shall we?"

Kathryn looked at the clock and nodded.

"I'll get the coats,"

He helped Kathryn into her coat. She moved as if to leave with him.

"Wait there, Kathryn, and I'll start the car and get a little warmth through it before we leave."

Kathryn felt warmth spreading throughout her body. She did not hear the car start. Her attention was diverted to the shadows of the fire as they flickered and danced through the room. She heard a whispered sound and turned her head to look in the direction of the door, thinking that James had returned. And then, as if by instinct, she knew that she was not alone.

James returned moments later to find Kathryn sitting on the couch, her coat removed, and staring wide-eyed at the fire. A slight smile on her face.

"Kath?"

"Please telephone Charlie and tell him we are running a little late."

"We are?"

"I need to relate something amazing to you before we leave."

As James dialed Charlie's number he was mystified by Kathryn's statement but felt the urgency of her words.

"Fine, James, see you soon," Charlie replied.

"Now, Kath?

"A moment, James, please."

He took off his coat and sat on the couch beside Kathryn. She turned and looked straight into his eyes.

"I have heard them, James!"

"Heard what, Kathryn?" Then the light went on. "You mean Oswald? And Margaret?"

"Yes, when you were starting the car. The voices in my mind. I thought that I too was Joan of Arc for a moment. The gentleness of Oswald's voice as he told me that I was not to worry. All would be well and that he would look after you. I thought . . ." James could see that tears forming in Kathryn's eyes. "He sounded so gentle and sincere. And then I heard Margaret's voice, woman to woman, as if to reassure me that she would do the same. I did not, or really I could not, say anything but they seemed to be reading my mind."

James moved closer and put his arm around Kathryn, expecting the tears to flow. He worried about the shock to her senses.

"James, it was so beautiful."

Her face had that look of contentment, as though a weight had been lifted from her shoulders. "James, my dear, if ever I doubted you, I am so sorry. Now I know what you have been going through."

She kissed him lightly on the forehead and before he could respond she added, "Let's go for coffee with Charlie and Sylvia."

The warm Jaguar glided through the Bridgeford High Street. A few of the villagers waved as they went about their tasks that also included shoveling snow from the paths. As the car slid quietly into the vicarage driveway, the gravel no longer noisy under the wheels because of the snow, the vicarage door opened. Charlie and Sylvia were eagerly awaiting their arrival. It was apparent that Charlie had cleared the snow from the front of the house. James and Kathryn entered amidst smiles and the general chitchat of greetings and the weather. Their coats were hung in the warm closet and they adjourned to the lounge. James took his briefcase with him. A pot of fresh coffee and a plate of fresh scones and containers of fresh cream and strawberry jam awaited them. Finally, all four were seated and ready to talk.

"Well, James, we hope all is well?"

"It is Charlie. But the reason that we wanted to talk is to get both of you up to date on events since Saturday."

As always, Charlie, suspecting that a several-cup conversation was in the offing, waved his pipe in the air. "Anyone mind?" No one answered so that the pipe was duly lit and once Charlie was puffing contentedly, he offered that he was sorry to have missed their return visit on Saturday but Sylvia had told him of the find. James and Kathryn took that as a sign to begin.

James opened his briefcase and suggested that they lay it on the table where all four could study it at the same time. Thoughtfully, Charlie extinguished his pipe but Sylvia suggested that they use the dining room with its convenient large table. Sylvia cleared away the remaining refreshments and all was ready.

The pages were laid out onto the table. Immediately, Sylvia noticed the faint numbers on one corner of each page.

"Well done, James, Kathryn. No danger of a mix-up if the diary is dropped."

Sylvia tended to be a purist where old documents were concerned and felt that they should not be marked at all. But James was pleased to hear her agreement with what they had done to maintain the chronological identity of the pages. Charlie and Sylvia started to make a close examination of the contents of each page. They had brought two magnifying glasses from Charlie's study to make the examination easier. James and Kathryn sat down and remained silent as Charlie and Sylvia commenced their work. Then Sylvia looked up.

"Please. Forgive us but if you would rather have coffee and relax in the lounge while we make our first examination of the pages?"

Without further ado, James and Kathryn did just that. They both knew that to disturb them, now that their interest was peaked, would be to destroy a golden opportunity.

As they sat in the lounge, James was pleased to see the relaxed look on Kathryn's face. Gone were the obvious signs of worry. It was as if the sound of Oswald and Margaret's voices had made her realize that James was indeed communicating with some one from the past. He could feel the absence of tension in her voice and general behavior. She was back to the Kathryn that he knew before all of this had started several months ago.

They talked. They laughed. They drank coffee and ate another two scones each. It took one hour before Charlie and Sylvia came into the lounge. Kathryn was the first to speak.

"Coffee? Charlie? Sylvia?"

"I'll get it," Sylvia offered.

"No, Sylvia," Kathryn was insistent. "Please take a moment to collect your thoughts. I know the state of mind that James and I were in when we first examined the document, or what we call a diary. Back in a minute." Kathryn left for the kitchen.

Charlie and Sylvia sat back. Both lost in thought. Sylvia smiled at James.

"Kathryn is such a dear person, James. Do you think—"

"Sylvia, my dear, please," Charlie interrupted.

James thought for a moment.

"No. Charlie. It is all right. Kathryn and I think a lot of each other and we have become such dear friends and we are very close to each other to the point where . . ."

At that moment Kathryn returned to hear the last few words that James had spoken. Her smile was radiant.

"Coffee, anyone."

Once more the four were settled with a cup of coffee each, and Charlie had his pipe lit.

"So, Sylvia, Charlie?" inquired James.

"Yes, James. Want to start, my dear?" Charlie turned to Sylvia who nodded as she momentarily turned over the words in her mind. Then she spoke.

"This is quite a find. I have not had the time for a detailed look, but I know of no other work that recounts a man's actions like this one. Perhaps Samuel Pepys's diary from the late seventeenth century, but these pages are a phenomenal record of an intimate and personal part of a man's life." She looked at James and Kathryn. "I know that you have been meeting with Dr. Alice Campbell so I am wondering if you have any further pertinent information?"

James and Kathryn looked at each other. Both decided that this was the time to make a full disclosure. Kathryn read James's mind and nodded in agreement.

"I would like Kathryn to tell the story. She has a somewhat less jaundiced and much more objective view than I do. She has read all of my notes and she can also offer some experiences of her own. So how about it, bonnie lass?"

Kathryn gasped at the unexpected request. Charlie and Sylvia smiled.

"James, are you sure?"

He nodded. "Certain, my dear."

Kathryn related the story and did not omit any of the details. She had read the information contained in James's computer and her near-photographic memory allowed her to give an accurate account to her audience. No one interrupted as she laid out one detail after another. There was hardly a breath in the room.

Sylvia spoke first. All eyes were on her. "It seems to me, James, that this fellow Oswald has an urgent reason for wanting to contact you. But why?"

"That is the part that I cannot tell you, Sylvia." James continued, "All I know is that he used the words indicating that they may have need of me. Soon."

"Now, let us sit back and think this out clearly." Charlie's thoughts had clarified in his mind. "I'll give you a point-by-point synopsis of my thoughts and let's see where they take us." Charlie looked at his audience, placed his pipe on the coffee table, and continued.

"First. Oswald died a tragic death in the sinkhole." Three heads nodded in agreement and three pairs of eyes focused on Charlie. "Second. He was loyal to his king. Third. Oswald's death occurred in December 1369. Fourth. He seems to have held a position of importance as a bodyguard to Edward III. Fifth. The year 1369 was one of the first years," Charlie looked at Sylvia, "correct me if I'm wrong, my dear, that Edward's health was coming into question. He was, in that year, 57 years old. Getting on in years for that time period. Sixth. All was set for his son Edward, also known as the Black Prince because of the color or sheen of his armor, to become Edward IV." Again, nods of agreement. "Seventh. But Prince Edward died in 1376, one year before his father. Richard, Prince Edward's son and King Edward's grandson, became king upon King Edward's death in 1377." Charlie gazed at the ceiling, as if to focus his eyes and his mind. "Good grief, could it be?" He reached for the pipe.

"What is it, Charles?"

James and Kathryn sat silent as Sylvia's question broke into Charlie's train of thought. Charlie continued.

"England entered into a very turbulent period. John of Lancaster, also known as John of Gaunt, became regent during Richard's minority. Gaunt was disliked by many of the nobles. Some of whom had convinced the king, Gaunt's father, that Gaunt's time would be better spent protecting the king's domains in France and other parts of Europe. So Gaunt knew that he was to be sent out of England for an unknown period of time. Otherwise, why send Oswald on this journey to protect his, that is Gaunt's, interests and his family's future? What with the Peasants' Revolt of the 1380s and other disturbances, it seems to me that England was close to revolution and that Richard and his close advisors, Gaunt excluded, were on the point of seeing a revolt. Richard would be blamed and the line of inheritance of the throne would be changed."

"And this period of anxiety ended," Sylvia interjected, reading Charlie's next thought, "when Richard and his advisors made the mistake of banishing Gaunt's son Henry Bolingbroke to France. But Bolingbroke returned with force, usurped and displaced Richard, and ascended the throne as Henry IV. So all's well that ends well and England then entered into a period of internal calm, although the war with France was very real. But, nevertheless . . ."

"What if," Charlie picked up the story again and looked directly at James, "your friend Oswald foresees this as well as other skullduggery on the horizon and requires help to keep everything on track and in the correct order?"

The room was filled with silence. Charlie's words seemed to be bouncing off the walls, repeating themselves in everyone's mind. Again, Sylvia broke into the silence.

"Are you really suggesting, Charles, that Oswald suspects or even knows of a plot to, for the want of a better expression, change history?"

"I believe that I am, my dear."

Kathryn spoke up, "But Charlie, I am a little confused. There is a general thought that one cannot change history. So?"

"I believe that is true. But when we speak of that issue, it is history, as we know it. Oswald may have stumbled onto something that he believes will change matters for the worse. What if Oswald has suspicions that, in the first instance, the death of Prince Edward was not an accident. What if our friend Oswald sees that the death of Prince Edward was a means to an end by which persons of a particular political persuasion were involved? In other words, an anti-Gaunt faction that wished to change the correct order, and assume control of the throne, to meet their own ends. Gaunt's assumption of the role of regent would only spike their guns for an interim period, say until Richard's death, by fair means or foul."

"Charles, do you not think that your idea may be . . ."

"A little far-fetched? Of course I do, my dear. But . . ."

James and Kathryn smiled at each other as they heard Sylvia and Charlie starting and finishing each other's thoughts.

"We have to start somewhere. And consider this. Gaunt, in 1369, suspects that something is afoot that is against himself and his family. He starts to prepare a hoard of wealth as a form of protection or to equip an army. In his prolonged after-life experiences, Oswald picks up on this and knows that he cannot handle this himself. So he contacts our friend James here," Charlie nodded in James's direction, "as a person that he can trust and rely upon for help. I think—"

"That we should have a break, a late lunch, and a spot of tea."

James and Kathryn stood up immediately. Ready for the break after the intense discussion.

"Sylvia," this time it was James who broke the silence of the moment, "I would like to suggest that we make it a very light lunch. We can talk here all afternoon and perhaps only get a little further than we have to at this point. We can speculate until the cows come home and perhaps make no headway."

Then Kathryn suggested, "If we dine very lightly and then go back into the crypt. There may be something else that we have missed."

All eyes turned to Kathryn at her suggestion. Charlie almost exploded.

"Well said, my dear. An excellent suggestion. Are we all agreed?" No one objected. "Then Sylvia, my dear, how about soup?"

Lunch arrived quickly and was soon finished. They sat around the table to relax for a while. Charlie fiddled with his pipe, threatening to smoke it but never quite getting to that point. Sylvia knew that he was on the verge of speaking, so she opened the gate for him.

"Charles, you are fiddling again. What is on your mind?"

"Well, m'dear, I am wondering how far we can go with this and what our next steps should be."

"Do go on, Charles."

"We have a situation in which two close friends," he gestured to James and Kathryn who both smiled in appreciation of his use of the words, "who have both had a remarkable . . ." Charles sought for the word that Sylvia provided.

"Experience?"

"Thank you, my dear. Yes, experience. That's seems to follow on directly from your accident last year, James."

The pipe was now lit and the odor of fragrant tobacco permeated the room. No one offered to interrupt knowing that Charlie's thoughts would be placed before them in a logical manner.

"As we discussed earlier," Charlie spoke the words through a cloud of smoke, "the time period of interest to us was one of several turbulent periods in English history where there were shifts in the monarchy. So, after thinking this out for the past hour or so, I am firmly convinced that your friend," he gestured to James, "Oswald was involved in preserving the correct order and now seems to be seeking your help."

"And let us not forget, Charles, that there seems to be the hint of a genetic relationship between James . . ." Sylvia now looked at James as she spoke "and Oswald."

"Good point, m'dear. So we have two options ahead of us. The first is that James must dig more into the possibility of genetic memory. I recall that you have had discussion with Dr. Spiller at Dryburn Hospital that result from his study of genetic memory. Perhaps a visit to him is in order? Might help to delve more into this. Followed by a search of the Internet to see what the latest developments are?"

"Good idea, Charlie," James nodded in agreement as he spoke "but . . ."

"What about the other option?" Kathryn had the light of discovery in her eyes as she spoke and followed on immediately. "Of course. Alice Campbell. She could help with the research of the papers in the Dean and Chapter Library and perhaps fill in some of the blanks related to the various events of the 1370 to 1420 period."

"But, Kath, why that period?

"James, did not Alice tell you that she thought that the scribe was still writing in the time of Henry IV or was it Henry VI?"

"Aye, lass, you are correct. And it was Henry VI." James nodded and smiled at Kathryn as he uttered his agreement.

"Thank you, James. So I propose that we follow up with Alice and look into what she has found!" James opened his mouth to speak but Kathryn followed up immediately. "The real estate market is a little slow right now and I feel that I am very involved in this mission, having also been contacted!"

"Charlie, do you mind?" James asked.

"Not at all, James, you know where the telephone is."

James left the room to return moments later. "Alice will see us," he looked at Kathryn and smiled, "tomorrow at ten. Charlie. Sylvia. I hope that you do not mind us moving ahead like this without you?"

"No, James, not at all." Sylvia spoke up immediately.

James was relieved at Sylvia's response but felt that courtesy dictated that he offer them the choice.

"So what's next?"

Kathryn smiled. "Forever the scientist, James. Always to the point." And the four voices spoke in unison. "The crypt!"

Dressed in warm clothing, they adjourned to the church and made their way to the spot behind the altar where the entry to the crypt had been concealed. Charlie and James moved the stone and entered the crypt first, then they helped Sylvia and Kathryn as they descended into the crypt with flashlights shining and lighting the way before them. Once into the crypt, Charlie lit the two lanterns that he had left on a previous occasion, instinctively knowing that they would visit the crypt again, and it was Charlie who broke the silence.

"Well, here we are again. What do you propose?"

"I think, Charles," Sylvia answered, "that we should search through the various documents and determine if anything similar to Oswald's diary exists. Perhaps we can find other clues?"

"Good idea, my dear. Kathryn? James?"

Neither Kathryn nor James had spoken since they entered the crypt. Kathryn had felt a chill and a shiver ran through her body so she held on to James's arm as though in need of protection. Finally, James spoke.

"We need as much information as we can find. It seems that this may be the repository of Oswald's effects but for some reason I feel that it is not only a storage place but I sense that it had been used frequently in times past."

"By Ranulf de Boise?"

James turned to face Kathryn as they disengaged their arms. "Yes, my dear. If we look around, we can see that the materials in here are placed in an orderly fashion."

"As though we are in a library or private study!" Kathryn added.

"That is the thought that I have been seeking and the sensation that I have been feeling," James stated.

"Then I propose," it was Sylvia who now broke into their thoughts "that you two, having had contact with Oswald and his dear wife, Margaret, let your thoughts and instincts unfold. You may, after all, be able to detect some clue as to the purpose of this room. Can you do that?"

"Not sure, Sylvia," James looked at Kathryn and saw the barely imperceptible affirmative nod, "but we'll give it a try. Kath, are you all right?"

"Yes, but my experience at your cottage," she smiled at Sylvia and Charlie and frowned at James as if daring him to comment, "after I heard the voices has made me a little wary and very nervous of what is to be next. I now approach this with a very different outlook. But as long as," she took James's hand in hers and smiled again, "we can go forward together I'll be all right."

"Well done, dear girl. We also have the protection of the Almighty in this church," Charlie exclaimed.

"All right, let's be at it!" James rubbed his hands together as if accepting the challenge and looking forward to whatever would come next.

"Charles, when we were last here we each looked around and that may be the most efficient or profitable way of searching for whatever it is that we seek. So I suggest that we use that tactic again."

"Good idea, my dear, but . . . back in a moment."

Charlie left the crypt and they could hear the diminishing sound of his footsteps on the stone slab floor as he left the church. Then Sylvia realized why Charlie had left. Soon, they heard his footsteps again as they grew louder and Charlie's voice penetrated the crypt.

"Look out below." Four cushions and blankets arrived through the opening followed by Charlie. "Thought these would help if we need to sit or need extra warmth."

"Thank you, Charles my dear. How thoughtful!"

Charlie went back to the crypt entrance and reached out into the church to collect some other items from the church floor. Extra lamps.

"Thought we could use a little more light."

As if by a prearranged signal, each one of the four sought out a different area of the crypt to examine the documents and other objects. The silence was complete. After about thirty minutes, Kathryn whispered to James.

"Where was it that you found Oswald's diary?"

"Back there," James gestured over his shoulder, "there's a small alcove that is difficult to see unless you shine the light directly on it. A small shelf is inset into the wall."

"Just going to prowl and stretch my legs. The cold is already giving me a few aches."

James agreed. He was also feeling the dampness creep up his legs, inch by inch from the floor. Charlie and Sylvia seemed to be unperturbed by the cool conditions and were intent on their work. Moments later, Kathryn reappeared.

"I need your help."

The trembling tone of her voice made the three of them look up suddenly from the respective studies. James was the first to sense the urgency of her voice. He stood up and as she moved closer to him, he put his hands on her shoulders, holding her in a steady grip.

"Kath, what is it?"

He could feel her shaking under the heavy coat. Her face seemed whiter in the glow of the lamps. She half-turned and pointed. "I heard the voices again. Mostly Margaret's voice. With the sound of Oswald in the background. Both trying to comfort me. Gentle words. Back there."

"Come on, Kath." As she turned, James put his arm around her shoulders. "Let's go see. Charlie? Sylvia?"

"We're with you. Bringing a lamp each."

One by one they entered the small alcove, the light from their lamps lighting up the area. And then they saw it. In the exact and same place where James had found the first package.

All four drew in a sharp breath. Kathryn, in surprise, put her hands over her mouth. Charlie coughed nervously. Sylvia opened her mouth to speak but the words did not emerge. James, the ever-vigilant scientist, reached out and picked up the small package from where it lay on the shelf.

"OK, everybody," he said, "let's get into the light and examine what we have found!"

*　　*　　*

CHAPTER 13

J ames carried the four-inch square package to the spot where he had been studying the documents. Kathryn, Sylvia, and Charlie followed him eagerly. He placed the package on the stone table and looked at his companions.

"OK, first we do nothing other than look at the outside of the package. Agreed, Sylvia?"

"Agreed, James. Just as we would when finding any artifact, may I?

"By all means, Sylvia, we'll follow your lead."

"Let's set up the lamps," Sylvia said, "so that we can better see." She looked at Kathryn, who seemed to be frowning. "Are you all right?"

"I'm fine, Sylvia. Just not quite used to being a modern-day Joan of Arc. The voices have disturbed me a little."

"All right, Charles, how about taking notes as I talk?"

Sylvia was a talented organizer and when she was in control of her field of expertise, she was unbeatable.

"Certainly my dear." Charles had a pencil and notepaper ready.

"Small package. Approximately four inches square. Vellum. That's odd." Sylvia paused as she examined the vellum. "It appears to be the best, made from calf skin, and not from the coarser materials that one so often sees. And it is quite soft as though it was recently made rather than that hard stuff that we see covering older books. It is quite a delicate color, almost white. Not too dusty considering the possible age. Marking on one side. Ah, ah!"

Her sudden exclamation as she turned the package over took them all by surprise. They leaned forward and could see the marking. James was the first to react.

"Oswald's mark but it's different," he said.

"Yes," Sylvia added, "there is a small cross at the bottom of the circle."

"Good grief!" Charlie exclaimed, "It is from Margaret, Oswald's wife!"

"Charles?" Sylvia looked at him quizzically.

"Look, my dear. The small cross. Remember, from Greek mythology, the circle with the oblique arrow transverse from bottom left to top right is the male sign, the shield and spear of Mars," Charlie took a breath then continued. "The circle with the cross attached to the bottom is the female sign, the looking glass of Venus. So, this small cross at the bottom of the circle of Oswald's mark signifies a female. Margaret. Who else?"

"Charles, my dear, you are brilliant." Sylvia glowed with pride at her husband's deduction.

"Well done, Charlie." James reached for the package. "May I?"

"Of course."

James allowed his hands to roam freely over the exterior of the package.

"I have a sneaking sense of what this might be!"

James opened the carefully folded vellum. As he unfolded each of the first two folds, his fingers became aware of something hard within the center of the package. He was conscious of the slow breathing of each of the other three members of the group. He opened the final two cross folds and there they were. Two small white chalklike tablets. He picked up one of the tablets and let it rest in his palm, then he sniffed the tablets, moistened the tip of the little finger of his left hand, and gently touched it. Before anyone knew what he was doing, he placed the tip of his finger onto the tip of his tongue.

"James! No!" Kathryn warned.

James smiled as he announced "Just as I thought. Aspirin!"

"James. You don't mean to tell us," Kathryn had sufficiently recovered from her outburst, "that those are the tablets that you . . ."

"Yes, Kath," James answered, "the tablets that I left with Oswald. I left a handful with him and how better to communicate with us than by sending us something that I left him. He, or perhaps I should say Margaret, is trying to show that she is able to communicate with us through this place. Perhaps you were the target of Margaret's communication. Just to let you know that all is well. Woman to woman."

Kathryn felt a sense of well-being with James's words.

"Well, it seems to me," Charlie broke into the conversation, "that it would be only courteous to send a sign back indicating that you have received the package. And I would not recommend that you merely use the same contents . . ."

"Let us remember," Sylvia added, "that this is a means of trying another route other than the voices. There must be an ultimate goal for Oswald and Margaret to try this tactic."

"And I am sure we will find that out in time." Charlie appeared to ponder the issue for a few seconds.

"You cannot write a note to Margaret," Charlie continued, "because if it is found by anyone else it might be construed as witchcraft! You know, the different handwriting and the language."

"I propose that I use a different sign," Kathryn suggested.

"And that would be, Kath?" James asked.

"Simple, James." Kathryn smiled as she spoke. "I place a small lady's handkerchief that can be folded thus," she took a small lace handkerchief from her pocket, "and fold it thus, rewrap it in the vellum and . . ."

"Bingo! Well done, my dear." Charlie could hardly contain his emotions. "Let's do it."

And so the handkerchief was wrapped in the vellum. The small tight package was placed onto the surface where Kathryn had first discovered it. Charlie smiled as he looked at the neat package.

"I think that at this point we adjourn for tea? What we have just done should determine if this area of the crypt is a bridge to the past, specifically to Oswald."

Sylvia linked her arm through Kathryn's and the two led the way to the exit. Leaving James and Charlie to understand that the answer to the suggestion of tea was a resounding yes. Charlie helped Sylvia through the opening. "Go on, Charlie, you next. I'll help Kathryn."

"Thank you, James."

Charlie scrambled though the exit. And then James helped Kathryn, allowing her to emerge through the entrance and into the church.

Charlie and James returned the large stone cover to its position, and they made their way from the church to the vicarage. They followed Sylvia into the kitchen. The kettle was filled, water boiled, and soon they each had a cup of hot steaming tea.

In the meantime, Charlie had recovered his pipe and was adding fresh tobacco to the bowl.

"It seems to me that we may have discovered a gate, a channel, a bridge, whatever, into the past."

"Let's call it a bridge, Charlie," James interrupted. "That is the word Oswald used when he spoke to me last December."

"A bridge it is." Charlie had lit the tobacco and now seemed stimulated by its aroma. "We may have discovered a bridge to the past, specifically to Oswald and Margaret. This has been done for a purpose. We do not know for what purpose. We need," he looked at Kathryn and James, "you to further our knowledge of the details of the fourteenth century. Or, to be more precise, as you suggested, my dear," Charlie nodded at Kathryn, "the 1370 to 1420 period. As we discussed earlier, the Peasants' Revolt of the 1380s, and other disturbances, have made it seem that Richard II and his close advisors, Gaunt excluded, were on the point of seeing a revolt. Should this have occurred, Richard would be blamed and perhaps the line of inheritance to the throne would have been changed. Had that happened, who knows what the result would have been? I for one prefer England, the modern evolution of the Western world, to follow along the path that we already know."

"I think that I see where you are going, Charlie."

"So if your friend Oswald needs help because of something that he foresees, we must give it to him. Whatever the cost. And there will be a cost!"

"Charles, my dear, do you really believe that?" Sylvia asked the question that was in their minds.

"The changes could be so drastic? That is an unknown, but I am sure that if we follow this path, there will be a cost to one or more of this small but elite group. In other words, one or more of us will change forever! By what force, I do not know. I just sense . . ."

Charlie allowed his word to trail into the pipe smoke. The only sound was the puffing of the pipe.

James raised his cup in a toast. "Well, for me, let me put it this way. Whatever we find, whatever it takes, we must do the right thing. A person must stand up and be counted for what he or she believes to be correct."

Sylvia looked at Charlie. Kathryn remained silent. Brows furrowed and a look of foreboding was in her eyes. Then James stood up and placed himself behind Kathryn and put his hands on her shoulders. He kissed her head.

Do not worry, Kath, my dear. We will discover what is going on. It may . . ."

"Be difficult and dangerous, James!"

As she spoke, his fingers sensed the slight shudder in her body. He squeezed her shoulders gently as if to reassure her.

"We can face this together." He looked at Charlie and Sylvia who nodded their agreement. "As the Duke of Wellington is supposed to have said to his guards at waterloo, 'Up and at 'em lads and lasses.'"

"James," it was Sylvia who spoke, "your paraphrasing of history is atrocious. But we all love you for it. So what is next?"

The tension left the air. James sat once more at the table.

"If I recall," Kathryn had regained her composure and she continued "we, James and I that is, have a meeting with Alice Campbell tomorrow and we can investigate what she has found. We will focus on all of the papers that seem to be related to Oswald. I certainly hope that she has been able to copy the papers that she found at the British Library?"

"I am convinced," Kathryn suddenly spoke up, "that there is a reference to the issue hidden in Oswald's writings. He seems to have had his finger on the pulse of the late fourteenth century, even though he was supposedly dead."

Kathryn seemed to have been transformed. She was now more forthright and willing to play a lead role in the investigation of the mystery. She was no longer the silent helper.

Charlie stood up, brandished the teapot, and broke the silence.

"More tea, anyone? And perhaps a few of your fresh scones, my dear. It's been a while since lunch and the coldness of the crypt."

Charlie and James made the tea, procured the scones from the cupboard, along with jam, and cream from the refrigerator. When all was ready, Sylvia spoke.

"We," Sylvia looked at Kathryn as she addressed James and Charlie, "have decided that there will be no further talk of this situation today. We will have a very pleasant tea and discuss other matters. Even football, if you wish. Kathryn and I need to break."

Charlie looked relieved. "Of course, my dear."

All four sat around the table, and the tea and scones were attacked with gusto. After having exhausted the topic of football, what else, and various other political and mundane items. It was already evening.

James and Kathryn left promising to keep Sylvia and Charlie abreast of any interesting happenings at the forthcoming meeting with Alice Campbell.

*   *   *

Kathryn arrived at James's cottage promptly at eight o'clock the next morning. As her Range Rover pulled into the driveway, James opened the door and stepped out into the coolness. He was dressed for the weather and ready to go. As she climbed into the vehicle, Kathryn moved across the front seat to the passenger side.

"Thought you would not mind driving, James, and since my car is warm."

She leaned over and gave him a light kiss on the cheek. "Good morning, my dear!" She placed her hand on his arm.

James smiled. "How about a nice hot cup of coffee in Durham?"

"Sounds great, James."

He reversed the vehicle out of the driveway and drove along the main street, of the village in silence. Minutes later, as the vehicle entered the Durham road, he could hold his silence no longer.

"Kathryn, are you all right?" James could sense something different in her demeanor. "You seem a little different today."

"I know, James. Did not sleep much last night. Yesterday's events kept my mind awake and I just could not settle. But I feel great. Almost rejuvenated by my experience of the presence of Margaret and Oswald. I just wish that I knew where I fit into all of this. I wish I knew how we both fit into all of this?"

"Don't worry, Kath, my dear."

She glowed inwardly at his use of the two endearing words. "I know, James. But I do wonder about it."

"Kath!"

"Yes, James. Time will tell. For the wrong reasons the right things happen."

James smiled, reached over, and squeezed her hand gently. She smiled and they settled into pleasant quietness for the remainder of the drive.

Forty-five minutes later, having parked the Range Rover in the parking lot, they were sitting in the breakfast room of the Royal County Hotel. They ordered coffee and now had the cups of hot milky liquid in front of them. As Kathryn stirred the coffee, she broke the silence.

"All right, bonnie lad!"

"Well, at least you did not say old lad!"

"What are we looking for when we visit Alice? We need to be very particular and our search must have a focus."

"Step or two ahead of you, me bonnie lass."

James reached down and retrieved his briefcase from where he had placed it against the table leg.

"Aha! Wondered why you had brought that!"

He extracted his notepad and gave it to Kathryn to study his handwritten notes. She quickly produced her reading glasses from her handbag.

"Busy last night, weren't you?"

"Yes, thought I'd get something down as a reminder!"

She did not answer but kept her gaze in the direction of the notes on the table and focused on the two pages.

After ten minutes, she looked at James. "I agree with your thoughts. We should first establish the identity of the pre- and post-1370 material that Alice has found that she credits to the same author."

"We need to establish that the post-1370 writing is that of Oswald?" James put his elbow on to the table and cradled his head on his hand, as he looked down at the stark white tablecloth. He was to be deep in thought.

"You will see, Kath, that the end of my notes contains a list of possible events and players who influenced major events in the late fourteenth century. But who knows? We may actually be seeking a lesser event that never became well known or we may actually be on a fishing expedition. Now let me tell you where you fit in."

"Awfully kind of you, dear boy." Kathryn teased.

James looked at his watch. The time had passed quickly.

"How about if we discuss this on the way to the cathedral? Are you in for a walk?"

They finished the coffee; James put his notepad back into his briefcase, collected their coats, and were soon outside in the cool air. He offered his free arm to Kathryn and they traced their route back along Old Elvet Bridge. The businesses were starting to open and the footpaths were busy with people.

James suddenly spoke.

"Kathryn, initially I did not want you involved in this because of the inherent dangers that might manifest themselves."

"But I am!"

"Also, you have a near-photographic memory for historical data in that pretty little head of yours."

Kathryn beamed as James went on.

"For this reason, we can read documents and compare notes. My hobby has always been history but you bring to this a clear mind that is unencumbered with preconceived notions. For that alone you will be of great assistance."

Kathryn stared straight ahead as they picked their steps carefully between the pedestrians. James continued.

"As I found out with the voices on the tape recorder there is much more to this issue than I had ever imagined. And now that Oswald and Margaret have made themselves known to you, you are involved. It is as though they were trying to tell us both the same message. We have to do this together. I am sure that Oswald and Margaret will look after you. But there must be a reason," James hesitated for a few breaths and then continued. "But most of all, I need you with me."

"Well, good morning to both of you."

They turned to determine the source of the voice coming from behind.

"Phillip. Good morning to you too."

"James, Kathryn. Nice to see both of you again. How are you?"

They stopped, smiled, and responded with similar greetings to Phillip Spiller, the young medical doctor who had treated James in hospital after the accident, and who also had introduced James to the concept of genetic memory.

"Off to the cathedral, are you?"

"Yes, Phillip, a little bit of work in the Dean and Chapter Library with Alice Campbell. You remember her?"

"Of course. Very nice young lady. I'm off in the other direction. Do you have an appointment for a check-up in the near future, James?

"I think that my next appointment is in June." James paused then saw that there might be an ulterior motive for the question. "Why, Phillip?'

"I have come across more information about genetic memory, if you are interested." James's eyes lit up. "And I see that you are, James. How about if we meet later."

"I was about to contact you on that issue!" James exclaimed, not believing the coincidence. "Lunch or dinner, Phillip?"

"I'll be in my office later this morning so why don't you call me." Spiller thought for a moment before he added, "Or let's make contact by e-mail. Save us playing telephone tag. Here, James."

Spiller took a business card from the pocket of his overcoat and gave it to James. It had his e-mail address on it, and his cell phone number.

"Must be off. Have a lovely day."

They bade him goodbye and continued the walk along Saddler Street to the Cathedral precincts. Fifteen minutes later they were in the outer office of the Dean and Chapter Library and had made the request to the receptionist to notify Dr. Alice Campbell that Mrs. Kathryn Stainsby and Dr. James Simpson were ready whenever she was available. They thanked the receptionist for the offer of tea or coffee but refused. Then Alice's voice came to them from the doorway adjacent to their seat.

"How lovely to see you both." Alice greeted them warmly with a hug. "Have you been offered tea or coffee?"

"Yes, thanks, Alice." James turned and nodded his appreciation to the receptionist. "But we just had coffee at the Royal County."

"So, you are ready?"

They followed Alice through the doorway and back into the room from where she had appeared. The room was a major part of the Dean and Chapter Library and held many of the large volumes that had come into the possession of the cathedral through the centuries. The rich leather smell of the bindings and the odor of the vellum and old paper made it a heady experience. Especially to James, a seasoned and avid book and document collector.

Alice took them through the library and into the large room that had once been the monks' dormitory. Part of it was used as a reading area for library users and was not accessible to the public. James and Kathryn were surprised that she did not take them to her office. Alice decided to explain.

"I have so much stuff to show you that I thought that the large table, one of the original oak dining tables used by the monks, would be more appropriate for what we need to do. We will not be disturbed by any of the public who visit the other side of the dormitory."

As they approached the table, James and Kathryn could see that Alice had been very busy prior to their arrival. Document after document was placed on the table so that the surface was covered. The documents were either a single page or a collection of two or more pages. The sheer number of pages took their breath away.

"I have arranged these documents in chronological order. They are either works that consist of a single page only and some of the works consist of several pages. Where would you like to start?"

"Where indeed!" James exclaimed. He had not taken his eyes off the table. He was mesmerized by the amount and splendor of the material. He could see the neat handwriting that covered the pages. Finally he found his tongue.

"Alice, can we start at the beginning with the earliest documents and perhaps you give us a summary of what you have found?

"Of course. Please take a pew. No pun intended but the chairs that you are sitting in were formerly pews until the eighteenth century when someone decided to make them into chairs."

James carried two chairs to the table, one for Kathryn and one for Alice. Then he retrieved one for himself.

"Alice, do you mind?" James brandished a tape recorder that he had taken from his briefcase. "It will help us remember what you say about the documents."

"Not at all, James."

"It will not be made public," James offered.

"Of course, James. If I did not trust the two of you, we would not be doing this." James nodded his appreciation.

James switched on the tape recorder and Alice worked her way verbally through the documents giving a summary of each group as to the time period when they were written and the subject matter. James and Kathryn remained silent most of the time. Two hours later, after a change of the tape, the receptionist entered and in a quiet voice told Alice, "All is ready." Alice smiled.

"This is a good place to break and it seems to me that lunch is ready in my office. Just a working lunch but the break will be welcome."

James and Kathryn were surprised at how quickly the time had passed, and since breakfast had been early for both of them, they were ready. They all adjourned to Alice's office. Lunch was set out on a small table. Tea with the necessary milk and sugar. Three small pork pies. Sausage rolls. Chutney. And a cream cake each for dessert.

"Alice, this is delightful. Where did you get these?"

"The cafeteria. When I told the manager, you remember her, Vera, that both of you were coming to visit and work with me, she offered to set this up."

After a thirty-minute lunch break, the table was cleared. All of the food had been eaten and enjoyed. The coolness of the stone walls of a medieval cathedral is a remarkable stimulus to the appetite. The last cup of tea was consumed and they were ready to go once again.

They reconvened in the dormitory a few minutes later and once seated at the table, Alice started her story again.

"The reason that the time to break was appropriate is that I had got to a point where the documents were all of a particular time period. The late 1360s, perhaps even 1369 as near as I can tell from some of the writer's commentary. But as you can see, our writer-soldier started his collection early, perhaps when he was still in his teens. There are descriptions of military actions. Missions for the king and other sundry events. There are medical descriptions of treatments that he seems to have given to soldiers and other who were injured at different times. And now we come to the remainder of the documents."

Alice gestured with a sweeping motion of her hand to the remaining twelve piles on the table. A section that she had not yet described. And then she announced, "I need to step into my office to check the mail and make several telephone calls that have accumulated. So this is a good opportunity for you both to examine these remaining documents in as much detail as you can. I would like you to form your own conclusions and we will go over it after my return in about an hour or so. Please also remember, James, the British Library has a collection of which some are very similar to these items that you are about to investigate."

Alice stood up, smiled, and turned on her heel, and left James and Kathryn to review and work on the documents. They looked at each other. Kathryn saw a smaller table at the other side of the room at the same time as James noticed it. They carried the documents to the table and laid out the pages, twenty-eight in all, in chronological order by group and consecutively within each group. All were written on large vellum sheets, the equivalent of a modern legal page in size. Kathryn inserted a fresh tape into the tape recorder and James started to translate the Latin and Old English into modern English.

One hour later Alice returned. James had barely made his way through eight of the pages. James stopped talking and Kathryn switched off the tape recorder.

"Well," Alice exclaimed, "what do you think?"

"It seems to me Alice that these documents postdate the late 1360s by several years or so. There are some references to personages that our soldier-scribe could not have known about if his writing stopped, for whatever reason, in the late 1360s. I would like to study these further in my own time but I am wary about subjecting such valuable material to the bright lights of a copying machine."

"Digital camera!"

James and Alice looked at Kathryn. Her outburst of two words had taken both of them by surprise.

"I don't have mine with me," James said regretfully.

"I have one in my office with more than enough memory on the storage disk." Alice left quickly and returned with the camera. "You can use my computer," she said, "to upload the images and put them onto disk to take with you."

They spent considerable time carefully placing the documents in the correct lighting to take readable pictures. Finally James was satisfied that he had what he needed for further research.

As they uploaded the images on to Alice's computer, James's mind was in turmoil, almost to the point of distraction. Alice had not detected anything wrong with him but as Kathryn had taped James's voice to record his translation to the tape recorder, his voice had changed again. He had assumed the voice that she now knew to be Oswald's.

Once more, James had made the transition from modern-day scientist-writer to medieval solder-scribe-medical man.

*   *   *

CHAPTER 14

James and Kathryn thanked Alice for her efforts. Just as they were about to leave her office, James turned, a questioning look on his face.

"Alice, one favor please."

"Yes?"

"If you come across any unusual events that occurred in the 1360 to 1400 time period, would you let us know?"

"Unusual events? It was a time of turmoil in England. So there is a variety of events that I can think of. Anything in particular?"

"Whatever seems to be the beginnings of a plot, even a murder of someone unimportant, a disappearance that still is unexplained. I am not sure what, just something out of the ordinary."

"Got it, James. I'll keep my eyes open. I am sure that I have told you that the best to talk to about that time period is Sylvia Kirkby. That is her area of scholarship and she does tend to have her finger on the pulse of that period of English history."

Kathryn broke into the conversation. "We have talked with her, Alice," she started to say but allowed her words to trail off so that she did not give any further details of the conversations with Sylvia and Charlie.

Alice responded immediately. "Let me suggest that you have a very in-depth close heart-to-heart talk with Sylvia. Prompt her. Jog her memory. Sylvia is an encyclopedia of such information but you need to, excuse the analogy, stimulate her to search her mental index pages. Only then will you find out how much she really knows."

James and Kathryn looked at each other. Then James spoke. "Just a matter of pushing the right button."

"Exactly, James. And make sure that Charles is on hand. He also is a wealth of information. Not to the same extent as Sylvia but enough to fill in some of the gaps that she may not recall."

Kathryn and Alice hugged each other promising to have lunch soon. James kissed Alice on the cheek and thanked her for her help.

As they left the cathedral precinct, James and Kathryn were locked in animated conversation. There was so much to discuss. Then Kathryn opened the door to their future actions.

"James, you have an extensive historical library so that is our starting point. We must go to Charlie and Sylvia well prepared with our own thoughts. You are a strong advocate of the Internet as a source of information on any subject that you care to research. I would find it hard to believe that someone somewhere has not posted on his or her Web page a commentary on the 1360 to 1400 time period."

"Fantastic, me bonnie lass. Let's try that route. But first, a coffee?"

A cup of hot milky coffee was consumed in a nearby restaurant where they could see the cobblestone street that sloped downward to Old Elvet Bridge.

As they drove back to Bridgeford, the shadows were lengthening and rush hour would soon commence. A good time to leave the city. The music of Johann Sebastian Bach on the car radio offered a soothing tone to the journey and they were soon entering the driveway to James's cottage. They entered the warmth of the cottage and Kathryn spoke as she took off her coat.

"Well, James, shall we start the research using your books and notes or have a cup of tea and then see where that leads us?"

James was about to respond as he closed the door when he noticed that the red light on the telephone answering machine was flickering in a pattern that told him that he had two messages.

The first was from Alice Campbell.

"James. It's Alice. Hope you arrived home all right."

Alice always liked to express the niceties of the moment. "I heard that there is snow coming in tonight. Dr. Spiller called just after you left, looking for you and asked that you telephone him as soon as you can. He'll be at the hospital until seven. Have lovely evening. Ta ta."

The second message was from Phillip Spiller.

"Sorry to bother you, James. But our conversation this morning got me thinking further about genetic memory. Did a little bit of work this afternoon and I may have something that could be of interest to you. You have my number. My cell phone number is also on my business card. Call anytime."

Kathryn had hung up her coat and James made the call to Spiller. It was answered within seconds.

"James, how are you? Thank you for returning my call. Caller ID by the way. I have some very interesting information about a fellow who has been working on genetic memory. Might be worth a talk. Lunch? Tomorrow? On me?"

"Sure, Phillip. What time. And where."

"My office at ten thirty. We can go over one or two interesting items that I have found and then we can adjourn for lunch. And do bring Kathryn with you if she is available."

"One moment, Phillip." James took the cordless phone into the kitchen and gave Kathryn the gist of the conversation, emphasizing the invitation to lunch. She nodded her head in agreement.

"Aye, Phillip, we'll be there. Got some good stuff, have you?"

Spiller did not answer James's question.

"Got to go, James. See you both tomorrow." The line was silent.

James made sure that the fire was lively, bought in more wood from the woodpile near to the garage, and Kathryn bought in two steaming mugs of tea. She took her appointment book from her purse and made a note in the book. They both seemed to have lost the power to concentrate. It had been a busy day. James wondered out loud if there was anything on television.

"Yes," Kathryn responded, "the latest version of *The Lost World*. The original story by Sir Arthur Conan Doyle. A four-hour movie."

James smiled. "Ah, yes." He thought. "Sir Arthur Conan Doyle. Along with H. G. Wells, Alexander Dumas, Daniel Defoe, Jules Verne, Mary Shelley, Bram Stoker, James Fennimore Cooper, all great authors but Sir Arthur is my favorite. They had stories to tell." The movie would be well worth watching, even though he had seen every previous version at least six times.

The movie was just what they needed to take a break from the concentrated research that had taxed their brains. Kathryn left after the movie, stating that she would return at eight thirty the next morning after a brief visit to her office to take care of any items that had cropped up during the day.

The snow that Alice Campbell had promised did materialize and in the morning two inches of fresh white powder covered the ground.

*   *   *

The next morning, Kathryn arrived on time. She accepted James's offer of tea instead of departing immediately for Durham. She commented that the temperature that morning seemed lower than usual, which had prompted her to wear a heavier coat. She was ready for a hot drink. She discarded her coat and sat on the couch in front of the fire. James appeared from the kitchen with two cups of hot tea. The coldness had penetrated Kathryn's winter overcoat and even the winter slacks and sweater and cardigan had not stayed the hand of Jack Frost.

"James, my dear, you do think of everything!"

The two teaspoons of rum that he had added to the cup of tea brought additional warmth to her body. She started to feel comfortable as the icy temperatures of the morning were banished. This gave them the time to go over in detail their recent discoveries and the most puzzling mystery of all—the changes that had appeared in James's voice yesterday as he read Oswald's document out loud in the Dean and Chapter Library. This was the same phenomenon that had happened as he translated Oswald's diary.

"James," Kathryn paused to place her cup and saucer on the nearby table, "it seems to me that the connection between you and Oswald is stronger than we ever imagined. The ability that he and Margaret have to call you back to their time was a shock to me. I was not sure what to believe until I actually experienced their presence the other day. And now, the phenomenon that I have experienced twice in recent days is the transposition of his voice to you. There is something . . . What is the word?"

"Spooky?"

"No, James dear, this is more serious than just spooky. This is not like a Stephen King story. This goes beyond spooky. It also seems to me that your conversation with Phillip Spiller about genetic inheritance might just be on the right track. Speaking of which . . ."

"Aye, me bonnie lass, time to go. Give me a minute to start the car."

Kathryn handed James the keys to the Range Rover, "Since it has been warmed up once already this morning . . ."

Five minutes later they both got in the vehicle, James behind the driver's wheel as Kathryn snuggled into the passenger seat.

The roads were not in the best of conditions and the drive to Durham took a little longer than usual. But they were able to talk, as two friends might without any specific agenda, and observe the countryside clothed in a white winter coat. It looked so bleak. James cast his mind back to those days of long ago when the Romans had tried to tame the inhabitants of northern Britain. Better tame the weather first, he thought. Kathryn's voice bought him back to the present. During the drive, she had deliberately refrained from touching on the subject of Oswald. Driving in winter was stressful enough without adding more stress to his life.

"James, I do not wish to sound presumptive, but I was wondering about your taking a break. You have been under such stress lately."

"Kath?

"Everyone needs a break, and you are not superman!"

"Let me think about it."

They were now entering the busy streets of the city of Durham and soon were parked in the hospital parking area. James knew Spiller's office number but asked the receptionist to let the doctor know that they were on the way to his office. She gave them directions to a different wing of the hospital, which surprised James, and volunteered the information that Dr. Spiller moved to a different office. They arrived at his office minutes later. Spiller shared a secretary with three other medics and James was about to introduce himself to the secretary when a door opened and Spiller appeared.

"James, Kathryn. Good morning. How nice to see you again."

Introductions were made, offers of coffee were accepted, and coats were hung on the rack. Then, each armed with a coffee, they entered the office. Spiller sat comfortably in the armchair. James and Kathryn were seated on the couch. James could not contain his surprise at the relative luxury of the office.

"Phillip, excuse me for being nosey, but . . . ?"

Kathryn could not resist a comment. "Do not listen to him, Phillip, he is naturally nosey and should not be excused."

"You are surprised at the apparent luxury of my office? Well, James, it seems that the powers-that-be like me and want me to stay, and no longer being the junior run-around or jack-of-all-trades, I requested a better office and got it."

Kathryn broke in again, "Then I believe that congratulations are in order?"

They stood up and offered their hands to congratulate Spiller on his unexplained promotion and settled back on to the couch.

"By way of starting our conversation this morning. Let me tell you that my background area—we have already talked of this, James—is in the field of genetics and the inheritance of specific traits such as behavior patterns and inherent knowledge. The hospital bigwigs seem to like this, as I believe that it may eventually give us clues to curing many diseases, cancer for one. Although I am not kidding myself that they like me. There is a lot of government grant money and commercial funding available for such work. Hence . . ."

Spiller stood up, waved his arms around to draw attention to his new surroundings, and sat down once more to sip his coffee. James spoke up.

"Don't underestimate yourself, Phillip, it seems to me that you must be very worthy of this or you would not have been chosen. This is wonderful for you."

Spiller put his cup and saucer onto the small coffee table. "Well enough of that but now to business. Let's get to the topic of the morning. You recall, James, that we talked about genetic memory sometime last December when we had a moment in the cafeteria?" Spiller did not wait for an answer. "In my recent searches of the medical literature, I stumbled across some work in a journal. The Internet is a wonderful source of information and you know how it is, James, scientists of different disciplines tend to favor their own type of journal and never consider what is happening in another discipline."

James nodded in agreement as Spiller continued.

"Well, I decided to use the Internet for a search beyond my own area of expertise and I came across some remarkable work."

Spiller looked at James and Kathryn over the rim of his cup before he drained the last drops of coffee from his cup. Then, an afterthought occurred to him.

"Kathryn, my apologies to you but this may become a little technical. In fact, it may become highly technical."

James and Kathryn looked at each other and smiled before Kathryn responded.

"Phillip, no apologies needed. Since I have come to know James, a renegade scientist he calls himself," she put her hand on to James's hand as a sign of reassurance and continued, "he is a good scientist, so much of the terminology and some little knowledge has rubbed off on to me. So, Phillip, you were about to say?"

"Yes, Kathryn. Thank you." Spiller thought for a moment as if collecting his thoughts. "The Internet!" he exclaimed before continuing. "I came across some very interesting work by a fellow called Hiroshi Takeyama. Used to be in Japan but moved to Hawaii some years ago. University of Hawaii at Manoa, that is. The university campus is just on the outskirts of Honolulu, as near as I can tell. Never been there, you know! Anyway, Takeyama has a PhD and several doctor of sciences degrees from different universities that indicate to me that his work has been appreciated worldwide. Seems that other faculty members in the department work with Takeyama and the department has the lead in this kind of research."

Spiller paused, went to the door of his office, mumbled a few words to the secretary that were inaudible to James and Kathryn, returned to his desk, and focused his attention on a pile of papers. Before he could reseat himself, she appeared with three more cups of coffee.

"Thought we could do with another one. Hope you don't mind."

James and Kathryn smiled in agreement and James focused his attention on the collection of papers in Spiller's hand. Spiller noticed his searching look.

"Ah, yes. I was able to download these articles from the Internet. All authored by Takeyama." He passed them to James. "In summary, Takeyama believes that genetic memory is a reality, not just one or two generations that we have seen in laboratory rats but over many generations. He feels that it just needs a physical or chemical trigger and genetic relationships can be rekindled."

James and Kathryn looked at Spiller. Then they looked at each other, with wide eyes.

James placed the stack of papers on to the coffee table and looked once more at Kathryn. Then he returned his look to Phillip.

Phillip, are you telling me that Takeyama has the theory that genetic memory can be acquired through several generations of related humans?"

"Yes, James, I am. He believes that as long as the major features of specific sections of the human genetic code, as might be evident in a family, are in place then the potential for genetic memory over many generations is a reality."

Again, James and Kathryn looked at each other.

"And what is more, I believe that from the suggestions in those papers, or reading between the lines . . .," Spiller nodded at the pile on the coffee table, "that Dr. Takeyama has more information on this subject. Much more than he is willing to publish. As I said earlier, my indications are that he is still at the University of Hawaii-Manoa and I do have the telephone number," Spiller smiled again, "the Internet is really a wonderful source of information."

Spiller went to his desk, consulted a notebook, and wrote a telephone number on a piece of paper.

"If my calculations are correct, Honolulu is eleven hours, no sorry, ten hours behind us. The Hawaiian Islands do not recognize the silly time change in autumn and spring that we have to go through every year. So, James, it might be worthwhile to give the department a call and see where he is."

Before James and Kathryn could even react to any of Spiller's words, he was standing before them, rubbing his hands together.

"Now, how about lunch? Just before you arrived, I had a one o'clock meeting sprung on me. So, if you do not mind an early lunch, we can go over some of this work or perhaps just have a nice chat. You may need time to think about what I have told you."

James and Kathryn stood up. Both felt the need to move. The information that Spiller had passed on to them had almost taken their breath away. Both of their minds were in turmoil. Because of Spiller's need to return before one o'clock, James suggested that they have lunch in the hospital cafeteria where, on previous occasions, he had found that the food was surprisingly good. Kathryn agreed. Spiller thanked them for their thoughtfulness and indicated that James could leave the collection of scientific papers on the table and they would collect them after lunch.

Lunch was a pleasant event. Neither James nor Kathryn broached the subject of the earlier conversation about genetic memory—such information would be a three-teapot discussion at James's cottage. However, they did enjoy catching up on each other's news. After lunch, they collected the scientific documents that had been thoughtfully placed by the secretary into a large envelope and retrieved their coats from Spiller's office. They thanked Spiller for the information and the documents, and as they bid their goodbyes, James promised to keep Phillip up to date on any additional information that he could find.

In no time they were on the way back to Bridgeford. There were very few words spoken during the journey and it seems that only moments later they were in James's driveway. He could not recall giving the command "beam me back, Scotty" but the journey seemed that quick!

Once more settled in front of the fire, with a pot of freshly made Lapsang tea at hand, James and Kathryn studied the package that Spiller had given them. Kathryn found that reading the abstract of each article presented much of the highlight and within an hour she had a good overview of what was contained in each article. James took longer, preferring to read much of each article for the scientific details. As he finished the last article, he looked at Kathryn. She read his mind.

"Yes, James. You should talk with Dr. Takeyama."

They both looked at the clock. In about four or five hours the offices at the University of Hawaii would be open. Kathryn decided that she would go to her office in Willington to clear up some paperwork from a recent sale and would return to be with James when he made the telephone call. She suggested that, in the meantime, he should relax, read, or perhaps watch television. He smiled and assured her that he would take things easy.

At shortly after seven in the evening, Kathryn returned bearing cooked ham for sandwiches, a baguette, a fresh cream cake, and a bottle of Riesling. After the refreshing meal, James picked up the telephone, taking the piece of notepaper from his pocket as he did so, and dialed the number written on the paper. After one ring, a very pleasant-sounding secretary answered James's call with the lilt to her voice that is common in the Hawaiian Islands.

"Aloha. Department of Microbiology. How can I help you?"

James gave his name and stated the reason for his call. The response was immediate.

"I am sorry, Dr. Simpson, but Dr. Takeyama is not in and may be on leave for a month or so. Please hold for . . .," the secretary gave the name of the department head and James heard a male voice introduce himself and ask how he could help.

"Well, Dr. Simpson, Dr. Takeyama takes leave frequently and is not physically in the department right now. He will return in a month or so. However, he can be reached in an emergency, but not by telephone. He resides at the north end of the Island of Kauai where he has a retreat, a place to relax."

James asked several more questions and was told that he would be welcome at the department anytime. There were other faculty members that he could meet and discuss the issues if he so chose, and perhaps it might be possible to meet Dr. Takeyama."

James's response was immediate. "I would like to make travel arrangements and get back to you. Possibly visit you soon?"

"That will be great, Dr. Simpson. Just let me know. Or if I am out of the office, my secretary will take the details."

Kathryn had heard the end of the conversation as she retuned from the kitchen where the teapot and cups had been cleared.

"Sounds like a trip to Hawaii is in the offing?"

"Might be, Kath. What do you think?"

"At this moment, James, I do not know what to think. Only that it may be for the best. I need to relax and think clearly. Would you mind if I just sit on the couch and relax."

"Go ahead, Kath. I have some calls to make."

Moments later, Kathryn was asleep. James covered her with a blanket and sat at his desk making the necessary telephone calls. After forty-five minutes he was finished and he was adding wood to the fire when Kathryn stirred. He looked at her and she looked refreshed.

"Earlier today, Kath, if you recall, you were telling me that I should take a break?"

"Yes. You are going to Hawaii?"

"Yes, we are."

"I can see to your cottage. Make sure all is in order. How long will you be gone?" Then the reality of his words registered in her brain. "We?"

"Yes. Hope you don't mind."

"Good grief, James. This is so sudden. When?"

"Can you be ready to leave for London on Friday? I made the reservations while you were sleeping."

"Well, I think so. But there is so much to do, and this is already Wednesday!"

"Kathryn! Listen.

"We leave on Friday for London. Stay at the Gatwick Hilton. Fly to Houston, Texas, on Saturday. Overnight at the Houston Airport Marriott. Fly to Honolulu on Sunday. Continental Airlines. I know that your passport is up to date."

Kathryn very rarely traveled abroad but she maintained an up-to-date passport, a habit started many years before.

James looked into her eyes. "So?"

"Wow! James, let me catch my breath. Sure is a hell of a rush!"

"Kathryn, such language. Where did you hear that sort of thing?"

"From you. Where else? But to answer in another way, certainly, James, let's do it. But why all of the stops?"

"All of the overnights?"

"Makes a journey halfway across the world easier to handle. Less stress and not such a disastrous effect of jet lag due to the time zone changes."

Kathryn hugged him.

"Now how much do I owe you? And how long is the trip?"

"Answer to the first question, nothing. Answer to the second question, not sure so I have open-ended tickets."

"But, James. That must be tricky to arrange flight schedule for the return trip?"

"Not when you fly first class or business first as Continental Airlines calls it."

Kathryn hugged him again.

"James, my dear, you are so full of surprises, all pleasant though!" Kathryn focused her mind on the present. "We have so much to do. The articles to read in more detail. We must inform Charlie and Sylvia, and because its winter, the cottage will need to be looked after. And my house? Heating systems do funny things in winter. At least at this time of the year, real estate is slow so I can arrange for someone to look after the business."

"It's all taken care of, Kath. I know that you have a housekeeper but if she needs anything, she can call Mrs. Nicholson, my housekeeper. John Anderson, our friendly police sergeant, and his constable, Bryan Jones, will pop in regularly to make sure all is well. John's contact at the Willington police station will look in on your place and so all is taken care of!" James smiled. "In fact by the time the other ladies of the village hear of this, no one would dare consider doing any mischief to this place or to your house. If there are any suspicious characters around, someone will take it upon himself or herself to sleep in our houses to make sure they have that lived-in look."

"You have been a busy person, James! But what about . . . ?"

"Oh, one more thing, Kath," James broke into Kathryn's thought, "Charlie and Sylvia will see us at eleven tomorrow and we will update them through lunch. So, me bonnie lass, it is all organized."

Kathryn's eyes lit up.

"Hawaii!" The realization hit Kathryn. "What will I wear?" she asked.

James's response was immediate.

"Nothing," for which he received a stronger-than-playful punch on his arm.

"James, we have work to do. Takeyama's articles."

"May I?" Kathryn asked as she walked toward the bathroom.

She disappeared momentarily to splash cold water on her face and then reappeared ready to do battle with the scientific articles that could throw some light on the chemical background of genetic memory.

Other than a break to make tea, the house was silent as the next two hours were spent in gleaning as much detail as they could from the scientific articles written by Dr. Hiroshi Takeyama. He was a man that they had to meet. And hopefully, they would meet him soon.

*   *   *

CHAPTER 15

Kathryn arrived breathlessly at James's door at nine the next morning. Just as he was opening the door to fetch wood from the woodpile, she was standing there, poised and ready to ring the doorbell.

"Good God, Kath, I didn't hear you!" James exclaimed as she almost fell through the door.

Kathryn recovered very quickly. "And a good morning to you too, James."

"Sorry, Kath. Good morning. You look absolutely stunning."

"In a heavy winter coat. Of course, James, but thank you anyway!"

"X-ray eyes and a wonderful imagination. Just let me get some wood and I'll be right back with you."

He saw Kathryn's Range Rover parked in the driveway and was surprised that he had not heard any sounds as she had approached the cottage. He returned with the wood to find Kathryn putting on the kettle.

"Tea or coffee, James?"

"How about coffee made with hot milk?"

"Sounds delightful."

And so the coffee was made, the fire rekindled, and all seemed well with the world as the heat percolated through the house. James broke the silence.

"Alice Campbell called just before you arrived. Seems that she has found some disconnects in the historical record. She seemed to think that it should be called the hysterical record!"

James took another sip of the hot liquid. Kathryn listened intently.

"Remember, we asked her to keep on eye open for any unusual events that occurred in the 1360 to 1400 period?" Kathryn did not respond to his rhetorical question. "Well, it seems that there are some unusual events related to the de Bohun family."

"The . . . who?"

"The de Bohun family."

"Humphrey de Bohun, the tenth of that name. He was the son of William de Bohun, Earl of Northampton. Humphrey inherited the earldoms of Hereford and Essex and the office of Chief Constable of England from his uncle, Humphrey IX, in 1361. Humphrey X died at the age of thirty-one and the circumstances of his death seem mysterious, if not very questionable. It is thought that King Edward III had Humphrey secretly murdered. It is also during the time of Richard II that the *disconnects* with this family seem to start. Alice is accumulating more detail to support her suspicions but she suggested that we talk with Charlie and Sylvia, Sylvia in particular, about the de Bohun family. I told her about the trip and she wondered if she could carry our bags! She will contact us by e-mail, if necessary."

"Timing is everything, James, as you tend to say. And since we are meeting Charlie and Sylvia at eleven . . ." Kathryn allowed the words to trail off as they continued to sip the coffee.

"Did you think any further about our reading of Dr. Takeyama's articles?"

"Yes, if I am reading between the lines correctly, he has found a way to reconstitute genetic memory through the use of selected drugs or chemicals. But it seems that at that point he may have gone into a different avenue of research. His papers became a little vaguer and tend to be evasive. Just as though . . ."

James refocused his eyes from Kathryn on to the far wall. Not sure what to say next.

"As though what, James?"

"As though he found the answer and moved away, possibly not liking what he found. But that is mere speculation on my part. It is just as though he was attempting to send a message in his most recent articles, which are now some three years old. There has been nothing from him, in the form of an article that deals with genetic memory, since that time. All we know is that he is alive and well and living in Hawaii. So I am very curious."

"Curious enough to make the trip to Hawaii."

"Worst case, Kath, me bonnie lass, is that we have a great time in the sun and surf but I suspect that it will be a learning experience that we will not regret!"

"Well, James, now that coffee is finished, how about a walk around the Bridgeford shops and say hello to a few of the folks."

"Sounds good to me." James got up from the couch to get his coat. "I'll warm up your car."

"And I'll wash the cups, and," Kathryn added with a poignant look to let James show that he was not being his usual tidy self, "your breakfast dishes."

Fifteen minutes later, the car was parked and they were walking, arm in arm, in the main street of the village.

They stopped to chat with Flossie Ambler, owner of the ice cream and coffee shop. Lennie Farmer, landlord of the Royal Duke, the village pub, was busy receiving a replenishment of beer in barrels for the coming weekend. Bob Fenwick the local doctor waved from his car as he left his surgery to make a house call.

Jackie Hall the butcher waved from his store and he and his wife Florence, a member of the Knitting Circle, came to the shop door to say hello. But both were interested in James and Kathryn's impending trip to Hawaii. News had already traveled fast and Florence wanted to be as up to date as she could be for the next meeting of the Knitting Circle. James always likened the Circle to Madame Defarge and her friends sitting at the guillotine in 1790s France waiting for heads to roll. Not quite that bad, but certainly aware of all events! Jackie's bull terrier looked at them from the adjacent house window, decided that there was nothing of interest, and withdrew to be closer to the warmth of the fireplace. Nonky and Alan Wood, the father-son operators of the local service station, waved and shouted their best wishes for a safe trip.

The villagers knew that James had been born in England, had moved away and become a Yank, but they all agreed, he is our Yank! They had not forgotten his role in helping to determine the person responsible for the wrongful deaths of Robbie Vardy and Tom Stiles who had, until their untimely deaths, been longtime village stalwarts.

James and Kathryn walked back to the Range Rover and drove the short distance to the vicarage. Charlie was already at the door waiting for them.

"Good morning you two. I hear that a trip to Hawaii is imminent."

Kathryn and James looked at each other and smiled. News did travel fast. They wondered who in the village would not know of this. No one!

"Good morning, Charlie. Yes, the trip starts when we leave tomorrow for London. Taking the plane from Gatwick on Saturday. But we need to talk with you and Sylvia."

"Come in. Take off your coats and we'll sit in the study by the fire. Sylvia has the kettle on the stove, just coming to the boil. So," Charlie continued, "you want to talk about William de Bohun and the de Bohun family." He noticed the surprised looks on James's and Kathryn's faces. "Just got off the phone with Alice. Ah, there you are, my dear." Sylvia entered carrying a tray that contained all of the items necessary for tea.

"Good morning, Kathryn, James."

It was only when all four had a hot cup of tea ready for drinking that Charlie started the conversation.

"Alice Campbell called and told us of her findings and that you would be off soon. She and Sylvia needed to compare notes before you got here. Make sure we are playing from the same sheet of music, my dear!"

Sylvia took a moment to focus her thoughts.

"It seems that Alice has found some very interesting disconnects in regard to the de Bohun family that may or may not lead to what your friend Oswald," she looked directly at James, "seems to be concerned about. Alice admitted that there is no guarantee that she is on the right track but she does think, and I agree, that she has got hold of something that is worth further investigation."

Sylvia paused as she looked at James and Kathryn.

"Let's start with William de Bohun, Earl of Northampton in the reign of Edward III. And he was related to Edward. William's mother, Elizabeth, was the seventh daughter of Edward I, so to be correct, William was a cousin of Edward III since both were grandsons of Edward I. Edward constantly employed William in military and diplomatic transactions and it was a great loss to Edward when William died in September of 1360 at the ripe old age of forty-nine. The title Earl of Northampton was passed to William's son, Humphrey, who also inherited the title Earl of Hereford and Essex as well as the title of Constable of England from his uncle."

Sylvia looked once more at Kathryn and James to make sure that she had not lost their attention. She was leading to her punch line.

"As Lord High Constable of England," Sylvia continued, "Humphrey was one of the highest officers of the Crown and next to the king, who was titular head of the army. Humphrey was actually the functional commander in chief of the army. As the older of two earldoms, he had considerable land holdings and could even challenge Edward's richest son, our friend John of Lancaster or John of Gaunt, whichever you prefer, as one of the richest men of the realm."

James whistled lightly under his breath. Kathryn sat motionless. And it was Charlie who broke in.

"Well done, m'dear." Charlie could not hold back any longer. "But wait, there's more."

Sylvia used the break to sip her tea and each of the listeners replenished their individual cups. Then she continued.

"And suddenly all was not well in the de Bohun camp. Humphrey died at the age of thirty-one in very mysterious circumstances. He was sent to France and no more was heard of him. It is thought that Edward had Humphrey secretly hanged or garroted, so much for family loyalty. Rumors abounded that during Humphrey's service in France, he was involved in the supposed poisoning of the Earl of Warwick. The Warwick family was close to the royal family and in the late fifteenth century, the earl of Warwick became known as Warwick the Kingmaker for his support of the claim of Henry VII to the throne. Henry was, of course, grandfather to Elizabeth I."

Sylvia sipped her tea and, sensing that her audience had comments at the ready, held up her hand indicating that she had more to add to the story.

"Consider this, James," Sylvia went on, "at the time that Humphrey was, let's say, murdered in 1373, Edward's health was failing and by 1372 his son Edward of Woodstock, the Black Prince or Prince of Wales, the successor to his throne, was forced to resign his principalities because of bad health. This left his brother, John of Gaunt, to attempt the impossible task of holding them for England."

"So," James tried to continue Sylvia's thoughts, "there are indications that some sort of skullduggery was afoot?"

Sylvia looked at the ceiling as she collected her thoughts and then went on with the story.

"So, let us consider this. Should the throne of England go to a child, Richard, son of the Black Prince, and who was a grandson of Edward III and a great-grandson of Edward I? Or should it go to Henry, the son of John, another child who was also a grandson of Edward III and a great-great-grandson of Edward I? Or should the throne go to an adult, Humphrey de Bohun, who was also a great-grandson of Edward I and also the son of a cousin to Edward III?"

The room was filled with silence as Sylvia's attentive audience sat motionless, lost in thought. Sylvia used the silence as an acknowledgement that she should continue and finish her story.

"The reason that I ask the question is that Alice believes that in some of the documents that she had dug out that might be ascribed to Gaunt, there is a hint of the question of succession to the throne with a suggestion of the dire consequences that might follow."

James's eyebrows went up in question to this last statement. Charlie and Kathryn remained silent. Sylvia responded to James's unasked question and looked directly at him.

"A civil war, James. The civil war of 1135 to 1253 between Maude and Stephen of Blois wrenched the country apart. After more than two hundred years of merely trying to kick the daylights out of the French, there were those who did not want another civil war. Oh of course, there were battles, minor engagements, murders, and all that kind of stuff, the usual for the time period, but no full-blown civil war. So . . ."

Sylvia allowed her words to trail into the silence that filled the room. Not a breath. Not a sound, until Charlie banged his pipe on the table to loosen the solid plug of half-burned tobacco.

"But, Sylvia," Kathryn's brow was furrowed as she fought to understand the exact meaning of Sylvia's words, "it seems that the whole issue went full circle from, let's say an attempt to displace Edward's immediate family, to a position where Edward's grandson became Henry IV."

"Yes, m'dear, where do we go from here?"

"I am not at all sure, Charles. I propose that we leave the story where it is at the moment. Alice will get back to me and it gives me more chance to mull this over. And we have two guests who are leaving on quite a journey tomorrow. So we need to spend time with them and have lunch."

"Well done, old girl. Capital idea."

Charlie announced that they should move into the dining room and that he and James would bring in the food and drink.

"Don't mind if I volunteer you for action, James?" Charlie asked as he led the way.

Sylvia had made a wonderful Scotch broth that was served piping hot with dinner rolls, followed by custard tart for dessert. Lunch allowed a full discussion of James and Kathryn's forthcoming trip. Charlie and Sylvia wanted to know all about Captain Cook's Sandwich Islands, as the Hawaiian Islands used to be called. James gave a brief description of his experiences, having briefly visited Honolulu some years before on a business trip back from Japan and on another occasion when he returned from another business trip, this time from Australia. In both cases his stay in Honolulu had been less than three days. But he remembered well the friendliness of the people, the pleasant temperatures, and the lush vegetation.

Sylvia and Kathryn entered into animated conversation about the various clothes that Kathryn would need and were really enjoying themselves.

There was no further mention of the issues that arose from Sylvia's story. When lunch was over, James got Charlie and Sylvia up to date on who was looking after the houses while they were away. Charlie and Sylvia promised to do anything to help.

"Just a telephone call is all that we need. Even getting on to e-mail soon," Charlie offered.

Soon after the meal, it was time for James and Kathryn to leave the vicarage. Charlie and Sylvia watched the Range Rover disappear down the driveway. Sylvia looked at Charlie and smiled.

"Don't say it, m'dear. I know. They do make a delightful couple. But we must not interfere."

"Oh, a little help now and again might not hurt!"

"Sylvia!"

"Yes, dear. I promise."

As James and Kathryn drove back to the cottage, the light of an idea went on.

"Kath . . ."

"Yes, James."

"We need to be up and about early tomorrow. So, let's go to your house, you can get packed, and we can return and stay at the cottage overnight. Saves running around early tomorrow."

"Sounds lovely, James."

"And what will you do while I am packing?"

"Watch television."

"And you promise not to interfere."

"Promise. Just want to make sure that you have your bikini!"

James did an about-turn at a convenient place on the road and they drove again through Bridgeford and on to the main road to Willington. Kathryn's house was on the east side. James could not help but contrast the winter countryside with the lush vegetation that they would see in Hawaii.

Although the trip involved work with a task at hand, he found himself looking forward to the journey. Kathryn would be with him. The number of journeys that he had made on his own was countless. He did not object to being alone. That has been his choice. He knew that Kathryn would make sure that he never felt lonely. He reached across and held her hand for a brief moment.

"James, what was that for?"

"Just a passing thought, Kath!"

He guided the vehicle into the driveway and soon they were in Kathryn's warm house, a two-story detached home on a spacious plot of land. The inside mirrored Kathryn's tastes. Just as she was immaculate with never a hair out of place, the home was the same; clean and everything neat and tidy in its place. James had been impressed from his first visit some time ago, and because of her full-time work that often occupied unusual hours, Kathryn also had a housekeeper who came regularly to make sure that all was in order.

They hung up their coats in the entrance hallway and James could feel the cozy warmth of the central heating system.

"I'll put the kettle on."

"No, Kath. You go upstairs and start your packing and I'll see to the tea."

The tea was made and James took a cup each up to the large bedroom where he could hear Kathryn moving about busily organizing her clothes.

"Ah, James, lovely." Kathryn took the cup.

"Me or the tea?"

"The tea of course!"

They both laughed and sat for a moment in two wicker chairs, enjoying the effect of the hot liquid. James looked at the pile of clothes on the bed, and the extralarge suitcase that would weigh a ton when fully packed! Kathryn saw his look.

"James . . ."

"I know I promised not to interfere, but . . ."

"I was going to ask you about the climate and general dress code in Hawaii."

"Temperatures are usually in the 70s and 80s, even at this time of the year. So shorts, cotton dresses, loose-fitting are suitable for the climate. Perhaps something a little more formal, if we have to meet persons officially, and a light jacket or cardigan. Also whatever you will need if we have some time to sit around a pool. Depends how much time we have."

Kathryn looked at the pile of clothes and quickly selected those that would be best suited. James sat and sipped his tea. He could see that she was excited about the trip. And then the case was packed, and she was ready. She also decided to take a suitable carry-on bag to hold last-minute items and spare clothes.

The sky was darkening by the time they returned to James's cottage. His main concern was his notebook computer. He made sure that all of his files were uploaded from his desktop computer and then he was ready.

Kathryn prepared a light supper. Bread and butter, cheese, fruit, and the ubiquitous pot of tea. They sat on the couch in front of the fire and settled down to talk about Sylvia's description of the royal politics of past time.

They did not see or sense that Oswald and Margaret were present in the shadows. They had listened to their conversation. Finally, Oswald looked at Margaret and put his arm around her. The thought passed from Oswald to Margaret.

"We must leave, my love."

Margaret nodded her approval. As their shadows flickered and decreased in intensity, Oswald looked at James and Kathryn. His thoughts were directed at James.

"*Deus vobiscum* . . ." (God be with you. For who knows what you will find on your journey.) As Oswald looked at Kathryn, his words were gentle and clear.

"Please take care of him. He will be out of my sphere of contact during your journey. Your James has become close to me these past weeks." And then the shadows were gone.

Kathryn looked at James.

"James, did you hear the voice?"

James nodded. "Yes my dear. I heard him."

As they talked, the lateness of the day seemed to come early and suddenly they were tired.

*   *   *

The next morning, James and Kathryn were up and about bright and early. By nine o'clock there were getting into the Range Rover for the journey to Durham, via the vicarage having decided to accept Charlie's offer of being their chauffeur and looking after Kathryn's vehicle. Charlie and Sylvia were ready and waiting.

"Thought we'd both go with you. Do a bit of shopping afterward and a spot of lunch with Alice."

The train pulled into Durham Station on time. James and Kathryn entered the first-class coach and Charlie helped with the bags. Once seated, Charlie joined Sylvia on the platform. Three minutes after the train had arrived, it departed. Charlie and Sylvia walked along the platform matching the slow speed of the train, they waved, and then as the powerful engine picked up speed they were still waving at a distance on the platform.

James and Kathryn settled into their seats for the remainder of the journey. They had brought individual reading. Two cups of coffee and three hours later, the train pulled into Platform 7 at King's Cross Station. James descended from the train, found a porter to help with the two suitcases, and minutes later they were in a taxi to Victoria Station. The train left Victoria Station for Gatwick Airport Station and with the help of another porter, they were soon at the airport hotel registration desk. The clerk recognized James from the times when he had made several return journeys from United States to carry out research for his early novels.

"Good afternoon, Dr. Simpson. It is a pleasure to see you again. Mrs. Stainsby, welcome. We have two very pleasant adjoining rooms for you."

"The bellman will bring your suitcase to your rooms."

The bags were delivered five minutes after they had entered their respective rooms. Within another two minutes, James heard a tap on the adjoining door. He opened it to see Kathryn's smiling face.

"Convenient, James!"

"You did not think that we would want to wander along the hallways to see each other, did you, Kath?"

The next morning seemed to arrive quickly. They did not take long to reach the airline check-in counter and they passed through security to the Continental Airlines Presidents' Club, where James had retained his membership. The flight across the Atlantic and into Houston Intercontinental Airport was on time and there was plenty of time to relax and enjoy the flight.

After a restful overnight stay at the Houston Airport Hotel, the eight-hour flight to Honolulu International Airport was pleasant and comfortable. Just before landing they had a delightful panoramic view of Waikiki beach. The flight touched down on time in the early Hawaiian afternoon. As James and Kathryn alighted from the aircraft, the warmth and the gentle breezes of Hawaii brushed their faces. They carried their winter coats over their arms trying not to appear like tourists, but failing miserably! Thirty minutes later James and Kathryn had checked into the Hilton Hotel complex that seemed to have everything that they needed without even leaving the hotel grounds and were in their respective adjoining rooms. Kathryn could see that James was anxious to get to work. But she had other ideas.

"James, my dear, it is Sunday. There will be no one at the university. How about a stroll or jog along Waikiki beach? Might help us get over our jet lag. After which we can relax for the remainder of the day."

James nodded his head in agreement. Kathryn could see the look of foreboding on his face.

"How about a jog?"

"Good, James. I am going to change. Back in a minute."

He quickly changed into his sweat suit bottoms, soft jogging shoes, and a soccer shirt. Kathryn reappeared moments later, dressed similarly.

She waved a pair of sunglasses at James. He picked up his sunglasses and also a sweatband for his forehead.

As they jogged along the sea walk, James could feel the tired groggy feeling leaving his system. They jogged the half-mile to the stone pier that jutted out into the sea for about fifty yards. At the end of the pier, they stood and looked around. Everything seemed so peaceful. The sea was clear and they could see small rock crabs scurrying about looking for any food that dared to invade their territory. Shoals of small fishes swam by, unconcerned that they were being watched.

As James and Kathryn stood at the end of the pier looking at the afternoon sun, James put his arm around Kathryn and kissed her cheek.

"Thank you."

Kathryn looked surprised.

"What for?"

"For being here."

*   *   *

CHAPTER 16

The next day, James and Kathryn were up early. By seven thirty they had read the papers that had been delivered to their rooms along with the pot of tea. Kathryn could see that James was ready to be on the move. The open-air cafeteria offered a buffet breakfast. The immediate landscape included several streams of water that were home to numerous ducks and swans. It was a truly restful and idyllic setting.

They started to plan the actions for the next few days, not forgetting that there was also a performance of light classical music scheduled by the Honolulu Symphony Orchestra scheduled for Tuesday that they planned to attend. Kathryn saw this as a chance for James to relax for three hours.

After breakfast, James made the telephone call from his room, with Kathryn standing by in case James had a question or needed pen and paper.

"Aloha. Department of Microbiology. How can I help you?"

James introduced himself again to the voice that he recognized from his first call some days ago and a half a world away.

"Dr. Simpson, how nice to hear from you again. One moment and I'll see if Dr. Johnson can talk with you."

The dean's voice came onto the line.

"Dr. Simpson, good morning. I hope that all is well in England. How is the weather?" Johnson was surprised when James told him he was in Honolulu. "Well, are you planning to visit us?"

"I would appreciate a meeting today, if possible," James responded.

The meeting was set for eleven that morning. Johnson gave James directions to the building that housed the department. Johnson finished the conversation with "I'm looking forward to meeting you, Dr. Simpson. But please be informal. These are the islands. We do things differently here!"

James replaced the telephone receiver into the cradle.

"So, James. When do we leave?"

"Kath, I wondered if . . ."

"Forget it, James. I am coming with you."

"You would like to accompany me to the university for my eleven o'clock appointment?"

"Love to, James. I would not have it any other way."

James smiled. Kathryn looked determined.

"And James my dear, what do you propose our story should be?"

James opened his mouth to respond, but Kathryn continued as she answered her own question.

"We need to have our stories coordinated but not word for word. Might sound suspicious. You are writing a book about a man who has the ability to present himself in different time periods. And you are wondering if there is a genetic base to this through memory. We can each say that in different ways without compromising ourselves. You can refer to your most recent novel that is about to be published as an indication of your thoughts. What do you think?"

"Kathryn my dear, to be compromised with you sounds like a good idea to me. Just what I was about to suggest!"

At ten minutes before eleven, via a taxi, they presented themselves at the departmental office to the secretary who warmly greeted them with "aloha and welcome to Hawaii."

"Dr. Johnson will be back in a moment. He is looking forward to meeting you."

"Dr. Simpson?"

The voice came from behind James and Kathryn. Johnson had entered the office from the hallway.

"Please do come in." Once in his office Johnson shook James's hand and offered his hand to Kathryn. "Jeffrey Johnson."

Kathryn introduced herself. As they sat on the comfortable couch, Johnson placed himself in an armchair opposite them. James opened the conversation.

"Kathryn is my friend and research associate in this work."

"I am not a scientist, Dr. Johnson . . .," Kathryn started to say.

"Please, call me Jeffrey. May I call you Kathryn?"

"Of course." Kathryn continued. "I am not a scientist, Jeffrey, but I have helped James quite a lot with his writing. We do a lot of work together."

James spoke. He was starting to recognize Kathryn's abilities.

"Also," James continued, "Kathryn has a memory that most of us would die for. Her memory is almost photographic and she can pick up scientific concepts very quickly. A truly remarkable lady and a treasure to me."

"Mrs. Stainsby—I'm sorry—Kathryn, then I can assume that as we talk you will understand our conversation?"

Kathryn responded, "I do understand that it may be quite technical, but if you do not mind I may have to interrupt to clarify a point or two."

"By all means, Kathryn."

Now that the introductions were made, the conversation flowed readily for thirty minutes. Johnson described the work of the department and their cooperation with faculty members in other departments. He focused on the Department of Chemistry, Pharmacology, and Zoology. Then he looked at his watch.

"In fact, I have assumed that because of the hour you will be available for lunch and I have arranged for three other faculty members to join us. A round-table discussion and then you can meet with each one after lunch, if you would prefer."

His raised eyebrows told James and Kathryn that the statement was really a question and Johnson was putting the question to them. James looked at Kathryn. Her smile gave him the answer.

"We'd love to, Jeffrey," James answered for them both of them, knowing that Kathryn would be willing for this opportunity. "As for the afternoon follow-up meetings, that will be great."

"So, if you do not mind a short walk to the Faculty Club?"

"Not at all."

The walk through the gardens was delightful and refreshing. Johnson casually pointed out various items worthy of note. The Japanese Gardens. The different types of flowers that were native to the Hawaiian Islands.

The dining room of the Faculty Club had a panoramic view of the university building and gardens. The tables were laid with white cloths and shining silverware. They followed Johnson as he made his way to a table where a woman and two men were seated.

Johnson introduced James and Kathryn to Dr. Agnes Mikule, head of the Department of Zoology, Dr. Paul Matsui, Department of Chemistry, and Dr. Arthur Chandler, Department of Pharmacology. Dr. François Ali of the Department of Microbiology had sent his apologies and offered to meet with James and Kathryn later in the day for tea.

When the preliminary introductions were complete and all were seated, it seemed that more detailed introductions were necessary. James was surprised that each person at the table had done a premeeting Internet search and knew about James, his scientific work, and his novels. Kathryn was the unknown person at the table. James made the same introduction to the group for Kathryn as he had done earlier to Johnson.

Lunch offered a variety of fruit and fish dishes and once all were seated, the conversation started. James and Kathryn took it in turn to explain their interest in genetic memory and gave an outline of the latest work in which they were involved.

The luncheon meeting went well. Each of the professors had something to add and two hours passed quickly. James was able to piece together the scientific aspects of genetic memory. As a result, he realized that this team of researchers was very close to coming up with a workable theory about that part of the chromosomal structure and the DNA sequence where memory was lodged. And they were also toying with several theories about the genetic structure of memory.

"Well, "James asked, "is it possible that within the area of the brain that is assigned to memory, one could recall events from past ancestors?"

The luncheon table became very silent. It was Agnes Mikule who spoke first as she placed her coffee cup back into the saucer. Her black eyes sparkled as she began to talk.

"I think that you have asked the sixty-four-thousand-dollar question, James. We," Agnes looked around the table, "have been thinking of such a theory for some time. But there is one part of the puzzle missing from this table. Well, two parts really, if I can refer to our colleagues as parts. The first part of the puzzle that is missing is Dr. Ali. He has worked closely with the second part of the puzzle, Dr. Hiroshi Takeyama."

James inwardly cheered. He had not wanted to be discourteous and mention Takeyama's name knowing that many researchers can be very proprietary and parochial about their respective areas of work. But here it was, out front at last. Agnes continued.

"I suggest that we make ourselves available for you and Kathryn this afternoon," she looked around the table to see the affirmative nods from her colleagues "and that we set the schedule. I suggest that you spend as much time as you need, mindful that we are now into the afternoon and that we wrap up tomorrow morning." Again there were affirmative nods from her colleagues.

"I would add," Arthur Chandler spoke up, "that we start with Paul, followed by myself, and finish the day with Dr. Ali. Then Agnes and Jeffrey tomorrow morning. I can see that each conversation could take an hour or so."

"I am not sure that I need to be present at all," Jeffrey interjected.

But Agnes would not hear of it. "Of course you do, Jeffrey. This may not be your specific area but you always have some constructive comment that stimulates my thoughts when we talk."

"So be it, Agnes. I will contact Dr. Ali and inform him of the plans. In fact, if you will excuse me."

Johnson stood up from the table and took the cell phone out of his pocket, using his speed dial.

"Now none of my faculty can escape me." His mischievous grin was interrupted as he responded to the voice on the other end of the call.

"François? Jeffrey. Just a moment to get you up to date and make sure that your schedule is open for this afternoon."

Johnson's voice faded as he walked away from the table to the lobby of the restaurant. He returned moments later.

"Dr. Ali is available any time that you need him," he said looking at James and Kathryn. "He did suggest that we keep each other up to date as the time goes on."

There was a chorus of "sure" from the remaining diners. For Kathryn and James, their schedule for the next twenty-four hours was decided.

"Many thanks to all of you for a delightful lunch and your help," James and Kathryn chorused.

Fifteen minutes later, James and Kathryn were seated in Arthur Chandler's office. For over an hour, the conversation focused on the chemistry of chromosomal DNA. Chandler gave them a good overview that might be called "the way life works." Kathryn took notes and allowed her memory to soak up the facts and Chandler's responses to James's questions. A few minutes before the hour had elapsed, Chandler excused himself and asked his secretary to let Paul Matsui know that they were running about fifteen to twenty minutes over.

As they were about to leave the office, James decided on one final question, not knowing how far he would be asking Chandler to stretch his imagination.

"Arthur, does anyone know if chromosomal memory can be altered by the application of specific chemicals or drugs?"

Chandler smiled.

"You are getting close to our way of thinking, James. We have carried out work on the targeted, not random, but specific reaction of DNA with various chemicals. I suggest that you go through the remainder of the afternoon with Paul and with François. Think about it overnight and bring that question to the table when you meet with Agnes and Jeffrey tomorrow."

James nodded his agreement with Chandler's suggestion.

"Will do, Arthur. And many thanks for your time."

Chandler continued, "It is always gratifying to talk about one's work and be understood. It is my thanks to you both for an enjoyable and stimulating time."

Chandler offered to accompany James and Kathryn to Paul Matsui's office since it was in a separate building, but they declined his kind offer telling him that the campus map would suffice and thanked him. During the ten minutes that they took to walk to Matsui's office in a separate building, they remained silent. As they entered the Chemistry Building, Kathryn spoke.

"Game plan, James?"

"Same as before, bonnie lass. Just let your imagination go into overdrive and run with the questions."

Matsui was waiting for them, having received a telephone call from Arthur Chandler informing him that they were on their way.

After a brief greeting, he suggested that they adjourn to the Department Common Room where they could talk in private and not worry about the mass of papers and books on his desk. He waved his arm toward the open door. James and Kathryn smiled at the pile upon pile of books and papers. They, being orderly persons, were taken aback at the sight. Matsui laughed.

"This makes me a legend in the department because I know the exact location of any item in any pile. My filing system is the pits but my colleagues tell me that my retrieval system is a miracle!"

James and Kathryn laughed.

"However, the fire marshal tells me to clean up every time he inspects the building. And he cites me for being a firetrap. Can you imagine that?"

Matsui led them into a very comfortable room that contained a variety of chairs, a table, and all of the necessary items for making hot or cold drinks. Kathryn and James accepted his offer and each settled for a tall glass of guava juice that they found pleasant and very stimulating.

The conversation with Matsui followed somewhat different lines to the conversation with Chandler as reflected by their different disciplines. There was some overlap, but Matsui focused more on the chemistry of chromosomal DNA compared to Chandler who had focused on the pharmacological effects of different types of chromosomal DNA when placed into a new host.

But to James and Kathryn, the story was starting to come together. James felt a little closer to Matsui than to Chandler because they had both been trained in chemistry. But he still did not discount some of the effect that Chandler had described. He was starting to see how each member of the team could make a real contribution to the team efforts.

Again, the meeting ran over the one-hour time but Matsui was very gracious and gave freely of his time and knowledge.

Finally, James and Kathryn were back in the building that housed the Microbiology Department where they learned that Dr. Ali had just returned from another meeting. He shook James's hand vigorously and kissed Kathryn's hand. Kathryn was surprised and beamed a smile that would have lit up a dark room.

"Mother was French and father was Algerian," he added by way of explanation, "old habits die hard!"

"What a gracious way to be greeted!" exclaimed Kathryn.

His office was smaller but much tidier than Matsui's office. As James and Kathryn sat in the available chairs, Ali volunteered that they could use the departmental office, courtesy of the department head who was on vacation.

Kathryn looked at James and read his mind.

"This will be fine with us."

"Mrs. Stainsby, Dr. Simpson, please call me François. Frank would be even better."

"And only if you call us James and Kathryn."

"So it is agreed. We drop the formalities and move on to the business of the afternoon."

Ali took a deep breath as he began to speak.

"Jeffrey did get me up to date earlier on the reason for your visit. So, if you do not mind, I will start in a very general way and please, ask any questions as they come to you minds."

Ninety minutes later, Ali drew the conversation to a close with a huge sigh. He sat back in his chair and folded his hands behind his head.

"It is some time since I had such an enjoyable session. Your questions, James, have made me think deeply about my subject and I appreciate that. Your questions, Kathryn, are quite remarkable for someone without scientific training and you are to be complimented on your background knowledge and the details that you have accumulated. Is there anything else that I can offer?"

James could not resist the opportunity to ask Ali the same question that he had asked Chandler.

"Frank, does anyone know if chromosomal memory can be altered by application of specific chemicals or drugs?"

James and Kathryn were surprised when the response was almost the same.

"That question is very close to the way that we think. I would prefer not to attempt an answer now but suggest that you ask Agnes and Jeffrey when you meet with them tomorrow."

As they were about to leave, Ali spoke.

"We had wondered if you would like to join us for dinner but we realize that we have given you a great deal to think about and you have just recently arrived."

"Thank you, Frank," James knew what Kathryn was thinking, "but we must decline your kind offer. We do have a lot to talk out between ourselves and we do have a lot of notes to get into the computer. On top of that we are still feeling jet-lagged. So perhaps we can make other arrangements?"

"I will advise my colleagues. What time tomorrow morning would you like to meet Agnes and Jeffrey?"

"Nine o'clock."

"Done." Then as an afterthought Ali asked, "How about a taxi?"

"Please."

The telephone call was made and Ali accompanied them to the door of the building. Minutes later, as the taxi drew up, Ali made a comment that struck home to James and Kathryn.

"It must be quite a novel that you are writing. The detail that you have been given through lunch and this afternoon must have brought you to a good understanding of genetic memory. You have been given a briefing that many scientists in this field would welcome, especially if they intended to use the information for practical purposes."

In the taxi, Kathryn looked at James and held his hand. "James, my dear, do you think that he knows or at least suspects?"

"He must suspect something but he cannot really know what we are doing. I think that he is more worried about scientific espionage. The pressure to obtain grant money is a tough competition these days. I suggest that we put him at ease tomorrow and offer the novelist's explanation. Might help."

"Might help a lot, James, but why wait until tomorrow?"

"Good point, Kath."

Once back at the hotel, James made a telephone call to Ali who was still in his office. After thanking him for his help again, James steered the conversation to the events of his most recent novel and explained in detail the reasons for their quest. Ali seemed quite satisfied that there was not a nefarious purpose to the visit by them. He even offered to join them for an evening drink at one of the several open-air bars at the hotel. He had further information that he felt they should know so his offer was accepted and suitable time was arranged.

Kathryn spent the time using James's notebook computer to enter the events of the day and fill in the scientific detail. He adjourned to the balcony to give himself time to think about what they had learned. Finally the balcony door opened.

"James, the work is ready for you to check. A few spelling mistakes but I believe that I have captured the substance to our visits today."

James read the words on the screen and was amazed at the detail. Kathryn stood behind him as he read her story. Finally, he was finished and as stood up from the computer, he put his arms around Kathryn in a gentle hug and kissed her.

"A lovely piece of work, me bonnie lass. Now we have an accurate record of all of the conversations and time to relax and shower before we meet our visitor in the lobby."

Kathryn beamed.

*   *   *

Ali arrived on time. James suggested that they sit in the comfortable chairs located in the open-air lobby. The conversation came straight to the point. James reassured Ali of his need for the information for his forthcoming book and even offered to sign a confidentiality agreement. In the agreement it would be stated that he, James Simpson, and Kathryn Stainsby would not divulge any of the information that they gathered from the ensuing conversation. James told Ali that he had a draft agreement in his room that could be signed and notarized here at the hotel. Ali seemed surprised but pleased at the offer.

"James, of all of the faculty involved in this program, I am the one who has worked closely with Dr. Takeyama. He was, and still is, my mentor."

James could see the fire of enlightenment in Ali's eyes. The passion that he put into his work was obvious.

"The reason for my hesitancy is that, about two years ago, we were approached by one fellow who seemed genuine but who turned out to be the representative of another group that was trying to steal our latest developments. I believe that is one of the reasons, if not the main reason, for Dr. Takeyama to disappear into the wilds of the interior of Kauai on a regular basis. I feel that signing such an agreement would have been worthless in that case. But, in your case, I have performed a background check and you are indeed the person that you purport to be. A simple handshake will suffice. You have my trust. And you also, Mrs. Stainsby."

They shook hands.

James looked at Kathryn who nodded as she read his thoughts. They were both feeling more comfortable. James suggested that they have dinner at the main open-air restaurant that looked directly on to the Pacific Ocean. That same restaurant where James and Kathryn had eaten breakfast. Ali agreed and they strolled appreciatively through the grounds of the hotel. The immaculate gardens and the lush vegetation were so pleasing to the eye. A black swan that regarded the territory as his and seemed to believe that it was his duty to keep the ducks in order offered good reason for them to smile at his antics. The hostess remembered James and Kathryn from her duty at breakfast and greeted them. They were shown to a table that overlooked the small pool and the ever-present ducks.

As the meals were ordered and delivered, Ali started to talk. He emphasized the need to talk with Takeyama. The mention of Takeyama's work that involved chemically induced changes to DNA had really caught James's attention. Ali said that he considered himself to be Takeyama's closet friend and confidante. But for the last two years, Takeyama had become more and more withdrawn when the subject of changes to DNA was discussed. Ali even speculated that Takeyama had gone beyond the bounds of any previous knowledge and was even beyond the realms of any previous work.

Throughout dinner, James and Kathryn had added comments to the conversation but they had remained silent whilst Ali talked. James knew that Kathryn's fertile mind would be soaking up this knowledge like a sponge. Ali pulled out his wallet but James would not hear of any offer of payment.

"Please, Frank. It's our way of thanking you for your time and the stimulating conversation."

Ali bowed slightly to show his thanks as James continued.

"Will we see you at the university tomorrow?"

"I should think so." After several seconds of silence, he spoke.

"I am perhaps the only person who has the means to contact Dr. Takeyama. If you have no objection, I would like to get him up to date on our conversation and since I assume that you would like to talk with him, I will broach the subject of a possible visit. That way, he will not be surprised and he is more likely to be willing to see you."

James and Kathryn inwardly rejoiced at the prospect of meeting the one person who could answer many of their very urgent questions. They heartily agreed.

Ali said his goodbyes and left.

*   *   *

CHAPTER 17

T he next morning, James and Kathryn followed the same procedure as they had the morning before. By seven thirty they had read the papers that had been delivered to their rooms along with the pot of hot tea and then went to the hotel restaurant for the buffet breakfast after which they took a taxi to the campus.

At nine o'clock they presented themselves at Jeffrey Johnson's office where Johnson and Agnes Mikule welcomed them with smiles and greetings. Moments later they were seated, Johnson's secretary arrived with a tray of chilled guava juice. After she had left the office, Johnson looked directly at James.

"Agnes and I have been talking," James smiled, "and it seems to us that we can tell you little more than our colleagues told you yesterday. Oh, by the way, Dr. Ali stopped by and left this book for you. A gift for you and Mrs. Stainsby."

James took the book that Johnson handed to him and noted the very simple title *The Way of Life*. As he opened the two-hundred-page book, James noticed that the easy-to-read text was illustrated with colored drawings of various primates and representations of the DNA double helix. The inside front cover was signed by Ali and given "With best regards to James and Kathryn." A nice touch, thought James as he passed the book to Kathryn.

"We'd like to thank Dr. Ali personally, if time allows."

"Sorry, James, he asked me to tell you that that he has to be off-campus for the day. Meeting with one of his funding agencies at the federal building. Sends his apologies."

Kathryn flicked through a few pages then placed the book on the nearby chair. James looked at the two scientists and raised his eyebrows as he asked.

"Well, what do you recommend that we do next?"

It was Agnes Mikule who responded.

"We," she looked toward Jeffrey, "realize that you are digging far deeper into this subject than the typical novelist might wish to go. Other than data that are currently between our clients and us, we cannot tell you any more. But we do suggest that you attempt to see Dr. Takeyama.

"I say 'attempt' because he is a difficult man to find. I detect that you need to go much deeper into this subject area."

She looked directly at James and then at Kathryn as if trying to read their respective minds.

"Call it intuition. That is why I am suggesting this next step. However, be prepared, you may not find Dr. Takeyama. He is very difficult to contact and no one seems to know where he lives. I was born and raised on the north shore of Kauai and spent my younger years prowling around the northern interior of the island but even I am unable to pinpoint his exact whereabouts."

Agnes sipped at her glass of guava juice as though thinking about how she would frame her next sentence.

"We," she nodded again at Jeffrey, "know that he will show up here after several weeks of being a recluse with a whole set of new ideas for research. After a short stay, he will leave once again for his reclusive home."

She paused then continued.

"Our friend, Takeyama, started on this course of absence some years ago. We are not sure why but it appeared that something or someone caused him to decide on this course of action. He will not tell us and we do not ask. We can speculate, but that would be grossly unfair to Dr. Takeyama."

Agnes paused to allow her words to sink in and waited to see what impact, if any, they had on her two enraptured listeners. It was Kathryn who spoke, seeing that James was deep in thought and not ready to talk.

"We do have a reason, other than writing a novel, to expand our knowledge in this area but we prefer that you do not ask as it is—"

"Very personal?" Agnes completed Kathryn's sentence as a question. She had noticed the disappointed look on James's face when it became evident that Takeyama was elusive.

"Yes."

Kathryn smiled at Agnes's perception. Jeffrey Johnson remained silent during the exchange as Kathryn continued. As she spoke she laid her hand on James's arm as if to give him reassurance.

"We do have a need to talk this over with Dr. Takeyama."

At that point in the conversation, James spoke up.

"We know that Dr. Takeyama was studying the pharmacological effect of chemicals on the body and had ventured to suggest that changes could be made in the DNA through use of specific chemicals."

"If you do not mind," Johnson said as he got up and closed the door, "I prefer that we talk more privately. Please continue, James."

James sipped the last of his guava juice as if to derive strength from the liquid. He looked at Johnson and then he continued.

"The last papers that Dr. Takeyama published in the *Journal of DNA Research* indicated that he was having some success with modifying the DNA sequence of the upper primates," James took a deep breath as if needing the additional air to continue, "and then, nothing. So I am of the conclusion that Dr. Takeyama had indeed learned, or was close to learning, the secrets of DNA modification through the use of drugs, or specific chemicals, if you wish to use that term."

The silence filled the room for a few seconds. James wondered what had happened and he looked quizzically at Kathryn. Finally, Jeffrey Johnson responded.

"I think that you," he looked at James and Kathryn, "have come as close as any of us regarding the nature of Dr. Takeyama's work. We have reason to believe that he was that," he used his thumb and forefinger to indicate a small distance, "close. He did try to withdraw his last two articles on the subject but it was too late. The journals containing those articles had already been published. So, it seems at that point he decided to make himself scarce and difficult to find."

Johnson appeared deep in thought as he rubbed his chin.

"And so," it was Agnes who broke into Johnson's thoughts, "can you imagine the implications of his work if it became known that he could change DNA by use of specific chemicals? Because of men like Hiroshi Takeyama, universities have remained the intellectual centers of the country in certain areas of scientific scholarship. Since World War II, many of the really important discoveries have come out of private companies. For example, the laser, the transistor, the polio vaccine, the microchip, the hologram, the personal computer, magnetic resonance imaging, CAT scans, the list goes on and on. We are thankful for the services of Dr. Takeyama and so we do protect him. Even more so, can you imagine the capabilities of Dr. Takeyama's mind? The DNA logbooks that we use here have to be kept on computer! DNA is such a large molecule that each species requires ten gigabytes of disk space to store all of the details of each iteration. Yet he can visualize the three-dimensional image of the DNA molecule. He prefers to be a recluse. If you find him, we ask that you also protect his work and whereabouts, as we do."

James looked at Kathryn and they suddenly realized the meaning of the conversation and the possible reason why that Phillip Spiller, the young doctor half a world away in Durham, had been informing them on that cold Durham street, only a week or so ago, that this man Takeyama was a great source of information for them. Kathryn continued the conversation.

"We appreciate your concern and we will honor your request. But if we go to Kauai, what are our chances of seeing Dr. Takeyama? Or should we return to England?"

"No, not at all," Agnes continued, "at this stage you have nothing to lose but a lot to gain. As you said, your reasons are personal but why come all this way and go home without at least trying."

Kathryn smiled as Agnes continued.

"I will tell you that Kauai is not like Honolulu or this island of Oahu. Kauai is the most northern island in the Hawaiian chain and is nicknamed the Garden Isle because of its dense foliage. Geographically, it is Hawaii's oldest and most mature island. When most people imagine a lush, tropical island in the middle of the Pacific Ocean, it is Kauai that they have in mind. It is easy to reach by air and only one hundred miles north of Oahu. But the people are much closer and more protective of each other. You will have to approach them diplomatically if you are to have any chance of them even acknowledging that they know Dr. Takeyama, let alone meeting him! If there is an answer to your questions, you will know in time. If we could, we would help but not knowing his exact whereabouts, we are not able to give you any further information."

Agnes shrugged her shoulders as if to indicate the difficulty of their position.

James looked at Kathryn and, with an unseen signal, indicated that it was time to leave. They both got up simultaneously. James offered words of thanks for the time that Agnes Mikule and Jeffrey Johnson had spent with them.

"If we can be of any further help," Johnson offered, "you have our telephone numbers."

James and Kathryn smiled their goodbyes and as they were about to leave the office, Johnson offered to call a taxi. They accepted the kind offer.

They reached the hotel in time for an early lunch. The trail of Dr. Hiroshi Takeyama was warm and they knew that if they could find him, several answers to James's physical and mental time travel might become very clear.

As they sat eating the refreshing tropical fruits, Kathryn reminded James of the plans for the evening. She had not forgotten the performance of light classical music by the Honolulu Symphony Orchestra scheduled for that evening.

The heat of the day that threatened them after lunch forced them to adjourn to the air-conditioned rooms. He sat at his notebook computer adding more notes as Kathryn talked him through the various details that had slipped his mind. She excused herself and he could hear her voice from her adjoining room as she talked on the telephone.

Five minutes later, she returned. Smiling.

"James, my dear. We have seats for the performance of the Honolulu Symphony tonight. My treat!"

But there was more. Kathryn had a very satisfied expression on her face as she announced, "We leave early tomorrow morning for Kauai. It's all taken care of and we have reservations at a hotel on the north shore, at a place called Princeville. They say it is very nice. And only an hour or so from the Lihue Airport."

"Lihue?"

"Yes, the main airport on the southeast shore of the Island."

"Kath, you are wonderful. How much do I owe you?"

"You owe me nothing, James Simpson. I also have American Express! The concierge has the tickets for us. The taxi to the airport is organized. This is my treat. So I propose that we spend the remainder of the day relaxing in the air-conditioning, then in the shade by the pool as the sun moves around. And tonight . . ." She left the thought hanging in the air.

James could see the twinkle in Kathryn's eye. He remained poker faced as he looked directly at her.

"The symphony!" he exclaimed. Then he raised his right eyebrow. "Did you have anything else in mind?"

*   *   *

The restful evening of music had been just what they needed to take their minds away from their intense research. Even better, the next day, all went according to plan. They ate a larger-than-usual breakfast, not knowing when the opportunity to eat lunch would present itself. The aircraft touched down at Lihue Airport thirty-seven minutes after leaving the gate at Honolulu International Airport. Kathryn had also reserved a car. They collected their luggage and were soon driving the car out of the rental agency lot.

The journey north to the Hanalei Valley was underway. Kathryn suggested that they stop at Kilauea Point to take in the spectacular views. They were approaching Kapa'a, a busy town north of Lihue airport, already awakened by the tourists looking for bargains.

"Sounds like a great plan, I'll have my camera poised and ready to go when we get there." James smiled to himself as he sensed the excitement in Kathryn's voice.

"I have the Kauai map and will look for the entrance road leading to the Kilauea Lighthouse. That's of course if I can draw my eyes away from this amazing scenery and give my camera a rest. From what I've seen so far of this island, I love it! Can't imagine what choice real estate would cost!" Kathryn exclaimed.

James stopped the vehicle a number of times so that they could take photographs between Kapa'a and Kilauea. The weather was ideal, lots of sun with gentle trade winds.

Before long the road sign appeared on their right showing that a short two-mile journey was between them and the lighthouse. The car wound its way to the parking area and they walked the remaining yards to the viewing areas encircling the lighthouse.

"This is fantastic, James. I'm so glad we stopped here," gurgled Kathryn as she oohed and aahed at each new vista from the headland.

The various shades of blue and green in the ocean were an artist's dream and made Kathryn wish she had paint and canvas and time to spend in this ruggedly beautiful place. The noise coming from the bird sanctuary on a rock below them interrupted the sound of the surf that prevailed along the precipitous coastline.

Not wanting to spend too much of their time in this one spot, they returned to the car and were soon on their way north again heading for Princeville and a leisurely lunch. James estimated that they would arrive at the Princeville Hotel around noon or shortly after.

On arrival at the hotel, they pulled up to the canopied entrance where a valet and a bellman met them. James and Kathryn walked unencumbered to the registration desk and James was surprised at the classical opulence of the hotel. He squeezed Kathryn's hand while they stood at the desk as the young woman read the message on the computer screen.

"Ah, yes, Dr. and Mrs. Simpson." Kathryn returned his hand squeeze. "We have a very nice suite for you, as per your request, Mrs. Simpson."

She looked at Kathryn, noting that she had made the reservation, as if to acknowledge the excellence of the suite.

"The suite has a large balcony and you have a wonderful view of the ocean. The bellman will help you with your luggage." She smiled. "Is there anything else?"

Kathryn, having made the reservations using her credit card, signed the registration card while James gave the bellman a handsome tip and then both decided to have lunch. The meal was served on a very large patio that was covered by an awning to keep out the effects of the hot sun. They sat in the shade and enjoyed a light sandwich that filled the gap left after an early but somewhat larger-than-usual breakfast. They were wondering about the next steps, when the waitress, clearing the dishes, asked about dessert and from where they had come.

Kathryn responded, while James looked at the ocean. His fingers drummed lightly on the table. Kathryn ordered desserts, pot de crème, for both of them. As the waitress approached with the desserts, Kathryn decided to take the plunge! She engaged the waitress in general conversation about the island and places to visit and then asked the question that she and James had in mind.

"I am wondering, Liza," Kathryn had spotted the name tag on the waitress's dress, "if you have ever heard of a Dr. Hiroshi Takeyama?"

The sudden stiffening of the waitress's body and her look of surprise told Kathryn that she had an answer to her question. James also perked up at the reaction.

"I am sorry, Liza, I did not mean to alarm you," Kathryn offered.

"No, ma'am. It is all right. I have heard of him."

Kathryn and James knew that her response was not that of someone who had casual knowledge of Takeyama. They did not push the question any further as the words of Agnes Mikule came to their minds. The conversation turned once again to places of interest to visit. James and Kathryn were astounded by the natural wonders of Kauai, the Waimea Canyon, the Fern Grotto, the Na Pali Coast, and the lush, green valleys that cut through folds in the mountains and opened out to the sea. But during lunch, they had seen a gathering mist blanket the inner mountain range and creep slowly toward the coast. Liza suggested that they drive to the end of the road into the reserve.

"I like this," Kathryn interjected. "Why don't we go there, James? It looks like it might rain later and now would be a good time."

James nodded his agreement and they took Liza's advice. They saw field after field of taro, a common crop in Kauai. The north side of the island was ideally suited for the taro crops, having constant rainfall. The first settlers to Kauai had, among other crops, brought taro to the island. Kathryn noted from her guidebook that millions of pounds of taro are turned into poi, a staple part of the Hawaiian diet.

On several occasions, James and Kathryn parked the car and walked along the sandy beach. The sound of the breakers was music to their ears. The seabirds added their characteristic cries to the sounds of the waves. It was so restful and peaceful after the hustle and bustle of Honolulu.

They returned to the hotel after three hours of rest and relaxation on the roads and beaches of northern Kauai, wondering why they would ever need to return to England. But there was a reason and they knew that this visit was transient. There would be times in the future when they could return.

For the first time that day, they entered the suite. The spaciousness and delightful decoration was accentuated by the vibrant colors of Hawaiian flora such as the yellow hibiscus, the red ohia flower, and muted green of Kauai's mokihana berry. The antique furnishings, original artwork, a spacious bathroom, and the picture window that allowed them a full view of the bay oozed luxury and took their breath away.

Just as Kathryn was about to express a combination of surprise, pleasure, and amazement at the accommodations, the sudden sound of the telephone startled them. James picked up the receiver and responded with a single "hello" and this was answered by a query.

"Dr. Simpson?"

"Yes."

"This is Liza. You know, the waitress." Before James could respond in any way, Liza continued. "I have made contact with Dr. Takeyama. He will meet with you, both of you, tomorrow. Please meet me in the lobby at eight o'clock in the morning and I will give you directions."

Before James could thank her, the phone line went dead and James was left open-mouthed. He wanted to know how she had made contact. Where did Takeyama live? How would they get there? And a host of other questions.

But it was not to be. The silence of the line told him that he would have to wait and be patient!

*   *   *

CHAPTER 18

James and Kathryn took the elevator to the hotel lobby at ten minutes before eight having had an early room-service breakfast. The elegant grandfather clock that stood against one wall of the hotel, next to the large portrait of Captain James Cook, started to strike eight o'clock and before it finished chiming, Liza appeared.

"Good morning, Dr. Simpson. Mrs. Simpson."

They responded with smiles and acknowledgements. During this part of the trip, neither James nor Kathryn had bothered to contradict anyone who presumed that they were married. Why spoil the thought?

Liza pointed to one set of the very comfortable chairs that were placed at various locations throughout the specious lobby.

"Shall we?"

Once they were seated, Liza took out a map that she had marked with a highlighter pen.

"This is the road that you are to take. You passed this road on your way along the north shore yesterday. As you cross the bridge on the sharp bend, instead of continuing to the right, look for the minor road on your left."

James nodded. He remembered the sharp bends and the one-car-at-a-time bridges. This bridge in particular as there has been a line of cars on both sides of the bridge with each driver courteously waiting for the one on the other side to cross. He had glanced at the side road and wondered out loud to Kathryn who lived in the area. Owners of the taro fields had been his response to his own question. Liza continued her description of the map.

"Take the road south from Princeville where you will pass the taro fields into the Hanalei Valley."

Liza looked at James and Kathryn to make sure that she had their attention. "My uncle lives beyond the Hanalei Wildlife Refuge in a modest dwelling."

Now she had their complete attention. At the two words indicating that she was a relative, two mouths opened in surprise. Kathryn was the first to recover.

"Your uncle?"

"Yes, Mrs. Simpson. Dr. Hiroshi Takeyama is my uncle on my mother's side. She left Japan as a young woman to marry my father who lived in Honolulu at the time. Three years later, just before I was born, they moved to this island to live with my grandmother. Two years after I was born, my parents were killed in an auto accident during a trip back to Honolulu. My grandmother raised me, you will see her house close by the entrance to the refuge. Stop there and please wait. My uncle will come to meet you."

Liza paused for a few moments and then continued as though she had a serious afterthought.

"Oh, by the way, wear comfortable walking shoes," Liza looked at Kathryn, "the runners that you are wearing now will be more than adequate, but I do not recommend shorts. The undergrowth where my uncle lives is hard on the legs."

Kathryn jumped into Liza's monologue with a quick "I have a pair of light cotton slacks?"

"That will do admirably, Mrs. Simpson."

Liza looked at James, and suggested, "If you have a similar pair of cotton slacks or Levi's that will suffice."

Liza continued to go over the details of the map and then added more information since the map did not show the precise location of the road that lead to her grandmother's house. The map did not even show the road! And then she made the move to stand up but thought better of it and sat back in the chair.

"I have given you the details that you need. Oh, yes, of course, please take extra clothes and your toiletries. I did check your Web page and biography, Dr. Simpson, after I got off duty at lunchtime yesterday so I am aware of your background. I do not normally give this information to strangers. There is a reasonable chance that my uncle may ask you to stay with him overnight. Also, the rain that can occur at any time in the interior could soak you to the skin very quickly." Liza smiled as she added, "I forgot to add that my uncle lives close to the wettest area in the world. The area receives more than four hundred inches of rain per year!"

This time, Liza did stand up and James and Kathryn raised themselves from their seats.

"Is there anything else that you need?"

James shook his head as he spoke.

"No thanks, Liza. Your directions to your grandmother's house are good and we should have no trouble finding the place. Oh, yes. What time?"

"Just leave when you are ready. My uncle will find you. Granny will make tea while you wait.

"I live with my grandmother and I did see my uncle last night. He asked me to pass on his invitation for you to visit him."

She noticed their raised eyebrows.

"My uncle visits my grandmother's house several times a week, so we do have frequent contact."

Liza smiled and extended her hand to them as she added, "I advise that you retain your room here. The hotel is playing host to a group of golfers who are visiting for a tournament that starts this weekend and the hotel will be full. I can advise the hotel management of your trip and they will give you a reduced room rate for the time that you are away."

Liza turned to walk to the registration desk and then remembered another point that she needed to add.

"And please do not be upset if the local people use the term *ha'oli* when they are talking about you. Literally, it means *without the breath* and it is not a derogatory term, but the term is applied to all of those people who are not local to the islands. See you when you get back."

James and Kathryn returned to the suite and packed the clothes and toiletries that they needed according to Liza's advice.

Kathryn broke the silence that had existed for the past few minutes.

"James, are you excited?"

"Tingling with anticipation, my dear," James responded. "But I do not know what to make of it. All of this secrecy seems to be going a little too far." He took a breath as he thought about his next words. "I can, to a point, understand the protectiveness of the people. After all, we are— what is the word Liza used?"

"*Ha'oli*, James."

"That's it." James smiled and looked at Kathryn. Her blonde hair told everyone that she was definitely a *ha'oli*! Then he continued, "There is a lot more to this than meets the eye. Or, as my friend Sherlock Holmes might say . . ." This time Kathryn finished James's sentence, "The game's afoot, Watson!"

"How about you, Kath?"

"I have not felt so excited since . . .," she fumbled for words.

"I first took you out for dinner?" James offered a response.

"Sounds about right, James." Kathryn kissed James affectionately.

They left the hotel grounds and turned on to the westerly road that would take them to the bridge. Kathryn had the Kauai guidebook and map in her hands and advised James of the various twists and turns in the road. He remembered that Liza had warned him to drive carefully because of the tourists who were not familiar with the narrow roads of the island. She had added, "This is not Oahu," referring to the island where Honolulu was located, "so please be careful as you drive, Dr. Simpson."

Kathryn had read that mixed groups of people live in the Hanalei area, among them were longtime residents, new age types, celebrities, and surfers. She could understand why, if for no other reason, Takeyama preferred the isolation away from the beaches.

The Hanalei Valley from the overlook was lush and colorful. Patchwork fields spread below them and they saw the winding road that they were to take to the home of Liza's grandmother. The road followed the course of the Hanalei River that gently cut through the taro fields on either side. The valley was ringed on all sides by the mountain range. Patches of mist hung over the higher peaks and ominous clouds flanked the interior of the island. They were not surprised that it was the wettest place on earth!

Liza had told them that the refuge was located on the floodplain of the Hanalei River, which received discharge from the Mt. Wai'ale'ale plateau. Kathryn and James had fumbled on the multisyllabic word but Liza released them from their efforts when she said, "It means Rippling Water." The plateau received an average annual rainfall of four hundred and fifty-one inches per year. Through a system of ditches and channels, the water was used to irrigate the taro patches and interspersed with ponds to provide a habitat for a diversity of waterfowl. Hawaiian farmers grew taro on the refuge and continue a tradition that stretched back at least one thousand years.

The road soon became unpaved and James was thankful that they had rented a four-wheel-drive vehicle. The paddy-field appearance of some areas made them wonder if the vehicle would take them to their destination without becoming mired in the swampy and waterlogged area.

Finally, after a drive of one-half mile beyond the end of the paved road, the route appeared to be taken over by the vegetation. Here, they reached a spot where James could park the vehicle. They decided to leave their bags in the vehicle, not knowing how far they would need to walk to the house, assuming that they were on the right track. But Liza's directions had been accurate to that point.

About fifty yards along the crude path and into the undergrowth, a small house suddenly came into view. As they approached, they could see an older woman talking with a man who had his back to them. He was wearing jeans, a dark sweatshirt, and his black shoulder-length hair was drawn back in a ponytail.

The woman saw them and indicated their approach to her companion. He turned to face them.

James and Kathryn saw that he was Japanese. Their exposure to the Japanese people was mainly through business meetings where very dignified business suits had always been the order of the day. As he walked toward them, he held out his hand to James and muttered an adaptation of those famous words that Stanley used to Livingston.

"Dr. Simpson, I presume. Mrs. Simpson. Or should I say Mrs. Stainsby? I am Hiroshi Takeyama."

Words failed James and Kathryn. They were facing Dr. Hiroshi Takeyama. A man who, as near as James could tell, should have been on the verge of, or perhaps even awarded, a Nobel Prize. He was a man who was also on the edge of understanding the molecular basis of memory and its integration into the DNA molecule. But he had opted for the quiet and peaceful island of Kauai rather than the hectic, and sometime cutthroat, world of molecular biochemistry

James and Kathryn made the supreme effort to keep their respective mouths shut and not gape at their guest as they shook hands with the elusive Dr. Takeyama. In the absence of words from James and Kathryn, he continued.

"Please call me Harry. May I call you James and Kathryn?"

"Of course, Dr . . . . sorry, Harry." James had found his voice. "We are pleased that you have agreed to see us." James looked at the old lady.

She exchanged words with Takeyama in a language that James and Kathryn did not understand but which they assumed to be Hawaiian since they were able to pick out the word *ha'oli*. Takeyama spoke again, in his perfect English.

"Allow me to introduce my late sister's mother-in-law. She does not speak much English and prefers the old Hawaiian language but she can speak Japanese and several other Oriental languages. She said that you may call her Mother." Takeyama looked serious before he added. "She does not give many persons that honor. You both behaved courteously to Liza and my niece speaks very highly of you, even though she barely knows you. Most important, both Liza and mother say that they can see the truth from your eyes. And that is why, now having seen you, Mother has taken an instant liking to you; she trusts you."

James and Kathryn nodded at the old lady who smiled, bowed her head slightly as if to indicate that they were welcome, and led the way into the house where Hawaiian fruit tea and delicious sweet bread were served. As soon as they were comfortable with each other, Takeyama started the conversation. It became very obvious to Kathryn and James that Takeyama knew much more about them, especially about James, than they could have imagined.

The conversation was polite and went back and forth about various aspects of James's work. Kathryn was not excluded from the conversation. He was surprised that Kathryn knew so much about his work, but as soon as she mentioned using the libraries and the Internet as a source, he understood. He was more interested in Kathryn's ability to understand the science of his work. He complimented her on her abilities. And then, when he saw that they were finished with the tea and were ready, Takeyama inquired,

"Well, James, how can I help you? I assume that your interest in genetic memory lies beyond the curiosity of the novelist. You are a scientist so I suggest that we begin at the beginning. If I know what specifics you need, then I will be able to answer your questions and help you in your quest."

*   *   *

CHAPTER 19

Takeyama stood up and suggested to Kathryn and James that they should accompany him to his house. After they had thanked Mother for the refreshments, they stepped outside and collected their overnight bags from the car. Takeyama looked at the clothes that there were wearing and nodded his head in approval. He led the way through the dense vegetation, and James and Kathryn were relieved that they had taken Liza's advice about what to wear. They could feel the vegetation along the little-used path clawing at their slacks and shirts. The perspiration from their bodies soaked their clothes and soon both Kathryn and James felt as though they had been swimming fully clothed. Takeyama strode on unconcerned.

After about one hour of strenuous walking, they entered a clearing and there was Takeyama's house. He waved his hand in the direction of the house as if in a grand gesture of introduction.

"Be it ever so humble, there is no place like home!"

The house was built predominantly of wood with many windows to allow light to enter the rooms. The vegetation was particularly thick and heavy and would not, unless the sun was at its zenith, allow much light into the area. Because of the high water table, the house had been built on a platform so that its base was above the ground.

James and Kathryn breathed a collective sigh of relief. Not wishing to appear exhausted, they had remained silent as their individual thoughts focused on an end to the journey. The vegetation had been so thick that they had wondered if the journey would ever end.

Takeyama smiled and invited them to enter as he stepped inside and held the door open.

"Please, leave your bags and have a seat. If you would like to have a wash and freshen up, the bathroom is along the hall to the right."

The inside of the house took their breath away. The room was furnished with antiques. Bookshelves lined the walls and they seemed to groan under the weight of hundreds of volumes. The subject matter of the books ranged from the classics to the more pragmatic mathematics, applied sciences, and the biological sciences. James was amazed at the sheer number. They could not resist examining the contents of the shelves. Takeyama stood and watched them. The heat and humidity outside were forgotten as they feasted their eyes on the multitude of volumes.

"You have an interest in my books?" Takeyama asked rhetorically, smiling as he spoke.

And from that point on the conversation never ceased. They felt a close relationship to Takeyama. Their initial nervousness at meeting him for the first time disappeared and their features took on relaxed expression, which pleased Takeyama. They were kindred spirits and the ice was broken.

They discussed books, his recent acquisition, the demerits of those who purchased books but never read them, and anything else that came to mind.

James and Kathryn suddenly realized that Takeyama's invitation to wash after their walk had not been accepted and decided to take up the offer at that moment. The heat and the humidity had caused them to lose a lot of water, and most of it had collected in their clothes and was obvious on their faces. James offered that Kathryn could go first. She agreed, with a big smile of thanks and relief.

In the comfortable living room, James and Takeyama relaxed and chatted. Then James, realizing how much more comfortable he was, commented on the air-conditioning. Takeyama pointed to the generator and its emergency backup that stood together outside of the bathroom window.

"Supplies all of the power for my needs, without it in this climate, it would be difficult to bear. But I refuse to be bothered by the standard telephone. I prefer the satellite phone. A notebook computer, yes! It is essential for my work. But I guard against invasion of my privacy. If I am to be accessible, it must be my choice," he explained.

James nodded, understanding that living off the beaten track did not always mean that there had to be an absence of amenities.

Kathryn appeared, looking much refreshed and changed into dry clothes. James thankfully took his turn in the bathroom and before long reappeared in the lounge wearing dry clothes and feeling much better.

Takeyama noticed them looking at a framed sign on the wall written in Japanese.

"Ah," he said, "you are interested?"

They nodded simultaneously.

Takeyama smiled as he translated: "Everyone brings joy to this room. Some when they enter. Others when they leave."

As he was translating, he carried pitcher from the kitchen that contained a mixed fruit juice. As they sipped the drink, they could feel the energy returning to their bodies. They were refreshed and awakened.

Takeyama sat in the chair, opposite to Kathryn and James. Beside him on the table he had placed several thick notebooks, compiled over many years. All of the information was written in miniscule Japanese allowing Takeyama to cram the pages with knowledge. Some of the information contained in the books had been entered into his computer files, but much of the work and notes in the notebooks predated his use of a computer. Thus most of it existed only here, among his private handwritten papers. There were dozens of hand-drawn diagrams, some mere hasty sketches of unidentified portions of the human DNA molecule. There were hundreds of queries that he had written to himself and a few formal articles that he had written and were published in scientific journals; extensive historical and bibliographical references; and a summary of the key findings in the area of DNA manipulation that he had collected over the years as well as a report of the recent work relating to the mapping of the human genome.

For years, even decades, Takeyama had been fascinated with function and order of human DNA. He had even wondered about the genetic changes that would be required to transmute species, the folklore, tales, and legends of lycanthropic events, the change of man into a wolf and vice-versa had even caused him to make a comment or two in his current notebook. But back to the human side of his work, Takeyama had never even considered wondering where his interest in the evolution of DNA had originated. Yet as one fascinated with human beginnings and development, the nature and function of DNA had always been there.

Many within the scientific community had ignored his work until it became obvious, to military and even to commercial interests, that there might be some significance to his results. He had been ignored, even shunned, by the traditional scientific community because of his far-thinking ideas. He had gathered about him a loyal network of students and co-workers, experts in a variety of relevant fields who were capable of initial thought with whom he had formed instantaneous and unquestioned friendship.

Now, James Simpson, this scientist had visited him who had the genetic background to move from one century to another. This was not the stuff of science fiction novels. Here was a man who had the capability of bringing a portion of the past to life.

Takeyama looked at James and Kathryn. They were genuine, he felt, and he would help. He would see to it that they were both coached in the necessary aspects of what they were about to undertake. There would be no shining the spotlight of international prominence. This was a personal event for two people who needed his help and who, in the short time that he knew them, he had come to like and trust.

He got up from his seat and walked over to a small cabinet on the shelf. "My apothecary's box," he stated by way of explanation. "Belonged to an ancestor. Rumor is that it was washed ashore after the fleet of Kublai Khan was sunk in 1281 by the divine wind or wind of the gods, you know the *kamikaze*, as he tried to invade Japan. It was protected from the ravages of the sea by a waterproof wrapping, almost like the material that you call vellum. One of my ancestors, an apothecary, was close to the shogun and was given it as a gift by the shogun. Since then, it has been in my family."

James and Kathryn looked at the wooden box. Perhaps made from cherry wood that had aged over the centuries. The writing was inlaid in gold on each drawer. The drawer handles were small and were made from silver. The box was approximately twelve by twelve inches and six inches deep with sixteen three-inch square wooden drawers. Takeyama opened a drawer and took out a cigarette.

"Allow myself one of these," he said brandishing the cigarette, "when I need to think. Hope the smoke does not affect either of you. If so . . .," he left the statement unfinished.

"No, Harry." James looked at Kathryn to make sure that the decision that he had made on their behalf was in order. She smiled in agreement.

James went over to the apothecary's box to examine it more closely. Takeyama could see his interest and continued with his story.

"The characters are Old Chinese and explain some drug recipes. That is how I received my stimulation for some of my work."

The looks on their faces were more than looks of curiosity and Takeyama hastened to explain.

"No, not from the drugs," he smiled as he could feel the thoughts passing through their minds, "from the translation of the Old Chinese. The writing on the front of each drawer is actually a recipe for the particular drug that is kept in the drawer with a description of the various doses to be administered and the effects of the drug relative to the dosage."

Kathryn's curiosity was awakened. She walked across the room to examine the box more closely.

"So each drug can act differently depending upon its partners in the recipe?"

"Yes," Takeyama responded immediately. "As you may be aware, many South American native people use curare-tipped weapons for hunting and for defense against intruders. It is not so much the weapon that kills but the curare. But curare, in the right dose, is used as a heart stimulant in many hospitals. Just a question of degree or the amount of the drug."

Takeyama shifted his focus from Kathryn to James.

"Now to the point of our get-together."

"The reason that I have allowed you to visit my home," again he swept his hands around the immaculately kept cottage, "is that I believe that you have a deep-seated issue that you wish to discuss with me. It is my opinion, James, from searching your background that you toed the line about as little as I did. We are two of a kind. We live for science and not the stupid politics and charlatans that we find so often these days."

Takeyama puffed at the remnant of his cigarette. Got up, left the room with the ashtray, and returned with it cleaned and sparkling again.

"Cannot allow the house to have too much odor. My niece, Liza, cleans the house for me once a week. She will not be too happy if she finds an ashtray full of cigarette ends. Might read me the riot act. Nice girl, though!"

Kathryn smiled.

"James, what is the reason for this visit? I realize that I am a stranger to you but please try to leave nothing out."

"I," James looked at Kathryn as he spoke, "we both feel that we can trust you. So here goes."

Two hours and three carafes of juice later, James had finished his story. The silence lasted for a minute as Takeyama thought about what he had heard from James with pieces of the story added by Kathryn. After a few thoughtful moments, Takeyama spoke.

"What you have told me does not surprise me. There are many tribes whose culture advocates that a man or woman can visit and talk with their ancestors. However, this usually occurs under the stimulus of narcotics and is more an illusion than what you may call a real visitation or transportation to the past. Excuse me."

He went to the box and helped himself to another cigarette. Lit it slowly and continued.

"Must not make a habit of this. But back to the point. Memory is not much more than a slurry of chemicals that can be manipulated. If the level of certain chemicals in the brain is changed, remembering certain events becomes impossible. On the other hand, manipulation of the chemical types in another direction offers the alternate result insofar as memory is improved."

Takeyama paused as if deep in thought and inspected his cigarettes again before he continued.

"On the other hand," he said, "by careful chemical manipulation I believed that genetic memory is a reality, not just one or two generations that we have seen in laboratory animals but over many generations. Genes appear to have the ability to store ancestral memories that can survive for hundreds of years. This can explain a specific attachment to a homeland or explain why a person can recall the actions of an ancestor without ever visiting the homeland or knowing anything about the ancestor. I believe that there is a specific chemical trigger from which a genetic relationship can be rekindled."

Takeyama puffed on his cigarette as he looked at James and Kathryn for a reaction. He had their full attention as he continued.

"I know of chemicals that occupy a specific three-dimensional space because of their structure that can assist in blocking certain chemical impulses thereby allowing the mind to direct the individual to the correct time period." Kathryn smiled and nodded her head in appreciation of the explanation.

"But—" James tried to interject, thinking that this was purely another drug-induced illusion. Takeyama held up his hand.

"No, James, this is not an illusion. It is an actual temporary modification of the three-dimensional structure of the DNA that allows the individual to transport himself, herself," he nodded to acknowledge Kathryn, "back in time without the use of H. G. Well's time machine or whatever term is used to refer to the time portal. The idea of traveling in a time machine, seeing the minutes, hours, and days go backward on a pseudo-scientific odometer is the pathos of fiction. This is real. And with modern DNA identification techniques I can identify the active sites. Although," Takeyama added, "it seems to me that you do not need any chemical stimulus to return to the past."

Takeyama smiled as he continued.

"I should imagine that even Mr. Wells would have been the first to admit that sending someone back in time to a different period would seriously influence the people involved. The Heisenberg uncertainty principle in another form basically says that as soon as one observes and studies an organism, the organism will change. And there are many examples where anthropologists studied a native culture and, without realizing it, brought about changes to that culture. The effect of just being there caused the culture to change. Or, watch children at play. As soon as they know that they are being observed, their play habits will change to be more appealing to the observers. So, a time machine, even if it was possible and it is not, is out of the question for the serious observer of the past."

Another two puffs on his dying cigarette and Takeyama continued.

"There are, of course, exceptions such as Jane Goodall, who studied wild chimpanzees, and Diane Fosse, who studied mountain gorillas. Both women exhibited extreme patience to become accepted by the respective animal communities that they studied and came as closer than any other human in terms of integrating themselves into animal cultures. This was, and still is, unusual and to do this in the past a modern man or woman must live and operate without any influence from his or her modern knowledge. An almost insurmountable task unless modern memories are erased and do not influence the time traveler."

Takeyama paused again as he extinguished the remains of the cigarette in the ashtray before continuing.

"But please allow me to become a little more technical to address some of the questions that I know you will ask."

Kathryn and James nodded their approval. Takeyama seemed not to notice and continued.

"Most of the time our DNA replicates with dutiful accuracy, but just occasionally—about one time in a million—a little piece gets into the wrong place. This might leave a person predisposed to some disease but, equally, they might confer some slight advantage such as increased production of red blood cells for someone living at altitude."

Takeyama knew that James would understand this because he had lived at an altitude of seven thousand feet above sea level in the Rocky Mountain region of the United States for several years. He continued.

"You, James have a difference conferred upon you because one of these little pieces that related to your genetic ancestors has moved into a place on your DNA where it can make a difference. And that difference allows a form of contact with an ancestor, who may also have a similar little piece of his DNA that has gone astray. Therefore, James, blood is the time machine by which you will travel. The Y chromosome that has passed unchanged from one generation of male relatives to another contains the genetic markers by which you are identified. In other words, your DNA is the historical document by which you are identified."

They all paused, wondering who would speak next. It was Takeyama.

"By the way, James, let me ask you something. How did your meeting go with my colleague, Dr. François Ali?"

"Fine. Seems a pleasant fellow and very courteous."

James answered the question cautiously, looking at Kathryn, wondering where it was leading. Kathryn nodded her agreement.

"Well, some years ago, François came to me with a similar story to that which you have enunciated. To cut a long story short, he became my student and protégé. And as you have deduced, seems to be a very fine fellow!"

Takeyama stared at them for a few moments and then the thought crashed into their minds at the same time. He saw the light of recognition in their eyes as James and Kathryn spoke together.

"You mean that—"

"Yes," Takeyama cut short their question knowing that a host of words would flow, "he was the first person other than myself who has made a journey. He needed to go across the bridge of time for reasons that only he and I should know. I, on the other hand, knew that such a journey could be perilous and that I alone should be the first to try to make such a journey. And here we are! Both alive and well and as far as we know feeling none the worse for wear."

"Now that you come to mention it, Harry," it was Kathryn who spoke, "François's words did seem a little strange at the time. As if he knew that we were looking for something other than research for a book."

Kathryn related the details of their conversations with Ali and Takeyama added, "François is very perceptive and he obviously sensed that which you seek."

As James and Kathryn digested this information, Takeyama looked directly at them.

"I have not made this theory because of the implications or fear that I have of everyone looking into his or her past and attempting to go back into the past on a whim. But my greatest fear is military use and the attempt to rewrite history. But I see that you are genuine, James."

Takeyama once more returned to the apothecary's box to open a drawer.

"So, James."

"Surely, Harry, you are not offering me a cigarette?"

Takeyama smiled as he responded, "No, James. I am searching for the means by which I can sample your DNA. We often use epithelial cells from the lining of the mouth."

Takeyama produced a swab and approached James. Kathryn looked on with interest, wondering what would happen next.

"But how, Harry?"

"Ah, my apologies, James, but I do have the means of sending the sample to François at the university. He can have the scan back to us within hours, but usually overnight since that is when he does such work. So by tomorrow morning at the latest we will have an analysis of your DNA." Takeyama smiled as he saw the amazed expression on their faces. He held up the swab. "Shall we?

James obligingly allowed Takeyama to take a swab from the inside of his mouth. Takeyama placed swab into a sample vial that he closed immediately. He smiled and walked to a door that had remained closed from the beginning of their visit. He turned to James and Kathryn.

"Come and see my lab."

The room was very simple. More of a study than a laboratory. The desk was covered with papers. But in very neat orderly piles. Takeyama inserted the swab into a machine and turned several dials. James and Kathryn looked on, with some amazement. Takeyama studied their faces before he spoke.

"Just a small lab, as opposed to the huge complexes that churn out data measuring anything and everything possible to measure without a specific hypothesis to guide them. I, on the other hand, with François, had a well-defined hypothesis. Our approach was simple. We focused on what we knew to be true and planned our work accordingly. But, thank heaven for satellite telephones. Without my phone connection, which cannot be traced, I would have no contact with anyone. The machine will give François a general introductory analysis of your DNA that will go directly into his personal computer. No reason to send this to his university computer." He looked at James and Kathryn. "Don't trust networks. Accessible to anyone with a purpose or with idle curiosity. François will send us his detailed structural interpretation in the goodness of time. I propose that we adjourn for tea."

Ten minutes later, they were seated comfortably again, sipping on an aromatic and strong-tasting tea that neither James nor Kathryn recognized. Takeyama smiled as he saw the curious looks on their faces.

"Made from the bark and leaves of the large tree just outside," he said. "Quite refreshing, don't you agree?"

James and Kathryn smiled and nodded in agreement. It was very refreshing. They could feel the hot liquid starting to relax their muscles. The effects of the walk to Takeyama's cottage were still evident.

"I thought that I would give you some background into my recent thoughts on the subject of genetic engineering."

Takeyama talked for almost two hours, as he realized that he had a genuinely interested audience. James or Kathryn would ask a question on occasion but for the most part, Takeyama continued uninterrupted.

"And so, as I became more and more involved in my work, I slowly started to realize its implications. At first, I was astounded. No, incredulous, at what I had discovered. This caused me joy and agony, almost at the same time. So I decided to remove myself unceremoniously from the university campus to comparative solace. In other words, I felt that I had to become unreachable."

He looked to see how James and Kathryn were receiving his words. They remained silent but amazed by his knowledge.

"There are those persons," he went on, "who are exceedingly able through ingenious cunning to acquire someone else's knowledge and use it for a nefarious purpose. I felt, no I was determined, that this should not happen. This game is simple, and it is played in all seriousness. I have the winning hand and I am determined to keep it."

Takeyama then stared at the ceiling.

"*Fuji san ni nobottara sazo tôku made miemasho.* It means, 'If I could ascend Mt. Fuji I could see far.' Your Isaac Newton had a similar saying."

"If I have seen further than others, it is because I have stood on the shoulders of giants," James said, remembering the quote.

"Correct, James. In other words, I may be one of the lucky one who has gone this far in the study of memory and its genetic relationships."

And so the conversation continued. The afternoon wore on and dusk started to fall, clothing the house in the darkness of the Hawaiian night. Suddenly, there was a sound from the study. Takeyama looked around.

"It seems like François is responding. Earlier than I expected. Please excuse me."

Takeyama returned with several printed pages that took all of his attention. He stared at it intensely and then burst forth with a word in Japanese. From his actions James and Kathryn guessed the meaning. One of surprise and joy. Takeyama brandished the papers in their direction.

"James, because of your natural tendency to return to the past, you are an ideal patient for this type of experience and it seems that there will be very little risk. Your DNA is ideal. It would take days to explain my reasoning and rationale, and I am perfectly willing to do this."

James's response was very simple.

"Let's get to work. I need to discover if my dreams are the mental records of a real experience of if they are merely dreams."

Takeyama nodded as he said, "I suspect that your dreams are real experiences and this event that we are now planning is merely a confirmation of that."

Kathryn reached over and squeezed his hand as she said, "I am with you, James my dear.'

"Well," Takeyama continued as he checked the data printed out at the bottom of the last page, "let me find the right drug to help us with your memory."

James and Kathryn were surprised by the directness of Takeyama's response. He sensed the tension in their silence.

"I know that this may be a shock to you but I believe that there is no time like the present. If you would like to sleep on it and have more time to collect your thoughts . . ." he left the sentence unfinished.

James stood up and looked at Kathryn. He paced the floor for a few moments before he spoke.

"Harry, the reason for my hesitancy and for Kathryn's silence," James looked and Kathryn, "is that I have an aversion to drugs. Many years ago, I was given a shot of morphine to deaden the pain from an injury to my left knee that occurred during a soccer game. A few minutes after administration of the drug, I was sitting on Saturn's rings counting little green men!

"However, Harry, I'm ready." James's simple words said all that was necessary. "What do you need me to do?"

"James?"

"I'll be all right, Kath, with you here." He looked at Takeyama for reassurance who nodded in agreement.

"Well, James, if we are ready then I would like you to make yourself comfortable. The principle is that the drug that I administer seeks out specific sites of your DNA. These sites are the source of your memory and if sites related to modern memory are blocked, your genetic memory will be initiated and you will imagine yourself to be in a locale that was very meaningful to your ancestor."

Takeyama took a deep breath and frowned. He thought for a few moments and then offered refills of the juice glasses. James and Kathryn accepted. Then he continued.

"I was wondering how to explain the next segment as it is complicated. Let me try."

Takeyama stared at James and Kathryn for a few minutes as he collected his thoughts and placed them in the right order.

"I call the acceptance of a molecule by the DNA molecule a *lock-and-key effect*. If you imagine how a key fits into a lock, that will help you to understand what I am doing. One of the first questions we tried to answer regarding the DNA receptor was why some drugs fit the receptor and caused enormous behavioral changes, while others, nearly identical in chemical structure, fit the receptor and resulted in no change. Then it hit me. Some keys fit the locks and open them; others fit the lock and will not turn or open the lock! Thus, I have key and nonkey chemicals. Moreover, if a nonkey chemical is put into competition with a key chemical, it will move the key chemical right off the receptor site. This was my first breakthrough as it told me that once I had made the change I could reverse it! And I concocted a system for testing this lock-and-key effect. So, there we are!"

Takeyama looked at them to make sure that they had understood his words, especially considering what he was about to do.

"But here I go," he continued. "The memories that you regenerate using this procedure will be related to your thoughts as you slip into the past. With practice you will find that you can recall specific memories that are caused by the thoughts and memories that you have as the chemical takes effect. In other words, you can self-direct yourself to any genetic ancestor that you chose. In your case, James, that is only one person. Poor François had to get beyond the effects of three genetic ancestors in his travels. It took some time but with practice he was successful."

Kathryn sipped her juice but James had caught on to one of the words that Takeyama had used. Deliberately perhaps?

"Harry, you used the word *travel*. I assume that was deliberate?" Kathryn paused between sips.

"Indeed it was, James. You are not going into a drug-induced stupor. Because of the interaction of the chemical with your DNA, you will essentially be transported back through time. Your body will remain here with us," he looked at Kathryn who gave him a very worried and forced smile, "but to all intents and purposes your mind and body will be transported back to the fourteenth century."

The silence was thick and heavy as Takeyama completed his explanation of the events that would affect James. He looked at Kathryn.

"Kathryn, it is as well that you are here. I see that you care for each other very much," Kathryn blushed lightly, "and I suggest that you both give yourselves a few minutes to accept what needs to be done. There is a danger to this, but I believe that all will be well and that you, James, will have answers and learn a lot about yourself."

James reached over and took Kathryn's hand. They smiled at each other and unable to contain his anxiety any further, James blurted out.

"OK, Harry, let's do it! What do you need me to do?"

"First, James let me ask one question of Kathryn." Takeyama looked Kathryn straight in the eye. "How do you feel?"

"Worried. But I agree that James needs to discover the reasons for the visitations of Oswald." She stood up, leaned over, and kissed James on the forehead. "Go, ahead Me Bonnie Lad. Let's see what happens. I will not leave you."

"Then it is decided." Takeyama rose from his seat. "Both of you relax while I make the necessary preparations."

He crossed the room to the apothecary's cabinet. He noticed that James and Kathryn, who was seated once more, held hands and talked quietly. And then he was ready.

"James, lie on the sofa if you wish. Kathryn, you may want to hold James's hand to maintain contact. This will be over in about five minutes."

Takeyama offered a glass of juice to James.

"No thanks, Harry. Enough juice for the moment. Don't want my first action to be that of seeking a medieval toilet!"

They all laughed. Takeyama persisted in his offer of the glass of juice.

"James, the juice now contains the necessary ingredients for your journey. The ingredients in the juice will help transport the chemical to the DNA sites where interaction can occur."

James took the glass, looked at it curiously, and then drank slowly. He lay back and made himself comfortable on the sofa. Kathryn knelt where she could watch him and took his hand. Takeyama sat on a nearby chair to observe.

James felt nothing at first. His eyes remained open as he looked at Kathryn. Her features were as crystal clear as the day that they had first met. Two years ago, he had been looking for a house . . . And then he knew that something was happening to him. Kathryn's features became hazy.

The functions of his brain slowed and his body temperature dropped to eighty degrees. His heart rate slowed below normal levels and his pulse rate dropped to fifty beats per minute. Suddenly he was being transported through time as the triggered changes to his DNA activated the metamorphosis and transported him back to a former time.

The chemicals induced physical changes to his DNA and replicated the life coils of his ancestor; he was taken back into the fourteenth century. The many portions of his DNA recalled the names of close associates and friends. And yet he knew, or was aware, of his modern life. His mind was in conflict as he attempted to separate his modern life from his past life. Then all recognition of his modern life disappeared and he could only sense his presence in his current surroundings.

*   *   *

CHAPTER 20

H e was back. He could see Kathryn once again. Smiling but had a worried look in her eyes.

"James, my dear, are you all right?"

"Of course, me bonnie lass."

"James could feel pressure on his other wrist. Takeyama was making a quick check of his pulse.

"Good. No elevated pulse levels. A very good sign," he pronounced with a triumphant smile. "Can we presume that you made your journey?"

"Yes, so it seems, Harry. I had an experience that I have not had before in any of the visitations from Oswald and Margaret. So it was not a recall from my current memories?"

"If it was new. It seems to have been a successful journey. I would add that a new experience confirms that your experiences with Oswald are not dreams. They are real journeys through time. Journeys involving your physical and mental state and not ventures into the dream world. Your relative is real and all that you have experienced is true and has a purpose. You are a unique person insofar as your association with your distant relative is all that is required to take you back to his time. As I thought earlier, you do not need the chemicals. Very unique, indeed!"

James attempted to rise but found a weakness in his limbs. Takeyama noticed this and suggested that he remain where he was for a few minutes longer. Kathryn hovered close by.

"James, I could not observe you as closely as Kathryn but I did sense some changes occurring."

Kathryn had not made any effort to move and her expression had remained unchanged, apparently emotionless since James had come back. She frowned as she collected her thoughts. Then she spoke.

"James, I watched as you made the transition, I know that you returned to the time of Oswald. I could see your lips moving but I could not hear the words. I sensed that you were talking with someone in a gentle voice."

James could see the tears in her eyes. He could feel the increased pressure as she held his hand.

Takeyama remained quiet sensing that she was about to make a major statement. James did not speak. Kathryn found the words to continue.

"When you first relaxed, your eyes remained open and continued to remain open throughout your journey. But you were not seeing anything or anyone in this room. Your eyes moved as though you were seeing and talking to someone."

"So, Kath, you agree with Harry that it was a successful journey."

"I do indeed, James. As the seconds ticked by, I could see the transformation occurring. You seemed to be a different man."

There was a moment of silence then James spoke.

"Kath, what are you telling me?"

"James, my dear, I am telling you that whatever was happening to you mentally, your physical shape had also changed." Kathryn took a deep breath. "You were transformed into Oswald or at least, as near as I can tell from my own visions, to a very close relative who looks like him!"

Kathryn's words hung in the air. Finally, it was Takeyama who interrupted the silence.

"James, the experiences that you have described to me are not dreams or, what is the word, visions! As you know I had anticipated a close genetic relationship to this man but it is even closer than I could have ever imagined. There is no doubt in my mind that because of this relationship you have actually experienced travel through time. And this genetic relationship is taking you into the past."

Takeyama rubbed his chin. Then he continued.

"Remember, on your previous journeys you were under the protective wing of Oswald. When you journey back on your own, things may be different and in fact, there is no guarantee that you will arrive whole!"

Takeyama saw the confused look on James's face.

"Let me explain," Takeyama added. "By 'whole' I mean being able to retain your personality. Kathryn has experienced the change in your physical appearance to the point that you may have looked like a close relative to the man, Oswald. From what you have told me, he was a scholar but, first and foremost, he was a soldier who would protect his king, whatever the cost."

He paused and then added his punch line.

"I doubt that you will take on his form but it seems that you will assume the physical form of a close relative to the extent where other may consider you a brother or even a twin." Takeyama held up his hand to forestall any questions and to show that he was nearing the end of his monologue.

"It is also possible," he said, "that a side of your nature that you did not even know existed may manifest itself. You will be a medieval man in all senses of the word. Your memories of the time from which you started your journey, the present that is, will at best be only vaguer flashes of memory for you that may be difficult to understand."

Takeyama knew that he had caused mental turmoil in their minds so he added, "I can see that you are very close to each other and your calling from Oswald may be a conflict for both of you. James, you will want to do what you believe is the 'right thing' and Kathryn will fear for your safety. This is a decision that you cannot make lightly and it must be a decision made by both of you."

The silence remained as James and Kathryn looked at each other. Finally, James found the energy to speak.

"Harry," James said as he looked at Kathryn, "I think that we understand what you are saying and we have talked about the subject of genetic memory but I am still not sure. It really does seem unusual if not impossible for such a thing to happen. I have wrestled with this for months now and I had begun to accept it as a series of occurrences, each of which was difficult to explain."

"Let me tell it this way," Takeyama said. "Very simply, genetic memory is alive and well. It explains the migratory memory of birds. Young birds that have never migrated know the way to their summer habitat. There is also the chromosomal memory of the lower animals. The simplest animal we know, the amoeba, is a single one-celled animal that occurs everywhere. It will respond to a stimulus. When it divides into two, both of the new offspring can recognize the same source of the stimulus and will respond automatically. Is that not a fine example of genetic memory?"

Takeyama looked at James as he took another puff on the still smoldering cigarette. He looked at the remains of the tobacco and muttered to himself but for James and Kathryn to hear.

"I wonder why I still smoke these things?"

He squashed the remains of the cigarette into a nearby ashtray and once more looked at James.

"If I am reading this issue correctly, James, it is my firm belief that your ancestor, Oswald, has a very good reason for contacting you. As I have already made it clear, this is no mere dream, but it seems to be an issue of the utmost importance."

"Even to the point where you assumed a form in which you bore a very close, let me say, family resemblance to Oswald." Kathryn interjected. "James, my dear, you really had changed physically! The loving look that you gave me was so real. Yet," Kathryn paused, "there was a deep sorrow in your eyes that I could not interpret. The aura that appeared around your body made me think of a white surcoat with lion emblems embroidered in red on to the upper left chest of the surcoat. That was the insignia of Edward III."

James finally recovered his thoughts.

"So, my feelings of reality during my meetings with Oswald were obviously true. I do accept the reality of what I have experienced!"

Takeyama answered, "You can be sure, James. Think it over as I make tea. I know that the English think that a cup of tea cures everything, even broken limbs. But let me make you both a cup of Lapsang tea to settle the nerves and give your brains time to rest."

Takeyama rose from his seat. Kathryn was also attempting to rise from her seat next to James.

"No, Kathryn. Please allow me. You sit with James and we can talk back and forward from the kitchen."

Takeyama carried the freshly made tea into the room on a tray and then the conversation focused on the various aspects of James's experience and continued for another two pots of the aromatic tea. Finally, James stood up and stretched to relieve the ache in his muscles.

"Well, it seems to me, Harry, that the only option that I have is to attempt to get to the bottom of this mystery. I sense, or I know, that Oswald has a need of me. I know that when I am away from Durham there is no contact."

"You must go back to your home," Takeyama interjected. "But before you do, I suggest that you and Kathryn remain with me for a few days. Enjoy the scenery and the fresh air. The rain, if you wish to walk a mile of so inland to the south. Have a pleasant break. Relax."

James looked at Kathryn and she nodded enthusiastically.

"My niece will arrange to have any luggage delivered here or placed into storage. If you have anything else that you need, she can make the telephone calls for you. As to the Hilton Hawaiian Village, if you have any luggage remaining there, she can also make the necessary arrangements for you to have your luggage stored there. If you need to make arrangements for your air transportation, use my satellite phone. I can even make myself scarce if you would like time alone."

Takeyama stretched out his arms in a gesture. "This house is much bigger than it appears," he said, "and you are welcome to use it as your own."

James and Kathryn could not resist such an offer. In fact they could not believe the unprecedented attention that Takeyama had bestowed on them, the true aloha spirit of Hawaii.

"Harry, this is an amazing offer that we cannot refuse. But we will not hear of your leaving your house. We do enjoy your company and would prefer that you remain here."

Takeyama smiled.

"So be it. I do suspect that we will have much to talk about over the next few days. I suggest that you, James, rest a while. Or enjoy the sun. I have a few tasks to take in hand."

*   *   *

Now feeling much better, James suggested to Kathryn that they go for a walk. They walked silently, hand in hand, along the path framed by luscious tropical plants. She could not see his eyes glow with passion as his thoughts blazed with the idea of discovering who he really was. He could not get the picture from his mind!

The thoughts continued to speed back and forth through his brain. He was in the midst of realizing that his ties to Oswald were real and he had not seen the larger picture, until now. He could barely maintain his focus sufficiently to begin thinking of conclusions.

The implications of this day's event were much more far reaching than he had imagined.

As they continued to walk, Kathryn became lost in her own thoughts, gazing alternatively, and very pensively, at the ground and at the foliage.

Suddenly, she sensed a change in James's demeanor and posture. He had made the decision. Kathryn squeezed his fingers gently and he looked at her, giving her a gentle smile in return. The nature of the decision she knew not, but she knew that he would tell her when he was ready.

Takeyama saw them returning to the house and greeted them by proffering a pitcher of the fruit drink. He could see from the looks on their faces that there was some acceptance of James's abilities but he knew that the consequences of this ability were not fully understood.

They would need time. And in that time, full realization of what needed to be done would emerge.

*   *   *

CHAPTER 21

I t was time for James and Kathryn to think about the journey back to England. They wondered out loud about contacting the hotel and the airlines. Harry would not hear of any of this.

"My niece, Liza, will visit us tomorrow afternoon before she goes on her evening shift. She will contact the airline to get you to Oahu and thence to England. She will also contact hotels and finalize your arrangements. Just let her know approximately what you require. In the meantime, we can walk and talk! I suggest that we enjoy each other's company and take in as much of the scenery as you can before you leave. But I do suggest that we stay in touch by telephone or by e-mail. And if I am not available, François Ali, whom you met at the University of Hawaii, will know where to find me," he reminded them.

The decision was made. James related the last item for their itinerary and that was to telephone Charlie Kirkby to make arrangements to be picked up at Durham Railway Station.

"Let's see what Liza comes up with for your itinerary and then it will be time to make your call. My satellite phone should suffice."

James and Kathryn could not refuse such an offer and a few extra days in paradise would serve them both well. They sensed that after the return to England, the game, as Holmes would have said, would be afoot!

Liza's visit went as planned and she was glad to assist them. She did say that, with the weekend looming close, her return would not be until the Monday. This news was accepted with smiles. The extra two days would be most welcome to them and Takeyama saw the chance to play host to his enjoyable guests.

The days that followed were energizing to James and Kathryn but at the same time, relaxing. Stimulating conversations were interspersed with walks through the lush vegetation and even into the rainy area. Often during their walks, a sudden shower would start as if indicating that they were entering the domain of the rain god. It was torrential at times. Visibility could diminish to a few yards with just sufficient vision for each of them to see the other. Then, as suddenly as the rain had started, it stopped. It would have been futile to run for shelter. They were soaked within seconds, such was its force and intensity of the rain.

* * *

Liza arrived at midmorning on Monday morning with the details of their travel schedule.

"Tomorrow you can stay at the Princeville Hotel. The day after, you travel to Lihue and then on to Honolulu. The day after that, the flight would be from Honolulu to Houston."

She had thoughtfully broken their journey to ease the pain of such a long journey by booking them into the hotel at the Houston International Airport. She even reported that she had a very friendly conversation with the young lady on the reservation desk and had managed to get them a suite for the price of a room. Liza smiled as she offered, "We hotel folks know how to talk to each other. Then it is on to London and home."

James rose and walked over to Liza as she rose from her chair. He kissed her on the cheek.

"Just a little thank you for your efforts, Liza. Now, how can I help you?"

"Anyone," she said looking from James to Kathryn, "who treats my uncle with the respect that you both have shown him is enough for me. And most important, Granny likes you. If you pass her inspection, you are all right with me."

"Liza, I need to say thank you in some way." Kathryn added, "Please Liza."

"Well, there is a Hawaiian Cultural Center that can always use extra funding."

"Done. When we get back to the hotel, the donation will be made in your name, Liza. As you may have gathered, I firmly believe that a person must defend his or her culture."

Liza beamed her gratitude. Takeyama moved to her and put his arm gently around her.

"See, my dear, I have told you that there are good *ha'oli!*" he said, using the Hawaiian word for outsider. He looked at Kathryn and James.

"Well, my two friends, it is time for a barbecue, Hawaiian style. Liza has brought the food and will lead us through the ceremony, that is what it really is, and we can all finish off this delightful stay in the true Hawaiian tradition."

Takeyama focused his eyes on James.

"Your friend, the priest or vicar, as you call him, will need to know your time of arrival so please make the telephone call and then join us outside."

James heard Charlie's voice after the first ring. Then realizing that it would be very early in the morning in England, he apologized for the early call. Charlie was unconcerned. Arrangements were made that James would call Charlie from London to let him know what time they would arrive in Durham.

"Say hello to Sylvia for us."

"Do it yourself, James, she's on the extension. Picked it up as soon as I said your name."

"Yes, James, Charles and I will be happy to meet you and Kathryn in Durham when you arrive."

James knew that Charlie was not finished with the conversation. The line remained silent for several seconds and then he heard Charlie's voice a moment later as he burst forth with the words that were foremost in his mind.

"And I do hope that you have a story for us!"

*   *   *

CHAPTER 22

James and Kathryn alighted from the train to the coolness of the railway station in Durham. The contrast from the Hawaiian climate caused them to shudder as the cold wind swept in from the north.

They saw Charlie was approaching them along the platform. He removed the pipe and a broad grin spread across his face. Moments later, Sylvia appeared, also smiling broadly. She reached them before Charlie. Her arms opened wide to give Kathryn a big hug. Kathryn reciprocated. Her arms circled Sylvia. James looked at the two women, so comfortable with each other. James shook Charlie's hand. Then Sylvia looked directly at Kathryn.

"Kathryn, my dear, hope you had a good time?"

"Lovely, Sylvia, and . . ." Kathryn looked at James.

"I'm fine, thanks too, Sylvia," James chorused. "How are you?" Charlie chuckled at James's intervention.

"Very well!" Sylvia focused her attention back to Kathryn. "Now, Kathryn, do tell . . ."

She allowed her words to trail into the wind knowing that Kathryn would sense that she had eager ears that were ready to listen to the tales of Hawaii.

Charlie smiled. "You are out of your depth, James, old man. You see, Sylvia did not even break her breathing pattern. Let's leave the ladies to their conversation and we can take your bags to the car."

Kathryn continued her conversation.

"And," she exclaimed, "we met the most delightful Japanese fellow."

*   *   *

As they turned off the main road onto the Bridgeford Road, James spoke thoughtfully to Charlie who had accepted the pleasure of driving the Jaguar.

"Would you mind if we went straight to my place. Just itching to see that all is well. We can have tea."

"And get us up to date on your travels."

Sylvia's voice came from the back seat of the Jaguar where she and Kathryn had been in animated conversation since getting into the car at the railway station.

James attempted to respond. But Charlie laid his hand gently on James's arm as if to remind him that the journey from Durham was merely the preliminary program in what would turn out to be very detailed conversation over the next several days. James took Charlie's unspoken advice that he should not interfere with the natural order of things. He did not say anything else other than "Sure, that sounds fine."

As they drove through the village, the main street seemed alive with people who were all inclined to wave to them. The members of the Knitting Circle, just happened to be outside of the ice cream shop that doubled as a teashop, saw the car returning with James and Kathryn inside. Flossie Ambler, owner of the tea shop, also took notice of their return. News of their return was now well known.

James smiled. "It's nice to be home, Charlie."

Charlie parked the car in the driveway and produced the house keys for James. As they alighted from the car, Charlie patted the door.

"Nice car, James, hope you did not mind me doing a little driving."

"Not at all, Charlie."

James walked to the rear of the car and patted the trunk of the car and just before he lifted the lid to retrieve their cases, he said, "Sturdy wench. Well-made old girl. Has never let me down and has remained in good order."

Charlie smiled and pretended to fiddle with his pipe. He took it from his coat pocket and smiled into the bowl. Sylvia looked away into the distance and allowed a soft giggle to escape from her lips. Kathryn was not amused.

Sylvia spoke up.

"Kathryn, you and I can see to the tea while the two men," Sylvia looked at James and Charlie, "find something to do."

James opened the door, allowed the ladies to enter first, and he and Charlie lifted the cases into the warm interior. The late February days cast more than a chill in north-east England. They entered the house and James was surprised to see the fire burning in the fireplace. In response to James's quizzical look, Charlie explained.

"Mrs. Nicholson has been in every day to monitor your telephone calls and the mail. As you see," Charlie pointed to the dining table, "she, God bless her, has performed a triage on your mail. There is a pile that requires your immediate attention, a pile that can possibly wait a while and is not serious, and a pile that can wait. Each of the envelopes has a date mark, courtesy of Mrs. Nicholson, to let you see when each one arrived and they are stacked in chronological order from the top. Your faxes are stacked neatly in the fourth pile, again in chronological order."

James surveyed the piles of mail and smiled. A housekeeper who also doubled as an office manager!

"And," Charlie continued seeing the look of satisfaction on James's face, "she has written down your telephone messages in chronological order with the return numbers. All ready for you to attend to when you are in the mood."

"Tomorrow, Charlie, but for now . . ."

"Let's have tea." It was Kathryn who gave voice to everyone's thought. "You two sit and do what you have to which, I suppose James, will include booting up your computer."

James looked at Charlie.

"I suppose, Charlie me old lad, we should make ourselves scarce and see that all is well with the heating and plumbing."

"Good idea, James."

Hours later, several pots of tea accompanied by a large plate of sandwiches, thanks to the efforts of Mrs. Nicholson who had left fresh sandwiches in the refrigerator, as the clear night sky started to show its pin points of light, Charlie and Sylvia bid their farewells to James and Kathryn.

The ladies promised to continue the story tomorrow. Charlie was about to offer Kathryn a ride to her home in Willington but Sylvia, sensing his action, pulled at the sleeve of his jacket and her look told him to be quiet.

Kathryn, reading Sylvia's action, looked at Charlie.

"James will give me a ride to my house so I can make sure all is well."

*   *   *

The next morning, Charlie was in a high state of excitement. Being of a curious nature, he had descended into the crypt, as he had often done since its discovery.

Sylvia heard his shouts as he entered the vicarage and ran to the door thinking that something was really amiss. He had a piece of vellum in his hand.

Ten minutes later, James and Kathryn arrived. James raised a questioning eyebrow as if asking about the need for such a hasty call. When they had settled into comfortable chairs, Charlie finally spoke.

"This is from him. From Oswald . . ."

Charlie gave the page to James who immediately started to concentrate on what was written.

"Were did you find this?" James asked as he continued to read.

"In the alcove, on the pedestal," Charlie answered.

James's attention was focused on the document. His three companions watched as his expression changed as he read line after line. Kathryn was the first to speak.

"Well, James?"

He looked at Kathryn unable at first to answer her question. Over the past few weeks she had contributed toward the gradual discovery of his new self. That part of him that was derived from Oswald. Now he found himself in a brand-new quandary. The sudden shock of the need to return to help Oswald now stared him in the face with a thousand very pointed implications. He now knew that his connection to Oswald was real. Even though he had accepted his dreams, the overwhelming reality had not struck a cord, until now. He was on the threshold of discovering proof, to his satisfaction, that his relationship to Oswald was true, and he was required to go all the way back to the fourteenth century to help solve an, as yet, unknown mystery. He placed the piece of vellum on to the table.

"Kath, I have to go back. There is treachery afoot that requires my help to resolve it. Something about King Edward, John of Lancaster, and protection of the throne. The Black Prince, King Edward's eldest son and heir to the throne, is dying and it seems that someone or other has designs on the throne and may attempt to change the line of succession."

His words were solid and spoke volumes. There was silence in the room. Then followed the most significant and vital question of all, from Charlie.

"Well, James my boy, when will this, your transposition into the past that is, occur?"

James shrugged his shoulders, "I do not know. But it seems to me that the situation is developing," he thought about the tense since he was talking about the late fourteenth century, "or has developed and if Oswald requires my help, I must be there for him. I cannot ignore his call."

"Well," Sylvia added in an attempt to explain what might be happening, "kingdoms rise and fall. On the horizon of history where the future is about to rise on a new era, destiny always plays a role. It seems that the late fourteenth century is one of those strategically selected periods that led to modern England. The hub, or critical point, focuses, as near as we have been able to discern, John of Lancaster who was the father and grandfather of kings and the originator of a dynasty. And so, James, considering the fortunes of the time, I am not surprised that you have been called by Oswald. Remember, he died tragically and so there are certain actions that his spirit, whatever you wish to call it, cannot undertake. He needs a surrogate that he can trust. You!"

"I am in complete agreement with you, Sylvia." It was Kathryn who now spoke. "It is becoming very obvious to me that the two of you are bound together in a genetic alliance that is unbreakable. I do not believe that you have a choice."

James and Charlie did not speak. They were individually considering the words of Sylvia and Kathryn. Words that had been unemotional, analytical, and difficult to refute. Finally James spoke.

"Well, before we get into my travel plans, how about another cup of tea?"

"James!"

Kathryn's exclamation indicated her frustration at sensing that James did not take the whole issue seriously.

"It's all right, Kath, my dear. I realize that this is a major issue for all of us, me in particular. But there are some things that we can change and some things that we cannot change. I believe that this is one of the latter. And I know that Oswald will contact me at the moment I am required."

"I sense," Charlie added, "that the moment will be soon, James. But you did say something about tea." He looked at Sylvia. "Shall we, my dear?" He nodded in the direction of the kitchen indicating that they should leave James and Kathryn alone for a few moment to collect their thoughts.

With Charlie and Sylvia's departure to the kitchen, Kathryn reached over and touched James's hand. A pause followed as they sat together in silence. Then she spoke.

"We cannot do anything until Oswald contacts you. I know, my dear, that you will prove yourself worthy of him. But I do worry about you. You are not . . ."

"As young as I used to be? I know, Kath. But this seems to be something that I have to do."

James put his arm around her to offer what comfort he could as they faced the unknown. They could hear Charlie and Sylvia in the kitchen as cups and saucers were taken from cupboards.

"James, dear, I now know that this is something that has been building up for the past few months. But please do not give me the John Wayne act that 'a man's gotta do what a man's gotta do.' I know that. Although I do prefer the Clint Eastwood line that 'a man's got to know his limitations.' You are going into an era of violence so," Kathryn sensed that she did not have James's full attention, so she tapped his cheek with her right hand, "be careful and do not try to be Mr. Macho!"

An extra loud banging of cups and saucers warned them that Charlie and Sylvia were about to return to the lounge from the kitchen. As usual, James, not being diplomatic, called out, "It's OK. You can come in. We're decent!"

Sylvia and Charlie entered the room, smiling. The cups and saucers were laid out and the tea dutifully poured into the cups by Sylvia.

A minute or two of informal chatting followed as they sipped the tea and it was Kathryn who brought the conversation back to the point.

"Sylvia, Charlie." She paused as they looked directly at her. "I have resigned myself to the fact that James will be leaving us for a while. I also have resigned myself to the danger that he will encounter. The thoughts give me the shivers . . ."

"It's no cause for fear, Kathryn my dear," Charlie spoke up as Kathryn appeared to collect her thoughts, and he looked at James, "but there is cause for vigilance. You will be entering the world of medieval politics and you must have all of your faculties at the ready!"

A hush fell over the room as each sensed the truth that lay behind Charlie's words.

Kathryn's voice broke through the stilled silence. The sound of Charlie fiddling with his pipe had also ceased.

"There is also a point that we are missing. What about the plague?"

"My God," Sylvia suddenly came to life, "I am so sorry, James, I had forgotten all about that. I was so carried away by the thought that you would be physically removed from us that . . ."

She looked at James who seemed very unconcerned about all of the fuss that was being made.

"Not to worry, Sylvia. You are still my favorite vicar's wife."

Sylvia smiled at the compliment. Charlie seemed to find the most interesting item in the bowl of his pipe but he was hiding a smile. Kathryn smiled at James. All seemed to be well so Sylvia continued.

"As you know, the plague is an infection caused by an organism known as *Yersinia pestis* that occurs in wild rodents and is transmitted to humans. In the mid-fourteenth century it was brought back from Derna, a Black Sea port by Genoese sailors where it spread through Europe like . . ."

"The plague?"

James smiled at his comment.

"Yes, James, and killed at least one-third of the population. It arrived in London in 1347 or 1348 and had the same effect in England. There was no known cure and no way of stopping the spread of the disease. In fact, it reoccurred very often until the nineteenth century. That is why the royal families had summer homes outside of London. They considered their chances of avoiding the plague that reoccurred every summer—the heat, the vermin, the fleas, you know . . ."

Sylvia allowed her words to tail off into nothing and then she became very animated.

"That may be your savior, James. You are going back, soon if we are to believe what we have derived from Oswald's notes, in a time where the winter season has not really emerged into spring. Perhaps . . . no, there is still a risk."

Charlie looked at the other three before he spoke.

"We are missing a vital part of our plotting and planning. Here in Bridgeford we have an expert in infectious diseases. Bob Fenwick—our local GP, medic, doctor, whatever we should call him—let it slip one day that he had worked for some government department or other in a laboratory in which the goal was to combat disease such as the plague, Hanta virus, Ebola, and all of those nasty little beasties. I can give him a call and arrange that you have a quick chat with him, James. Not to disclose the whole shebang but to ask advice on what to take and what he can prescribe for a forthcoming visit to some county or other where such diseases exist."

"You are all such dear people worrying about me like this. But does it ever occur to any one of you that I will be all right?" James questioned.

"No!" the three answered in unison.

"Well, consider this. Do you believe that Oswald would invite me back into danger? Do you ever wonder why Oswald never caught the plague, even though his wife and son died of that dreadful disease? Do you ever consider that Oswald may have visited the village where his wife and son had died and the disease wiped out the entire populace of the village? Perhaps, just perhaps, he had a genetic disposition that allowed him to survive the plague and perhaps and I have that same genetic disposition."

Kathryn, Sylvia, and Charlie were not convinced and the looks on the faces showed James their disbelief.

"All right, Kath, my dear, Charlie, Sylvia. I will see Bob Fenwick. But only if he can see me now, even though it is Sunday, and you," he looked at Charlie, "come with me."

James then looked at Sylvia and Kathryn. "This, ladies, is a men-only thing. I suggest that you . . ."

"Knit!"

James knew from the tone in Kathryn's voice that she was not amused and that he would hear about it later.

"What a smashing idea, light of my life."

Kathryn blushed. Sylvia smiled. Charlie, who had left the room to make the telephone call to Bob Fenwick, returned with the words.

"All done. James, get your coat. Bob is available right now."

*   *   *

One hour later Sylvia and Kathryn heard the car in the driveway. They met the two men at the door, even before James and Charlie had time to take off their coats.

"Well?"

The question came from Kathryn, hands on her hips, and daring James to make light of this whole situation. Sylvia looked equally formidable. Charlie spoke first.

"Well, ladies, as we make our way into the kitchen I will explain as you make tea. Bob did not even ask where James was going, but he gave him good advice about the symptoms as well as a series of drugs to take with him. Bob even had drugs on hand, samples he called them, which he gave to James. Streptomycin sulfate with a tetracycline and chloramphenicol and strict instructions for the dosage. James can substitute the latter in case the tetracycline makes him nauseous."

Charlie paused and smiled to himself and then he continued, still smiling, and with a light but very polite clearing of his throat.

"Since James is not pregnant," Charlie looked at James who nodded negatively, "the instructions are fairly easy to follow. I have recommended to James that he write instructions for taking the drugs on the bottle in an old English calligraphic hand of the fourteenth century so that, if his memory should play tricks, he can read it and follow his own orders."

"Charles, my dear, that is a brilliant suggestion." Sylvia could not help but wonder at the simplicity of the thought.

Charlie looked at James who had remained silent throughout this explanation. Kathryn knew that he had something serious on his mind.

"You know, my dear," Charlie looked at his wife, "I think that this has been a tiring day for James and Kathryn and we must let them rest. So without further ado, let them take our leave."

Charlie and Sylvia stood at the doorway, waving to James and Kathryn, as the Jaguar left the darkening driveway.

*   *   *

CHAPTER 23

"I am coming with you!" Kathryn declared.

"No, Kath. We don't know," James fought for words, "what effect this could have on you. I cannot allow you to do that."

"Dr. Simpson!"

James knew that formal sound of Kathryn's voice told him that he had lost the argument. Kathryn focused her eyes on James and he started to melt under her withering look.

"Dr. Simpson," she repeated and her voice softened as she continued. "James, my dear, I realize that we do not know the effects that such a change will have on me and we do not even know that I can go with you. But remember I have seen Oswald and Margaret, and that is a positive start. Whatever will happen, we will face it together."

Kathryn breathed deeply as she started to speak once more. "I do not care, James. I do love you and to see you disappear from my life now is not acceptable. I am coming with you. If we have to remain in the past, so be it! We will do it together. But you are not leaving without me!" she said emphatically.

James thought for a few moments.

"Kath, I cannot agree with this. Your life may be in jeopardy. I am not going to allow you to put your life in danger. You mean too much to me."

"So, I mean so much to you that you are willing to say goodbye forever and leave me here?"

"No, Kath, that's not what I meant."

"What did you mean, James?"

He was lost for words. Kathryn took the opportunity to continue with her thoughts.

"If you think that you can leave me here wondering where you are, waiting for some sign that you may have lived, oh no, my dear James, you have made a serious mistake."

"Kath, I just wanted to make sure that you will be safe."

"Then I will be with you. That is the safest place that I know."

James realized that he had lost the argument and that concession was inevitable. Their love for each other had blossomed and thinking that one would lose the other had been too much for either to accept. They stood before the fire, arms around each other. Not knowing what the future or the past held for them. But determined to face it together.

"James . . ."

"Yes, Kathryn, my dear."

"We have plans to make. How will we handle this? What will Oswald say? How and when should we tell him?"

"I know, Kath. But first, a quick question."

"Yes, James."

James sensed that she was ready to start with the plans and he had better not get in the way. The emotion of the moment was intense. He decided that it was time to follow through with his desire of the past few weeks.

"Kathryn, will you marry me?"

"Of course, James, my love."

They fell into each other's arms and kissed passionately as if nothing else mattered. And then Kathryn suggested, "Let's call Sylvia and Charlie with the news. I can't wait until tomorrow morning!"

Charlie was surprised to hear James's voice over the telephone. "Of course you can come here now. Any hint of the subject matter?" Charlie asked.

"Only good news, Charlie.

Minutes after arriving at the vicarage, James and Kathryn had explained the reason to Charlie and Sylvia why they had need to see them immediately.

"Well done, James, Kathryn," was Charlie's way of offering his congratulations. Sylvia sniffed in her handkerchief before she crossed the room to Kathryn who stood up from the couch to meet Sylvia's outstretched arms. Both hugged each other as Sylvia added, "I am so pleased for both of you. I really was hoping this would happen!"

Kathryn turned to Charlie and James spoke her thoughts.

"Charlie, we would like you to marry us. As soon as possible."

This seemed to awaken Charlie out of his deep thoughts and Sylvia voiced her plan out loud.

"If my dear husband so much as mentions three weeks for the Banns of Marriage to be read, I will do him mischief!"

"Glad to, James. But in response to my dear wife's comment, the reading of the Banns of Marriage in the church need not take three weeks but they must be read three times, preferably on three separate occasions. The banns were originally put into place to make sure that marriage was not taken lightly. Gave the prospective bride or groom time to back out!"

Charlie was now well under a head of steam and his pipe let forth clouds of aromatic smoke.

"I propose that we go to the church, read the banns, clear the church, reenter, and read the banns again. In ten minutes, it is done. Then tomorrow we can commence with the ceremony."

All James could say, under the circumstances was "we shall need witnesses."

Sylvia moved to volunteer but Kathryn stopped her short, "Sylvia will be a much better attendant of honor."

"Get your coats." Charlie had an idea. "I know where there are many witnesses. Even too many to count."

They left the vicarage in a flurry of coats, scarves, gloves, and Charlie's pipe smoke. Charlie led them to the Royal Duke and as they entered he scanned the faces for the landlord, Lennie Farmer, who was asked if he would be so kind to call for silence. Lennie did so by banging a sturdy pint pot on the counter top. Charlie had center stage.

"Dear friends," Charlie announced. The silence fell like lead weight. Utter and immediate. "Two of our own have requested that I perform the ceremony of marriage for them." He looked at James and Kathryn and held his arm in their direction to the accompaniment of loud cheers. "Who will stand with them as witnesses for this glorious ceremony?"

The resounding chorus of sounds that could only be interpreted as "we will" told Charlie that the whole village was ready and willing. Charlie looked at the faces in the crowd. He pointed his finger in the general direction and added, "Everyone is invited to the church at ten tomorrow morning!"

*   *   *

The next morning presented an amazing spectacle. The mass of humanity took the form of a snake as the villagers were emerging as one from their homes and places of work and moving in the direction of the church.

By the time that the crowd had reached the church the villagers who had not been in the Royal Duke had received the word and were there also. John Anderson, the police sergeant, and his constable, Bryan Jones, knowing what was happening had offered some form of crowd control but had given up as they too joined in the march to the church.

Once inside the church where silence, other than a whisper here and there could be guaranteed, told the congregation that was, in fact the whole village, the plan. And thus the Banns of Marriage were read three times after which Charlie, in his usual manner, performed the ceremony with dignity. James, in a dress suit, and Kathryn, wearing a pale blue dress, were the center of attraction. The absence of a wedding ring caused only a minor delay until Sylvia produced a dress ring for Kathryn to wear as long as she wished and in good health.

Then a final hymn was sung. Announcing the hymn, Charlie admitted that it was not the usual hymn for a wedding but that all would join and sing "Abide with Me."

Kathryn looked at James as the words of the hymn filled the church. The tears started to flow as her thoughts moved into what could be a great adventure from which there was no return.

*   *   *

After the service and at Lennie Farmer's suggestion, the Royal Duke was offered for the reception with no charge for the drinks. Other villagers chipped in with food and the other requirements for a wedding reception.

James offered to pay but Lennie countered with "James me lad, you are one of us and we would have it no other way. Besides, how will the brewery know the truth when I tell them that a barrel or two of draft beer was damaged in transit and burst." Lennie spread his arms wide to include everyone within hearing range. "I have my witnesses."

The sounds of mass agreement responded to Lennie's words. James smiled and shook his head and through the noise mouthed the words "thank you" to Lennie.

Charlie puffed on his pipe. Sylvia smiled. Kathryn glowed. All was well for the moment.

James knew that it would be soon. His senses were telling him that Oswald was close to calling him. What would Oswald say when James had a companion?

*   *   *

Kathryn looked at James, she was curious about his thoughts. He looked at the food that had suddenly been set before him, courtesy of the villagers. He had two deliciously looking pieces of meat covered by a blanket of rich dark gravy, with vegetables on the side.

A delightful aroma assailed his nostrils and his mouth began to water. He chewed a piece of the meat slowly, surprised that he had an appetite after so much excitement and he fought to answer Kathryn's quizzical look.

"You know, Kath my dear, this meat is very good," James stated as he took another forkful, finding himself hungry for another piece, and then another.

Kathryn smiled and waited. It was only a matter of time before James would respond to her questioning look. Suddenly he placed his knife on the plate and looked at her. He saw that she had hardly touched her meal.

"Great food, Kath, I was ready. All right, my dear. I see from your plate that you are not in an eating mood. You have questions?"

"Yes, my dear James, I am worried. I cannot eat with the thoughts lingering on that we may be on the edge of an adventure that we cannot even begin to describe."

James looked around the room. Charlie and Sylvia, realizing that James and Kathryn needed time to talk over their inner thoughts, had managed to secure a quiet spot for them and the reception continued as if James and Kathryn were not there.

"I sense your concern, Kath. If you have any doubts, we should face them together, but I feel that I cannot change what is about to happen."

"I just have that fear of the unknown. I am not sure where it will lead us."

"Ah," said James quietly, "that is an unknown to me also."

"Yes, James," Kathryn put her fingers to his lips, "and we shall, as you say, face the dangers together."

"You know, James, I suddenly feel hungry. What is this meat? Is it beef?"

"No," said James, "it is lamb."

"Lovely," responded Kathryn and she proceeded to attack the lamb as though she had not eaten for days.

Charlie, seeing from the other side of the room that Kathryn had become animated and was also eating, decided to join them.

"Ah, you two, how are you doing?"

They both returned Charlie's question with a smile. Charlie knew that they had resolved their inner thoughts

"You look like two fragments of isolation sitting here. The music will start momentarily. Kathryn, when you have finished your meal, would you care to dance."

Kathryn looked up as she responded, "Love to, Charlie."

"And Charlie," James cut further into Charlie's words, "I would love to dance with Sylvia."

The Royal Duke was full. The regular patrons, mostly the men of the village, and their families filled the Duke to capacity. The dancing area was filled beyond capacity.

"This is incredible," James said to Sylvia as they danced next to Charlie and Kathryn, "Oops, sorry, Sylvia, that was almost a pleasure," James commented as the tight crush of fifty people, attempting to dance on a floor made for twenty, made close contact a necessity. Sylvia giggled.

"Behave yourself, James," Kathryn said and then she looked at Sylvia, "Watch him. One has to wonder about these author fellows."

Sylvia flushed lightly, "Charlie will vouch for me. But it is such a lovely way to celebrate your wedding. The whole village . . ." Sylvia allowed her words to trail off as she thought about the conversation from earlier and what might happen to Kathryn and James.

Charlie, seeing Sylvia's discomfort, suggested that they sit at the table where Kathryn and James had eaten.

They waved away the offer of a drink from Lennie.

"Do you know," Sylvia asked as she and Charlie faced James and Kathryn across the table, "the inevitable result of this day? It sorrows me to think that . . ."

Charlie put his arm around Sylvia, "Now, my dear, this is a happy day. I suggest that we take up Lennie on his offer of drinks and make a toast to Kathryn and James and pray that all is well for their future."

"Charles," Sylvia responded, "you have been such a dear to me all of these years. You always seem to have the right words for the occasion."

Charlie fingered his clerical collar. "That is what I am here for, my dear."

*   *   *

Lennie, who had been keeping an eye on the four of them, saw James's look and miraculously appeared at the table as he materialized from the crush of bodies. He bent over to hear James's whispered words in spite of the noise all around. He disappeared and within a minute reappeared with two glasses of Oban single malt scotch whiskey for James and Charlie and two glasses of Bristol Cream Sherry for Kathryn and Sylvia. Lennie smiled as he shook away James's offer to pay for the drinks.

"No, bonnie lad, this is your day. None of us," he waved his arms around indicating that villagers filling the Royal Duke, "will accept a penny from you. We," he waved his arms around again "are taking care of this."

James raised his glass to Lennie, who smiled and left to dispense more of the various brands of liquid cheer.

James leaned back in his seat and mused how his life had changed since he had come to Bridgeford. The quality of life and the people made it all so delightful. And now he was married! He smiled to himself. Kathryn, sensing his thoughts, moved closer and she could feel his warmth.

Their friendship had become something of a ritual. Several times a week they would meet, usually at his cottage, for a meal or from there they would depart for a social outing. James had changed her life. Since her husband's death some years ago when the stadium had collapsed during a soccer game, she had shunned contact with the opposite sex. But for James she had felt that there was something different about him. He always behaved as a gentleman. She had grown to like his dry sense of humor and appreciate his more serious side that grew from being a scientist. First he had become her friend and now he was her husband. She was determined not to lose him.

"No, Charlie," James was saying as Kathryn focused her thoughts once more on the present situation, "we have made this decision. We are, as you might say, footloose and fancy-free. We do have dear friends," James raised his glass to Charlie and Sylvia and then to the whole crowd in the Duke, "but we must do this. I do wonder whether it would not be more tactful to gracefully withdraw from this quest but a man who appears to be a distant ancestor has asked for my help and I cannot refuse."

"Just remember, James," Sylvia ventured, "there are treacheries afoot in the historical worlds. All that we ask is that you look out for yourselves. And please do try to maintain contact with us, you know, as we suggested. Use the crypt as Oswald has done with you."

James nodded and looked at Kathryn. She had regained her thoughts and smiled.

"Of course, Sylvia, we will do our best. Wherever we may be." The tone of Kathryn's voice changed, "I suggest that we move beyond this conversation and enjoy the remainder of the evening."

"I'll drink to that," James and Charlie chorused.

James got up and walked to Sylvia's side. He bent over and kissed her on the cheek.

"Do not worry, Sylvia me bonnie lass, we will be all right. Now, shall we mingle?"

"James, my dear, shall we dance?"

Kathryn smiled as James stepped forward, the love in his eyes so apparent.

As they danced, more than a hundred people sat at table or stood about in the Royal Duke, looking on, talking and drinking. The women drank from smaller glasses, usually a port or a sherry, while the men drank their Newcastle Brown Ale from tall pint glasses.

Occasionally, a pair of the guests, who were also dancing, would inch toward Kathryn and James to have a brief word and wish them the best of luck for the future.

As the time allowed and having no intention of leaving the reception this early, James and Kathryn talked over the issues that they faced. Possible travel back to Oswald's time? The health issue that James had to face. The transposition of modern bodies into an alien and violent century. General health issues, including the plague and other illnesses. Plus anything else that could arise.

Suddenly Kathryn increased the pressure of her hand on James's hand. Her eyes seemed to lose their focus and looked as though they were about to glaze over. James held her close hoping that they would not stumble. Her eyes returned to their focus and she was Kathryn again.

"Did you hear him?" Kathryn asked. "In fact, both of them?" she asked.

James shook his head and looked round wondering what Kathryn meant by her questions.

"It was Oswald and Margaret! They made themselves known to me."

James frowned at Kathryn's use of the words.

"What was the message, Kath?" James asked. "Please repeat it word for word as you heard it."

Kathryn stepped back a little way so that she could see James as they continued to dance.

"Word for word?"

James nodded.

"Do not worry, dear lady. We ask that your husband help us in a just cause. It will be no dishonor if you refuse but we need him for an honorable task that will serve my lord."

James looked at Kathryn with wide eyes, his hand moving her closer and his mind focused on what Kathryn had said. He could feel her body quivering with anticipation.

"And then," she continued, "since your husband is a relative, or cousin, of my husband, I trust him beyond all others. He is an honorable man who always wishes to do the right thing. Can you accept this, wife of my cousin?"

James could sense that Kathryn's body temperature was rising as her instincts told her that she had indeed talked with Oswald.

"You did not respond," James said rhetorically.

"But I did, James," Kathryn whispered.

"I spoke in as steady a voice as I could," she said. "I saw his face as I told him that what must be done. I saw his lips turn into a smile, as did Margaret. He moved suddenly toward me but I was not afraid and he touched me as if to say 'thank you' for my decision to go back with you. All of my instincts told me that Oswald and Margaret were testing me, as I have never been tested before, and I felt my body grow ready for whatever we must face."

The music continued to play as James and Kathryn took a few more steps around the dance floor. Kathryn continued.

"And then he asked me if I could accept that, if I am with you, it could be dangerous and would I have the courage to fight as a woman. He also asked if I could accept the fact that I might become someone I might not recognize and whose behavior was different to my usual self."

James misstepped and almost stood on Kathryn's toe.

"He said what?"

Kathryn repeated the last sentence. For a moment he did not say anything, his eyes unfocused and lost in thought. He was conscious of the music. He sensed Oswald's closeness.

"James, it is fine woman that you have married." Oswald's voice was clear. "Listen to my Oswald, James," Margaret spoke, "I talked with her and explained the dangers in what must be done."

"It is over, Kath," James blurted out. "the decision is made. It is too dangerous for you."

"And that, Dr. Simpson, is rubbish!" Kathryn was not amused. Her forthright whispered tones told James that she was serious.

"Kath!"

"I will not stand by and see you leave without me. That is my decision! And you will not stop me. After all," Kathryn smiled, "now that we are married, Oswald is also my relative. I may have to ask his help!"

James relented. Perhaps they could face this together better than he could face it alone. A mist filled his vision as he tried to refocus his eyes on Kathryn's face. He was, as the term goes, vanquished! They decided to sit out the next dance. This one had been quite exhausting. And the efforts were reflected in their faces.

"The sight of you two dancing out there, so gracefully, is a memory that will always stay with me," Sylvia commented as they returned to their seats.

Charlie, at James's request, brought cups of tea so that they might sit, sip, and chat. Outside, the day was drawing to a close as the afternoon turned to twilight and soon the fading twilight would yield to the night.

"Charlie," James said when they were settled, "it seems that our plans might have changed."

Charlie raised his eyebrows and Sylvia reached across the table and touched Kathryn's hand.

"In what way?" Charlie asked. And James got Charlie and Sylvia up to date on the latest visitation from Oswald.

"Goodness gracious," Charlie exclaimed, "and all of this happened while you were dancing?" Charlie looked at Kathryn. "It seems my dear," he said, "that you may be going back into a rather sticky situation!" Kathryn smiled gracefully in response to Charlie's words.

James looked at Charlie. "You know, Charlie," he said, "you are a master of the understatement."

"Yes," added Sylvia, "my Charles is worthy of that title."

Charlie smiled and started to work on another pipeful of tobacco.

"Well," he said, "my instincts are telling me that this venture of yours, James, may be even more dangerous than we thought. It seems to me that you are no longer going back as an—what is the word," Charlie thought for a moment, "observer but as a fully fledged participant."

He checked his pipe to make sure that the tobacco was packed correctly and then he looked at Kathryn.

"And you, my dear, will play an equal if not greater role than James." Charlie tried to light the tobacco. "I am not a gambling man, terrible waste of one's money, but I would bet on this one!

The tobacco lit and Charlie was happy. He puffed a cloud of smoke into the air and had the smile of satisfaction, like the proverbial Cheshire cat.

*   *   *

CHAPTER 24

Hiroshi Takeyama had been feeling uneasy for the past several days. In fact, he had sensed, from the time that James and Kathryn left to return to England, that he was being watched!

He sat drinking tea and as he put the cup to his lips he glanced up and looked at the window. Was that a shadow that he had seen? A change in the intensity of the light coming through the window made him wonder if someone was out there.

"I must take control of this situation as I have done many times before," he decided.

He got up, made sure the door was locked, and looked out of the window. He gave a sigh of uncertainty then closed his eyes as he contemplated his next move. When he opened them again, his next move was to contact his associate. He picked up the satellite phone and dialed the cell number of his friend and colleague, François Ali.

"Thank the gods that you are available, François," he said. "There are some things that we must talk over. I am pleased that I did not have to leave a message. I think that we have a problem."

They talked for a while as François had realized the seriousness of Takeyama's call. Ali tried to put Takeyama at ease and soon they were laughing and joking. But there was an uneasiness that Takeyama could not get out of this mind. He felt claustrophobic.

"I am certain, François," he said, "that I am being watched and I have made as much effort as I could to find out who it might be."

"You are absolutely certain, Harry?" Ali asked knowing what the answer would be. His mentor was the most cautious person that he had ever known and once his thoughts or suspicions were aroused, the answer was a foregone conclusion.

"In fact, Harry, now that I think of it, I am not sure if I, too, have not been followed. I have seen two or three new faces on campus that appear in places where I frequent. The cafeteria. The bookstore. The student's union building. And these are faces that have become visible over the past two weeks or so." Ali paused leaving the line silent then he continued. "I had thought to confirm my suspicions, but now that you mention it, I believe that we may be under scrutiny. Any idea who?"

"None, François. But I am wondering if your work is not raising some eyebrows again in certain boardrooms and backrooms. It did not take long for Dr. Simpson to put two and two together and see where we were going with this. But I know that he would not say anything and I doubt that he was followed here."

"Damn!" Ali exploded. "After taking as much care as we always have."

A worried look transformed Ali's otherwise peaceful face in to mask of worry and he passed his hand through his black hair.

"So, Harry," he continued, "what do we do next?"

"It is my thinking," responded Takeyama, "that we may not be able to draw out this person or persons to see who is behind this. I am a little concerned with the various attempts to produce new technology for military uses now that the cold war has been over for some years. The shifts in power to small countries may not be in the realms of developing a nuclear arsenal. In addition, commercial interests controlling certain technologies can make a lot of money. And so, you and I may need to resort to alternate options!"

Takeyama excused himself for a moment while he walked over to his apothecary's cabinet and picked out a cigarette. As he lit it, the aroma of cigarette drifted into other parts of the room. He felt comfortable again. The room glowed warm in the candlelight of the early evening. His words seemed to echo in the empty room.

"However, François," he went on, "I am at the stage where I am concerned for the welfare of Mother, you know my late sister's mother-in-law, and my niece, Liza. If my fears are correct and someone is prowling around, they could also be in danger. Liza will be here tomorrow morning, at about breakfast time, and I am wondering about talking this over with her. But . . ."

Before he could finish the sentence, Ali spoke up.

"I know, Harry, you do not wish to alarm her. But I feel that she must be prepared for what may happen to us."

The line was silent again as both men applied their thoughts to the issue and what to do about Liza.

"Is this, as Holmes would say, a three-pipe problem?"

"No, François," Takeyama smiled, "but I would say that it is a three-pack-of-cigarettes problem!"

"Harry, you know my thoughts about those things!"

"It seems to me," Takeyama continued as though Ali had not spoken, "that we may be in a difficult situation. What if," he paused for a moment as he inhaled the cigarette smoke, "these people are after our work for the wrong reason? I doubt that these men, whoever they are, are contract auditors. We can safely assume that, since they would not be creeping around in the bushes!"

The end of the cigarette glowed as he inhaled more of the smoke. And then he went on and spoke his recent thoughts out loud.

"They will have difficulty in attempting to understand what we have done. Even my notebooks that I have here are sufficiently coded that interpretation would be difficult, even for someone fluent in Japanese. I have modified the characters to such an extent that the codes of the Navajo Wind-Talkers of World War II look like child's play. So, my friend, it is not only the work that these persons seek, I fear that it is we who they seek!"

Another two puffs on his cigarette and Takeyama spoke again. His mind was racing with ideas.

"François, you should be leaving for home soon?"

"Yes, Harry, but . . ."

In accord with Ali's answer, Takeyama nodded assent and went on.

"We may need to pool our efforts and since the location of my place is known to whoever these people are, perhaps you would like to come out here and we can move farther inland together. I know a shack where we can reside until this situation ends. And then we may be safe."

"But, Harry," Ali interrupted, "it may take us no further than we are now. We need to formulate another strategy in terms of judging the focus of our program, especially in light of these events."

"That would be admirable, François, but the implications of our work appear to be known to those who would use it for their own purposes."

"I will, Harry," Ali said, "give it some thought but I do need time to consider the implications. In fact, we both do. Can you imagine our work in the hands of a rogue government or a megalomaniac? Changing history to meet their demands could cause havoc."

"True," Takeyama agreed, "so we need time to get our thoughts clarified and plan out next moves.

"One suggestion is that we let our friend or friends out there take some information that will be incomplete and then we make our homes elsewhere."

They both laughed and there was something of relief in their voices.

"You trust Dr. Simpson, Harry?" Ali asked.

"Yes, I do." Takeyama exclaimed. "James is not the type of person to talk about our work with anyone else. He had a genuine personal interest in our work and he will not use it for other gains. I was delighted to meet him and Kathryn and to hear of his adventures. I found that he was forthright with me. He showed no other interest that you would expect from an author researching his next novel."

Takeyama took a last puff on his cigarette.

"All right, Harry. I will talk with you again soon. Tonight, if I can or at the latest, early tomorrow morning."

"All right, my friend," Takeyama concluded.

Takeyama sat back in the chair forming his plan of action. He knew that François would also be forming a plan of action. Their carefully worded conversation was needed because François's telephone was not as secure as his satellite phone and prying ears were everywhere. And he had protected James and Kathryn.

For now, the words "formulate another strategy in terms of judging the focus of our program" that François had used were the key. He knew now what he had to do, and he would do it as soon as possible. Time was of the essence.

*   *   *

Takeyama thought of, and smiled at, the term *hara-kiri*. The expression that literally meant stomach cutting, suicide by slashing the abdomen, was not practiced any longer in Japan. But only *gaijin*, foreigners, refer to it as *hari-kari*. The official term of *seppuku* denotes a highly ritualized performance, as complicated as *chado* (tea ceremony). The principal difference is that at the end of *chado*, one is merely nauseated from too much green tea, whilst at the end of seppuku, one is dead.

The first thing to do is to recruit an assistant, a *kaishakunin*. And he had done this. The coded words "talk with you soon" in his conversation with Ali meant that his friend would even now be making his way to Honolulu Airport to get on the next flight to Lihue.

Contrary to what is thought, almost all forms of seppuku do not technically involve suicide, but merely inflicting fatal injury upon oneself. The *kaishakunin* does the actual killing and one can appoint one's own *kaishakunin*.

He had already laid out his white robe. Whiteness expressed purity of intention and he would sit in the *seiza* position, his legs drawn up under his body so that he was actually sitting on his heels. The *sanbo*, an unlacquered wooden table, was already in place. When he was ready, a sake cup, a sheaf of *washi*, paper handmade from mulberry bark, writing accoutrements, and the *kozuka*, the disemboweling blade, would be in place on the table.

He would empty the sake cup and then write a death poem in the *waka* style that involved five lines of five, seven, seven, five, and seven syllables. The poem would be graceful, natural, and here would be no reference to his death.

At this point, he would remove his outer garment, the *kamishimo*, and tuck the sleeves under his knees to prevent him from doing something undignified like slumping to one side. It would soon be over and any finishing that needed to be done would be performed by his *kaishakunin*.

Following tradition, blood should not be allowed to spray across the floor; only low-class criminals were treated in this manner. There would be sufficient blood on the floor to show that a deed had been done.

As the day drew to a close and the shadows had long since lengthened to signify the disappearance of the sun, he was ready. He sat back in the recliner and waited.

He heard the heavy running footsteps on the wooden floor of the porch and the door was flung open.

"Ah, François, my friend. Come in." He saw the worried look on Ali's face. "Do not worry, my friend. We have planned for the arrival of such a day. But first, I suggest that you close the door and we will have a cup of tea to steady our nerves and help us in our quest. Are you ready?

"I am, dear friend and mentor."

The tea ceremony took a little longer than anticipated. There was much to talk about and many reminiscences were called to mind. And then they were done.

Takeyama took his position before the table and looked at François. They smiled at each other.

"As you can see, all has been prepared. You know what needs to be done, François?"

"Yes I do, Takeyama-san. May God be with you. I am sure that we will meet again."

"*Insha'allah*. As God wills it," Takeyama responded in the native language of Ali's father.

He looked once more at Ali before he drew the knife across his flesh. The blood dripped onto the floor.

*   *   *

CHAPTER 25

James and Kathryn were talking with John Anderson, who reminisced about his own wedding, when they saw Charlie approaching.

"Excuse me, John, but I do need to have a word with James and Kathryn." Charlie smiled a disarming smile that could not be refused. Anderson smiled and moved away toward the bar as Charlie led James to the door. Kathryn and Sylvia followed.

"James," Charlie said once they were out of earshot, "just been back to the vicarage and as you often say 'timing is everything,' there was a telephone call for you. Young woman by the name of Liza called. Seemed in a bit of a pickle and seemed very distraught. Wanted to talk with you immediately. Told her that you would get back to her whenever you could. Here is her number, a cell phone she said so you can reach her any time."

James and Kathryn looked at each other wondering why the call. Perhaps a wedding wish but who, outside of the village, had known of the wedding?

"I think, James," Kathryn offered, "that you should call Liza. Perhaps Harry needs to talk with you?"

"And," Sylvia added, "you can call from the vicarage rather than leave for your cottage."

James's eyes narrowed, suspecting that all was not well. He had never even considered that he would hear from Takeyama again. He could hold back no longer and agreed to make the call.

"Only if," he said "you three join me in case I have need to talk something over with you."

Charlie made their apologies to the crowd, promising that they would return momentarily. Minutes after entering the vicarage, James had the telephone connection to Liza's cell phone.

The cautious "hello" told him that all was not well.

"Liza, James Simpson," he introduced himself.

"Dr. Simpson, thank you for calling. There was no one else that I could think of who might be able to help."

He exchanged glances with, and rolled his eyes to, his three-person audience to indicate that the tone of her voice did not bode well. Charlie pushed a chair closer to the telephone and indicated that James should sit down.

"Go on, Liza. I am all ears."

"This morning," he could hear the worried tones of her voice, "I visited my uncle as always but his house was deserted. I have no idea of what has happened but the whole house looked as if someone had broken in and had been searching for something. I have no idea why, but there is something very frightening going on. And I am scared! My uncle," she continued, "is a gentle man and to have this happen is such a shock."

James could hear the tremor in her voice as she managed to speak the last words.

"How about your grandmother?" James asked.

"Granny is all right," came the immediate response "and knows nothing of this. I am sure that if I tell her it may be hard for her to take. I cannot even imagine what it will do to her."

James pursed his lips as he thought for a moment.

"Have you called the police?"

"Yes, Dr. Simpson, and they have looked at the house and are investigating my uncle's disappearance. I am not sure what to call it right now."

Then, the thought struck him.

"What about Dr. Ali? He and your uncle were close friends and colleagues. Does he know anything? Or the faculty on the University of Hawaii campus?"

His words drew more interest from Charlie, Sylvia, and Kathryn who leaned forward to try to hear what was being said on the other end of the telephone. Kathryn had used the last minutes of time to get Charlie and Sylvia up to date on the relationship of Liza and Ali to Takeyama. They continued to lean forward, interested despite not knowing the *dramatis personae*!

"Well, Dr. Simpson, that is the problem. It seems that Dr. Ali has also disappeared!"

"Good lord," James exclaimed, "When?"

Kathryn could see the change in James's body language and she knew that something was very wrong. James tried to remain calm in his words, not wishing to panic Liza and have her think the worst.

"When was Dr. Ali last seen?"

"According to the police and the faculty, sometime the night before last. He told his colleagues that he was taking a day or so off to write a book review for a journal and that he would return by the end of the week. This," she said "is the reason why I am worried. For the two of them to disappear at the same time is very suspicious!"

She started to sob. It sounded almost out of control and James could almost visualize the violent movements of her body as the sobs came out. The dam had broken. The strain was too much.

"Liza, I am asking my wife," he motioned his head to Kathryn who smiled at the words, "to pick up the extension phone and join us."

James looked at Charlie and Sylvia who nodded in agreement. Sylvia led Kathryn into the next room where the extension phone was located.

"Liza? This is Kathryn."

"I am so sorry, I couldn't help myself. I am worried about my uncle. He does not do things like this. I did not know who else to call."

"Liza," Kathryn said, "we are pleased that you took it upon yourself to call us. We are here to help you all that we can. Collect your thoughts and we will talk. Tell us all that you can remember, and do not worry about what you have already told my husband, I can sense from his words what you were saying. Not wishing to worry you but I must say it, this is rather strange. As you say, this is outside of your uncle's usual behavior. How much have you told the police?"

"Very little, Mrs. Simpson. But the police seem to think that robbery was the motive. Some of my uncle's valuable costumes and swords have disappeared. There is also . . ."

"What kinds of costumes and swords, Liza?" James asked.

"Oh," she thought for a moment, "a samurai costume and two swords that he valued a great deal. Always did like to think of himself as a samurai warrior. They were," she hesitated as she thought about the time that Takeyama had purchased them and shown them to her, "seventeenth-century items that he said were authentic. The costume and the sword were his prize possessions."

"Anything else, Liza," Kathryn asked being very suspicious.

"Why yes, Mrs. Simpson. Funny you should ask. You know that he had a large number of notebooks that he kept for his work?"

"Yes," Kathryn answered cautiously.

"They too have gone! And," she hesitated as she took a deep breath, "the police found drops of blood on the floor, enough to make them suspicious that something more serious had happened. They are doing a DNA test on it now to see if it is my uncle's blood."

The hair on the back of James's neck was starting to stand up and he feared the worst for Takeyama and perhaps Ali. He remembered Takeyama's immaculate house and the way in which he kept things neat and tidy. He also remembered what Takeyama and he had discussed about the implications of time travel in the hands of the wrong people. The chance to alter history, which James did not believe could happen, was still an unknown and unresolved issue. Even though many theoreticians had indicated the possibility of changing history through time travel into the past, James was not a subscriber to this theory. The best or worst that anyone could do, James had reasoned, was to delay the inevitable. He recalled the basic premise of chaos theory that no matter how well you planned under current conditions and with current knowledge, the unexpected was inevitable.

"This, then," James said, "is more than just a robbery. It is robbery with intent. Who would break in and steal a pile of notebooks that were written in Japanese? I can understand theft of valuable Japanese artifacts but the notebooks, no! It seems to me, Liza, again not wishing to worry you unduly, that you need to go back to your grandmother, collect her belongings and whatever else you may need, and disappear until this blows over or is resolved. Can you do that? I think that your safety is of the utmost importance."

"Yes, Dr. Simpson. I can. There is a cabin well into the interior that my uncle liked to use to get away from it all," James smiled since Takeyama's cottage was already away from it all, "and which my granny likes. We can go there."

"Liza," Kathryn spoke up quickly, "do it as soon as you can. And the telephone that you are using, it is a cell phone?"

"Yes, Mrs. Simpson. One of the cheap ones."

"Dispose of it as soon as we are done with this call."

"Good girl," James thought but did not say the words. Kathryn's idea of traceable phones was not as outlandish as it might seem to some.

"And, Liza," James said, "we have to leave for a while but you can leave messages for us at this," he looked at Charlie who nodded, "this number." James gave Liza the number. "And please let the reverend or Mrs. Kirkby know if your uncle or Dr. Ali returns. If you do, keep all calls short and use a disposable phone if you can."

"I will, Dr. Simpson. And thank you."

The line went dead. James waited several minutes and then redialed the number. There was no response. Liza had probably destroyed the telephone as had been suggested to her.

Charlie stood by as James replaced the receiver. He had been watching James's action, listening to his response, and putting two and two together as much as he could. Sylvia and Kathryn arrived from the other room.

James and Kathryn filled in the gaps in Charlie and Silvia's perception of the conversation with Liza.

"Well, James," Charlie summed up, "to begin with, there is something incredibly wrong. Two men disappear. Items are stolen to make it seem like a robbery but a whole pile of valuable notebooks also go missing. I can attest to the fact that this whole situation does not bode well for Takeyama and his friend. The coincidences are uncanny. Uncanny, indeed!"

"James, Kathryn, my dears," Sylvia continued Charlie's thoughts, "How do you propose to handle this when Oswald needs you?"

James and Kathryn looked at each other.

"We must go, Sylvia." James answered.

"Ah," said Charlie, "that seems to be without option. I am not sure that there can be any benefit to refusing Oswald's request. Whatever the case," Charlie continued, "it is you who possess the ability to help Oswald. No matter what happens on the other side of the world. I agree with you, James, and I see that you have no choice."

"Well," Charlie said looking round at them, "not to reduce this issue in importance, I think that we should rejoin the party and, all being well, we may be able to continue this conversation tomorrow. A night clearing our minds might help."

As they entered the Royal Duke, there were smiles and words of congratulations all round. The music from the band was lilting, soft, and pleasant, and everyone seemed a little mellower than when the four of them had left. The food and drinks were taking their effect.

"Ah," sighed Charlie, "no man has better taste in beer than the Northern folks. Newcastle Brown Ale rules the world!"

As soon as it was generally known that James and Kathryn had returned, the round of toasts started. Many of the villagers had something that they wished to say, and all were different. Kathryn's eyes sparkled with a soft blue light that complimented her blonde hair. When the toasts were finished, it was the turn of Kathryn and James to speak. James declined other than a brief thanks but Kathryn took up the challenge.

"Now," she said, "there is one thing I wish to say to all of you tonight."

Kathryn smiled stunningly to everyone in the room. They could all see the pleasure in her face. For her, this was a very meaningful time.

"When my husband was injured last year," she looked at James, "you gave me, even though you did not know me, immeasurable support. For this I say thank you. The depth of my gratitude to you cannot be measured. And now you have accepted me into your hearts as you have already accepted my husband."

Kathryn fought hard to retain her composure as James reached up to her and took her hand.

"I sat, silently, for many an hour," she continued "praying that James would pull through after that terrible injury. Your prayers helped me. For that you have my undying gratitude. And now I propose a toast."

The villagers stood up as glasses were refilled. Kathryn looked around and saw the anticipation on the faces. She raised her glass of sherry.

"To the people of the village of Bridgeford!"

The tumultuous sound told her that all accepted her toast. Her vision blurred as the tears began to well up in her eyes. She looked at James who smiled at her. Charlie, Sylvia, and the villagers were joyous. Her throat was tight with emotion as she mouthed the words "thank you" to all who were present.

*   *   *

CHAPTER 26

Kathryn and James left the celebration to return to the cottage. No one seemed to notice that they were leaving except Charlie and Sylvia who knew the reason. Charlie took James by the arm.

"James, if there is anything or any way in which we can help?" Charlie raised his eyebrows indicating that they would be available, whatever the need.

"No, Charlie, this is something that we have to face ourselves. And also, I am concerned about Takeyama's disappearance. Perhaps we can talk about this tomorrow. But I can sense that Oswald is close. Perhaps tonight? I do not know but I just have this feeling . . ."

"But," Charlie added, "if it should be tonight and considering what we have talked about, we must have plans to maintain contact. How . . ."

Charlie's words trailed off and the light went on in his eyes and he answered his own question.

"Of course. The crypt. You can contact us as Oswald contacted you." Then Charlie looked thoughtful. "Do be careful, there are many dangers out there that we cannot even begin to think about let alone know. Of course, we will pray for your safety."

James looked at Charlie. This dear man was so concerned for them both. He shook Charlie's hand and patted him on the shoulder.

"Charlie, me old lad, do not worry. All will turn out for the best."

With that James followed Kathryn and Sylvia to the vehicle. The two ladies said their tearful goodbyes and James and Kathryn left for the cottage.

The cottage was warm and comfortable. James turned to Kathryn and took her in his arms.

"Well, Mrs. Simpson, how does it feel . . . ?"

"Wonderful! Just wonderful!" she cooed.

They took off their coats and settled onto the couch. The rekindled fire burned brightly and the glow filled the room. James looked pensive and then he spoke.

"He is close, Kath. I can sense it. We may be on your way tonight. This will be some honeymoon. In my wildest dreams I never expected anything quite like this!"

Kathryn smiled and touched his hand reassuringly. James continued with his thoughts about the preparations that they must make.

"I suggest that we prepare ourselves as best as we can. The long robes. We can wear our sweat suits underneath. Warm layers of clothes would be best. The drugs that I got from Bob Fenwick, suitably marked and wrapped in vellum, will serve for both of us. And I also recommend . . ." he collected his thoughts for a moment but Kathryn was too fast for him as she continued the sentence.

"That we stick some extra generic drugs into the pockets of our robes and sweat suits!"

"Yes, Kath. One never knows! Plus," James continued after a moment's thought, "that we forego the use of glasses and use the contact lenses that we have. Mine for general wear, yours for reading."

Kathryn was about to protest since she, like James, had never felt comfortable wearing contact lenses. They did help her reading activities but were not for constant use like those of James. She agreed after giving thought to the surprise and comments that the use of modern eyeglasses for reading in a fourteenth-century setting would cause. She agreed and offered to make sure that both pairs of lenses were clean.

"Oh," James said, almost as an afterthought, "for some reason these," he reached into a drawer and produce a full bottle of aspirin, "might just be of some help."

"And," Kathryn added, "speaking of clean lenses, I think that we should take a shower. One never really knows when the next one will be available."

"Good idea, Mrs. Simpson. I'll join you."

"And no funny business, Dr. Simpson. You never know who is watching! And a rest will do you good," she added. "By the way, you really think that tonight is the night?"

"I do, Kath."

"That is the second time today that I have heard those first two words, and I like them."

James smiled. He kissed her on the forehead and went to start the shower and get the hot water running.

The shower was relaxing and after toweling each other to remove the last drops of water, Kathryn and James dressed as they had planned and walked toward the front room.

"You go and sit in front of the fire and I'll make tea," James offered as he went into the kitchen.

The silence was broken only by the sound of the tea utensils being assembled on the tray.

And then he heard Kathryn's voice, shouting for him.

He ran into the room and there in front of the fire stood Oswald. It was the first time that Kathryn had seen him clearly and the surprise had caused her to cry out. He wore the clothing of a soldier with the surcoat of Edward III.

Eyes of deep blue looked at her out of a face rough-hewn but handsome. His features were strong and his skin was the pale healthy color that one imagined of the Saxons. He was smiling and she could see well-set visible teeth and prominent cheekbones that all combined to enhance the image of force, vitality, and supremacy. Thick blond hair came down slightly over his forehead. His eyebrows, likewise thick and fair, accentuated the eyes to yet an even greater dramatic and imposing effect.

He was just as Kathryn had imagined from what James had told her. He was indeed a man of imposing stature and carriage who would command attention wherever he went. His face and build were true to the vision of the transpersonification that James had undergone in Takeyama's cottage.

Oswald took Kathryn's hand and held it while he looked at James and spoke in the dialect of the North.

"I would say, my cousin, that you have made the right decision, and I congratulate you," he looked at Kathryn, "on joining our family."

Kathryn was in awe. She composed herself and spoke to Oswald.

"I do understand as I also speak the dialect."

"Of course," Oswald responded.

"Thank you, dear Oswald, for accepting me," she said. "I am pleased that you consider me as one of the family."

"As it should be, Kathryn." He looked at James. "You know why I am here?"

"Yes," James answered, "Kathryn and I have expected you and we are ready."

"Then we did understand your feeling correctly to allow Kathryn to come with you. But," he looked at Kathryn, "you know that you may have to face unseen dangers. You should also know that you might undergo a change in personality. James, here," he motioned to James, "takes on the role of the quiet physician when he comes back to me but I suspect that there is an underlying personality that has not yet emerged."

He held Kathryn's hand as he continued.

"For you, dear Kathryn, I am not sure. But you do have a look of some warrior women that I have seen. Who knows what physical form you may take or in what form your personality may emerge? Finally, your memories may not be sharp and you will in all probability only have fleeting glimpses of this life in which you were born and raised."

Oswald appeared to think for a moment and then, still holding Kathryn's hand, he held out his other hand to James.

"James, my cousin, you have done this before. But even you will find changes that you may not understand."

Oswald looked directly at Kathryn once more.

"Kathryn, hold on to me. James has his own power. You do not. Feel the strength of my hand. Let the energy flow from me to you. Do not resist and do not worry, all will be well."

Kathryn felt the power of his hand and then an overwhelming sense of tiredness came over her. She wanted to lie down and sleep.

James took her other hand, gently kissed her fingers as if he was a young beau seeking her attention in some previous past time and then her eyes closed.

Kathryn smiled as her body started to relax. A pleasant numbness descended upon her.

*   *   *

PART II

ACROSS THE BRIDGE

CHAPTER 27

Kathryn felt giddy as she turned and swayed in the cool air. The events of the day had been sudden and tiring as the evening turned into night. It was as if the drinks at the Royal Duke had clouded her mind and she was in a dream. Her feet seemed immobile in the darkness and she felt herself stumbling, as if she was once more a young girl on the dance floor. She raised her head to see what was happening but there was nothing. Only darkness.

She realized that she was standing in a doorway and as she looked out from the doorway there was only darkness. Was that a light she could see? She caught her breath as the light moved closer.

She could see the dim outline of the man who carried the lantern. He seemed to be bigger than her James. Her instincts were telling her to protect herself. But she had no means of doing so. Who was this man?

"Kathryn?"

She could hear a voice. Questioning as if he was asking how she felt. It was the voice of James. He was with her. All would be well.

James squeezed her hand in reassurance. He knew that they had reached their destination. It was the city of Durham in the year of our Lord? The question remained in his mind. He did not know the day or the year and put the thought out of his mind, for the moment.

In the dim light James saw Oswald. He was tall, well over six feet, of supple frame, instinctive agility, ready to react when the occasion required. He appeared to be about forty years of age. Oswald looked round as though looking for something or someone and then he smiled and uttered the simple words.

"There you are. Come to me."

Kathryn sensed rather than saw the other man but she did hear his words.

James moved her out of the shadows, as though materializing from nothing and first appearing as a shimmering light.

She placed one foot in front of the other. Gently. Timidly. She could walk. Strong arms continued to support her. As she stepped into the road, she looked up and now she could see a moon and objects that were starting to become visible.

"Kathryn and James," she heard the voice, "welcome to my world. Stay close to me. Especially you," he looked at Kathryn and in reference to her size and hair color added, "Little One."

"I had to come this day, as you guessed, James, because the time is near. I can feel that evil is afoot and it does not bode well for England."

"But who is the other man?" the question shot through Kathryn's mind. "Is he not someone who is known to my husband?" She asked herself, "Why is he here with us? What has caused me to get into this situation?" Had she realized that it was Oswald, all of her questions would have been answered.

Her self-directed questions remained unanswered but she was not bothered. There would be answers later.

Her memories lingered. Possibly because everything that transpired that night was still in the active part of her brain. Or because of the way that the day had changed to become the happiest day of her life and embodied all that would come after. She now had a husband. After the tragic death of her first husband, she had wondered if ever there would be anyone else. If someone all of those years ago had told her that in the future she would marry again to a man who had ventured all over the world and who encouraged her to study the past with him, even venturing into the past herself, she would probably have laughed.

Her first husband had been such a dear man and the tragic accident that took his life that black day had made her a widow. She would not lose her new husband.

"I will protect him," she vowed silently, "even if it should cost me dearly, even my life!"

Her mind flashed further back in time to a life when she had been a warrior queen. Had she not fought enemies before to protect her children after the murder of her husband? The pictures of armies and battles flashed through her mind. She could hear the clash of metal on metal and the screams of dying men in her mind. There had been men who had tried to kill her but she had killed them.

"Yes," she answered her own question. "I will fight them in any way that I can. My James is precious to me. I will not let him go. I will not be a widow again!"

A light at some distant point attracted her attention in the dim recess of the darkness. It was faint, almost imperceptible, and at times hidden. Just like a star. She tilted her head and looked around, seeking a glimpse of anything that she could recognize. The darkness seemed to engulf her, almost beckoning to keep her within its folds. In that moment the real world seemed far away and memories of them whispered through her mind. Memories that she had not recalled before, speaking to her of times past, actions that she did not recognize, and men speaking with foreign tongues.

She shuddered as she felt a chill, as if a cold icy hand stroked her flesh. There was a sound but she could not see any light to fix her position. She cast another quick glance around and saw dim forms of men and women as they moved like shadows behind a gray curtain.

Slowly, she returned her gaze to what was in front of her and tried to see the outlines of the men who held her hands. She knew that one was her beloved James. But she could not recall the other man.

"Hello!" she exclaimed and then asked, "who are you?"

She felt a comforting squeeze of her hand as her eyes searched for the hidden form of the man. He must be an apparition. But she could feel his hand. The power that came from him sustained her.

"Hello?" she asked again, and then her breath caught in her throat, another light appeared, as if in answer to her words. She felt herself drifting slowly down and forward. And then he was moving just beyond the edge of the light. She shivered and felt strong arms enfold her, as if to ward off the chill.

"Ah, my dear James is with me."

Her words were thoughts. She could not speak. She sensed that she was standing at a bridge between two worlds.

"Across the bridge," she thought. "I must go across the bridge. The crossing might not be easy," she continued to herself, "but this is where I am needed. And no one told me that it would be easy!"

Kathryn could feel her heart pounding. The cool night air invaded her lungs. With trembling fingers she reached up and tried to uncover her eyes. But they were uncovered.

"Kathryn!"

She heard her name and allowed her hands to fall to her sides. She could hear her name called again in the darkness.

She looked around and only saw the darkness. She raised her hands to trace the face of her husband in the darkness.

"I have you," she said, "and I will never let you go."

The darkness started to turn to gray and she could see the outline of her husband. He looked at her and smiled; even in the gray darkness she could see the curve of his mouth and the laughing eyes.

"James, I knew that you were here with me."

"Where else would I be, Kathryn?"

The reassuring tones of his voice made her feel sleepy again. But where was the other man? Who was he?

*   *   *

It was the time of full moon and even though the sky was partly covered by cloud forms, James could see that ordinary objects were becoming visible.

Kathryn could hear the other man as he spoke to her husband, giving James the facts about the city of Durham, the fortified peninsula that enclosed the castle, the cathedral, and the priory that was known as the city of Durham. It was a citadel, an exclusive concentration of religious and political power.

For the most part, Oswald ignored Kathryn. He could see that she was in a state of transience in which her mind and other senses were not able to focus on her surroundings. He held her hand and indicated to James that he should do the same. Kathryn looked at them out of unseeing eyes and was happy to hold on to them.

"Do not worry about her, James. She will feel better after she has walked in the cool air," Oswald said. Then he continued his description of the city.

"Within the castle walls lie the bishop's palace and his cathedral church. Beyond the cathedral is the Benedictine monastery, the successor of the Community of Saint Cuthbert and custodian of his shrine. After the holdings of the bishop, the priory is the greatest landowner of the palatinate and a major influence on the life of the city. The dwellings of the palatinate officials and the castle garrison are in the outer bailey. Or as some now call it the outer yard."

Oswald looked at James who nodded to show that he understood. Kathryn walked dreamily along holding their hands. It was as though she was seeing objects, as they would have appeared on a film negative. She remained silent.

She felt that she was dreaming. But the dreams were real. She could feel her hands being held. The change had been a shock to her system and she was finding it difficult to adjust to her surroundings. She made the effort to control her breathing, worried that she would hyperventilate and did not want to bring attention to herself. She fought to gain control. The other man was still talking.

"We are not within the citadel now but we are just outside of the walls, on the north side of the city. When you have the opportunity to walk within the walls, you will realize that you are walking in a fortress town. Wherever one enters or leaves the city, he or she must pass through one of the gates, beneath ever-watchful guards who are positioned on the walls. There are no shops within the citadel, they lie outside the walls but the wall has been extended beyond the north gate to include the marketplace. This wall also forms a second line of defense that can only be entered through the north gate. That is the only part of the city that is not protected by the step incline of the hill. Most of the shops are to the north but some on the east and a few new settlements on the west. It is a busy place, James."

"As you will see," Oswald continued, "the focus of the activity of the shopkeepers and trades people is the marketplace, where military personnel and religious clients buy goods. The marketplace is only accessible to those who were willing to subject themselves and their produce to the most detailed, and in some cases, intimate searches."

Oswald smiled at James's expression.

"How intimate?" James asked.

"I recommend that you do not try to find out!" Oswald retorted. "You may be in for a surprise. And make sure that your Kathryn is not subject to such procedures. I trained the guards to be very thorough!" Oswald smiled to himself and then he continued.

"Although the city offers a livelihood to local traders as well as its prime purpose and that is security against Scottish raiders, the protection provided by the castle and its garrison to the surrounding population in times of strife encourages the development of trade. In some respects, the city is a market community but the self-imposed isolation of the city on its hill-island, Dun Holm, as was called by Saxons and by Vikings, has necessitated the development of settlements on neighboring riverbanks that led to the spread of the city."

Oswald looked around at the houses as if collecting his thoughts.

"James, I hope that this is not boring you?"

"No, Oswald," James cut in as he looked at Kathryn to make sure that all was well with her. She still had a dreamy unfocused look in her eyes. "I need to know," James continued, "what the city is about if I am to make my way around and help you."

"Good," Oswald acknowledged. "That is precisely the reason why I am telling you these facts. So, every day, the city bustles with so much life and activity that cellars and attics have to be used as dwellings for the poorer inhabitants. In the past, the demand for property was such that houses started to encroach on the castle precincts until laws were passed forbidding dwellings to be built within specific distances of our river-island. As you may have guessed, James, such dwellings would give cover to an enemy army as it approached the castle. Trees are also forbidden on the river-island and the dwellings across the river are built at a specified distance from the riverbank. Unlike other cities, and because of its fortress nature, the growth of the city of Durham has been controlled by the king's law."

Oswald looked at Kathryn. "How is the little one," he asked rhetorically.

"Still not quite with us," James replied. "I am not sure why," he could not recall what had caused Kathryn's lapse, "but she seems to be moving along much better than she was. It is as though," James thought carefully, "that she has had too much wine but she is not a heavy drinker so I am at a loss to explain her condition."

"She will improve with time," Oswald assured James.

Oswald adjusted his hold of Kathryn's hand to make sure that she was comfortable and understood that they were walking. She looked at him and forced a smile. Then Oswald continued.

"The River Wear is one of the greatest influences on the city. Bridges, Framwellgate on the west side and Elvet on the east side, were built a century or more ago and they have allowed development of separate communities outside of the city walls. However, unlike many other cities, the townspeople know better than to use the river for drinking water. Wells and piped water, carried to the citadel by lead pipes, provided the necessary supply. But, much to the joy of some and the disappointment of others, the river served the town as an open sewer for all refuse. Good, insofar as the garbage is carried away from the city. Bad, insofar as one must not enter the river on the downside of the sewer discharges. To do so is to ensure a quick death from disease. In fact, a shopkeeper died two days ago from an accidental fall into the river. He developed the bloody flux and was dead within one week after his fall into the murky waters. Do not, my cousin," Oswald turned and smiled at James, "consider entering the water for whatever reason or do not allow yourself to accidentally fall into the river!"

"So, James," Oswald concluded, "you have come to help me resolve the mystery that had been in my mind for these past several months."

*   *   *

CHAPTER 28

Kathryn could hear his voice but she still could not see clearly. As if dark clouds had moved over her eyes causing a blurred vision. She did hear his command and she could hear other voices but the sounds were not clear. Through mist that clouded her eyes, she could hear sounds of activity. Her husband's voice talking with the man who had met them was clear and resounded in her ears. She frowned and held on to the hands that led her along the road. She could feel changes to her body as she walked. Changes that made her feel as though she had been on a long trek and exercised every muscle in her body.

Through the dim mist she could just see a fallen form, sprawled in the boot-sucking mud that tried to hold her feet. Was it an old man or old woman? She did not know as the form picked itself up and moved off stumbling, into a doorway. She wondered if she would see any familiar faces as they moved forward.

She felt that she needed to dust herself off but, as she pondered this thought, rain started to fall from the clouds that had collected themselves into an ominous sheet and blocked out the light from the moon.

"Why is there dust in the rain?" Kathryn asked herself.

She felt that her body was starting to adapt to her surroundings as she gathered her senses and tried to shake off the dust that blocked her vision and had prevented her from seeing clearly. The strengthening winds that carried the rain should help.

She tried to speak but the words would not come. Gently as a mother with a child, she held the hands near to her. She could see her husband, a warm and friendly smile spreading across his face. The she saw the face of the other man as he looked at her. His smile was warm and friendly and he looked a lot like her husband. He was staring at her. She gave him a sideways glance and moved her fingers in his hand. She smiled.

"James," he said, "I think that she is becoming conscious of us."

Then she heard voices from the crowd that had appeared from nowhere.

"Pretty, isn't she?" a man's voice from the shadows came to her.

James laughed. "Of course," he said, "that is why we are husband and wife."

"If only I could see clearly," she whispered to her husband and to the other man.

"It will come in time," the man said. "Rest yourself by leaning on our arms and we will have you home soon."

"Then can we spend some time talking?" she asked finding her voice. "I need to know what is happening to me."

"I promise, my love," her husband answered. He kissed her cheek. "In fact, I promise that we can talk as much as you wish. We will have tea and something to eat."

"Thank you," she replied.

"Good," the other man said. "It will be soon."

He turned so that she could see him smile.

She adjusted her arms to make the walk easier. She did not require them to take all of her weight now. The strength was returning to her legs. A strange mix of feelings was running through her. Her husband and the other man seemed at peace and were gentle with her.

She narrowed her eyes into slits and tried to focus on what lay before her. She was still hardly able to see the road beneath her warm boots. Her loose hair whipped around in the wind and she could feel her forehead starting to cool. She searched in the pocket of her robe for a long, narrow strip of . . . ? She was not sure but it was a long narrow strip of something. Finding it, she automatically pulled her hair into a ponytail and bound it. The two men watched her and smiled at each other.

"Yes," she could hear her husband's voice, "she is coming round."

It was at that moment that she sensed that her faculties were returning. Dark shapes loomed out of the doorways. Debris filled the streets.

They stepped to one side as a horseman passed by. Another man shuffled past carrying a package on his back. He wore tattered clothes that were pulled tightly around his frame and his hood was pulled low against the wind and rain.

And then Kathryn saw the large double-edged sword that the other man carried. It was sheathed in a leather scabbard and strapped across the man's back. He watched her eyes as they roamed over the sword.

"James," he said to her husband, "it seems that our Kathryn is taking notice of me."

They stopped in the roadway, both men looking at her. Then they turned and continued their walk in the wind and rain. The sound of the rain hitting the thatched roofs was persistent and almost musical. Kathryn's mind was starting to clear.

And then the thought that she had been seeking came to her and she was able to answer the question that had been persistent in her mind.

"The other man is Oswald," she declared to herself. But she could not stop thinking of the sword that hung on his back. She wanted to look at it closer. The large blade was unlike anything that she had seen before.

She started to notice other features of Oswald's stature and appearance. He seemed to be a man of some substance who walked with dignity and posture, like her husband, and his clothing was clean. Not like a lot of the others she could now see, whose clothing was dirty and worn. It was odd to see someone like Oswald among all of these other people.

"Well," Kathryn mused as she allowed the wind and rain to brush against her face, "there is one good thing about the wind and rain—it is a good awakening."

At last they veered away from the main street toward a side street. Kathryn looked into the street, and her blurred vision returned.

"Why is it," she asked herself, "that streets always seem so long when you are trying to get home?"

Then suddenly, she could see much better, for although the wind and rain continued, the dust that had plagued her eyes disappeared. Deep ruts that were filled with mud marked the streets. She continued to feel stronger. Her legs were able to support her weight fully, a testimony to her returning strength.

The shadows in the doorways gave her an uneasy feeling as she looked upon them, for what lay waiting in the shadows, she could not even guess. It was if she had passed from another world and she had walked through shadow after shadow, her vision limited to her immediate surroundings.

She always imagined that dark, mysterious people lurked in the shadows, waiting patiently for opportunities to do mischief.

Kathryn looked around and sighed. Why was she worried? She was with her husband and Oswald.

As they walked, she was able to see human figures that were drifting slowly out of the various houses toward the tavern. They had an alien and unnatural appearance. It did not please her to think that she would be mingling among all of these people. Had not she been warned about something like that? But she could not remember who had warned her of the dangers of such contact. It was as if her memory had been erased.

She saw great houses as well as hovels. Many of the houses were of wooden construction with two rooms, one above the other, and a thatched roof. Those in poorer situations lived in rooms built within tenements that could be found down the narrow alleys between wide thoroughfares. The upper floor of these small houses protruded into the street itself so that little of the sky could be seen between them. Many of the smaller houses had been built of wood with thatched roofs, still reflecting the appearance of Saxon or early Norman construction.

The street under the shadow of the nearby bridge was not a friendly place. Sounds of human suffering and other activities reached her ears. The slow-moving river grew black and foreboding as darkness had descended on the city. A thin fog began to creep shoreward along the water's surface. Kathryn shivered as she felt the dampness penetrate her clothing, bringing with it a numbing cold.

She was conscious of the many faces that seemed to stare at her. The people were on their way to an evening meal or to a tavern and cared little for the three strangers. But she was conscious that as they passed by some glanced curiously at them. A man with prominent eyes stood still and tried to interfere with their pace. One look from Oswald and he was gone back into the shadows from whence he came. Kathryn moved closer to Oswald and James and took a firmer hold of their hands so that they might not lose her. She started to feel comfortable as her body and mind adjusted to the new place. A place that she thought she remembered but could not recall the date or time when she had visited the city.

For the most part, the men and women who appeared in the street from time to time did not even look at them. They were merely three people, one of whom was Oswald, a soldier. He was tall and very well armed. In the changing light, the passersby did notice that the clothes of other two were unusual but no one asked any questions. The soldier looked formidable.

"Walk on," Kathryn told herself, "you are in a city, among the people."

She was conscious of hoping that in a short time she would be able to rest. The lane held the smell of the people and the cold darkness was heavy with the sounds of their activities. Candles brought dim light to the rooms and she could see through some of the windows that had no coverings. Through one window she saw a man mending a pair of boots. Through another window she saw a woman holding a baby. Through another window, a family was sitting at a table eating.

Suddenly, Kathryn was jerked out of her semidreamy state when she realized that they had reached their destination.

"And this," said Oswald, "is our house or hideaway as you may call it."

James and Kathryn stood before a square wooden facade identical with the others that extended from across what seemed to have been a gap between two other houses in the deserted street. A glimmer of light showed behind heavy curtains.

Before she could think of what movement to make, the door opened and a light shone into the lane. For a second or so she stood as rigid as a post and then she heard James's soft whisper in her ear. She followed him into the room. Her eyes took a few moments to become accustomed to the light from several candles and then she saw Oswald's wife, Margaret. Margaret smiled and the warmth of her smile made Kathryn feel that all was well. Her smile matched the warmth of the log fire that burned brightly in the hearth.

The lower room that opened upon the street was the living room and kitchen that contained chairs and a folding table. On the walls they could see kitchen utensils, tools, and weapons. Among them were a frying pan, an iron spit, and several metal pots. There were plates, cushions, and curtains that were hung before the doors and windows to keep out the draughts. Glass windows were not practical in this part of the city and nailed wooden boards closed the windows spaces. Rushes had been spread on the floor to collect the dirt. The back of the room contained chairs and looked more like a sitting room in which there was an open wooden chest that held blankets, linen sheets, tablecloths, a coverlet, and several aprons.

The upper floor consisted of two smaller rooms and was reached by means of a ladder. Each room contained a thick straw-filled palliasse or mattress for sleeping and two pillows. There was a multicolored rug on the floor that was soft to the touch and added warmth to the room.

Clothes that had been taken out of wooden chests and hung on the walls consisted of three surcoats, several robes each with a hood, and two suits of leather armor.

James and Kathryn stood still for a few moments and it was Margaret who broke the silence.

"Welcome, my two cousins. It is a pleasure to see you. I have hot mulled wine for you that will take the chill from your bones. And then we will see to your clothes."

"This," Oswald announced, "is a home without pretensions. Because of our situation, it is perhaps most important that we remain unseen and unheard. We go about our business without any fuss or bother and we are not disturbed by anyone.

"Probably a useful idea, but may I ask why?"

"Aye, James my cousin. You have the curiosity of those who always seek the truth. And I shall tell it to you."

Oswald looked at Margaret and she nodded her head in agreement with the decision that her husband had made and offered, "Kathryn and James are here to help us, Oswald, and we must honor their willingness on that score. After all, is James not your cousin? I see in him many of the traits that drew me to you."

On the wall that faced the door was a small religious painting on vellum in a brown leather frame. The colors had artistic merit and were strong and rich in their representation of the Virgin and Child. It was the emblem of the Priory Church of Christ and Blessed Mary the Virgin.

Oswald was about to speak when he saw the astonished look on James's face as he noticed the painting and read the words underneath.

"Yes, Cousin, you are in Durham. The year," he paused, "is 1370."

Again, James gasped at what he was hearing. Oswald continued.

"As you may have gathered, Margaret and I have been given an extension of our lives. We think that we are here to attend to some specific task that will be for the good. We have filled our time by helping the sick and ailing people of this city. But these last few months we have begun to realize the nature of that task. It is our belief, or the thoughts have been imprinted on our minds, that a plot has been hatched to bring down the king. The time is near!"

James nodded to show that he had heard but he was not sure that he could fathom the true nature of the problem.

"Oswald, if it is our help that you need, so be it. For a variety of reasons I feel very close to you and," he looked at Margaret, "to you also. As if we are indeed cousins."

Oswald held up his hand to show his appreciation and continued.

"When we enter this house we leave the insanity of the outside world and it is as though we are rejuvenated. Whatever the year, the month, the day, or the hour, we find ourselves restored in spirit and by dignity, which seems to be a lost quality of our time."

James smiled.

"You make it sound more like a hideaway from the horrors of the world than a mere dwelling place."

"Indeed it is, James. Indeed it is," Margaret spoke for Oswald. In the flickering light of the candles and the fire, Margaret looked at her husband and then to James she said, "We are unable to appear before those who were close to us before," Margaret paused, "our death."

She looked at James and Kathryn for any reaction but there was none and she continued.

"As Oswald has indicated, we help the sick, aged, and infirm. We take happiness and health to those who need it. I think that you can understand this and I know that we have not made a mistake in extending this invitation to you and asking for your help. There is no one else that we can trust."

James was pleased by Margaret's words. But he turned his eyes to Kathryn who still seemed to be suffering the effects of her journey. As though the realism of what was happening was not acceptable to her mind. He was worried about her and he was impelled to make some display of his feelings.

"My dear Kathryn seems to be taking this rather badly and I am wondering if we can make plans for her recovery?"

With his blue penetrating eyes, Oswald tried to put James at ease by insisting that they have a warm drink.

"James, you are the sole person who can help Kathryn. We can help you as relatives and appreciative friends. She will come around but she must do it of her own accord. She will feel that she has a part of her mind locked in a room from which she cannot release it. It will take a little time, James my cousin."

James felt relieved by Oswald's reassurance.

Margaret busied herself with food and drinks while James and Oswald faced Kathryn across the table and peered curiously at her. The candles and the fire provided the only illumination and threw such a deceptive light that emphasized her tiredness and the strain was obvious from a mere glance at her. She clasped her white hands tightly together and her entire figure and face wore every mark of weakness and physical exhaustion. But her eyes belied her physical condition. Her brain was alive and ready for action.

The change came slowly over Kathryn as they sat in the warm room and the strained look gradually left her face and her eyes once more started to take on the light of awareness. James moved to the other side of the table and sat close, putting his arm around her, knowing the strain that she must have experienced. As Kathryn slowly recovered, James breathed an audible sigh of relief.

Margaret laid food on the table and the aroma of the hot broth that contained meat, vegetables, and barley assailed their nostrils. The mulled wine had stimulated the feeling of warmth in their bodies and the broth would add more energy to their tired bones without causing undue strain in their stomachs.

"I knew that she would come around," she said, "but we must watch her for a while. Have you noticed the look in her eyes?"

Oswald and Margaret, sitting across the table from James and Kathryn, were happy and relieved that Kathryn was looking better. They had not known what effect the change would have on her and now they feared that the decision to bring her back might not have been the best one. Oswald started to speak but James shook his head indicating that silence was the best course of action. As they watched Kathryn he could detect changes that were occurring in her demeanor. Her eyes started to take in the surroundings.

Suddenly she threw out a faint smile and looked at James. He smiled in return and the warm glow returned to Kathryn's face. James wondered for the thousandth time how she could possibly love him and by what earthly miracle she had come to accept him.

They were about to rise from the table when Margaret, at a sign from Oswald, rose from the table and returned with more of the hot mulled wine. As they drank the hot liquid, Kathryn became more aware of her surroundings. She saw James and leaned over to touch him. Oswald smiled. She had made the transition.

Oswald got up and went to the back of the room to return soon with heavy robes and boots for both of them. He carried four heavy woolen black robes, all with hoods.

"My Oswald thinks it better if you don the robes of the Benedictine monks. These will make you less conspicuous than if you continue to wear," Margaret thought for a few seconds, "those robes."

She also convinced them that the sweat suits should also be discarded for the time. Breeches and a jerkin would suffice. She looked at Kathryn and shook her head as if having a serious of second thoughts.

"Kathryn, you will do better to wear this half chemise under your jerkin. It is light and you do not need heavy clothes under the robes. The wool is closely woven and will not only protect you from the cold but will also keep the heat in."

Margaret looked at Oswald and no words were spoken but Oswald knew what was required.

"James, we need to look away from your lady while she dresses herself in the garments that my wife has ordained should be worn."

James could not help smiling when he realized that he was included in the request.

They were allowed to turn around again when Kathryn was finished dressing. James observed to himself that no one turned the other way when he dressed. Oswald caught his look and smiled as if to say "C'est la vie!"

As James folded his clothes to pack them away, he felt something hard in one of the pockets. He took it out. It was a glass bottle containing small white tablets. He looked at it curiously and frowned, unable to understand what it was. He felt that his mind was slipping away from items that he should have recognized.

"Ah," said Oswald noting James's expression, "you have them! These are very good for reducing fevers. Perhaps we should each carry some? One never knows when they may be of some use!"

James looked quizzically at Oswald who only smiled. He nodded his head in agreement with Oswald's suggestion. There were several small packets that had writing on them to explain the intent of the contents. He looked at them, read the writing on the packets, shrugged, and placed them into the voluminous pockets of his robe.

Then the look on Oswald's face became serious. It was time to explain what he needed from James and Kathryn.

"James," he said and despite the low tones, his voice was powerful, "we need to attend to a grave matter."

"Yes, Oswald," James replied between sips of the mulled wine, "let me hear what you have to say."

"Well, it seems to me from what I can determine that there is a plot to bring harm either to King Edward or to someone close to him. I know not who will be the target of this violence nor who will carry out the deed."

"King Edward! You mean," Kathryn suddenly spoke up as her senses returned and she was able to focus on the conversation, "but who would wish to kill the king or someone close to him?" She thought for a while and added, "I am not surprised. Men are such strange creatures when they are after something, especially power."

Oswald looked at Kathryn. James smiled. She was back!

"You have spoken correctly. I believe that it is indeed someone who seeks or lusts after power. I have my ideas who that might be and which family would be willing to sponsor such a deed but these are just ideas and I have no proof."

"What do you propose, Oswald?" It was Kathryn who spoke again.

"I have given you the robes of the Benedictines for a purpose. This city is full of monks of the Benedictine order. Just a short distance away from us is the Priory Church of Christ and Blessed Mary the Virgin."

Oswald looked at them for some reaction but there was none. Perhaps their memories had faded away as a result of the journey back?

"So," he continued, "what better disguise than to wear the robes of the Benedictine order. However, Kathryn, you may be conspicuous because of your size so we will have to pass you off as a novice or as your husband's apprentice. Your stature could easily be taken for that of a young boy who has been accepted by the order. In fact, young novitiates are often apprenticed to physicians. But I recommend," Oswald frowned as he formed the next words, "no, you must not speak. It will be thought that you have taken a vow of silence until your novitiate is over."

Oswald stood as if to emphasize his words.

"There is a murderer among us. There are many murderers out in the street but we must face the fact that one in particular has a vicious task to perform. I am easier in my mind now that you are here. Our goal is to find this man and as we track him I know that we will also be in danger. It is not a happy or peaceful place for you."

He sat down again to face James and Kathryn; Margaret joined him and they sipped on the hot drinks. His instinct told him that danger threatened. Danger that was hidden away in the centers of intelligence and, once it asserted itself, could lead to murder and chaos.

"That is why I have need of you. I am not able to do this myself or with my dear wife," he smiled at Margaret," so I need people that I can trust. Kinsmen. Cousins." Oswald took a deep breath and added, "If you do not see that danger that I foresee, I can return you to your origins."

Kathryn and James were a little uncertain of what he meant by origins. As Oswald had already observed, their memories were not fully functional and so the means by which they had been brought to him and from where were not obvious to them.

"The place from whence you came," Oswald added. James and Kathryn nodded.

"You are under extreme stress, my cousin," James spoke, "but we are here to help you. The cunning of your enemy may exceed normal bounds when the prize is the king or someone close to him."

Kathryn's voice was gentler.

"You said that you needed us. So, we stand with you," she reached over and touched James's hand. "We have a job to do. If we are unable to continue our daily life, so be it. You have no choice, Oswald. We are here, and here we stay."

James was surprised at this outburst. Kathryn was adamant. He had not seen her this way at all before. As if she had taken control. He smiled inwardly. But she was not finished.

"Your enemy," the words burst out of Kathryn, "is our enemy." Oswald smiled his thanks as Kathryn continued, "Do you know the identity of your enemy?"

"I can tell you not, Little One," Oswald once more referred to her small size and hair the color of ripened corn.

"Then," Kathryn added, "I can tell you that we will find him and stop him in his tracks. That I promise."

James looked at Kathryn thinking, "Who is this woman? She speaks like a soldier with a dedicated purpose?"

He turned and looked at her. Their eyes met and he had no doubt of what he saw in them. She looked at him. He could discern from the look in her eyes that a fire burned from within.

"Perhaps this is everything for which we have lived and worked?" she thought to herself.

James was proud of her and it showed in his face. He sensed that there was danger ahead and he wanted no harm to come to Kathryn. He would do whatever he could to protect her. "After all, are we not husband and wife?" he asked himself.

During the next two hours, both Kathryn and James experienced vague snippets of memory from their modern lives but these memories were vague and fading quickly. As Kathryn's memories faded into the dark recesses of her mind, she became very interested in the potential for action that would involve crossing paths with a potential assassin. She examined Oswald's weapons with great care and as she held the different weapons in her hands she felt that she was accustomed to them. She felt particularly comfortable holding a short sword, a falchion, one of two that Oswald owned. They were constructed for close quarter fighting in cramped places and had a short, slightly curved blade with a convex cutting edge and a sharp point that could penetrate armor and chain mail.

She tested the sword for weight and it felt right. The six-inch handle and the twenty-four-inch blade were the right size for her. She looked quizzically at Oswald.

"Kathryn, if you are comfortable with that weapon, you may carry it. For self-defense," Oswald offered not fully understanding the changes in Kathryn's thought patterns, "I have a belt that you can use to secure the sword to your waist." She smiled and nodded in agreement as Oswald continued. "The length of my arm permits me to strap my sword to my lower arm under the sleeves of my surcoat. That would be no good for you, Little One. I suggest that you wear it under your robes with the base of the scabbard secured to your leg. Stop the sword flopping around and reduce the potential of being observed. That way you are always armed." Oswald stopped and frowned as if in deep thought then he asked, "Can you use both hands?"

Kathryn answered immediately.

"Not as well as James but well enough to be useful."

"Excellent," said Oswald. "The Norsemen were ambidextrous and to be able to shift weapons from one hand to the other was an admirable trait. A two-handed swordsman is a formidable enemy!"

Kathryn flipped the sword from one hand to the other several times getting the feel and balance of the weapon. Then she looked directly at Oswald, smiling.

"Oswald, my tall cousin, you have my permission to call me Little One. But please remember that I can still hold my own if needed. This little body has a lot of fight in it!"

Margaret laughed and looked at Kathryn who smiled back, her eyes filled with laughter.

"My cousin, what weapon would you like to have, for protection?"

Oswald added the last two words almost as an afterthought. James looked at the array of choice on the table.

"I prefer the two long-bladed daggers."

Each dagger was about fifteen inches long and sharply pointed.

"I can conceal them about my person but I may also have medical use for them. One never knows . . ." James allowed his response to trail into silence.

Oswald helped James and Kathryn with the belts and scabbard that would allow them to carry their weapons safely.

Oswald looked at Kathryn in wonderment as Margaret helped her strap the weapon to her waist. He still could not fathom the changes that were coming about in her personality. She met his look and he knew that she had a question. He raised his eyebrow in an invitation to ask the question.

"Oswald, dear cousin, you have told us that you do not know the identity of the murderer or assassin, but do you have any information about this fellow? His habits? Where he goes to relax? Anything at all that will help us define his mannerisms and modus operandi?"

Oswald responded, "I can answer that by pointing out that the type of person who undertakes such work and has some success is of above-average intelligence. He may even be educated, but often has an ego that makes him believe that he cannot be caught. That is where he makes his mistake."

Kathryn and James looked at Oswald and admitted that there was some fact behind what Oswald was saying.

"Let us assume," he continued, "that to be the case. There are also often associates that the assassin uses in various ways. Many of them are sacrificial lambs that are used to cause a diversion or a series of diversion in which they die. They do not sign on to die but are left by the assassin in some form of trap while he completes his work."

"But," asked Kathryn, "doesn't that make the assassin vulnerable since one of his associates may talk. If they visit taverns . . ."

Oswald broke into Kathryn's thought.

"No, my dear little one. He will keep them all under tight rein and not allow any to wander until the task is done. He believes in complete control and has full authority over the members of his group. Any of his associates that are allowed to go out and about will have been told a story that is far from the truth. If caught, they give out the wrong information under hot irons for they know no other story."

"I fear," Margaret added, "that we must not confuse the deceptive action from the true action. Otherwise we will fail. But I prefer not to acknowledge the chance of failure."

She thought for a moment as she brought all of her thoughts together in a coherent form. Sensing what she was doing, her three listeners remained silent. And then she continued.

"The true assassin, though glutting himself with power and ego, requires a wider and wider latitude of task to stir his senses. In fact, one might say that he takes on greater risks to give himself that thrill. But the very nature of the assassin's task is simplicity. The assassins of Caesar were such men. They carried out their task in broad daylight. And they would have successes had it not been for Marcus Antonius wanting to right their wrong and also for the ambition of Octavius."

"So," Kathryn continued Margaret's thoughts, "by alternating between monk and searcher we may be able to maintain a delicate balance that will allow us to overcome the possible violent actions of this man. In that manner, we can use our most precious quality, the element of surprise. After all, who would suspect three Benedictines," Kathryn looked at Margaret, "four?" Kathryn questioned but Margaret shook her head negatively, "three Benedictines," continued Kathryn, "of trailing an assassin?"

"May I ask," said James, "why you regard this man as capable of being found and assailable? Surely he must have deep motives and planned his moves carefully? Have we not heard that from Oswald that he is a very dangerous person? That his motives may be personal as well as professional? What about such mundane reasons as he may not wish to be found. In a city like this," James gestured toward the door and beyond, "where there are thousands of people, how can we hope to find him."

"James my dearest," Kathryn walked over to him and in a show of affection that surprised Oswald and Margaret, took a gentle hold of his head and kissed him fully on the lips, "because of his ego. He probably believes that, after so many successes, he cannot be caught. He will be careful but he can also slip. Then we will have him!"

Kathryn pronounced the last few words with so much conviction that she surprised everyone.

James smiled but shook his head.

"If and when we meet this man," he said, "we, possibly except Oswald, will understand at once that he is not the man to take on under his terms. As a matter of fact, my guess is that he is well versed in the art of weaponry and," James hesitated then added, "what say you, Oswald?"

"I believe," Oswald stated, "that he is an amazing man and, although I hesitate to use superlatives, he may, to my way of thinking, represent a man at the apex of his career, if we can call assassination a career!"

"Then," offered Kathryn, "we will topple him from that apex!"

Margaret smiled at Kathryn's statement. Oswald and James looked at Kathryn. Their eyes met and they both showed the signs of wonderment at the change that had overcome Kathryn in the past two hours. Her revival was nothing short of amazing. But her personality seemed to have undergone a significant change. She had adapted to the weapons and was now talking openly in a manner that to James, recalling items from the back of his mind, was totally out of character.

Oswald saw the look on James's face and smiled as he mouthed the words "I told you so!"

*   *   *

CHAPTER 29

L ate in the evening of the next day, Kathryn, James, and Oswald, clad in their Benedictine robes, were seated opposite two men on the floor of a plain small room in a simple house that has been built, with many other similar houses, in a narrow street that passed close by the north gate of the walled enclosure of the castle and the priory.

One of the men, a monk, sat on the coarse wool blanket that was his bed by night and smelled of dust and human odors. His tonsured head had lost its once thick crop of side hair at about the same time as his girth had added an accumulation of poundage. Beside him lay the bowl from which he had eaten his lunch of stale bread and a pungent vegetable soup.

His mind had wandered back to the good old times of ten years or more ago when he had continued to enjoy the pleasures of the ladies in the local parish that was situated to the north of the monastery. As it had been in every monastery that he had been assigned. But he had made one mistake. He had been caught. His dismissal from the monastery and the parish had taken time. His actions had to be debated by his brothers and by the various powers that were in the monastery. In fact, he had continued his ways until the villagers from one of the fishing villages on the coast had threatened him with death. A quick resolution was reached and here he was. Lonely. He was no longer a monk, although he continued to wear the habit as he tried to ekee out a living by gathering and selling information.

The other man, a Frenchman whose taste ran not much further than boiled onions, which was evident from his breath, had been unable to eat the stale bread and soup. Now, with his stomach rumbling and being able to smell the soup on the old monk's breath, he wished that he had accepted his invitation to eat.

The months since the old monk had last had a commission or some assigned activity that would give him an income that allowed him to live in the style that he preferred had been difficult. He was accustomed to wrestling with rewarding activity and his brain accepted weighty problems with relish. The more complex the activity or the problem to be resolved, the bigger the challenge and the better that he felt. Although, he had an uneasy feeling about his current activity.

He had seen death many times since he had left the monastery. He had always escaped death, but then it intruded so close and with suddenness, the effect on him was indelible. And now he wondered if the activities that he had accepted might not bring to him the finality of death.

The Frenchman was a testimony to many men like him. His skin was sallow and dark, either from the weather or from dirt or perhaps from both. His long hair that acted as a haven for lice was sleek and black, which, with his narrow face, gave him an animal-like appearance. And he was homeless. Available for hire to do any kind of work. But for the most part it would be illegal work.

It was obvious that he subscribed to a popular notion that there are three times in a man's life when he should wash and these start with the first wash at the time that he is born. The second wash happens when he is married, and third wash is when he dies and he is being prepared for the grave. Many men, such as the Frenchman, did not receive the honor of burial. Bodies were hurled into a river, a midden pit, or left by the roadside and soon gave sustenance to the carrion that abounded and thrived on human remains. And finally, there is also a fourth time when a man should wash and that is when he is knighted. The likelihood of the Frenchman being knighted was very slim, even non-existent!

He was also irritable. And he was tired of picking the bedbugs out of his clothes after a miserable night of being jostled by filthy strangers in the sagging beds of a series of wretched inns and houses. As a result, he was not in a good mood for this meeting. In fact, he wondered why he was meeting with an old monk and three Benedictines? At the worst, he looked them over thoughtfully, he could kill them and steal anything of value.

The Frenchman's day had been a day of mixed pleasures. There had been two events that he had watched. The first involved a thief who had been nailed by his ear to a cartwheel. The soldiers had given him a knife, but he had not had the nerve to cut himself free and the Frenchman had watched him squirming under the taunts of the onlookers and listened to his squeals for an hour.

Then he had watched a murderer dragged on a hurdle to the gallows whilst the executioner walked alongside poking him in various parts of his body with a hot iron. The murderer was delivered to the scaffold to be hanged, drawn, whilst still conscious of what was going on about him, and quartered. He had finished his life with a long anguished scream for mercy. Mercy was not forthcoming. The Frenchman was pleased at this event.

In spite of what the Frenchman thought about the old monk, he did appreciate that while he was no longer a man of the cloth, he was very successful at what he did. He was a listener and gatherer of information from a variety of sources that he put together to form a coherent story. He was probably the most successful person who could do this. The stories and rumors that abounded in England, one of the most powerful kingdoms in Western Europe, were at the tip of the monk's tongue. He had the ability to think clearly, at a time when many of his colleagues in the cloth imagined that they were chosen to eat, drink, and control the populace by the power of faith and the strength of voice. But the monk knew that he needed help.

The three strangers—whose names unknown to him were Oswald, James, and Kathryn—sat before him showed no emotion. The hooded robes of the Benedictine order hid the determined look in their eyes.

The three of them had approached the monk and the big one, Oswald, had expressed the desire for a meeting. After he had told the monk the subject of the meeting, the monk had sought out the Frenchman and drawn him into this gathering. The Frenchman was an assassin and the monk had approached him as the person who would know what was about to take place. And it was momentous!

From the pieces and snippets of information that the monk had recently gathered, he knew about the unexplained deaths of a dozen prominent people in several English and French cities. He had not dismissed this information lightly and the trail had led to Durham. Now he sought to make capital of it.

The monk had thought about this and he had reasoned that there were usurpers afoot who wished to see Edward and his son, John of Lancaster, cast forever into the realms of forgotten history. Usurpers who saw gain for themselves and who would follow their chosen successor to

Edward until the time came to place themselves in power. The monk knew that he had to do the right thing and stand up for what he believed.

The enemies of King Edward and his son, John of Lancaster, would not listen to reason. They were both to be killed at the most propitious moment. The Frenchman did not have the skills to perform the act of assassination, but he had agreed to be an instrument bringing together those who were more capable then he was.

And so, here they were. The Frenchman did not know the three strangers and it turned out that the monk knew very little about them. There was the tall muscular one who walked with an air of authority that could not be covered by his monk's habit. The other two, one of medium stature, James, and the shorter one, Kathryn, were unknown to the monk and it was unlikely that he would ever know their names. The Frenchman fingered his long assassin's dagger under his robes. He had a feeling that he needed caution if this was to turn out right for him.

The monk, at last, opened his dry lips. The Frenchman and the three strangers leaned closer fearing to miss a word.

"The king," said the monk, "must not be harmed in any way nor must his Lordship of Lancaster. To do so would turn the country into a civil war that would outdo in terror and killing in those times when Matilda and Stephen fought over two hundred years ago."

He referred to the years between 1135 and 1153 that finally resulted in a truce in which Stephen assumed the throne but could not start a dynasty. After Stephen's death, the throne was occupied, as agreed, by Matilda's son Henry who became Henry II, King of England and started the Plantagenet Dynasty.

The Frenchman did not catch the last few slurred words and it took him a few moments to understand what the monk had said and the reason for the almost incomprehensible words. He handed a container of water to the monk who nodded his head in thanks and sipped the liquid to moisten his cracked lips.

"Edward must live," the monk said, "and so must John of Lancaster."

The Frenchman looked at the three strangers, seeing nothing because of the hoods that covered their eyes and most of their faces. The little one made him think. Was it really a man? The form under the robe could not be defined but there was something about the style of walking. And if it was a woman, what courage! The Frenchman was starting to enjoy himself. If the little one was a woman or boy, did he really care?

Oswald interrupted the Frenchman's thoughts as he spoke in a loud tone that bespoke of his ability to command. And he spoke French in a dialect that the Frenchman could understand.

"Only one question, perhaps two. And I require honest answers."

The Frenchman nodded his head in agreement. But he knew that honesty might not be the best policy and cause him harm.

"Who hired you for this work? And when do you meet him again?"

Oswald did not show any emotion. James raised his head and fixed the Frenchman in his glare as if to warn him about the consequences of being dishonest. The Frenchman swallowed with some difficulty as he realized that he no longer had command of this situation. He seemed to lose command as soon as Oswald had spoken. He looked at Kathryn. She had also raised her head and the hood of her robe had shifted and he could see cold blue eyes that showed no emotion whatsoever. They showed coldness that the Frenchman could not interpret in any way other than unfriendly.

"I know not. All negotiations were done through others that forbade me from knowing my sponsor. All I know is that the intermediary is not my sponsor. He is of France with an English tone about his voice, as though he has lived in England for some time. I was given subsistence money, but my contract is that I be paid in full after I have accomplished my task."

Oswald smiled. He had the information that he needed and it was apparent that the Frenchman knew little else.

"Now," Oswald asked himself, "what should I do with this piece of human flotsam?"

The sound of thunder and the dark sky signaled an approaching storm. The rooftops of the houses formed nondescript and haphazard lines against the sky. By morning, the roads in the city would once more be muddy bogs.

* * *

Unknown to Oswald, James, Kathryn, and the monk, four men hid in the darkness just outside the door to the midden. They had been witnesses to the conversation and awaited the Frenchman's word. These were men who looked as equally disgusting and dirty as the Frenchman, their ersatz leader. Their ragged clothes, scarred and pockmarked faces, and missing teeth were a testimony to their lives. They were not men who were devoted to dignity! Their task was to kill and they had no intention of being killed. They knew not the reason for their goal, nor were they concerned; kill and be paid was the simple creed that they followed. They had not been told any reasons for the kill and as they crouched in the darkness, holding their weapons in their hands, they awaited the signal from the Frenchman. This was the perfect setting for an ambush.

Leaning against the side of the house, braced by one arm, the man closest to the door attempted to listen to the conversation, awaiting the word that would command them to jump into action. It would be swift and bloody. What resistance could three Benedictines and an old degenerate former monk offer? So the old one had played with women, little boys, and little girls? He deserved to die. The others? Why not? He looked back at his companions, watching and waiting.

He could feel the tension in his own body. It would be soon, very soon. He felt no sense of right or wrong. It was a job that had to be done.

*   *   *

Thinking that he was safe with the knowledge that his companions were sufficient to the task of killing his audience, the Frenchman relaxed. He had not given anything away in his conversation with the monks. "And," he thought, "what use will the information be to them? They will die in a very short time."

He knew that his companions were poised for his word and the resulting actions would preserve his life. He looked at Oswald knowing that this one was not what he seemed to be. Perhaps he was a soldier whose presence was necessary to preserve the safety of the other two Benedictines. The Frenchman smiled. Perhaps he would spare one of the monks to satisfy his curiosity about the gender of that one. Perhaps there was sport to be had before he returned to report the night's work?

The Frenchman laughed out loud at his good fortune. He felt safe in what he had planned.

The wind had strengthened and whistled through the gaps in the wooden boards that made up the door and made it difficult for the assassins to hear the signal. Mistaking the Frenchman's laughter for the signal, they sprung into the room prematurely.

*   *   *

The creaking of the wooden door and the wooden panels that formed the wall caught Oswald's ears. The sounds seemed to be magnified by the emptiness of the room that occupied the whole of the ground floor of the house. These sounds were not natural and could not be caused by the wind and rain. His keen senses told him that danger was near.

Oswald's shout "To arms, a trap!" brought an awareness to Kathryn and James. They were about to fight for their lives. Oswald and James quickly disrobed, weapons drawn, feet apart, and ready. James held a long sharp dagger in each hand. Oswald held a shorter sword, not his usual long sword, but it was to his advantage; the long sword would have been cumbersome in the enclosed space of the room. Oswald and James formed a two-man wall between the Frenchman, his intruders, and Kathryn.

The old monk was not surprised at such a turn of events but he was now worried about his own safety. Being a man who would not participate in such dangerous activities, he scampered into a dark corner. The Frenchman noticed the old monk's withdrawal and nodded thinking, "I will attend to you later, monk." The old monk mistook the meaning to conclude that he would be safe and allowed to leave after this deed was done.

Kathryn exhaled a brief grasp. Although the thought of treachery had crossed her mind she had hoped that it would not come to this. She quickly untied the drawstrings of her robe and allowed it to fall to the floor.

The guttural throaty sounds from the Frenchman, his cutthroats, and the old monk were audible. There in the midst stood a blonde woman, the likes of which they had never seen before. They took in the sight of the woman who now stood before them. She was of short stature, feminine, clean, wearing nothing but breeches and a chemise shirt, muscular, and with a falchion in her right hand. The blade glistened in the dim candlelight.

She shouldered her way into line with James and Oswald, never taking her eyes off the ruffians who stood before them.

"Well," the Frenchman spoke in his native language, "this is interesting. Who will die first? And you," he looked at Kathryn, "I have plans for you. You will die slowly and at my pleasure."

Kathryn, understanding the words that he had spoken, stared back at him. Unblinking. Knowing as if by instinct what must be done.

"Come," she said, "prepare to meet your fate."

Before Oswald or James could react, she darted forward swinging the falchion. The curved blade caught the Frenchman in the throat. The sound of metal cutting through flesh and tissue filled the room.

The strike was so swift and unexpected that it took the Frenchman by surprise. He attempted to smile but he realized too late that his throat had been cut as the life-giving blood escaped on to his chest. His smile was lost in the grimace of death as he dropped his sword and attempted to stem the flow of blood by holding his hands to his throat. But it was all to no avail. As she stepped back, he fell to his knees, the surprised look of death on his face.

"*Couchon!*"

"Pig!" she exclaimed, "that is the closet that you will ever get to me."

His head lolled forward onto this chest and he fell face down on to the floor. And so the Frenchman died.

Seeing their leader fall, the four intruders faltered but Oswald and James using the moment of uncertainly that Kathryn had created stepped forward.

"Put down your blades!" Oswald commanded but he could see that his words were futile. He glanced at James who stood ready by his right side. Kathryn, stepping back from her action stood on his left side.

They stepped forward, filled with determination. This was their opportunity for justice. To allow the intruders to escape would be foolish and it was unthinkable for the intruders to turn and run. Word would soon spread around the city that two men and a woman had bested them in a fight. To a man, the assassins knew that this was unthinkable.

The men started to inch toward them. With a quick movement of his arm, Oswald stepped forward and opened up the chest of the nearest intruder. The man looked at Oswald with wide eyes, hands clutching his chest. The dark red blood welled between his unsuccessful fingers as he crumpled to the floor.

James moved his gaze back to the three men who remained. They had backed up to the wall and escape was impossible.

"Gentlemen, what do you propose to do?" James spoke first in English and seeing no recognition followed up in French. There was recognition of his words but no response. The evil in their eyes told James that there would be no mercy if these three were allowed the upper hand.

"By the way that you looked at my wife," he continued, "I sense that you had thoughts about the outcome. So what should we do? Do you fear to fight two monks and a woman?"

Their lips turned into snarls at the taunt. James, expecting Oswald to move with him, was surprised when Kathryn appeared at his side. He smiled as the three men raised their blades. The intruders attempted to step forward but James and Kathryn shifted their stances to meet the attack. Suddenly, James moved forward and, with mesmerizing movement of his two daggers, dispatched the closest man to him.

"That should even the numbers a little, my cousin," Oswald's voice echoed in the room as he smiled. "Call if you need me!" He stood back two paces to make sure that all went well.

Kathryn and James felt that they were being tested and they could feel their senses grow ready and alive.

One man moved to Kathryn. He was so close that she could smell his foul breath. He pushed her backward and his strike was so fast and so strong that all she felt was a ringing pain that shot up her arm as his blade struck the falchion and almost knocked it from her hand. She gasped but held her ground. He attempted to move closer to bring his body nearer to hers. For a moment Kathryn appeared to falter, seeing his eyes burning with hatred, and then feeling the strength return to her arm she took the universal action of protection that is available to all women. She raised her knee, driving it into his groin. She hit him hard and as the breath left his lungs, he staggered backward attempting to move away but, again, her falchion again opened up a man's throat.

He fell to his knees, watching his blood spill to the earthen floor, the pain in his groin forgotten.

Seeing Kathryn handle the situation amazingly well, James moved toward the other man who glanced fearfully around the room. His eyes rested on the daggers that James held in his hands. He felt a deep longing to get out of this place.

He cried out suddenly, springing forward toward James. A powerful kick from James slammed the man backward into the wall. He attempted to recover his stance but it was too late. The dagger entered his body and sliced into his heart.

"You will never, ever," James looked into the man's eyes, "insult a lady again."

All of James's rage poured into the thrust. And then he stopped just as abruptly, leaning up against the wall as cold sweat trickled down his face.

The man slid down the wall and came to rest on the floor. The look of surprise had never left his face.

Oswald cleaned his blade on the Frenchman's robe. He spoke as he inspected the blade, determining that he would clean the weapon thoroughly later. And then he turned to the monk who still cowered in the corner wondering if death was to be his visitor.

"If any word of this gets out, monk, you may be having a conversation with your maker sooner than you had planned."

The monk nodded in agreement, showing that he understood the threat and that he would obey. He had heard of this one who thought nothing of showing a disloyal subject the road to eternal rest. Then Kathryn spoke and for the first time the monk heard the soft delicate tones of her voice. She spoke in speech patterns that he was unable to identify.

"My dear cousin, that was quick. I do admit that I suspected foul play but was not prepared for it when it came."

Oswald looked directly at Kathryn and James.

"Yes," he said, "you acquitted yourselves well. I am sure that within the hour others would have known of this meeting. We could not afford such a risk and the opportunity presented itself when the henchmen burst through the door."

James, who had remained silent and unemotional through this exchange, put his hand onto Kathryn's arm.

"I too suspected treachery."

She turned to look at James and the old monk thought that he could see the vestige of a smile on her face. Then she looked at Oswald.

"The Frenchman did not say anything about his employers. So where do we go from here?" Kathryn asked.

The old monk saw his opportunity. He needed to ingratiate himself with these three lest he also fall foul of them.

"There is a group that I have heard who wish harm to the king and Lord John."

There was quiet respect and resolve in his voice, as he looked at the remains of the assailants, blood oozing from their bodies as they lay quite still and quite dead on the floor.

"I may have the answer for you in a day or so."

The monk looked at Oswald, not knowing his name but now realizing the seriousness of the matter at hand.

"Do I have your permission, sire?"

Oswald looked at the monk through his clear blue eyes cut off the question by fixing him with a stare that would have stopped a charger in full gallop.

"Do not address me in that manner."

The monk nodded knowing that he had looked into the cold eyes of a trained soldier and one who was probably very good at his job, as he had witnessed in the past minutes. Oswald continued.

"You have my permission. But . . ."

The monk saw the threat and spoke quickly.

"I have no wish to pass along the same road as these men," he looked once more at the bodies, "at least not for a few years," he looked skyward, "God willing."

"It is not God who you must fear. He has nothing to do with whether you live or die. It is I and my cousins," he looked at James and Kathryn, "who will make that decision. And God will have nothing to do with you by the time that we are finished with you."

The old monk saw his life pass before his eyes and he could only nod his head to show that he understood.

"Yes, go your way."

Oswald held up his hand to forestall the question that he knew was on the tip of the monk's tongue.

"You will be contacted and informed of the meeting place. And you will be alone. Bring friends and you die with them."

Again, the old monk nodded his agreement. Oswald lifted a hand to forestall any further conversation from the monk.

"Do as you are told and all will be well. You may even be rewarded on this earth as well as in heaven. But . . ."

Oswald did not complete his sentence. The monk needed no further explanation of the consequences of any covert actions.

"There can be no betrayal." Oswald continued. "Make sure that your sympathies lie with the king and with the Lord of Lancaster."

The monk gave him a look that was filled with pride but fear of this man lurked in his mind.

"I love the king and our Lord of Lancaster as much as you do. You have nothing to fear from me."

His three listeners nodded their heads as he continued.

"I will not allow these pretenders and assassins to be successful. They hate their country, their king, and their lords. I will do all that I can to help you to make sure that they are doomed."

*   *   *

The old monk watched as they all arose and walked out of the room, out of the house, and into the blackness of the night. He was not even tempted to follow. He knew that the consequences could be final.

"It is possible," he thought to himself "that they may just be able to do it. They might just be able to keep the king and his son, the Lord of Lancaster, from the hands and blades of the assassins."

He started to sweat, realizing what he had just been through. He looked at the Frenchman's body.

"Yes, my friend, this is what happens when you get in above your head. Farewell, my friend," he made the sign of the cross over the body, "I have much work to do. And why should I worry about what happens to your earthly bones?"

*   *   *

The old monk shuffled out of the house and into the street. There was a light rain and he pulled the cowl over his head to protect himself. He could not see the three figures in the shadows as they watched him depart. He was not to be trusted. At least not for the moment.

As the old monk walked thought the muddy streets, he allowed the events of the night to tumble through his mind. The Frenchman had surprised him by coming alone. Whether he directed affairs from behind the scenes or whether he was not supposed to be present, the monk did not know. Whichever it was, the Frenchman had paid for his treachery with his life. As had his companions. Their deaths, bad news for him but good news for others, was a fair warning to him.

The monk was pensive. The big Benedictine had even suggested that his silence was a matter of life and death. The monk did not like what he heard and was determined to be on his best behavior.

And this was not the behavior that one would expect of a member of the Benedictine order.

*   *   *

As the old monk continued his journey through the dark streets to his humble resting place, Oswald, James, and Kathryn were once more sipping hot herbal tea that Margaret had prepared for them to keep away the chills from the dampness that the latest rain had brought upon them.

"No, James," Oswald said as they all focused their thoughts once more on the present situation, "by this action we have made this decision. We are, as you might say, caught in the web of treason and intrigue. We are no longer free to do as we wish. We do need to be cautious. As yet, we are uncertain of the involvement of others who might be in high places. We do know from the words of the late, and unlamented, Frenchman that one of them was English."

James attempted to speak but Oswald held up his hand and would not allow James to voice an opinion and he continued.

"If, as you suggest, my dear James, we report this to whoever we think is the correct person, we may be leading ourselves into a trap. I cannot talk to those that I knew," he paused before adding, "before. And if you try you will certainly be seen as a stranger and perhaps be considered as a part of the plot. Then how will I explain your demise to," Oswald looked at Kathryn, "your dear wife?"

James nodded to Kathryn and Oswald to show that he saw the logic of this reasoning.

"I think," suggested Oswald, "that we should gather our thoughts about next steps and where we go from here."

"Good idea, Cousin," Kathryn and James chorused before James continued, "what do you have in mind?

"Let us sit and ponder this while we prepare food and during supper we can all speak our ideas out loud."

Margaret raised herself from the table and went to the kitchen where a cauldron of hot vegetable broth simmered on the stove. Freshly made oatmeal cakes stood on a platter close by. Much to her and Kathryn's surprise, Oswald and James offered to serve the meal to be accompanied by a hot fragrant tea. When all was done, they carried the food and tea to the table and joined the two ladies.

Oswald started the conversation.

"This world contains many treacherous hills and valleys where men plot and plan. What better way to secure your position than with one of the most successful plotters. Already, a group may have formed that is close to the king and understands the workings of the court. This would allow the plotters to know the movements of all members of the royal family. Not a good thing."

"So," James broke into Oswald's thoughts, "there was obviously everything to be gained and nothing to be lost by retaining our anonymity. Perhaps after testing the attitude of various persons to whom the old monk can find for us, we should have a better idea of the cast of characters. Thus far, it seems that the main character has not made an appearance."

Kathryn leaned over the table to pick up a piece of the soft white bread from the plate and as she did she held it in her hand for the briefest moment of time. Then she put her thoughts into words.

"Tonight was the first meeting of its kind," she looked questioningly at Oswald who nodded in agreement before she continued and was surprised to sense that her heart was pounding with expectation.

"So, we offer bread, bait that is, to draw out the assassin. Even perhaps draw out those who sponsor this man," she finished her statement by looking at Margaret who sat next to her. The women smiled at each other.

Across the table, Oswald and James beamed with delight. They also felt the elation pounding in their chests at the thought of laying a trap.

"That is it!" Margaret's voice startled his three listeners such that at least two almost leaped from their seats. "The triumph of all times!" She continued. "And faced by the right bait, the assassin would not be able to resist. In fact, he would not dare resist. He would be concerned that he might miss something and he would fail to achieve his goal."

"How can we be sure of that?" James asked.

"How? Because of his ego, my dear love," Kathryn placed her hand onto James's hand. "He could not afford the embarrassment. Add to that the air of omnipotence and invincibility that he may have," she looked at Oswald acknowledging his analysis of the man's temperament.

They looked round the table at each other. Smiles of anticipation on four faces filled the room.

"That is the way it will be done," Oswald announced. "Thanks to your thoughts, Cousin," he looked at Kathryn, "we can have the element of surprise, providing that our friend, the old monk, values his life."

"Or," said Margaret, "provided he fears us more than he fears the assassin!"

James inclined his head slightly to the side.

"We must follow up and determine the number of persons involved in the actual deed." He looked at Oswald, "I am not sure how we can do that."

"It will take time, James. We will have to see what evolves over the next few days. The old monk may, within limitations, be of some help. If he survives."

Oswald made a gesture with his arm outstretched showing that no one could guarantee the old monk's behavior or his loyalties.

"But again," James said, "what if, as has already been said, we make the old monk fear us more than he fears the assassin? That very portly old man would certainly take sides very quickly, if he has not already made his choice?"

"I think that he has come to that point," Kathryn observed. "The death of the Frenchman and his cronies may have been the first killing that he has actually witnessed for some time. Perhaps even for an entire decade more likely. In fact, on recollection, I do not think he's witnessed many killings. Cast your minds back and see if you," Kathryn looked at James and then at Oswald, "can recall the expression on the monk's face when we were done. I watched him carefully and I would be surprised if he had not emptied his innards at the sudden shock!"

"Then you have it," announced Margaret, "we have our first plan of action. I propose that we discuss it over fresh tea and then we rest with these thoughts."

The words flowed as they talked over the next actions. No one monopolized the table. There was no monologue. Tea was sipped. The fire offered warmth to the room. Their eyes glittered in the flickering light of the candles. Oswald with his long sleek hair, the color of ripened corn that was swept back from his smooth forehead, smiled at Margaret who smiled back, as if at peace. James and Kathryn also exchanged smiles as if they were coming to terms with their present situation and what they had to accomplish.

*   *   *

CHAPTER 30

J ames and Kathryn spent the next day resting and allowing their bodies to become even more acclimatized to their new surroundings. As day turned into night, there had been no word or sign from the monk. Kathryn had retired to rest and was comfortably asleep when James's voice jerked her out of peaceful slumber.

"My dear," she could feel his hand gently squeezing her arm, "we need to rise. It seems that the old monk is meeting with someone in a tavern nearby."

Kathryn rose and shook the sleep from her eyes. She splashed cold water onto her face from a nearby dish and gave herself the awakening that she needed. The room was warm. She looked around.

"Where are Oswald and Margaret?"

"They had to go out," responded James, "and will be back shortly. We need to ready ourselves before they return."

As they sat in front of the fire that James had rejuvenated in the hearth, the door opened quietly and James and Kathryn turned their eyes to Oswald and Margaret. Oswald tried hard to put aside the excitement that showed on his face. James could not resist the question.

"Oswald, what has happened?"

"We were able to learn more. I did wonder," Oswald said, "what the old monk would be doing as this day drew to a close so we followed him from his dwelling to the tavern. It looked to us as if he was waiting for someone. We felt that we needed to watch him very closely."

"And so," Margaret smiled as she spoke, "I have taken care of things. One of the tavern maids was very open to my suggestion that she do something for us. Money had to change hands, of course, but she will watch what happens and report anything that she hears to us."

Kathryn smiled so broadly and her face glowed in the candlelight.

"But what kind of woman . . . ?" James was trying to ask when Kathryn dug her knuckles into his ribs, "Oh, I see." He had no further questions.

Margaret smiled at the interaction between Kathryn and James and then she continued.

"We cannot take on the world, if that is the way it has to be, by not having the information that we need. But we can use cunning and deception. This woman will do her job because there was the promise of further work if she remains loyal to us. She has no other means of support and must feed her children. So, if she discovers a secret, she will share it with us. She considers it just a matter of good business."

"Then in the light of all this," James persisted, "and considering all the conventions that may be imposed on this woman, she will do what it takes to get the information that we require?"

"That, my dear cousin," Oswald smiled as he answered James, "is precisely what we have done."

Their ears detected the sound of a light tapping on the door. As if by magic, four hands instinctively reached for weapons.

Oswald placed his forefinger over his lips to indicate silence and went to the door and looked though a small peephole that he had made. He opened the door and stepped outside into the darkness. Moments later he returned.

"That was the tavern maid. There is action afoot. Prepare yourselves with weapons. We leave now."

*   *   *

The old monk's understanding of the dialect of the North was fractured and often lacking many words and phrases. The guttural tones were foreign to his ears. But he had a quick ear for hidden meanings. That was why he was allowed to move freely in the dark foreboding alleyways and taverns of the city and that was also why he was still alive. Now he was alone and at the mercy of the big blond soldier, and he was a soldier who spoke the Northern dialect and the English language of the south, as well as French and Latin. The monk instinctively knew that he was no ordinary soldier and that he, Baldur of Winchester, had better produce reliable information or he would join the Frenchman and his cutthroat associates in meeting his maker. And bidding the Lord good day would be much sooner than the old monk had planned.

As he sat in the dark corner of the tavern, caressing the warm mug that contained the hot mulled drink, his thoughts went back to the good times. This past day had not been one of life's highlights for him as a monk. He had searched high and low for a contact and only late in the afternoon had contact been made with those he believed were involved in the conspiracy even more so than the Frenchman who had died twenty-four hours previously.

The tavern was filled with the usual riffraff of the city. The man sitting at the next table was ready for his ale. He was fidgety and the monk wondered if he was his contact but this was not so. The tavern maid came over and sat next to the man. He smiled and seemed to make himself comfortable.

A giant of a man lolled across the bar. His jutting jaw and apelike posture suggested that he would not take kindly to anyone who gave him offense, and that would not take much of an effort. His eyes flickered over the monk but passed on. The monk raised his head toward the ceiling and muttered a quiet "thank you" to an unseen benefactor.

He began to ponder on past memories. He had the satisfaction of knowing that he had several living illegitimate sons and daughters in a number of parishes throughout England. But what did it matter if they did not know? To all intents and purposes his lineage terminated. And now he was too old. Well, perhaps not too old, but what kind of woman could he attract?

He thought of the woman who had killed the Frenchman. There had been something that he did not quite understand. He had wondered about her from the beginning. Her mannerisms were not what he had expected. And she was a competent killer. He had looked into her light blue eyes and what he had seen there had made him shiver. The coldness of her eyes. She looked even more determined than the big blond man, until she spoke to her two colleagues and then there was softness toward both in her speech, especially to the quiet one that would act when needed but preferred to hold his own counsel.

The monk's thoughts about the Benedictines terminated as he inclined his head in an attempt to hear any meaningful conversation above the noise of the tavern crowd. He was startled as he felt a presence behind him.

"So, priest. You have need of me!"

It was a statement and not a question. The monk recognized the voice and he knew the speaker. He hesitated, aware of its presumption, aware too that his answer better have a ring of honesty or the result might be pain. The old monk smiled as he turned to look at the man who had joined him at the table.

"Ah, Gervais, who but you could appear like that? Unseen and silent?"

"No one!"

"Gervais, my friend, I am not a priest," the monk started to respond to Gervais's first words, "I am only a lowly monk—" but he was interrupted.

"That has been excommunicated and has nowhere to go." Gervais looked at the monk through eyes as black as the halls of hades! "You can only go further down. But let us speak freely. And I am not your friend but you are what I chose to call you."

The monk knew that his life was in the balance so he carefully chose his answer and deciding that discretion and valor were not related, he chose the former.

"As you wish, Gervais."

"Have you ordered a pitcher of ale in advance?" Gervais asked.

"No," said the monk, and his face took on the look of one who is in a permanent state of financial embarrassment.

"Then let us do so now," commanded Gervais. "You seem to have something to tell me and listening to you can be thirsty work."

Gervais smiled at his own touch of humor. The monk was not amused but he could feel the undercurrent of fear as his legs started to tremble. He found the energy to wave to the tavern maid, got her attention, and she bounced jauntily over to the table. Her movements seemed to offer so much, to the delight of monk's companion.

"Yes, Father?" she asked.

She leaned a hand on the table as she attempted to speak a clearer and understandable form of English knowing that the monk was not fluent in the dialect.

"What can . . . ?"

She started to ask the question but her words were cut short as she felt the hand of the monk's companion on hers. She attempted to withdraw her hand but it was in a vicelike grip. He smelled even stronger than her other patrons.

"Bring us a pitcher of ale then do not bother us," Gervais nodded in the direction of the monk, "unless you see me looking for you."

"But before you go, tell me," he asked leeringly, "what else are you serving this evening?"

The woman tried to hide her contempt for the man. "There is bread and cheese and," she thought for a moment, "and a hot broth."

Gervais's face fell into lines of impatience. "That is not what I meant," he said in an emotionless voice that frightened the woman.

He looked at her through dark calculating eyes that gave no clue as to his ulterior motives. His pockmarked skin, the well-formed lips, a hard face that showed no emotion, and the brown hair that peaked from under his woolen cap marked him as one to be feared. She retrieved her hand and hurried to the bar. Soon she returned with the pitcher and two tankards, filled the tankards, and set them down on the table.

Gervais gave her a coin that more than paid for the ale. She dared not look into his face but could not avoid it since he decided to raise her head by placing his grimy hand under her chin. She could do nothing else but look directly at him and she saw a face of evil.

She had seen many faces in her life but this one filled her with fear and she felt a sudden chill down her spine, as if she had been touched by the devil. She could not speak. The words were trapped in her throat. She nodded to show that she understood. He allowed her to move away.

"The sooner I am finished with these two," she thought, "the better," as she left to see to their needs.

Neither of them observed her departure from the tavern nor did they notice her re-entry into the tavern minutes later. She had a promise to keep that she had made to a woman who had approached her earlier.

Gervais waited for the monk to speak. The monk shifted uneasily on the bench as he attempted to find the words that were suitable to the occasion. Gervais, another assassin, but from Flanders rather than Paris, suspected something. The monk knew better than to signal the need for a meeting unless it was a matter of life or death. And he also knew that if he called for a meeting it had better be with good reason.

Gervais could smell the fear. He knew that the monk was a very successful gatherer of information. Every city that he had visited became a new source of knowledge for the old monk. He was useful to Gervais because the information gave him the power that he needed for his quest. Knowledge was the cutting edge of his profession, if assassination could be called a profession. He had been trained well in his youth. He armed himself with the weapons of silence. The dagger, the garrote, and poison. His profession did not allow him to fight with a sword in the open. Such action was taken only under extreme situations where his own life was in danger.

In the name of power, which was the personal cause of everyone who had ever hired his services, Gervais had killed many times. A cousin of the French king in Paris, children of an Italian aristocrat, the wife of an eastern potentate who had threatened to expose him, a Spanish cleric on his way to Rome to be given the cardinal's red hat, and so it went on. He was not even involved in any of the politics of those he had killed. It was a job, and it meant that he would not only earn money but also reap the pure enjoyment of the work.

The holy man meant little to him but he knew something of Gervais's life and background. The monk was the spiritual leader of no one. He would not be missed. But, for the moment, the information that he provided was of paramount importance. Hence, Gervais needed him.

"When the time comes that the priest is no longer useful . . ." Gervais smiled inwardly as he allowed the thought to trail away into the recesses of his mind. And then, continuing his silent thought, he smiled, "Perhaps finding and killing the old monk might be a suitable task for one of my younger colleagues who needs the experience?"

The monk saw the glimmerings of a smile on Gervais's face and took it as a sign to speak. He finished the remains of his first drink and at last, he opened his moist lips.

"There are those," he said, "who appear to know that something is afoot. They do not know what. But the Frenchman and his men are dead. Killed last night."

The monk stopped short. Something told him that to give more detail could be to his disadvantage. He then related part, but not all, of the story of the events of the day before. He focused on Oswald and left out much of the role played by Kathryn and James. Gervais listened, wondering what the monk was holding back and finally satisfied himself that he knew all that had transpired at the meeting that resulted in the death of the Frenchman.

"So," Gervais thought, "there are those who would follow me? With the Frenchman gone, I am one step further removed from anyone who can identify me." He smiled, pleased at the added layer of insulation that the Frenchman's death gave him.

Gervais knew that the Frenchman's death, if not fortuitous at the moment, was inevitable. The sponsor of this plot did want any trails that could result in his discovery. Even he, Gervais, did not know the identity or background of the man who would be king. He snapped his thoughts back to the monk and handed him a piece of coarse vellum on which was drawn a rough plan drawing of the castle. The monk frowned in question.

"Tell them to meet me beneath the wall of the upper moat, the place marked, at this time tomorrow. We will see whether or not they are truly monks of Saint Benedict. Now finish your drink with me."

Gervais was starting to enjoy himself, the old monk was sufficiently afraid of him. There would be no problems with the message falling onto the ears of the three Benedictines. If they agreed to the meeting the following night, there would be a time of reckoning and he would discover their real motives. He put his hand on the waist of the tavern maid as she went past taking drinks to other customers. She had kept her promise and had been rewarded handsomely. Now, once more at work, she tried to smile but could not hide the look of fear in her eyes. Gervais knew that he was in control.

"Bring us broth."

His words were curt and to the point. The woman nodded. He turned once more to the old monk.

"Remember, not one word of who I am or what I am."

"Of course. You can be sure of it."

The monk's voice quivered with emotion. The monk wondered if he had overstepped himself this time. Gervais was not a man to be exposed. But, then again, had he not dealt with worse criminals during his life of information gathering? Had not the monk's habit protected him? But would it protect him from Gervais? He thought not. Perhaps it was time to move to another city?

"You disapprove of what I do?" Gervais asked.

"I am ambivalent," the monk responded.

"There can be no sitting on the fence." Gervais scowled, making the old monk squirm.

"Were you ambivalent," Gervais asked smiling like the proverbial fox in the henhouse, "when you committed those acts against the church and its women?"

The monk looked worried, wondering what Gervais would say next.

"Consider the subtle advantages of knowing that there are those who suspect what I am about to do? They have limited choices in the manner in which they can react. They can weigh their limited choices and make easy decisions that they will ultimately come to regret. The effect of all this is a tension on their part that, however slight, must make for my pleasure."

Gervais sipped more of the ale. He was starting to feel warm in the knowledge that he would outthink his opponents. Had he not done the same many times before? Was he not still alive and his opponents dead? He smiled as he continued.

"Also, consider this. Instead of a hurly-burly of sweating soldiers rushing about in a frenzy to find me, I have the advantage of knowing what they will do and then I can bring all of my talents to bear on one task, with all assurance of a complete triumph!"

Gervais was extremely pleased with himself. He saw the surprised look on the monk's face. Then he continued knowing that he had made a major point.

"Who else knows of me?"

The monk shook his head to indicate that, as far as he knew, no one was aware of the presence of Gervais in the city. Gervais knew that he could only trust the monk as far as he could throw him, not too far. So he decided to continue his verbal attack. This would add an element of fear that would keep the monk loyal until it was time to dispose of him.

"Did you not think that I would know of you? I am aware of all of your actions. The actions that you and your fellow monks were engaged in.

Women and children were not safe in your presence. The very ones that they trusted abused them. That shows how sick you and your fellow churchmen were, and even continue to be!"

"I am not ashamed of what I have done," the monk exclaimed suddenly finding courage where before there had been fear, "I should have been allowed to continue my work. After all, it is a way of life among the clergy. So why should I suffer?"

Gervais felt a rush of pleasure. Now he had the monk where he wanted him. After the work was done the old monk was doomed.

"How many tavern maids are there here?" Gervais asked.

"Seven," the monk replied, "but the landlord does not encourage members of the fair sex to enter the premises other than those who serve the tables. And I tell you, his methods of removal are effective and final."

The monk looked into his tankard as though recalling memories from the dark liquid.

"I had the experience of seeing two women get a taste of his methods not too long ago. They sat at that table," he motioned with his head in the direction of a table in the corner, "for a few moments before the landlord noticed their presence. He walked over and picked up both at the same time and threw them out into the dark street and into the mud."

Gervais nodded. ""Did anyone seem concerned?"

"Two men tried," the monk smiled at the recollection, "but they too ended up in the mud and rain. They also had broken noses for their trouble." He paused again. "The landlord does not take too kindly to others who try to poach on his territory."

Gervais smiled. Obviously the landlord had an arrangement with his tavern maids that would result in money changing hands. Gervais would recall this fact. One never knew when such snippets of information could be useful. Like the monk, Gervais was a collector of information.

The tavern maid reappeared with a tray bearing another pitcher of ale and two bowls of broth that she set in place before them. Gervais dipped his spoon into the broth and tasted it with some curiosity. It was delicately flavored. "Bland," some would say also and add, "and on the verge of tasteless." He preferred the broth of his homeland that would be pungent and highly spiced. This bland English food was not to his liking. Gervais looked up from his broth and saw the monk's eyes on him. Willing to compromise his own tastes to reduce some of the fear that he saw in the monk's eye, he hesitated, smiled, and indicated the broth.

"Excellent," he said.

The monk, feeling easier, returned his smile.

"I thought that you would have found it not sufficiently tasteful?"

"To my surprise," Gervais added, "I find it pleasant."

The monk continued to smile thinking that a new Gervais was emerging from this meeting. Perhaps he was getting to know the man.

The tavern maid came back with another pitcher of ale. As she busied herself clearing a nearby table, Gervais lowered his voice significantly.

"You will find," he said to the monk "that your abilities to collect information is but one of several noteworthy characteristics that made me seek you out. And now I must be leaving. You can have my ale. You may need it!"

He smiled at the private joke and as he stood up he caught the tavern maid by the waist. The fear in her eyes made him feel strong. If she knew who he really was, she might be friendlier.

"My friend here," he nodded at the monk, "needs your help." He gave her a gold coin, "see to it that he is not disappointed."

The monk had started to sweat. Gervais looked down at the sweating monk. How was it that a country that produced such sturdy soldiers could also produce such men as the monk? They were not dependable, inefficient, and a burden on society. He turned once more to the tavern maid.

"The monk has some work to do for me, so you make your own arrangements with him."

The monk looked at Gervais. "I will take your message to them," he said. "Where will you be so that I might find you?"

"I'll find you. I know where you will be later tonight."

The old monk knew that Gervais did not like him. But he did not care who had recruited and trained him. He did not care about Gervais's exploits. He was a realist. A weakling who still liked women, food, and liquor, but above all he liked money and life. He could always be bought but he did realize that he could be outwitted. He was not invincible. Gervais was staring at him. The monk sensed that Gervais's plans for him might not be beneficial to his health!

The monk sat alone and finished the pitcher of beer.

*   *   *

It took time for the monk to settle his nerves but the fear never left. Customers came and went as he tried to ease his mind. Finally, after he had finished the beer, he got up from the table, smiled at the tavern maid, and muttered, "I'll be back." He had to play this out until the most opportune moment.

The monk moved silently across the tavern floor. His dark robe made him almost invisible against the darkness of the walls. He exited the tavern to breathe the open air. It still had a foul stench but, in keeping with the times, was better than the air indoors. A wagon bucked through the rough street, stirring up the mud that splashed everyone and everything within several yards.

The monk's thoughts turned away from the mud to the job at hand. He had to deliver the message and try to assure his self-preservation. He did not know the whereabouts of the three, who he still preferred to call Benedictines. But he did remember the words that the authoritative one had spoken.

"You will be contacted and informed of the meeting place. And you will be alone, bring others and you will die with them."

He could not have known that he was observed all of the time since the departure of Gervais. His meeting with Gervais was not only observed but everything that had been said had been heard. The unkempt-looking man sitting at the table two paces away, and who seemed to be on the verge of an alcoholic sleep, had been a silent witness to the meeting. He followed the monk from the tavern and tottered his way into the street.

Once into the darkness, he straightened himself to his full height. He looked in the direction where his wife, Margaret, and two cousins, James and Kathryn, were concealed in a doorway, nodded to indicate that all was well and that they should return home, and then he continued to follow the monk. As he walked, he discarded his loose outer clothes and threw them into doorways where beggars lay and argued about how to divide their newly arrived gifts. These doorway beggars were coming up in the world!

Oswald quickened his pace and once he had determined the path that the old monk would follow, he took another route. It was a circular route that joined the street at a point where he knew the monk would walk. Below the castle walls but out of sight of any possible observers.

The monk was not aware that he had been followed, not until a figure came out of the shadows and stopped him in his tracks. Oswald once more wore the robe of the Benedictines.

"Well, sir monk. How went your meeting with the assassin?"

The monk looked stunned and swallowed hard as he realized that at least some parts of his meeting might have been observed. He could not find the words to respond. Oswald continued.

"I do hope that you did not let him know about us?"

The monk finally regained his voice.

"No, sire!"

"Do not call me 'sire.'"

Oswald's stern voice was intimidating, and the monk had experienced more than the usual dose of fear for one night!

"No, I did not tell him anything about you. But he does want a meeting."

The monk related the details to Oswald who remained silent throughout the monk's tale as he compared his words with what had been said at the table in the tavern. Finally Oswald nodded.

"Yes, tell him that we shall see him at the appointed time and place. Go back and give him that message and see your tavern maid."

The last words filled the monk with dread. He knew that the conversation had been overheard. But how?

"Do not worry yourself about us. Do your job. Remain free from trickery and you will fare well. Now go!"

The monk turned and walked away from Oswald. After a few paces he turned to mutter a question about when they should meet again but Oswald was gone.

>From the shadows, Oswald could see the monk hurrying away. It was a few moments before he moved again. The streets were not a safe place at night and in light of the developments, extreme caution was necessary.

He would return to where James, Kathryn, and Margaret awaited him and prepare them for the day ahead.

*   *   *

Seated once more in the warm house, they were curious about Oswald's arrangements and when he told them that a meeting might take place in a tavern, they were surprised. He saw the look on their faces and thought it better to explain.

"My dear cousins, you think of the lack of privacy in a tavern. But there is more privacy in a public eating place than in most rooms in any palace or castle that you could name. No one will inquire about of your business; no one will ask about the intimacies of your life. In a tavern, the business is eating and drinking. Those who frequent the taverns are not curious about names and where you live or the reasons for the coming and going of the customers. The landlord and tavern maids will welcome you when you are there and will have no regrets when you leave. That is the simple answer."

James was startled by the simplicity of Oswald's thinking, but he knew that Oswald was correct in his logic.

Kathryn ran the tip of her tongue over her lips as she also brought her mind to bear on the issue.

"I follow what you are saying, Oswald, but are we not in danger? He may have friends."

"Perhaps," responded Oswald, "but do not let me give you the impression that it is so simple. We will have the advantage in that he will not know how many of us there are in the tavern or, for that matter, waiting outside. He will never believe that there are only three of us. And his friends, should he bring them, will be hampered by the crush of the people."

Kathryn put her forefinger on to her chin. A memory flicked through her brain as she thought of a situation that she had been in some time ago, she could not remember the day or the time, when she had been in a crowded tavern and was hardly able to move. "But that was a happy time," she thought.

"But I invite your questions because it will help the four of us to think our way through this." He saw Kathryn's pensive look. "You have a thought, Kathryn?"

"Oh, nothing, Oswald. Just a passing memory that I cannot place. Do not let me interrupt you. I see that being in a tavern can offer us some degree of safety but we must take all precautions. Nothing is guaranteed. Only death and taxes."

Again Kathryn put her forefinger to her chin wondering from where she had heard the last four words. Her mind remained blank and she had no recall.

"I like that, Kathryn," said Oswald, "a very good saying and I shall remember it."

Suddenly, James slapped his hand on the table.

"Good grief! That's it," he said. "Now let us look at what we have. Has anyone outside of yourself and Margaret ever talked of this?"

Oswald looked up. "No one. We are unable to communicate with those that we once knew."

Oswald looked at James then at Kathryn, wondering if they could remember that he and Margaret were no longer in the living world but remained on earth to minister to the sick and infirm. He continued, "You, both of you, as very dear friends are the only ones that know."

James studied his fingernails noting how black they had become, and started with recognition.

"Then," he said excitedly, "that is precisely the game that we need to play. This obviously is a very close-guarded secret. It seems that anyone who gets to know outside of a small circle has the potential to suddenly disappear."

"Of course!"

Kathryn almost shouted the words then looked around by instinct to make sure that she only had three listeners. There were no other listeners. The door was thick enough and sufficiently well fitted and the windows were shuttered with stout wooden boards to prevent prying ears from hearing anything that was discussed in the house.

"And to think," she continued, "we have been assuming that a whole gang was in on the secret. Without even realizing it we have probably talked our way into seeing what is really happening. There are two men, who obviously know what is about to happen, the assassin and his sponsor."

Oswald's face took on an even more serious look.

"And so," he said" "you are both thinking that it is more politic to search out and follow anyone who appears to be associated with this man?"

"Yes, that is the way that it should be done," Margaret affirmed.

Kathryn and James sipped their hot tea as they contemplated the picture and then Kathryn spoke.

"We all recognize that this will end in a confrontation. And that should," she emphasized, "be on our terms!"

With the arrival at this juncture, Margaret got to her feet, as did Kathryn, to set about making more tea and serving food. Oswald and James talked in low tones, of nothing in particular, just an attempt to clear their minds and think everything out. This would be a very serious commitment that could cost them dearly.

Margaret and Kathryn appeared with the food and set various dishes on the table. His eyes alight with curiosity. James lifted the lid from the first dish and sniffed at the fragrance. Then, taking great care not to lose a single drop of gravy, he filled four platters with chunks of dripping meat. He sat back in his chair, breathing happily.

"Ladies and gentleman," he said, "to our good appetite in protection of King Edward." Oswald looked around the table before adding, "And now, I propose that we leave the conversation as it is, enjoy our food, allow the thoughts to percolate through our minds, and I am sure we will come to a satisfactory resolution."

*   *   *

CHAPTER 31

G ervais had returned to the house where he knew the three men awaited him. The darkness of the early hours of the day, shortly after midnight, had cloaked his movements in secrecy. He sat with two other men and listened as the leader, another Frenchman by the name of Bernard who had been involved in battles and skirmishes throughout Western Europe, gave them their instructions.

Gervais looked at Bernard wonderingly. Bernard was threatening, ill mannered, bad tempered, and plagued by a speech impediment. Bernard's specialty was overseeing torture and attending personally to burnings where he readily taunted the victims with a lisp so heavy that it obscured many of his words.

Gervais knew that the sponsor of this plan would have seen Bernard as someone who could be used to lay a trail, albeit false. He was expendable. That would become obvious as the night wore on.

Bernard and the other two men wore the robes of a nondescript order seeking the privacy that was often accorded to an itinerant monk. Also the fear of catching the plague from travelers still remained in the minds of many people. This guaranteed that they would not be bothered and offered some privacy.

Gervais's position with the group was not officially recognized, although the other two men, like Bernard, knew that he was an assassin. The men had mixed emotions about Gervais. The older one considered Gervais's ability to penetrate personal defenses and kill the prey an admirable trait. The younger one considered Gervais to be of lower station than the common soldier since he did not face other men in battle. Bernard accepted Gervais for what he could learn from the local taverns and street corners.

Now that he had listened to Gervais as he had recalled his meeting with the old monk, Bernard gave instructions to his three-man audience. Then, feeling the effects of the recent meal and the nondescript food that he had consumed earlier in the day, Bernard nodded to Gervais, slung his sword across his back, and headed for the crude toilet that took the form of a narrow midden ditch in the corner of the backyard. Gervais, knowing the reasons for Bernard's nod, went with him and waited by the ditch, as if on guard. Bernard, seeing Gervais standing at the ready with his sword unsheathed, removed his own sword from his belt and gently pushed the sword into the moist earth an arm's reach away. He lifted his robes, loosened his drawers, and holding up the robes, he straddled the ditch. He knew that he was vulnerable but did he not have Gervais watching his back?

Gervais smiled at Bernard's partial nakedness and fallibility as he squatted above the ditch. Almost lazily and without any sudden motion, Gervais lifted his sword and cleaved Bernard's head from his body in one quick and very smooth, horizontal stroke. The disembodied head had a look of surprise on the face as the body fell over sideways into the filth that half-filled the ditch. Gervais looked at the head as it lay unmoving on the well-trodden ground in front of him. The dead eyes, although unseeing, seemed to accuse Gervais of the deed. He kicked the head into the ditch. Death was quick and who would care if a body remained in the ditch.

Gervais smiled to himself. He had now insulated their sponsor even further from the group of killers. Secrecy was of the essence and now that the deed was accomplished he, Gervais, would be paid a bonus for his work this night. He returned to the interior of the house.

"So, it is done?" asked the elder of the two. "You have rid us of the cur by putting him where he deserved?"

"I have," was the simple response from Gervais and with a frown as if in deep thought, he added, "now, we can follow the task that we have been given."

"It is up to us now," the elder of the two companions said as he nodded to his younger counterpart who went to the front door of the house to make sure that they would not be disturbed. Only silence filled the empty rain-soaked muddy street.

Gervais looked once more at the two of them.

"No one must know of this. Those who hired me ordained the action. Our friend," Gervais turned slightly and nodded his head in the direction of the backyard, "has embarrassed my employers."

He stared at his two companions through hard eyes that showed no emotion and continued.

"He failed to bring about the demise and untimely death of Lancaster in Calais. Those who aspire to power are not convinced that allowing Lancaster to live is in their best interests. You will not say anything of this to anyone. Not even to the women with whom you take your pleasure."

The younger of the two looked at the floor while his elder companion held up his hand in a conciliatory gesture. He knew perfectly well what Gervais intended if they strayed from their chosen actions.

"You have nothing to fear from us. You are paying us well and we will get the task done."

Gervais nodded to show that he was satisfied. And then he sensed. The sound of a woman and her companion passing the front of the house had caught his attention. The woman giggled and muttered words in the Northern dialect that seemed to hold a lot of promise for her companion. Gervais and his two companions quietly drew their swords from well-oiled leather scabbards. The soft leather scabbard was most useful when stealth was essential. They moved silently toward the door, ready, muscles tensed, awaiting a possible incursion into the room. But the sounds of the woman and her friend gradually faded into the distance. Gervais and his two companions breathed normally. They were safe.

Gervais signaled them to sheath their swords and frowned as he wondered about the man and woman outside but one body in a midden ditch was sufficient for one night.

They sat at a rough table and ate the spartan dinner that he had acquired earlier in the day. Gervais remained aloof and silent. There was no small talk. The two companions watched his every move. It was hard to tell what they looked like under these robes, but Gervais knew that they could be trusted. After all, they had been highly recommended. Gervais had watched their actions in taverns before their first meeting. He knew that they would not be distracted from any orders that were given to them. He had even bribed several tavern maids to make tempting offers but neither the old one nor his young companions had succumbed to the temptation. He was pleased with what he had seen.

He now took a chance, which really was not a chance. He needed to find out how far he could really trust the pair. He stood up and leaned against the wall as he untied the sword and the scabbard from his belt. He threw the sword to the younger one.

"Clean this. Take the fowl odors of that dead scum from my blade."

The older one nodded to his young friend who finished his meal and proceeded to fulfill his task. When the job was done, the sword and scabbard were duly returned to Gervais. He smiled. He knew that he could trust these two. They had seen him take a chance by giving up his sword and had done nothing to threaten him.

The two companions had not known that Gervais had visited the house earlier and placed two swords in the room, each one in a dark recess so that they were always within his reach. His suggestion that candles not be lit was more for this reason than for security. He had planned all the moves of this night, knowing Bernard's habits. If the swords had been discovered, Gervais had a simple explanation that would have satisfied all. "It is better to be prepared than to be sorry," he would have said, "we must be watchful and have extra arms at hand."

Gervais had seemed to take a chance but the dice were rolled in his favor. He had lived too long to jeopardize his life by such actions.

He placed the cleaned weapon into the sheath and secured it on his belt as he looked at his two companions.

"You have been chosen for this task," he told them, "because you can be trusted. We will accomplish what we set out to do. There is always the possibility that we may die but I am not willing to accept such an outcome. That is all." He paused as he carefully formulated the next words. "It is better that we not remain together. Two companions are acceptable. Three men together are suspicious."

Gervais paused as he thought of the three Benedictines that were the companions of the old monk.

"Yes, very suspicious indeed," he added. "You will hear from me, as I need you." He saw the quizzical looks on their faces. "I will know where to find you. But, a few words of advice, do not try to find me!"

They nodded to show that they understood his meaning and took their leave quietly, going out of the front door and into the deserted street.

Later, as Gervais inspected his cleaned sword, he nodded in satisfaction at the job that the younger of the two had done. He had watched him perform the task carefully and in detail. Perhaps he would make a valuable ally when it came time for the older of the two to retire. Gervais knew that his thoughts had no meaning. The man would not retire. He would be removed, as his employer preferred to use the word.

He shook himself back into the present. He cleaned up the remains of the meal, throwing the remnant into the midden ditch then he looked around once more for any telltale signs of their occupancy of the house. Nothing! He had tarried too long. He picked up the two swords from their dark corners, strapped them loosely to his chest where they would be hidden by his long cloak. He opened the door to the street and looked furtively to either side, then quickly stepped out, closed the door, and left the house.

*   *   *

Gervais did not see the man and woman huddled close together in the dark doorway two houses farther along the street. They had taken a risk, hoping that he would turn in a direction away from the bridge that would have allowed him to cross the bridge and enter the city.

There had been another distraction that took Gervais's mind off anyone who may have been watching or following him.

Not far from the entrance to the house that Gervais and his men had used, two figures struggled in the darkness. They swayed back and forth and suddenly tumbled into a writhing heap on to the road.

Gervais saw that the men were of no consequence by their clothes and the air reeked with the stench of ale. He was about to step past them when he stopped, as though he was in deep thought and one, thinking that Gervais had stopped to give aid, shouted "Help! This man . . . drunk . . ."

"Drunk am I . . ."

The two men got to their feet and continued to struggle, moving around the road until they bumped into Gervais. He considered this an attack on his own person that triggered a natural instinct and sent him into immediate action. Without a sound he seized the shoulder of the nearest man, and drawing his dagger at the same time, finished the move that, within the blink of an eye, had cut the man's throat.

"Let go of him," the other one shouted as he leaped at Gervais, attempting to punch and kick Gervais's face and legs. Gervais was not surprised by the attack, he merely avoided the man's rush and he too received the same treatment as his companion. He staggered back in shock as he fought to take breaths. In the next instant he joined his pugilistic companion on the muddy road.

A piteous gurgling could be heard as the men struggled to take their last breaths. For no reason, other than they had too much to drink and were disagreeing over who the attributes of a tavern maid, the men had seen their last moments on earth.

Gervais looked at the two bodies and wondered. Then he smiled as he recalled that there had been a man and a woman outside of the house earlier. He looked around. There was no sign of a woman. He wondered about the old monk and the tavern maid. And then the thought passed from his mind.

Gervais was pleased with himself. He had killed three men this night without any one of the three being able to resist. He allowed himself a brief smile as he continued on his way but he did not approach any of the city gates. The guards had strict orders not to allow anyone into the city after the lockdown at the approach of darkness.

Gervais could enter the city at any time that he wished. There were passages that a knowledgeable man could take that would bring him into the center of the city or any other part that he chose.

                    *   *   *

James and Kathryn, dressed in their monk's habits, witnessed the two killings and watched Gervais as he disappeared into the darkness. James looked at Kathryn and smiled in reassurance in the darkness of the doorway. He reached out and allowed their hands to touch. Oswald had advised them of what actions to take if they were questioned. The people of the city of Durham had sympathy for monks who spoke the local dialect. Kathryn, as instructed by Oswald, would remain silent and James would indicate that she, a young novice, was mute.

Kathryn heard James's whisper.

"All right, my dear?"

"Always, when I am with you. That man had the body language and movements of a trained of a killer. Were there not four men who entered the house?" she asked.

"Yes, indeed. Three have since emerged, and with the house in compete darkness, we can assume that one of the original four is remaining somewhere in the house never to see the light of day again."

Rain was starting to fall steadily. Once they were sure that Gervais had gone from the immediate area, they made their way along the wet muddy streets.

*   *   *

A short distance away, the old monk hurried along the dark street that lay just across the river to the west of the castle. He was ready to sleep in the hovel that he used but he was worried. The rain had started suddenly and was quickly becoming a soaking downpour. However, it was not the rain that worried him. As he realized that the three Benedictines were not really what they claimed to be. After all, a woman who was supposedly a Benedictine monk? But why not? He had heard rumors of a female pope some centuries before the present time. He shrugged. "What is the world coming to?" he asked himself.

He knew from their style of speech that they were from this area and had probably lived in or close to the city of Durham all of their lives. But the manner in which the Frenchman and his comrades had been dispatched was efficient and accomplished swiftly and professionally. That was it. Professionally and there was only one such group that was trained in those methods—they were secret soldiers of King Edward, or more likely, John of Lancaster. But the little one, the woman, how was she connected to this? And why?

He considered these thoughts instead of paying attention to the streets. Or least to the inhabitants of the streets. The hand came out of the darkness from behind and circled his mouth. He felt himself lifted off his feet and carried into a dark alley. Oswald's voice whispered in his ear.

"One word, monk, and your neck will be broken."

"I did not hear you," the monk mumbled through Oswald's fingers. Then, for safety, he added, "I will not cry out."

"As it should be" was the response from Oswald as he released his grip on the monk, lowered him so that his feet once more made contact with the mud.

"What do you have to tell me, old man?"

The monk explained that he had made contact with one man who was willing to meet with Oswald and his two Benedictine companions. The man, Gervais, did not appear to be too worried about meeting with three monks but he was suspicious. There would be danger. The monk appeared to think for a moment.

"I believe that this man has been trained in the art of killing. Much like—" the monk did not finish the sentence as Oswald cut his words short.

"Much like me?"

The monk remained speechless.

"Lost your tongue, master monk? From where comes this Gervais?"

"Possibly France. His speech reminds me of the accents of the Parisians."

The monk loved to listen but he also liked to talk. And he was finding that he could trust this tall blond Benedictine-soldier or whatever he was. His eyes seemed to be sincere. So he started to tell Oswald all of the events that had occurred since they last met.

He was unable to see the other two figures in their Benedictine robes approach. Nor did he see Oswald give the sign with his hand that they should remain some distance away.

"Lancaster is to die," the monk whispered, "are the words that I hear. Do you know what that means?"

Oswald looked down at him with piercing eyes. He had known the old monk for less than two days but he had come to recognize the man's desire to live. He knew instinctively that the monk was telling the truth.

"Who is going to kill the duke?" Oswald asked.

"Perhaps it is Gervais who has been hired for the task? I heard that he has hired others like him. There is word that it will happen when the duke returns from France and pays a visit to this city."

"Who has hired this Gervais?" Oswald remained calm as he asked the question but he felt the inner turmoil as his worst suspicions had been confirmed.

"That I know not," the monk answered.

"Do you have a description of this Gervais?"

"No. I only saw him in the shadows and he goes by various names. Although I do believe," the monk scratched what remained of his hair as he appeared to turn the thought over in his mind, "that Gervais might be his real name. The story is that he can change his appearance to match his surroundings. Like that lizard . . ."

"You mean a chameleon," Oswald prompted and the monk nodded before he continued.

"Yes, that is the name I was looking for. This Gervais has all of a killer's behavior patterns. He has silence, stealth, contempt for all, including women, and anyone who opposes him."

"What good is that?" Oswald thought. "If I cannot recognize him, I am vulnerable. If he can change his appearance, I will not know until he is behind me and then I am in danger." Oswald rubbed his forefinger against his chin.

"So," he said to the monk, "maybe that is not so bad after all. He knows nothing of me other than I am a monk with two companions?" Oswald allowed the statement to become a question.

The old monk nodded in agreement.

"You have done well," Oswald said. "Now go and arrange a meeting. Here are my instructions. You will arrange for us to meet at the specific place at a specific time."

"I will try."

As soon as the words left his mouth, the monk knew that he had not spoken well. Oswald glared at the monk.

"No, monk, you will do it. Now begone."

"What about your companions?"

"My companions are my concern. Not yours."

The monk looked into Oswald's eyes. Blue and penetrating.

"How will I find you?"

As the words left his mouth, the monk realized that his question was unnecessary. He knew the answer.

"I will find you. As I have done this night. Now go!"

The monk left the alley and disappeared into the darkness.

Oswald turned around to stare after the retreating figure of the monk. "It is, perhaps, best that we sever our relationship soon," he mumbled. He was not sure how much further the monk could be trusted.

James and Kathryn, seeing this, approached Oswald who looked at them and smiled.

"Well, how goes it, Cousins?"

They were ready to tell him before they realized that the question was rhetorical. He smiled and indicated that they first seek the shelter of the house that they called home. Warmth and food would resuscitate their senses.

*   *   *

Once inside the warm house, they took off their heavy robes and settled in front of the fire that Oswald had encouraged, by adding more logs, to spread warmth to the room. Soon, they were sipping hot tea and eating oatmeal cakes laced with honey. James and Kathryn started to talk and told Oswald and Margaret of their adventure.

"You are both all right? He did not see you?"

"No. We are sure of that, Oswald," James answered.

"Well done."

James nodded his head in acceptance of Oswald's praise while Kathryn beamed with pride.

"Now to a plan of action," Oswald continued. "The duke is my friend and we will do our best to save him. We," he looked at his wife, "have talked this out."

Margaret nodded as she took the cue to continue.

"I've been trying to think this out more clearly," she said. "What bothers me," she continued, "is that this man, Gervais, is uncontrollable. He does as he pleases and does not appear to respond to anyone. To tell you the truth, I hope that we have read him correctly and that we can catch him soon, and I think that we simply cannot delay anymore. I do hope that when the time comes, there will be no mistakes or regrets."

Oswald smiled at his wife's concern, "My dearest, there will indeed be no mistakes," he said as he turned to James and Kathryn.

"Well," Oswald said, "how do you feel now? You have seen what we have taken on as an enemy."

"Oswald," James whispered, "just as the two of you are committed to this task, so are Kathryn and I. We feel for some reason that we owe this to you. And this is our way of repaying you for unknown deeds in the past."

Oswald looked at them with some amazement. He knew their backgrounds and that he had saved James when he had suffered a major head injury as a result of an automobile crash in his own time. Oswald knew that James would not remember any details but his senses were telling him of Oswald's role as a lifesaver.

Oswald shook his head firmly. "James and dear Kathryn," he said. "I appreciate your words so let us get on with our work and we will not discuss this again."

Kathryn did not stir an inch, but her voice rose slightly as she looked directly at Oswald.

"By the body and blood of our Lord, we will help you even if you do not wish it. Do not consider us as mere observers. We," she reached to James and held his hand, "will trade our lives for yours."

"As you wish, dear Kathryn." Oswald smiled. "So be it. We are in this together!"

Margaret laid her hand on Oswald's arm.

"This is an opportune time as ever that we rest," the soft voice seemed to fill the room. "It seems to me that all questions have been answered."

Oswald's teeth showed in a broad grin.

"But of course, my dear. Do I not always take your advice," he said as he took her hand.

"No, you do not!"

"Ah," he said looking at James and Kathryn, "I am faced with a dilemma of great proportions. As I am sure that you are, James."

"James has no such problems," Kathryn broke into the conversation, "as long as he listens to what I say, he is happy."

James raised his hand in mock protest. "With that, I do believe that Margaret is right. It is time to rest. I foresee some busy days ahead."

"I, like you James, see it as a great adventure. And then, too," he became more serious, "we cannot forget the ferocious nature of the man that we must stop. So, we leave you for the night as we take to our respective beds."

Oswald held out his hand and James held it for a few moments.

"Until the morning, my cousins." Oswald said. "I hope that you will rest well as I feel that there may not be much time before we need to strike at King Edward's enemies.

"*À demain!*"

"In the morning!" James and Kathryn chorused as they made their way to their sleeping area.

As they lay down on the straw-filled palliasse, James held Kathryn's hand. The warmth of the room made their eyes heavy.

"My dearest Kathryn, I am so proud of you. I know not what makes me say that but you have the courage and fight of a score of men!"

She leaned over and kissed him.

"Of course. Am I not here to protect you?"

James smiled as sleep closed his eyes.

*   *   *

CHAPTER 32

I t was night and there was a freezing chill in the air. After a day of rest, Oswald was leading James and Kathryn to the house where he knew they would find the old monk. Kathryn was immediately behind Oswald with James following her as they worked their way toward the back door of the house. The odors of the midden were strong in the still night air. By a series of hand signals, Oswald advised them not to stumble and fall into the ditch!

Kathryn and James watched the shadowy figure of Oswald as he moved toward the house. All was silent. He cocked his head to one side as if listening for the slightest sound. The silence seemed to hang heavy in the air. Oswald stopped, and in the dim light, Kathryn could see Oswald place his forefinger across his lips in the universal language for silence. She turned and gave the same signal to James. As she turned to face Oswald, he bent over to accommodate the differences in height and spoke to Kathryn in a low whisper.

"I thought that the monk would be asleep at this hour. Be on your guard. I sense that someone is afoot. It might be the old monk, which I doubt, or he may have been followed. But we have no way of knowing, for the moment, who else is abroad this night. I will find out. If you hear a commotion," he seemed to pause as he thought abut his next words, "men make a commotion as they die, get out. Neither you nor James must attempt to show any heroics."

Oswald looked into Kathryn's eyes, as he beckoned James closer so that they both might hear his words.

"Kathryn, please make sure that my cousin here," he nodded his head toward James, "leaves this house in safety."

Kathryn nodded her head to show that she understood and poked James in the ribs to make sure that he had heard and understood Oswald's words. In the darkness, she could see his head move showing that he also understood the seriousness of Oswald's words.

She smiled at James as she placed her hand lightly on his mouth so that he should also remain silent. She could feel the movement of his lips, in the form of a kiss, on the soft flesh of her palm.

Oswald disappeared silently into the darkness and reappeared a short time later. To Kathryn and James, the moments seemed like hours.

"A matter that needed my attention."

Oswald looked through a crack in the wooden door and saw the monk wrapped in his coarse well-worn blanket on the floor. There did not seem to be anyone else. But always suspicious was even more vigilant. Oswald made the sign to Kathryn and James to remain where they were. He could see the shadowy outline of the monk as he moved in his sleep. Oswald inched open the door without any sound as it swung on its leather hinges as he moved ahead into the room. James and Kathryn followed, and at Oswald's signal, closed the door and waited by it.

As they entered the house, the silence remained. The sleeping monk had not been disturbed by their soft footsteps as they crossed the floor to where he lay. And then, he thought that he heard a rat scratching on the floor.

"A rat," the monk decided, his senses coming alert. "Christ's bones, a rat," he mumbled. He knew that several persons had associated the plague with rats and was immediately aware of the possible danger.

Oswald had spoken in Latin and James translated to Kathryn as they moved from the door to kneel by the shadowy Oswald.

The monk stirred and started to become aware of his surroundings as the sleep cleared from his tired brain. The blanket seemed to offer no protection from the cold and he wondered if he would ever feel warm again. His old bones did not take very well to the coldness of the early morning. It was at that moment that he felt Oswald's presence. He started to sweat.

"Not one word until I tell you to speak, monk," Oswald's ordered, "or that word will be your last."

The monk shivered in fear at the sound of Oswald's voice. He nodded his head to show that he understood Oswald's words.

"Well, sir monk," Oswald whispered into the monk's ear, "how goes this night? I see that you had a watcher outside. He was any easy target and will follow you no more. Who else follows you?"

The monk nodded his head as he attempted to show convincingly that he had no knowledge of being followed. The monk realized that it would be Gervais who had him followed. So, the monk reasoned, he must be on a short list for a knife in the ribs or through the throat, courtesy of Gervais.

"I know not. But . . . ?"

"No," Oswald preempted the monk's question, "there is no one else. You may light a candle. But wait and do nothing until my command."

Oswald rose and made sure that the window and the crack in the door were sealed and that the light would not escape from the house.

"Now, arise and light a candle, monk."

A sputtering of the flint and the candle showed its dim light in the darkness. Baldur saw the soldier and the other two, the woman and the silent one. Both stared at him, eyes unblinking and the monk was even more unnerved. He could not tell who would be the more deadly. As before, they wore their Benedictine habits and he feared all three, equally but perhaps for different reasons.

"So, what news do you have for us?" It was Oswald who spoke and broke into the monk's thoughts.

"News?"

"Be careful, monk. I know that you met with the leader of the new group who calls himself Gervais. Try not to manipulate us or . . ."

Oswald left the remaining words unsaid. The unspoken meaning was clear. The monk trembled at that then he sighed, wondering if there was no trust left in the world.

"Yes, his name is Gervais. He seems to have a task that involves the death of someone in high places. I cannot guess who it is but it may be someone close to King Edward. I am not party to when or where such a thing will happen, but I believe from the urgency in Gervais manner that it will be soon."

The flickering dim light of the candle allowed the monk to clearly see the faces of his visitors. Fear ran through his mind. The Big One, as he referred to Oswald, could kill him as a soldier kills, face to face and with no emotion. The Silent One, as he called James, could be equally deadly and probably would kill him with no other thought than he was to be killed. The Little One, as he referred to Kathryn, looked at him and the monk knew that she could also kill him without a second thought. She, the monk had observed, had a familiarity with weapons that made the monk shiver. She also had the look about her of a warrior. The monk sensed that she would dispose of him without even a blink of her blue eyes. He had read such tales of female warriors in the past and they always seemed to be deadlier than their male counterparts. The monk was starting to feel depressed!

"Gervais," he started to say, "seems to be one of a group that came from Paris. He has two other companions who also seem . . ."

"Seem? Or are?" Oswald's words cut into the monk's story.

"Are," the monk corrected himself and then continued, "from the continent. The reasons for their venture are unknown to me. But someone of a very high standing has hired Gervais. He, himself, also has the bearing at times, of a highborn person. Who he might be or who has hired him, I know not."

The monk paused and rubbed his lips. He searched the darkness as Oswald regarded him with suspicion. The monk reached out and picked up a bottle.

"By our leave?"

Oswald took the bottle, uncorked it, and sniffed the open top. His nose was not assailed by any suspicious odor.

"Here, sip your bad wine and continue your story."

The monk tilted the bottle to drink part of what was left and then placed the bottle on the floor close to his pallet. He did not wish it to be perceived that he would use it as a weapon. He looked at Oswald.

"I do have several comments to make from what I have been able to glean from Gervais's actions and from the word in various dark places."

The monk paused to take a breath. He looked at Oswald who gave him a reassuring nod to proceed.

"It seems that there are those in France who have designs on the English throne. I have reason to surmise that with Edward, Prince of Wales, being in ill health, there is not much hope for a long life for him. Who will succeed after the death of King Edward is unknown. Will it be John of Lancaster? Whether or not it will be Richard, the young son of the Prince of Wales, is not known. Our friend Gervais may be here to make the change in the line of succession. There may be those who are of the opinion that the boy Richard will make the better king because of the manner in which he can be manipulated. And should that be the case, I fear for the life of John of Lancaster."

The monk looked at the three listeners. Again, there was not a show of emotion or feeling of any kind. Silence pervaded the dim light. The only noise was the sputtering of the candle as it fought to throw its light into the room.

"Gervais seems," he looked at Oswald, "to be very well trained and has the techniques of various schools that allow him to be a formidable foe and an expert killer. Several of the deaths of those in high places in European court circles can be credited to his efforts. But he very rarely leaves proof and what I say is speculation."

"Well," it was Oswald who spoke, "I have heard of such a man and perhaps Gervais is that man. He appears to be fearless and ruthless, pursuing his goal without concern for anyone else. Anyone who gets in his way must prepare to die. His actions are instantaneous and final."

"You say he has two companions?"

"Yes, there was another one who was supposed to be the leader until Gervais removed him from his exalted position. He now lies at the back of the land in the midden trench where the house is situated."

"You're telling me nothing that I would not have guessed or might have known, monk. What about a meeting with him?"

The monk reached for the bottle.

"Leave it and answer my question."

The tone on Oswald's voice worried the monk.

"Yes, of course," he responded, "I was getting to that. He is willing to meet but I caution you that it may be a meeting from which only Gervais emerges. I believe that he considers you a threat . . ."

"He will consider anyone a threat until the task is complete," Oswald interjected, "go on."

"There is another house that Gervais has set aside for such a meeting."

"Good. We can watch it," James blurted out.

"No, that may not be wise," the monk added. "He will have it surrounded and watched by as many cutthroats as it takes to remove you from competition."

"You are learning, monk," Oswald added in praise of the monk's thinking. "But go to him and see what he is willing to recommend. Then we," Oswald looked at James and Kathryn, "will decide how best to approach this situation."

Oswald's mind was racing but he was in control. He had separated the team into two groups, Gervais, his two henchmen, plus any cutthroats that could be hired to accomplish the task, whatever it might be. The cutthroats would be men who were thirsty for their chance to earn money killing for pay and enjoying it.

He had indeed heard of Gervais, a displaced man of power who went by several names but whose tactics only slightly vary from killing to killing. How he had come across his two companions Oswald cared not. But they would have had similar training, perhaps with not as much experience as Gervais and they would be dangerous. All in all, a formidable trio. The weakness in Gervais's plan would be if he was an idealist and had something to gain, other than money, from the completion of his task. Perhaps lost power would be restored. A high place in a new government or new lands and income would offer some comfort.

Either way, the task ahead for them was challenging, to say the least, because it was not just money that motivated Gervais but the unique services that he could provide.

"I have a very important job for you, old man," Oswald said. "Everything, I mean everything including your life could depend on your success."

"I will try to do my best," the monk responded.

"No, monk, you will do your best." The monk nodded. "You will meet once more with Gervais and tell him that a bargain can be struck. Tell him that there are those who are willing to double or even triple whatever he is being paid."

"Now tell me, how does he contact you?"

"Much like you," the monk responded.

"Then," Oswald added, "make yourself available so that you can be contacted by Gervais. If there is any mention of the man outside who now resides with the devil, you know nothing. I have made it appear that he was killed for other reasons. Do my bidding. I will find you."

The monk turned to reach for the bottle. There was at least one good gulp of the sour liquid remaining. The room was suddenly cast into darkness. The monk turned in shock wondering what would happen next. He thought about removing his old body from the pallet for protection, as if a change in position would help. But there was nothing. The three Benedictines had left the house and he was alone once more.

In the darkness, he felt around for the bottle and his greasy fingers soon closed about it. He shook the bottle. The sound of a small amount of liquid sloshing around came to his ears. He smiled in the darkness. Pity to waste it. He drank the remains of the acidic liquid and discarded the empty bottle. Then he pulled the blanket across his body.

As his eyelids closed, thoughts flashed through his mind. If he was to be killed, so be it. Why worry? He could do nothing for the moment. Once the chance arose, he would move to another city. If he bolted now, his actions would be judged to be suspicious by both sides and that would not be good for him. He would stay in Durham and make his escape at the most appropriate time, when he was most likely not to be noticed or not required anymore by either side of this struggle.

After all, his brain was working overtime, if he could change the inevitable, he would, so why worry about it? If he could not change the inevitable, there was nothing that he could do, so why worry about it?

The monk had become quite a philosopher in his old age and wine in any form, good or bad, helped his philosophical moods. He smiled to himself in reassurance and was soon fast asleep.

*   *   *

Gervais sat alone in the house, his mind brimming with thoughts and questions. The justification for murder was in danger of vanishing. Murder offered a change in the status quo and a vision of the future with the potential for control over enemies and over the natural laws. Since he had become involved in murderous deeds, the supply of victims had never waned. In fact, it had grown to levels not before seen, even greater than that he had observed as a young boy in his native France.

Men in dark clothing, claiming to be healers of the sick, sold their services to the highest bidder and used poisons to accomplish their goals. The job should be done and a getaway made before the victim succumbed to the sickness that many poisons created. Gervais was not of this type. He preferred to see his victim die. Then he could be sure that the task was accomplished. Even if he had to cheat and lie to his colleagues.

It was this world of murder that Gervais had seen and that had made his career choice so much easier. But he remained determined to perform his job with professionalism and not to leave any witnesses. This is the way that he had always done things and would continue to do so. It was his past, present, and future.

And as for the three Benedictines that the old monk had told him about, he would take care of them. He would seal their future, or termination of any possible future, at the right moment. And that moment was close by!

As he allowed the thoughts to cross his mind, he could hear the voices in the background. Just like the old days when he had been among different men in diverse places. Men who were not afraid to fight for their beliefs.

The results of the next few days, if they went the way that he predicted, would help him make his decision. But the thoughts of those damn Benedictines were lurking in his mind for some reason, even when he felt confident about the next few days, would not leave him. There was something about them . . .

He got up from his sleeping pad and walked to the door. He needed some air. The city was still wrapped in the coldness of night. The sun had long since disappeared. As he looked out of the door, after having extinguished the lone candle, he saw an empty street, long and deserted. He could see the dim lines of the castle across the river. The white stone walls reflected what little light there was back to him.

This was a fine city in which to complete his task. Perhaps even the best city in which he had ever worked. It was a city of churches that was populated by monks and priests. The general population catered to their every need as well as to the needs of the church. There were libraries and all the essentials that go with this being a cathedral city that was presided over by a prince bishop.

If he was questioned, he had all of the necessary documents that explained who he was and his reasons for being in Durham. He was a traveler who came in search of knowledge. He carried the weapons of a soldier because he traveled alone and needed the protection that the weapons afforded. But it was the emphasis that his letters of introduction placed on his scholarship that pleased him. A scholar. He smiled and that made him feel very comfortable.

He reassured himself that this was far better than London. There were fewer nosey people around and fewer soldiers. He was unlikely to be discovered. But the thought of the three Benedictines still worried him.

He knew that there was nothing else in the world like the work that he did. He had complete secrecy. He had free rein about the countryside and always could look to his sponsor, as long as he, Gervais did not betray a trust. There were thousands of ways that he could hide in a city until his job was done and it was time to leave.

Battle among opposing armies was no longer his concern. In earlier times, he recalled from the stories, it took the form of dueling between champions of either side. Now the battles were pitched battles with very little semblance of order in which a soldier killed as many of the enemy as possible before being killed or wounded himself. But there were strategies emerging.

Had not William of Normandy used the ruse of retreat to fool the Saxons of Harold and draw them from the higher ground of Senlac Hill near Hastings? And there were many other examples but in an age when communication between the various units of an army was limited to the king sitting on high ground or runners between the units, the battle appeared to be utter chaos, and so it was to all soldiers. The idea of an assassin penetrating their ranks was almost unknown. They were used to being confronted by enemies who did not hide.

He knew that he had various nicknames but the one that gave him the most pleasure was *Monsieur La Nuit* or *Mr. Night* by those who had heard of him but had never seen him. It was to them, as though he always worked at night and in darkness so that no one ever saw him. Without the services of *Monsieur La Nuit*, there would have been no meaning to the lives of some of Europe's most powerful families. And these were families who gained their power as a result of his work.

But he knew that somewhere within the archives of those families were the answers to questions about his identity and his deeds, questions that have perplexed men for many years.

Did the German prince strangle his wife Isabella on her marriage bed or did he hire someone else to do it?

Who was the sainted man that had entered the French castle and never been seen again to answer questions about the death of the cousin of the king of France?

Who was the coarse-looking woman with her long blond hair who had been present at the death of the Danish nobleman? Was she, in fact, a nun?

What secrets are hidden in the walls of the castle at Caen? Was it really the ghost of William the Conqueror who had been seen before the death of the bishop? A bishop who had been advocating insurrection against the French.

Gervais wondered what was to be his payment in the next world. What was the payment required for the absolution of sin? For the necessary exemptions from ecclesiastical law?

"In the meantime," he asked himself, "what can I acquire in this life? What comforts can I collect to serve me in those years after the hairs on my head have turned gray?"

*   *   *

He turned his mind once more to the task at hand. He knew about an entrance to the castle that would lead to a small room from which he would make his sortie to accomplish the killing. In that small room he would not be disturbed. The guards very rarely inspected the room, for reasons unknown but he guessed what the reasons might be since the room was unused and being in the lower parts of the castle, was not to their fancy.

The only meaningful part was to make sure that his maps, drawn long ago by the architects and collected in many volumes, were true and that no more walls had been built to separate the room from the upper floors. He had no way of checking and the unknown made him uncomfortable. But he had a simple plan for his escape. He would go back along the tunnel from the room to the outside.

Gervais was not a gambler but he felt that, for him, this was a gambler's chance with fortune on the side of the gambler. It was what made the job so enticing. The thrill as he found his quarry. The killing and then the withdrawal with no one any wiser about him. It was worth the effort. The money would help him to smile. Perhaps even laugh about it at a later date!

He knew about the rooms in the castle that had been closed in the past twenty years. Permanently closed but none that affected his plans. He had made friends with a junior stonemason who had the misfortune to disappear after he revealed all that he knew to Gervais. His body was never discovered and it was believed that he had left for London in the company of a woman of pleasure or at least that was the story carefully planted by his newfound friend, Gervais.

Gervais remembered his rule. Be as sure as you can about your prey and their habits.

"Without this rule," he muttered to himself "more than three quarters of the men who set out to kill are themselves killed."

Gervais looked once more into the street.

"Thank God for a brain that gives me the knowledge to handle these things. Saints be praised."

He closed the door and went back into the house. He was very confident. The task was about to begin and in a short while he would begin the initial moves and that would result in his success.

Yes, he was very happy!

*   *   *

CHAPTER 33

L ater in the morning, as the light of day had overcome the darkness of the night, a man and a woman, posing as traders in pots and pans, left a note with the monk. They wished to meet with Gervais. The monk, who was also up and about at what for him was an extremely early hour, had seen them loitering near the marketplace and had wondered about their purpose.

They told the monk that they would be available every morning at the same time and they had camped outside of the city to allay any suspicions.

There were rumors that they were foreigners from the continent, possibly Flanders. They had in their possession a list of prominent persons who were going to be assassinated if their sponsors had their way. Unfortunately for the two foreigners, they strayed beyond the safety of the city into areas that were not always defendable by the soldiers and they were captured by a band of Scottish raiders who were in the area.

The raiders were not interested in them or in any list, had they even known about it. They were interested in the horses and the wagon. The raiders could not afford to take prisoners that would slow them down, and the prisoners had nothing to offer; even if they did try to bargain their way out of captivity, the woman died quickly after a short debate about their worth. The list remained concealed on her body, even as she was left sprawled on the ground where she had fallen. The man was tortured; more for sport and to see how much he could tolerate rather than as a search for information. He too was left on the ground; his broken limbs sprawled in the loose attitude of death. The animals would eventually dispose of their remains.

In the city, no one asked about the foreigners since it was assumed that they had left for another destination.

Gervais did think that it was unusual that the two did not return with any message for him. The opportunity had not arisen to pass on the list. And he had more pressing matters that required his attention.

*   *   *

Oswald, James, and Kathryn left the house and moved toward the house where Oswald knew that they would find the old monk. There had been a light rain earlier and the chill in the air made Kathryn and James glad that they had taken the precautions of wearing extra clothes under their robes.

From his movements, they knew that Oswald was suspicious! He seemed to be taking extra precautions as they moved silently through the darkness. He could sense the men who were hiding in the shadows of doorways. The drunken voices of would-be singers as they moved from tavern to their respective homes were of little consequence to him. There was some other mischief about!

Four men wrapped in cloaks hurried by the spot where the three friends stood concealed. Oswald watched as they disappeared around the next corner. The sounds of a scuffle came to Oswald's ears. He motioned with his finger across his lips for silence. The sounds ended as quickly as they had begun. It did not seem that robbers were about and Oswald suspected something more nefarious. He looked at James and Kathryn, and gave them a sign to remain where they were and he slipped away from the security doorway. He returned moments later and gave them a sign to follow him.

*   *   *

The old monk had made himself visible in the usual taverns but with no success. Oswald had not contacted him and he wondered if Gervais had found the three Benedictines and exacted some form of revenge or punishment on the three. Although the monk did realize that there was no other punishment than death. The time that it took to die could be a punishment, he thought.

He awakened the old monk from another alcohol-induced sleep. In his semiconscious state, he thought that he heard a rat scratching at the floor or wall. But after the previous night, he knew that it was not a rat. It was a noise made to awaken him and he was better prepared this time and ready with his story and the piece of vellum.

Oswald took the grimy vellum from the monk who offered it to him and read it by the light of a shaded candle.

"An address. Whoever wrote this, writes well," Oswald announced and continued, "I wonder if he plans as well as he writes?"

Oswald looked around and the monk seemed to remember an insignificant detail. He coughed lightly to show that he wished to speak. All three visitors had his attention.

"This," he said pointing to a wooden keg in the corner of the floor, "was left for me yesterday. Perhaps we can open it and have a drink?"

Oswald became suspicious.

"Let us take the keg outside," he ordered, "I have ascertained that we are not being watched."

Once outside, he started to work on removing the stopper, carefully with his knife, rather than hitting it hard with a hammer, as was the usual practice to open a keg. He had seen landlords splashed, sometimes doused, much to the amusement of their customers, with the alcoholic contents of such kegs. As he loosened the tight stopper, his nose twitched and he motioned the monk, James, and Kathryn to step back. He gave the stopper a few more twists with his knife and stepped back as the stopper was forced out of its resting place by the contents. The liquid sprayed outward several feet from the keg and a powerful odor assailed their nostrils.

No one spoke. They returned into the house and Oswald reached over and took the bottle of wine from the old monk and moistened one corner of the vellum with it. Holding the vellum by the moist corner, he held it in the flame of the candle. James's nose twitched at a foreign odor and he looked at Kathryn wondering about Oswald's action. The sudden flare as the candle flame touched the vellum caught them by surprise. Oswald smiled.

"As I expected, it seem that our friend Gervais was hoping that I would do as much. My nose told me that there was an odor of the liquid that makes Greek fire in the room and the vellum had the same odor. As did your nose also, Brother," he looked at James using the term that one monk would use to another rather than cousin, the term of their relationship. James nodded his head to show in agreement.

"Well, my friends, this may be Gervais's way of saying that he does not consider us a threat," Oswald announced with finality, "so we will play along with his game. He assumed that we would be sprayed and some incident with the candle would cause the fire."

Oswald thought for a moment then smiled, "Remain here. I will return soon. I have packages to collect."

They went into the house and waited. Moments later, Oswald returned and announced that there were now four bodies in the backyard, close to the midden ditch.

"Earlier, when I left you in the doorway, I was suspicious about the sounds that arose when the four men in cloaks passed by us. It seems that, for whatever reason, they had been dispatched in the alley," he said by way of a perfunctory explanation to Kathryn and James. "They are lying in the backyard. And now, we must pull off the switch so that no one suspects. If we do it right, Gervais will believe that we perished tonight. We will burn the bodies but we will not burn the house. To do so would cause untold damage to nearby houses and kill more people. You," he looked at the monk, "will die with us!"

The monk felt his heart beating wildly. So this was it. He was about to meet his maker. He knelt on the floor ready to make his peace.

"Stand up, monk. You will not die in that sense, only in the sense that someone has already died for you."

The monk's face started to return to its normal color.

"It will," Oswald continued, "be assumed that the Greek fire took us by surprise and because of our proximity to each other, took hold on our clothes but we were able to get out of the back door before we died. Hopefully, no one will be any wiser. Gervais is getting closer to us. So we have four bodies. Help me lift the bodies into place."

As the work started, Oswald turned to Kathryn.

"Little One, please direct the monk to spread the liquid from the keg onto the bodies while we," he looked at James, "prepare the house to show that the event took place as Gervais planned."

*   *   *

Gervais felt pleased with himself. He was talking with his two companions. While outside of the house, there were cutthroats with knives and daggers standing guard. He had lost another three men. Their lives were worthless in the normal scheme of events let alone when compared to the ultimate scheme of events. Most of all, he had got rid of the old monk and the three inquisitive Benedictines, whoever they were. The bodies could not be identified and Gervais was pleased with the damage that his Greek fire had wrought. The result was a little more drastic than he had planned, but very successful. Three bodies were scattered in the backyard and one was in the midden ditch. All were burned to a cinder. The scorch marks in the room told him where it had happened, just as he had planned. Somehow, they had managed to stagger into the backyard before they died. That was of no consequence to Gervais. They were dead and now he could focus on completing that task for which he would be rewarded handsomely. Very handsomely indeed!

*   *   *

Oswald looked at the old monk.

"I think that it is time that you depart from here," the monk wondered what was coming next as he listened to the soldier's words, "so I will help you escape to a safe haven. Might I suggest that you once more seek the solace of a monastery?"

The old man stuttered, "If you think . . ."

"Whatever I think, this is the best course for you. I have a contact who will see that you are well cared for and can have a restful and pleasant end to your days on this earth."

The old monk nodded and smiled, "I thank you. When?"

"As soon as we have rested. After daybreak, when the scum disappear from the streets, my two friends," Oswald nodded to James and Kathryn, "will take you to my friend who is in the priory. He, Brother Thomas that is, will see that you are re-admitted to the order and accepted by the other brothers. They have no need to know of your past. You will take a vow of silence so that if anyone should recognize you, you have no need to deny everything. The prior will see to that for you."

The old monk looked at his three companions. Tears had formed in his eyes and were rolling down his cheeks.

"I know not who you are," his eyes moved from one to the other, "but I thank you whoever you are. You," he gestured to Kathryn, "I . . ."

Oswald interrupted before the monk could express himself.

"Keep your words to yourself, monk, and all will be well. If you become too curious, you may not survive into old age."

The old monk took the suggestions courageously and bowed his head in acknowledgment of Oswald's words.

*   *   *

Some hours later, when the service of matins was in progress, he was introduced to Brother Thomas at the priory.

"*Pax vobiscum*," he said to Kathryn and James, as he made the sign of the cross, and he looked at the old monk.

"I have been expecting you. I know of you and you are welcome here, Brother. Your repentance is welcome, Baldur of Winchester."

Thomas took the old monk by the arm, "Come with me and I will see that you have the comforts as befits one of your age."

Thomas smiled at Kathryn and James who returned the smile as they looked for one last time on the countenance of the old monk. He seemed to be at peace with the world and with himself. Brother Thomas led him into the priory precincts.

"Bless his shiny tonsured head," James thought as Brother Thomas and the monk disappeared from sight. They left the area to walk back to the house where Oswald and Margaret awaited their return.

They sensed that the adventure had begun.

*   *   *

Margaret greeted James and Kathryn as they entered the house. She looked pensive as she saw that Oswald was not with them.

For the first time, James and Kathryn observed how Margaret was dressed, as if she was celebrating an event. Just as though their senses were becoming accustomed to their situation. Over a gown made of a bolt of sky blue silk, Margaret wore a tunic of darker blue with long tapering sleeves. A girdle of wrought gold filigree circled her waist; on her bosom lay a small gold cross set with pearls and rubies, made by an Italian goldsmith.

Suddenly Oswald appeared in the doorway. Margaret beamed as she saw him. He was her love and companion and would remain so forever. They sat down at the table to talk over the events of the day.

"Mea culpa," Oswald said as he smiled at Margaret. "It is my fault that I am so late. There were issues that needed my attention."

He did not elaborate but Margaret knew that he had been in danger. Oswald, sensing her worry, spoke to her in soothing tones as she shook herself free from worry and listened to his deep rich voice with the Northern English accent.

"Margaret, my dear. You should not worry so. Come, a cup of your hot tea will cure everything. What say you, James, and you, Kathryn?"

The familiarity of Oswald using her name made Kathryn warm to being with them in this strange place. It made her head swim and sent a shudder through her body. She could not understand her reactions to this situation. Oswald was so much like her James and like James, he always had that mischievous look in his eyes. But it was his eyes; boring into and through everything! So intense that she wondered if the pot might melt. But when her James smiled, the warmth and friendliness that he seemed to exhale with every breath made her forget that reoccurring thought that she was in another world.

Margaret smiled and soon delivered the pot of the aroma-rich tea to the table. Kathryn's nose was becoming sensitized to the various odors and she detected the presence of cloves and lemon in the hot liquid, to which honey had been added. James finished his tea and for some reason felt the need to write. He asked for writing materials to make notes on what they had done over the past few days.

Oswald looked steadily at James and read the look on his face and in his eyes. Smiling he asked, "You wish to make a journal, James?"

James nodded. Was he not a physician? Was he not used to recording his actions with various patients? But he had not seen any patients for at least . . . He sought for a timeline and could not remember how long it had been since he had last tended a sick person.

Oswald agreed to James's request and asked if he might help, suggesting that James could talk and he, Oswald, would write. Oswald winked at Margaret and Kathryn as he stood up.

"My dearest wife, I am now a scribe. Can we not think of other things for me to do?"

Margaret blushed. She remembered that first day when they had met at her father's apothecary stall in the marketplace in this very city. Oswald and his friend Ranulf de Boise. She blushed and her legs turned to jelly. She watched his deliberate, purposeful walk as he went into the back room to set up the writing table at which he and James could work.

Oswald took only a few moments to assemble the writing materials, to sharpen the goose quill into a pen, to make the ink from a dried ink stick by adding water, and so as not to feel encumbered, he removed his Benedictine robe and the weapons held by his belt. He was ready. He beckoned James into the room.

"*Carpe diem*, James. I am ready."

The Latin words meaning "seize the day" or "seize the moment" or "let's do it" were familiar to James's ears as he followed Oswald into the room. This was a room into which James and Kathryn had not ventured. It was much bigger than James had imagined.

Oswald seated himself at a long oak table that had rolls of parchment and books bound in vellum on it. Parchment scrolls and leather-bound books filled ironbound chests that were positioned next to the walls.

James wondered about the roll of yellowing parchment in the room. He knew that they had done this before. Perhaps even many times in the past. Not only here but somewhere else. Far away. Many years ago, yet he could not remember.

As he started to talk, Oswald looked and asked him to speak slowly. The pen made from a goose feather and the ink was not conducive to writing as quickly as he talked. Why not? James wondered. Had he not given dictation before without slowing his speech patterns?

The words flowed from James as if he could not stop. Oswald wrote down the words dutifully.

Margaret and Kathryn talked busily in the kitchen area and seemed to be happily huddled over more cups of herb tea.

As he talked, James recalled an incident when he had tended to a young man who was sick and so hot that he might die. The man got well soon after he took the two small white tablets that he had swallowed with the water to which he had first added a small amount of sour wine. The young man had slept all night without any repeat of the sweating, heat-searing hours that had brought him to his state. When James and Oswald—yes, Oswald had been with him—visited the house the next day, the young man was sitting up and eating broth.

He had awakened the next morning, weak but feeling much better; the bedding soaked by her perspiration. His parents were at the bedside with cool water, boiled first, just as he had instructed. Standing there, smiling, and crossing themselves, hoping that they would not be accused of witchcraft, determined to remain silent now that their son had survived. If giving him life was witchcraft, so be it . . .

These thoughts were not new. James had seen them before but he could not remember when. He stopped pacing and smiled.

"Oswald do you recall . . . ? Oh never mind," the question was not complete as he passed on to other thoughts for Oswald to write.

And then, James remembered. He was the man the young man's mother and father had called a "doctor."

He was the man who had been born . . . His name slipped his mind. What was his name? The man who would be known to the modern word as . . .

A few words form Oswald, and James shook his head to clear out the strange thoughts.

"Yes, Oswald, it is a good idea that we do this whenever we can. There may be some facts that I need to record to help me with future patients."

James looked over Oswald's shoulder. He could see the neatly written lines that had accumulated on the pages that Oswald had continued to write. The writing style looked familiar but James could not place it. He knew that he had seen the writing somewhere. The doodles that Oswald had made as he adjusted the new pen to his grip were also familiar. The circle into which Saint Cuthbert's cross was placed, as if for protection. Where had he seen it?

James looked at the table and the collection of books. One was wrapped in oilcloth. He looked at Oswald.

"May I," James asked.

Oswald smiled and nodded.

James unwrapped the oilcloth. Inside it lay a leather-bound book, with heavy metal clasps set with semiprecious stones. Even though the pages were yellowing, there were still the bright colors of startling illuminations.

Oswald saw James's inquiring look and said, "A gift to me a long time ago from Brother Thomas. It is one of my most prized possessions. That book had been with me ever since I began service to King Edward."

James rewrapped the book in the oilcloth.

"A very fine book, Oswald. A breviary I believe?" Oswald nodded as James continued. "The illuminations are spectacular."

"How are you men doing?"

Margaret and Kathryn appeared at the entrance to the room. Curiosity had motivated them.

*   *   *

CHAPTER 34

O swald and James had completed their start on James's journals and were once more sitting with Margaret and Kathryn at the table. The conversation focused on Gervais and they realized that there was only one way to stop him and it had to be final. Gervais had to die.

The rumors were, as near as could be determined when conversation with the old monk were recalled, that whenever Gervais was in the streets, which was not often, he was seen to be accompanied by at least two of his companions with several more of the cutthroats at various distances away. As with the stray dogs that abounded in the streets, other members of the pack protected the leader of the pack. No man trained like Gervais, in the technique of the assassin, would allow himself to be approached, harmed, or killed. His men were strategically placed so that any potential killer would have to get through two or three layers of defenders. And such a task was unlikely to succeed; such was the planning of Gervais.

"But," Oswald thought, "I am the protector of the king and his family. Perhaps I can be the wolf in sheepdog's clothing, herding this sheep to his death. It is time."

He smiled as James and Kathryn returned his look. Kathryn gave him a puzzled look. Had he no regard for what was about to happen?

Oswald looked into his cup at the steaming liquid. He knew that the streets would be snarled with people going about their business, noisy horse-drawn wagons and donkeys that seemed to bray for no reason. The quiet oxen were not used too much in the city. Pity. Durham was a busy city, a gem in the northern bastion that kept the Scots under control and prevented a major invasion of England. Occasional forays by marauding bands did occur, as the two Flemings had found out the day before.

Oswald stood and walked around the table to the side where James and Kathryn sat.

Margaret returned from the kitchen with a tray of oatcakes. They stood together, in the form of a communal hug, for that golden moment when each knows the thoughts and feelings of the others.

"Now, my friends, we must get ready for the most important actions of your lives. We are about to catch a killer."

Oswald took some clothes out of his bag. He gave them to James and Kathryn. "Even though we are supposedly dead, Gervais will be very suspicious if he hears of three Benedictines walking around the streets of Durham. You, my dear," he looked at Margaret, "need to join us. We need to change our stature. You, Little One," he looked at Kathryn, "need to grow in size and we can do that by the use of thick soled boots. You will wear this mask and if anyone approaches we will say that you have had contact with some disease, the pox. Your skin is too precious to allow these rogues to look upon you."

James and Kathryn decided not to question Oswald's words. The decision was made and they were more than willing to take his advice.

"James, you need to reduce your stature by walking with bent knees so that you appear to be much smaller. I will also use the same tactic and our voluminous robes will cover this tactic. You, my dear," he looked at Margaret, "use the same ruse as Kathryn and also wear a mask. You will be two journeying monks that have just arrived and the pox masks will support your stories. But you will be journeying monks who also, unknown to others, have weapons concealed about you."

Once adorned in their masks with the new boots, Margaret and Kathryn did appear to be inches taller. James simulated a walk with bent knees and neither Kathryn nor Margaret could find fault with his new posture. Oswald had been correct. The voluminous robes covered his ruse. Oswald turned and looked at them both.

"Now you look very much the part. But you are too clean. Wrap this bandage around the lower part of your face," he handed the bandage to Kathryn, "and pull the cowl over your forehead."

James helped her tie the end of the bandage so that there was no fear of slippage and disclosure of her looks.

"Good," Oswald declared. "Much better. In fact, it does not even look like you."

ELIZABETH JAMES

"It's my winning smile that you can no longer see," Kathryn offered.

"Even better," Oswald said softly, "your voice is completely masked and not recognizable as the voice of a woman, much less high-pitched."

"You too, my dear," Oswald looked at his wife but she was already going through the motions of completing her disguise.

"Now," Oswald looked satisfied, "I believe that we are ready! But, my dear wife and dear Little One, please take off the cloths from around your mouths until we leave the house!"

"So, how do we go about this task," James asked as the two ladies freed their mouths from the confines of the cloths.

Oswald explained that the plan was to draw Gervais out of hiding and away from his protectors. He might even find his guards and eliminate them one at a time. The quicker the better.

"Since it is Gervais that we are after," Kathryn offered, "it could be quite a task to find out his habits and where he lives."

"Aye, Kath," James threw his ideas into the pot, "we need a good reliable source who may have had a relative, a victim of Gervais's killings or perhaps one of the oppressed who needs money to support his family for a decent standard of living. Or is that too idealistic?"

"No, Cousin, your words ring true. Gervais has no friends and I may know of such a person."

The light came on in Oswald's eyes and he turned on his heel.

"Do not stray from here. I will return in one hour."

Margaret took the empty teacups into the kitchen and left James and Kathryn to their thoughts. James held Kathryn's hand, realizing the danger that they were about to encounter. They looked into each other's eyes and remained motionless as their hands comforted each other. Kathryn had just leaned forward and kissed James lightly on the lips when they heard the sound of Oswald returning.

He carried with him a basket of food. Fresh food that they had not seen for several days. Margaret smiled but before she could speak, Oswald filled the gap of silence.

"To continue our conversation, I do have such a person," he said. "I just needed the time to think clearly. I needed to weigh the advantages against the disadvantages. And it is done."

"Great," James almost exploded. "When do we meet him?"

"Yes, Oswald when do we meet—" Kathryn was about to repeat James's question when Oswald cut her words short.

"Her," he said.

The one word took Kathryn and James by surprise. Complete surprise. They both muttered the word at the same time. Two pairs of eyebrows were raised in question.

"Her?"

"Of course, her. Here she is."

Oswald gestured toward Margaret who smiled sweetly as if she was not at all concerned.

"Margaret! You. But why?"

Kathryn could not contain her words or her curiosity. James felt the same but Kathryn had beaten him to the question.

"My dear wife has her own reasons . . ." Margaret put her hand onto Oswald's arm before he could continue and then she spoke.

"I do, but there are also other reasons. Whenever, my husband needs me, there I shall be. No matter what the dangers, I will be with him. We do not know our fate but I do know that the extra time that we have been given is precious and I will not spend it apart from him. Nor will I leave him alone in his hour of need. Just as you are doing for him, dear James and Kathryn, so shall I."

She looked into their eyes and they saw the sincerity and love that Margaret and Oswald felt for each other. Kathryn reached out and held James's hand. Before she could speak, Margaret spoke.

For the remainder of the daylight hours, they talked, ate, laughed, and tried to relax. And they were successful. From time to time they returned the name of Gervais to the discussion and then Oswald explained his plan.

"It is my firm belief that the target of this plot is John, Duke of Lancaster. He bears the most threat to those who would acquire the throne through the child Richard, should his father Edward the Black Prince die. And that seems very likely. His health has deteriorated over the past few weeks. And he continues to attempt to subdue the French. He has had success but at a great personal cost to himself. So, I have assumed that he will not survive many more years and may even die before his father, King Edward."

"But what about other targets?" James asked.

"They are all," Oswald thought for a moment as he chose the correct word, "what I would prefer to call minor events or diversions. I am more and more convinced that it is John of Lancaster who Gervais must kill."

"Then why does he delay?" James continued with a question.

"To kill him in a particular place, for a particular reason," offered Margaret. "It seems," she continued, "that this man will have a reason for his actions and he must always leave some doubt or conjecture about the death of his target."

A silence fell. It was stifling in the room despite the coolness of the air outside. The noise of the city, a loud cacophony of voices, sounding like an out-of-tune orchestra, came to their ears.

"Are we ready?" asked Oswald.

Each of the three nodded in agreement.

"Perhaps we should sleep," Oswald suggested although it was more like a command. "The days ahead could be very busy for us and allow us to sleep only when action is not required."

Darkness had descended and settled around them. The candles were extinguished as they retired to their respective paliasses and slept.

Two hours later, James felt the gentle awakening shake of Oswald's hand on his arm. As James came out of the depths of sleep, Oswald placed his hand across James's mouth indicating the need for silence. Once fully dressed, James went into the kitchen where Oswald had prepared hot tea, he spoke to James in a whisper.

"We need to be about this night. There is something that troubles me regarding our 'assassin' friend. He may be ready to move."

James nodded. They armed themselves and left the house. Neither Margaret nor Kathryn had stirred.

*   *   *

CHAPTER 35

The same night that Oswald, Margaret, James, and Kathryn had discussed their plans and had reached the conclusion that John of Lancaster was the target of the assassin, Gervais paced the floor of his house in deep thought. His thoughts went back to the many times that he had responded to the many calls for his services, which had taken him to various parts of Europe. And now he was involved in what might be his last, and most ambitious, task. The assassination of John, Duke of Lancaster. He might consider retiring after this one. But then, what would he do? If he was successful, there would be a monetary reward and the gift of land that would need managing. Other than his sponsor, no one knew that. Gervais had requested that the secret remain between the two of them.

He decided that he needed to leave the house and sought out the younger of the two Flemings.

"I know that you want to come with me," Gervais said, "but this night is not for you. I am saving you for the real work."

It was always a relief for Gervais to speak French. The guttural English of the North was not an easy language for him. He mixed up the words and, not wishing to seem foolish in front of those that he commanded, he spoke only when absolutely necessary. The success of this task lay in his followers understanding that his authority and command were absolute.

The two Flemings were from the northern part of Flanders and they had been sent to him because they were skilled assassins. The older one was very good with the knife and it was he, so Gervais had been told, who had been instrumental in the deaths of several men of noble birth in France, Spain, and Italy. But never in Flanders. Never send a man to do dirty work in his own country where there was the high risk of disclosure through a familiar face. The younger one had also performed several tasks but his skill lay with the sword. He was not as proficient with the dagger or knife as his older companion. That was a definite disadvantage to the art of assassination where the ability to handle a sword, however proficient, in a confined space offered limited success.

The two Flemings were expressionless. They looked directly at Gervais. They knew that he had come to a decision. He needed to be alone on the street and they would respect that. Previously, one of the cutthroats had attempted to follow Gervais as he left on a nightly excursion. He had not returned but his body had been found in a place where the others could see it and heed the warning. And there were others who Gervais had sent out to watch the old monk and the three Benedictines who had also failed to return. Their fate was unknown but every member of Gervais's entourage suspected what had happened even though their bodies had not yet been found.

But like all who were ambitious, the young Fleming thought that he was an aristocrat of the killing order. He wanted to be involved in every step of the operation. But he had almost caused a disaster when Gervais had released, rather than killed, the fourteen Italian dignitaries and the eight women that they had seized as hostages when they traveled from Rome to Florence. The young Fleming had decided that one of the ladies was to be his prize. Gervais could not allow this, and he had a large investment in the plan being carried out successfully. He had almost killed the young Fleming then. So now Gervais was torn between the two poles of a major decision. How long could the older Fleming last in this work? How far could he trust the young Fleming? He had already decided that the older one was a man to be trusted; his younger companion had the potential to jeopardize the mission. He could even cost Gervais his life! And so the decision was made within a few steps of the house. The only question remaining about the death of the young Fleming was related to the timing of his demise.

Gervais looked at both of them as though summing up his thoughts and his distrust of the young Fleming.

"Remember," he said, "you must follow the plan of the mission. You are not to diverge from the plan. This must be a clean and accurate kill with no survivors, if there should be anyone else in the vicinity."

The young Fleming looked back at Gervais with cold eyes. He had planned his words carefully.

"When we have killed the target," Gervais had not told either of them that the target was John of Lancaster, "if he is as close to the king as we suspect, we will be lucky to get away with our own lives. And why must the timing be so perfect? The commotion will allow others to know that something of a major significance has happened. And then we will be in danger."

Gervais smiled and responded.

"After we have done the deed, I have men placed to create a diversion. That will protect us to a point. But we will need to be quick about ourselves to remove ourselves from danger."

Gervais smiled again. He now knew the timing of the demise of the younger Fleming. His body would be left close by the scene of John's murder. After all, someone would need to take the blame. And who better than a Fleming who had died from wounds caused by the knife, belonging to the Duke of Lancaster of course, sticking from his chest. Gervais grinned with anticipation.

This operation would be a success and the body of the young Fleming found close to the corpse of Lancaster was a little something extra, perhaps a bonus, to let his sponsor know that he should not be slow in forthcoming with his reward. Gervais liked this final part of his plan.

Gervais did not bother to add anything more to the conversation. The Flemings both believed that all would be well. They heard Gervais mutter something about lambs to the slaughter and then all was silent.

Moments later, Gervais got up from where he had been sitting and announced that he would finally take his nightly walk. He announced that he was leaving for a while. There was surprise in the eyes of the young Fleming. His older companion remained unperturbed as though he knew what Gervais had decided. Gervais looked at both of them.

As he left the house he felt that he was in full control. The operation was planned in detail and he now had to take care of the last-minute thorn in his side. The young Fleming.

At last he was on his way to recouping the castle and lands that he had lost when John of Lancaster, during one of his forays into France, had captured and Gervais had been lucky to escape with his life. And the irony of all this was that his sponsor wanted John removed for another reason and he, Gervais, was being paid handsomely to perform his own act of revenge. Such is life. Or death. He allowed himself an almost silent chuckle.

Two men watched him from the shadows. Both were clad in the long dark robes of the Benedictines, but these were monks with a difference. They were fully armed and their faces intent on the actions of their quarry; they remained still. They knew that the slightest sound and Gervais would be alerted. It would take only moments for his companions to exit the house and surround them.

From beneath his robe, Oswald drew his killing sword. A double-edged weapon that had a blade about eighteen inches long, in the style of the Roman gladius, which allowed Oswald the luxury of full movement in enclosed spaces.

Gervais disappeared quickly into the darkness of the night. Oswald was about to sheath his sword when the young Fleming also emerged from the house. His actions showed that he was intent on following Gervais. Oswald, ever vigilant, held the sword at the ready. It was a timely move.

The sharp eyes of the young Fleming sensed a movement in the shadows and realized that two men were standing there. Rather than shout for help and with the confidence of youth, he decided to be a hero. He challenged the two monks to show themselves, at the same time brandishing a sword. He discerned the individual shapes and thrust his sword toward James. Seeing the imminent danger, Oswald's knife bit deeply into young man's throat. There was no time to call out to his older friend or to any of the other companions in the house. His words were drowned in the blood of his throat. His legs took on the rubbery feeling of death and collapsed under him as he sank to the ground. The last words that the young Fleming heard before his eyes closed forever were spoken in a strange accent by one of the men.

"Oswald, my cousin, that was smooth. Not even a sound or a gurgle. Now I suggest that we remove ourselves from this spot before we are discovered."

"Aye, James, let's leave this traitor here for his friend to find. Perhaps it will make them think twice about what they plan to do."

No one in the house had heard anything nor did anyone suspect anything. The action had been silent and final.

*　　*　　*

As he returned from his nightly excursion, Gervais sensed that something was amiss, and then he stumbled in the darkness. He muttered a single curse when he realized that he had almost fallen over a body. He ran to the house and alerted his companions, demanding that they bring a candle. For one of the only times in his life, Gervais felt the cold shiver of fear pass along his spine when he saw that the body was the earthly remains of the young Fleming.

"Did you not hear anything?" Gervais asked the older Fleming.

"Nothing." The response was immediate. "I did not even know that he had left the house. He told me that he had to take care of himself in the backyard at the midden ditch."

"Well, my old friend, it seems that we are being watched. I do not see this as an accident. This has the look of a deliberate deed. The way that his throat is cut. Beautiful. Very professional. I could not have done better myself."

Gervais looked at two of the others.

"Move the body and bury it in the backyard. We," he looked at the older Fleming, "need to talk."

They seated themselves in the middle of the main room. Gervais indicated, by a wave of his arm, that they were to be left alone. The other followers acknowledged the sign and went into the backyard. They were less conspicuous here in the middle of the night than they would have been on the front street.

Gervais broke the silence. The Fleming had kept his mouth shut, wondering if he might be accused by Gervais of shirking his duty.

"I can only assume the worst," Gervais said. "Your young friend must have stumbled onto someone who was watching us. I am wondering if the old monk has not been as silent as he should have been."

The older Fleming added to this thought.

"Perhaps there are tongues wagging on the street and in the taverns. Should we retire from this task for a while?

"The world is nothing but talk and noise," Gervais added in his flawless Norman French and the dialect with which the Fleming was most familiar, "how great is the price for a man to betray us?"

The Fleming was pleased at the question since it told him that, for the moment, Gervais needed him. On the other hand, Gervais had carefully thought out the role that the Fleming could now play; he was satisfied that he should live, for the moment. Simply put, in Gervais's mind, the older Fleming now took the part of his formerly expendable younger countryman. The plan was still very workable.

Gervais closed his eyes. What a sensuous thing was the silence of the night. He had always enjoyed the nighttime hours when questions were not asked. He could relax, no matter what he was doing, as if the best aromatic oils were massaging his body and mind. Without opening his eyes, Gervais reached over and put his hand on the Fleming's shoulder. He knew how much he would enjoy the killing. He had given the Fleming no clue to his intentions.

"Now we know for sure that they are after us," said Gervais. "I suspect that it is one of a team that I heard of some time ago. He was a sworn protector of the king and his family, but I had thought that he died in an accident close by this city."

"I also have heard of such a man," added the Fleming. "But his whereabouts is not known to me. Perhaps he did die in the accident of which you speak."

He removed his hand from the Fleming's shoulder and sat thinking for a few moments. The Fleming watched as Gervais focused his eyes on the mud floor and became lost in his thoughts. Suddenly, Gervais looked up at him.

"I have several men left," he motioned his head in the direction of the backyard. "They should be sufficient to get this job done."

"You have also the two Italians and several of their followers who are due here?" the Fleming paused as he searched for the answer.

"Within the day," Gervais was quick to finish the Fleming's sentence.

"Surely they must be of some value and can be used?" The Fleming frowned as he asked the question.

"They are good at their work but I am only using them because they are the favorites of my sponsor who does not understand what must be done. Italians dancing around with their short but very sharp knives that they call stilettos can be so irritating and ineffectual. If the man who killed your companion is as good as I think, the Italians will last only a matter of minutes. But they can create a useful diversion for us."

"If your sponsor insists that they be used, who are we to question how they be used."

Gervais smiled and reached over and slapped the Fleming's arm. He was starting to like this man. Perhaps he would not need to die. But he needed to lay another false trail. The older Fleming had to die!

"I know more about the contract of requirements than you do," Gervais said as he reached for a bottle of wine that lay nearby. He was feeling good enough to drink, something that he rarely did until a task was completed. He took a gulp from the already-opened bottle, left by the now-deceased and almost-forgotten young Fleming, and passed it to the Fleming. As he drank, Gervais looked at him.

He realized that the Fleming was becoming more and more useful. Among the persons with whom he had worked over the years, this one had been the best with every kind of weapon. He spoke perfect Norman French and several regional variations and, to Gervais's surprise, he even wrote Norman French. His only pastime seemed to be maintaining his weapons in good condition and practicing.

Despite his age, Gervais had observed that the Fleming was strong in the arm. In a training exercise it had taken five men to slow him down but not one could get near enough for the simulated kill. He was as adept with his hands as he was with his weapons. He had the calm fearlessness of the true professional killer. Since he had decided that he could not allow the Fleming to live, Gervais offered him some comfort with his words.

"Let us sleep for a few hours before the dawn. I sense that tomorrow will be an eventful day!"

The Fleming dutifully obeyed. He did not nod or say anything. He lay back and closed his eyes. It was as if he had become a stone.

*   *   *

CHAPTER 36

G ervais inspected the weapons while the Fleming slept and the other members of the group, that were awake, watched with interest. They very rarely cleaned their weapons and were watching Gervais as if they were uncertain of what was expected of them. The quasi-leader of the group offered to help Gervais but his offer was quietly refused. The group sensed that something major was about to happen and that they would be involved. It never occurred to any of them that they were expected to die to allow Gervais and the Fleming the luxury of success.

Finally the weapons were clean, sharp, and ready for use. Gervais was proud of his work.

The Fleming, who had awoken from his brief sleep, looked over Gervais's shoulder and smiled at the sight before him.

"Well?" Gervais asked.

"Very clean and ready," responded the Fleming. It was four of the few words that the Fleming had spoken for some time.

The other men, sitting and standing around, were all equipped with weapons of their own choice and they varied from a dagger to swords that were all in various states of disrepair and sharpness. One of two even carried a mace fitted with a short chain. Some of the men wore chain mail that was battle-torn and even patched in places with newer rings. Rust showed in places. Some carried shields and one single-bladed axe. The weapons had been purchased new, but had been taken from bodies of the dead and kept for personal use or sold, depending on the preferences of the mercenary.

A variety of scars decorated the faces of the mercenaries. Some were the results of the pox but most were battle scars. Gervais thought that if he had a gold coin for every scar on the faces and the bodies of the mercenaries, he would be a very rich man.

Neither Gervais nor the Fleming approved of such a varied collection of weapons. They were only good for close quarters and not for general skirmishing. Even then, at close quarters, how much damage could a blunt dagger do? The Fleming looked at the group and quietly acknowledged to himself that these men were back-alley thieves and vagabonds. Not equipped for what they had been asked to do. But well equipped to cause a diversion as they died. The group did not know any of these thoughts and were pleased with themselves for the apparent show of force that they believed was their image.

They moved away from the group to talk in quiet tones close by the place where the Fleming had slept.

"Our weapons will be sufficient for the task that we have to perform," Gervais looked at the Fleming as he spoke. The Fleming nodded affirmatively and then added, "The swords should be enough and we need to make sure that we do not weight ourselves down. Mobility is the key."

Again, Gervais was surprised at the number of words that the Fleming had found in his vocabulary; he had become quite a talker. Perhaps nerves before the action Gervais wondered.

The Fleming continued, "Let us remember that the main thing is the timing of our action. I will approach the target upon your signal and hold my hand out to him in greeting."

"And I," Gervais interjected, "will approach from the other direction. Any person in my way will die and then I shall dispense my justice to John."

"Your justice . . . ?" The Fleming was puzzled.

"A slip of the tongue, my friend. Meaning that I will send him to meet his maker." Then, lowering his vice so that the others would not hear, he added, "Then we must leave the killing place as soon as we can and in different directions. We will meet at the other house, known only to you and me, lest any of our ruffian friends who might survive, will lead the soldiers back here or give out information under the hot iron."

Gervais turned to the group and they actually stood and came to attention when he looked in their direction.

"Let us go over the final arrangement of this night's work. The target is in a building close by the castle. We," he nodded at the Fleming, "will approach the target from another direction and you," he nodded at all of them, "will offer us protection from any frontal attack. After the deed is done, you will disperse to allay any suspicion that several men together might cause and make your way back here. Understood?"

A series of nods told him that at least they had ears. Gervais looked at their equally unkempt and dirty quasi-leader.

"What is your name?" he asked.

"Hugo."

"All right, Hugo, you will take your men straight to the building close by the north gate of the castle. There you will find about twenty Scotsmen awaiting you. If not, disperse your men to watch the castle gate. I have arranged for the guards to be looking in another direction so entry will be easy. You will start your actions when you hear the bells of the priory calling the monks to *Prime*. I will meet you inside the gate and from there we will proceed to our task. Any noise that you make could wake up the rest of the castle guard, who do not know of this venture, so I advise caution and silence."

"It will be done as you wish." Hugo smiled at Gervais showing a line of crooked and blackened teeth.

Gervais looked at the Fleming who nodded and remained expressionless. They both knew that the castle guard would not be subject to bribery. Gervais and he would slip into the castle by another route, known only to a few persons. Where Gervais had got this information, the Fleming did not know. But he did know that the commotion nearby the north gate might draw soldiers from their posts.

Since the day of his arrival in Durham, the Fleming had been watching Gervais carefully. He was not a man to trust others lightly but since the death of his young acquaintance he realized that Gervais needed him more than ever. He had even believed that Gervais might have a plan for his untimely death. He even slept lightly so that any sound or movement would awaken him and he would be ready. He doubted that Gervais could have overcome him without taking some form of heavy wound. Now he felt that he could relax his guard a little and allow Gervais some iota of trust.

Gervais handed the Fleming a red band with a golden lion rampant, the emblem of some of the Scottish kings. It would fit across a helmet.

"Wear this at all times," at all times Gervais told the Fleming, "I want you to be recognizable and if there is any doubt afterward I want those who see us to lay the blame on the Scots. I also have one for my helm."

The Fleming could sense his chest heaving as he listened to Gervais. It was warm inside of the chain mail that he had donned under his cloak. And now they would walk to the castle. A short distance and the cool air would revive him.

*   *   *

Oswald and James, having observed the commencement of activities at Gervais's house, returned to awaken Margaret and Kathryn. Margaret could see from the look in Oswald's eyes that he sensed that the hour was near.

His lordship, John of Lancaster, had been in the castle for a few hours. His arrival had been sudden and unexpected, except for a few persons who needed to know. Oswald had seen John enter the castle but John had not seen Oswald.

James reached out and touched Kathryn. She struggled to awaken and arrived in the kitchen in a semi-awake state. Margaret touched Kathryn lightly on the forehead and she was immediately awake.

Oswald looked at his wife and his two cousins. The dim light of the candle showed the determined looks on all of their faces.

"We know what we have to do." It was a statement from Oswald. The time for questions was over. The three nods told him that all was understood. "Then let us be about our business."

Margaret and Kathryn carried the lighter falchions. James and Oswald, having been out in the night, already carried their swords and Oswald took from the sackcloth package his trusty axe. He looked at James.

"Thank you, dear cousin, for returning my friend to me." Oswald raised the axe and kissed each of the two blades. "He and I have work to do this night."

James smiled and took Oswald's hand in his.

"As long as we have a just cause we will succeed. I have no intention of leaving my dear wife," he looked at Kathryn, "a widow."

"You had better not," chorused Margaret and Kathryn in one single voice.

Oswald smiled.

"You see what I have had to endure all of these years."

"But he did it with a smile," added Margaret, "and when he got out of hand, I would tell him so even if I had to stand on a chair to meet him eye to eye!"

Oswald reached out to Margaret and drew her closer and kissed her. "Caution, my dear. Danger is abroad this night. I doubt that we can be hurt but we have our two cousins to help us and we must watch for their safety."

Margaret smiled at James and Kathryn who had exchanged a tender kiss.

"Methinks that they will be all right as well. But I will be alert. And please, Oswald, my dear, no heroics! You are not as . . ." she allowed the words to trail away into the silence realizing what she had been about to say was not an issue to either of them.

Oswald looked at James and Kathryn.

"Are you ready, Cousins?"

"Aye, we are." Kathryn answered for both of them. James nodded.

"A few words to both of you. You win by killing the enemy. Fair play, as you may call it, is not our lexicon. Kill before you are killed. You understand me?"

Kathryn and James nodded.

"Then let us be on our way."

*   *   *

Gervais used his knowledge of the terrain to ascend the hill on the west side of the castle. The light was dim in the early-morning hours. Dim enough to offer some cover but light enough to offer guidance up the steep slopes.

The Fleming was not surprised that Gervais had chosen this route. He was surprised when two other men, both well armed and not known to the Fleming, joined them at a point about halfway up the hill. They rose from the low vegetation and their armor had been blackened so as not to reflect any meager light from the moon or other sources. The Fleming was alert as he saw the two shadows. He pulled his sword partway out of the scabbard. Gervais turned to him and made no sound, only a head signal to the Fleming to show that this was anticipated.

The two newcomers followed in line behind the Fleming, who started to feel very uncomfortable having two strangers behind him.

"So," thought the Fleming, "our Gervais still does not trust me. I have another two that need my attention."

Gervais found the marker stone that he was seeking. It led him to a point on the wall where there was a gap between the stones. The gap had been made some years before during an attack by the Scots. A messenger had left the castle and ridden to York to bring word of the attack. The Scots, who had settled in for a long siege and were determined that the castle should fall, were surprised when a relief army appeared. The blood lust was high and the Scots were slaughtered, almost to a man.

The gap in the stones was sufficient to allow one man at a time to enter the tunnel that led under the wall. The Fleming followed Gervais along the tunnel, making a mental note of this feature. The odor was almost unbearable. It seemed that the tunnel was in reality a sewage outlet and the Fleming cared not to think of the foul sewage laden with disease that flowed around him. They were under the wall by at least the height of a man and then Gervais found the mark that he was seeking. A sharp turn and the grayness of the early-morning sky became visible above their heads.

Gervais led the way out of the tunnel and into the dungeon area of the castle. They were one step closer to the target.

The Fleming slithered feet first into the basement room, clumsy in his wet chain mail and surcoat. The front of his helm was fouled and he could hardly see. He removed the helm to get the fresher air to his mouth and nose. The other two were also out of the tunnel gasping for air. He suddenly realized that all was not well. Gervais was looking at him in a manner that could only be described as mistrustful.

"It seems, my friend, that it is time to part company," Gervais announced. "You have served my purpose very well. I had toyed with the idea of letting you live. But your death here will throw those who try to follow me off the scent. And what a scent it is!"

Gervais smiled at his play on words and he held his nose between thumb and forefinger to show his disgust.

402

ELIZABETH JAMES

"My friends and I will finish the job. And those who follow can seek me in Flanders!"

Gervais nodded at the two newcomers who knew what his signal meant. The Fleming had outlived any usefulness for which he had been hired. Like the others of the group, now at the north gate, he had also been hired to die and to lay a false trail.

Gervais stripped off his wet surcoat and replaced it with a dry one that he carried in his pouch. As one watched over the Fleming, the other two did the same in turn.

"Relieves the odor somewhat," Gervais offered by way of explanation. "And now, my friend, it is time to bid you *adieu*. Forever."

One of the two strangers raised his short dagger to dispatch the Fleming. As he did so, a voice called to them. He half-turned and slipped on the grime that had clung to his boots. As he slipped his dagger caught the Fleming in the hip, piercing the flesh to the bone. The Fleming was in severe pain as he fell and caught his head on the hard surface of the tunnel base. The pain of his pierced hip muscle and the confusion his head rendered him almost senseless. Thinking that the silence from the Fleming was a sign that his knife had stuck home, the darkness preventing a close look at his victim, the assailant rose to join Gervais and his other companion.

*   *   *

At the top of the stairs that led to the level above and toward the room where John lay sleeping stood two figures wearing the dark robes of the Benedictines. Gervais smiled.

"I know who they are," he whispered to his companions, "there should be a third. They are Benedictines. And they have been trying to find me for some time. This night we can put a stop to their activities."

Gervais heard the mocking laughter.

"God's teeth. They are women. This is even better than I thought. We can show them that women die as easily as men."

Gervais and his two companions walked slowly up the steps to reach the next level. Gervais licked his lips in anticipation. There was something about a woman dying in battle or being put to the sword that he found stimulating. This would be an enjoyable night. They faltered only momentarily as the two women pulled swords from under their robes.

"Did you sharpen these yourselves?" he asked.

The one on the left responded in an accent that Gervais did not recognize. Taunting.

"Come to me, Frenchman, and let us see what you are made of." Her high-pitched laughter ground on his ears. "Do you really eat snails?" She continued. "Well after this, the snails will feed on you!"

Gervais made the mistake of allowing his anger to rise. Such insults. And from a woman. He could see her light blue eyes. Icy. And serious. "Well, anyway, what could a woman do," he asked himself.

He looked at his two companions and nodded. The narrowness of the stairway prevented a concerted rush by the three men. Gervais led the way. As he approached the top the two women stepped back to allow him to enter the spacious landing. His two companions were close behind. The slime that still coated the bottom of Gervais's boots caused him to slip and stumble ending up on his knees. His two companions tripped over his sprawling legs.

They each felt pain as the two short swords, wielded by the two women, pierced their chain mail and entered the flesh. Not serious wounds but just enough to enrage. The darkness and the confined space prevented a full counterattack.

Gervais cursed and rose from the floor. He saw that the women had disrobed and were wearing the short jerkins and breeches that were common to the soldiers. Two pairs of cold eyes stared at Gervais. Two swords were held in the ready position. Gervais licked his lips again. As did his two henchmen. The stimulation of seeing women girded for battle was sending thoughts ripping through their brains. Their target, John of Lancaster, was almost forgotten.

"Well, my dears, it is a pity that you have decided to stand against us. We will deal with you and then we may have use for you later. A cut to the rear of your beautiful legs, the Achilles point I believe it is called, and you will be powerless to do anything. We will leave you here and my companions and I will enjoy your company later. And then you will die!"

"We are not the ones to die, Frenchman!"

It was the other who spoke. She had the accent of the North and her cold eyes dared them to move.

*   *   *

CHAPTER 37

O n the other side of the castle, at the gate, Gervais's men heard the priory bells ringing for *Prime*. The monks started the chants and their voices could be heard throughout the castle grounds. This was the signal to start the attack.

The men that Gervais had picked to start a diversion did just that. They attacked the building near to the north gate of the castle. Thinking that all would be well and they would overcome any interference from the few guards that were on duty at that time of the morning, but they were surprised and it was too late. The guards were well prepared. Oswald and James had joined them and given an indication of what might happen. And in order that they should not appear suspicious in front of the other soldiers, he and Oswald had discarded their Benedictine robes in favor of surcoats that were marked with the emblem of King Edward. As a result, no one had even thought to question Oswald's authority.

As Gervais had told him, the Scots were in the house. They had entered the area under cover of the dim light of the late evening and had been awaiting the arrival of Gervais's men. Hugo nodded to their leader, exchanged a few words, and led the men from the house toward the castle gate, thinking to overcome the few soldiers on duty. But he was mistaken.

Bows were quickly swung into position, arrows knocked, and let fly at the assailants. Several went down in the first salvo as the other arrows continued to take their toll of the attackers. Oswald and James, with some of the castle guards, moved outside of the gate to corner those attackers who had sought the safety of the dead space next to the wall where bowman on the walls could not aim accurately. One of the attackers grabbed at James, and without thinking James kicked him in the groin and thrust his sword into the man's chest even before he could double up with pain. James had surprised himself but the penchant for survival was strong.

"Welcome to the world of chivalry, James my cousin," Oswald acknowledged James's effort.

James turned to face another attacker. This one, seeing his colleague down, thought better of it and decided upon a tactical withdrawal only to be halted in his tracks. Oswald had seen the man approach James and as the man stepped back he had the great misfortune to skewer himself on Oswald's sword. Blood flowed from the man's surprised mouth, his face disintegrated in pain, and he died without uttering a sound. Oswald pulled the sword from the body as it fell away from him and toward James. Seeing that the remaining attackers had opted for flight, Oswald wiped his sword clean on the clothes of the dead man. He looked at the one that James had felled.

"James, you are more of a warrior than I thought. And from the look on your face, killing enemies becomes you. Well done!"

James unsure of himself and his feeling could only mumble.

"Aye, me lad. That's what scares me. I enjoyed it."

Another attacker rushed at James, who, surprised at his newfound agility, stepped quickly to one side and as his attacker overshot his mark, James thrust the sword into the man's left side, piercing the heart.

"Another one who will cause us no further worry," James thought.

To repel the attackers, other soldiers had been called from the barracks and ran to the defense of the castle. The fight continued with the deafening din of sword blows on helmets, shields, and corselets accompanied by the tumult of shouts, grunts, oaths, and screams.

Limp, severed bodies lay where they had fallen. Other men were writhing in the mud as death approached. The sickly sweet smell of spilled blood pervaded the air. The acrid odor of fear was everywhere. And then, it was over.

James and Oswald watched carefully as the bodies of the attackers were collected and laid out for identification. Later, they would be dragged to the outside wall and placed in a trench where they would be burned for fear of contagion.

Oswald and James looked at each other.

"You know, James, none of these men seem to me to be the type that we could call outstanding citizens with the capability of planning such an attack."

James walked to where Oswald inspected the bodies and as he looked he could not help but make the comment, "There is an appearance of malnutrition, of vitiated body fluids, and of general ill health in these men. As a physician, I naturally think of soldiers as being fit and healthy. These men are not. They could rightly be called the scum of the earth!"

"And," James, Oswald followed on with his thoughts, "would our assassin be here to die in what is nothing more than a foolish and futile effort to enter a castle through a well-defended gate?"

Oswald looked pensive as he pondered his question.

"James, we have been fooled. As I expected our assassin is a very clever man. There is another way into the castle and I believe that is where we will find our assassin. And what worries me is that I know not where our ladies are amidst all of this."

*   *   *

Kathryn threw her sword to Margaret and stripped off her jerkin. The heat in the lower parts of the castle was often unbearable and she could feel the discomfort. She felt better in the coolness of her waist-length chemise and the breeches.

The three men licked their lips. What a piece of fortune. Two Benedictines had suddenly become two women.

One of the companions looked at Margaret. He smiled thinking about how he would enjoy himself later. He spoke in coarse French.

"*Alors, ma cherie. Vous êtes une belle dam aussi! Comme celui là?*" (Well, my pretty. You are also a fine woman! Like that one there?)

"*Et vous monsieur, vous êtes un couchon. Venez ici, et je vous mourir.*" (And you, sir, you are a pig. Come here and I will kill you.)

Margaret's taunting words were too much for the man. His emotional lunge with his sword caused him to miss the target. Margaret's light sidestepping made his lunge seem so clumsy and useless. The sword in her hand came alive. His lunge caused him to stumble toward her and he was about to right himself for another lunge but she used the falchion for its main purpose, cutting and slashing. Each time she drew blood. He attempted to right himself again when her sword entered his throat in a sideways slash that felt no resistance. There was no time for surprise or emotion or pain. The man died instantly.

Gervais did not like what he saw. His face was hard and immobile. Above the three-day stubble that had grown on his face since he had last shaved, his eyes formed tiny slits. This was not the way to tackle these two women. He should taunt them. Tire them. Get them to make rash moves and then he would pounce. He looked at them. Yes. He would play their game and he would win.

The other man was enraged and he faced Kathryn. Margaret whispered to Kathryn across the space between them.

"Guard yourself, my cousin. Be cautious, my cousin. His sword point may be envenomed with poison brewed from toads."

Kathryn's eyes narrowed as she focused on the Frenchman. Margaret's voice offered her another suggestion.

"Remember the Norsemen. It will be to your advantage!"

Kathryn smiled as she heeded Margaret's words and she flipped the sword into her left hand. Her profile would give the assassin a smaller target while she would have a full target for her cut-and-slash tactics.

"Use what you have."

Kathryn smiled again. She knew what Margaret meant. The man was staring at her chemise. She allowed herself to move around the room as Gervais watched Margaret, wondering if he should attack. The pause cost him another companion.

The man, now engaged with Kathryn and not wishing to believe that he could be defeated by a woman, stared at her. The look of a killer had returned to his eyes. He had seen his companion die quickly and he knew now that this was no game. These women must die.

He began, methodically, to move toward Kathryn while Gervais decided that Margaret was to be his target. Kathryn raised herself on to the balls of her feet. The sword in her left hand looking menacing. The Frenchman made the mistake of glancing at Gervais. A knowing smile on his face, indicating that he thought this would be an easy match and there would be no further surprises.

Kathryn stuck. She moved in under his guard and slashed his right arm with the falchion. He dropped his weapon but recovered it with his left hand. Kathryn gambled that he had never taught himself to use his left hand. So he would be weaker on that side. And his handling of the sword told her that her thought was correct.

"*Maintenant*," Kathryn smiled at the irony of the situation, "*Nous avons égalité. En guard, si vous pouvez!*" (Now, we are equal. Defend yourself if you can.)

Kathryn's lightness of foot surprised the Frenchman as she continued to move around him striking when she could and he had not laid a blade on her.

She feigned a slip and he smiled in pleasure. In his mind's eye he could see her on the ground bleeding in her death struggles. And already in his mind he could hear her shrieks of panic.

But Kathryn had no such vision. As the Frenchman rushed in to finish her, he suddenly realized his mistake. Her hand was so close to his chest that he knew it could only mean one thing. The pain shot through him as she twisted the sword to make sure that survival was not an option. She withdrew the blood-covered blade. And then it was over. He stood, tottering on unsure legs, looking at her through unseeing eyes and fell to the ground.

And now it was the turn of Gervais, who Margaret and Kathryn had seen to be the leader of the other two.

His eyes riveted on Margaret's face as he attempted to mesmerize her with his intimidating stare.

"So, my lady, you think that you can use your sword against me and win? I am not like the other two idiots who did not see your plan. I will tell you that you can wave your sword about all you wish. I am only interested in planting my sword firmly into your chest. Then we will see who is the better. And then, my lady," he turned to Kathryn with a leer on his face, "it will be your turn."

Gervais was making things difficult for Margaret, even though she was poised and ready. He now realized that he had two enemies, both women, who had killed his two companions and who could just as easily kill him. How had he allowed this to happen? He quickly reconnoitered his position as he managed to keep Margaret at bay. The other one, with the chemise and the very strange accent, was standing watching, as if she was enjoying it. She had not yet made any effort to help her cousin, as they had called each other.

Margaret circled as she sensed that his thoughts were distracted for the moment. He had a look in his eyes that told her that his thoughts were elsewhere.

At that moment, Gervais charged as he suddenly brought his senses back to the moment at hand. Margaret backed away and he slipped on the blood of the first man to be killed, hitting his shoulder against the wall. The pain was intense; his shoulder was dislocated. Margaret also slipped and stumbled backward. Even with his dislocated shoulder, Gervais saw his chance. He lunged toward Margaret only to have his sword halted in midstroke.

"Damn," he muttered, "the other one."

Kathryn had parried his blow and foiled his attempt to harm Margaret.

Gervais smiled through his pain. He sensed that this one, light on her feet that she might be, was not as adept with the sword as her companion. And the flimsy chemise would not distract him! He would finish her and then turn his attention to the other one, as long as they did not launch a concerted attack. It seemed that they preferred to fight one at a time. However, his dislocated shoulder would not allow him the luxury of completing his task. Things had gone wrong and this was difficult for him to accept.

He tried circling the women and attempted to disregard the pain in his arm, at the same time making sure that his back was not turned to the other one. He had them both in his sight. He felt confident that he still had the situation in hand. He would enjoy seeing this one die and then he would take care of the other one, who sat with her back to the wall as if enjoying her rest. The women looked at each other and smiled.

"So, you see humor in me."

"No, just death," Kathryn said without emotion.

This one was annoying him. Her coldness was an obstacle to his thoughts. She had to die. He looked at her as she stood relaxed, holding the sword by her side, as if deciding what her next move might be. Her eyes remained emotionless. Was she preparing for her own death? Pity. She had really looked to be of interest to him. As had the other one. He looked at

Kathryn and knew that the time was his as he prepared to make his move against her. He shifted his weight so that his painful shoulder would not cause him to be off-balance. He saw the blow in his mind's eye as he raised himself on his toes to bring the sword down onto her head.

The other one would do just as well for what he had in mind. Dislocated shoulder or not he would manage.

*   *   *

CHAPTER 38

"**J**ames, I should have known that something was afoot. I should not have allowed myself to be fooled by this action. It was an act of deception!"

All of the attackers lay dead before them. The castle guards had not suffered one casualty and were now in the process of removing the bodies.

"But, Oswald, where would the others be? How would they gain entry to the castle? It seems as if the attack was to start with the chants for *Prime*. So any others must be within hearing . . ."

The light went on in Oswald's eyes.

"I know of such a place. It is my belief that our ladies foresaw the events of this night and are there already."

They hitched the bloodstained surcoats up to their waists and ran to the west wall of the castle. Oswald knew exactly where the sewer entered the castle and he knew that would be the point of entry for the intruders. They could enter the castle only a short distance from where John would be sleeping in an upper room.

They reached the top of the stairs and sensed the death. They inched forward and Oswald, placing his forefinger over his lips in the universal sign for silence, turned to James. They moved slowly, step by step, down the stairs without a sound. And then they saw them. Two bodies lay on the floor, their own blood pooled around each body. Margaret stood with her back to the wall watching the movement of the two combatants. Kathryn, one of the combatants clad in only breeches and chemise, was holding a man at bay. Margaret started to circle the man to try to get to his side or even behind him. At the same time, Kathryn and Margaret saw Oswald and James. Their faces showed no sign of recognition and remained fixed without any emotion. It looked as if the man was about to strike Kathryn. James wanted to rush into the small room that formed the landing between two sets of stairs, but Oswald held him back in a grip that would not allow any movement.

Kathryn was taunting the man. They thought that he looked familiar. Perhaps he was the assassin? The one the monk had called Gervais? If so, he would be a very dangerous and unpredictable man. He seemed to be hurt. He was favoring his left shoulder as though it was dislocated and he had several cuts in his clothes that showed signs of bleeding.

The odor of the area was almost too much for James. The age and dampness had mildewed the massive stonewalls and the whole place stank unpleasantly.

They could hear other sounds coming from different parts of the castle. Obviously people were now awake to what was happening. The diversion had worked as no one was descending into this level of the castle. The noise carried through the slit windows above from the castle yard.

"Well done, Little One," Oswald thought. "I have to wonder whether or not you are a reincarnation of Boudicca, Queen of the Iceni, who held the powerful Romans at bay many centuries ago." Oswald pretended to think before he added, "Or perhaps you are a reincarnation of Penthesilea, Queen of the Amazons?"

Oswald and James silently stepped out from behind the wall where Kathryn and Margaret could see them. James made the sign for silence and not even the flicker of an eyelid in recognition. He moved behind the man silently and lethally. Oswald remained behind James in case there was a need for James's defense.

Gervais grinned and showed his teeth in the final look of triumph. He would show these two women who was in command. One would die now and the other would serve his pleasure and then she also would die. But only after he was completely finished with her!

*   *   *

"Hello, Frenchman. You're a long way from home!" he whispered. "And so shall you remain."

The whispered voice from behind surprised Gervais. He did not hear all of the words and tried to turn around to see the newcomer.

And then he felt the discomfort. It was not his dislocated shoulder. And the discomfort turned to pain. He could not turn. He looked down and saw the point of the sword, someone else's sword, protruding from his chest. At first, he did not know what had happened. The sword had entered his back as the man's arm went around his neck. He could not move. He was held in a vicelike grip. He felt the sword entering his body and he was powerless to stop it as it sliced into his chest and through his organs, destroying them as it went.

His groan turned into a high-pitched scream as he realized what had happened. He stood straight, at attention, as he attempted to relieve the pain. But it did not help. His eyes went out of focus. All he could see was the outline of Kathryn's chemise.

"Damn the woman," he thought. "Why did I allow myself . . . ?"

He did not finish his thought. The sword turned in his body and was pulled free. His muscles started to relax and he sank to his knees.

The blurred outline of a tall blond man appeared before him with a companion. Oswald had recognized Gervais. His eyes cleared for a moment and he saw that the tall man's companion looked similar but was not of the same height and his hair was darker. Through the haze, he could see a resemblance. His mind remained focused on the pain that coursed through his body. He could feel the blood running through his fingers as he held his chest at the point where the sword had exited. The blond man spoke.

"Hear me, Frenchman. You have failed. Take that knowledge with you as you die."

The blond man smiled as he continued.

"Also, take this with you. You have been beaten by two women. Two women that you would have not thought capable of killing you and your men."

In a gesture of defiance, Gervais attempted to stand. The hand on his dislocated shoulder would not allow him. He came to rest once more on his knees and then he toppled onto his back. But, strangely enough, he now felt no pain in the shoulder. The blond man looked at him to show him the contempt that he deserved.

"You lived like a dog. Now die like one," the blond man said.

Gervais attempted to speak but could not. His head hung forward and he stared at the floor through almost lifeless eyes. The blond man read his thoughts, knelt by him, and whispered in his ear.

"You have nothing that we need, Frenchman. So die."

Gervais could not feel anything as the paralysis took over his whole body. His last act of this world was to move his head so that he could see the two women who had led to his downfall. No emotion on their faces.

"The damned Benedictines!" Gervais realized that his enemies were none other than the Benedictines that the old monk has mentioned. "There were only three. Why are there four?"

Gervais could not answer his own question as he lay onto the stone floor and died as he had lived, alone and with no one to care about him.

Oswald, James, Kathryn, and James looked at each other. They heard footsteps. At a signal from Oswald, the two women donned their Benedictine robes. Oswald and James remained in their surcoats.

*   *   *

The soldiers and the young sergeant entered the small room and saw the two men in surcoats with the two Benedictines. The sergeant recognized the two men from the events at the north gate and both had acquitted themselves extremely well. They wore surcoats with the king's mark. "Obviously," he thought, "these men are soldiers who were trained to protect the king and the duke." From the stature of the two Benedictines, the sergeant assumed that they were boys, probably novices.

He bowed his head in deference to the two men, as he surveyed the scene and the three bodies.

"You, sirs, have acquitted yourselves very well tonight. Can I help you further in any way?"

The taller of the two men responded.

"No, sergeant. We thank you for your courtesy. If you would be so kind as to clean up the mess in here, we would like to adjourn to make sure that all is well with the king and the duke."

"Aye, sir," the sergeant responded quickly. "The heads will be mounted on the wall for all to see. It will be a warning to anyone who attempts to follow in their footsteps. The bodies will be impaled and left for the crows."

"Also, sergeant," Oswald added, "have your men check the tunnel by which these," he gestured to the bodies on the floor, "gained access."

"Immediately, sir."

Well done, sergeant. We thank you."

The sergeant nodded to his men and the cleaning process began. Oswald, James, Margaret, and Kathryn left the area and once more entered the fresh air of the morning. It was light and the sun was journeying across the sky.

*   *   *

CHAPTER 39

James was shaken from his sleep by a heavy hand. Kathryn moaned beside him, not wishing to be disturbed.

"James, my cousin, I have need of you. Quickly. Kathryn, you also!"

"Oswald, good grief . . ."

"It will be grief if you do not move quickly. The sergeant found my friend, Ranulf de Boise, in the tunnel. He lay there severely wounded by a knife to the thigh. Had the sergeant and his men not found him, he would have surely died. As it is, I fear for his life. I cannot attend him. I need you. In your physician's clothes."

James and Kathryn jumped up from the bed where they had lain on the floor. The exertions earlier in the day had taken their toll. Weariness had set in, leaving James and Kathryn no option but to sleep. Margaret approached the bed and stood next to her husband.

James looked at Oswald and Margaret. "How bad is it?"

"A knife in his thigh that caused some considerable loss of blood. The point may still be in there. It appears that my friend was stalking the same Gervais that we met earlier. He seems to have survived the weeks spent with Gervais but may have been turned upon as they approached the castle. James, it seems that I am always asking you for . . ."

"Oswald. Shush," James bade Oswald be quiet and then he turned to Margaret, "I always wanted to do that but he is so much bigger than me."

"Never mind, James, I do it often." Margaret smiled. "Now drink this and warm yourselves before we leave."

James turned back to face Oswald.

"Oswald, my cousin, I will do what I can. Now take us to de Boise."

*　　*　　*

They left the house and a few minutes later came to the north gate. The gate, one of the main gates to the city, had double doors of heavy oak reinforced with iron. Atop the massive walls that surrounded the city, guards armed with spears, bows, and arrows, and sundry other weapons carefully watched the throng of people coming and going.

Oswald explained the business that they had to the guards and were admitted immediately. Once through the gate, they stopped at the walls of Saint Nicholas's Church. Oswald and Margaret hesitated. Oswald took hold of James's sleeve.

"You know that we cannot come with you," Oswald said, "It is forbidden that I appear before anyone close to me before my death."

Oswald still found it difficult to accept that his death had occurred the year before. He knew that he was on the earth for some purpose. Perhaps he had just gone through it. But he felt that he still had a mission to fulfill.

"I understand, Oswald. You will be with us in spirit and with Kathryn as my assistant . . ."

"Wait a moment, James. Me?"

"Of course, Kath. I could not do it without you. I need a pair of hands that I can trust."

"But the sight of blood . . ."

"Kathryn. For someone who just . . ." James was about to refer to Kathryn's role in the death of Gervais and his companions.

"Sorry, James, my dear, reflex action as though . . ."

"We were home? I know, love. Shall we."

James turned to Oswald and Margaret. They were gone. But Oswald's voice was clear.

"James, my cousin, I have faith in you. Do your best for my friend, Ranulf."

James whispered, "I will."

Kathryn took the pose of a young assistant who might also be a novice Benedictine and followed James at a discreet two paces behind. She carried James's leather satchel of medical supplies while he had a similar satchel, containing his instruments, slung over his shoulder.

The temperature had dropped and felt glacial. They were both pleased to have the heavy black robes. They quickened their pace and after a short walk they were at the gate where James announced his reason for being there to the guards. The guards suggested that they should be checked for weapons. James could almost feel Kathryn's tension. He knew that she would not be in favor of having a castle guard prod and probe her body looking for hidden weapons. James almost smiled as he thought how she had handled herself against the three Frenchman earlier in the night. But as he thought it out, he would not be too happy either having someone prod and probe his Kathryn!

"No, you will not. I am a physician and surgeon. Of course I have knives. They are a part of my profession. And my assistant here," he nodded in the general direction of Kathryn, "does not yet know one end of a knife from another. In fact, he cut himself earlier this morning attempting to shave his almost hairless face."

The guards laughed. This physician with a strange accent amused them. But his arrival was anticipated and they knew that he was needed urgently.

Another guard was called who escorted them to the room where de Boise lay. The foul odor in the room was the smell of the sewer. James beckoned to the two attendants and ordered them to attend to him as he cut away the clothes from de Boise leaving him, after a minute or so, naked on the bed. Blood had soaked through his clothes and onto the bed linen.

A poultice of some unknown foul-smelling mixture had been applied to the wound. James stripped it away and saw the cause of the trouble. But at the same time he was smiling inwardly with relief. He ordered the attendant to bring hot water as he inspected the wound. It was deep and there was the remnant of a knife blade embedded in the flesh next to the bone. As near as James could estimate, the knife had missed the artery by less than the length of a thumbnail.

De Boise lay on a table that was about waist height. As James inspected him for any other wounds, he saw that de Boise was a good-looking man of above-average height with a rather round, clean-shaven face. He had a broad forehead, slightly hooded brown eyes, dark hair, and a mouth that added to the character of his face. He looked at James; his faced showed a faint ironic twist.

"You may be too late, Physician. I am not sure if I have much time left on this earth."

As he spoke, James could see the pain and anguish in his face that flowed from the wound.

"Please let me be the judge of that, sire."

"They were French, you know," de Boise offered as if to explain his wound and his current circumstances. "I was on their track as they were up to mischief," de Boise attempted to explain his actions.

"Who, sire?"

"The men who did this to me. Caught me unawares. Must be getting . . ."

"Old, sire," James cut in with a smile trying to relieve the tension that he saw in de Boise's face.

"You know, Physician, you have a quick tongue in your head and you remind me of someone. Who are you?"

James ignored the question. De Boise continued to fill the vacuum of silence as James started to inspect the wound.

"I don't trust a Frenchman as far as I can throw him. And some are difficult to pick up!" De Boise smiled at his attempt at humor. "They say," he seemed to be thinking out loud since James and Kathryn were not really listening, "that if one of them takes your hand in a sign of friendship, have someone watch your back and then count your fingers, murdering thieving bastards."

De Boise had lost a lot of blood but the good news was that, in spite of the poultice, the bleeding had kept the wound clean. It was in his favor that de Boise had slept and given his body the chance to start the healing process. James looked at the attendants once more and asked them a question in the Northern dialect that few could understand. They stared back at him dumfounded. He asked them the same question in Norman French. They understood and responded. Kathryn realized what James had done and that he would be able to converse with her and give her directions in the dialect. If she spoke, her voice would give her away!

Kathryn helped James prepare a sleeping draught of jasmine, honey, and essence of poppy was mixed and given to de Boise. As she cradled his head in her hand to administer the sleeping draught, his eyes opened wide and he smiled at her then the relaxed look came into his eyes. The draught was starting its work. He would struggle a little as James did his work.

James asked her to light the incense in the bowl to reduce the odor of the room. He used a mix of gum benzoin with oil of cinnamon and the oil of calamus roots dissolved in olive oil. The fragrant odors imparted a healthy and pleasant smell to the room.

James knew what he had to do and set about his task. He motioned Kathryn closer so that she stood on his right side, ready to be of assistance. James washed the area of skin around the wound with a solution of vinegar, knowing that it would sting. He opened up the wound with a clean knife that was honed to razor sharpness, and probed for the broken knife blade. He found it, as he expected, deeply embedded in the thigh muscle, next to the bone, but accessible through the open wound. Kathryn reached over and washed away the blood that continued to flow through the open wound. James looked at her and smiled his thanks. The blade had broken on impact and had folded itself under the skin and lay at an acute angle to the femur bone. If it was not removed, de Boise would surely die from infection from the dirty blade. And any slight movement would cause the loss of too much blood and might even cause damage to the artery. It was essential that de Boise remain still.

James's eyes did not wander from the wound as he carefully cut through the layers to find the offending piece of metal. But his mind was active. As he worked he thought of why he was here. In this place.

The knowledge of human anatomy was scanty indeed. How else would it be possible to probe the body for a piece of metal and remove it to save a life? Despite the doctrines of Mother Church, there was the need to cure men of wounds without allowing them to die, blood oozing from their broken bodies as their life moved through its final chapter.

Successive monarchs and their bishops were very concerned about the spread of knowledge among the lower classes. The use of medical techniques to prolong the active life of people and spread knowledge away from the crown was threatening to the church and to the royal physicians who might otherwise be known as superstitious quacks. Control would be lost with this spread of knowledge and the shackles of fear and ignorance would be loosened.

A movement to his right brought James back into focus. Kathryn had sensed that his mind was wandering so she had lightly tapped him on the arm as a reminder.

James nodded his head in thanks and continued with his work. Cutting. Cleaning. Swabbing and sewing until the bleeding was stopped, the wound was clean and closed. He washed the blood from de Boise's leg with warm water and again with vinegar. Then came the job of sewing the wound to close it from further loss of blood and infection. The two attendants were in awe at his technique. They had never before seen anyone use a needle on another person.

The sewing finished and the wound was once more wiped clean. James smeared a paste of the extract of witch hazel onto the stitched wound to help the wound heal without infection. He bound the wound with linen so that movement would not open it. To his surprise, de Boise opened his eyes and, in spite of being in pain, raised himself onto his left elbow and looked straight into his eyes. He then looked at Kathryn.

"I know not who you are. Yet you have a look of someone who was close to me but is no longer of this world."

De Boise looked at James through squinting eyes. Trying to focus on James's face. Then he continued.

"But I do know that I still have a leg that I hope will be useful to me and not whither and die like the limbs of so many of my comrades. They followed those limbs into the grave as surely as if they were anchored to the grave."

De Boise's breathing was labored and there was tiredness in his voice as he spoke through tight lips. The effects of the poppy extract had worn off. After all, James realized from the light outside and the position of the shadows that it was more than two hours since he and Kathryn had entered the room. De Boise was coherent. The authority started to return to his voice.

"But I believe that you are a good man. Not one to be afraid of the superstitions of the priests. I thank you. Wait." He cocked his head to one side. "I heard the soldiers of the prince bishop approaching. Probably instigated by those idiots who call themselves medical men. I would not trust them with a dead cat, let alone with a live man! Let me handle the old goat so that he will not dare to complain."

"I hope that you were not talking about me and calling me an old goat!"

The booming voice with the slight quiver of age resounded throughout the room.

"Sire."

De Boise attempted to rise but could not.

"Be still, Ranulf. You have suffered enough this past night. We had bad thoughts when we heard that you were wounded and found lying in the sewer ditch."

James realized that he was now in the presence of Edward III, King of England. Edward was tall and resplendent in a crimson tunic and black hose; a black cloak lined with fox fur was thrown over his shoulders.

He looked at James and at Kathryn then fixed them with a stare that could freeze water.

"Physician! Do you and your assistant not bow before your king?"

At the sound of Edward's commanding voice, the shaggy deerhound that had accompanied Edward into the room moved away for the king and lay in the corner, head on its paws, mournful eyes fixed on James.

"One false move and I'll have you," the dog seemed to be thinking.

"Sire," out of instinct James chose to use the same term that de Boise had used, "We forgot since we were busy attending to Sir Ranulf."

Edward continued to stare at James.

"By God, man you have a tongue in your head."

Edward stopped and paused for a few moments as if remembering some long-forgotten item.

"Look at us, Physician," he commanded.

James looked straight at Edward. The light eyes and the blond hair made Edward a very imposing figure, even at this late time in his life.

"You have a look of someone who was once close to us but is no longer of this world. He also had a tongue in his head. I used to call him . . ."

"Blondie, sire?" offered James.

"Physician, you interrupt us! But how did you know?"

"My cousin, sire."

"Then Physician, you have our confidence and we know that our Ranulf de Boise is your good hands. Do your job well, Physician, and you will be rewarded. But, Physician, guard your tongue."

"Sire, if I may be so bold?"

Kathryn could have kicked James. Why not let it go? We need to move before Edward suspects something.

The king's booming laughter filled the room.

"A cousin of our dear Oswald asks if he may be so bold? You two must be very much alike. Go ahead, Physician."

"I do this because I believe that what I am doing is right. And I do it for my king and for his family. No reward is necessary, sire."

"We will be the judge of that, Physician. But I like your words. We will . . ."

Edward stopped as he heard footsteps. He turned and smiled when he saw that it was his son.

"Ah, John. It seems that our Ranulf is in good hands and will survive the attack. At least that is what we are led to believe by this physician. A cousin of our dear Oswald."

And now James and Kathryn were face to face with John of Lancaster. Tall and blonde like his father. The typical Plantagenet look. Slimmer than his father but also looking very fit.

John first looked at de Boise to make sure that all was well with his adopted brother then he looked at James and Kathryn. He frowned and then his eyes lit up as he exclaimed.

"I heard that someone of your description played a role in stopping our enemies this night past. Do you know anything of this, Physician?"

"Sire," replied James, "I can only know what I am told."

Edward and John were taken aback by this answer and then joined together in laughter.

"Physician," Edward spoke, "you seem to be truly a man of your word. We will trouble you no longer. I only ask that you see Ranulf to good health. Come, John, we must talk abut your earlier discussion with Ranulf."

James and Kathryn bowed their heads. The two attendants were still kneeling. Edward was about to leave the room when he returned and looked at the attendants.

"Out."

They left quickly. Edward looked at James.

"Physician, why do you cover your attendant in such long unflattering clothes? She," Edward emphasized the word to show that that he knew that a woman was under the robe "seems to have much to admire."

Edward's laughter filled the room once more and they could hear him laughing as he walked along the hallway.

James and de Boise looked at Kathryn who threw back her hood and blushed.

"That robe makes me itch anyway."

De Boise smiled again and watched James and Kathryn as they washed the implements in hot water, wrapped each one carefully in a piece of goatskin, and placed them in James's satchel. He then washed his own hands before he opened up a smaller pocket of the satchel.

"Why is it that you cleanse everything if you are to use it again under similar conditions of blood and dirt?"

It was James's turn to smile.

"Kathryn," he said requesting that she answer.

"Sire, I can only tell you that dirt in a wound causes it to fester and the limb to turn black. And then you will not only lose the leg but you will also lose your life. Because it is clean," she indicated the vinegar-soaked cloth, "you will feel some discomfort because of my crude methods of cleaning the wound. But rather some discomfort than the pain of losing the leg and then death."

"Your tongue is also strange, of the North I suspect like Oswald's cousin. It is good that the king spoke to you before those idiots of medicine color his mind. Before you leave, Physician, your name?"

James smiled again. He did not answer de Boise's' question. Preferring to continue as though the question had not been asked.

"I will leave more of this extract of tree bark, which you call witch hazel, to apply to the wound lest it begin to fester. You will not walk on that limb for one week. I will return at least twice each day until you are well enough to walk again." James looked at de Boise. "I need your word that you will follow my instructions—sorry, sire—advice."

James decided that he should not give instructions to de Boise. It would be most unusual to do so and he could not predict the consequences of such actions.

"You have it, Physician! Now, who are you?"

James and Kathryn picked up their satchels and prepared to leave. Kathryn placed her robe and hood back in place as she prepared to leave the room. They looked around at de Boise.

"You shall know me when I return. As I have said, I shall visit you and make sure that your wound heals. I will visit you and I will see that you recover. For now, we take our leave, Sir Ranulf de Boise."

"Wait, Physician." It was a command that James could not, or dare not, refuse. "Before you came to me," Ranulf breathed slowly as he carefully adjusted his position to ease the discomfort and as he thought out the next words. "I have been in conversation with Duke John and we both feel that more information is needed. As you now know, I was with the Frenchman pretending to be someone other than my real self, and I can swear that he was well prepared. We, Duke John and I, need to know who was aware of the details of the structure of the castle to give the Frenchman information about the tunnel. Perhaps it could be someone of a high order or was the existence of the tunnel known by others?"

Ranulf shifted himself again as he continued.

"We are of the belief that only the original builders of the castle knew of the tunnel. And they died long ago. Because of your relationship to Oswald, we feel that we can trust you. So, the duke will see to it that you have access to other sources of information. Such may be found in the secret archives of the priory library. The duke will talk with the prior and with Brother Thomas, who I am led to believe was also a friend of your cousin, to ensure that you have full access to the material contained in the archives."

Ranulf shifted once more to make himself more comfortable. He was prepared to continue but James cut him off from further speech by holding up his hand, palm toward Ranulf.

"Sire, I must stop you."

James knew that any further movement might cause the wound to open leading to a further loss of blood. James sensed that there must be additional medication that he should apply to facilitate the healing process.

"You must stop me, Physician!"

"Aye, sire for you life. You have too much movement that can open up the wound again. If you lose more blood . . ." James raised his eyebrows as he left the remainder unsaid.

"Sire," Kathryn's voice cut into the heavy silence, "please listen to what you are told."

Ranulf smiled as he realized that they were correct.

"Yes, Mother," he said imitating the way in which a child would speak to its mother, "as you say, Mother."

"Sire!" Kathryn's tone advised silence from Ranulf as she moved toward him.

James smiled. "Well done, me bonnie lass," he thought without daring to speak out loud.

"You are to take this," she preferred a small amount of the opiate in a cup. "It will help you to sleep and allow you the time for your body to start on the way to recovery."

"Yes, Mother," Ranulf smiled as he responded. "I know not from whence you two came, but I am pleased and I am pleased that my late friend Oswald continues his work through you."

Kathryn cradled his head and shoulders as he swallowed the mix followed by drink of water to help the drug into his stomach from where the effects would spread to the remainder of his body.

Kathryn laid his head gently on the pillow and moved to replace several items into the satchel. They stood at the foot of the bed and looked at Ranulf as the drug started its effect.

"I feel the need for rest," Ranulf said drowsily, "and I thank you again for saving my leg."

James and Kathryn smiled and bowed slightly with a nod of the head and then they were gone.

Shortly after, the soldiers of the prince bishop entered the room. De Boise momentarily shook off his drowsiness and stopped them with a motion of his hand.

"You will find no one here but me. The king and my brother John have just left. Return to your bishop. I need to sleep."

Ranulf lay back. As sleep overcame his weary body, he thought of Oswald. That dear friend of many years who had so tragically lost his life in the mudhole. And yet here was the physician, cousin to Oswald, who looked sufficiently like him to be a brother. And now he owed him his life also.

And so it was done. Ranulf finally succumbed to the effects of the rug as sleep found him.

*   *   *

CHAPTER 40

J ames and Oswald discussed the next steps and decided that James needed to search the archives of the priory library for additional information. He sensed that he could not afford to allow de Boise to die because he was uncertain of the follow up treatment of the wound.

And there was another issue. The Frenchman and his cronies, strangers to Durham, had known about the tunnel that allowed them entry into castle. It had almost caused the death of de Boise and could have caused the death of John, Duke of Lancaster.

James wondered about the advisability of taking Kathryn with him but decided against it. The chances of Kathryn being discovered for what she was, a woman in monk's robes, were high and it was a risk that could not be taken. So, he left the house with Oswald and they walked along the road toward the castle.

There was a deep blue sky that was fleeced with streaks of white cloud and the crisp and cool morning air carried a hint of cleanliness and the promise of spring. There was something familiar about this road and he felt that he had used it on many an occasion in the past. But his memories were dim and he could not recall the exact circumstances. He could only think of a young boy walking to the priory to take a meal to his father as he worked.

James looked up at the castle as he approached the gate from the bridge. On each side of the road, through the gate and stretching away in both directions as far as the eye could see, was a great wall composed of large stones. He knew from Oswald that it was at least eight feet in thickness and several times as tall as a man.

As arranged, Oswald did not approach the gate or attempt to cross the bridge with James but backed away and stood behind a nearby building from which he could watch James's progress.

Once across the bridge, James reached the gate and, as luck would have it, he saw that one of the guards on duty was the same man who had asked if he carried any weapons.

"Enter, Physician," the guard said with a smile. "I hear that Sir de Boise is all the better because of you."

James smiled as the guard stepped aside and mumbled a few words by way of explanation to his colleague.

James stopped and decided to chat with both men. He could see that they were feeling the cold and offered some help when he said, "I suggest that you bring with you containers of hot herb tea. Perhaps your captain might oblige by seeing that it is renewed every hour so that the cold will not penetrate your bones. In fact, I will mention this to whoever I see of consequence once I am inside."

Both men smiled their thanks and allowed him to pass into the castle.

"What is he doing?" Oswald wondered as he saw James talking with the guards. "This is taking too long!"

Then all appeared to be well as the guards smiled and allowed him entry. Oswald left his place of concealment and walked to the house where Margaret and Kathryn awaited him.

James walked through the yard and to the priory. The reputation of the priory scriptorium was worldwide, from Northumbria to the lands of the Mediterranean Sea and from the kingdom of the Franks to Ireland.

"Hold," the voice took James by surprise and brought him out of his daydream. He turned and saw John of Lancaster within twenty paces coming from toward him.

"Hold, Physician, I will speak with you."

"Sire," was the only response that James thought proper.

"What is your destination, Physician?"

"The library, sire. I need to read some items that are of interest to the health of Sir Ranulf."

"I will walk with you." It was not a question but a statement.

"As you wish, sire. It will be my pleasure."

"Physician, my father tells me that you are not a man to accept payment for your efforts. It seems that you are one of those few men who believe in doing what is right."

"Aye, sire."

"See to the continued good health of Ranulf. Do your best for him. He is very dear to my father and to me."

"Aye, sire. You have my guarantee."

They were now at the priory door and John led James through the building and the scriptorium and then into the archive. No one would stop the duke. After introductions were made to the librarian, whom James recognized since it was that same Brother Thomas to whom James had delivered the old monk, John looked around and said, "I must leave you now. My father has business with me."

James nodded and then remembered something.

"Sire, I do have one request."

John raised his eyebrows in question. James realized that there was no guarantee of the request being granted so he related to John the story, with much feeling, about the guards being cold. He followed it up with his request for the hot herb tea. John smiled.

"It will be much better than some of the stuff that they drink and it should keep them alert. I will see that it is done. For all of the guards? At regular intervals?"

James smiled and nodded his agreement to the questions.

"Thank you, sire."

John waved his arm to acknowledge James's thanks then turned and walked away. As he walked away, James suddenly realized the implication of his words. He had guaranteed to John, Duke of Lancaster and son of King Edward III, that all would be well with Ranulf de Boise!

Accompanied by Brother Thomas, James entered the library. As he looked around he saw shelf after shelf lined and groaning under the weight of books, ancient and recent. The subject matter of the books ranged from the classics of Virgil, Suetonius, and Livius, to the more pragmatic mathematics and applied sciences. It was one of the most magnificent collection of books that he had ever seen. He doubted that any library, even the library at the abbey in London or the priory at York, could compare with this. Durham was truly an outstanding center of learning. The library contained the books from Lindisfarne that had been salvaged before the Viking attacks as well as the books from the library at Jarrow that had suffered the same fate as the Lindisfarne Library.

"*Mens sana in corpore sano*," muttered James.

"A healthy mind in a healthy body," Thomas translated. "I agree with you. A good thing to remember, Physician." Thomas thought for a moment, "In order to allow your search to be uninterrupted, I have told my assistant to give you a free hand in here. If you need any help, he will be sitting at the door."

As he led James to the section dealing with medicine, he said, "I have also been told by the duke that you may seek other information. Such may be found in our secret archives," Thomas pointed to the shelves in a locked room. "Here is the key," he took a large key from his belt and handed it to James. "The archives are open to no one," he continued, "except the prior and I. You have full access to the material contained in the archives." I must now go to see to my students. Without me watching over them, who knows what might happen."

James nodded his appreciation, placed his bag on one of the carrels, and took out his parchment, ink stick, and goose quill pen.

Oswald had told James that there was nothing else in the country like the secret archives of the priory library.

Row after row of shelves stood full of books stacked one on top of another that constituted thousands of volumes. These volumes gave a real picture of the history of Durham and of England.

James felt that somewhere within these books lay the answers to his questions. What additional medication should he apply to de Boise that could stop any degeneration of his wound? Who else knew of the intimate details of the structure of the castle? Who gave the Frenchman information about the tunnel? Was it someone of a high order or was the existence of the tunnel generally known?

The secrets would not be hidden in the thousands of weighty volumes but should be available in specific places. Who were the builders of the priory? Who were the builders who might know of such outlets through the walls? What in the way of personal allegiances did any of these men owe to others? Was there really a plot to murder the duke? Or was it a last-minute improvisation that allowed them to be caught? Were they seeking the treasure of the castle and priory? According to Ranulf, the answer to the last question was a definite no. So, why did Duke John have to die?

James knew that he needed the answers to these perplexing questions. And the truth was probably somewhere within these volumes. He looked at the bound volumes. Some bound in leather and others bound in vellum.

The medical book collection was phenomenal. Dioscorides' *De Materica Medica* that described early medicine, Pliny's *Historia* that described plants and their uses, Strabo's *Hortulus*, Albert Magnus's *De vegetabilibus*, Trotula's *Passionibus Mulierum Curandorum* that described the diseases of women and the cures, and Ibn Botlan's *Tables* (*Taqwim*) that dealt with Arabic medicines. James also saw a copy of the forbidden works of Arnold of Villanova, a thirteenth-century physician, occultist, and alchemist who employed occult conjurations, mystic symbolism, and magic potions in his medical practice. There was also a copy of the *Mappae Clavicula* that contained descriptions of the nature and preparation of various minerals, herbs, woods, stones, and chemicals.

He even came upon books that that denied that the earth is what it looks to be, that is an expanse of land and waters stretching limitlessly east and west between the forever-frozen north and the forever-sizzling south. Those books averred that the earth is a round ball meaning that a traveler who has left home and went far enough eastward would eventually find himself approaching his own home, but from the west! This is what all the far travelers who have wandered over this world have found it to be. A memory stirred in James's mind as he thought to himself, "Is the world not truly a round ball that circles the sun?" But the origin of that thought did not come to him.

There was nothing in this part of the collection that James could use. Frustration was starting to get the better of him but he pressed on further.

As he walked around the shelves, he saw a collection of documents that were not bound in book form. They were wrapped in coarse vellum and bound with a cloth tie. The individual collections lay, like the individual books, on the shelves, one on top of the other with a descriptor or name written on the edge so that identification was facilitated. And to James's delight, they were arranged alphabetically.

Of all the folders, as James preferred to call each collection of documents and they seemed to be innumerable, there was one marked with the simple word *Miscellanea*. This collection was in several folios and filled one shelf. Its contents seemed to be collected randomly and placed in the package without any form of order. James decided not to investigate.

It was all part of his background that allowed him to know the kinds of material that could possibly be found in the archives. And he knew that in this vastness of books and folders that he would find what he needed. But the time that it would take might be a serious disadvantage.

He knew that to examine the uncataloged and unstudied contents of this room would require two persons working on nothing else but their contents for a considerable time, more time than he had available. He would need someone who had the ability to remember . . .

A thought was triggered from the deep recesses of his mind. Kathryn? She did have a wonderful memory that allowed her to understand and remember what she had read, to the word. He could not understand how the thought came to him but it would be worth the risk of bringing her with him on the morrow.

"First and foremost," he thought, "the medical papers. Sir Ranulf's wound is in the most urgent need of attention."

James decided to take the chance that the medical documents would be in this room rather than on the shelves in book form. If he could find them, his visit to the secret archives would have been well worth the effort.

After two hours of fruitless searching for medications and cures, he felt frustrated. It was at that moment that he found himself in front of the shelves with the folders marked *Miscellanea*.

He reached out and carefully unwrapped the documents and began to recognize some of the writings. All in the same hand and marked at the end by a circle containing Cuthbert's cross. One was even marked *Oswaldus Dunelmensis*! Notes belonging to and written by Oswald! But when? James decided not to dwell on this question. He started to read. One hour later he found what he was looking for; the answer to his quest for further treatment of Ranulf's wound. It was yarrow, or bloodwort as it is often called, and said to be an excellent poultice for wounds that would not stop bleeding. A favorite herb of the Anglo-Saxons who used it to heal burns and the bites of insects. The fresh leaves were also chewed to relieve toothache.

James smiled to himself. He had the answer. His anxiety that the wound would continue to bleed inside could not be quashed, but he had the necessary items in the satchel that Oswald had given him.

In half an hour he was once more in the room where de Boise lay, having been recognized by the guards and allowed access. He nodded to the attendants who sat at one end of the room to make sure that the fire remained healthy and that de Boise's needs were satisfied.

James approached the bed with a smile on his face. De Boise had heard his footsteps and raised himself on his elbow to see his visitor.

"Ah, Physician, you seem pleased with yourself. To what do I owe the pleasure of this visit?"

"A slightly different treatment, sire. I need to add a new poultice to your wound. If you will allow me, sire?"

"Go ahead."

James gave the attendants instructions for making the poultice. He supplied the ingredients and told them the method, step by step. When he was satisfied that they could do the job correctly, he approached the bed. De Boise was still resting on his elbows watching every move that James had made.

"Where is your . . .," the hesitation in de Boise's voice was obvious, "helper?"

"Unable to be with me today, sire." James did not use any form of description for Kathryn. The attendants would be all ears and gossip in the castle was a thriving occupation.

"There are medications to prepare, sire," James continued, "bandages. The usual work for a medical apprentice."

De Boise smiled seeing how James had handled his answer to maintain his and Kathryn's secret.

"Medical apprentice, my foot," de Boise laughed as James smiled in return, "No sire, your leg!"

The attendant were stunned at James's familiarity with de Boise and were even more surprised when they both laughed at some apparently private joke to which they were not privy.

"I have the poultice, sire," one of the attendants addressed James.

James took the prepared medication and turned to look at de Boise.

"But I am curious," de Boise said, "about your origins, Physician."

"I have lived in this area most of my life, sire, apart from short times when I lived elsewhere," replied James. His memories were telling him that this was indeed the truth and he thought no more of his answer.

De Boise then decided to tell James how King Edward had taken him as his ward after the death of his father during the defeat of the French at sea battle of Sluys. He recalled how he had grown up with the king's children and considered them his brothers and sisters and they treated him with the same familiarity. Then he had met Oswald at Crécy and from that time they had been firm friends. They had even become relatives through marriage when a daughter of de Boise married one of Oswald's nephews.

James worked as de Boise talked. He had successfully taken de Boise's mind away from his wound thereby allowing him to work without interruption.

James removed the bandages, and to his delight, the wound was clean and then he added the freshly prepared poultice and rebound the wound with clean bandages.

"Again, you use clean materials, Physician."

"Aye, sire. To use unclean items would infect the wound and bring on a reoccurrence of the infection and a fever."

"You are leaving now, Physician?" de Boise asked as James and the attendants cleared up the unused items and threw the used bandages on to the fire. "When will you return?"

"Every day, sire."

"I suggest, Physician, that you and I talk about the events that led me to this condition as soon as we can. I fear for the safety of Duke John, and with the king here also at the castle, who knows what may happen?"

"As you wish, sire, but I do recommend that we wait a day or so for you to regain your strength."

Ranulf nodded his head to show agreement with James's suggestion. The tired look in his eyes betrayed how he really felt.

"Before you leave, Physician, one more thing."

James stopped, his satchel slung over his shoulder wondering what de Boise would ask.

"What is your name?"

"My name, sire?"

"Yes, Physician. Your name? The one that your parents gave you when you were born. I assume that you were born?"

"Aye, sire. I was." James paused as he looked straight into de Boise's eyes and saw the questioning look there.

"My name, sire, is James."

*   *   *

James hurried back to the house to discuss his findings with Oswald, Margaret, and Kathryn.

He had barely left the castle gate when a figure materialized out of the shadows of a nearby house. James must have visibly jumped but became calm when he heard Oswald's voice.

"James, we were starting to worry about you."

The look on James's face told Oswald that all was well. Perhaps even better than they had dared to hope.

Once they were seated in front of the fire with the food and tea laid out on the nearby table, James told his story. De Boise would survive. The wound was healing nicely and there was additional ointment to ward off any possible infection. He would treat de Boise every day and they would converse about the events that led up to this attack. James then required that Kathryn should accompany him to the library tomorrow.

All was agreed upon and the remainder of the night was spent in quiet conversation about Kathryn's visit to the library and how she should behave so as not to attract any attention.

It was decided that Kathryn would dress, like James, in the black boots and robes of a physician. They were not unlike the Benedictine robes but looked a little more sumptuous and formal. Oswald inspected their robes and nodded his satisfaction. Then he smiled.

"Kathryn, after your performance in the castle against the Frenchman and that of my dear wife," he looked at Margaret and smiled, "I am not sure that you are the right person for the job. There is an old saying from the time of the Saxons that I remember from my parents. When the fox preacheth, keep an eye on your geese! After your prowess with the sword, I am not sure that you fit the role of physician."

Oswald and James laughed. Margaret and Kathryn remained serious and allowed the witticism to pass on unnoticed.

Kathryn looked at them and decided to bring the conversation back to sanity and to the present.

"Now, my two fine specimens, I am expected to go into the library on the morrow and assist my dear James and perform as if I am used to it. First I do not look like a man in this close-fitting robe. If I bend over . . ."

James and Oswald rolled their eyes and smiled. Kathryn and Margaret glared at them again.

"I am sure that some wide-eyed Benedictine will notice that I am not built like his colleagues. After all, did not King Edward notice my differences?"

James and Oswald ceased their smiles at Kathryn's words.

"Plus," Kathryn continued, "if you two can be serious for a while, when I have to use the privy there may be few unpleasant moments if another monk walks in."

It was decided that Kathryn would redress in her voluminous Benedictine robes and Margaret adjourned to the back room where she could give Kathryn a woman's advice. When they emerged once more, Margaret gave James exact instructions on how to behave and care for Kathryn under such circumstance.

"Now, if we can get back to the matter at hand," Kathryn indicated that she was not yet done, "I am supposed to go into the library and help you," she looked at James, "to find certain items from the book. I must remind you that the books are probably all in Latin," James and Oswald nodded to show agreement, "and also in a script that may not be familiar to me."

Oswald and James nodded again and realized what had to be done. But Kathryn spoke again before they could respond.

"If you," she looked at them, "will teach me the basics of word recognition as well as the type of writing, it will help. I seem to recall, from where I know not, that I will be able to remember what you tell me and show me." As an afterthought, Kathryn added, "Oswald my dear cousin, I may need some of your writing materials with which to practice as a means of remembering what you tell me."

As the night wore on, Kathryn adapted herself to reading Latin written in various styles. Unknown to her, the photographic memory that she had recently begun to develop helped and made her a willing pupil.

She found that she could look at several manuscripts that Oswald had in the house and not only recognize the style of writing but also read and translate many of the words. As a final test, Oswald led her to the table. Kathryn looked down and saw several old manuscripts that had been written in different forms of cursive hand. The marks on the vellum were a curious mixture of Oswald's doodling as well as the doodling of other unknown writers. Kathryn was able to recognize all of the signs and letters.

"Well, James," Oswald announced, "your Kathryn is ready!"

Margaret smiled at Kathryn's accomplishment and took her hand.

"You will do well, Kathryn."

*   *   *

CHAPTER 41

As they left the house with Oswald, the mist that had appeared just before dawn wrapped them in a soft gray cocoon. Margaret had made sure that they consumed the hot tea and nourishing oatmeal, with honey, before leaving. The food, and the fact that they wore long robes, kept out the cold and the dampness. After escorting James and Kathryn to within sight of the castle gate, Oswald bade farewell and watched as they approached the gate. They were relieved to see the same two guards who had been on duty the day before.

"Good day to you, Physician," said one of the guards, "I see that you have your helper with you today."

James nodded and he was about to pass through the gate with Kathryn when the second guard stopped them. James's silent prayer to heaven ceased in midsentence.

"We would have words with you, Physician," the guard said, looking at his companion.

James stiffened in anticipation. Had they noticed something about Kathryn? She had walked a pace behind him. What could they have detected? James's thoughts were brought quickly back to the current situation as the other guard spoke.

"We thank you for your promise, Physician. It seems that the Duke of Lancaster took heed of your words and has given order that all guards are to be supplied with hot herb tea, day and night. The word has spread that it was a physician who speaks with a strange accent who prevailed upon the duke to do this. We have been asked by all of our comrades to thank you."

James was surprised and thankful for the guard's words. He was also amused as it was such a small effort that he had made. He patted the guard on the shoulder, "You are very welcome, my friend, and offer my sincere thanks to your colleagues. I also offer my services to all of you. No matter what the ailment, you can find me every day within the castle."

The guards nodded in appreciation, stepped aside, and allowed James and Kathryn to pass.

Again, Oswald wondered what was going on.

"Why does that cousin of mine talk so much?" he had asked himself when he saw that James and Kathryn were allowed to pass through the gate.

Then, a curious thing happened. The guards went into their small gatehouse and stepped back out immediately with a cup in their hands. The rising vapors told Oswald that the liquid in each of the cups was hot. He smiled.

"So that is what he has done, made sure that the guards have hot drinks to ward off the chill; just as I might also have done under the circumstances. Such actions create friendships and loyalties that may be useful some day."

He walked away smiling. He could not wait to tell Margaret the latest escapade of his sometimes-strange cousin.

*   *   *

James and Kathryn walked across the castle yard and when they were only a short distance away from the library, they met John. James acknowledged his greeting with a smile. After pleasantries were exchange, John looked at Kathryn and smiled.

"I see that you have your friend with you today, James."

"Do not worry. My father and I have no secrets and my brother de Boise told me of your name last night when he and I talked."

John reached over and raised Kathryn's hood with his forefinger.

"You are a very beautiful woman, my dear," he looked at James, "protect him as I believe that he will be of great value to us."

Kathryn felt the redness rising in her cheeks as she looked at John's fairness and blue eyes. John then addressed James.

"Ranulf seems to be progressing well. He also told me that you and he will talk in a day or so."

At that point, John was about to leave when he stopped.

"Wait! In case of any problems, although I do doubt it, I will escort you to the library. To my knowledge there has never been a woman, other than the nuns, in the priory and I would not wish it that you were discovered. I will make sure that you are not disturbed. Brother Thomas is a good man and will see to your needs."

At the entrance to the library, the introductions were made once more and John took his leave.

James and Kathryn were left alone to settle into what was to become a routine for the next several hours.

Kathryn looked at shelf after shelf of books, examining the contents, deciding if any further examination was required. James could see the surprised look on her face as she examined the books and realized how much of the language that she actually understood. James remained close to her in case of any inquisitive monks.

"Ah, Physician, good to see you." Brother Thomas had appeared as if from nowhere.

"Brother Thomas, I hope that you are well this morning."

"I am, and are you finding what you need?"

"Yes, Brother."

Thomas seemed to be in deep thought for a moment and then he continued. "If you need anything, I will be available."

As he left, Kathryn let out a breath that she had held during the minutes of Thomas's visit.

"It is all right, Kathryn. He was just letting us know that he is here and we can contact him whenever we need him. Are you . . . ?"

"I am fine, James," Kathryn relaxed. "It was his sudden appearance that made me nervous."

As the day progressed, they examined numerous books and documents and they spoke in whispers about the events that had taken place over the past few days. It was an interesting day, but their searches did not provide any specific clues to the possible sponsor of Gervais, the Frenchman.

"Shall we go, my dear," James whispered as the afternoon wore on. "I must visit Ranulf to see how he is doing."

She nodded her head in agreement and making sure that the hood of her robe covered her face, picked up their satchel and left the library.

A quick walk across the castle yard and they had arrived at the room where Ranulf lay. Or, actually, was sitting. He had raised himself up on his bed and had his back supported by two boards. He was reading.

He beamed as he saw them. "Finally," he thought, "people who will talk to me rather than standing motionless and lifeless as my two attendants."

James was becoming, in the short time, his favorite visitor; he offered another form of companionship. And he had Kathryn with him.

Ranulf looked at the attendants.

"Leave us. Go feed yourselves in the kitchen."

The attendants did not need any further encouragement. Their footfalls could be heard as they ran along the hallway toward the kitchen.

"So, Physician, you have with you your assistant!" Ranulf said as he looked around, as if checking for unseen visitors. "We will be alone," he continued, "unless John and the king decide upon a visit, so you can relax in whichever way you wish."

Kathryn bowed her head, "I would like to remove my hood, sire."

"As you wish." He looked back at her but addressed to the question to both, "Have you eaten?"

They both shook their heads.

"Before you start with me, partake of the food on the table. I will join you, if you would bring it to me."

Kathryn placed tasty morsels of food onto a platter that she took to Ranulf.

His charming manners and informality put her at ease. She sensed the warmth spreading through her body as she watched him eat. Without even asking, she knew what he would request as she shook herself back to the real world and delivered a cup of the hot aroma-rich tea.

"So, James, and . . . ?"

The inquiring look told her that he did not know her name.

"Kathryn," she said.

"So, James and Kathryn, we have much to talk about."

"Sire," James interjected as if to stop de Boise but Ranulf held up his hand.

"I feel well but I suggest that you examine my wound first, and if all is well we will talk. But let us finish our meal first."

The chicken, smoked fish, and fresh fruit were just what James and Kathryn needed. And soon they felt revived. When the meal was over, James removed the bandage that covered de Boise's wound. He was surprised, even amazed, at the condition of the wound. This man had remarkable healing powers. The wound was closing under the stitches. There was no sign of inflammation or discoloration. Kathryn carried a dish of warm water to the bedside and washed the area around the wound as James prepared another poultice. He applied the poultice and clean bandage and when he declared that he was finished, de Boise again suggested that they talk.

"As you wish, sire."

"I have addressed you as James and Kathryn, out of earshot of course, so you can call me Ranulf."

The familiarity of using the first name of a man so close to the king felt strange, but at the same time, it was an unexpected honor. They nodded their heads in agreement.

James suddenly realized the reason for their nervousness. Now that he was healing, James noticed that de Boise's eyes bored into and through everything! Yet, when de Boise smiled, there was a warmth and friendliness that transformed his face.

James finished cleaning his instruments and left two knives on the table so that, if someone should suddenly enter the room, he could make a pretext that Kathryn was putting them into his satchel, after having finished cleaning them.

De Boise looked at James and Kathryn. He did not really know them and yet he was willing to trust them. It was the James who caused him to question his thoughts; it was as if they had met before. It was Oswald who was the connecting link but there was something about this physician that puzzled de Boise.

Perhaps it was the pain. And then the pain disappeared at the hands of the physician. The drink that he had been given by the physician the day before had caused him to sleep deeply without any of the dreams that had been his companion during the nights when he had been a member of the Frenchman's gang. De Boise felt that he had visited the underworld during those weeks. Now he knew. It was the physician who had been one of the Benedictines that the Frenchman had feared.

De Boise had awakened that morning, weak but feeling much better; the bedding soaked by his perspiration. The attendants had been at his bedside with cool water, boiled first, just as the physician had instructed. Standing there, smiling, and crossing themselves, hoping that they would not be accused of witchcraft, determined to remain silent now that Sir Ranulf had survived.

"Yes, that was it," de Boise thought to himself and then the thought was gone.

And Kathryn? Of course. De Boise realized who she was. She was one of the two women responsible for killing the Frenchman and his two companions in that small room at the end of the midden tunnel. The same tunnel where he had been left to die. Yes, this was the woman who was the source of the rumors. She was a reincarnation of the powerful Boudicca, Queen of the Iceni.

"Yes," thought de Boise. "I can trust these two."

He had made his decision. He looked squarely at James then at Kathryn.

"All right, if you are ready, let us talk."

*   *   *

"William de Bohun." The name rang in their ears as de Boise made the pronouncement.

James and Kathryn looked at each other, puzzled looks on their faces.

"Perhaps I should explain."

They both nodded in agreement.

"William de Bohun," de Boise went on, "was a full cousin to King Edward. They were both grandsons of the Great Edward, he being the first Edward of that name. De Bohun was Earl of Northampton and he died on the 16 September 1360. I remember the date since I attended the funeral. So you can see that de Bohun was of illustrious birth."

He studied their faces before continuing.

"Without going into great details, de Bohun served the king well until his death. His loyalty to Edward, eminent abilities, and undaunted prowess were qualities that fitted him well in his position as cousin to the king. He was elected to the Most Noble Order of the Garter after September 1349 and the public records attest the constant employment of this earl in military and diplomatic transactions of the highest importance down to the period of his death, which happened on the 16 September 1360. His remains were interred in the abbey of Walden (Essex), on the north side of the presbytery."

De Boise halted again, not only to study their faces but also to take several sips of water from the container close at hand.

"De Bohun's only son Humphrey, the tenth one in the family to be given that name, succeeded to his father's estates and dignity in 1360, and to the earldoms of Hereford and Essex, and the Office of Constable of England upon the death of his uncle, Humphrey IX, who was unmarried and childless, at least that we know of. In 1365, he was honored with his appointment to the Most Noble Order of the Garter. So far, Humphrey X's life has been unspectacular but I do know that there are several questions that have come to my mind since the plot against Duke John has become evident to me."

"So," James cut in, "Humphrey de Bohun had a distant claim to the throne that could stand him in good stead at some future date?"

"I would not go that far," said Ranulf, "but I do believe that you may be getting close to my way of thinking."

"Oh, what tangled web we weave . . . ," Kathryn added and allowed the words to trail off for effect.

"Kathryn," de Boise looked puzzled, "I am not familiar with that expression."

"Nor me either, sire. But it was ringing in my mind. I cannot recall its origin!"

"It certainly does seem appropriate," de Boise added, "But, listen, I do have more."

Ranulf took another few sips of water. James and Kathryn waited in silence until he was ready. He had caught their attention.

"Now we come to the interesting part," de Boise continued, "the health of Edward of Woodstock the Prince of Wales is weak. There are those who believe, or even hope, that he will not survive the next five or six years and that he may even predecease the king. The king is sharing the effective government with my brother John, as you may have noticed when they visited me the other night. They are very close and the king enjoys the company of John. However, there are also those who fear John's influence."

James raised his eyebrows as a reflex action. The information that Ranulf was placing before them was now starting to make sense. De Boise noticed this and smiled.

"I see that you are thinking ahead of me, James. But I will continue."

The light in Kathryn's eyes told both men that she was with them in their line of thinking.

"John is very forthright," de Boise said, "and will tolerate no fawning idiots. His exploits in France are well appreciated but there are those who spread rumors about him being a failure as a commander. John offers no response but allows his deeds and success to stand as evidence; because of this, in some quarters, John is hated. He is not a corrupt man and tries to be fair so to get back at him, there have been rumors that he is corrupt and in an attempt to discredit him, he is said, unjustly, to have designs upon the throne."

Ranulf stopped and looked at Kathryn.

"I think," he said, "that I would like a break. I feel a slight discomfort from sitting in this position on my bed. So, Kathryn, would you please make a cup of that delicious herb tea."

She nodded indicating that she would. The water was continually heated on the fire so that the tea could be made almost immediately.

"And James, would you please examine my wound. I am hoping that I have not irritated it to the extent that I have done some damage to your stitching."

James removed the bandages from the wound, and examined the wound.

"All is well, sire." James replaced the bandages carefully. "If you wish, sire, we can return later or on the morrow to give you time to rest."

"James!"

"Yes, Ranulf!"

They both smiled at James's use of the familiar name. Ranulf got his point across. Kathryn brought the tea and Ranulf continued with the story.

"The Prince of Wales has a young son, Richard, who may be the next heir to the throne but the rumor is that Duke John will dispossess him of his heritage. The Prince of Wales has many friends, who I consider to be friends of convenience. One of these friends is Humphrey de Bohun.

Recently a letter that is a bitter lampoon against the government of King Edward and John has been circulated."

"Is that not treason?" Kathryn asked between her sips pf tea.

"That, it is," Ranulf responded, "and if we knew the author he would suffer for it. But he remains unknown, concealed behind a veil of words.

"The letter is written in Latin and to my thinking," Ranulf said, "it is clearly intended for an informed and limited circle of readers. To avoid censure, the letter has been written in the guise of a prophecy that was, supposedly, composed early in the century. The prophecy is that Edward's reign would decay through his own profligacy and neglect and would reach its present nadir as a divine punishment for sin, until rescued by the accession of the prince. The prince is supposedly Edward, Prince of Wales, or if his health continues to deteriorate, his son Richard."

Fire was in his eyes as de Boise continued. Kathryn and James could see that he was ready to leap out of bed and pursue the wrongdoers.

"I will not tolerate such an attack on the king and my brother!" The tone of his words could not cover his emotion.

"Well, it does seem to me," Kathryn's voice sounded clear and concise in the silence that followed Ranulf's last outburst, "that someone, perhaps Humphrey de Bohun, sees himself as the power behind the throne should the Prince of Wales die and Richard succeeds to the throne after his grandfather."

"And," James eyes shone with anticipation, "if the path to the throne is only connected by the delicate thread of distant lineage, what better way to seek power than to be the power behind the throne?"

The silence was heavy as they each retraced their individual thoughts and put the whole story together.

"All right, Ranulf, if I may use your familiar name?" Kathryn asked and de Boise smiled and nodded. "What do you see as the next move?" Kathryn asked.

"First," de Boise said, "I must recover and be able to walk again. Second, I need you to help me. Third, it is my belief that somewhere in the works contained in the priory library are the secret archives," he raised his eyebrows in a question and James and Kathryn nodded to show that they were aware of the archives, "perhaps even in Oswald's papers."

Kathryn and James were surprised that de Boise knew of Oswald's papers. He saw the questioning look on their faces.

"Yes, I know of them," he said, "after all it was me who donated his papers to the library to be retained by the prior in the archives. I am sure that there are items in that collection that will provide help, if not proof, of this conspiracy."

"You may not be aware of this," de Boise continued, "but Oswald was a prolific writer. Everything that he saw he wrote down, ever since my father made him an unofficial scribe to the army. But, back to the focus, Oswald may not have realized it but he may have written down some description that could give us a clue to this conspiracy."

James and Kathryn nodded.

"We will start our search tomorrow," Kathryn had made the decision. "Brother Thomas will probably expect us at the usual early hour."

"A word of warning. This is a basket of snakes that you open. Humphrey de Bohun may be the force behind the conspiracy, or he may be the unknown pawn used by others for their greed. Be cautious and no one should know of your quest. My brother John must be told and I will see to that."

Kathryn and James nodded in agreement.

De Boise looked at them

"You amaze me," he said, "a physician and his assistant who show no fear and are ready for battle. Well done, but be careful. One wrong step and you may give John's enemies the pretext that would allow them to hang your dead bodies from the castle wall!"

"We heed your words, sire," Kathryn said. It was a statement made without any emotion. Her eyes showed no fear.

"You see, sire," James added, "we must do what is needed to protect the throne and make sure that it stays in the rightful hands."

*   *   *

CHAPTER 42

J ames and Kathryn had two pressing matters on their minds as they hurried back to the house to meet Oswald and Margaret. Their thoughts even eclipsed the news that Ranulf was recovering very well and should be on his feet soon. His fever was no longer evident.

Their minds were distracted momentarily at the execution of a marauding Scot on the castle green. He had been separated from the other members of his band the day before and he had been caught one mile to the west of the city. He was not to know that the other members of his band were dead to a man. He was the only survivor, for the moment. The soldiers would have killed him out of hand, but their captain had restrained them thinking that the prisoner might have useful information that he would give up with some persuasion. It was a correct assumption.

James and Kathryn were stopped in their tracks as the procession of guards dragged the wretched fellow to the gallows. He had been dragged unconscious from his cell, or in reality the torture chamber, and led to the gallows in that same state. A bucket of ice-cold water was used to revive him on the gallows platform.

"We'll have a public spectacle," one man within earshot of James and Kathryn announced, "to teach these Scots to have respect for our lands and our women."

A nearby sergeant growled his agreement, and the man puffed himself up to let everyone around know that he had been involved in the killing of the other members of the marauders as well as his involvement in the capture of this one. He wanted all to know that he was serving his king and country. The life of the would-be bandit was almost over.

As the prisoner started to revive from his stupor, he suddenly realized his situation. The wide-eyed worry in his eyes betrayed his true feeling about death. Especially about death in this manner. He felt threatened by the close assault of the spectators before the gallows.

"Hang him!" one member of the crowd demanded and the shout was taken up by several others.

The prisoner's eyes opened wider. Had he not been told that if he gave information he would be given a quick death? The thoughts of death were sufficient enough to cause him pain. But the idea of being hanged, drawn, and quartered was even more unpleasant.

Now able to stand on his own, the prisoner attempted to straighten himself to his full height. The pressures of the rack and the pain that they left were still real. He looked around and started to shake. He did not realize that he was truly alone until he glanced to his right and was conscious of a movement behind him. The sword was swung at him horizontally by the executioner and the prisoner's head left his body. His life was extinguished by that single swishing blow.

The crowd groaned out loud. They were not amused and the men started to shout in anger. Their women had been threatened and that could not be tolerated. As far as they could tell, the prisoner had come across the border with his companions into the county palatinate of Durham, having evaded several troops of soldiers, until the day before. He should have paid the penalty for them all.

More than one of the bands of Scottish marauders sallied forth into the palatinate and they were not always caught. The crowd felt that they had been cheated of a show and were demanding that the matter be referred to a higher authority. At that moment, the Duke of Lancaster appeared on the platform and the crowd immediately fell silent. He told the now-silent audience that his word and rule was absolute. He had recommended to the king that this prisoner be dealt with swiftly as he had the information that he needed. He made sure that the soldiers who were responsible for doling out this justice were showered with praise for their courage and fortitude. The now subdued crowd applauded John; such was his power over the people.

James and Kathryn stood still for a few moments amazed at the influence that John had over the crowd. One minute they were demanding a show. The next minute they were quietly leaving to go about their business.

"Physician, a word."

They turned to see John approaching them. Two soldiers accompanied him and from the insignia on their surcoats, James knew that they were members of the king's elite bodyguards.

"Sire," James greeted John.

They stood, two paces back, warily looking at James and Kathryn thinking that these two men, one a good size the other a small fellow, might have other business that could harm the duke.

"I am grateful to see you," he said. His words were, as usual, courteous to them even though they were, after all, below his rank.

The execution had now passed from their minds as though it was an everyday event that they had witnessed.

"Walk with me," John commanded in a gentle voice. He turned and nodded to the guards indicating that they should follow at a discreet distance.

"It seems to me that the situation that occurred the other night goes deeper than I thought." He rubbed his chin with his forefinger as he thought out his next words. "Our friend on the execution platform there," he indicated by a nod of his head in the direction of the gallows, "had more to say than we believed possible. My guards have learned that an army was gathered just north of the border to invade and take and hold Durham on behalf of persons unknown had I been killed. But he had no knowledge of the persons behind this scheme. And we only caught him because his stupid leader thought that they would pick up some quick booty before the remainder of the army arrived."

"Sire, if I may," James requested. John nodded.

"We," James looked at Kathryn, "had some discussion with Sir de Boise and we are ready to work with him as soon as he recovers. In the meantime, we are looking into this for you and attempting to discover who is behind the plot."

John stopped and looked at them.

"Well done, James," he added in a whisper, "and Kathryn. You are a plucky pair. Say what you like but my father and I are grateful. At time like this I do miss Oswald, but you are so much like him that I feel a good level of comfort by your presence." He looked at Kathryn again. "Both of you."

He thought for a few moments and said, "I am on my way to see Ranulf and he will get me up to date on your conversations?"

"Aye, sire," Kathryn whispered, trying to deepen her voice. John smiled. "You have a brave woman with you, James," he said and could not see Kathryn's blush under the hood.

"I will also tell him about the news that the prisoner gave to my guards."

John turned and marched with his guards toward the part of the castle where Ranulf lay. Or, at least, James hoped he lay resting and was not walking around and abusing his injured leg.

"This, my dearest," he whispered to Kathryn, "is getting more interesting with every hour that passes. I am now very inclined to agree with Ranulf and to believe that there is much more to this than meets the eye."

*   *   *

Kathryn was the center of attention as she related the events of the day to Oswald and Margaret. She described every action in detail and repeated every word faithfully as it had been said. Between sentences, she munched on hot oatcakes and sipped the herb tea; finally she had completed her story.

"So," Oswald summed up Kathryn's words, "we have here a plot that is much more widespread that anyone could have believed."

He scratched his chin as he thought about the reference to his writings.

"I do not even recall being in the presence of Humphrey de Bohun. I did meet Sir William on more than one occasion. But nothing comes to mind that would have led me to believe that he, Sir Humphrey, might be behind this skullduggery."

Oswald knew that the chances of the now-dead prisoner being privy to information about the leader of the plot were nonexistent and that the guards had been able to get the information that they did was an achievement. He looked at James and Kathryn and he knew that his request that they come to his aid had become a monumental task and not a short visit to his world as he had first thought. He could not understand why James and Kathryn were taking so well to this venture and wished that he had not had to bring them into this danger. He wanted to do more to help, but under many circumstances, that was not possible and his actions were limited.

As the night turned to a bitter cold, their conversation grew more thoughtful and less animated. Words seemed to freeze in midsentence as they realized the nature of the work that lay before them. Finally, Kathryn, with soft words and a partly stifled yawn, suggested that it was time to rest and refresh themselves for the coming day.

James smiled as Kathryn looked at him. Such a dear man, this physician that she had met, and she could not for the life of her remember when or where or how she had come to this end. She knew that she had lost one husband because of an accident rather than because of an illness, and it was more than she could bear to think of losing James.

Through her tiredness, she found the energy to say a silent prayer.

*   *   *

"James," Oswald suddenly said at breakfast, "I have given some thought to the contents of my papers that Ranulf lodged in the secret archives. And," he continued, "I can think of nothing relevant to this latest event."

"Oswald, we . . .," James started to speak but Oswald continued.

"I know that you will work tirelessly to find something of relevance but I was hoping to pinpoint a shortcut for you that will take you quickly through the many pages of material. But I can think of nothing that will help. I suspect that whoever is at the head of this plot will have covered him with layers of deception so that he remains unknown. To be known is certain death!"

"Oswald," Kathryn spoke knowing that he would allow her to speak, "I propose that we go on doing what we did yesterday. If there is anything, we will find it."

"That is sound thinking, Kathryn," said Oswald, "in the meantime, Ranulf may be able to give you some information as his memories are recalled."

"Well," said James, "we shall be about our business."

Margaret wrapped some of the oatmeal cakes in a napkin and gave to Kathryn with the word, "to keep away hunger."

Margaret looked at Oswald.

"We," she said, "have other business to take care of today. A young boy is sick and needs our attention."

"What are his symptoms?" James asked.

"Fever and chills," Oswald responded.

"Here," said James, as if speaking by instinct, "give him two of these," he offered Oswald a container of small white tablets, "leave six so that he can take two every four hours."

Oswald smiled. "I think that these cured someone a short while ago. Do you remember?" he asked James.

James looked mystified.

"Oswald, I do not know why I did that. Perhaps it was instinct. I do not even know what is in the tablets only that they will control fevers."

They took their leave of each other and went their separate ways in pairs. As they reached the bridge to the city, James looked at Kathryn.

"My bones tell me that it is going to be another very interesting day!"

Kathryn did not respond. She had her own thoughts to consider. And she would have not used the word "interesting"!

*   *   *

Once they were in the library, having bid a "good morning" to Brother Thomas, they delved into the task at hand, to find something related to a plan or plot to be the power behind the throne.

Kathryn and James worked tirelessly but they were unsuccessful. They took several breaks and it took many a cup of hot, spiced wine to restore their spirits.

Another execution took place on the castle green, but this time the prisoner had a heavy escort of soldiers for protection. It seemed that the duke was not willing to risk having to make any further speeches to a semihostile crowd. He did not wish the anger to be turned against him. But there was no incident. The man was a murderer who, strictly speaking, deserved to die.

James and Kathryn remained in the library; there was so much work to be done. They did, however, visit Ranulf to check the status of the healing process and change the bandages.

They had not even reached the halfway point of searching Oswald's documents when Kathryn's eyes lit up.

"James, my dear," she whispered looking around to make sure that she was not overheard, "did we not decide that we needed to look at the construction maps of the castle as well as the architect's plans?"

James turned from his work and nodded.

"We have a mystery before us," Kathryn continued, "of how a plot against Duke John could originate and I feel that we are moving in the wrong direction. Eventually, we may need to examine Oswald's journals but they were written with his experiences in mind and not with the idea of saving the duke from his enemies. And," she added, "did not Brother Thomas tell us that records were kept of those who read the construction maps and architect's plans?"

James knew that Kathryn was indeed on to something. Her appearance was more striking than usual and he hoped that no one would enter. It would not be at all difficult to see that under the robes was a woman. Her blue eyes had the look of the successful hunter as he carried the game home to feed his family. He could see the movement of her slender fingers as she placed Oswald's papers back into the correct folders. She was definitely on the scent of the prey!

Her thinking was entirely logical. She had devoted her time to thinking out the problem. Now she realized that Oswald's papers were a collection of journal entries for his own personal use, she was able to bring the concentrated mental force of her mind to bear on a real question. How had the Frenchman known of the tunnel leading into the castle? Given that this question was the real issue, she knew that they had to focus on this information for a possible answer.

"Well done, Kath!"

"James, my dearest," she questioned, "why are there times when you shorten my name?"

James looked at Kathryn, trying to remember. But he could not.

"I do not know. It just seems at times to be the most natural thing in the world, as though . . ." His words trailed off.

"As though," she finished his sentience, "you have used that name many times."

"Aye, lass." He looked at her smiling. "Now for the diagrams and maps. I suspect that we should ask Brother Thomas or whoever he has left in charge?"

*   *   *

The lower level of the archives was cold and damp. Brother Thomas led the way carrying a flickering candle that threatened to go out at any moment.

"Perhaps we should have brought a lantern," he said out loud as an afterthought?

But then he had made the decision and did not want to go back up to the library level and fetch the lantern. It was a while since he had been at this level but he knew where he was going. He planned to help the physician and his assistant find the drawings and plans. Then they could return to the more comfortable upper area rather than this damp cold place.

They progressed quietly along the passage and entered a large room. He paused at the door and listened. There was no sound except for the steady, regular breathing of the two visitors and Thomas's somewhat harsher breathing from the exercise. He unfastened the double locks with two keys with scarcely a sound, attesting to the good conditions of the locks. Thomas entered the room, located the candles that had been placed in holders on the wall, lit each candle in turn, and then they entered.

James and Kathryn walked into the room. The center of the room was clear but the shelves that lined the four walls were filled with documents of all sizes and shapes. Some documents lay flat in neat piles. Other documents were tied together in bundles. Others were rolled and tied with leather thongs. A makeshift table and a chair stood in the center of the room.

Thomas looked at them as they took in the room and its contents. He still could not see the face of the Little One. Thomas was curious about that one, but he was anxious to get the business done and get out of the place.

"What exactly is it that you seek?" Thomas asked the physician.

James described what he was seeking and Thomas scratched his head before responding.

"The castle and the priory have undergone renovations almost continually since the original building that was started at the time of Bishop Ranulf Flambard almost three hundred years ago. However," Thomas scratched his head again, "my guess is that the midden tunnel was placed into service about fifty years ago. So . . ." Thomas thought for a moment then walked over to one of her shelves, "this is the most likely place for what you seek."

James and Kathryn moved to the shelf that Thomas had indicated. James turned and saw Thomas standing immobile.

"I must," Thomas offered by way of explanation, "remain here. We came in together, we must stay together, and we will leave together."

James looked at Thomas and raised his eyebrows in the inevitable question.

""This," Thomas explained "is the personal archive of the prior and I am under oath not to allow anyone into this room without my continual presence." Thomas held up his hands as if to say, "Sorry, but I have no choice."

James nodded and responded to Thomas in the Northern dialect, which caused Thomas to look at James curiously. James apologized and repeated his statement in Latin.

"I was telling my assistant that we will continue and that we will search the shelf until we have found what we need, if that is all right with you, Brother Thomas?"

Thomas nodded. The physician was unusual. He seemed to have a command of several tongues, especially the dialect of this part of northern England.

"I will," James continued in Latin, "need to converse in the dialect as my assistant understands that better than the other languages."

Thomas nodded and smiled his agreement indicating that he would not be offended if a language of which he had no knowledge was spoken.

Kathryn understood what James was doing. And he had, unknown to Brother Thomas, told her to keep silent.

The search that they made was thorough. Not one inch of the shelf or any manuscript was overlooked. And then Kathryn found it. James could tell from her body language that she was on to something. A flash of inspiration had caused her to look on the adjoining shelf and there it was. She untied the leather thong and as she unrolled the plan she knew that this was what she was seeking. She passed it to James. Brother Thomas had been occupied sitting at the table and reading his newly acquired missal by the light of a lantern that had been left in the corner by a previous visitor.

"Brother Thomas," James announced the find by calling out the monk's name. "May we?" James gestured to the rough table that looked very unstable.

"Of course."

After a moment of careful handling, James unrolled the document and saw a strange shape in the light of the lantern.

"Ugh!" James exclaimed. Kathryn stood silent and unmoving. Thomas also exclaimed his disgust.

James saw that the document had been the coffin to a dead rat. His eyes narrowed and he kicked the loathsome creature out of the cell into the hallway. Brother Thomas moved away. Fear seemed to be alive in his eyes as he watched James's successful removal of the rat from the room.

"They tell me," he said "that it is the rats that brought the plague."

"Only partly right, Thomas," said James. "The fleas from the rat," he saw Thomas's quizzical expression and added, "the rat's body lice," in language that Thomas would understand, "carry the disease from the rat to humans. But this rat is desiccated, has no blood, and the fleas have long since departed. Almost as if the already dead rat was placed there by someone who thought that it might . . ."

James allowed his words to trail off. Thomas looked at him in disbelief.

"How do you know such things, physician? The rat's body lice carry the disease. It is, as you said, desiccated? I am not familiar with such thoughts and words."

"One picks these up in travel," said James wondering where he had actually gained this knowledge. He could not remember. Then, suspecting that for whatever reason he may have said too much, James turned his attention to the plan that had recently been the rat's domain of death.

"This is interesting," James exclaimed. Thomas moved closer.

"Apparently the midden tunnel must have been built later than we thought. There is not sign of it on this plan." He looked at Brother Thomas, "Could someone have built the tunnel without marking it on here?" he asked Thomas.

"No," came the quick response. "The prior, and more lately, Bishop Hatfield, would not allow such secrecy. All modifications must be marked on an updated plan and shown in detail. Anyone who does not follow this rule, no matter who he may be with the exception of the Duke of Lancaster, would suffer Bishop Hatfield's wrath and most likely be punished. Physically!"

Thomas emphasized the final word as if to indicate that with the one exception, there were no exceptions!

Thomas went to the next shelf along the wall shelf and pulled out another plan. He unrolled it just as carefully as James had unrolled the previous one.

"No," he said, "it is not there. And," he looked at the lower corners of the plan that he had just unrolled, "this plan is a record of the last

458   ELIZABETH JAMES

renovations done in that area of the castle. Just five years ago in fact. The midden ditch is as recent as five years ago! I know the man who did the work and he is as honest as . . ."

Thomas thought for a few moments as he searched for the correct word.

"As a monk?" James suggested.

Thomas smiled. "Well, at least as honest as one of our monks," he responded. "I know this man personally and he would not falsify any such document! In fact, you may know him," Thomas looked at James. "He is a brother-in-law of your cousin Oswald, having learned the trade from Oswald's father and married a sister of Oswald. No, he is an honest man."

James did not know any relatives of Oswald but he sensed that they would be of the same honest stature as Oswald. He was satisfied with Thomas's assessment of the family.

"Brother Thomas," James asked, "could there be any other plans?"

"None could have been made without the knowledge of the prior or Bishop Hatfield. Absolutely none."

"Well, I suppose," James said, "that we should return these and take our leave. We appreciate your efforts and thank you for your patience."

Thomas smiled. "Patience is a quality that we are trained to acquire, if we do not already have it when we enter this priory. I am pleased to have been of help, although you were not successful in your search."

James smiled at Thomas and then spoke to Kathryn asking that she help him roll up the plans, tie them securely, and return them to their places on the shelves. James helped Thomas place the rat in an old wrapping and it was ready for disposal. Neither he nor Kathryn made any sign of their disappointment as they followed Thomas to the upper level and out of the cold dampness.

James looked at the sky through the windows of the library. The time had passed and it was time to leave.

The hour had grown late and darkness approached. Clouds had collected and the snow was in the air. Old Man Winter was still proving his presence and vitality as they wrapped themselves in their warm robes and started the walk back to the house.

James turned to Kathryn after they had left the castle gate, "It seems, Kathryn my dear, that had we been able to find some definite evidence or the names of the plotters, it would have been too easy. Who was it who said to me once, for the wrong reasons the right things happen."

The snow was getting thicker.

"Let's quicken our pace, James, before the storm really starts," Kathryn suggested as they walked in the gathering gloom.

The finer snow fell first followed by the bigger flakes and by the time they got to the house the dark muddy streets were covered in white.

Margaret and Oswald had been watching for signs of their return, anxious since he had heard reports of the snow.

*   *   *

CHAPTER 43

When Oswald looked out of the door he saw the two figures plodding up the street against the face-freezing snow. He let out a sigh of relief that brought Margaret to his side.

The welcome warmth of the house and smiles from Oswald and Margaret greeted James and Kathryn and enveloped in the arms of heat. The robes that they wore were heavy and kept out most the cold. But their boots allowed the coldness in and made walking uncomfortable.

Margaret fussed to make sure that their cold boots and snow-laden robes were taken and placed in a warm spot to dry. James and Kathryn knew by eye contact that Oswald and Margaret would not be disturbed if they sat around in their breeches and jerkins.

During the meal of hot broth followed by tea, they discussed the happenings of the day. Oswald, like James, saw an ulterior motive in the placement of the rat among the plans.

"As if," Oswald expounded, "someone expected others to be looking at the plans and did not want the word to spread of the apparently recent construction of the midden tunnel. If the rat carried the plague, the one who left it there would expect you to be dead in three days."

"Oswald!" Margaret exclaimed. She did not wish his blunt words to frighten James and Kathryn.

Kathryn smiled, "It is all right, Margaret. The rat did not seem to have any body fluids left in it. It was as flat as an oatcake."

Oswald and Margaret also had news for Kathryn and James. Margaret indicated that Oswald should tell the story.

"It seems," he started the story, "that there has been a minor skirmish in the south, as though someone is attempting to start a pattern of general unrest throughout England and Scotland. The outlaws in Cheshire have always been a thorn in John's side. It seems to me," Oswald ventured, "that the king should have been firm with this rabble. King Edward is a strong monarch. Some would say that he is harsh in his judgments or even cruel, but neither he nor John ever seemed to get to grips with these bandits. But now," Oswald smiled, "even without King Edward and John, it seems that the bandits have been killed and those who were not killed are dispersed. John's younger brother, Edmond, Duke of York, led the king's soldiers. I heard that there are bodies hanging from gallows throughout the region to set an example for anyone else who may wish to cause trouble. But," Oswald continued, "I do wonder if there is not a coincidence between these bandits and the army that was marshaled to the north of the border?"

"However," James continued Oswald's thought, "the cessation of this minor revolt is not an indication that our prayers have been answered. I believe that the danger is not yet over and we must maintain our vigilance."

"It seems to me," Kathryn's voice sounded shrill after the two deep voices of Oswald and James, "that, if anything, our friend Gervais failed in his mission thereby causing the army in Scotland and this skirmish in Cheshire to be mistimed and futile."

Kathryn's eyes twinkled and her usually pale skin glowed with excitement and cold.

"I agree with both of you," she looked at James and Oswald, "that the danger is not yet past. And . . ."

Margaret jumped into the conversation as she read Kathryn's thoughts.

"But we have," she said "gained an advantage. I should think that all who knew of us, perhaps this was only Gervais, may not be dead. So we remain undetected to whoever else is involved. We can use that to our advantage."

"I propose that we rest now," Margaret continued, "and that we go about our business as usual tomorrow. We," she looked at Oswald "will visit the sick to do our healing work and see what else we can find. While you," she looked at Kathryn and James, "should talk with Ranulf."

*   *   *

As usual, after a breakfast of hot oatmeal and hot tea, James and Kathryn made their way through the knee-high snow to the castle. After they had given the guards greetings and told them to stay warm, James looked at Kathryn.

"Well, my dear, let us see what words of wisdom Ranulf has for us today."

As they approached the door of Ranulf's room, the sergeant of the guards stepped forward.

"Good morning, Physician," he did not address Kathryn nor even look at her. She was the physician's assistant. "Sir Ranulf," the sergeant continued, "has been awake for some time and he is asking for you."

De Boise was sitting upright in a high bed with no covers on him. Pillows supported his back, his face was healthy, and he was smiling. His hair was brushed and the residue of fever seemed to have disappeared. The attendants were clearing away the remnants of a bed-bath session. Fragrant herbs burned in censers to remove the odors from the room and the scented smoke gave the impression that it was a misty morning along the riverbanks. He saw James and Kathryn and eased himself up even further.

"Physician," he spoke softly and then looked at the attendants. "Leave us. Get yourselves something to eat," de Boise commanded. They took the bowls and clothes and left the room.

"Those two young men love to eat," he said by way of explanation. Then he added, "James, Kathryn. My greetings to you both."

They approached the bed and James saw the bandage on de Boise's leg. Kathryn opened the satchel to remove the poultice ingredients and the materials for bandages. She turned and saw clean linen strips hanging on a chair near to the fire.

"My lord," said Kathryn but before she could say more, Ranulf's raised eyebrow cut her short.

"Ranulf," she continued, "I see that bandages have been washed and scrubbed."

"Yes, Kathryn," replied de Boise.

"Was the water boiling?" Kathryn asked.

James rolled his eyes and smiled. "Do not worry, Ranulf, I get this all of the time. The easiest way to handle such a question from my dear Kathryn is to answer simply yes or no."

Kathryn took no notice of this exchange but with more questions satisfied herself that the bandages had been cleaned correctly and were, subject to the final inspection, suitable for further use.

"Ranulf! You do look well."

The voice took all three by surprise. It was King Edward. James and Kathryn attempted to go down on bended knee.

"Get up, Physician, and you too young woman. You do not fool me. If you are anything like your late cousin, God rest his soul, you are only pretending. You do me homage in the way that you treat my adopted son Ranulf."

Edward was beaming at Ranulf. James and Kathryn moved away to allow them privacy. Edward turned.

"Where are you going, Physician?" he asked

"Giving you privacy, sire," James answered.

"We will tell you when we need privacy, Physician. You too, young woman. Go about your business for we only have a few moments to spend with Ranulf."

Ranulf's eyes were bright and alert, and his voice was steady. James was pleased. Kathryn continued her work with the poultice and bandages.

"We must leave you now," Edward announced. "Our son John will see you later in the day. Fair you well, Ranulf." Then, turning to James and Kathryn, Edward said, "Take good care of him. He is dear to us."

Edward gave them both a long, piercing stare. His blue eyes sparkled, he was composed and in command, then he left, smiling to himself.

"James and Kathryn," de Boise started the conversation. "I am truly feeling much better today. I feel that my condition has not allowed me to be at my best."

"Ranulf," Kathryn exclaimed, "I knew that you would recover. Once my dear husband had his hands on you I had no doubt about your recovery. However, I am sure that James," she looked at James for confirmation, "will recommend that you do not overtax yourself too much in these early days. You must rest your leg and give it time to heal fully!"

The words came much easier to Kathryn than they had in the past. She was recalling phrases that she had heard James use.

"Well, it seems that your assistant is taking control, James." Ranulf smiled as he continued. "But you both have my thanks. I am being well cared for and that is fine with me!"

Kathryn carried the warm poultice and clean bandages to the bed where James cleaned the wound and nodded when he saw that the scar tissue was starting to form without any sign of infection.

"I will be up and about in no time," Ranulf pronounced "but for the meantime, we must give consideration to our next steps." He looked at James. "Have you found anything that would help us in our search?"

James, with frequent additions that Kathryn could recall from her excellent memory, got him up to date.

Kathryn's happy tones were infectious and Ranulf felt persistent buoyancy in his spirits. James's words and appearance genuinely impressed him. The thoughts racing through Ranulf's head were far removed from the matters related to his estate west of the city. As soon as he could, he needed to be up and about. He felt stronger but he knew that he had to heed their words. He had brightened visibly as a result of King Edward's visit. He knew that soon, moved by sheer determination, he would be completely recovered.

Delighted with this thought, Ranulf was in good spirits.

*   *   *

The days passed quickly as James and Kathryn settled into the daily routine of visiting Ranulf, helping Oswald and Margaret whenever they were able. James found that his bottle of small white tablets were depleting and he became known as *Doctorus Tablati*, the Doctor of Tablets. James and Kathryn used herbal medicines, and they also learned about new medicines that they had never used before.

It was during these days that James decided to keep a medicinal journal that he could use as a reference. At the end of each day, the four of them having returned to the house, James would sit with pen and any pieces of parchment or vellum that he could acquire. Most of the writing materials were given to him, courtesy of Brother Thomas.

Sitting at the table after supper, the four friends recalled the activities of the day and James made notes after which he transcribed into the format of his *De Medicinae et Chirurgiae*, a text on medicine and surgery.

He started with a description of the wound that de Boise had suffered and the method by which he cleaned and treated the wound. He added notes on the recovery of Ranulf.

Other pages described a variety of cures. Women who did not wish to conceive were given a piece of sea sponge cut to the right shape and dipped in a mixture of lard and hemlock. An alternate method was for the woman to cleanse herself with gall, a mild solution of vinegar in water. For the termination of pregnancy, wild thyme was used as was yellow dock or horseradish. The extract of colchicum, a poison that can cause serious if not fatal vomiting and diarrhea, was used in milder doses to prevent gout.

For scrofula, a disease of the skin on the hand and neck, he gave the patient pieces of sea sponge that had been soaked in iodine. The only other so-called cure was to have the king touch the infected area. James knew that King Edward would not be too happy with such a recommendation!

For a cough, he prescribed the vapors of antimony. The steam caused the lungs to expand while the antimony would loosen the catarrh. Antimony was also often used to ward off infection. It was a powerful purgative and emetic, and again, James had to learn from Oswald the fine line between curing the patient and driving the patient into further depths of sickness.

James was a frequent user of poppy and mandrake to induce deep sleep and subdue pain. He found these particularly useful when he had to perform surgery. The patient slept through the pain, did not struggle, and he was able to perform complete and clean surgical procedures.

He also prescribed rhubarb syrups for constipation, borage for phlegm, theriaca against the plague, preparations of sage against the tertian fever.

A farmer claimed that his family had suffered from a mysterious illness since the autumn when he had harvested his grain and used it for bread. James advised him to destroy the remaining grain by burning it. "Examine the seeds for any trace of blight. Do not even let it lie to fertilize the fields. It is this that has poisoned your family. And when the new crop comes from the seeds that you have used, burn that also." Afterward, James arranged with Brother Thomas and John that the man would be employed at the priory until his fields were clean and he could work them again.

He refused to believe what he had been told by several monks, after leaving Ranulf one morning, that "sickness was the finger of Providence. God used illness for a multitude of higher purposes . . . as a punishment." James countered with the statement that sickness was a result of the conditions under which the people lived and God gave rise to the herbals to help cure sickness. The monks had no response to this. They told James that they would pray for guidance.

Another man claimed that the water from his well was causing sickness in his family, whereupon he produced a sample and offered it to James and Oswald to drink. James knew from one sniff, as did Oswald, that the well was too close to the moat or to a midden ditch. The sour water seeps into the well from underneath ground and the man was told, not advised, to move his well.

As the days passed, the number of pages grew until the collection was substantial.

*   *   *

"Are you sure that you are strong enough, my lord?"

James and Kathryn heard the words as they were about to enter Ranulf's room. They smiled at the guards and walked into the room to see two very worried attendants supporting de Boise as he tottered from the bed to the table. The sight made James and Kathryn wince as they thought about possible damage to the wound.

The attendants stopped in their tracks as they saw them. The furious look that James gave them induced shaking.

"Sit Sir de Boise down, now."

Ranulf grinned as much to say "You see, I am not a child to be confined to bed all day."

"Out," was James's next words, "and close the door. We have business with Sir de Boise!"

The expression on James's face told them that they had better not incur the wrath of this physician. The attendants hurriedly left the room.

Kathryn looked at Ranulf through eyes that were not too friendly. Her bottom lip quivered in anger as she started to remove the bandage, and then she said.

"Ranulf, it is of the utmost importance that you rest and, as difficult as it may be for you, these first days are critical to your complete recovery."

"Yes, Mother," he said with feigned meekness, but his inner voice told him to speak with care.

Kathryn then brought the freshly prepared poultice to the bedside. James had changed the ingredients slightly so that the poultice was more appealing to the nose by adding a scented flower extract.

"Good grief, James!"

Kathryn's exclamation made him look up suddenly. Fearing the worst he took three hurried steps to where de Boise was sitting. Kathryn was examining the last vestiges of the wound that had healed remarkably well.

James looked at Ranulf in a brotherly way. He was typical of what one should expect. A man used to fighting and who was not going to be restrained by a leg wound, even if it tried to kill him.

James beamed when he saw the wound. He told de Boise that it was almost healed and he doubted that any bleeding could start. He would watch for discoloration over the next four days and there being none, he would declare Ranulf fit to walk.

"James, I thank you," de Boise responded.

"Ranulf," Kathryn looked at him, "we feel that you are also a friend to both of us." Ranulf smiled and Kathryn added, "So behave yourself and no overexertion, you still need healing time," as she kissed him gently on the forehead.

James and Ranulf smiled at her comments.

"James," Kathryn asked "shall we cover the wound again for at least another day? I think that it would be wise to do so. I also recommend that we give our friend Ranulf a bed bath!"

"As you say, Mother."

The three of them filled the room with laughter. James's words and the beaming smile from Ranulf when she had kissed his forehead tickled her long-repressed sense of humor.

"Who, may I ask, will do the bathing?" Ranulf looked worried.

"Of course you may ask, Ranulf. Surely you know that we," Kathryn looked at James as she spoke, "are fully qualified to perform such duties? So, we will give you the bath, clean you up, and at the same time we can determine the effects that any slight movement may have on your wound. So if you would be so kind as to request hot water?"

Ranulf shouted for the attendants as James and Kathryn once more pulled the hoods of their respective robes over their heads. A guard entered the room to inform de Boise that the attendants were in the kitchen and that he would fetch them.

The attendants duly appeared, looking less hungry than they had looked when they were ordered out of the room. Instructions were given and hot water was brought to the room. The attendants were told to go back to the kitchen. Scented flower extract was added to the water and de Boise was bathed.

As they cleared up after the bathing session, Kathryn looked at the two men as they chatted about their plans for the next few days. She sensed that beyond the next days, they would encounter several incidents before this whole mystery was cleared and John is safe once more.

James was her husband and she was bound to him by love and by marriage, she told herself. In the eyes of God, Ranulf was a lord of the manor, a knight of the palatinate, and adopted son of King Edward.

She knew that a hard road lay ahead and that she had to protect these two men, first her husband and then Ranulf, even in a life and death situation.

*   *   *

Three days later, James pronounced Ranulf's wound healed and that he was well enough to exercise in the room. De Boise was elated. As the days passed and de Boise grew stronger, he was clearly in a good mood to laugh and smile with James and Kathryn but decorum and the need for secrecy prevented this while others were present. De Boise held their attention with stories of Oswald, in particular, stories of those times when they traveled together with the army. They had shared food, drink, and friendship. And then, suddenly during one of their conversations, de Boise became deadly serious.

"I am of the opinion that we need to act as soon as possible. King Edward will be returning to London soon and we must resolve this issue before the king leaves and John departs once more for France. You have nursed me to health and allowed me to take a position where I can do something to prevent what might be planned. I do not know how I'll ever be able to repay you."

James smiled.

"You owe us nothing, Ranulf. As we have already said," James looked at Kathryn and she nodded, "we are here to help you. You will not be alone!"

"It is time," he thought to himself as he stood up and looked at James and Kathryn.

"*Ic eom gearu*! I am ready!" He continued to look at them. "I use the words that I learned from Oswald. And," he added, "there is only one thing to be done: whether because of our actions we shall end up in this world or the other, we must start on our work to resolve this mystery and remove the danger from John and King Edward!"

*   *   *

CHAPTER 44

Kathryn and James had returned and over a light evening meal, Kathryn had repeated what had taken place during the day.

Oswald and Margaret had listened intently, hanging on every word. Oswald wanted to be involved with the plans but could not, and it showed in his disappointed expression. He stood near the corner of the room that had darkened as the last crimson shafts of the sunset departed for the night.

"Let's have a cup of tea," was all that Kathryn could think to say. Her words diffused the situation and Oswald was back to his usual self.

"Ah, Little One, a cup of tea cures everything," Oswald said smiling once more. "And I do apologize for my frustration, but to have this going on and not to be a part of it . . ." He allowed the words to trail into silence.

"But Oswald," Kathryn asked, "will we not have you watching over us? That is good enough for me and," she looked at James, "for my dear husband."

James moved from his seat and next to Kathryn. The colors of their clothes, the robes having been shed, showed shades of green, and red that were darkened in the dusk and the candlelight. As James placed his arm around Oswald's shoulder, their likeness to each other became more obvious to Margaret and Kathryn. James even seemed to add an extra few inches to match Oswald's height. Margaret and Kathryn gasped at the apparent transformation. Suddenly their two men looked as if they were twins.

"The Frenchman died because he could not combine reason and violence, at least on this occasion," Oswald told them. "But," he continued, "we are not so sure of those that controlled the Frenchman. That is the source of my worry. But you, Cousin, seem to have it in you to bring about justice. You have my full support and my blessing."

James said, "Fantastic!"

After the most searching look at each other, the two men were ready for tea.

"Where is my tea, woman?" James spoke to Kathryn in a commanding voice. Oswald smiled. Margaret smiled.

"On your head if you do not use a civil tongue, your lordship," Kathryn responded sweetly. Margaret laughed.

"Well," offered Margaret as they sat with the hot tea in mugs before them, "it seems to me that we should relax and play a game of chess. Two women will play against two men. And we will, of course, defeat you!"

"My dear Margaret," James said, "there are expressions that are forming in my mind and I do not know their origins. But one stays firmly fixed on my tongue and I must say it." James paused.

"Do not keep us waiting, Cousin." Oswald spoke. "Let us hear it."

"Fat chance!" James allowed the words to explode from his lips.

"It seems to me," Margaret spoke as she realized that now her challenge had been accepted, "that those words might mean something derogatory about our playing skills. Come, Kathryn, let us show these mere men that we women are made of stern stuff."

James and Oswald looked at each other in the flickering light of the fire. In the corners of their Saxon souls they knew that the game was serious. The ladies had rebelled, and these little pieces of ivory on the chessboard would determine the victors.

"All right," Kathryn's voice spoke commandingly. "Are you two ready?" She looked at James and Oswald. "The board is set." She beamed at Margaret.

"Ladies first! Pawn to king-three."

* * *

CHAPTER 45

I t was the morning of the next day. James and Kathryn had just arrived and were ready to check Ranulf's leg when he let forth with the outburst.

"Get out!"

James and Kathryn were almost bowled over by the two attendants as they fled the wrath of de Boise. As James and Kathryn entered the room he gave one command, "Close the door!"

De Boise gripped the arm of the chair in which he sat. Then he spoke, and his voice was low and thrilling.

"I have heard from a very reliable source that Sir Humphrey de Bohun has been in the castle for these past three weeks!"

"My dear Ranulf!" James exclaimed as he blew a long, slow whistle of astonishment.

"It is true," Ranulf emphasized. "I heard it this morning from none other than my brother, John. Could it be that de Bohun has been waiting here for the insurrection to begin? If there is proof, I know that my father, even though he be the king, would think nothing of showing Sir Humphrey that his head is not a permanent attachment to his body. And he would willingly swing the sword himself!"

De Boise seemed wound up to continue indefinitely, but Kathryn, who had stood quite still and was ready to remove the bandages, was shocked by the flow of profane adjectives.

"I appreciate your emotion, sire," she used the formal term so that de Boise would look at her as she pushed the hood of her robe back onto her neck. She met his stare equally and saw gentleness in his eyes.

"Ranulf," Kathryn continued, "we use this to our advantage. It is very important that we maintain our secrecy. Now more than ever, no one can know of the remarkable recovery that you have made. We then face the task of discovering the extent of de Bohun's involvement. And if he is involved, we need to know to what extent and who is with him. By the way, how is your book?"

Kathryn pointed to the book that was on the floor, having been thrown there no doubt by de Boise when he assimilated the seriousness of the news.

"The book, I take it, is readable?"

"James," said de Boise in a smiling tone, "where did you find your good lady? She fights, so I am told, like a tigress and then has the words of diplomacy in her vocabulary."

James, who had been standing by and knowing what would happen, shook his head in wonderment and the two of them laughed.

"Now, listen to me, you two," Kathryn commanded as she started to undo the bandages, "it would be impossible for de Bohun to hide his actions if he is watched carefully. Ranulf, do you have men of the king's guards that you can trust?"

Kathryn knew by instinct what the answer would be. And she was not disappointed.

"Yes," de Boise responded. "In particular those who were trained by Oswald I would trust with my life. And," de Boise added for emphasis, "I have done so on several occasions." He appeared to be deep in thought and then added. "In fact, if I am not mistaken, the men who are with the king and John were all trained by Oswald and so . . ." He allowed the words to trail off since he knew that James and Kathryn would know the meaning.

Kathryn looked at James and since she was concentrating on making sure that the wound was clean, took over the conversation.

"Then, Ranulf, we propose," James had read Kathryn's thoughts perfectly, "that you place these men in key positions and that there are sufficient to protect the king and John from up to one dozen intruders. We believe that it is very important that you do this. We may even consider setting a trap."

Ranulf was about to protest when Kathryn cut him off.

"We know, Ranulf," Kathryn said, "that we cannot even think of using King Edward or John as bait. We need someone of equal importance. A man who would give his life for his father and brother!"

"Kathryn, you are a little fox! "Ranulf exclaimed. "Of course you may use me as bait!" He looked at James. "You, Physician, are also a fox!"

"We," Kathryn looked at James as she spoke, "need to have the word put out that your wound is regressing. I think that we can trust John with this news and he should be up to date on all aspects of the plan. But I worry that . . ."

"My Kathryn," James jumped in at Kathryn's slight hesitation, "is worried that if the king gets wind of this situation, he may take matters into his own hands!"

"I will talk with my brother," Ranulf offered "and he will decide the best moment to talk with the king."

Kathryn bathed the wound and wondered why she was doing that. The wound was clean.

"I think, James," she said, "that we should cover the wound to maintain its good health and then overlap with bloodied bandages to effect a bloodstain. I hate the thought of using blood that might carry disease but . . ."

"Wait, Kathryn," de Boise interrupted, "What if we use a piece of red cloth that is then covered with a top layer bandage? Do we reduce the risk of infection from the bad blood?"

"Ranulf," Kathryn commented immediately, "Good idea. We shall make sure that the red dye is fixed and will soak into your bandages."

De Boise pointed to the red cloth hanging on the wall by his sword. The emblems of the king were prominent. "That is an undercoat that I use at times. No one will miss it."

Kathryn soaked the red cloth in warm water, did not see any evidence of leaking dye, and then placed the cloth under the topmost layer of bandage. The redness was obvious through the bandages and the water allowed the cloth to appear that it has no definite outline.

"You know, Ranulf," said James, "that this requires that you remain in your bed. If you decide that you must move make a show of great pain and effort. Even to your attendants. They will certainly spread the word throughout the kitchen staff and thence to others."

Ranulf nodded.

"Now I have more news for you that tell me that we may be close to a showdown with de Bohun or whoever else is behind this plot." He nodded his head in thanks as Kathryn passed him the hot tea. He took a sip and then continued, "Information has also reached me that a band of men are encamped a short distance away from here. John and I are the only ones who know of the existence of this group. We have reason to believe that the numbers are substantial, many hundred of men. They may, it is surmised, be awaiting the arrival of the army from north of the border."

Ranulf paused to sip his tea and then continued, "They are led by Turstin Fitz Malet, a man of no means and of no importance who is looking for rewards greater than he dares to hope. And can you believe it?" Ranulf continued the conversation as he answered his own question. "They are encamped at the Red Banks: some now call it the site of the Battle of Neville's Cross, which is hard by my estates. Either they know not of where I live or they are fools to think that no one would tell me or my brother of a group of men playing at hiding in the bushes!"

"Then Ranulf," James aid, "we may, for a moment, have the upper hand. Do you know if Fitz Malet is in league with de Bohun?"

De Boise shook his head as he replied.

"What I have told you is the current extent of my knowledge. But it seems that the remainder of the horsemen with Fitz Malet are also men of no means but who may have been positioned to control segments of the Scottish army and thereby lay their claims to lands here and farther south. I need not add that if they had succeeded in killing John, anarchy and chaos would have been the result. I would have gladly died a thousand deaths for the privilege of stopping their little game."

"Dear me," said Kathryn, "it must indeed be a cutthroat band and from your description, I gather that an out-and-out fight is not within the realm of chance?"

"No, Kathryn. John and I have thought of that," said de Boise, "but if we withdraw men from the castle, the defense is weakened and we may play right into the hands of these brigands."

"I assume that we will not play a waiting game?" Kathryn asked. "Knowing what the answer would be."

"You are correct, my dear," James responded immediately. "The combined forces of . . ." James thought for a moment to recall the name, "Fitz Malet and any that, assuming he has a role, de Bohun can muster would be too much to handle at a later date. We must," he looked at de Boise, "set the wheels of our plan in motion as soon as possible."

"You are anxious, James? And you Kathryn?" de Boise asked looking at them both keenly. Before either could answer Ranulf's question he spoke again. "My God!" he said, rolling up his eyes and clapping his hands, "Do you suppose . . . ?" Once more he allowed his question to trail off into silence.

"Yes," James interrupted as he read into Ranulf's unspoken question, "It is a move that we must assume. The force led by Fitz Malet may only be a small part of the total force available in England. We cannot put aside that notion. But you know too well the difficulties of hiding such a number of men without being spotted. Indeed, only very greedy, and perhaps foolish, men would attempt such moves in an attempt to purloin the throne."

Ranulf took the water flask that stood on a small table near his elbow and drained it at a gulp, and then he continued his thoughts.

"I have it. As I have said, your cousin Oswald," he looked at James, "trained his men well. They are trained to loyalty. Much against my wishes, as I would rather be the one for this task, I will send a sergeant and four men, heavily armed, to spread the word, quietly and effectively. They will pass on orders to other units of the guards to engage and kill as many of the insurgents as possible and by whatever means they must use. Any that survive must be the leaders so that we might ask them a few questions. And after I am finished, they will regret that they had survived."

Ranulf smiled as he added, "I will call for food and drink and then let us talk over your plan of using me as bait. I look forward to action again!"

Within minutes of de Boise calling the attendants from where they stood outside of the door and giving them instructions, they returned carrying trays with beef stew and fresh bread as the main course with custard tarts for dessert. Hot tea, prepared according to Kathryn's direction, but given to the assistants by de Boise, was also brought.

When the meal had been concluded and the remnants cleared away by the attendants, with Kathryn and James sheltered from prying eyes by the hoods of their robes, de Boise made himself comfortable in a chair that was close to the bed. He screwed up his nose as though attempting to get the words in correct order. Kathryn and James remained silent in an agony of apprehension.

"First I ask that you do not interrupt until my thoughts are organized. Once I have the details placed before you, we can then talk." Kathryn and

James nodded their heads in agreement and he continued. "It seems to me that I must, possibly through John, let de Bohun know that I am here in this room and I am incapacitated. Almost, we might say, at death's door."

Ranulf paused for a moment to collect his thoughts.

"If de Bohun is involved," de Boise continued, "he will be worried about my possible role and he will make every effort to visit me. Then when he has satisfied himself that I am not in any way fit to walk or take any other action, he will strike. On the other hand, if de Bohun is not involved I must expect other visitors. And my guess is that they will be men who are of a more unsavory nature than de Bohun. I do think that I will be the first target. John will be the second target. Other targets will be anyone else who gets in their way."

"Why must you keep us waiting, Ranulf?" Kathryn whispered lest the excitement in her voice carry through the door to the guards. "Tell us, at once, please, who you think may be involved." Her voice trailed off into silence as she awaited Ranulf's answer.

"In my mind, the criminal," said de Boise smoothly, "is . . ."

A knock was heard on the door and one of the attendants, without putting his head around the door announced, "Sir Humphrey de Bohn to see you, sire."

Kathryn and James quickly donned their hoods and stood up from their chairs. De Boise quickly lay back on the bed and with a wink at Kathryn and James, took on the pose of one who is near death. At a signal from de Boise, James opened the door for Sir Humphrey de Bohun who entered looking pale and ill. As if by a nervous reaction, he started to talk immediately.

"Forgive me for intruding, Ranulf," de Bohun spoke quickly, "I had heard of your recent mishap and thought to pass on my best wishes. I have been much upset by the news of your misfortune," he said, looking directly at de Boise. "They say that you foiled a plot to harm John."

He seemed to lean nervously against the chair that was placed at the foot of the bed. James and Kathryn did not feel any pity for de Bohun's apparent discomfort. Ranulf remained in his pose of the mortally wounded man. He lay still looking at de Bohun through half-closed eyes and then seemed to recognize him.

"Oh, Sir Humphrey," Ranulf's voice sounded weak as he looked at James, "why did you send for Sir Humphrey?"

"Because," said James taking up Ranulf's cue to show that de Bohun was one of the trusted few, "I thought that being the Constable of England and close to the king, he needed to know what had happened to you."

"Sire," James turned to de Bohun and whispered quietly to give the impression that de Boise should not hear the words. "I believe you have not been told as yet that Sir Ranulf is gravely ill. The fate of his leg is not yet known. I had hoped to save the leg but Sir Ranulf's condition has taken a turn for the worse and I may have to remove it. We can only hope that all will turn out well," but James rolled his eyes at de Bohun, as if to indicate the unspoken seriousness of de Boise's condition.

"What about," de Bohun asked in a low voice, "the fate of Sir Ranulf?"

"He is weak, sire," James continued to whisper, "and I am not sure what I can do to protect him from the worst."

"Do your best, Physician," de Bohun commanded. He appeared to fumble with the chair and then he sat in it.

"Should you not," de Bohun continued to whisper "have taken the leg earlier if it looked beyond saving?"

"Sire," James whispered, continuing in the mode that de Bohun had set, "Sir Ranulf's leg improved for some days after the wound was inflicted and lately it has deteriorated to a point that may be irreversible. I was suspicious of the remarkable progress but the wound seemed to have done more damage that could be determined."

Sir Humphrey nodded, apparently satisfied with the response from James. He looked at the diminutive figure of Kathryn.

"I see you have a young assistant. Is he any good?"

James nodded, "Excellent, sire."

Sir Humphrey looked at Kathryn again. "When will he be ready for work on his own?" Kathryn tried to hide her slight shiver under the robes.

"In about three years, sire," James responded cautiously.

"I may have need of a personal physician. So I may contact you again."

"As you wish, sire," was all that James could say.

"This is a very curious situation that has developed," said de Bohun in his normal voice and returning to the matter at hand. "There are rumors of a plot against the Duke of Lancaster. Have you heard anything about that, Physician?

"I have not, sire," whispered James. "I do not mingle with the servants or the soldiers. All I know is that I was told to attend Sir Ranulf until he improves."

"Physician," said de Bohun turning his back to de Boise and signaling to James that he should face him, "no one needs to know that I was here. You are not to repeat any part of this conversation. Do you understand?"

"Aye, sire."

"And, Physician," de Bohun said, "your accent is strange to my ears. From where do you hail?"

"Many places, sire, but," James chose his words carefully, "originally from a small village close by this city, sire. The village still remains and is about a half-a-day journey from here. To the east," James added to indicate the direction.

"I do not know of the villages in this area," observed de Bohun, "My home is many days journey to the south. Take care of Sir Ranulf and let me know how he progresses. Immediately."

The look on de Bohun's face told James that he would also want to know immediately about the any less-palatable events. "Such as Ranulf's death," James thought quietly to himself.

"Aye, sire," James was about to say more but stopped suddenly as de Bohun looked at Kathryn and he appeared to be about to move in her direction, but he changed his mind and walked out of the room. At a signal from James, Kathryn closed the door and returned to stand by Ranulf's side.

"You did just fine, James," said de Boise, "that took courage!"

"I was wondering if I should have done something?" James queried.

"There was nothing that you could have done. Short of killing him! And then there would have been the bothersome issue of his body and having to explain to my father why his constable had suddenly died. No, James, there was nothing that you could have done." De Boise looked at Kathryn, "What say you, Little One?"

"I agree," Kathryn answered quietly, "although I did have the same thoughts as James. There is something about that man that makes me feel that he is very untrustworthy but I cannot put my finger on it precisely."

"And so," de Boise added, "he is innocent until proven guilty. We have nothing other than supposition. I was surprised to have him visit me!"

"You are right," James said, "In these situations, the best thing you can do is remain calm and behave normally. Well, Kathryn my dear, what about you? Would you like to be de Bohun's personal physician? I can put in a word for you!"

Kathryn's response was to reach over to James and pinch his cheek between her fingers. Ranulf laughed quietly. A dying man should not be heard laughing and enjoying himself.

"This," Ranulf got over his laughter and whispered, "is very suspicious. I find that the guilty ones, instead of fleeing the scene, often stay close to the crime. Perhaps it is to divert suspicion from their own person. And I am very suspicious, even more than I was a short time ago, of our friend de Bohun!"

"He acted," Kathryn added, "as though he was in a state of shock to find you alive."

"Yes," de Boise agreed, "it is a mystery."

"Even though he did nothing and practically said nothing," James added, "he was very nervous in your presence, Ranulf."

"That is the curious circumstance," de Boise added. "Sir Humphrey spent his time here with difficulty and for the Constable of England to behave in such a manner is extremely suspicious!"

"Ranulf," Kathryn said, "this has raised my curiosity to a higher level. Let us spare no pains to find out the truth of this matter!

*   *   *

CHAPTER 46

Ranulf gazed intently at them from the bed and, looking at James and Kathryn, he knew that over the years he had not, with the exception of Oswald, permitted himself the luxury of friends.

"There is no doubt about it," de Boise reiterated, "the crime that was planned, in which John would see the end of his days sooner than expected, is a possibility but it does require perfect timing, total commitment, and the perfect criminal to perform the act."

"Of course," James spoke up in agreement. "We suspected de Bohun and he may be one of the plotters but he does not seem to me to be, as you put it, the perfect criminal. So, we must find the person, whoever he, or she, might be."

"Naturally," assented de Boise with a shrug, "but the perfect criminal is a mythical person whom we may never meet in the flesh."

"Precisely," Kathryn added her words to the conversation, nodding her head.

De Boise sipped again from the mug and adjusted his hair as if in deep thought. "I admit that I have not encountered him as yet, but I am always hopeful. However, I do know of one person of that caliber." De Boise paused, as if for effect.

"And," James asked, "who might that be."

De Boise laughed and said nothing. James and Kathryn looked at each other and then the light went on.

"You mean to tell us, Ranulf," Kathryn said, "that you are such a person? But how . . . ?"

"Kathryn's question started to trail away as de Boise spoke.

"I served my father for many years, almost twenty years in fact, to maintain order in many disordered courts and manor houses. There were times when his life was threatened and he needed someone that he could trust, me that is, to remove a possible assassin from this earth. And many times there was also the need to remove the assassin's sponsor from this life into the afterlife."

"And, Ranulf," Kathryn smiled as she spoke, "I always thought that you were a very nice gentleman!"

"But I am, Kathryn!" Ranulf responded. "To those who are loyal to King Edward and to those who respect his laws."

"We will, as you will see," de Boise started the explanation, "be able to tax the limits of their endurance. We have already seen the effect that my survival has on de Bohun, assuming that he was shocked to see me living. We have to use your talents, James. You, are a physician *extraordinaire* insofar as you use all of the information at your disposal to treat and cure sickness, even wounds. You found a different poultice to stop internal bleeding. You use clean bandages. In other words, you are precise in your work but you are also a critic of yourself and you are not happy until you have the answer to your questions. Am I correct?"

"Of course, Ranulf," James replied, "but that is my way . . .," he paused and then he added quickly, "A hit-and-miss approach is bad enough and can lead to death of a patient but in this case it is much worse. It is the assassination of the duke!"

"So, James," de Boise carried on with his previous thoughts, "think of yourself as being involved in a game of chess."

Kathryn smiled at Ranulf's words. Had she and Margaret not put James and Oswald to shame by winning the very game the other night?

"And," de Boise continued without realizing the reason for Kathryn's smile, "it is not the immediate move that counts but you must think three, four, even five or more moves ahead to have a chance of beating your opponent. Heaven knows," Ranulf crossed himself, "and even then, victory is not assured. So, let us assume that our assassin or assassins now believe that the way is open for them to commit their crime. They believe that they will never be discovered unless they wish it."

"But," Kathryn's eyes gleamed, "they do not know about us. Our friend de Bohun thinks that you," she looked at Ranulf," are incapacitated and close to death. You, my dear," she looked at James, "are a mere physician and the only weapons that you have are your surgical knives. I am sure that no one knows of the way in which you dispatched Gervais."

Ranulf suddenly sat bolt upright.

"Well done, Kathryn. A shipment of gold coin and plate was lost due to an unfortunate circumstance that was also related in the death of my dear friend Oswald. It happened on the north end of my estates. So, this would be quite a haul if the plotters could find it. A very handsome source of funds for their misbegotten deeds. So, by all means we will use me as the bait."

De Boise held his chin as he continued.

"They will want to get the location of the coin and plate from me. But even I do not know precisely where it is. We may even get a pleasant surprise when we find out who comes to take care of me and help me on the way to my maker."

"The risks for you are high, Ranulf," James said, "but no risk no gain! And," he added, "we must make arrangements to quietly move in without drawing too much attention."

James stroked his chin in further thought.

"You know," he said, "who has more need of a physician than a dying man?"

"And," Kathryn finished the thought, "we are going to quietly take a room next to yours so that we can watch over you like your proverbial falcons." She saw the look on Ranulf's face and added, "Do not protest, Sir de Boise. You have no choice. It has been decided that we are your guardians as you are, if we are correct, the first target. My dear James," she looked at James, "will make arrangements with those who own the house that we're using to not expect us to be there every night."

*   *   *

By now it was early afternoon. James and Kathryn had talked the whole morning with de Boise and decided that it was time to leave for their house and to let Oswald and Margaret know their plans. They were hungry.

De Boise, who knew that he had to feign weakness, called for the attendants who bought food. Everyone was cautious and acted in the correct manner so that the story of Ranulf's weakness would get about the castle.

Gradually, settling down after the meal, Kathryn spoke, thinking of the practicalities.

"I am worried that we do not know when an attack or attempt on Ranulf's life will occur. So, I propose, James, that you return to the house and do what you must." As an afterthought, Kathryn added, "I do not have a weapon. My knife," she brandished it, "is of little use other than to cut vegetables. So if you could . . ."

De Boise cut into her conversation.

"What type do you prefer, Kathryn."

Upon hearing her preference, he pulled a sword of the type that she had used against the Frenchman and his cronies from under the bed. "And here is a belt and scabbard," he added as he gave her the sword.

Kathryn tied the belt around her waist and tested the sword for balance. The sword disappeared into the scabbard and her robe was wrapped around to cover the weapon.

James was just leaving as John was announced by one of the attendants. The first item that John noticed was the red bandage. His eyebrows, raised in question, were put to rest by de Boise who related their plan.

"Well done. Well done, indeed!" was John's reply.

James felt no need to remain and, after excusing himself, continued on his way, closing the door as he left.

"And what role would you like me to play," John asked.

"None, sire," Kathryn told him. "You are to remain as far away from this room as possible."

"It is a while," John remarked, "since I had a lady giving me orders. The last, I believe, was my dear departed wife, Blanche, may God rest her soul!"

"My apologies, sire," Kathryn added hurriedly, "I forgot my station."

John and Ranulf laughed.

"No, my dear," John said, "I understand your forgetfulness. We are living in interesting times, are we not? You are truly a remarkable young lady. And I thank you for your diligence."

"I will see that my father," John continued, "is fully aware of your plans. I would not want him to find out by accident and decide to take up arms again. It would be a fearsome sight!" John smiled at the thought.

"I presume that at sometime you will need additional guards secreted close by?"

"Aye," Ranulf responded, "but we will get to that as time passes. I would not want to arouse any suspicions at this time."

"I will take my leave, Ranulf, Kathryn." John smiled and then added in a serious voice as he opened the door, "It is such a shame to see that your wound does not bode well and my brother, I am sad that you do not look as well as you did at my last visit. God be with you, my brother."

The door closed and Ranulf smiled at Kathryn.

"That is the way that I wanted it to go. I know my brother well. We will now rest until James returns and make sure that we are prepared to attend to any unwanted visitor."

*   *   *

"Ah, James." Ranulf's voice seemed to echo throughout the room, "I'm glad to have you back."

James smiled and looked at Kathryn as if to say, "All is well. Oswald and Margaret are aware of your plans."

"Took me a little longer than I thought, it seems that there is a banquet being planned for three days from now and the announcement has just been made and the castle is thronged with workers getting the great hall ready for the event," James said by way of explanation.

"That is it!" de Boise exclaimed, "they will make their move against me when the banquet is well under way."

Kathryn immediately saw the possibilities to lay the assassins to rest, "John will be prominent at the banquet while you will be here alone, except for us. So, I suggest, Ranulf, that we make it known that you are spending your last hours in peace and solitude and have the guards take up positions that are well hidden."

"In other words, Kathryn," de Boise continued with her thought, "let us pull the flies into our spider's web. You agree, James?"

"Aye," James said, "the opportunity that we have talked about has been thrust upon us. Let us tell John of this plan. And let us prevail upon him to omit no one from the list of invitations. That way, we can be sure that all will be present." Then James added, "Let us find out who had ordered the banquet and under what circumstances. That will guide us closer to the plotters."

"Excellent thought, James," Ranulf's eyes glowed in anticipation of the night to come. "We have a day to prepare as I doubt that anything will be initiated tonight. A killing under the noise of a banquet is an easy thing to do."

James and Kathryn were surprised at the conviction with which de Boise made the last statement.

"But we must," Kathryn said, "make sure that we are not the ones who are killed!"

De Boise smiled at her.

"You are right. So we must prepare well. Now," de Boise exclaimed, "for weapons!"

*   *   *

Night had fallen but the hustle and bustle of the preparations for the banquet continued and would perhaps continue throughout the night until the crow of the cock welcomed the start of a new day.

This was to be one of the biggest banquets that the city had seen for many years. And there was money to be made from the sale of produce. Wagonloads of food and many a cask of ale would be consumed.

*   *   *

Turstin Fitz Malet smiled to himself in the darkness. Thanks to the early advice of the forthcoming banquet, he and nine of his followers had been able to gain entry into the castle grounds. They had entered in the guise of food carriers, without weapons, but they would be provided with them in due course. There had originally been Fitz Malet and ten of his followers. One had panicked at the last moment and had attempted to flee the soldiers at the gate, instead of stopping for the security check. He had paid for his flight with an arrow in the back and was dead before his body hit the ground. He did not even have the time to utter a groan as the arrow brought an end to his miserable life.

"It was as well the fool died," Fitz Malet thought to himself, "I am better off than one who panics for no reason."

From the rumors, Fitz Malet knew that getting into the correct place in the castle to complete the task would be difficult. He had heard that his predecessors had got into the castle but had died at the point of entry. There were rumors of a man, or a man and a woman, or two men and two women. The rumors were endless and could not be true. Whoever thought of women fighting with the ferocity to kill intruders? The fools had probably run into six or seven guards and they had paid the price for poor planning.

"I," he thought, "do not intend to be so foolish. And if there did happen to be a woman involved, she would die very quickly on the point of his sword. A woman indeed. Such rubbish!"

He shuffled his way through the tents and fire braziers on the castle yard. He could bed down again in the same tent that he had used last night. The owner was dead on the road east of the city. The body was buried in a shallow grave in the field behind Saint Giles's Church and out of sight of the castle walls so that the prying eyes of the guards could not have seen him.

As he walked past one tent, a bony old woman peered out at him after seeing his shadow cast by the fire on the side of the tent. She looked at him as best as she could through half-closed eyes, spit in the dirt, and withdrew once more into the tent. Fitz Malet ignored the intrusion into his thoughts.

He saw other members of his band as they also occupied tents, gained by similar actions that he had used. If someone noticed a sudden high number of dead bodies in shallow graves after their job was done, so be it. Everyone was too busy with the activities of the moment to notice any such thing. The fields were not due for tilling for at least another month. Let the farmers find the bodies as they tilled the field and prepared them for another summer crop. They would find a very early crop! Fitz Malet laughed inwardly at his own humor. For the moment, he was in good spirits but he was also on his guard.

He reached his tent. The nearby fire had died down and the water in the pot was only lukewarm. He added more fuel to the fire and sat watching the flames as they increased in activity. The water heated quickly and he made himself a hot drink of herb tea. He could never understand why the English had such a love affair with herbs boiled in water. The stuff tasted like the perfume some of the ladies applied. Why not a hot mulled wine or brandy? He frowned as the hot liquid went down his throat. At least it warmed him but the taste! His meal was also another point for annoyance. His victim had packed oatmeal that was also to be added to boiling water and swallowed without any other additives. The English and their tasteless food.

"How had they survived so long?" he wondered. It warmed his stomach but there was no taste.

He sat, waiting for the dawn, wondering if he would sleep but thinking that a series of naps might serve him better. He needed to be watchful.

He wrapped his outer garment around him to retain the warmth. At least the English wool was thick and kept out the cold and the rain. Fine linen or silk garments may look well at court, but there was nothing like the homespun English wool for protection from the weather. Still holding on to his robe, he noticed some movement of people among the tents. That was of little bother to him unless one became very curious about him. Then he would have to take further action to protect himself. It was the continuous train of ox-carts and horse-carts moving around within the castle yard, their movement and accompanying noise would not help induce sleep!

He thought he must have dozed for a while, but in fact, he had slept for several hours. The cold and tiredness had been too much for him. A group of workmen moving through the tents came toward him as he shook the muscle-numbing effects of the deep sleep from his body. They were cathedral workers, craftsman who carried the tolls of their respective trades in large heavy satchels. He placed his hands in his robe to . . . there were no weapons. He felt naked without a sword a dagger. That would change with the passage of time, as he would be allowed to arm himself once more.

He gathered his cloak about him once again and turned away as if seeking sleep once more. The workmen muttered with scorn about those who slept beyond the dawn and two of them almost caught him with their feet, as if to remind him that there were those who rose with the sun to go about their work. He quivered with rage, but he did not dare say anything since his accent was not of the area. The men were all North men and he barely understood their words.

At last they had all passed. He shook himself to ward off the chills and put more fuel onto the fire. He could only look forward to "another mug of hot water with the tasteless herb and another bowl of the tasteless oatmeal."

Time was passing and more people were on the move. It was, he estimated, only another day until the morning of the banquet and once more he would throw organization into the mud. He would help change the power in England. He did not care about the whys and the wherefores. He cared little about the outcome. Whether or not the new power was to restore order among the barons or to crush the rabble with an iron heel, it was not his business. In Europe, two centuries of unrest had just passed, particularly in his native France where the English had taken land and allowed the peasant a little more say in their lives than the French would ever even consider.

The armed peasants had even threatened the French throne and had attacked nobles whenever they traveled. All at the instigation of that damned Henry Plantagenet, whom the English referred to as Henry II. The terror of a mob let loose when they had the effrontery or encouragement to arm themselves rocked the foundations of French society. Someone had needed to take the reins in his hand. But that was not possible because of a series of foppish idiots who occupied the throne of France. So what better than to put into power those men who coveted the throne of England. At the same time, his plan would end the frequent incursions into France that were led by the powerful Duke of Lancaster. He, Turstin Fitz Malet, would put a stop to this. He would no longer be the unwanted fatherless waif who had grown up in the small settlement, not even a village, which was given the name Malet after the seigneur who lived a half-day journey away in his fine house.

This would shut the mouths of those in the settlement who could remember him. Although he doubted that anyone could remember the boy who had left with a priest to, supposedly, enter the church. He had discovered that the priest had no intention of schooling him for the church. The priest's thoughts were on a more worldly use for the boy. As it happened, the priest became his first victim, his rotting body might even be discovered someday buried, ironically, in a local churchyard.

After he had completed his task, Fitz Mallet would pay his respects to others who, throughout his life, had scorned him for his low birth.

For the reminder of the day he had to be a hardworking, gratuitous deliverer of food. He would talk with any idlers and loafers that he saw.

They were always ready to deliver information to the right questions, without even realizing what they were doing!

If his plan worked, the country would be bereft of a leader and ready for a take-over. The nobility would attempt to make compromises. They would vacillate, but it would be too late!

It was going to be a good day. A very good day!

*   *   *

CHAPTER 47

An hour later and a short distance away from where Turstin Fitz Malet had his feelings of well-being, Ranulf de Boise also sensed that the day was going to be a good day.

De Boise lay on his bed ready to assume the posture of someone close to death should the door open. James and Kathryn talked quietly as they sat on chairs close by the fire. Ranulf looked up at the narrow windows wondering what was going on outside of the castle in the yard. The high windows filled with thick glass and the stone walls did not allow any sounds to enter. Nor did they allow any sounds to escape.

He was one day closer to the banquet and the festivities would start in the late afternoon or early evening. Thos guests who had not yet arrived would start arriving in the midafternoon.

It would be a very grand affair. John knew that his father's flair for putting on a show would come to the fore and that all who attended would talk about the banquet for years to come. He hoped that the reasons for remembering that banquet were not the reasons planned by others. The windows allowed light from the sun to enter. He had heard that it was cold outside and that there had been more snow. But underneath, in the depths of his mind he wanted so badly to walk about and make sure that his leg could take the pressure of walking. If they were attacked at the time of the banquet, as he was sure that they would be, he needed to know his capabilities.

The banquet would take place no matter what the weather and de Boise did not wish to miss this opportunity of seeing the enemy face-to-face and ending this attempt on John's life once and for all.

The morning wore on. De Boise dozed several time.

James had acquired ink, pen, and writing materials to continue to make his notes. He had even treated several of the guards for minor ailments, much to the pleasure of Ranulf and Duke John.

There business took them away from the room several times, but James and Kathryn would only leave one at a time so that Ranulf was never left alone. Much to Ranulf's displeasure.

During the noon-interval, James had left the room to acquire more writing supplies and returned one hour later with a crutch and clothing slung over his arm. The crutch was a simple T-shaped pole that would fit under Ranulf's shoulder.

"Ranulf," James said, "it seems to us that you grow restless. Kathryn and I have decided that it is time for you to exercise. Being forced into action if, or I should say, when we are attacked will tax the strength of your leg."

De Boise muttered with delight. This was exactly what he needed. At last, he could move without having to put his arms around the shoulders of James or Kathryn. They could control him that way and no, he would have the freedom of his own movement.

"But there is more, Ranulf," Kathryn added, "We have also decided that it is time that you took a real walk."

She raised one eyebrow at the questioning look on Ranulf's face.

"Who decided?" he finally asked.

"We did," responded Kathryn waving her forefinger at James and herself. "I mentioned the idea to Duke John on one of my forays out of here earlier this morning and he agreed. So," Kathryn smiled, "you now become a Benedictine monk."

She picked up the robe that James had placed on a chair and held it up and examined it carefully.

"Quite clean," she pronounced, "no signs of lice and should fit you quite well." She walked over to where Ranulf sat. "Let's get this on you and make sure that you are covered."

Kathryn inspected de Boise as he made hard work of getting to his feet.

"Ranulf, please! Not such a show!"

De Boise attempted to look puzzled.

"Come, come, my dear Ranulf," Kathryn was quick to respond to his efforts, "James and I know that you have been walking around in our absence. My memory has observed several items in the room that have been moved that could only have been moved by you. We have not allowed the attendants to be in the room unless we were here. So . . ."

De Boise looked at her with that sheepish smile of being guilty and being caught. Kathryn brushed off the look and continued.

"You know, Ranulf, you will make a good Benedictine. But it will be more fitting," Ranulf looked at her and smiled wondering what was coming next, "if you take the guise of an old monk, especially one who is frail and in need of a crutch to help his aging legs. Your hood will cover your face all of the time, and you must bend a little to reduce your height."

Cheered by his ability to walk comfortably with the crutch, de Boise walked back and forth across the room. He was determined to show that his leg was fully functional and ready for use.

James walked alongside de Boise in case of any mishaps that might cause him to stumble as Kathryn looked on with benevolent satisfaction. She knew that de Boise was capable of anything that he set his mind to, but one fall could undo all of the healing work that had gone on for the past few days.

Ranulf sensing Kathryn's apprehension looked across the room at her and smiled, "See, Kathryn, I think that all seems to be working well." She returned his smile.

"How about . . . ?" de Boise was about to ask a question of James but Kathryn cut him short by her quick response.

"James, my dear," she said, "I think that it is time that we gave our friend his walk! We will have a light meal first. It is cool in the hallways and hot tea with hot broth should help maintain the warmth in our bodies."

De Boise was not about to complain, as walking around the room had generated an appetite. To Ranulf, the meal would be a celebration! He was able to walk comfortably, sit with Kathryn and James in front of the fire, talk without straining his back to sit up on the bed and face them. It was a fresh experience that he enjoyed. They talked quietly so that they would not be heard by the guards or by any passersby.

They left the dishes on the table and, dressed in the robes of the Benedictines, moved to the door. James had neatly stacked several additional blankets under the cover on the bed so that, to the casual observer looking into the door, de Boise would appear to be asleep.

Once outside the door, de Boise was introduced to the four guards as Brother Cedric, a Benedictine monk and teacher who had known de Boise for about twenty years. The guards nodded, seeing the old monk bent with age and hobbling along on a crutch.

James also added, "Sir de Boise is not to be disturbed by anyone, save the Duke of Lancaster. No one to leave their posts while we are gone. Is that understood?"

The guards nodded quickly to show that they understood. Not one of them was about to disobey this physician who was known by King Edward.

They walked slowly toward the great hall, more from curiosity than anything. The sun streamed through glassed-in windows and added warmth to the cool hallway. For the last few years, ever since the day of his wounding, de Boise had not seen such a glorious sight. He had lived in his room, eaten all of his meals there, and been personally attended by James and Kathryn. Now he was out again! The walk brought the color to his cheeks and he felt healthy. His leg caused no pain.

The banquet had captured the attention of everyone. They looked though a window that overlooked the castle yard and were surprised at the number of tents that had been pitched since de Boise had last crossed the yard and since Kathryn and James had last visited the priory library. Despite the hectic pace of the preparations, groups still found the time to lounge and gossip, news and compliments are exchanged, opportunists looking for more work were engaged in laughter and the delights of the open, if not cool, air.

Without making it obvious, de Boise looked down from the second-floor hall window at the crowd of bodies in the yard and wondered if there was anyone that he would recognize. It was the largest crowd that had collected, or been allowed to collect, in the castle yard for some time. Quite an audience, de Boise muttered to himself. Quite an assembly had collected round that one particular tent, ten men in all, and it was obvious that this group were not the usual workers.

De Boise, ever on his guard, was suspicious of what he saw. One of the men was speaking to the others who seemed to listen intently. Could this be men who were here for work other than the banquet? The man continued to talk. His moves were not animated, merely careful and seemingly calculated. He was certainly able to hold the attention of the group, de Boise observed.

He allowed his eyes to scan the other groups in the yard. For the most part they seemed to be vendors or farmers who had come to sell the produce of their fields and give themselves a comfortable living for several months at a time in the year when sales were usually low and income sparse.

"I think," Ranulf observed out loud to Kathryn and James, "that we have a group of men yonder who do not seem to be the usual vendors or farmers. Methinks that they are here for another purpose."

He motioned with his head in the direction of the suspicious group. James and Kathryn indicated that they had spotted them also.

"We live," remarked de Boise as his hand disappeared under the hood to scratch his chin, "'in a time of abortive plots and attempts at revolution."

They focused their eyes on the group just as the leader looked up at the window. Fitz Malet saw the three monks looking out into the yard and wondered why anyone would ever wish to become a monk. Missing out on all the earthly pleasures. He continued to speak to his men, never giving the monks another thought. His attention was now focused on the task at hand. The time was drawing close.

Ranulf could sense Kathryn and James's tension.

They turned and walked slowly back to the room. A few of the castle staff who had business in the area hurried passed them thinking that they saw three Benedictines, one small, one very old who walked slowly using a crutch to support his old legs, and another one. They reached the room and addressed the guards.

"If you need a break," James said to the oldest man, "I suggest one at a time so that three of you remain here."

The guard nodded. They would follow that suggestion. It would be a pleasant relief from standing for four hours at a time.

The room greeted them with a glow from the candles and the warmth from the fire. It was pleasant and de Boise saw it in a light that he had not noticed these past days. It was also a fortress within a fortress. All along the stone walls there were high with stone out-juts of utilitarian construction for candleholders. "These," he thought, "will serve us well, I am sure."

"That was refreshing," Ranulf said to Kathryn and James. "And," he continued, "I am pleased for the respite from this room and my bed." He looked at them, "I sense that the group of men that we saw may be the ones that we seek."

"Should we not inform John?" Kathryn asked.

"I think not, my dear," de Boise responded. "There is little that he could do other than arrest them and it would be unwise to tip our hand at this stage. I look to using them to help us identify the forces behind this plot."

Trembling with excitement, and concealing his secret satisfaction at having spotted a very suspicious group, de Boise felt that he was active once more. He would finish what Gervais had started. His annoyance at not being able to leave the room had disappeared and given way to the feeling of being in a gala mood. He had felt energized during the past hour and the sight of the suspicious figures in the crowd gave him much to think about. He instinctively knew that he was on the right track.

*   *   *

The sun was well into the heavens as the vendors continued their work. Minor arguments arose. Two vendors quarreled about a missing box of fish. They were told to resolve it by a sergeant of the guard or he would resolve it for them and they would be outside of the gate in short order. Several clerks took up their positions just outside of the main door to the hall. Ready with their writing materials and lists to make sure that there would be a record of the attendees. The officials started to move quickly and efficiently around the hall. In their nervousness, they pushed benches into the correct position and arranged any other items that needed to be moved.

They had heard that Thomas Hatfield, the prince bishop of the palatinate of Durham had recently retuned from his latest journey and would also attend the banquet. He would not miss a function that was central to the affairs of the palatinate.

Guests and the city dignitaries arrived throughout the late afternoon, and were still arriving as the sky darkened. They came by horse and in wagons. They brought their baggage, their servants, their retainers, and their bodyguards, all of whom had to be billeted within the castle area. When it was known that King Edward and his son, John, would be at the banquet, all of the would-be powers in the palatinate were clamoring for an invitation.

Palatinate officials continued to file into the great hall in greater numbers than any one had imagined, and the castle staff received them graciously. Adversaries became friends in the public eye since they knew that King Edward took a very dim view of personal quarrels at such affairs.

The castle accommodations could support only a limited number of the guests and dignitaries, so tents had to be pitched on the castle green to accommodate the servants, their retainers, and their bodyguards. Fires were lit in braziers as the cold was expected to continue and extra provisions were needed, and the city of Durham became depleted of goods! The castle staff bustled with activity and the castle area took on the look of a very busy market. The guard at each of the gates and on the walls was doubled as an automatic precaution, as what happened whenever such an event took place. It was as if all that mattered was happening in the castle and the world outside of the walls was of little consequence.

On the morning of the banquet day, the gates to the castle were closed with the exception of the north gate that led into the marketplace from the Claypath Road. Anyone entering was carefully screened by name and by the nature of his or her business at the castle. It was cold, and the snow blew in light wisps around the people as they formed a line at the gate. On the castle green, the fires were stoked regularly and kept alive with wood and the black rock that they had called *coal* in English and *charbon* in French. The various bodyguards soon established gaming areas and hot drinks were provided for all by the castle staff.

The skies remained leaden throughout the whole day as if promising heavy rain or snow, just to remind everyone that winter had not yet left the region, but to the people in the castle yard and to the staff of the castle, they were too busy to feel cold.

Inside the great hall, a pile of logs, each the length of a man's height, blazed on the hearth. Braziers were spread around the hall to keep the heat even. As the guests collected, the braziers would be removed. The heat generated by the large body of people would be sufficient to maintain a level of warmth in the hall. A light smoky haze filled the hall but the majority of the smoke was drawn to the chimney and out through vents above the windows.

The floor was covered with scented rushes to add a light cheer to the room and to remove the persistent odors that remained from previous banquets and revelries. As the night wore on, the rushes would become ale-sodden and dogs would be fighting and snapping over the scraps dropped by the guests. Only John's deerhound maintained the dignity of its station and refused to join the other snapping yapping curs.

At a prearranged time, the north gate was closed for the night. Anyone arriving after the gate closure would be denied access to the castle. The guests started soon to fill the hall as the light outside diminished. Each guest and his wife or companion were seated at assigned places at the rectangular table. Those of higher importance and rank sat at points where they would be closer to King Edward and have his eye. After one hour, all of the guests were seated and awaited the arrival of the king and his son. Mulled wine had been served lavishly to the guests, and the room started to warm up. As if by a prearranged signal the noise of more than one hundred guests was suddenly hushed. King Edward and his son John, Duke of Lancaster, had entered the hall and were taking their seats at the head of the table and at a spot where the warmth of the fire was focused.

The banquet itself was sumptuous and a marvel of medieval cooking. The guests commented over and over that they would never again sit down to such a fine array of food and drink. The staff struggled under the weight of platters, trenchers, and silver dishes piled high with a variety of meats that were placed in front of the king. There were capons, ducks, geese, haunches of venison, and suckling pigs that had been roasted whole. In the kitchens, younger members of the kitchen staff turned two whole ox carcasses on spits to add to the feast. Thick slices of beef were cut at regular intervals to be placed on the tables to supplement the mountains of food. On the castle green, two more whole ox carcasses were roasted to feed the attendants who had accompanied the various guests. Kitchen staff ran back and forth carrying platters of beef to feed the soldiers standing guard on the walls and at the gates.

Custard pies, other pastries, and fruit completed the food. Apples and pears that had been carefully stored over the winter were heaped in bowls placed on the tables.

Bread was also plentiful as baskets full of freshly baked loaves were carried into the hall and offered to the guests by young boys. Casks of ale that had been set on supports behind the guests, against the walls, as well as in the corners of the hall provided ample drink. The king, John, and his close guests each had a tankard of wine. They wished for their heads to remain clear. They were uncertain of the turn of events that might occur that night.

To add to the confusion, musicians played a variety of lively tunes but it is doubtful that they were heard by anyone in the hall. As the ale flowed in torrents down the throats of the guests, the conversation became louder and louder as the behavior deteriorated into fights and arguments.

As the time wore on, many of the guests were showing signs that they were starting to suffer, if not already suffering from, too much food and drink. But they had the spirit and will to carry on. The eating and drinking were their way of leading for winter to end and for the start of good weather that would herald the coming of summer. The coldness and the light wisps of snow outside seemed to be winter thumbing its nose at their revelry.

*   *   *

Secretly, John wished to leave and be with Ranulf. His wish was realized when Edward leaned over and whispered that it was time for him to leave. He would feign tiredness. John had personal knowledge of his father's habits and he knew that, for the moment, Edward was strong and healthy. The king had dictated that he would play the game, only if he could have a meeting with the plotters before they were brought to trial and hanged, drawn, and quartered.

John signaled for the attendants and two fully armed knights to escort his father to the rooms on the upper floor.

John's thoughts remained on de Boise and he wondered again about the possible move against Ranulf. He stood and bowed to his father as the attendants assisted the king to rise from the table.

The activity and revelry had, as many of the guests surmised, overtaxed the king's strength. They had heard earlier that the king's physician had not approved the idea of the king attending so much revelry, but as always,

Edward had refused to listen. He was known to keep late nights, many times drinking too much and eating rich food. It was, the guests thought, an attempt to recapture old times.

John's focus was to make sure that Ranulf fared well. There was no obvious attack in the halls so John knew that Ranulf was safe for the moment but he needed to be sure. John silently prayed that all was well and a fleeting thought that had Oswald been here he would have had less cause to worry.

"There must be a way to stop these plotters," he mused, deep in thought. John was keen to get this business settled.

His eyes narrowed as he thought about the plan that Ranulf had described to him two days ago. He knew that the two newcomers, James and Kathryn, fitted into Ranulf's plan, but John was unsure of their abilities. Although, he thought, did they not remove the Gervais and his henchmen from this life?

And he was led to believe Kathryn, who had showed herself to be a fierce fighter in a pitched battle, did it quite professionally. John had been told by the soldiers that James had entered the room shortly thereafter, calmly walked up behind Gervais, and ended his life with the calculated thrust of his sword, a masterful stroke.

John was sure that Ranulf would protect himself well and there was a surprise for anyone who had evil deeds in mind. Ranulf was very much alive and certainly not at death's door as most believed.

John felt comforted by these thoughts. His father's display as he had left the banquet room had played out well. Many guests had shown surprise at Edward's poor condition. But, all being well, his father would appear before the population of the city looking fit and healthy when the plotters were thwarted and killed. He considered words that Oswald had once voiced, "No matter how well you plan under the current circumstances, the unexpected is inevitable!"

The antics of some of the guests at the banquet table had confirmed John's fear that vigilance was till a prime requirement. He had his agents seated at strategic locations under the pretence of being further under the influence of ale than their seating companions. The constable, Sir Humphrey de Bohun, was under very close scrutiny but had not acted suspicious in any way. He appeared to be quite relaxed and amiable throughout the festivities. John's real fear was that he did not know who was involved in the plot.

"Sergeant," John turned to one of the guards, "send two of your men to see how Sir Ranulf fares."

The sergeant nodded, "Sire, it will be done immediately," and left to see that John's command was obeyed.

Some of the guests had passed out under the tables but the majority continued to eat and drink. "As long as that happens and the festivities continue," John thought, "all will be well. The ill omen is the cessation of the festivities and night descending on the castle."

*   *   *

CHAPTER 48

F itz Malet knew that he had to wait until the effect of the food and wine distributed at the banquet took effect. He sat on a low seat absorbing the warmth of the fire from the brazier. The members of his group had done their work and now sat with him. To all observers, Fitz Malet intended that they look like a group of men resting after the labors of the past two days. The next two hours would be key to the success of his plans. He allowed half of the men to sleep in his tent while he and the remainder stayed vigilant. The sleepers would be woken in one hour to allow the others to rest for an hour. He would not sleep. The plan could go awry when the leader was not fully cognizant of his surroundings. He did not intend this to happen. He sipped his hot drink, gave a grunt of satisfaction, not at the taste but at the plans for the coming action.

The meeting earlier in the day had gone well. But time was drawing closer and he needed to be sure that his men knew what was expected of them. They would be provided arms one hour after the second group was awakened from their slumbers. And at that time they would move into their positions, seek out the target, and execute the plan.

He had pledged to himself that this venture would be a success and he had made similar guarantees to his sponsor. He had gone over the plans several times with the sponsor in order to explain any last-moment changes that were required. Any incident, however trivial, did not escape his consideration. Simply, he was a thinker and a planner and he did not intend that any incident, trivial or major, especially incidents whose importance has been exaggerated out of all proportion, did not escape his thoughts.

But all this fervor does not bring a task to succeed. As far as Fitz Malet was concerned, taking action at the right moment was what counted.

*   *   *

The man sitting next to Fitz Malet had been with him on several missions and he knew that some of them would not survive the night. The other who escaped would be hunted down if all aspects of the plan did not fall exactly into place. He even wondered about Fitz Malet's sponsor. How reliable was he? Would he have them hunted down and killed? Perhaps he would prefer that no witnesses would survive the actions of the night.

And once Fitz Malet realized the true nature of his thoughts, the chances of survival diminished. Fitz Malet was known to kill followers at the completion of an action because they had doubted his word.

The man admitted to himself, "Fitz Malet is also a planner. We have heard that John of Lancaster's closest friend and adopted brother, Sir Ranulf de Boise, lies close to death from a wound that has festered, continued to bleed, and turns black. It seems," the man continued his thoughts, "that we are to kill de Boise and then take care of the remaining business."

He looked at his companions. Faces full of determination. "Perhaps this would not be such a bad mission after all," he thought as he drained the last of the hot liquid from the mug.

*   *   *

De Boise lay on the bed, sleeping comfortably. Kathryn and James had been pleased with the progress of the wound on Ranulf's leg. The walk had not affected it and the leg looked strong and healthy. Thanks to his unauthorized walks in the room during their absence, Ranulf's leg had gained strength and was normal once more. The leg could bear his full weight and his maneuverability was restored. There had been some muscle soreness after the walk but a soothing bath, with help from James and Kathryn, had relieved any discomfort. He had also been given two small white tablets that seemed to take away the ache in the muscle and relaxed him sufficiently so he could sleep.

Kathryn and James now sat in front of the fire and she listened intently to James as they whispered their innermost thoughts to each other. Her body was bent forward in an attitude of extreme attention, her robe on another chair as she stroked her hair with her fingertips. They whispered to each other about the coming hours. De Boise would have to be removed if the way to John was to be clear for the assassins.

They wondered how they became involved in such a volatile and dangerous situation. Their memories were dim beyond a certain time. And yet they both had knowledge of the use of weapons and medicine. They realized that they were different.

"Different in what way and why?" they asked each other. They knew not.

James had built up respect from his medical activities and Kathryn as his assistant, but in the eyes of Ranulf and John, her fighting spirit and abilities were equivalent to any knight in King Edward's court.

What puzzled them most were the little white tablets that were capable of taking away aches and pains as if by some miracle. The source of these tablets and the bottle with its peculiar top, which had to be removed by turning, remained a mystery. The bottle had been in the pocket of a robe that James had worn some time ago. The material from which the robe was made had a strange texture as though it had been made by some process other than weaving. James knew not the origin of the robe or the bottle containing the tablets.

They could not even remember where James had received his medical training. Was it in Durham? Or London? Or was it in some city in Europe? They knew not. They knew that they had come, or returned to Durham only a short time ago.

Realizing that time was of the essence, Kathryn pronounced, "Let us see to the weapons and prepare ourselves. Anyone can die," Kathryn said as she tested the edge of her short sword, "but living is an art and takes some learning. And I," she looked directly into her husband's eyes, "intend that you and I, my dear, continue to live and learn!"

*   *   *

Fitz Malet beckoned to the man next to him to indicate that they walk a few steps away from the remainder of the group so that no one would hear their conversation when they talked about the immediate plans.

Fitz Malet had reasoned that, even with help from the inside, he could expect to lose six of his men. One thing he had surmised was that he did not intend to be one of the six. But he did not tell this to his companion.

However, like Gervais before him, Fitz Malet saw himself as a very rich and powerful man when all was accomplished.

*   *   *

Kathryn heard the sounds from the bed. "Ranulf is stirring," she said to James.

James smiled.

"Good," he said, "that gives us time to prepare."

"There is, however, one thing," she said, "that I must do and that is," she took a step toward his chair and kissed him on the cheek, "no matter what happens to us this night, my love, I have no regrets that we are here nor do I have any regrets that death may descend on us. We are, after all, doing what we believe to be correct."

James stood up and took her in his arms.

"I will make sure that we pass through this night unharmed."

He looked at Kathryn and saw a tear in her eye.

They stood quite still, arms around each other for several moments, and then they heard the voice.

"I leave you two alone for one minute and look what happens!"

De Boise was awake.

Despite the fact that he was the focal point of the forthcoming attack, he appeared to be less concerned.

"How about," Ranulf asked, "a cup of that stuff that is prepared by boiling some kind of herb in water?"

For the first time since de Boise had awakened he looked at James. It was an incredible scene that greeted him. As James released Kathryn from his hold, de Boise took a deep breath. It was a shattering experience. All of the happenings since his wound could not be compared to what he had just seen. James, the physician who had nursed him back to life, no longer stood before him. His hair was different. His stature had changed. De Boise felt as though he was in a dream. It was not James who stood before him. It was Oswald!

"Oswald?" Ranulf tentatively asked.

"No, Ranulf, it is me, James." The answer came back immediately.

De Boise sighed, closed his eyes, and opened them again. He arose from the bed, rearranged his breeches and undershirt, and walked over to the table where Kathryn was making the tea. He remained preoccupied as he took the container of hot liquid in his hand. Not for one single moment did he doubt that Oswald was in the room. He had failed to recognize James, or had he? His mind was fully occupied thinking of the last time that they had met. He walked to the fire to sit in one of the chairs.

"Ranulf," he heard Kathryn's voice and turned to look at her. He did not dare look at James. He feared that the wound affected his mind.

"Yes, Kathryn," he said.

"How do you feel?"

"Very well, thank you."

"Let me ask the question again. How does your body temperature feel?"

"Very comfortable, Kathryn. Thank you," he responded carefully wondering what was coming next.

"Good," she said. "I think that any attack will involve men who are dressed for fighting. You know, heavy clothes, perhaps chain mail. They will be hot and sweating!"

"Kathryn, you are beautiful." De Boise could not contain himself. "You are suggesting," he said, "that we make them even more comfortable by adding fuel to our fire and maintaining the temperature in this room."

"Yes. We are used to this heated room. They, as you say, have been outside huddled against a fire for at least two days to ward off the cold. So, let us give them heat!"

"Well done, Kathryn," de Boise heard James's voice but it was not James's voice. It was Oswald. "How could it be?" he thought.

Mechanically de Boise sipped his tea and stole the occasional glance at James. He wondered if had woken up. Perhaps he was till dreaming? He looked at the stature of the man in the room. It was as though the physician had left the body and Oswald had taken over. Kathryn added more logs and coal to the fire and the heat started to spread throughout the room.

James took off his jerkin as did Kathryn. De Boise was surprised and shocked at the transformation in their bodies; both very muscular and fit, and ready for action.

And then they heard the sounds.

They looked at each other and passed out the weapons. Kathryn took two of the shorter swords and a dagger, the latter in her belt and the former in her hands. She bound her hair with a ribbon so that it would hang behind her check and was unlikely to cause any difficulty with her vision. She smiled at James as he chose to take a long sword and an axe; the former tucked into his belt, the latter cradled in his arms. De Boise chose two long swords, one he held ready and the other was placed in a scabbard that hung from his belt.

De Boise looked at James. "For reasons that are not clear to me," he said, "I knew that you would pick the axe as your first weapon."

James smiled back and said, "In this space I have the room to use it, as did my forefathers!"

*   *   *

The weapons had been delivered and Fitz Malet was pleased with what he saw. He did not ask questions of the two hooded men in their heavy robes who silently distributed the swords and daggers to his men, after which they disappeared into the darkness and were not seen again. The night was quiet and cold. Fitz Malet had allowed the fire to die down in case any inquisitive person would see the weapons and wonder what was happening.

Fitz Malet stood at the opening of his tent and listened for any unusual sounds. There were none. The wind had shifted slightly and his tent was filled with stinging smoke from the fire as it attempted to rejuvenate itself. His men had retired to their respective tents to await his command. Strong-boned, bull-necked men, equal to any situation, were busy checking the condition of their weapons.

Fitz Malet stood for a while, looking at the tents, and then he looked up at one of the windows. Yes, a light flickered as it would in the rhythmic swing back and forward behind the window. It was time. The entries to the castle would be available and there would be no guards. His sponsor had assured him of that.

It was time for action,

He wiped his eyes free of the smoke that still swirled around the front of his tents and gave a quiet signal to show his men that it was time for action. The men had wrapped their weapons in sackcloth to muffle the sounds and they moved as one toward the castle.

*   *   *

The guests lay where they had fallen in the great hall. Soldiers who might have been standing guard seemed to have disappeared to the more comfortable pallets to sleep in their barracks.

Fitz Malet thought this unusual, but he knew that when King Edward put on a banquet, it was a showpiece and no one would feel left out. Obviously he had wined and dined his guards. After all, the plot on the life of John had been thwarted and nothing else remained, only the celebrations.

Fitz Malet looked around and beckoned to his men to follow him. One of them was standing close to one of the guests who was on the verge of waking. Fitz Malet gave the briefest of signals to his accomplice just as the unprepared guest opened his eyes. His sudden gasp was not sufficient to disturb any of the other sleepers. A coarse hand covered his mouth as he attempted to rise but a knee was placed firmly onto his belly keeping him on the floor. A soft sound betrayed the thrust of a dagger into the unfortunate man and he was silenced, never knowing why.

The dead man was half seated, propped against the wall with his head on his chest. A blanket was used to cover the wound and the inevitable trickle of blood that stained his shirt. For the moment, should anyone else see him, there would be no suspicions. He was, to all intents and purposes, asleep.

*   *   *

They had just made themselves comfortable in the hot room by dressing as Kathryn had suggested and de Boise was about to ask a question when Kathryn spoke, "Shush, I hear sounds!"

The rhythmically thudding footsteps echoed from the hallway. There were no challenges from the guards. As requested, John had removed them from their posts. He would see to any follow-up that was necessary.

De Boise saw James, or was it Oswald, and Kathryn smile at each other as if looking forward to what lay ahead. They imagined the ill-boding, numbed faces of the attackers hardly believing their good luck, when the guards were not visible. Or would the intruders suspect a trap?

Kathryn, James, and Ranulf stared at the door. They listened carefully to the mouselike sounds outside of the door. It was then that they heard voices. Kathryn, James, and Ranulf rose from their seats. They could hear the sound of metal against metal and the general noise that accompanies the approach of armed men.

And then all was still.

They waited for the door to open and the intruders to enter.

The door opened slowly, the hinges deliberately left without oil for the last few days so that they would creak with movement. Four men entered the room only to be halted in their steps as Ranulf said amiably, "Come in. Is there anything we can do for you?"

Four mouths opened wide in surprise as they beheld the three armed people before them, but the shock turned to confidence when they saw that one was woman.

For a moment, they stared at the three armed friends. One of the attackers even leered at Kathryn. She noticed that he was starting to sweat and was looking extremely uncomfortable in his heavy clothes. She glanced over to James and Ranulf and winked, as if to say, "See, I told you what would happen!"

The man approached Kathryn warily. Looks are deceiving. He had a wide, good-natured face covered with freckles; the way he carried himself made him look rather attractive, if he had been washed. Kathryn looked at him and he started to smile, and then he spoke showing a mouthful of bad teeth.

"Well, we have a fine one here. Such a pretty little thing. My friend here," he gestured to the one who had leered at Kathryn, "needs your attention."

James and Ranulf smiled at each other.

"You know not what you say. My wife will not tolerate such thoughts from scum such as you!"

The man became inflamed at James's words of warning. He extracted the ball and chain from his belt and stepped toward Kathryn while the other three stood *en guard*, ready for action.

"Go ahead, scum with the breath of a pig," Kathryn taunted, "let's see what you can do!"

That was too much for the man. He swung the ball and chain as he shouted, "I can tackle you with one hand! *Chienne!*"

The ball and chain became entangled on one of the iron brackets in the wall behind him that was used to hold a torch. James stepped closer and swung the axe.

"First, you said that could take my wife with one hand, so be it. You have one hand!"

The blade went cleanly through the man's lower arm leaving the hand attached to the handle of the ball and chain and hanging from the wall. In the initial moments of the strike, the man did not realize that he had lost his hand; the cut had been so clean. Then his body told him that there was an imbalance and he realized that his weight had shifted. He saw his disembodied hand.

"Second," Kathryn said as she moved closer to him, "do not call me bitch!"

She stepped closer so that she was within three feet of him. Her sword thrust was true. The blade entered the man's abdomen and she twisted it before withdrawing it from him to make sure that he died.

The other three were quiet. They had just seen their comrade go down so easily.

This blonde woman had used her skills to taunt their comrade before he was killed.

Ranulf broke the silence, "Come join your comrade," he said.

The mercenaries looked at each other warily and then they prepared themselves to do battle.

*   *   *

CHAPTER 49

The heat emanating from the fireplace had greatly increased the room temperature. Blood on the floor, where the dead man lay, would make footing treacherous so Kathryn and James moved back; Ranulf was already on dry footing.

Carefully and without bringing undue attention to their moves, Kathryn and James slowly placed themselves between the door and the three remaining intruders. Ranulf moved only slightly so that he was in the flank of the three.

To protect themselves, or so they thought, the three Frenchmen stepped back to the apparent safety of the wall opposite to de Boise.

One of the men, a lean little fellow, moved threateningly toward Kathryn and appeared as though he was about to lunge at her. James looked at him then and nodded to Kathryn. This seemed to take his attention and then de Boise moved in quickly and kicked the man solicitously in the groin. The man bent in pain.

The other two men quickly dragged their colleague out of farther reach of de Boise, to relative safety. The man took a few moments to recover.

Kathryn, James, and Ranulf stood watching and waiting. Who would make the first move?

"Where are your colleagues," Ranulf asked. The men looked surprised. "I saw ten of you talking in the yard yesterday. And I assume," he continued, "that your leader is close!"

The men smiled with the comfortable thought that they had advantage of help nearby. De Boise read their smiles perfectly.

"I doubt that your colleagues will survive. A very warm reception awaits them when they attempt to attack the duke."

Their faces took on a more somber look as they moved farther back toward the wall. The colleague who had been kicked was well enough to rise to his feet. They remained quiet and then the man who had been kicked looked at James.

"We seem to have reached an impasse . . .," he started to say but James cut him off from further speech.

"No, you have lost one of your colleagues because he insulted my wife. Soon another, then another, and then you will share the same fate. You thought that you could assassinate the duke!" James laughed and put his hand on Kathryn's shoulder.

The three intruders stood still, clustered in silence as James looked back at them. The man looked as though he was to going to speak again.

"And now what shall we do with you?" James asked.

The three intruders looked at him and at their fallen colleague. Their eyes were quiet and attentive. James liked that. Knowing what the response would be, Kathryn, James, and Ranulf rose up onto the balls of their feet, without any haste, and stood ready for action. Kathryn shook her head so that her bound hair fell into place at the back of her neck.

As expected and as if by some preconceived signal, the three intruders rushed at Kathryn assuming that she was the weak link. By immobilizing her, they hoped to gain advantage of the situation.

They underestimated Kathryn! Taking a sword in each hand, she sidestepped the rush killing one with a sword thrust into the throat and wounding the other with her second sword. She bent beneath the sword swing of the third intruder. His face showed frustration but that was the last look that he was ever able to express. James and Ranulf dispatched him and his wounded colleague within seconds. The wounded man shouted for mercy but all to no avail.

They looked at the four bodies and were about to lock the door when detachment of guards arrived, sent by John.

The guards looked at Ranulf and James with some surprise but were relieved to see that de Boise was unharmed. They looked at Kathryn with surprise. Her small stature, the two bloodied swords one in each hand, were the most unusual sight for them.

"Gentlemen," Kathryn responded to answer their staring eyes, "surely you are not going to tell me that you have never seen a woman before?"

The sergeant was about to respond, looking at Ranulf, "Address the lady. She asked you a question," Ranulf commanded.

The sergeant bowed his head slightly to acknowledge Kathryn and told her that he had never seen a lady before in such clothing.

Kathryn smiled as she said, "Thank you, Sergeant, and we," she looked at James and Ranulf, "do appreciate your efforts to help us. But we are done here." Her tone changed immediately. "How goes it with the duke?" she asked.

"All is well, ma'am," the sergeant responded. "I will send a man to offer your respects."

"That is quite all right, Sergeant, we will move in that direction ourselves. If we can leave the clean up to your men that will be helpful." The sergeant nodded in agreement.

"Thank you," Kathryn added.

The bodies of the intruders lay in the twisted and agonized attitudes of death. At a signal from the sergeant, the guards started the clean-up activities. After the bodies were removed, maids were called to clean the floors and to return the room to its original condition once more.

*　　*　　*

"James, Kathryn," de Boise's commanding voice got their attention very quickly, "we have other work!"

"Show us the stairs to the duke's room," de Boise commanded the young guards in the hallway.

Without any further words, and at the best speed that de Boise could muster, they hurried to the upper floor where the room was located. The solid heavy door of the room opened as they approached and they saw the serious face of the duke.

"Ah, there you are," he said breaking into a smile.

Kathryn and James looked at each other. "Have we not heard that somewhere before?" their expressions seemed to be asking.

"Do come in," John offered. "All is well. These fellows," he gestured to the five bodies on the floor being moved by the guards, "came along uninvited and were dispensed by my guards."

John continued, "I asked them if they would yield voluntarily but one of them had the nerve to suggest that we prepare to die. This was not an option that I or my guards felt we should recognize!"

De Boise spoke in earnest, "But where is the tenth man. He was possibly their leader. I saw ten men talking in a group yesterday in the castle yard and I believe these are the men. Where is the one who appeared to be their leader?"

"Guards, please," Ranulf spoke to two of the guards who held torches to spread light on to the faces of the dead."

"There was one who did not come into the room and appears to have fled," John said, "so my estimate is that he has fled to better pastures."

De Boise swore so violently that his voice took on a higher pitch. "If we can catch him, this may be over. But I think that he has fled to his mercenary army that was close by, perhaps north of the castle."

"Guards," John yelled and more guards ran into the room. They had swords and shields at the ready, fearing another attack.

"Lower your arms," John commanded, "we have much to do." He looked at one of the guards, "Robert, summon Geoffrey. I have need of him for planning."

The guard turned and left.

"It would seem," John said as he turned to Ranulf, "that law and order have deserted us for a while. I have heard of that mercenary army. Perhaps the one that you mentioned, Ranulf, is in the vicinity of the city. I must believe that the one who escaped from here is already with them. He may even be the leader of that group."

John addressed James and Kathryn, "Are you with us?"

"Of course, sire," James exclaimed.

"We would have it no other way, sire," Kathryn added.

"Stay close by me and by Ranulf," John commanded, "and use caution as we draw near to the mercenaries. This will be different to fighting on your own terms here in the castle. Out there," John motioned with his head toward the north side of the castle, "anything is possible. True, Ranulf?"

"Yes, John, very true. But I know that my friends will acquit themselves well."

Ranulf frowned as he spoke the last words. The most sensible thing for James and Kathryn would be to remain in the castle. He knew that the horrors of a pitched battle were to descend upon them. And they would be outnumbered.

Ranulf was not happy with the situation, but he also knew that James and Kathryn would not remain behind.

*   *   *

Three hundred of the king's guards left the castle by the north gate and marched in time to the field one-half mile to the northeast of the city, close by the point where the River Wear once again turns to the north. After much discussion, John had prevailed upon his father to remain in the castle to command the garrison. Edward had smiled at his son and recognized the ruse to keep him out of the way.

Fitz Malet's army of mercenaries had ridden from their camp in the western part of the county and their path had brought them aimlessly through hamlets and by-paths. They had sent out patrols, who reported that peasants and field workers had fled at their approach. Their animals had disappeared from the fields, and since it was the early part of the year, there was not any grain for food. Since their arrival more than one week ago, they had eaten little and were close to desperation.

As early afternoon wore on, the mercenaries had made camp in the fields within sight of the north gate. The mercenaries preferred to fight on foot and were not skilled in the ways of the charging knight on horseback, and their horses had been left behind a hill in the care of ten mercenaries. Water had been boiled and any herbs that they could find had been added. As the afternoon wore, on dusk fell, no one moved. The mercenaries were loud and they seemed to be uncertain about their next moves.

The sight of the guards moving into position on the high point had caused some concern. The sounds of the guards' swords beating in cadence against shields had made some of the mercenaries swallow hard as they wondered what they were doing in this cold place. They had enlisted with Fitz Malet for the sake of pay, daily rations, and booty. So far there had been a little pay, very few daily rations, and no booty. And the weather always seemed so cold, much colder than the south of France where many of the mercenaries had been recruited.

The guards had moved in formations that had made their numbers difficult to estimate by the mercenaries. Fitz Malet put the word that there were only about three hundred guards and that they, the mercenaries, outnumbered the guards by about five to one. He did not give any details of what had happened in the castle but allowed his commanders to think that he had left his companions in charge and that all that was needed now was to defeat the inferior numbers that faced them. The city was theirs for the taking; booty, food, and women would all be available in large quantities. The mercenaries were willing to endure the pangs of hunger for another night, if that was to be the case.

Two hours after sunset, no action had been taken. The moon was young and offered very little light. Fitz Malet had posted pickets to watch for any preemptive action by the guards. Close to midnight, a commander approached Fitz Malet as he sat before his fire and he had with him a breathless man who walked with a limp. The man wore tattered clothes and said that his name was Walter Gifford. He was, according to his story, from a village just to the south of Paris and he had lived in the Durham for three years. Several soldiers had broken into his home that night in their search for French sympathizers and beaten him. He told Fitz Malet that the castle was well defended but confirmed that they numbered about three hundred, with no archers, and if the mercenaries prevailed in the forthcoming conflict, all other resistance would end and the city would be theirs. Fitz Malet smiled and thanked him. After which Gifford inquired whether there was any reward for his information.

Fitz Malet felt inclined to kill him but he had his ambitions and the man was allowed to live.

"We will discuss your reward on the morrow after we have entered the city," Fitz Malet responded to the question as he thought to himself, "And your reward will be to have your dead body burned with the others."

Fitz Malet looked at the man squarely in the eyes. "For the moment," he told Walter, "find yourself a place to sleep and tomorrow I will make sure that you have a more conformable place to retire."

Walter Gifford smiled his thanks but knew that his life would have an extremely short tenure if he remained at the camp.

The camp continued its night of silence. Fires burned. Torches flickered and smoked in the gentle breeze. Were it not for the flickering flames, the camp appeared dead and deserted

*   *   *

After the conversation with Gifford, Fitz Malet felt more comfortable with the numbers of his opposition. And the fact that there were no archers made him feel elated! His number had been an estimate based on the number of guards that would be left to secure the castle. He beckoned to one of his commanders who approached quickly. A few whispered words and the commander left.

Minutes later, after receiving instructions from their commander, two mercenaries slipped out of the camp and made their way in the inky blackness to the outskirts of the guards' camp. They crept slowly and silently across the cold land until they were within paces of the guards' picket lines. They could hear sounds, as voices approached, so they lay flat on their stomachs to reduce the chance of discovery.

At one of the fires, three men were in animated conversation with a fourth man. One looked like the Duke of Lancaster. "But how can that be?" one of the mercenaries thought, "Fitz Malet was supposed to kill him hours ago."

Time passed and the conversation finally seemed to be drawing to a close. Three of the men bowed their heads to the fourth. It must be Lancaster! One of the men walked with a limp. The mercenaries realized that they had seen him a short while ago in their own camp. It was a trick. Lancaster lived and a spy had been in their camp. They must report to Fitz Malet.

They attempted to rise but were unable to do so as a foot was placed firmly on the neck of each man forcing their faces into the wet ground. The remains of the snow forced its way into their mouths and nostrils. Speech was not possible. They attempted to move, but the two soldiers who held each man down were in no mood for any action.

The last words that they heard were "Silence them. Cut their throats."

"Was it not was a woman's voice that I heard giving the command?" One of the mercenaries had a last thought. The soldiers produced knives, raised the heads of their captives only briefly enough to perform the task. It was done.

Kathryn looked in the direction of the mercenary's camp and asked her four companions to place the bodies in a slight depression in the ground. There was less chance of them being seen in the light of day.

This being done, they walked away quietly in the darkness and returned to the guards' camp.

*   *   *

Fitz Malet was worried. He had not had a report from the men who were sent out to spy on the enemy. It was two hours since he had given the order for the surveillance and the dawn approached quickly.

"And where is that damned man with the limp?" he asked himself.

Fitz Malet left the fire and looked for his commander. He told Fitz Malet that there had been no sign of the two men and feared the worst.

"The worst!" Fitz Malet almost shouted, "Explain yourself."

"The men have both been discovered and taken captive or killed or . . .," the commander hesitated.

"Or," Fitz Malet said, his voice becoming high-pitched in anticipation.

"Or," said the commander, "they had left us."

Fitz Malet was not pleased with this answer. He walked away muttering and, if this was true, how many more men would leave before the morning?

*   *   *

In the dim light of the early morning, Fitz Malet ordered his commanders to get the men stirring. He had a score to settle and wanted them ready.

The mercenaries woke to a cold morning with very little in the way of warmth. Many of the fires had died during the night and fuel to relight them was in short supply. The voices of the men could be heard over the field and in the guards' camp. Men were kicked in the rump to get them moving. There was no need to dress. They had slept in their clothes to try to keep out the cold.

Fitz Malet called for his captains and demanded that they quell the chaos. He was particularly verbose about the two men who had still not returned.

"Damn their souls to hell and damn all cowards from here to hell. Get the men moving to ward off the chills of the early-morning air," he ordered. "Otherwise the guards will attack, and high numbers that we have, it will not bode well for us."

He turned to the fire to warm his hands.

"All fires that are burning must be kept alight by whatever fuel we have," Fitz Malet ordered. "Have the men gather around the fires for measured intervals until they are warm."

He summoned his commander who stood close by.

"This is the day," Fitz Malet said, "that we become known for our work. I want nothing left to chance. All men are to check their weapons, and spread the word among the captains that the men are to form ranks of two hundred men each. We will advance on my command. As we move on the guards, the men in each of the two end ranks will, upon my signal, form a flanking movement and we will capture the guards in a pincer movement. After that, it should go well for us."

Fitz Malet was pleased with his plan and the commander, seeing new confidence in Fitz Malet's face, turned away to carry out his instructions.

"Wait," Fitz Malet ordered, "tell the men that we cannot afford prisoners, and at the end of it all, if the Duke of Lancaster is present, I want to see his body!"

At the end of the day, he would have command of the castle and his men would patrol the walls. He may even have King Edward in custody. He, Fitz Malet, the urchin of the settlement of Malet, would welcome the Scots army with open arms and be hailed as a hero.

*   *   *

As the gray fingers of dawn were starting to tinge on the sky as the day approached, John and Ranulf stood together and looked toward the enemy camp. They heard a sound and turned to see Kathryn approaching in the company of a man with a limp. They halted a respectable distance away, and on John's signal, they approached. Kathryn introduced Walter Gifford and related Walter's adventures and findings from the night before.

"You knew of this, Kathryn?"

"Aye, sire, we felt that we should know the enemy and Walter volunteered. But, sire, there is more!" She looked at Walter and her eyes told him that all was in order for him to speak.

"Sire," Walter addressed John as he was about to finish his story, "there are fifty men, all old codgers like me, who are willing to stand with you."

"I appreciate your loyalty, Walter, but . . ."

"Sire, forgive me," Kathryn interjected, "what Walter is trying to tell you is that they are archers!" She nudged Walter, urging him on.

"Sire," Gifford responded to Kathryn's nudge, "we stood with your father when he was victorious against the French at Crécy twenty-four years ago and when he was again victorious against the French at Poitiers, ten years after Crécy. We may be old but we can still pull a bowstring, sire."

John looked at Ranulf. He had a plan in mind. The look of recognition in Ranulf's eyes was immediate. Seeing this look, John nodded and smiled then he turned to Kathryn.

"How are the men?" he asked her.

"In good spirits, sire," James replied.

"A little surprised at me, sire," Kathryn smiled as she spoke. "It seems that rumors have been spread about my prowess. One even called me by the name Boudicca! And I was flattered."

John and Ranulf laughed.

"Aye, Little One," John said, "you already have a name and my guards will look out for you."

Kathryn bowed her head to acknowledge his words.

"Walter, I thank you." John looked at Gifford. "My brother, Sir de Boise, knows my thoughts on this matter. Please give him your full attention then muster your men and listen to his words."

"My companions, sire," Walter grinned as he responded, "are at the gate and await my signal."

"Well done, Walter. Well done, indeed!" John had suddenly become very enthusiastic about the day ahead.

*   *   *

The guards drank hot herb tea and ate oatmeal cakes that had been freshly on the fires. The camp was strangely silent as they started to contemplate the business at hand. The order of their camp was very different from the disorder that was apparent from the sound coming from the mercenary camp.

John gave the command to assemble the men. Once assembled, he stood on a large stone so that all could see him.

"They say," he began, "that they have greater numbers than us. But we have training, we have discipline, and we have archers! Those bowmen of this city who fought with my father stand with us. We will succeed in quelling this rabble. They are ready to engage us," he said. "Look to your captains and do your best. God be with you."

All grew quiet. The guards checked their weapons for the last time and arranged themselves into a battle order.

The snow and ice still covered the grass and sparkled in the early-morning sun. James and Kathryn stood side by side, close to Ranulf and the duke. After a while James, deep in thought, turned toward Kathryn.

"My dearest, I do not consider it an option that we should die today. Should we be separated, look to yourself. I will find you."

Kathryn stood on her toes and kissed his cheek just below the line of his helmet. They had opted for helmets with nasal protection. Kathryn's hair was braided and tucked under her helmet. They had been provided with coats of mail but Kathryn found hers too big and opted for a strong leather jerkin that was a better fit but offered less protection. She stood flanked by James and by Ranulf, small in stature, her head at the shoulder level of each man.

"We will start soon," Ranulf leaned over closer to Kathryn, "I sense movement in the mercenary camp."

The guards were ready. John took a position in the center of the line and signaled to his commanders that all was well.

"This," John thought to himself, "is going to be a very interesting day!"

*　　*　　*

CHAPTER 50

I n that morning mist, the guards took their positions, ready for battle. The Duke of Lancaster was in command and, seeing that they were outnumbered by about five to one, walked along the lines speaking softly to the guards. He knew that he could trust his guards to stand and fight.

As soon as Fitz Malet saw the battle lines of the guards, he told his commander to pass the rod to the captains that it was time to advance. He surmised that the battle would be fought using swords and any other hand-carried weapons that the mercenaries had. And he had the overwhelming odds when it came to men against men. He would see that this field became a graveyard for the guards. He saw a slight movement in the guards' ranks but gave it no further thought. He knew that all men are uneasy before a battle.

The movement that Fitz Malet had discounted was the guards arranging their formation so that the archers were hidden behind the row of guards.

Now, as Fitz Malet and his men watched, the front rank of the guards stepped to one side and the archers moved forward and became the front tank. The strings of the archers' longbows were already in place and the long-shafted goose-feathered arrows were set and unleashed upon command. The goose feathers flickered in the early sunlight and hissed as the arrows arched gracefully through the air and fell into the ranks of Fitz Malet's army.

Confusion reigned. Grunts from the victims and then screams of pain rose from the ranks of the mercenaries as they realized that this was their fate. The promises that Fitz Malet had made meant nothing to the arrow-pierced men, many of whom were dead before they hit the ground.

The bowstrings continued to hum their deadly tune as more flights of arrows were released into Fitz Malet's lines. Gathering momentum as they fell, the arrows pierced heads, arms, and breasts. Whatever armor the rabble were wearing was ineffective against the metal point. Arrows that at first did not find a target hit the ground and skied along the moist grass until spent or until they pierced legs and bodies. Mayhem was well under way. Men were shouting in disorder, pain, and in the violent throes of death.

One man managed to get shelter under his shield only to have his arm pinioned to the shield by an arrow. As he attempted to free himself from the steel point, another arrow pierced his knee. His scream of pain as his kneecap splint asunder was cut off with an arrow into his mouth. The force of the hit took him over backward and pinned his head to the ground. Another man staggered as he was hot by one of the feathered messengers of death. Then he was struck again by three more arrows and fell to the ground with a crash of mail.

Fitz Malet, arrows hissing all about him, looked from behind his shield and saw the archers and the effects of their arrows, he flew into a rage and ordered the charge. Suicidal as it may have been, Fitz Malet's men needed to move and felt that anything to get away from the hails of arrows was better than standing and waiting to be hit. As they moved forward, James and Kathryn were able to see that almost one-half of Fitz Malet's men remained where they had fallen. Arrows sticking youth of them as if bristles on a hedgehog.

There was massive confusion among the mercenaries. The shrieks of and groans of dying men could be heard all over the field. Men who did not have the protection of shields tried to run from the arrows and tripped over each other. This probably saved their lives, at least for the moment. They fell to the ground and were sheltered from the arrows by their colleagues who still stood in rank and received the arrows into their bodies. As bodies continued to fall to the cold earth, the snow and ice became tinged with red until the whole area took on the look of a field tinged with the pink blossoms of late spring.

Through this onslaught, the rhythmic cadence of the guards' striking shields with the flats of their swords increased to an ear-splitting crescendo.

"Kathryn, my dear," James looked at her, the helmet just about covering her eyes, "it seems that the odds have been somewhat evened. They seemed to start with five times our number and now it is much less! Thank the Lord that our guards know how to use the longbow."

Kathryn looked at him and winked. "Aye, my dear, now let us wait until the odds are even better before we take on this rabble."

The move by Fitz Malet's army made little difference; the archers who changed the flight profile of their arrows and killed even more as they attempted to reach the lines of guards. The men in front ranks, if they can be called ranks, continued to fall and when they went down, they fell in front of their colleagues and caused further chaos.

"The odds, my dear Kathryn, are definitely in our favor," James said. "I think," he looked around at Ranulf, "that we should go and do our best. Stay by me, my dear. It seems that the policy is to let the mercenaries approach us because of our lower numbers."

The cadence stopped and a drummer was heard about the shouts and screams of dying mercenaries. At that signal, the ranks of the guards split themselves into two groups so that the mercenaries approached a V formation with the two arms of the V ready to encircle the mercenaries. One arm of the V was commanded by de Boise, the other by the duke. The archers, dispersed throughout the line of the guards, continued to fire at Fitz Malet's men until, at a signal from the duke, they ceased their withering fire. The guards now started to close in as the mercenaries struggled to maintain any sort of formation and discipline.

"Sheep led into the fold," Kathryn murmured to James. But suspecting trickery, they took twelve guards toward the rear of Fitz Malet's men expecting to find the leader in a position to leave. And they did. Fitz Malet had surrounded himself with a similar group to those that had attempted their attack in the castle. They were heavily armed and prepared to fight their way out no matter what the cost.

Some of the mercenaries attempted to break though the lines, but the guards were up to the challenge and fought with confidence on the frozen ground of the meadow. Attempts by the mercenaries to leave the field were cut off by the guards in the long arms of the V and had them surrounded. Many mercenaries died close to the place where their two colleagues had died the night before. The ground formed a small trench and the attempt to form a defensive line as a last bastion of defiance against the guards was unsuccessful. They died falling into the trench; many were unaware of the blow that killed.

A young man, a member of the duke's personal guard who was fast on his feet, saved the duke from a charge by five mercenaries who had slid past the defensive line that surrounded the duke. He sprang to place himself between the attackers and the duke. Back-to-back they fought off the attackers until help arrived.

James and Kathryn pressed their way into the melee with one goal in mind and that was to capture or kill Fitz Malet. The ground was thick with the dead and dying mercenaries. Kathryn forced her way toward Fitz Malet and James last saw her disappearing into a crowd of men fighting for their lives. She had lost her helmet and James had last seen her blonde unhelmeted head disappear into the turmoil of steel-covered heads.

James could not attempt to find Kathryn. Three mercenaries attacked him at once but he managed to retain his footing on the slippery grass. He sidestepped their rush, and by a swing of his axe, forced one to stumble into the others and all three fell to the ground. Ranulf saw the intent of the three and came to help James dispatch them. One man had recovered from his fall was about to chop his sword down onto James's head when Ranulf rammed his sword into the man's back. The man arched, shivered, dropped his sword, and fell lifeless to the ground. James chopped his sword down onto the neck of the second man and all but severed the head from the man's shoulders. The third one attempted to rise but was sent to meet his maker by a timely sword thrust from de Boise.

The guards continued to fight in with precision and order. Shouts of men rose in pitch and the guards started to make headway into the ranks of the mercenaries. Bodies piled up in the grim attitudes of violent death.

James looked around.

The battle had started to slow as Fitz Malet's men diminished in number and were surrounded by the guards. Above the noise, James recognized a voice that he knew and loved.

"I have him," Kathryn yelled and her voice was heard no more.

James listened but there was nothing to hear. Men milled around, arms and swords continued to rise and fall. And then there was the high-pitched, wordless cry of a man in triumph followed by a shriek of pain.

The sound of a man shouting for mercy came from the mercenaries and it was echoed by a dozen voices. The guards drew back from the general mass and reformed on its flanks. Some mercenaries laid down their swords while others broke off into groups, turning to the left or the right as if seeking a means of escape. Others formed a new line on the far side of the field.

"This battle is finished," a guard commander shouted, "lay down your weapons."

Most of the mercenaries had no stomach for any further conflict. They threw their weapons to the ground as if disgusted with them.

"The battle has ended, sire," Ranulf said as he approached the duke.

*   *   *

De Boise realized that there was something amiss. He looked for James and Kathryn, and James saw him standing close by. Alone.

De Boise put his hand on James's shoulder.

"What of Kathryn, James?" he asked.

"I am not sure, Ranulf," James responded with a worried look on his face, "the last I heard, she went in that direction to find Fitz Malet."

"Then, we shall find her," De Boise said.

They made their way to where James thought he had heard Kathryn's last shout. Bodies lay on the ground with their limbs spread in the awkward angles of death. James shouted Kathryn's name but there was no response. The groans of the dying remnants of Fitz Malet's army shrouded any sound. This was where the most intense fighting had occurred. James looked around, seeing nothing but dead bodies, feeling despondent but still full of hope. He muttered a silent prayer that Kathryn would be safe. Or at least only suffering from a wound that he could treat. He searched the bodies but there was no sign of her.

*   *   *

In the heat of the battle, Kathryn had become disoriented. She and four of the guards were fighting their way to the place where Fitz Malet had last been seen. And then they saw him. Disheveled and directing his men.

Above the shouts of men fighting and dying, Kathryn yelled at the top of her voice. Fitz Malet picked out the high-pitched sound, looked around, wondering at the source of such a sound, and then he look directly at her. An evil smile wreathed his face as he moved in her direction. Her four companions were occupied fighting and killing Fitz Malet's mercenaries. They had formed a back-to-back square that was impenetrable and deadly for those trying to separate them.

Kathryn moved toward Fitz Malet but she suddenly flung herself sideways. Her helmet had fallen to the ground earlier. "The thing is a poor fit anyway," she had told herself. Peripheral vision had saved her life and the sword missed her head by inches but it was so close that she felt a rush of air as it swept past. Kicking out, she caught the other man's ankle with her foot and the man jumped backward with a startled oath. He did not jump quickly enough. He attempted to steady himself for another stroke when Kathryn struck. The blow was hard enough to stagger him, but he felt no pain and did not realize at first that he was dying until he saw the bloodied blade of her sword as she withdrew it from his midsection.

And then Fitz Malet arrived with two others. Kathryn realized that they knew their trade and would not be easy prey for her. One grabbed for her arm, not seeing the other sword and died for his impatience. Fitz Malet and his remaining companion closed in on Kathryn.

For a few frenzied moments, Kathryn felt the waves of panic that sweep though soldiers in battle. These two were fierce fighters and the fleeting thought that she might not be up to the challenge did cross her mind. But it was only fleeting.

The man with Fitz Malet, seeing her an easy target, decided that he wanted to be the victor of this fight. "How long can this woman last?" he asked himself. And then he smiled, "I have killed women before, but I have never killed a woman in battle. She is tired and weakening. She is mine!"

But desperation and the adrenalin pumping in her veins had lent Kathryn strength that belied her appearance.

The mercenary saw his chance and moved in for the kill, almost knocking Fitz Malet out of the way as they made contact. His off-balance slip on the slippery grass and subsequent fall took Kathryn by surprise. The man seemed to trip and suddenly he was not there anymore. But he was more dangerous. His slide took him into contact with Kathryn and she also fell. The sword in her left hand was pointing to the ground as she fell. It penetrated the mercenary's neck and he died.

Kathryn heard a loud shout and a snarl as Fitz Malet saw his chance. He leapt over the body of another mercenary and tried to assume a commanding role as he towered above Kathryn as she lay on the ground. She kicked wildly at his ankles and managed to catch him on the shin. He felt the leg-numbing pain and started his fall. His mouth opened to shout his revenge but she had already withdrawn her sword from the mercenary's neck and she held at full arm's length. Her aim was true and Fitz Malet fell onto her sword. He too died quickly.

His lifeless body landed on top of her. She fought frantically to get free, but each time the body of Fitz Malet seemed to become heavier. She did not see that other bodies were being added to the pile. She tried to gulp air into her lungs as she felt the weight increase. The ground around her was rapidly turning red and then she felt that she was spiraling down into darkness.

She could feel herself slipping into unconsciousness and her body fought to survive even as her brain clouded and she battled her way back to consciousness. Gasping for breath, she had no strength to resist. Her body started to relax under the weight and the lack of air. And then she could hear voices. Someone had called her name.

"Damn," she thought, "I am not ready to meet the saints. They can wait. I will meet them in my own time!"

*   *   *

"*Jacques, qu'est ce que c'est?*" (James, what is that?)

De Boise, in his excitement, had lapsed into French. He pointed to a pile of bodies from which protruded a diminutive boot, which they recognized immediately; it was Kathryn's boot.

James was uncertain of what had happened except that he knew that he needed to get to her as quickly as possible.

"Kathryn?" The boot did not move. James rolled one of the bodies away from the pile and saw movement. Then, after moving another body, there were two leather boots and both were moving of their own accord!

"Will you please get this smelly, sweaty idiot off me!" It was not a question but a command.

"God be praised," de Boise looked at the blue sky and offered a brief thanks to the Almighty.

They rolled two more bodies away and helped Kathryn to her feet. Her clothes were bloodied and her face covered with mud, grime, and blood. Her blonde hair was in no better condition. But she was smiling.

"Kathryn, my love," James exclaimed, "I was so worried."

"Of course," she said smiling. "Now would you please retrieve my sword for me?"

"Where is it," de Boise asked as James hugged Kathryn.

"There," she said pointing, "sticking out of Fitz Malet's neck."

Fitz Malet had died instantly. Ranulf retrieved the sword and cleaned it on Fitz Malet's clothes.

"Do you know," Kathryn said by way of explanation, "he had the effrontery to suggest that he and I . . .," she left the words unspoken and added, "ugh," and shuddered at the thought. "So," she continued, "I decided that he should never speak again! The nerve of the man!"

"Kathryn, your other sword?" James asked.

"Oh," she thought for a moment scratching her head and adding more grime to her hair, "sticking in someone else who thought that he could get the better of a mere woman. And," she added, "the things that some of these men said to me!"

James and Ranulf laughed.

*   *   *

Kathryn, James, and Ranulf surveyed the field. It was over. The remaining mercenaries had flung down their swords and sat on the ground, waiting to see what would happen next.

The guards collected all of the arms and carried them to a central spot for shipment by cart into the castle. The surviving mercenaries were told to pile their dead in a narrow depression in the ground. When that was done, the pile of bodies was set alight and burned, with the exception of the body of Fitz Malet. The duke intended to display him on the castle wall as a lesson to others who might have similar ideas. The guards picked up their own wounded, there were no deaths and carried them to a spot close by the wagon.

Ranulf went to see how John had fared while James started to attend to their wounds, with Kathryn by his side. They looked at the mercenaries who had surrendered.

"John, what are your wishes for those men?" Ranulf asked jerking his head in the direction of the captives, who sat on the cold wet ground as they had been instructed. Their legs were crossed to prevent any sudden movement or dash for freedom.

"We will take them back to the castle," John answered, "and there we will decide their fate. The captains will be asked questions to see how much they know and then their body parts will be used to decorate the walls of the castle as well as the castles at York and Berwick. The warning will show what happens to those who take up arms against my father. The display at Berwick will serve as a warning to their Northern cousins."

John placed his hand on his chin as if in deep thought.

"The others," he continued, "shall be at the disposal of the people of the city of Durham. It is their lives and homes that were threatened; they will decide and see that justice is done."

Some of the mercenaries heard John's words and attempted to plea for mercy. John, hearing the murmurs of discontent, turned and said.

"You took up arms against King Edward. The question, therefore, is not whether you will die but how you will die." That was John's final word.

John approached Kathryn and James as they tended the wounded guards. Seeing them approach, James said to John, "Nothing serious, sire. All wounds can be cured by treatment and rest."

John smiled and said, "It seems, Kathryn, that you have acquitted yourself very well. Very well, indeed."

James and Kathryn looked at him.

"Sire?" James asked as Kathryn remained silent.

"It seems, from what my brother Ranulf and I can gather from the guards who fought alongside Kathryn, that things were starting to slip away in that part of the field. But she mobilized her colleagues to secure the advantage. Then, she stood foremost in the line, sustained violent assaults, and displayed skill that would have done honor to the most experienced guardsman with two very sharp swords, one in each hand, fighting with great courage."

John took a drink of water from a flask handed to him by de Boise and then he continued.

"She led them out of the pocket they were in and successfully fought their way to find Fitz Malet. She then took on Fitz Malet and several others, taunting them that she was a mere woman and that she would feed them to the worms. And by God's blood, she did!" John exclaimed.

"But what interested me even more is that," John continued, "my guards tell me that the two of you fight using the same fighting as dear Oswald, and I must say that your resemblance to him, James, is remarkable!"

John turned to Kathryn and smiled at her appearance.

"Kathryn, wife of James, I bow to you for exhibiting great courage on the field. Take this with the thanks of my father, my brother Ranulf, and all of your colleagues. You are one of us. A true soldier in arms."

She was greeted with thunderous cheers from the guards, who picked her up and placed her sitting on the shoulders of two of the larger men so that all could see her. James glowed with pride. She was carefully lowered to the ground to stand next to James. They moved away to tend the wounded once more.

"I would suggest that if you two are both caring for our wounded," Ranulf offered, "that you clean yourselves first."

James hugged Kathryn muttering, "I am so proud of you, my love!"

Two of the guardsmen appeared miraculously with buckets of water, and to the pleasant surprise of Kathryn and James, a cake of soap. James and Kathryn washed themselves and then started to take care of the wounded.

One guardsman swayed a little as he attempted to walk and he was holding his right arm across his chest, with his left hand supporting the wrist. James stared at him. The guard's face was blackened with mud thrown up from the field.

"Got hit by a rock, did you?" James asked.

"Sword handle," the guard said pointing to the dent in his helmet. "Might have done worse if I had not deflected the blow with my arm, sire."

"No need to call me sire." James put the man at ease "Physician will do fine. And your opponent?" James asked.

"He was sorry for it," the guard said, "now he is over there," indicating with his head the funeral pyre of the dead mercenaries.

The guard sat quietly as James tended to his injuries. At one time he raised his head to look at James, "Doesn't hurt at all," and he stretched out his arm for James to finish bandaging where the skin had been broken. When James had completed his work, he gave instructions to Kathryn for an ointment that he needed.

James straightened himself to his full height to ease his back and looked down at the guard.

"You will be fine and your wounds will heal within the week. If your headache persists beyond the next two days, come and find me and I will give you medicine."

The guard nodded his thanks.

"Saw your friend," the guard blurted out, "Would not want to get on her wrong side." The man looked at James, as if searching for his next words. "You can be proud of her, si—sorry—Physician. And I hear that you did well yourself."

"Thank you," James told the guard as he smiled at his use of words, "Now sit here and I will have someone bring you tea to clear your head. I am proud of my wife and I will pass your very kind comments to her."

"You know," the guard continued his comments, "she did not want any help and even saved the lives of two of us. Dare say had it not been for your wee lass, this dent in my helmet might have been much more serious."

"Aye, lad," James said, "that's my Kathryn!"

Kathryn returned with the medicine to the beaming smiles of James and the guardsman.

"Been talking about me, have you?" she asked.

"No ma'am," the guardsman responded, "after seeing the way you handle yourself with the two swords, no one would want to talk about you behind your back."

They all laughed and she bent over and touched the guard's cheek.

"And you," she said, "I know who you are. You covered my back for a long time and probably saved me several times." Then she asked, "Where is your friend, the one who stayed close by you."

"Over there, ma'am," he answered, "he may be badly hurt."

"Wounded in the thigh, lad," James gave him the information.

"Will he die?" the guard asked.

"Already looked at him since his wound was more serious, and he will be as right as rain in two or three weeks." James thought for a moment then added, "Give yourself a little time for your head to clear and then go and see him."

Kathryn gave the smiling guard his ointment with instructions on how to apply it and they left to tend to another wounded man.

Ranulf found Kathryn and James. The look on his face told them that he had an urgent matter to discuss with them.

"I am used to a little pain and stiffness after a battle," Ranulf said, "but . . ."

"Your leg?" James butted into the sentence.

"It seems to me, James, that we are not done here. The sponsor or money behind these assassins remains unknown and there is an urgency to catch him before another attempt is made. I have," he continued, "talked with my brother and with my father."

"The king is here?" Kathryn asked.

"Oh, yes," Ranulf replied, "he watched the whole thing from one of the castle towers. He even threatened to have his advisers hang from that same tower if they attempted to keep him within the castle walls. He arrived," Ranulf gestured with his hand, "only moments ago. He wishes to talk with his guardsmen."

"So," Edward spoke from behind them, "this is a fine group that we have. Is it not? Wasting time talking."

Edward was not a man to keep his presence unknown. His laughter let all of the guards know that he was present.

"We hear from our sons and even from some of our guardsmen that you, Physician, and you, Little One, did well for yourselves on the field. You have our gratitude and thanks."

James and Kathryn bowed their heads in respect.

"Peace is my desire," he continued, "but whosoever is behind this has other supporters who may have already slipped away to other parts of our realm. It is also painfully clear to us that Charles of France, who cowers in Paris, may also have his hand in this. He very rarely leaves the city since we embarrassed his predecessor Jean at Poitiers and his earlier predecessor Philip at Crécy."

Edward appeared to be lost in thought as he considered his next words.

"We would like to have both of you present at a meeting with John and Ranulf. Our advisers are of no help so they will be excluded. Ranulf," Edward turned to his adopted son, "when the time is set inform James and Kathryn."

James and Kathryn were thrilled at the use of their names.

"Now, my son," Edward looked at Ranulf, "if you would be so kind to give me your arm and help me back to my horse I will return to the castle."

"Sire, if I may be so bold, I suggest that a wine posset will help you to relax. If you sleep and awake hungry, a tasty chicken broth will restore your energy. These have been trying times and I can think of nothing better for you."

Edward raised an eyebrow and looked at James. Ranulf continued to support the king on his arm.

"Physician, you have much about you of our beloved Oswald. He also presumed to tell us what to do. But I see as much good in you as I saw in him. We thank you for your advice. It is sound."

"And now, Ranulf," Edward looked at de Boise, "let us remove ourselves from these physicians lest they give us more orders!"

*   *   *

CHAPTER 51

James and Kathryn sat in close proximity to the warmth of the fire in the rooms that they had been assigned as sleeping and living quarters. It was only a short distance along the hallway from Ranulf's room. The closeness had allowed them to monitor his condition during and after the time that he had been wounded. They had not used the rooms to any great extent because of the fear Kathryn's gender may be discovered. But now, it did not matter. Kathryn was recognized by all and was accorded the mixed tribute of being a fine soldier and a lady guest of King Edward and Duke John.

They had just finished bathing. Seeing the servants struggle into the room with a large bath had caused them to smile. John and Ranulf had instructed the servants to provide all that was needed.

And now, the bathing being over and the bath having been cleared away, clean clothes washed and dried in the interim, they felt relaxed and refreshed. They were clean and wholesome again.

As sudden knock on the door brought them alert.

"Yes?" James said.

There was no response. Kathryn moved to pick up her sword as James stood by his axe.

"*Oui, entrez.*"

The door slowly opened and a man popped his head around the door. He was dressed in the robes of a monk.

He introduced himself and inclined his head toward Kathryn. His eyes opened wide when he saw the sword that she held and even wider when he beheld James's axe. He apologized for his lack of understanding of the English language and spoke in rapid Norman French to James. He told him that he was from the Monastery of La Trappe in Normandy. He had known King Edward for many years and that he was a friend of the duke. James translated the words to the ever-vigilant Kathryn.

She looked at his eyes and fingered her sword. The man smiled and said to her through James.

"Fear not, my daughter, I come only in peace and on an errand from Duke John."

Kathryn nodded and spoke to James in her Northern dialect. She did not wish to have the monk understand her words.

"My wife," James translated, "says that she understands but is naturally cautious with strangers."

The monk smiled. He bowed to Kathryn.

"*Votre mots êtes très sage, madame* (Your words are very wise, madame), and I respect your caution but you have nothing to fear from me. I am the duke's confessor and I bring you a message from the duke."

"And that message is?" Kathryn asked.

James did not need to translate. The monk read her expression and understood what she was saying.

"There is to be no celebration this night. It will be as though the incident this morning did not occur, for which I thank both of you."

He paused and looked at Kathryn.

"Especially you, madame," Kathryn and James bowed their heads to show that they appreciated the monk's compliment.

"It is to be a normal night. No revelry. The king and the duke will dine together. Sir Ranulf will join them and King Edward requests your presence."

James and Kathryn looked at each other.

"Did you say," James asked, "the king requests our presence or commands our presence. I may not have heard correctly. Sometime the words are not clear to me."

"The king requests your presence." The monk repeated his words. "And he added, he also requests that you wear the robes that I will provide for you."

"What robes?" Kathryn asked.

"You, sir," the monk looked at James "will be in the guise of a monk. And you, madame," he looked at Kathryn, "shall be in the guise of a nun." Before Kathryn or James could make any comment, the monk added, "The robes are rather large and should you wish to carry anything underneath strapped to your belts, it will not be noticed. And King Edward has no objection to your wearing your present attire . . ."

"Under our robes," James finished the sentence and translated for Kathryn.

*   *   *

Within the castle, there was no sign of de Bohun. His whereabouts had not been discovered no matter how carefully the guards had searched. His absence pointed to a role in the plot and that, by implication, he may have entered into an agreement with one or more malcontents.

The citizens thronged the marketplace that had been chosen as the site for execution for the captured mercenaries. Executions would occur the following morning but for the moment the full occupancy of the pillories gave the citizens some sport. Additional pillories had been quickly constructed so that all of the mercenaries could be accommodated. The word had been put about that the mercenaries were allied with those who supported the Scottish king, David II, who had been held in custody for eleven years but had been released on payment of a heavy ransom. The citizens remembered well that he had attacked the area in 1346 and had been defeated at the Battle of Red Banks, now undergoing a name change to Neville's Cross, just a short distance from the city. To make matters worse, word was also out that the Scots were in league with the French. And so the French-speaking mercenaries were in greater trouble than they had ever imagined. They had been offered an option. Speak up and tell of the whereabouts of any other mercenaries or leaders or advise of the whereabouts of any bands of Scottish invaders and they would have a quick death. Otherwise death would be slow and painful. There were no speakers. They knew nothing other than that they had been hired to fight.

On hearing of their denials, John had stood in front of them as they were secured to the pillories and made the announcement.

"You have advised me that you know nothing of this plot. Yet you must have known the nature of the task for which you were hired. I do not have the time to dally with you here and listen to your repeated denials. The first of you will die as the soon as the sun has provided enough light. The citizens will decide which of you is to be the first. Then we will continue in this manner until you are all dead. If you hear any sounds coming from the room yonder," John pointed to a door of the castle, "have no concern. It is only the executioners drawing lots for who will die by what means. Other than that, think upon your death!"

The citizens who heard this short speech cheered knowing that they would be a part of the decisions and the executions would be in the form of a show. Entertainment had been very sparse these last few days. The citizenry of Durham were looking forward to the morrow. John turned and walked across the castle yard to the cathedral. He had business with Bishop Hatfield.

The citizens liked John. He avoided too much or overuse of his power and a steady, effective dialog always kept them informed. Even after a long journey whether it be through England, Flanders, or Calais and into France, he always had time to acknowledge the soldiers and the citizens.

He walked toward the cathedral with the aroma of food being cooked in his nostrils. The monks ate in their own dining room, but the kitchen on the west side of the castle was where the food for the soldiers and staff was cooked. The smells were tempting, but he decided to show restraint and continued on his way. The soldier at the gatehouse acknowledged his entrance.

There was no sign of Bishop Hatfield in the cathedral so John walked to the far end of the massive structure. A man stood in the shadows between the windows of the cloisters. He was not wearing the vestments expected of the bishop. Then John realized that it was not the bishop. It was de Bohun.

He stood still, not making any effort to move. John approached him cautiously although de Bohun had not been a proven member of any plot, and church law forbade drawing a weapon within the sanctity of the cathedral or priory.

"Well, Humphrey," John addressed his second cousin, "how are things with you? We had missed you this past day. Where have you been?"

"I decided that in the light of the events of the past few days," de Bohun answered, "that it would be better for me to spend some time in this house of the Lord."

"Do you have worries, my cousin?" John asked, as he looked at the well-dressed man who had turned his head to look at him, his sleek black beard seemed to shine in the gray morning light of the cathedral.

"Have you considered," John continued, "that my father and I might have had need of you?"

Humphrey knew that this was a very leading question. His uncle, King Edward, who was the first cousin of de Bohun's dead father, was an irascible old man who could not be trusted. Just like the first Edward, the current Edward would make an agreement one day and if it fitted his goals or mood, he would violate the agreement within the day, sometimes within the hour!

Humphrey stepped closer to the window to allow his eyes to adjust to the brighter light.

"I needed the time to think and pray," Humphrey said. "These are difficult times for me. As Constable of England I should be keeping the peace but these mercenaries were a surprise. And I knew that they would not offer any opposition to your well-trained guards."

John did not ask how Humphrey had come to know that the men were mercenaries. He would leave that question for another time. He merely filed it away in the back of his mind. No need to arouse any further suspicions too soon.

"Well, Humphrey," he stuck his thumbs into his belt, "I would that you had been with us. This I can tell you, Cousin," John decided to open up some thoughts to see if he could make the rabbit run for the hounds to pursue, "there is a suspicion about you because of your absence. If anyone else here was to be asked about you, the response might not be favorable. So, why not come with me and make your peace with my father? An explanation for your absence would suffice."

Humphrey saw through the invitation. He was able to recognize John's ruse to remove him from the church precincts. He foresaw an ambush as soon as he left the precincts. A group of guards would be waiting for him. He did not realize that John was as surprised to see him in the cathedral just as much as he was surprised to see John. He had been considered to be in flight, perhaps for France or another part of Europe. Although John had told Edward that he considered France the most likely place because they believed that the French king Charles, the fifth one of that name, to have his fingers very deeply in this pie.

John looked at Humphrey's unemotional face. His eyes were averted, so perhaps there was reason to suspect the man. He would try another approach.

"You know, Humphrey, that I leave for France very soon. Activities there are going to become increasingly hostile again and my father wants me to command the forces there. I would be happy if you would come with me as an advisor."

Humphrey looked at John inquiringly but could not detect anything suspicious in his expression. John was a Plantagenet through and through. Like his forbearers he was clever enough to cover his emotions.

"I had thought that as Constable of England I would be needed here to assist the king in maintaining peace, and in case our Scottish cousins decide to invade again."

"An admirable thought, Humphrey," John responded, "but I fear that there may be a greater need for you in France. Your father acquitted himself very well in France and your uncle, constable before you, was honored likewise. The family name is to be upheld and in France the family honor maintained."

Humphrey placed his forefinger on his chin as if in deep thought. He involuntarily scratched at his beard. He was trying to manipulate his way out of John's invitation. He preferred England.

De Bohun was really uncertain where he wished to be. England was his home, although he had estates near Calais. He was worried that the perception of any impropriety on his part could lead to imprisonment and, eventually, death. King Edward was not merciful to those he suspected of any disagreement with his policies and decisions and these latest events were more than a disagreement. They were treasonous. Life was very short for those convicted of treason and death that followed conviction was very painful.

Humphrey was in a quandary named thoughts tumbled through his mind, "It is my duty to help England, but do I want to lead England's armies into battle against the French? I could stay here and discourage Scottish attacks from north of the border. If John intends to go back to France, and that seems a certainty, I for one will be happy, yet his message is that I should go with him. I will be in constant danger, as I see that I am already on the wrong side of John. He'll be watching for the first opportunity to take me to task about my activities these past few days."

"Yes," John was saying as de Bohun focused once more on his words, "Humphrey, your help in France will be invaluable."

Again, Humphrey put his finger on his bearded chin and bent his head to think over John's latest comment.

"I dislike him," de Bohun thought as he folded his hands and tried not to look directly into John's eye. He looked at the ground as if in deep thought. "And yet," his thoughts continued, "I am not the only one who dislikes him. There are others in line before me. I know that I cannot possibly dislike him as much as Charles of France. I wonder who else knew of the mission. Care must be taken so that no one discovers what it is about. It is the accession that we question. The need to secure the accession is of paramount importance."

Humphrey finally looked at John. He had made up his mind.

"I may be able to join you in France in a short time. At the moment, I prefer that I remain here in England to secure some items of major importance that need my personal attention."

"The fatherless only son of a . . ." John cut the silent curse short lest he give away his feelings.

"That will be adequate," he agreed reluctantly.

Humphrey nodded. "It will be interesting to know the plans that John has formulated for France," he thought. "I need to know his whereabouts to make myself secure."

John smiled inwardly, "Any plans that he hears from me will be truly false." At that moment, John saw Bishop Hatfield and Prior Fossor approaching from the other side of the cloisters. They walked with purpose and determination.

"Good day to you, sire," Hatfield said out of courtesy to John. As the prince bishop, he had seniority over John in the palatinate. Fossor gave John the same greeting but with a polite bow of his head in respect to John's station.

De Bohun turned to greet both men. Humphrey knew that he was now in an awkward position and hoped that the conversation could end quickly without any embarrassing question.

"We are on the way to see your father," Hatfield told John. "We have urgent business that we must discuss with him."

Hatfield looked straight into John's eyes as though begging him not to ask the nature of the business. John understood the message and they would talk later. Perhaps sooner!

"Of course," John said. "Please go ahead."

Hatfield and Fossor walked away at the same brisk step as when they had arrived leaving John and de Bohun to finish their conversation.

"Now, where were we?" John asked de Bohun after the bishop and the prior had departed.

"We were discussing my arrival in France."

"Ah, yes. When do you think you can be there? I need to complete my plans and inform you where we can meet."

Humphrey thought for a while, nodding his head from side to side as if counting days, and then he gave John the answer.

"I can meet you in Calais in two months. I will have my affairs settled here sufficiently so that I can attend to matters in France for the summer."

"Excellent," John exclaimed but meaning, "Now that I have a commitment from you, I can really start planning."

"You will of course send me word before you depart so that I might advise you of my position?"

Humphrey nodded his agreement.

John had decided to ask Humphrey if he had sought sanctuary within the cathedral and the priory. Sanctuary that could protect him from the king's justice. John smiled. If de Bohun thought that the privilege of sanctuary, or asylum from charges of treason, would protect him from King Edward, then he had thought wrong. Edward had, as a younger man, made a thorough study of the various legalities of sanctuary and he also had an excellent understanding of the law.

"Give them sanctuary," Edward had once proclaimed to his older son Edward and to John, "by all means let us honor a man's request for sanctuary. Then I know where he is and he will keep very well in a monastery or church for years until I am ready to deal with him and design the punishment accordingly. And do not forget, my sons, if you know who your enemies are and know where they are, you can control them!"

If de Bohun had claimed sanctuary from the bishop and the prior, he was in a situation where he could be controlled. And John was in no doubt that Hatfield and Fossor had requested an audience with the king to discuss that very issue.

John looked at Humphrey and smiled like a fox that has just gained lawful entry into the henhouse.

"I must needs take my leave now, Humphrey, there are other issues that require my attention. I will send you word when we can meet before I leave and we will make more specific arrangements for meeting in France."

"Was that a look of relief on de Bohun's face that I saw?" John asked himself as they parted. "Is the man that worried? If so, what has he been doing to put himself into such a fear for his life?"

John let the matter drop from his thoughts. He went and heard the singers practicing the chants for the forthcoming mass. The energetic voices filled him with a sense of peace as he sat in one of the wooden seats at the rear of the cathedral and listened to the music.

He had accomplished a lot in the past hour.

Then he heard someone behind him, it was Ranulf.

"What did you say, Ranulf?" he asked.

"I said, my brother, that our father is not in a good mood. We are lucky that there is not to be murder done in the cathedral this day. Hatfield and Fossor had an audience with your father. And that was the start. When he heard their words, he jumped from his seat and I thought that he was going to physically throw or kick them out. His anger was terrible. His face became wild and very emotional, almost out of control, and his words were not pleasant to Hatfield and Fossor."

"Well, I do have some understanding of the possible reason for his anger," John said. "Let us go to Father to make sure that he does not have any kind of fit. And you know, Ranulf, I was thinking that this was a good day. Silly me!"

*   *   *

Edward was livid! He had ordered Hatfield and Fossor to appear before him once more, and both men feared for their lives. They were vociferously proclaiming their innocence from any and all forms of collusion that Edward could throw at them. And then John and Ranulf appeared. They walked to the dais where Edward sat in his chair and bowed showing great reverence and respect. Edward was the king. He was their father.

"What do you two want?" Edward's question was sharp, curt, and angry.

"Sire," John approached the dais, "we request that you allow Bishop Hatfield and Prior Fossor to go about their business."

"Who is this we? Do you have a mouse in your pocket?" He paused for a moment and looked at Hatfield and Fossor. "You two, stay where you are," Edward thundered. "You can leave when we give you permission to do so!"

"Sire," John decided to start again, "Ranulf and I request that you allow Bishop Hatfield and Prior Fossor to go about their business."

Edward fixed John and Ranulf with a glare that would have felled Goliath. He thought for a moment.

"You two," he looked at Hatfield and Fossor, "out!"

They bowed and scraped and left as quickly as they could.

"Now," Edward focused on his two sons, "did you see the look in the eyes of Hatfield and Fossor? We still scare the you-know-what out of them." Edward was smiling. "What story do you have for me?"

"Father," John spoke first, "I have a sense of the news that the bishop and prior brought to you." John took a deep breath; his father was still a formidable opponent, physically, mentally, and verbally. "I have talked with de Bohun."

John relayed the details of his meeting and conversation with de Bohun. Edward listened intently, asking a question now and again that was related more to de Bohun's physical and mental state rather than to the actual contents of the conversation.

"Well done, John. Ranulf," Edward looked at his other son, "the way that you left here quickly is appreciated. It gave the two priests a thought that their last days had come. And that is precisely what I wanted. Well done, my boys!"

Edward smiled at his two sons. Grown men and successful in their own right but to Edward they were still his boys.

Edward took a sip of the water that was on the side table. He remembered when Oswald had told him that a container of water with about five or ten parts vinegar per hundred parts of water would help keep the water pure. He had followed this advice from many years, ever since they had landed on the Normandy beach some weeks before the Battle of Crécy.

"Father!" Ranulf had become worried when he saw the dreamy look in Edward's eyes. John stepped onto the dais to hold his father's hand.

"All is well, boys, just a memory or two of . . ."

"Oswald, Father."

"Yes, Ranulf. He is difficult to forget. He touched our lives in a way that will not be forgotten. And such a fighter!"

"Well, Father," John spoke up, "we," he looked at Ranulf, "feel that James and the Kathryn are adequate for the task that must be done. They can never replace Oswald but we see Oswald in James."

Ranulf nodded and added, "Had it not been for them I am doubtful that I would have survived the leg wound. And here I am fit and fighting again. And Father, there are times when I am talking with James that I think I am talking with Oswald."

Edward put down the glass.

"All right, my sons, just a little memory of times past." Edward straightened up in his seat. "Now here is what we will do."

"Winning is not always due to superior weapons or superior numbers of men," Edward said, "As you found out brilliantly yesterday. The winner had the best strategy, and, many times, the luck on his side."

Edward continued to talk and the plan was laid out to them over the next hour. There was nothing on paper. Just the thoughts that poured out of Edward's mind, one after the other and in order. Edward had thought out the details with painstaking care. Not a piece was omitted.

The hour went by. Finally he was finished. He took another sip of water and then he asked the question.

"What do you think?"

There was no response.

"John! Ranulf!"

They looked at each other.

"Well, Father," John began and Ranulf added, "Do you mind if we make a suggestion?"

"Why do you two always respond as though you were twins?"

"Like father like sons, sire. We have had the best teacher!"

Edward laughed.

"Go ahead."

Edward listened intently and watched them as they spoke. They looked at each other and then at their father; there were no blustering or lost words. It was all straightforward. Then they stopped. Took a glass of water each from the large container and slaked their dry throats.

ELIZABETH JAMES

Looking through their eyes, Edward could see the points that they had made and their reasons. They liked the challenge of such mental work. It was their instinct. In their active minds, mental sparring was second nature. "Aye," he thought, "they have learned well!"

Silence fell. Edward looked at them as they waited for his response. They had courage. And they had brains.

It was easy for Edward to respond.

"Well done, my boys. We will proceed as we have discussed. Now bring the new Cistercian brother and the new Cistercian sister to us."

*   *   *

CHAPTER 52

James and Kathryn sat down as Edward requested. The table was laid simply but well for the five of them, Edward, John, Ranulf, James, and Kathryn. Edward sat at the head of the table, and at John and Ranulf's request, Kathryn and James sat next to the king. Two trusted servants stood near the door, out of hearing range, and were not privy to the conversations that followed, but Edward, merely by a look in their direction, could bring them running to his side.

At John's request, Kathryn and James removed their robes and their weapons. Edward looked and raised an eyebrow.

"You too seem well prepared, although come to think of it, after the latest events, you need to be."

Kathryn and James bowed their heads in respect. Kathryn responded and raised her head to smile at Edward. "We have learned a lot from your two sons," she looked at John and Ranulf.

Edward was silent for a moment. They all contemplated the table. The food was fresh and appetizing.

"You said something, Kathryn?" Edward asked.

"Aye, sire. I was thinking that fighting gives me an appetite and had not realized that I had spoken my thought out loud."

Edward and the others laughed.

"James," Edward said, "how do you feel?"

"The same, sire. We," he smiled at Kathryn "think alike and do a lot together. We would have it no other way."

Edward looked at the spread before him.

"James, please bless this food for us."

James intoned the blessing in Latin and then they helped themselves to portions of the food on the various dishes. Mutton, beef, boiled onions, boiled leeks (that the king loved), peas and beans, fish brought in fresh from the coast, white bread, and butter.

The servants had provided place settings for the meal that included a cup, bowl, spoon, napkin, knives, and a plate. The plates were in place of trenchers, the thick slices of dried bread that were used to soak up the juices and gravy, which were more common for casual meals in the king's household.

James and Kathryn listened to Edward, offered comments when asked, and were pleasantly surprised that he had a demeanor that could adapt to any occasion. He was courteous, but they knew that he had a temperament exactly like that of a warrior and he could change within moments.

"It seems," Edward finally got to the point of the dinner, "that you are both equally well schooled in learning and soldiering. But I have only little knowledge of you. John, Ranulf," Edward looked at his two sons who had been adding to the conversation but not with the same intensity as their father, "what say you?"

John spoke first. "It is reasonable for me to say, Father," John said, "that we can trust James and Kathryn with your lives."

This was precisely what Edward wanted to hear.

"By God, John, you have sharp eye. I am assuming that you," Edward looked at Ranulf, "have the same opinion?"

"Yes, Father."

"You have always given me sound advice, "replied Edward. Then he turned to look at James and Kathryn. "Sit at one side of the table so that I can see both of you at the same time, otherwise my head will be swinging from side to side so much that I may lose it!" Edward thought for a moment then laughed at his inadvertent joke. "And," he said, "I have no intent to lose my head to those who would have it placed on the tower gate!" He thought for a moment before he spoke again. "Now, since you have our trust, there is one or two things that we need you to do for us," Edward said as he looked at James and Kathryn. He did not require an answer but continued talking.

"Edmund Mortimer, the son of Roger Mortimer," Edward did not mention Roger Mortimer's adulterous relationship with his mother Isabella that led to the death of his father Edward II, "has lately come under our suspicion. This young earl, powerful on account of his possessions and hereditary influence in the Welsh marches, has been become more important when he married our granddaughter Philippa, the daughter of our son Lionel. We believe that he may have designs on the throne at some future time and may be priming himself for such a position. He seems a little too confident of his positions at our court!"

James and Kathryn continued to look at the king. Edward scratched his chin, as if in deep thought, before continuing.

"For some reason, it seems that our Mortimer has deigned to make it known to all and sundry that he is in our confidence. And as Marshal of England, he has been seen to be in the frequent company of our friend Humphrey de Bohun. And we are not sure of their relationships with the damned French. They had never," Edward said by way of an explanation, "forgiven me for wiping the floor with the cream of their nobility and their ineffective armies at Crécy and Poitiers! So," Edward concluded his story, "we have need of two persons that are unknown to Mortimer that we can trust. And you," he fixed his eyes on James and Kathryn, "are those persons! What say you?"

James looked at Kathryn knowing that a negative answer to Edward was not politic, and besides, they did feel that it was the right thing to do. The bowed their heads and chorused, "As you wish, sire."

Edward almost fell off his chair laughing.

"Where did you find these two?" he asked John and Ranulf, who were also smiling. "As we wish has nothing to do with it. But I assume that you have given me an affirmative answer?"

"Aye, sire, we have," Kathryn said.

"Ah, Little One, good to hear your tongue." Edward smiled as he answered Kathryn.

"Fortuitously or not, Mortimer is here in Durham. We are not sure of the reasons for his visit. Although married to our granddaughter he is not in our confidence." Edward looked at de Boise. "Ranulf, give directions to our two monks to let them know where they may find Mortimer."

*   *   *

James and Kathryn stood outside of the room that was situated on the other side of the castle from where the king has his apartment. He had asked to be allowed to speak with Mortimer, and after a brief delay was shown into the room by one of Mortimer's guards.

"I am of the Benedictine order," James announced to Mortimer. "I am called 'Physician' and this is my assistant."

"You are a practitioner?" Mortimer asked.

"Yes, sire."

"With the king's mandate?" Mortimer asked.

James was still for a moment. Then he nodded. "Aye, sire, and with the mandate of the Duke of Lancaster for it is in the palatinate of Durham and in the duchy of Lancaster that I do most of my work. I also work in London and wherever my travels take me. All with the mandate of King Edward."

"And what do you do?" Mortimer looked at Kathryn. "Small fellow, isn't he?" he commented in the form of a question.

Kathryn remained silent, her bowed head covered by the hood of her robe.

"My lord," James answered for Kathryn, "my assistant was struck dumb as a child. A fever sent his body into convulsions and the brain was unable to cope. That is the reason for the inability of my assistant to speak. We communicate through signs, by writing, and by drawing."

"And it is your request that you spend time here before you leave on your travels to . . . ?

"I return to London, sire."

"Then you indeed have my permission to remain here. Remain as long as you wish, and if you insist on practicing, there are a number of ailments in this castle and town that could benefit from your attention. But remember, Physician, magic is the province of those trained under the king's mage and none other. I expect healing from you and no magic!"

"Yes, my lord."

"Good."

Mortimer looked down from the dais where his chair was placed and his eyes looked straight into James's eyes. He was unable to see Kathryn's face because of her hooded robe.

James hesitated, wondering if he should remain. They bowed their heads, turned, and made for the door.

"Physician."

They both turned. A thin smile moved over Mortimer's features.

"With whom did you serve to get your medical knowledge?"

James thought for a moment as an answer formed. "Slowly," he thought, "do not give anything away. He will check."

"From the works of various master physicians and from books," he said at last.

"I studied at Montpellier in the south of France and worked in the hospital there, one of the hospitals that were required by Pope Innocent III to be established in every diocese. I am familiar with the works of Arnold de Villanova, the *Compendium Medicinae* of Gilbertus Anglicus, the *Rosa Anglica* of Joannes Anglicus, as well as the works of John of Gaddesden."

James looked at Mortimer who continued to watch them closely. He made no effort to speak so James continued.

"I am also familiar with the texts of Hippocrates, Celsus, Galen, Dioscorides, and a Haly Abbas. I consider the *Medicina Antiqua* to be one of the most significant books of its kind. The *Theatrum Sanitatis* of Ububchasym of Baldach is also a worthy book. The textbook of surgery written by Abu al-Qasim Khalaf Ibn Abbas az-Zahrawi is the leading handbook in this field of medicine. Then the Tacuinum of Ibn Botlan is also worthy of study."

James took a deep breath as he watched for any signs of disagreement or other emotion on Mortimer's face.

"I see, Physician," he said, "that you include Arab authors in your readings."

"Aye, sire. One can learn much medical knowledge from other countries and we can use their knowledge to advance our knowledge of medicine."

"Oh, really!"

"Yes, sire. What a bitter irony when one uses Arab medicine to treat the wounds of Christian soldiers."

"You have a point, Physician." Mortimer smiled. "And you have a smooth tongue in your head."

"Where have I heard that before?" James thought to himself.

"Will there be anything else, sire?" he asked.

"Come back on the morrow and we will talk."

Mortimer waved his hand in dismissal and James and Kathryn, smiling inwardly, left the room and made their way to the chapel that lay across the castle yard.

"Books," James whispered to Kathryn, "I feared that I would not remember any of the texts that I have read. I wonder if he believed me?"

"You gave him a lot of names and I know, my love," Kathryn whispered, "that you have read all of those books. Often the truth makes for the best lie."

They paused when they reached the marketplace. It was late in the day and many of the mercenaries had been dealt justice of the citizens' choice. James threw his hood back off his head to allow the cool air to blow through his hair.

"Do I not look the part of a monk?" he asked Kathryn.

"Of course you do. You are the subject of curiosity and even fear. You are a physician who has the power to heal wounds and cure sickness."

They walked quickly past the scaffold as the last victim of the day was meeting the justice of the moment. It was painful. The citizens cheered.

"I am thinking, my dear Kathryn," James continued to whisper in case the words could be heard by any passerby, "that it is time for a visit to our friends."

He replaced his hood as a group of citizens hurried away from the scaffold. They had not missed any of the activities that afternoon and now were returning to their homes outside the city walls. The gates would be locked soon and any unauthorized persons within the castle enclosure could spend a very cold night in the dungeon.

He saw her nod in approval. She took his medical satchel and hung it on her shoulder.

"After all, my dear James," she whispered, "what good is an assistant if the assistant does not assist?"

*   *   *

Oswald stepped back from the window, opened the door, and looked along the street, in the direction of the castle. The skies were darkening and night was close. He looked at Margaret, and reading his thoughts, she nodded her approval.

"She is the only one," he thought, "who knows the true extent of my powers."

They wrapped the heavy woolen cloaks about themselves and left the house to walk to the castle in the direction of the north gate.

Oswald started to walk with purpose but his long strides caused Margaret to fall behind. She touched his arm as a reminder that she could not keep up. He smiled and slowed his pace.

And then, in the dim light, they saw Kathryn and James as they left the castle by the north gate. Or at least it looked like Kathryn and James. The size and walk were the same. Or was the man bigger than James? They wore the robes that they had been provided.

As the monks moved closer they looked directly at Oswald and Margaret. The faces were unmistakable. It was Kathryn and James. They immediately embraced each other.

"Welcome home," Margaret said. "You seem to have had some interesting adventures!"

Kathryn smiled weakly. Suddenly the tiredness and the effect of the previous days were starting to catch up with her body.

"First," Margaret looked at them, "let us hurry home and get you something warm. Then we can talk."

Once back at the house, a mug of hot tea sufficed. James and Kathryn refused any food. They had already eaten! They brought Oswald and Margaret up to date, and immediately, plans were formulated for the next steps.

*   *   *

Sensing Edward's displeasure with them and John's suspicions of de Bohun, de Bohun and Mortimer did not take long to arrange a meeting.

"Reason? What reason does Edward need?" Mortimer's voice took on a higher pitch than usual.

Humphrey de Bohun sat beside him in the cloisters, his tousled hair showing the signs of the strain that he had been under in recent days. Having to remain within the cathedral and priory precincts was starting to wear on him. The seat was built against the wall and no one could approach them from the rear by surprise. They had a perfect view of the central square of the cathedral.

"Well, considering that you are little more than twenty years old and already the Marshall of England and master of much land! That may be reason enough."

"Perhaps, Humphrey. Perhaps."

Mortimer tried to smile. "Now I'm held at a standstill," he said. "I have exhausted all my contacts."

Humphrey bent over and rested his chin on his hands. After a pause for thought, he again looked at Mortimer and spoke.

"There is no proof of anything that you have done, Edmund. If you flee to France, Charles will take you in. They do not call him Charles the Wise for nothing. He will do anything to get back at Edward."

"But it is the old law, my friend," said Mortimer, "I feel that there is more to be had by remaining in England and not tipping my hand. Flight is for those who have no other way out and are deemed responsible for treasonous actions."

"Tell me, Edmund. Why do you fear that word so much?"

"Flight?" Mortimer reached into the pouch at his side and fished out his small, wooden statuette. He fingered it and murmured a soft word. His eyes lit up and he sat back to rest his shoulders against the wall. "This," he said, "is the source of my belief. My father, this is his image," he proffered the statuette to de Bohun, "was this close," he indicated a small distance using his thumb and forefinger, "to the throne. He and Isabella forced the abdication of her effeminate husband, Edward, in favor of their youngest son, the future Edward III. Following Edward, my father acted as regent and was the virtual ruler of England. Then he was falsely arrested and murdered by execution at Tyburn in London."

He paused but de Bohun did not offer to speak and Mortimer continued.

"We of the Mortimer family are descended from Roger de Mortemer of Mortemer-sur-Eaulane in Normandy, a supporter of William the Conqueror. We have been close to the kings of England since that time and I believe that it is my legacy to move to a higher level. A man is a master of the powers he wields. Because of the family power, people are starting to think of me as a greedy man."

"Surely no one thinks of you like that, Edmund?"

"I'm not so sure, Humphrey."

"People like you, Edmund. You are a relative of the king . . .," de Bohun started to say when he was interrupted by Mortimer.

"Through marriage, Humphrey. Through marriage to his granddaughter."

"But you have a following. Had it not been for those idiots who got themselves killed in the castle and on the battlefield, that following could have been even greater."

"Aye and little good it's doing me right now."

De Bohun sighed and shook his head.

"Nothing is certain," he said.

"Thank you for your counsel, Humphrey."

"It is just that you have so much, Edmund. A rich home in the southwest, much wealth, land holdings that are beyond the dreams of many nobles. It is just difficult to see sometimes why you still hold desires."

"Power, my friend. Power and my rights for years of service by the family. I would be lying if I said it was anything else."

"Are you sure that you want more?" de Bohun asked.

"My potential is great, Humphrey," Mortimer continued. "Perhaps my potential is not as great as yours. You are a great-grandson of Edward I. You have as much right to the throne as many others."

They sat in silence for some time. De Bohun focused on the stones in the wall. Mortimer stared out of the windows at the central square.

"Tell me something, Edmund."

"Yes, Humphrey."

"If you are restless here, if you feel bound to what you see as your future, why do you stay? Edward is suspicious of us all now. I even hear that de Boise, older and wiser now, is taking up his old occupation of assassin-to-the-king!"

"De Boise? It is true then?"

"Yes, it is true. Edward is determined on revenge. And you know that his anger knows no bounds. Anyone who he even thinks had a part in this attempted assassination will suffer."

"My parents left me the family name, titles, and lands. That is imprinted on my mind more firmly than anything else. The family name is my heart and soul. Without it, there is nothing to my life. Nothing!"

De Bohun was surprised at the vehemence of Mortimer's outburst. He shifted uncomfortably on the seat as Mortimer continued.

"Out there," he gestured to the open area that lay beyond the cathedral, "out there is the realm of England. That is real. The losses that we have suffered in France are also real. Even though I pretend friendship with Charles, I seek to regain the lands in Normandy that are my birthright. Knowing that I will do all in my power to bring that about is what lets me sleep at night."

"You? Sleep?" de Bohun seemed incredulous. "Now that is something that I would like to see!"

Mortimer smiled.

"It is late. We should both retire and see what the morrow brings."

*   *   *

Kathryn blinked her eyes open. It was then that she heard the sounds. As her eyes focused, she could see a dim light beyond the window. The stretched pigskin that covered the window to keep the cold and wind out only allowed a certain amount of light to penetrate. Where was James? She felt around the pallet and there was no sign of him. She sat up and rang her hands through his hair. She felt refreshed, as if she had slept through the night. Then she heard the sound again. She reached out and found her sword, just where she had left it at the side of the pallet. She jumped out from underneath the cover.

"Damn, it is cold," she thought realizing that she was clothed only in her undergarments.

She readied herself in the dark, relieved that her eyes had become accustomed to the gloom. There was a light tap on the door. And then the raucous laughter started. James entered holding a candle and a mug of steaming tea. Oswald followed with Margaret, who carried a tray of food.

"You really do not need that sword for your hot oatmeal, my love," James said as he attempted to diffuse the situation.

"Out!"

Margaret's command was even more final and they had no choice. James put the candle onto a small table and Margaret gave Kathryn the hot oatmeal. Oswald pretended not to look. They left the room.

"I told those two . . ."

Kathryn put the sword down.

"Thank you, Margaret. I seemed to have slept for some time."

"Yes, it is morning, although somewhat dark. And James told me the reason for waking you, an appointment with Edmund Mortimer."

Margaret took her mug of tea from the tray and sat in the chair. Kathryn sat on the other side of the table. Margaret looked at Kathryn, reached over, and gently brushed her hair from her eyes. She went to the pallet, picked up a blanket, and placed it over Kathryn's shoulders.

"Sometimes, Kathryn my dear cousin, I regret that we have brought you to this. It has been different for you and fraught with danger."

Kathryn looked quizzically at Margaret.

"I know not of what you speak, my dear Margaret. All I know is that I am with my husband. I am protecting him as he protects me. As you and Oswald protect each other. I sense that James and I have been together for a long time and yet I also sense that we are just married. I know not from where those feeling arise."

Margaret got up.

"I will bring you water to wash. And we can spend time together while you eat the oatmeal and drink your tea.

Kathryn felt better after she had eaten, washed, and dressed.

*   *   *

"Well, gentlemen. How are we this morning?"

Her bright and breezy entry into the main room surprised Oswald and James.

"We are well, Kathryn. And you?"

"Well, thank you, Oswald. And thank you for the breakfast and tea."

Kathryn felt that she had been doing this all her life. But now her mind was in turmoil. Visions flashed before her eyes. There were sights that she could not comprehend. Kathryn shook her head as if she was removing a feeling of lethargy.

Outside of the house the city was coming to life. Traders and other workers were making their way to their respective places of work. Braziers were lit at some street corners to take away the chill of the morning and to heat water for hot drinks. Soon there would be an avalanche of people in the streets going abut their daily work.

Once again, Oswald and Margaret accompanied Kathryn and James to within easy reach of the gate. Before they parted company Oswald offered a few words of advice.

"Kathryn, I sense that you are uncomfortable. Rest as much as you can and we will talk tonight."

James, who had also noticed Kathryn's discomfort earlier, mouthed the words "thank you."

*   *   *

They walked along the busy street and gained entry into the castle area through the north gate, since the guards recognized them as trustworthy victors.

The scaffold was being cleaned for another day's work and people were already moving around busily inside the castle. People seeing the two monks took no further notice. After all, what was the presence of two additional monks in a priory to them?

Several minutes later James tapped on the door of the room where Mortimer resided. They had passed by several pairs of guards but there were none at this end of the castle building.

"Physician," a man shouted, running up to them from behind. They allowed him moment to catch his breath. "My Lord Mortimer will be in the cloisters and requests that you join him there."

James thanked the man and they walked in that direction.

"What is he up to," Kathryn whispered when they were out of earshot of others. "Why the cloisters?"

"I think that your questions will be answered soon enough, my love."

"Ah, Physician, there you are." Mortimer seemed to be in good voice this morning, James thought to himself. "Come let us talk some more."

And then James saw the second man. It was de Bohun. The very same that they had met when he had visited de Boise to discover the nature of his wounds.

"Damn," James whispered to Kathryn. "Keep your head down. It is de Bohun who stands with Mortimer!"

De Bohun was the only man who could recognize them, if he had seen their faces during his visit to Ranulf's room. James doubted this but could he take the chance? It was too late. He could sense Kathryn's uneasiness. She gave the satchel to James and put her hand inside her robe. James knew that she would have a sword hilt in either hand. She was ready.

*   *   *

CHAPTER 53

J ames whispered the words "de Bohun" to Kathryn and she knew by instinct to keep her head down.

Mortimer had his back to James and Kathryn and as they approached but de Bohun could see them clearly and he muttered something unheard to Mortimer who turned to greet them. The look on Mortimer's face told James that he had a calmness about him. His voice was strong and clear as he welcomed them.

"Good morrow and welcome, Physician. You know my friend Sir Humphrey de Bohun, of course."

James nodded. No one took any notice of Kathryn. She was a physician's assistant and did not hold a high place in their pyramid of life.

"Sire?" James inquired.

"As you are no doubt aware," Mortimer spoke as de Bohun watched intently, "there was a battle outside of the castle walls yesterday. Because of our sojourn here," Mortimer waved his hands around to signify that they were within the precincts of the cathedral and the priory, "we were unable to participate."

"On behalf of the king," de Bohun added.

"We," Mortimer spoke up to include de Bohun, "hear that all of the mercenaries were killed or are about to be killed."

"Tell us, Physician," de Bohun said, "were there any persons of note and position captured?"

James bowed his head to de Bohun in respect of his position as Constable of England.

"No, sire." James responded. "It is my understanding that the mercenaries were led by a French fellow, name of Fitz Malet, who seems to be a person of no consequence."

Kathryn remained still with her head bowed. Mortimer started to stare at her, as did de Bohun.

"Physician," Mortimer began.

"Aye, sire," James acknowledged.

"Your assistant," Mortimer continued, "seems to have little to say. From his size, I assume that he is a boy in learning? An apprentice?"

"Aye, sire."

"Has a good aptitude for learning, does he?" Mortimer asked.

"Aye, sire."

James could see where the conversation was going as Mortimer half-turned and smiled at de Bohun.

"And what is the background of your assistant? I may have need of a personal physician and from what I hear of your talents, your assistant may be such a person."

James was about to respond when he saw the figure quietly approaching through the shadows.

"Ah, there you are!"

The voice of the Duke of Lancaster rang through the cloisters. They had not seen him approach. He carried no weapons and his boots were of soft leather. His approach had been as silent as a ghost.

John stepped forward and Mortimer and de Bohun parted, allowing John to stand between them.

"Good morrow, my lords," John spoke as de Bohun and Mortimer responded with a bow of their heads and chorused the word "sire."

"It is amazing how sound carries within these cloistered walls. Almost, as if one was in a cave."

John stood next to James so that de Bohun and Mortimer were unable to see Kathryn clearly.

"I heard that you are attempting to take away one of my father's physicians?"

John smiled knowing that he had now put the fear of God, or even worse the fear of King Edward, into both of them. James lowered his head not wishing that either one should see him smile. The fear of the king was indeed the sum of all fears!

"I thought, my lord," Mortimer bowed his head, "that the physician's assistant might be available for an assignment with me. Of course, now I realize that may not be the case, I withdraw my offer."

"That is a very wise decision, Edmund. And you, Humphrey," John looked at de Bohun, "you have no designs on my father's physician or on the physician's assistant?"

"No, my lord. It was a misunderstanding as neither of us knew that the king held their services dearly."

John looked over them both. He could see them swallow hard. John was starting to enjoy himself. He had almost forgotten that James and Kathryn were present. Sensing this, James gave a light cough to serve as a reminder of their presence. John turned to face them.

"Wait for us yonder," he said, pointing to an appropriate place where they could sit. Then he turned once more to de Bohun and Mortimer.

"Have you tried others who might be available for service?"

"No, sire." Mortimer responded for both.

"My father suggests that you might try France. He has heard that other physicians who used to serve French nobles in the lands which my brother Edward now controls may be available for service."

"Sire," de Bohun started to protest.

"No, Humphrey, listen to me," John commanded.

"As you know, we have not found any ringleaders of this assassination attempt."

"Sire, we can assure you . . .," Mortimer started to speak but was interrupted by the metallic sound of weapons as a mail-clad figure approached.

"Ranulf, my brother, welcome to our gathering."

Ranulf de Boise smiled at John and bowed his head.

"John, you have need of me?" de Boise asked.

"No we were almost finished here. But," John added, "stay with us."

"Ah," de Boise thought, "John needs a witness."

"So," John continued the conversation, "because of your absence from the field of battle and your failure to declare support for him, my father no longer has confidence in either of you."

Mortimer and de Bohun paled at John's words.

"And so," John continued, "I was summoned and commanded to offer you safe passage to France. You will fall under the jurisdiction of my brother Edward. You will obey him as if you were obeying my father, the king."

John hesitated to make sure that he had the full attention of both men. De Boise stood on John's right side and slightly to the rear. His hands were free to use his weapons if needed.

"You will depart to Calais on the morrow. Your personal effects will be collected for you and sent to you within the week. In fact, teams of men have been dispatched to your respective dwellings and are on the way at this very moment."

John held up his hand to forestall any words of protest.

"The decision has been made. It is irrevocable. Unless, of course, you wish to protest directly to my father?"

Neither de Bohun nor Mortimer wanted to accept that option. The last person who had protested a decision to Edward had not been seen again.

"Do you understand?" John asked.

There was no response.

"Then I shall leave you in the care of my brother Ranulf." De Boise put his hand on his sword. John turned to leave.

"Sire . . ." Mortimer spoke first. He looked at de Bohun. "Our homes are here in England. We would prefer . . ."

"You would prefer!" John exclaimed. "Your preferences are of no account in the scheme of things. My father does allow that you shall be buried in England. The timing of the burial is yours to choose. Sooner or later. And I assume that you would prefer later? Show me that you understand," John commanded.

Both men kneeled before John.

"In the absence of his majesty, King Edward," de Bohun intoned, "we recognize your authority as his regent and we depart this place as commanded. We accept the mercy that the king has shown us. And we leave without protest and with undying fealty to his majesty."

John looked down at their heads. He was not impressed.

"To which majesty do you swear undying fealty?" he asked.

His hand felt the long sharp-edged dagger that rested comfortably in the scabbard on his belt. De Boise saw the movement and had his sword half-drawn when Mortimer and de Bohun replied individually.

"To his majesty, Edward III of England."

"That will suffice, for the moment." John said. His dagger remained in its comfortable scabbard and de Boise returned his sword to its resting place. "But we have one last formality to complete."

Mortimer and de Bohun rose to their feet. They nervously looked at John and at de Boise wondering what was next. Ranulf's reputation for solving issues that were displeasing to King Edward was legendary and his methods were final.

John turned to where James and Kathryn had been sitting quietly, out of earshot, as they awaited the outcome of the conversation.

"Physician," John commanded, "approach with your assistant."

James and Kathryn approached. They bowed their heads as they approached John.

"Do you have writing utensils?"

"Aye, sire."

"Then let us repair to the scriptorium yonder where you can undertake a task for my father. You two," John looked at de Bohun and Mortimer, "follow me. Ranulf, shall we?"

They walked to the opposite end of the cloisters where the south-facing scriptorium was located. As they entered, the monks busy at the writing carrels looked up at the sudden sounds.

"Brothers," John announced, "we have need of your scriptorium for a little while. Please leave us."

Only the sound of goose quill pens being replaced into the channels and stools pushed back from the carrels was heard as the monks exited the scriptorium.

"Now, Physician," John looked at James, "I have words to dictate that our friends here," he looked at de Bohun and Mortimer, "are willing to sign. And you, my dear," he looked at Kathryn, "can now remove your hood so that you can comfortably assist your husband." John turned to de Bohun and Mortimer. "Have you met *Katrina Dunelmensis*? She is the wife and assistant to *Jacobus Dunelmensis*, physician to King Edward. This is the assistant that you tried to lure away from my father's physician."

Neither de Bohun nor Mortimer responded; they were surprised and speechless.

"Now, James, are you ready to be a scribe for my father?" John asked.

"Sire, I am ready," James replied.

A lantern was moved closer to the carrel to provide extra light for James. Kathryn busied herself making additional ink and ensuing that sufficient goose quill pens were available. She searched the carrels for the best vellum that she could find. James pinned a piece of vellum in place and looked at John to show that he was ready.

John thought for a moment.

"English I think, rather than Latin or French?"

James started to write the words on the vellum that John dictated. John's voice was clear in the stale air that was laced with smoke from the many candles. Mortimer and de Bohun ran their tongues over dry lips as they heard the words. They were banished from England until their death after which time they could, at their own individual options, be buried in England. The words bound them from any further action against Edward or the English crown. To do so meant that they would forfeit their lands, titles, and family rights. Too well did they know that Edward was more than capable of carrying out the threats contained on the vellum He was the sole guardian of power in the kingdom and holdings in France.

When James was finished, he looked at John to show that he had made a faithful recording of his words.

John then walked to the door of the scriptorium and addressed one of the monks who waited outside.

"Brother Thomas, how nice to see you. Please request that Prior Fossor present himself here as soon as possible."

"Sire," Thomas replied, "one of my brethren has been searching for him during the time that you were busy. He has been found and hurries to join us."

Within the space of several heartbeats and before John could respond, Prior Fossor appeared.

"You have need of me, sire?"

"Yes, Prior Fossor. I have need of six of your monks to make copies of a document for my father. More specifically, I need monks who are skilled in writing English."

John Fossor nodded and looked at Brother Thomas, who in turn looked at John.

"All of our monks are skilled in reading and writing English, sire. I will pick six of my brethren and we will do as you request."

The monks were duly chosen and as they seated themselves at their respective carrels with fresh vellum laid out, new goose quills cut, and a pot of ink each, Thomas looked at the duke.

"May I, sire," he asked. John passed the document to Thomas. "I propose reading the document out loud to my colleagues who will write what they hear. Will that be in order?" Thomas asked.

John nodded. "As long as the words are written out fully and not shortened."

Thomas looked at the document, read it, and remained silent for longer than John expected.

"You have an issue with the writing, Brother?" John asked.

"No, sire. The style took me by surprise."

"How so?" John asked.

"It reminds of the style of someone that I knew from years past. In fact, I taught him to write. He was called . . ."

"Oswald," James spoke up, "he was my cousin."

Thomas looked at James and saw the look in James's eyes that reminded him of the young boy so long ago. Tears welled up in Thomas's eyes as he fondly remembered Oswald. Then he jerked himself back to the present.

"Brethren, shall we?"

Thomas slowly and carefully dictated the document. He stopped and repeated words and phrases to make sure that the monks did not miss a word or mistake the meaning. The temperature in the scriptorium rose as the sun ascended into the heavens and shone brightly through the glass windows. Thomas wiped his brow to make sure that there were no beads of sweat that were likely to enter his eyes or, even worse, drop onto the master document. Thomas, along with John, Ranulf, James, Kathryn, de Bohun, and Mortimer stood and watched the documents emerge as the monks worked steadily.

John looked at de Bohun and Mortimer.

"How little they know," he thought. "Their sojourn in France may be short!"

The scratching of the goose quills continued to respond to Thomas's clear voice. And then, the monks, almost in unison, sat back from their hunched positions over the carrels. They had completed their tasks. The heaviness of the stone in the walls seemed to lend itself to the seriousness of their work.

Thomas looked around and asked the monks to exchange their pieces of vellum and check each other's work. Then he collected the copies and checked each one individually before approaching John.

"My lord duke," Thomas said, "the work is completed."

John looked at Thomas.

"Well done, Brother Thomas," he said. "Well done, brethren. Now you may leave. Thomas, please provide wax and pens for my two friends."

Thomas bowed in obeisance and soon returned with the materials needed.

"Gentlemen," John announced, "you will sign these declarations that carry the seals of the king and of the priory. If you renounce your oaths as written on these documents, you not only renounce the authority of the king but you also renounce the authority of God."

The realization, sudden and complete, of what they were about to sign showed in their faces as de Bohun and Mortimer approached the carrel where the documents lay. Their signatures and the seals were added to each of the documents in turn. The silence was only broken by the goose quill pens, as both men scratched out their signatures. How easily it could be destroyed but only at the perils of king and God.

"I will sign for my father but," John spoke up when all was complete, "it seems that we must have a witness, two preferably. Perhaps more, to show that these documents were signed without coercion."

Ranulf looked on seriously waiting for any last-minute protests that might be made. No such protests occurred. He looked at his audience. Everyone stood motionless, wondering what John was about to propose.

"Kathryn, you are a person of good standing. I am sure that your signature will bear some weight and authority. Would you sign the document if you feel that what I have said is the truth?"

Kathryn bowed her head. She raised her head, smiled, and nodded to the duke to show that she understood.

"Certainly, sire. I sign of my own free will. And I attest to what you have said that there was, to my knowledge, no coercion. Your word is good for me."

John looked and spoke to Ranulf and James in turn, who also agreed to co-sign the documents as witnesses. And then he turned to Brother Thomas.

"Brother Thomas, our brother in Christ, I ask that you do the same and I give my word to you that there has been no coercion of any sort to get Sir de Bohun and Sir Mortimer to sign these documents."

Brother Thomas agreed.

"I now make these documents official and binding using my father's ring, the official seal of the kingdom."

When the seal had been impressed into the hot wax, the documents were official and only the king could revoke them. Then, suddenly, all was completed. The six versions, with James's original version, had all been signed and had the seals attached.

"These documents," John said and he stepped toward de Bohun and Mortimer, "shall signify your privilege to remain in France under the care of my brother Edward." John gave one of the documents to de Bohun and to Mortimer. "Do not," he whispered, intending the words to be so soft that only their ears would hear, "take advantage of your positions. You have families to protect. There is death in my words, my lords." John continued. "Let these words haunt you and control your actions for the rest of your days."

John nodded his head and de Boise walked quickly to the door. Four guards entered and followed Ranulf to John's side. They faced de Bohun and Mortimer.

"Now," John said, satisfied that all work had been completed, "adjourn to your quarters, collect what you may need for the journey, and you will be escorted to the seaport on the coast, Wearmouth I hear that it is called, and from there you will be taken by ship along the English coast to Dover and thence to Calais where my brother awaits you."

"Sire," de Bohun began but John held up his hand.

"I want to hear nothing from you lest my patience wears thin. Your retainers are safe and on the way back to your respective estates here in England. Your families remain safe and have the right to journey to visit you in France as they may choose. Your wives will be informed as soon as messengers are dispatched and that will be within the hour."

John paused for a moment as he thought out his next words.

"When you arrive in France and meet my brother, you will pay respects to him as my father's regent in France. He will expect that you deliver to him the document that you each hold in your hands. I will retain four here. James! Brother Thomas!"

John retained the original document and he gave a copy to Brother Thomas.

"Brother Thomas, since the document bears the seal of the priory, you should lodge one in your library for posterity."

Mortimer and de Bohun shuddered visibly. They were tied to their written and signed oaths. There was no way out.

John had been swift and sure in his timing. There was no turning back. The way was cleared and well marked for de Bohun and Mortimer. The degree of their guilt had not been established. Except in Edward's thoughts, and he would not tolerate distrust. They were lucky to escape with their lives.

Then came a sound to John's ears. It was a low, deep rumbling, and then a retching sound. De Bohun lost the contents of his stomach to the cold stone floor. His pressure point had finally broken.

"Good Lord, de Bohun," John exclaimed. "Are you ill? Was it something that you ate?"

John handed de Bohun a piece of cloth that he had carried in his sleeve. Mortimer attempted to support his friend as de Bohun fought to regain his composure. Brother Thomas summoned two of his brethren who waited outside the door to fetch water and cleansing cloths.

"My apologies, sire," de Bohun offered. "Indeed, my stomach has been in dire straits these last several days."

"Well, Humphrey," John attempted to console de Bohun, "think of this sickness as a cleansing river. It has removed all of the impurities stuff from your system that were causing you distress. You will pass into better health soon. What say you, James?"

"Aye, sire. In fact my assistant," James looked at Kathryn, "my wife," John smiled, "has a mix that can settle Sir Humphrey's stomach. A tincture of mint."

"I have tried most potions, sire," said de Bohun through gulps of air, "but nothing has worked."

Kathryn presented a small vial to de Bohun, but he was worried that the physician's wife might be giving him a mix of mint and poison. John was insistent that he take it.

"Would the duke dare to poison him in front of these witnesses, one of whom was a churchman?" de Bohun thought.

Deciding that he must take the risk, he took a deep breath then took the vial from Kathryn and tipped the contents into his mouth, quickly swallowing the mint-flavored liquid.

"Tasty," he said.

"And you will feel better in a short while." It was the woman who spoke. "The movements in your stomach will stop and there will be no more sickness."

Mortimer continued to support de Bohun as he became steadier on his feet. He looked about, took one more breath to steady himself, and took a step forward.

"I can feel the ease already. Thank you, sire," he said to John.

"Thank the lady physician. You should be obliged to her."

De Bohun shrugged.

"I am obliged to you, Madame Physician."

Kathryn smiled to acknowledge his words.

"I believe," John's words cut in, "that it is time to bid you farewell, gentlemen."

The four guards stepped into positions on either side of de Bohun and Mortimer. Another four guards had miraculously appeared and waited at the doorway of the scriptorium.

"My brother, Sir Ranulf de Boise," John said, "will lead your escort to the coast. Farewell, gentlemen. I doubt that we shall meet again!"

Kathryn closed her eyes for a moment as a vision of pale, broken bodies came into her head. She reached out with one hand and steadied herself against the wall of the scriptorium.

"James," John noticed Kathryn's position, "Kathryn needs your help. She seems to be unsteady."

"No, sire. I am all right. I suddenly felt very tired."

James helped steady Kathryn. He could see in her eyes that all was not well. Limp strands of hair fell away from her ashen face.

"Is there anything you can do," John asked.

"Perhaps, sire, if I can take her to a bed where she can rest."

Kathryn closed her eyes as she felt James's arms around her. She felt enclosed by the sounds and the heavy darkness. She could see images of the bodies. All of the sights and feelings churned in her mind, urging her to turn and flee into a different world that she could not identify.

"Brother Thomas," John asked, "might you aid Kathryn and James?"

Thomas nodded.

"Ranulf," John looked at de Boise, "we shall see you when you return late tomorrow?"

De Boise nodded and led the procession of guards with de Bohun and Mortimer out of the scriptorium.

"Take her to a resting place, James. I will see that my father is told of the events that happened here. Return to us when your good lady feels better."

"Aye, sire," James responded.

*   *   *

"And here they are!" Oswald muttered. He could see James supporting Kathryn as they walked through the city gate. "And, good Lord, that is Brother Thomas."

Oswald remained unseen until Thomas left James and Kathryn. He stepped from the doorway and walked to Kathryn and James. Kathryn's weak smile told Oswald that all was not well.

"Come let us hasten to the house and then you can tell us what has happened these last days. We have awaited your return for some time now."

Oswald sensed what had happened to Kathryn. The passage through time was now having a reverse effect and she needed to go home. He was left with little choice. Otherwise Kathryn could suffer. He looked at Kathryn, her slow, inexorable steps through the mud. It might be too much for her to remain. But he needed to know what had transpired. From inside a pocket in his jerkin he took a small piece of herb.

"Chew this, Little One. It will make you feel better."

Kathryn allowed Oswald to place the herb on her tongue. She felt the rush of energy as the chemicals from the herb started to enter her bloodstream and take effect. She gathered her senses and organized words and thoughts until she could feel her flesh tingling. She locked her eyes onto James and smiled at him.

They wasted no time in getting back to the house. Once more, Margaret was there with a warm welcome and that changed to concern when she heard about Kathryn's lapse. She sat Kathryn into the chair and placed her hands on Kathryn's head. Kathryn could feel the tiredness disappear at Margaret's touch. As if the strangely swirling waves in her brain had been allowed to breach a dam and flow away.

"You two," Margaret commanded over her shoulder, "make yourselves useful and brew some tea." Her eyes never left Kathryn's face. "Kathryn," she said, "come back to me. Stay with me."

Tears glistened in Kathryn's eyes as she acknowledged Margaret's words. She put on a brave face and nodded.

"Where is my James?" she asked.

Then she saw his face behind Margaret. And the face of Oswald. She looked away from the faces as if to focus her eyes. She could see more clearly, as if mud had been cleared from her eyes.

"I would like to stand up."

Margaret helped Kathryn to her feet. The ground under her feet seemed to be treacherous. She leaned forward and took a step. And then another. She felt stronger with each step. And then she felt James's arms around her. She blinked and stopped.

"How about a nice cup of tea?" she asked. "I hear that it can cure all types of ailments."

Oswald smiled at Margaret and then at James.

Kathryn was back. But for how long, he wondered.

Oswald looked at Margaret and they read each other's thoughts. They sensed that Kathryn was starting to regress to her previous time, and they had to do something about it to protect her. Otherwise the consequences could be fatal.

Together they began to exchange thoughts and a plan of action formed in their minds.

*   *   *

CHAPTER 54

T he night had passed without incident. James and Kathryn had told their story and had not even noticed the time. It was the small hours of the morning when the tale was completed.

"So," Oswald said as James finished relating the events of the past days and the fate of de Bohun and Mortimer, "that, I hope, is the end of the threats against the duke's life. It looks as though the succession is in place and will prevail."

Oswald looked at James, and he could feel the deep blue eyes penetrating his mind.

"Do you realize that Kathryn may not be well? You have described her behavior as, let's call it, that of a warrior queen. But it is the sudden appearance of tiredness and reduced activity that indicate to us," he looked at Margaret who nodded in agreement, "that she needs attention. Perhaps even a change of location to get her away from here and the politics of the moment."

Oswald looked at James then once again to Margaret. She knew that they could not disclose the real issue to James. The transition to the thirteenth century had taken years away from James's and Kathryn's physical appearance and Oswald hoped that this would not have any adverse effect on their conditions when they returned.

"Faith, my husband," Margaret's thoughts came to Oswald, "will bring back their health when they return and their memories of this time will be lost in the dark recesses of their minds. In a wink of the eye they shall pass back to their time and will be caught up in their lifestyles once more. But . . ."

"Yes, my dear," Oswald responded to the pause in Margaret's thoughts as James looked on, unaware of what was transpiring between them. James's attention was fully focused on Kathryn who seemed to be in good spirits as she drank the herb tea.

"The biggest threat, dearest husband, may come from within. I sense that all is not well with James as though his body is degenerating while his mind lives on."

"Perhaps that," Oswald answered as he continued to use the mental thought process, "is the reason for his unexpected tiredness while Kathryn, up to this point, has shown remarkable energy. I did suspect that something was not in order with my dear cousin." Oswald thought for a moment before he continued and then he said, "I am hoping that the tea made from herbs that we have been giving him can help. Nevertheless, I will see what I can do before I send them back to their time."

James briefly turned his attention away from Kathryn and looked at Oswald and Margaret.

"Very quiet over there."

They smiled back at him.

"It may be fitting," James continued, "that I visit the duke today and make sure that all has been settled in the manner prescribed?"

"Yes, but first," Margaret answered James's question, "it is better that Kathryn remain with us and that you have a few hours of rest before I allow you to set foot out of this house."

Oswald looked at James. "Mother has spoken," he said. "Do as you are told, dear cousin, or you will be in serious trouble!"

Margaret reached over and slapped Oswald's hand.

"And so will you, dear husband, if James does not heed my advice."

*   *   *

Six hours later, James was in the castle yard. The marketplace was still busy with the execution of the mercenaries. The citizens did not seem to tire as one mercenary after another was executed. The walls of the castle were starting to fill up with hanging bodies. The monks offered prayerful words that the saints in heaven would receive the souls of the mercenaries.

The monks did not want to offend God and hoped, perhaps grudgingly, that he would accept the souls of these sinners into His domain. With other ambitious nobles always seeking power, they knew that this would not be the last. If they could not be ransomed, the king took a terrible vengeance on those who would oppose him. The monks genuinely feared for the souls of all of those who departed this life.

The citizenry of Durham did not care about the spiritual well-being of the mercenaries. There had been a good haul of horses captured after the battle. The duke had offered a good price for the horses and the money was to be shared equally among all citizens, and in many cases, the money would be the equivalent of six months' living for families.

James presented himself to the guards at several points. He was recognized by all of them, some asked about the welfare of his lady. He responded courteously and thanked each one for their kind questions. He sensed that regardless of Kathryn's bright and breezy appearance when he had left, there was a dark foreboding thought in his mind that all was not well. Oswald and Margaret had assured him that she would be all right and that it was just fatigue from her exertions during the battle that had caused her "tiredness," as they had called it. James was not so sure.

*   *   *

After a short walk, James reached John's apartments and was admitted immediately.

"James, welcome," John greeted him, smiling as he rose from the table where he was enjoying a light meal and refreshment. "You will join me in something to eat?"

James was not sure if John's words were an offer or command but he accepted John's offer to sit down.

"It seems," John continued when they were both seated, "that we have a controversy that may divide the feelings of those who hear of the fate of de Bohun and Mortimer. Not that I care and I will leave it to the good Lord to lay upon the hearts of men and they shall decide for themselves when they hear the full story. There will always be those who are not satisfied with the status quo. So be it. But I do have a request to make of you."

John stopped and looked around as if missing something or someone. He frowned and asked.

"Where is your dear lady?"

James explained that Kathryn was resting and generally seeing to other duties among the people.

"There are," James added using Oswald and Margaret's duties so that he would not lie to the duke, "those who need attention for minor ailments."

John remained silent.

"Sire," James decided to jog his memory, "your request?"

"Ah, yes, James. It is my father's wish that there be a record of the events that have transpired over the past days. You seem to have the best overall knowledge of all of the events, starting with the wounding of my brother Ranulf. I also believe that he may have told you about his part in the initial discovery of the plot. He is expected to return this evening. So my father asks, he does not command that you collect your thoughts and write them down?"

"I will be honored, sire."

John smiled as he said, "That is precisely what my father and I predicted that you would say. We thank you, James. When would you start?"

"Immediately, sire. I will work the remainder of today and perhaps tomorrow Kathryn may accompany me to make sure that all is included. In the meantime, I will need writing materials . . ."

James stooped as John held up his hand.

"I have spoken with Brother Thomas and he had agreed that you can have two monks to write as you speak. There is something, so Thomas says, about you that makes him trust you, as though you remind him of someone. If you make your way to the scriptorium, one of the monks will fetch Thomas and you can start as soon as you wish."

"Sire," James rose, "I will take my leave now."

James bowed his head and walked to the door.

"James!" John called out, as he was about to leave the room. He turned to face the duke.

"My father and I thank you. All that we ask is that you, through your writing, paint a picture of the events that occurred here. It should be faithful and true and reflect what you believe to be the reasons for the actions that occurred. Otherwise there will be no record and rumor will be the key to what occurred."

James nodded to show that he agreed with the duke's suggestion. He turned to leave again but was stopped once more.

"James, where can we find you when you leave the castle?" John asked.

James thought for a moment and the responded. He needed to protect Oswald and Margaret.

"The exact address where I stay is unknown to me. If you would, sire, please send four soldiers to stand at the northern head of Saddler Street. I will be able to see them from the house."

John nodded. "It will be done."

*   *   *

Brother Thomas was in the scriptorium working with the monks when James arrived. He looked up from his work and smiled.

"James, good day to you." Thomas greeted James and then continued with a smile. "I believe that you may be here for a purpose?"

James nodded.

"It seems, Thomas, that you have been expecting me?"

"Aye, James," Thomas smiled. "You remind me so much in stature and looks of your late cousin Oswald that I had no doubt that you would agree to the king's request. And you must be privileged! The king does not make many requests. He commands. And people obey!"

"Well, Thomas, what do you propose?"

"My two brethren here," Thomas looked at two monks seated at their respective carrels, "are prepared with all of the necessary materials. When all is done, we will check the order of the pages and we can form a book, if I may call it that."

James nodded in agreement at the arrangement. He had a feeling, he knew not why, that the time to do this might be limited and the sooner they started the work the better. He added, "When I return tomorrow, I will bring Kathryn with me to check my words. Is that permissible?"

Brother Thomas nodded in the affirmative.

"She will be most welcome. Now shall we . . . ?" He allowed his words to trail off into the question.

James began to dictate. The monks worked tirelessly to write down every word. As the day drew to a close, the pile of pages had increased and his story was coming to an end.

James left the castle in the darkness and walked through the marketplace noting that the citizenry and the crows had indeed been busy. As he was about to leave the north gate, the sergeant of the guards spoke.

"I have orders from Duke John to see that no harm comes to you. The darkness can be a friend or foe. My men," he indicated with a nod of his head, the four guards standing close by, "will walk with you to the head of Saddler Street. From there you can proceed to your home in safety. If you require them to take you to the door of your house, they will do so."

James nodded his appreciation to the sergeant and smiled at the guards. He turned to the sergeant.

"Sergeant," he said, "I thank Duke John for his kindness."

The walk from the north gate to Saddler Street was short and James felt safe with the guards. They chatted about health, minor ailments, and especially about the hot tea that they had been receiving since James's arrival. That seemed to be more welcome than his attention to their other ailments.

Moments later, James bid the guards good night and walked the short distance to the house.

Once he had entered and closed the door, Kathryn flung herself into his arms and showered him with questions. Oswald and Margaret smiled. When she was able to loosen her grip around his neck, he held Kathryn at arm's length. She was clothed in her breeches and short chemise. The look of tiredness that had ravaged her body and taken the color from her face was gone. Her golden hair shone in the light of the candles and fire. She looked the picture of health.

"May I assume," James asked, "that you are feeling better?"

"The way she attacked you, James," Oswald said with a twinkle in his eye, "I believe that the answer is yes."

"God has responded to your prayers and given Kathryn strength. She has been under our examination all day and will be all right. But," Margaret looked directly at James, "we should also examine you to make sure that you do not suffer from the same malady as did Kathryn."

"Of course, dear cousin," James said. He gave Kathryn a kiss on the forehead and rose to leave. He looked at Margaret and Oswald, "Whenever you wish."

"Let us have supper first and then you can rest," Margaret said as she busied herself at the table. "And we would like to hear of your adventures today."

It was as if Margaret and Oswald preferred to act as nursemaids, even though he and Kathryn were perfectly capable of looking after themselves.

When the meal was finished, they all sat back to relax before the fire. James related the request that he had received and his offer to take Kathryn with him the following day. And then it was time to sleep.

*   *   *

James dreamed that he was a child again. He was able to see waves crashing onto the rocky coast from where he stood on his high vantage point. He knew that he would make a new life in a place far away from where he stood. It was his birthright and he knew that it lay beyond the sea. The very thought brought a smile to his face.

He could feel himself aging as his body started to ache. There was much ground to cover. He shook his head wearily. He knew that he would have to force himself into action. But he was not sure that he was up to the task. He felt as though every fiber of his body ached. And then he could feel the pain of breathing. He strove to surpass the pain and aches in his body. Then he felt strong hands massaging his aching body.

Where was Kathryn? For her sake, he knew that he must fight until his last breath was spent. He rejected the thought that he would be immobile. His body would respond. The aches and the pains would disappear. He started to feel a relief from the pain that was sapping away his strength.

The pressure of the hands on his body eased. Where am I? James thought that he had a fever. He could see the ocean once more. He was able to breath easily again, without pain and without effort. Kathryn was calling him. He smiled. All was well.

*   *   *

"James. James." Kathryn shook him gently awake. "Drink this."

He reached out in his state of semiconsciousness at Kathryn.

"It seems that my massage has done our James the world of good," Oswald observed.

"He is much better," Kathryn announced.

James sat up so that he could touch her hair, as he often did. Kathryn now looked fit and she was smiling. There was so much he wanted to thank her for, so much love he needed to declare, but never had he known the right words. He sipped some of the tea and then rose from the pallet. He cleared his throat.

"I think that we should adjourn to the castle. There is a task to complete and then, perhaps," he looked at Kathryn, "we should leave."

"Where?" Kathryn asked.

"I am not certain, but it seems . . ."

Oswald interrupted to say "You will be needed elsewhere." He looked at Margaret who smiled in return. "Persons with your abilities to help others are always in high demand."

Kathryn gripped James's hand. She could feel that something was about to happen. The thought of leaving had been in her mind for the last day. Oswald and Margaret had noticed that a whimsical look had appeared in Kathryn's blue eyes and they knew that her recollection of another time had sent images into her mind.

*   *   *

The work that day in the scriptorium was to complete the document. Kathryn had devoured the information that the monks had produced, assimilated it into her memory, and quickly made some minor suggestions. There was not a detail missing when she had finished. Brother Thomas thanked them and told them that two copies would be made, one for the king and one for the library. Of course, a third copy could also be made for their own private use. James and Kathryn were nodding in agreement when a messenger arrived and craved forgiveness for his interruption but the king requested their presence.

"You had better go," Brother Thomas said. "I certainly would not like you to keep King Edward waiting." Thomas smiled. James and Kathryn did not understand his smile. Then Thomas looked at the messenger and asked, "Where does the king wish to hold this audience?"

"If the gentleman and lady would come with me I will lead them to the king," the messenger replied.

"Would you like me to fetch a cloak, my lady?" the messenger asked.

"No thank you. My robes are sufficient to keep me warm. The air is blood-stirring and I enjoy its freshness."

"More like bone-chilling," James offered.

Brother Thomas smiled at this exchange.

A short time later, James and Kathryn stood before King Edward in the cathedral. His tallness made Kathryn realize why he had christened her Little One.

"We have decided, James and Kathryn, that you may wish to reestablish your marriage vows." He did not wait for a response but continued as though no one else was there. "And so you shall, before us, our family, and God."

James and Kathryn stared at the king. Their mouths were open. They were unable to speak.

"Well," Edward exclaimed, "for once we have made you speechless! We could not make your dear cousin speechless, even when he was commanded to be so! We suggest that we all move to the high altar. As they walked along the nave following in Edward's footsteps, John and Ranulf appeared from the shadows of the pillars, and Bishop Hatfield joined them in procession. Moments later they stood before the altar.

There was no wedding finery, no snow white dress or ermine robes. James and Kathryn stood there in their monk's robes. Even with such clothes, James only saw the woman who had laughed with him, fought with him, and had shown that she was ready to die with him. Kathryn looked at him and smiled her contentment. She could have wept, knowing how close she was to losing him, but instead she looked forward to the future, knowing the sort of life she would have.

"Our son Ranulf," Edward said, "is a justiciar, and, as such, has our authority to act as my legal representative in this palatinate and can pronounce you man and wife. We presume that you will be satisfied with such an arrangement."

"You presumed correct, sire."

Kathryn dug James in the ribs to stop him going any further. They were, after all, in the presence of one of the most powerful kings in Europe.

"Ah," Edward smiled, "we see that the tongue has returned to your head, James." Edward looked at de Boise. "Ranulf, please continue."

In the face of the church and in the presence of King Edward, the Prince Bishop of Durham, Thomas Hatfield, the Duke of Lancaster, and Brother Thomas who had also been summoned to be present as guests and witnesses, they were married by Ranulf de Boise, justiciar and legal representative of King Edward. They recited their vows willingly and happily.

James and Kathryn looked at their guests and smiled with content. King Edward, standing as guardian and surrogate father of Kathryn, gave his consent and was proud of the part that he played. The Duke of Lancaster and Bishop Hatfield played equally important roles as they stood in to support James in his petition for marriage. Ranulf looked at the group standing before him and wondered when the cathedral had last seen such a group of important guests at any wedding or at any service for that matter. He performed the best service of his life.

The ceremony was over. The king, the duke, and the prince bishop signed the three copies of the marriage document. Each copy was dated and formalized by the wax seal of the prince bishop, the wedding having taken place in his palatinate. One copy would stay at the church. Another copy would accompany the king to London to be lodged in his archives. And the other copy would go to the bride and groom.

As the group, including members of the king's guard who had miraculously appeared at the south end of the nave, walked along the aisle to leave the church, only James and Kathryn noticed the two figures in the shadows. Although they were well covered by their hooded robes, James and Kathryn recognized the forms of a man and a woman.

The bride and groom turned their heads and nodded in their direction, knowing full well that Oswald and Margaret were there to give the marriage their blessings.

They left the cathedral. It was a perfect day.

*   *   *

When the day drew to a close, Kathryn and James made their way, under the protection of armed guards to the house that they had shared with Oswald and Margaret. It was cold and Kathryn drew her robes closer, shivering enough for the two of them.

"Just a short while, my dear, and we will be home," James said to ease the chill that he knew Kathryn would be feeling. "Then warmth and hot soup," he added.

"I'm all right," she replied. "It is such a whirlwind day that it has almost taken my breath away. Our first wedding . . .," she paused and then burst into tears. "James, my dear, I cannot even remember the day that we were married. There is something in my mind about a crowd in a building, drinking ale, but that is all. But," she said, "this is a day that I will not forget."

James thanked the guards gently for escorting them home and they walked into the house to find Oswald and Margaret all smiles.

"In the name of all of the saints," Oswald said as he and Margaret helped James and Kathryn cast off their heavy robes, "that was exceptional. King Edward thinks very highly of you to do that. Did you ever think that you would be married in the presence of the king?"

"Far be it from me to question our king, the motives of men are confounding enough," Margaret said with feeling, "but when the king does this, you are in his favor."

"Well, be that as it may," Oswald said as Kathryn and James warmed themselves in front of the fire, "I propose that we have a meal and toast the bride and groom." Oswald added, "If your plans are what I perceive them to be, you will be leaving us soon."

While Kathryn pondered Oswald's words, intoxicated by the thoughts of the moment, James sensed that something was about to happen. He knew not what but his thoughts had been following Oswald's thoughts and it was as though Oswald was transferring messages to him.

His thoughts became clear. They were to undertake a journey that would not be of the usual kind. Not the usual several-day journey on horseback. The images that he saw rallied his spirits. They were going home. He knew not where that might be.

Oswald smiled reassuringly at James, who allowed his mind to relax as his body warmed to the temperature of the room. Kathryn sat chatting with Margaret as she sipped her mulled wine, but James savored the ideas and thoughts that Oswald had placed in his mind, and he knew that all would be well.

For Kathryn's sake, he needed to keep a level head. After all, what could he tell her? Nothing. Except that all would be well. They were in Oswald's hands and he would protect them. Here was a situation where his spiritual strength and trust in Oswald was needed. He would truly believe that this trust would be turned into a blessing.

James mentally backtracked. He was trying to focus on home, and where it might be. He could not. Oswald's thoughts came into his mind.

"It is not where, James, my cousin, but it is when?" the unspoken question entered his head.

James and Kathryn started to relax under the effects of the mulled wine. James resolved not to struggle any more with his thoughts.

Oswald looked at Margaret. "It is time," he was telling her, "for our cousins to depart. James understands and Kathryn is well enough to make the journey back across the bridge."

"You ladies appear to be enjoying this glorious day," Oswald said, "but I fear that the hour grows late."

"Aye," James replied, "and I've enjoyed it all the more seeing my wife's health is better." He looked at Kathryn. "Perhaps it is time for us to rest."

She nodded her head, indicating that she was ready.

"Something weighs heavily on your mind, Kathryn?" Oswald asked. "Perhaps you'd care to share it with us?"

Kathryn looked at Oswald and then at Margaret.

"Tiredness," she replied. "And this feeling that I am about to go on a long journey."

Oswald smiled. Her perception was uncanny, but slightly off the mark, because she did not know the true nature of the journey. She and James had fulfilled their mission.

*   *   *

After James and Kathryn had retired to their pallet and fallen into a deep sleep, Oswald and Margaret sat before the warm fire and he looked into her eyes. He could see that she shared his concern for them, especially for Kathryn.

"We must," he said to Margaret, "restore them to their time without delay. They are in need of attention that we cannot provide. Kathryn's mind and her thought processes and her physical well-being, seems to be deteriorating. They must go back across the bridge."

She nodded and added, "Also, my dear, they undoubtedly have friends who will be wondering and worrying about them. We should send a sign."

Oswald agreed and Margaret allowed the final glimmer of a smile to cross her face.

"And," she added, "I know the sign!"

*   *   *

CHAPTER 55

S leep came easy to Kathryn and James. Within minutes of lying down, they lapsed into the realm of Morpheus, an unconscious sleep where they would know nothing and Oswald and Margaret would not be disturbed as they made their preparations.

The celebration at the house had, unknown to Kathryn and James, been a farewell celebration. Oswald had honored his tryst with James and the attempt to overthrow the king had been thwarted. The light evening meal of bread, mutton, and chicory salad with the mulled wine had allowed a calmness to overtake Kathryn and James that assured there would be no interference as they began their return journey. Oswald hoped that the journey back would be as easy for them as it had been when they had first arrived. Kathryn's prolonged disorientation had surprised him but she had come out of it very well. But her reactions these past two days had been a cause for worry.

Eight hours later, the sun had been shining gloriously in the sky and was already making its westward journey. Oswald had finished replenishing his medical satchel and as Margaret sat by the fire, he placed his hand on her shoulder. She looked into his face and met his gaze, knowing that it was time, and nodded her head. She went to the pallet where James and Kathryn slept and gently touched them in turn, calling their names. After a few moments, they sat up in a semiconscious state but gradually shaking off the effects of the deep sleep and suddenly realizing how remarkably refreshed they felt.

Margaret and Oswald offered fresh water for a wash; clean breeches, jerkins, and shirt-chemise were also provided, then they helped Kathryn and James into the heavy Benedictine robes. The clothes that they had worn when they first arrived had been destroyed.

James looked around. He could hear the sounds coming from outdoors that told him that the city was awakening. People were starting on their daily schedules, some coughing and wheezing as the cold morning air invaded throats and lungs. A talkative merchant setting up his stall, trying to coerce serving maids to buy his goods while a group of young men, from the tone of their voices, imitated his attempt at sales. A pair of fishmongers argued about the quality of their fish, one accusing the other of encroachment on his selling place. It was, all in all, a typical city waking up and preparing for the business of the day.

Oswald looked at Margaret and smiled. Then he looked at James and Kathryn. They returned his smile, somewhat uncertain but seemed, by instinct, to know what was in store for them.

Margaret stood on her toes and kissed James on the cheek bidding him farewell and a safe journey. She looked at Kathryn.

"Your James is so much more like my Oswald than I ever realized. God speed to you both."

She hugged Kathryn, who returned the embrace as though one sister was saying farewell to another.

"I know that we will meet again, Kathryn, my cousin. You have served us and your king well."

Kathryn and James were filled with emotion and there were tears in Kathryn's eyes. Oswald moved so that James was on his right hand side and Kathryn on his left side. They stood looking at the interior of the house that they had come to know so well. James and Kathryn looked at each other.

Oswald spoke in a calming voice, "We have done this before, even if you have no recall, but heed my words and all will be well." He held out his hands to them.

"James and Kathryn, my cousins, hold on to me. Once again, I ask that you feel the strength and heat of my hand. Let the energy flow from me to you. Do not resist. All will be well."

James took Kathryn's other hand and kissed her on the cheek. She allowed her eyes to close as she heard James say, "We are going home."

Realization of what he meant came to her as she felt the energy from Oswald's hand surge through her body. An overwhelming sense of joy came over her and she smiled as her body started to relax. A pleasant numbness descended upon her. She opened her eyes to see what was happening but there was nothing.

"Kathryn . . ."

She could hear James's voice. He sounded concerned.

"I am well, James. Oswald is with us."

As if to reassure her, Oswald increased the pressure on her hand slightly to show that he could hear her words.

Her memories were still clear. She remembered fighting with swords and the battle. Her brain was active. There had been the very happy day, yesterday, when she had been married in the presence of King Edward, who had been her surrogate father. That day had been the happiest day of her life.

The sense of movement ceased and she felt her feet touch hard ground. Stone ground and the air was cool around her. She pulled the thick robe closer to ward off the chill. Oswald and James still held her hand.

The light in the building was gray. The high narrow windows shed little in the way of sunlight.

Oswald held up his forefinger to his lips.

"I will look around to make sure that all is well. Remain here." Oswald held his head to one side as if listening. "Shush. Someone approaches!"

He drew the sword from its scabbard. The metal caught a ray of light from one of the high windows and gleamed. Kathryn and James, by instinct, stood at the ready.

Oswald looked at them and indicated that they should stay back in the shadows. He moved to stand in the middle of the nave. He allowed the sword point to rest on the stone floor but he kept both hands on the hilt.

*   *   *

CHAPTER 56

Ranulf de Boise drew his sword quietly as he walked toward the house with his troop of guards. He had missed James and Kathryn these past two days and wondered if anything had happened to them. There had been no word or sign that they were about the streets and alleys of the city, and their visits to the castle had stopped abruptly after the wedding ceremony. He felt certain that they would have said something before he left. Unless some foul event had befallen them.

Earlier in the day, de Boise had talked with the soldiers who had observed the comings and goings of the physician and his assistant through the north gate. Then, at noon, one of the soldiers had approached him and offered that he had, by chance, heard of a physician who lived close by the castle walls, only a short distance from the north gate. De Boise had commanded a sergeant, who was close at hand, to pick twelve men for a foray into the town.

The early afternoon saw the streets bustling with townspeople going about their business. They stepped aside as the de Boise approached with his sergeant and twelve guards. A few people stopped to discuss the reason for such an important fellow as de Boise marching through the streets with a purpose.

De Boise and his men turned into a narrow street. He felt drawn to this place as though a spirit was guiding him from within. De Boise turned to the young soldier who had offered the information.

"Well done, Walter. My senses tell me that we are close. Which one?"

Walter bowed his head in acknowledgement of de Boise's compliment, and then walked partway along the narrow street and stopped outside one of the houses.

"This one, sire," he said turning to face de Boise.

"Back in line, lad," the sergeant commanded and then added, "well done, lad."

De Boise nodded to the sergeant and the men.

"Here, by me," de Boise ordered and the soldiers formed close formation around their commander. They moved to the front of the house.

De Boise felt a presence around him. He uttered a silent prayer for James and Kathryn, and also for his men.

"Sergeant, if you would be so kind?"

The sergeant nodded to two of the men and the three cautiously entered the house. Minutes later, they reappeared.

"Nothing, sire," the sergeant reported, "an old house that does not appear to be lived in. Maybe abandoned. There has been talk of a house in this area that the townsfolk fear." The sergeant looked around. "You," he called to one of the onlookers, "approach."

The man walked cautiously not knowing what was required of him.

"Who lives here?" the sergeant asked.

"No one!" The response came back quickly.

De Boise was suspicious. He had seen abandoned houses before but not in the good condition that the front of this house suggested. Abandoned houses were often rat-infested and not used because of the plague that had killed the occupants. "No," he thought to himself, "there is something about this house that is different!"

The man spoke up. "Sire," his fear made him shake as he responded to the hard look from de Boise, "it was occupied until recently by those who were unknown to many of us." He shuffled uncomfortably and his worn boots made scraping sounds on the cobblestones.

"It is said," the man continued, "that there was a former soldier, his wife, and lately they were joined by a physician and his wife." He looked uncomfortably at de Boise. "That is what I have heard from others and I know little else, sire. There has not been a sign of anyone for these past two days. As though . . ." The man's words faltered and stuck in his throat.

"As though . . . what?" de Boise asked words impatiently.

"As though they have disappeared into thin air!"

The man gasped as he uttered these words. De Boise looked pensive, if not annoyed at the response. His inner feeling told him that this was not so. There had to be more to this than an empty house. He had heard stories of demons that lived in abandoned houses but he had never believed such stories. The townsman had just related stories of strange goings-on and de

Boise wondered if there was a basis in fact. "Or," he thought to himself, "is it fiction?"

He looked once more at his informant, took a coin from his inner pocket and flipped it in the direction of the man. The man caught the coin deftly, looked at the sparkling silver of the newly minted coin with wide eyes, touched his cap, and raised his eyebrows in the universal question.

"Yes," de Boise responded to the raised eyebrows, "you may go."

De Boise signaled to the sergeant, who automatically placed his men in strategic positions on either side of the door. The sergeant also sent two men to the rear of the house to cover any possible exit from that side.

After a second search, the sergeant declared that both floors of the house were deserted. De Boise told the sergeant that he alone would now enter the house. The sergeant was about to accompany him, but de Boise insisted on entering alone.

"No, sergeant. Have your men remain standing on alert and keep watch for me. This is something that I feel I must do on my own."

"Aye, Commander." He turned to his men. "V formation, lads, starting on both sides of the door. I'll be middle point."

De Boise entered the house and it was, as the soldiers had reported, truly deserted. It had not even been deserted long enough to become a nesting site for insects and/or small birds that enter through any available orifice. At the back, the remains of a cultivated garden were still evident, with a variety of plants, edible and decorational, where, he surmised, the occupants must often have spent many an evening away from the hustle and bustle of the street. On the ground floor, he saw a fireplace and stove that seemed to have been used recently but only several oddments of furniture remained. One of which was a table that appeared to have seen service as a desk. Ink stains that had penetrated the wood and feathers, possibly goose quills, lay on the top of the desk. A small piece of vellum lay on the floor close to the desk. There was no writing on it but de Boise, having picked it up, guessed that it was part of a larger piece that had probably been used at some past time and cleaned for future use. On the upper floor, a mattress was all that remained to show that there had been habitation.

He looked around; this was not a plague house. The odors of torment and death that always accompanied the plague were not present. He was

walking toward the door when he sensed that he was not alone. He had
heard of resident spirits who inhabit a dwelling after the occupants had
died and the shadows on the wall were playing tricks with his eyes. He
turned and saw the reason for the shadows. A healthy fire now burned in
the fireplace and the house seemed to take on an air of lived-in warmth.
Even his fortitude was tested. Had he not seen this for himself, he would
have denied the story.

"Perhaps," he thought, "there are resident ghosts that wish to contact
me. Ghosts be damned," his thoughts continued, "no such thing!"

He could feel a strange presence and a sinister coolness in the air, in
spite of the fact that the fire continued to thrive in the fireplace.

He felt a nudge on his left shoulder. At first he thought it was his
imagination, but when he was nudged again, he began to feel an intense
cold, unlike any that he had ever felt in his life. Not even when he lay close
to death in the sewer tunnel had he felt so cold. His head ached with the
feeling of words coursing through his brain. He could not speak. His lips
felt frozen. It was time to leave. What would he tell the sergeant and his
men? How could he explain the feelings that had passed through his body?
How could he explain the fire that burned vigorously in the fireplace? As
he turned the shadows moved and danced on the wall.

Then an incredible picture appeared before him. The shadows
gradually formed in the shapes of two people, and it seemed to be a man
and a woman. The man's form took on that of a soldier in full military
clothing. The woman was very striking in her beauty and attire and held
the man's arm, as a wife would do with her husband.

Ranulf stood still, holding fast to his ground, and tightened the grip on
his sword. He did not call out. His eyes were fixed on the apparition before
him. The outlines of the shadows became firmer and then he heard the
voice.

"Have no fear, my friend Ranulf. Indeed I have never known you to
show fear. We are here to wish you well."

And then the shadows took on human form and he saw Oswald, and
standing with him, he saw Margaret.

"My dear Ranulf," Margaret's gentle words formed in his mind, "it is so
nice to see you again after all of this time. Please, there is no need to grip
your sword so tightly."

"How does she know," Ranulf asked himself but he had no answer and Margaret continued.

"We mean you no harm. We visit you as friends. As we have been and shall always be. We bring you good news that you will hear but then forget as time goes by, but for now we will set your mind at ease."

He slid the sword back into its scabbard without taking his eyes away from the two figures.

"There must," he thought, "be a reason for this visitation, or perhaps it is a dream."

Had not James done the impossible and returned him to health after the incident that caused the serious wound to his leg? Had it not been for James, the killers would have succeeded in sending him to an early meeting with his maker.

Margaret continued to look upon de Boise with tenderness in her eyes. The silence thickened and then she spoke again.

"The church that you are building to the memory of my Oswald," she looked at Oswald as she spoke his name, "is a true tribute to our friendship and we both thank you for your thoughts."

"How does she know," Ranulf asked himself another unanswerable question.

"We would ask of you one further kindness." De Boise nodded showing that she should proceed with the request.

"As you can see, we have another form of life. We do not know the reasons why we have been granted this existence but we are committed to making a contribution to the good of the people." Margaret paused to make sure that he understood her words before continuing. "Whether or not this is a superior form of life, we know not. We do know that we are to expand and propagate knowledge. We also know that we may assume various forms and that we will survive for centuries to come. Names that are currently unknown to you will have our spirit. It is for this reason that we need a permanent home."

Margaret paused and Oswald took the cue that it was his turn to speak.

"Ranulf, my friend, the church that you build could have a crypt that would be ideal for us. A base from which we can work that will serve us through the centuries. It can be our home. As much as we can never enjoy a home again."

De Boise was stunned. Ghosts or sprits making such a request? Unbelievable! And then his faculties returned. Before he could speak Oswald continued.

"I know that you have doubts. But let me put your mind at ease. I will relate to you an event of which you and I only know the details."

De Boise nodded, waiting to hear the words. But he did not hear words, only sensed them in his mind.

*   *   *

Ranulf was once more in the marketplace in the city, walking with his friend Oswald. A shout had gone up as a man in the crowd discovered that his purse had been removed from his belt. The thief who had cut the purse from the man's belt had made the mistake of seeking his escape by choosing to run past the apothecary's stall where Ranulf and Oswald were standing. Oswald's sword appeared with lightning out of the scabbard, and the hilt hit the thief full in the face. A broken nose and blackened eyes were the thief's only rewards that day. The purse was promptly returned to the rightful owner, and the cutpurse was turned over to the custody of two soldiers who had been on duty nearby; he would learn his fate later. Oswald and Ralph turned back to the apothecary to continue their conversation once again.

The apothecary was standing there with his mouth agape. As Ranulf and Oswald turned back to continue their conversation before the interruption occurred, Oswald became aware of the presence of some other person. He looked up, and it was then that he saw her.

Ranulf drew his sword. "Oswald, are you hurt," he asked.

"My God, she's beautiful," Oswald mumbled.

A low whistle escaped from Ranulf's lips.

"Ah, gentlemen," said the apothecary, "allow me to introduce my daughter, who is also my assistant."

Greetings were passed back and forth as Margaret was introduced. Cedric, the apothecary, told them that she was a widow whose husband had been killed three years prior by a runaway horse.

Ranulf nodded as the memory flooded his brain. It was, Oswald reminded him, the day that he had decided he would take Margaret as his wife, if she would have him, and also the day that Ranulf decided that Durham was the place in which he would settle. Ranulf knew now that this was no dream or vision.

*   *   *

"Oswald, my friend, it is truly you and you. I will do as you ask."

"Ranulf, my friend, may you have a long and fruitful life. I am in your debt."

"No, it is I who am in your debt."

"There is one last thing that I must tell you, Ranulf. I know that you are concerned for his safety and for the safety of his lady wife, but I can put you at your ease."

The spoken words came clear to de Boise and not through whispers in his mind. He nodded, almost willing for Oswald to continue.

"The physician, James, who healed you," de Boise nodded again as Oswald continued, "is not of this time. He is, in fact, a distant result of the marriage of your daughter to my nephew." Oswald paused to allow time for the surprise to leave Ranulf's face. "You are not to know this, but he is successful in his own right and there was a need for him to stop the actions against your father, the king. His lovely wife, the warrior woman, came with him at her request. It is through them that much good has been done. You can be proud of the man that our lines have produced! So my friend, we bid you adieu. We will be with you always and we will watch over you."

The shadows started to shimmer again, as they had done when they first appeared. De Boise saw Oswald and Margaret smiling as they disappeared into the shadows of the afternoon. The fire died in the fireplace and the house returned to its original condition when the two soldiers had first entered.

"Commander! Commander! Is all well with you?"

He could hear the sergeant's voice calling him.

"Aye, Sergeant. All is well."

As he walked outside, he could feel the peace and quiet, but he was also starting to feel the tiredness as it began to creep through his body. The strain was telling on him.

"Commander."

"Yes, Sergeant?" de Boise replied.

"Are you all right?"

"Yes. Just a little tired. This has been a long, long journey, from the time that I joined the mercenaries to now. It is almost as bad as a campaign against the French."

"Aye, Commander. What are your orders?"

"There is nothing here. Just an empty house. I feel that our work here is over and that I shall return with you to the castle. Pay my respects to my father, and thence to my home, west of the city. My journey is over."

"If I may, Commander, I, for one, am pleased to hear it. Your work should be turned into a well-earned rest with your family."

De Boise turned to the sergeant and gave him a rare smile.

"Thank you, Sergeant. You have done well!"

*   *   *

PART III

THE RETURN

CHAPTER 57

It was the Saturday of Easter weekend, that time of the year in England when new buds are appearing on the trees. Crocuses had already made their appearance and had given way to daffodils and other spring flowers. The winter had passed and the earth was about to celebrate a new season of growth and happiness.

Charlie and Sylvia were very preoccupied. They had cleared away the breakfast items and were finishing a last cup of tea before Charlie needed to go to the church. They were strangely silent. Charlie fiddled with his pipe trying, as always, to make sure that the tobacco was packed correctly in the bowl. Sylvia looked into her teacup as if attempting to count the errant tea leaves that had made it through the filter.

"I do worry about Kathryn and James," Sylva said as she looked up from the cup at her husband.

"There had been no sign or message so far since the time that they had left. Even though they had suggested the possibility of using the church crypt as a means of communication as they had done with Oswald." Charlie sat, seemingly not quite at ease, as he continued to give the pipe his full attention. Sylvia felt exasperated. Charlie had not talked much since contact with James and Kathryn had been lost.

"Charles, my dear," she said gently, "I will take a hammer to that pipe if we do not talk."

He looked at his wife.

"I just wish," he said, "that there was some sign or at least if we had a clue as to their well-being. We do not know what has become of them. No message in the crypt. James's cottage remains undisturbed. So I am at a loss what to think or what to do."

Sylvia looked at her husband. His sleek, gray hair seemed to have turned several shades grayer in the weeks since James and Kathryn had left, or perhaps disappeared was the correct word.

"Charles," she said in an attempt to comfort Charlie, "I am not sure what to think. I remember James once saying that for the wrong reasons the right things happen."

Charlie smiled at her and continued as if she had not spoken.

"The latter half of the fourteenth century was a very troublesome period. We do not know if James and Kathryn became involved in battles against French armies. There seems to be no doubt that this Oswald was authentic. I hope that they are not in any danger, physical or mental danger. Being on the wrong side of a time line cannot be too healthy." Sylvia remained somber for a moment then her face changed as the gem of a new idea came to her. "How about," she said, "if we quickly organize the altar flowers for the service tomorrow and then we have a day in Durham? Perhaps afternoon tea at the Royal County Hotel might help take our minds off this business."

Charlie nodded in agreement.

"That is a lovely idea." He got up from the table. "I will go to the church and make a start."

*   *   *

Sylvia was completing her work in the kitchen when Charlie surprised her by his sudden return. His emotion, she could see, was beyond excitement and bordered and euphoric agitation. He waved the lace handkerchief in his hand. It was that same lace handkerchief that Kathryn had sent back to Margaret some weeks ago to test their ability to communicate with each other.

"Sylvia, my dear, they are alive! This," he offered the neatly folded handkerchief to Sylvia, "was on the pedestal!

Sylvia looked at her husband and smiled at his excitement.

"I suspected as much, Charles, but this is the first proof. God be with them wherever they are and in whatever they must do."

"Well, Charles," Sylvia was smiling and wiping away the tears of joy, "we must return to the church and see to the flowers. As for our day in Durham, I am not sure. After all of this time, I find it unusual that we receive a sign at this moment."

It should not have taken long to arrange the altar flowers, but they deliberately slowed their actions and then stood and looked around the church. All was as usual. There were no flickering shadows to occupy their attention, just the coolness of the church ready for one of the most important days in the church year.

On impulse, Sylvia suggested that they walk out to the back of the church to where the centuries-old headstones and grave markers lay. Inspections of these headstones and markers had been a hobby of Charlie and Sylvia since they had discovered them some years ago, shortly after Charlie's ordination as the parish vicar. They were not sure why they were suddenly, and at that particular moment, feeling the urge to walk through the old cemetery. Sylvia was now convinced that the earlier discovery of the lace handkerchief had something to do with their decision. They could see the fourteenth-century names on the headstones. But none of the headstones indicated that the remains of any one person by the name of Oswald lay beneath the fertile earth.

As they walked, the idea of tea in Durham was forgotten. Then Charlie noticed the old wooden picnic table with attached seats that stood under the ageless oak in the northwest corner of the cemetery.

"You know, my dear, we obviously are not going to have tea at the Royal County, perhaps a picnic tea here? The weather is so perfect and it is so quiet . . ."

As always, Sylvia read her husband's mind and quickly added the words to complete his question.

"Charles, an excellent idea. I will get the tea and sandwiches. Back before you know it. You just sit and collect your thoughts about James and Kathryn. I am sure that they will be thinking of us."

Charlie sat at the old table and pondered the events of the past weeks. Who would believe the story? Two dear friends had disappeared. Seemingly, they had transported themselves back to the fourteenth century. While Charlie was mulling over these thoughts, Sylvia arrived with the thermos of tea and the sandwiches. They sat, drank the tea, and nibbled on the sandwiches as they continued to discuss the fate of their two friends. In frustration, Charlie dug his heel into the ground where he sat and to his surprise, a circle of earth the size of a pie plate caved in to a depth of several inches.

"Good grief, m'dear. Looks like a hole below. I hope we are not having subsidence problems. You know, the mines that have been in the area for centuries may be the cause."

They stood up and moved the table so that they could inspect the spot where the earth had caved in.

"Charles," Sylvia said, "it looks like there is something below."

"Back in a moment, m'dear. But please stand away just in case any more earth collapses. Cannot afford to lose you, m'dear."

Sylvia smiled at Charlie's words. Always tender and with feeling. Without any comment, she stood several paces back from the hole. Charlie soon returned with a spade. He removed his jacket and as he started to remove the earth carefully, a one-foot square stone came into view, eight inches below where the depression had first appeared. Sylvia was the first to see the marks.

"It looks as though there is writing on the surface."

Charlie got onto his knees to inspect the object and as he rubbed the dirt away an idea came to him.

"Please pass me the flask, m'dear. That tea might be just what we need!"

He swished the tea around the markings until he could see clearly that it was writing that had been chiseled into the stone.

"We've found him, my dear! Take a look."

Charlie moved aside as Sylvia got on to her knees. She could clearly see the Latin words and she proceeded to translate them.

"*Oswaldus Dunelmensis* . . . Oswald of Durham. I searched and I found you. Now rest in peace, old friend, in the earth of your ancestors. The signature, if you can call words in stone a signature, appears to be that of Ranulf de Boise."

Charlie and Sylvia were speechless. But it was Sylvia who spoke first.

"Well it seems that Ranulf found Oswald's body and allowed it to remain buried somewhere in this vicinity," she said reflectively. "Charles, what do you propose?"

"I suggest that we take steps to protect this site and leave Oswald in peace. I am assuming that his remains are below since de Boise claims to have found Oswald's remains. We will never know unless we despoil this site by digging, and I suggest that we do that."

"Yes, Charles, you are right. By disturbing this plot of ground we may disturb more than we can imagine. Let us leave him to rest in peace."

Charlie offered his blessing to the site and then replaced the marker into the hole before he leveled the earth. As he smoothed the ground, his spade struck another solid object.

"These rocks are a menace," he said out loud to Sylvia.

But when he tried to dig out the rock, as he moved the damp earth he found it to be another marker.

"Sylvia! Look here!"

Charlie lifted a second one-foot square stone marker out of the hole and placed it on the ground. Being out of tea, Sylvia hurried back to the vicarages for a bucket of water to remove the earth that stuck to the marker. As she washed away the earth, the words gradually became clear. They were in a form of Middle English. Sylvia read them out aloud.

"This marker is dedicated to a physician, *Jacobus*, and his wife, *Katrina*, who helped us through unmentionable troubles that allowed us to retain our heritage. These cousins of our dear *Oswaldus Dunelmensis* have protected a heritage that we will pass on to our sons and grandsons. To the physician and his wife, wherever you may be, we bid you farewell and may you always be happy. *Edwardus Tertius, Rex.*"

Sylvia wiped a tear from her eye as she looked at Charlie.

"This had to be James and Kathryn. The Latin forms of their names are very prominent. They are capitalized along with the name of Oswald and that means that King Edward III has given them equal stature to himself."

Sylvia looked at the marker. Then her eyes lit up.

"And look," she exclaimed, "the stylized initials *Johanus Lancastrensis* and," Sylvia frowned then continued, "RD? John of Lancaster and . . . ?"

"Ranulf de Boise," Charlie cut in and answered Sylvia's questioning look.

"Oh, Charles, I do not know what this means but I feel so worried. It suggests that James and Kathryn were alive and then disappeared!"

Charlie put his arm around his wife's shoulder. He could feel the sobs that made her body shake.

"Look on the bright side, my dear. Edward, John, and Ranulf thought it fit to give them a marker. But they did not know their whereabouts. So, anything might be possible."

Charlie continued to look at the marker on the ground as he held Sylvia. He was not sure that he believed his own optimism.

*   *   *

Slowly and with heavy thoughts, Charlie and Sylvia returned the vicarage to wash their hands after which Charlie walked back to the church in a much lighter spirit than he had experienced for some time. He could not understand it, but he felt as though he was walking on air. The handkerchief was, to him, a sign that James and Kathryn were well. This should be a cause for celebration and hope, but as he entered the old stone building he felt that there was something different about the church this time. His emotion turned from joy to caution and the hair on the back of his neck was distinctly uncomfortable. He could sense a presence. He looked around. Nothing. No one.

"Must be getting old, Charlie me boy," he muttered to himself and then he asked silently, "let's see, what was I doing?"

The flowers stood proudly in their vases on the altar and looked magnificent. The church was cool and the flowers would maintain their glorious bloom for at least five more days.

"What a spectacle for Easter Day," Charlie thought.

Just then, he detected a movement near to the wall. His peripheral vision had always been good. But there was no one there. He looked around again, and then he saw the visitor.

The big man stood alone. He was wearing a light-colored coat. He seemed to be resting on an umbrella that he held in front of him. And he wore some kind of rounded hat.

Charlie was about to speak when he heard the hurried footsteps coming from behind.

"Good grief," Sylvia exclaimed as she saw the man. She had felt the need to follow Charles to the church, almost as soon as he had left the vicarage. "Who on earth are you?" she asked.

As the visitor stepped forward, both she and Charlie could see that he was not wearing a light-colored coat. It was a white surcoat with the three red lions embroidered above the left breast. And it was not an umbrella; it was a sword. It was a very large sword. And he was a very large man, approximately six feet four inches tall as near as Charlie as Sylvia could estimate. Always the gentleman and wishing to protect his wife from the unknown, Charlie moved so that he stood between Sylvia and the man.

Charlie found his tongue first. "Can I help you?" he asked.

Not being a shrinking violet, Sylvia stepped forward so that she stood shoulder to shoulder with her husband.

The man looked at them and walked slowly toward them. As he entered the light, they could see that his hat was in fact a helmet with the nasal piece that ran from the edge of his helmet, at a position in the middle of his forehead, to just below the tip of his nose and made his face look very intimidating. The light blue eyes were emotionless. His long blond hair hung below the helmet on to his shoulders. He looked at Charlie.

"Yes, you can help me, Priest."

He spoke in a language that was unknown to Charlie, but Sylvia picked up the form of Old English immediately and responded.

"My husband does not understand your form of speech but I do. So let us . . ."

"No," the man replied, "let us talk in whichever language makes you feel comfortable. Latin? French? English?"

"English will be fine, thank you," Sylvia said as she nudged Charlie.

He looked at them for a moment and then replaced the sword into the scabbard that hung from his belt.

Charlie took a cue from Sylvia's nudge.

"Can we sit?" Charlie asked.

"You may. Especially the lady," he nodded his head in the direction of Sylvia. "I will remain standing."

Sylvia smiled weakly, still wondering about him, and then she looked at him closely. This was a man who would fight when necessary. He was a soldier. He would seek battle regardless of the cost for a just cause. She could imagine him in battle, the darting bodies trying unsuccessfully to overcome him. There was strength and fire and an unflinching courage in him that she admired. She could imagine him in battle. Strong arms wielding his sword, the sharpened point that would spear through vitals as men died before him. Sylvia caught herself and shuddered at the thought.

"He means us no harm," she thought, "in spite of his warlike appearance. Just like James . . ." The thought trailed away into silence.

Her eyes opened wide. She reached out and got hold of Charlie's hand.

"My God!" She exclaimed. "You are Oswald. *Oswaldus Dunelmensis.*"

Sylvia put her hand over her mouth, as if to stifle her exclamation. But could it really be him? He could not be the man who had died and who had visited James over and over again in his dreams. Surely, it was not possible for me to see him? Here in Charlie's church?

"Yes, I am he," the man said. "And you are the priest, Charles, and his wife, Sylvia, who are friend to my cousins." It was not a question, a simple statement of fact. A response from Charlie or from Sylvia was unnecessary.

Oswald looked at Sylvia.

"Your thoughts do not convey that you believe me, dear lady."

Sylvia was surprised that he had read her thoughts.

"I can assure you," Oswald said, "that I am he. And all being well, you will have your proof by the by . . .," he paused, "in fact, you already have proof of me. The handkerchief that you found earlier."

"You sent it?" Charlie asked."

Oswald nodded.

"How can we help you?" Charlie asked.

"There is no way in which you can help me. But you can help my cousins. You seem to have their trust. And if so, I can also trust you."

He looked at Charlie and Sylvia as if daring them to say anything to the contrary. They nodded in agreement.

When Charlie looked into his eyes, he could see a resemblance to James. Or should it be that James resembled Oswald? Oswald's frame was large and muscular but he moved with an athletic grace.

Oswald spoke again. "I came here first in their place. I needed to determine if all was in order. They have been through troublesome events. And I am sworn to protect them. Do you understand?"

Charlie and Sylvia nodded again. After all, who would not understand a man of such size?

"If all is well," Oswald continued, "I will release them from my care and they can return to you."

Oswald looked at Sylvia then at Charlie. His blue emotionless eyes stared at them. Charlie and Sylvia wondered what his next move would be.

"So be it!" Oswald exclaimed. "You shall have them."

Charlie and Sylvia smiled their thanks to Oswald. They could not see beyond him. His form blocked the way and the line of vision.

"You cannot see James or Kathryn from here," Oswald said sensing their thoughts. "You see me because I chose that it be so. You will see my cousins shortly."

Oswald then pointed to the gray stones of the church wall on the south side. A buttress had been built there for support at a time past when the church was young. There were only shadows that flickered in the dim sunlight. A gentle breeze outside blew the tree branches in between the window and the sun and gave the shadows a living appearance.

The shadows thickened and two figures emerged from the grayness of the wall. One almost as tall and as broad as Oswald, the other, more diminutive but standing straight, erect and ready. They had swords in their hands. Not the long sword that Charlie and Sylvia had seen in Oswald's hand, but shorter swords.

The figures stepped away from the wall and looked at Oswald. Their features were impossible to see as heavy hooded robes covered their heads and masked everything. Charlie looked at Sylvia wondering what was about to happen. They continued to watch the two shadowy figures. As the grayness became light, the two figures threw their hoods back. Two friendly faces appeared. From the shadows and into the light they could see the faces of James and Kathryn.

Charlie and Sylvia were unable to express themselves. Kathryn ran straight into Sylvia's arms. James tried to restrain her but could not.

"By the saints, Charles and Sylvia," James said, "it has been a while since we last set eyes on you. It is good to see you both again."

Charlie noticed that the words were not the usual words spoken by James, but there was no mistaking the voice.

They turned and looked at Oswald. He smiled at them and said,

"Now that I have seen you into safe hands, I must leave you. My Margaret is waiting for me to return."

Kathryn disentangled herself from Sylvia and stepped toward Oswald.

"My dearest cousin," she said, "we have much for which we must thank you. My memories grow dim. I send my love to Margaret and . . .," she paused, "I forget but I know that there were others."

James also offered his thanks to Oswald and with a hug of brotherly love they said their goodbyes. And then he felt the words coming from within him. Kathryn's look told him that she could also hear the words.

"James Simpson, my cousin, you are now to carry both of us into the future. You hear my words just as your woman will also hear the thoughts and words of Margaret and myself. We are one."

James tried to speak but Kathryn squeezed his hand. Gently. Oswald looked at them and continued.

"We will be with you wherever you go and we will make changes that will change darkness into light."

"How . . . ?"

"James, my cousin, please listen. Together we will be men of the future, great men of science and medicine. The names are unknown to me but known to you. This is our destiny."

James and Kathryn turned quizzically to Charlie and Sylvia but when they turned back to Oswald, he was gone. They could hear his soft laughter as it echoed through the church. And then there was silence.

"You heard him?" Kathryn asked Charlie and Sylvia. They nodded their heads.

"And we saw him!" Charlie exclaimed jubilantly.

"Now, my dears," Sylvia tried to speak calmly but the quiver in her voice betrayed her joy of seeing Kathryn and James again. "I suggest that we get you into the vicarage and share a pot of tea while we catch up on what has happened to you."

"Yes," Kathryn spoke, "good idea. Someone once told me that a cup of tea could cure anything!"

*   *   *

When Oswald returned to her, Margaret smiled and spoke of the plan that she had in mind.

"Well, Oswald my love," Margaret said then she asked, "shall we start?"

"Yes, my dear Margaret. I have so much to record. Perhaps one day someone will read this and know who we are."

He moved over to the table, sharpened a quill, prepared the ink, made sure the vellum was clean, and started to write.

After making a note of the date, the first day of Advent, in the year of our Lord, 1370, his first words were thus:

"It was in the year of our Lord 1347 that a great plague came to this England . . ."

*   *   *

CHAPTER 58

J ames and Kathryn walked hurriedly to the vicarage with Charlie and Sylvia. Had anyone seen them, they would certainly have wondered why two monks were walking with the vicar and his wife.

"Now," Sylvia said when they were comfortably inside and in the lounge, "take off those heavy robes . . . Wait." Sylvia appeared to be thinking. "I assume that you can take them off without suffering any embarrassment?"

They proceeded to take off their robes. Charlie and Sylvia were unsure what to expect but had not expected that their friends would be wearing breeches, shirt-chemise, jerkins, and soft leather boots.

Since their memories of the events were dimming as the minutes ticked by, Kathryn and James were, to a point, also surprised. They had been overwhelmed by the return into the church and had not realized their mode of dress. Kathryn briefly recalled when she had first donned the garments but could not recall the time or the place. As they stood in the lounge of the vicarage, they stared in surprise at each other's garments, uncertain how they came to be dressed in such a manner.

Sylvia, always ready to be of assistance, said, "I will get you both a bathrobe and you will feel more comfortable."

Kathryn smiled and looked at James as she said, "Good idea, Sylvia."

Charlie coughed lightly. He had found his pipe.

"What about that tea?" he asked.

It was such a relaxing afternoon. Sylvia had produced a tureen of veal broth, placed it on the table, and ladled it into dishes.

"There is more if you wish," she disclosed.

Charlie and Sylvia listened intently as James and Kathryn tried to recall their adventures. But their memories grew dim as the day wore on. At the end of the afternoon, they had exhausted all memories.

"What is it?" Charlie asked as James and Kathryn suddenly held their heads.

"Tiredness, Charlie. I feel a little disoriented. It will pass," James whispered and looked at Sylvia. "I just feel we need to rest." He paused and then started to say, "If you can give us a ride . . ."

"No such thing," Sylvia was adamant. "You will stay here at least for tonight and then for as long as is necessary for you to feel better. Charles will go to your home," Kathryn smiled at the use of the word "home" instead of "cottage," "and get the clothes that you need."

Sylvia got up from the chair and faced Kathryn and James who were sitting on the couch.

"A good hot bath and a good rest is what you both need."

"You know," Kathryn said, "I have a memory of us having a bath together in a room with a large fire. The two men who organized it for us were friends. But for some reason the memory is incomplete."

Sylvia smiled.

"Well, Kathryn my dear, our bath is big enough as is the shower, if you so wish."

The hot bath was indeed relaxing and within moments of toweling themselves dry, James and Kathryn were asleep in the large bed of the guest bedroom.

Charlie returned with the clothes in record time and Sylvia, much to her delight, was examining the clothes that James and Kathryn had worn during their return.

"You know, Charles," she said as he walked into the kitchen, "these clothes are genuine fourteenth century. What a treasure to be able to examine such fabrics and study how they were made. The robes are made in such a way with the wool woven so closely that they are waterproof! And look at these swords. They are the same style as the Roman gladius or short sword but much better."

Sylvia was happy.

James and Kathryn slept for most of the next five days.

They slept so deeply that on Easter Monday, Charlie felt that the local medical doctor, Bob Fenwick, should be called in. He could find nothing wrong with either of them. The vital signs were in order and Bob even suggested they appeared to be in a better state of health than when he had last seen them at their wedding! He told Charlie to let them rest but to keep him informed and he added, "When the two sleeping beauties awaken, please call me immediately."

James and Kathryn finally awoke in the afternoon of the Thursday following Easter Monday.

*   *   *

James sat up in bed so quickly that his head was spinning. Kathryn awoke moments later and sat up. Their questions to each other were continuous but mostly related to "where are we?"

"Are you decent? I hear your voices!"

They answered affirmatively to the light tap at the door and Sylvia's question. She walked into the room and looked at them.

"Well, not quite as decent as I thought. Charles will be here soon with tea and toast."

James wrapped a sheet around himself and Kathryn did likewise moments before Charlie entered.

"How do you feel?" he asked and offered that it was "quite a sleep that you had!"

"How long, Charlie?" James asked.

"Most of the time from last Saturday afternoon until this evening. It is Thursday!" Charlie answered with a smile to their questioning looks. "Must have needed it," he said. "We have checked on you several times and you were so still we called in Bob Fenwick on Monday to make sure that all was well with you. And it was. Bob commented that whatever both of you have been up to seems to have made you very fit and healthy!"

"Easy now, James," Charlie commented as James made the effort to walk to where Charlie had set the tray on the small table.

"Don't move if it causes you dizziness. You too, Kathryn," Charlie said and after looking at the desolate fireplace offered, "stay in bed and we will set up the tray for you to drink your tea and eat your toast without getting out of bed. If you require more blankets, let me know, for warmth or we can start a fire in hearth."

James looked at Kathryn and then nodded.

"No, Charlie, we'll be fine. I think that a cup of tea, some toast, and a shower would be very welcome."

"Yes," Sylvia answered, "towels are ready for you in the bathroom suite that adjoins this room. We did not have the time to explain the layout since you seemed so tired on Saturday."

"Well then," Kathryn said, "how about if we all have tea together and then a shower." Her eyes twinkled. "The shower does not include you or Charlie, Sylvia."

"You know, James," Charlie said smiling, "that was worthy of you. But I see that your humor is well honed, Kathryn. Oh, and I do have clothes for you. Picked them up at your home. Sylvia," he looked at his wife, "felt that you needed fresh clothes so she has washed and pressed everything for you."

The tea and toast were consumed. Charlie and Sylvia withdrew while James and Kathryn retired to the shower.

With the shower, they felt as though the dust of centuries was being washed from their bodies. Dressed in fresh clean clothes, they left the bedroom and joined Charlie and Sylvia in the lounge with a fresh pot of tea.

"I do have a very big favor to ask of you both," Sylvia said when everyone was seated.

James and Kathryn looked at each other.

"The clothes that you wore for your return are genuine fourteenth-century clothes. And the swords are magnificent. I was wondering . . ."

James cut Sylvia short in her question.

"Of course, Sylvia. They are yours to do with as you please. With our love and regards for being such great friends."

Sylvia beamed. Charlie had the smile of the proverbial Cheshire cat.

"After all," Kathryn added rhetorically, "where would we be without both of you? But," she added as a serious afterthought, "the means by which we acquired the clothes and the weapons are hazy and the memories are dim. We can provide you with very little information."

Sylvia offered her thanks profusely until Charlie interrupted.

"While you were in the shower, I made a call to Bob Fenwick. For the next few days, it seems to us," he looked at Sylvia to show that they were both of the same mind, "that you should stay here until we and Bob can make sure that all is well. Bob knows nothing of your little adventure. And oh, by the way, he will be calling in to see you tomorrow morning after his outpatients have left. Probably about ten thirty?"

It had all been arranged.

*   *   *

Exhausted after their experience, James and Kathryn spent their time walking in the fresh air of early summer. James did not even use his car to drive outside of the village. The temperature was pleasant, as expected in the late spring or early summer in England. They walked along the village streets, along the trails on the outside of the village. The aspect of the country was rural and relaxing.

It was reassuring to their ears, not knowing why, to hear the continuous buzz of the villagers' voices speaking in the local dialect that they knew so well. It seemed to be a different language from that to which they had been accustomed, and yet they did not know the reason for their thoughts. There was something very pleasing in the manners and appearance of the people of Bridgeford.

The villagers had not realized the nature of their experience having thought that they had been traveling on their honeymoon. Charlie and Sylvia played a role in helping them to readjust to village life once more and arranged that they should have tea or a meal together as often as possible.

As the days passed, Charlie and Sylvia gave them their special attention. Then, one day, Sylvia put forward the suggestion of a day in Durham. She reminded herself that that was what she and Charlie had been planning the day of James and Kathryn's return.

As they approached the city, Charlie and Sylvia encouraged James and Kathryn to talk about their feelings. They did have visions that reminded them of what they had almost forgotten. One memory in particular was that Durham had, for them, lately been the city in which extraordinary events had taken place. Nothing could be more memory jogging than the distress of a battle in which men were killed.

As Sylvia prepared dinner after their return to the vicarage, James and Kathryn spoke of fading memories. There were only remnants, which allowed thoughts to be embellished only by their imagination. Just as day faded into night and the dawn gives birth to a new dawn, their journey was over.

*   *   *

CHAPTER 59

A world away in distance and time, Hiroshi Takeyama sat quietly and finished his meal. He had left modern time weeks ago, under the pretence that he had taken his own life, in order to escape his pursuers. These were men who did not have his well-being in mind. They wanted the secrets of DNA manipulation and time travel to support their own nefarious purposes.

Takeyama had sent himself back to the seventeenth century into the golden age of the samurai. But he had not taken on the guise of a samurai, as he had first thought. He had taken the guise of a healer because the samurai, rather than attempt to kill him, would protect him. Nothing was safe from these bands of wandering displaced knights who were not responsible to anyone, only themselves. He was a thinker and the samurai loved to talk with thinkers. That is how they found out about activities that might bring them profit.

Takeyama was fully aware of his surroundings and of his past. Several samurai had visited him over the past weeks. They had been courteous and he had graciously allowed them to join them in his cave. It had surprised him that each samurai had showed a courteous demeanor. But they were still dangerous and could be amenable one minute and deadly the next. He had returned their courtesies and took tea with them, exactly in the manner of the wise old man that he had portrayed. He bowed, he smiled, but he never once gave them any information. Instead, he had talked in riddles, allowing them to depart thinking that he had provided valuable information in the form of a puzzle. He knew that once his mannerisms were intolerable, he would die like so many of the other samurai victims. His head would be removed from his body in one swift cut from a sword.

Takeyama's instincts told him that it was time to return. He missed the company of his niece and his conversations with François Ali. He wondered about the fate of François, his former student and now his colleague. The last time he had seen François had just been at the time of his supposed suicide. François had mumbled something about "one thousand and one Arabian nights" and had taken samples from Takeyama's apothecary box to start his own journey back into time.

He looked at his precious apothecary's box. "Never leave home without it," he thought to himself with a smile. And then his face became serious.

"I wonder how my friend, James, and his lovely lady are progressing in their search?"

He knew that his niece Liza was to warn them of the situation but she was to do this to them in a noncommittal manner so that anyone eavesdropping on her telephone conversation would believe that she had nothing to do with his disappearance. He smiled again.

"Liza is better schooled than many at the game of subterfuge. She has more than a passing knowledge of my work but who would suspect her?" He knew that it would be a mistake to make a rush decision and allow his emotions to get the better of him. This would be a major mistake and it was a time for a calm head. He closed his eyes and allowed his mind to flood with pleasant thoughts. He took the time for his pulse to go below its usual rate and then he allowed it to return to normal. He stood up slowly, his back arching as if he was on parade, and then all was peaceful and calm.

He looked up. "Now is the time." He had made his decision.

He opened a drawer of his apothecary's box and took out one of the plant specimens. He ground the plant between two stones until it was in small pieces. He mixed it with hot water into a paste. He poured part of the mixture over his tongue. It was still hot, but not scalding. He allowed the paste to lodge under his tongue and to contact the delicate mucous membranes of his mouth. This would encourage the passage of the chemical into his bloodstream and into contact with his DNA. He took another sample of the mixture and smeared it onto his arm. Using a carefully sterilized, fire-heated needle, he pricked himself twenty times to allow the chemical to enter his bloodstream. His efforts seemed to have tired him and he sat back onto his makeshift chair. He made sure that his apothecary's box was secured to his waist by a strong cord as he held it in his arms. He issued orders to himself.

"Easy. Rest easy now. Do not move. Feel the warmth of the fire. Bring yourself to a semiconscious state and allow time to carry you on its wings. Yes, yes. That is it. Now you can feel the sensation of time."

He could feel himself floating. The walls of the cave blurred before his eyes. The apothecary's box was heavy in his arms. As he let it go he could see it floating with him, attached by the cord. He smiled. He was on his way.

He felt as if he had suddenly been gripped strongly by the throat, as if someone was pressing a thumb into his windpipe so that he could not cry out or make a sound.

* * *

"My uncle is not here. The police believe that he was murdered by a person or by persons unknown. I am sorry but I cannot help you."

Liza closed the door as the journalist left in his four-wheel-drive vehicle. That had been one week ago. They had seemed to appear every day and she never knew which ones were genuine and which ones were bogus, trying to find out information about her uncle's whereabouts. Most visitors, whatever their reasons for the visit to Takeyama's house, seemed to accept the story of his disappearance. The stories and conjecture about his disappearance had been in all of the newspapers, and the police had expressed their frustration at not having any suspects.

She turned her head and looked about silently. She stepped backward with her hand over her mouth, as if in deep shock. The sobs came and shook her body. The stress that she had been under these past few weeks was starting to show.

"I know that you are here, Uncle," she said through her sobs. "Please show yourself to me. Give me a sign. Please."

The last words exited her body as a cry for help. And then she stopped sobbing.

"What's wrong with me?" she whispered hoarsely. "I know what he has done and he will be well."

She put her hand over her mouth again to stifle any further sobs, but her eyes were calm.

It was fearful to know that her uncle was in another time. He would return but not, she hoped, as he had before. To see him convulse on the floor, as if someone had driven a dagger into his intestines, was more terrible than anything she had ever known. He was such a gentle man and did not deserve such pains.

She had dipped towels in hot water, wrung them out, and laid them over his neck, shoulders, and stomach. As quickly as they cooled, she had removed them and dipped again. She felt that she has given him a hot towel bath and that she had almost boiled him in the process. She sat by him to make sure that he did not convulse any further until his body temperature had reached normal levels.

He had warned her about a second seizure and that, if it occurred, she should make him drink as much water as he could. She would have to force a green stick the size of her thumb between his teeth, to keep him from biting through his tongue. If it got any worse, she would have to use poppy juice to ease the pain. She knew about the effect of opium and its potency and that too much would kill. Then she would allow him to sleep and get over the effects of exhaustion.

She sat in the chair and waited. She was almost asleep when she heard the words.

"Liza, what is wrong with you?"

The words were whispered in Japanese and she had heard them several times before she realized the source. Her heart started to pound.

Takeyama was slumped over on a stool, near to where she lay and he was shivering.

"Uncle!" she cried.

He raised his head and smiled weakly.

"They tell me," he said "that there is a young lady here who can help me!"

She cradled the graying head into her arms. "Of course there is, Uncle."

"I have a stiffness in the muscles of the jaw and throat as well as my arm," Takeyama said as he put his hand to his throat and rubbed his neck several times, as if he had a cramp. He repeated the process on his arm.

"Come on, up you get. But first let me untie you from this precious box of yours!"

Liza picked him up and helped him into the bedroom as if he was a rag doll. He felt so light in her arms.

"Now," she said placing him gently on to the bed, "lie there. Behave yourself and I will bring you round."

Takeyama smiled at his niece.

"Open your mouth. Let me see."

He did as he was commended.

"Ah, good," she commented. "No signs of tongue biting. And there have been no obvious attempts to swallow your tongue. Perhaps the worst is over."

Takeyama smiled again.

"You catch on quick, my girl. Just like . . ."

"No, Uncle, leave her as a memory."

She knew that if he brought up the memories of his late wife, he might not be strong enough to cope with the emotion.

His eyes were closed, his voice a mere whisper. Then he sat up as if he had heard a call to arms.

"Uncle. No!"

"I'm only a simple scientist," he said, "but I suddenly feel fine." He yawned.

"Uncle Harry! Simple scientist, my foot!"

"Liza!" Takeyama found his niece's outbursts interesting at times. She refrained from using more outlandish words having great respect for his age and their cultural differences.

"Does that put my feelings in a better light, Uncle? You are the top scientist in your field so please do not use the poor-absent-minded-scientist routine with me. You are my uncle. I will take care of you."

He sat up slowly so that they were face-to-face.

"What option do I have," he asked smiling.

"You have two options," Liza replied. "You can do it my way, the easy way, or . . ."

"Or?" he asked

"We can do it the hard way, your way. Your choice, dear uncle."

He felt as if a lion had breathed in his face. He was about to lose his argument. An argument, as far as Liza was concerned, that had not even started.

"All right, you win, my dear. But can I talk?" he asked meekly.

She nodded her head and then went to attend to the moist towels and medications that she needed to remove his aches and pains.

"Anyone spying on you?" he asked when she returned.

She turned to look at him and nodded her head. Liza told him of the visitors that had occurred almost daily until the last one had shown up about one week ago. Since then, there had been no one and the plant life surrounding the house did not show any signs of disturbance.

Takeyama smiled and Liza knew the reason. The plants around his house had not been for aesthetics only. These plants were fragile variety and would show any signs of disturbance.

"Now, dear uncle," Takeyama lost his smile. Liza had that commanding sound in her voice again. "You will lie here until I tell you that you are well enough to move."

He nodded. He had his orders. And though he would not admit it to her, she was right. The rest would be very welcome.

And then he would contact James Simpson.

*   *   *

CHAPTER 60

Kathryn and James were having a morning coffee in the cottage when the telephone rang. The voice was strange and accented and then James recognized the voice as that of Harry Takeyama.

"Harry," James said excitedly, "Good to hear your voice. How are you?"

The last that James had heard, he recalled that Takeyama had disappeared under very suspicious circumstances. In fact, the police believed that he was dead, even though a body had not been found.

"It seems, Harry," James continued, "that there might be a need for caution."

"That is all right, James. We have time to talk. I am using a throw-away cell phone that cannot be traced during the time that we are talking."

"Harry, if we have time I'd like to put you on the speakerphone. Kathryn would like to have a word."

"Go ahead, James," Takeyama responded.

"Harry, this is Kathryn," the speakerphone was on. "Are you all right?"

"Yes, I am fine, Kathryn. And my heartiest congratulations on your marriage."

Kathryn smiled at James and touched his hand. "Thank you, Harry," she said.

The niceties of the call having been accomplished, Takeyama cleared his throat and said.

"Now to business, James."

"Go ahead, Harry."

"First, my apologies to both of you."

"For what, Harry?" Kathryn asked.

"For leading you to believe that I was dead. Liza knew what was happening but had to make the call to you to let those listening think that their goal had been accomplished."

Kathryn and James looked at each other quizzically.

"François and I had been uneasy for some time," Takeyama said. "Knowing that we were under scrutiny. As I indicated to you during your visit here, there are those who would love to send a man or men back through time to attempt to change the inevitable for their own gains. Now whether or not such a gamble would pay off is unknown. Would the traveler's memory sustain such travel? Would he have the power to accomplish his goals? No one really knows. There are many theories but no one really knows if an isolated event can change the future. But, be that as it may, my technology is sought after by the government and commercial interests."

Kathryn raised her eyebrows.

"Harry, is it really that bad?" she asked.

"Yes, Kathryn," he responded, "to the extent that François and I feared for your lives. Hence, the elaborate efforts to make my demise appear real. But to answer your question, can you imagine what might have happened if Hitler had known about the atomic bomb being built in the United States? He would have tried to rush his prototype into production and tried it on London. Or can you imagine sending someone back to 1929 or to 1940 to buy specific stocks? The owner could be worth billions! In fact, the potential questions that I can ask and answer are limitless."

"I see," James said.

"Well, James, to add more," Takeyama continued, "the last two decades have been the decade of greed and there are those who would stop at nothing to reach their goals. My technology could be a typical setting for the intersection of illicit commerce and politics."

"So what are your plans, Harry?" James asked.

"I am just talking out loud to both of you as I am presently uncertain of my plans. But I do have a germ of a plan in my mind."

Takeyama paused to collect his thoughts. Kathryn made a sign that she would put the kettle on and make tea.

"Harry, before you go on," James said, "Kathryn is making tea but she can still hear you on the speakerphone."

Takeyama nodded to himself and spoke.

"First, I could remain here and possibly put myself and Liza in unnecessary danger. I could ask for police protection, but if those attempting to acquire my technology are serious, police protection would be of limited value. That would be a matter of pride. Foolish pride. And when pride is foolish, it can have a very severe human cost."

"It seems like you have another option that may be your germ of ideas, Harry," James said. "Sorry for the interruption, Harry. Please go on."

"I do not," Takeyama said quietly, "believe that such a choice is a real option in keeping my world together. Even when the news media get hold of this, my and Liza's safety would be in jeopardy. Public life offers a perfect place for accessibility and the profusion of lunches and dinners that I would, no doubt, have to attend are perfect places for those who wish to strike at me. Pardon my paranoia, James."

"No apologies necessary, Harry. Ah," James paused Kathryn has returned with the tea."

"Did you catch my words, Kathryn?" Takeyama asked.

Yes, Harry," she said. "And I do see your only option."

"And that is?" Takeyama asked prompting Kathryn's thought process.

She paused to sip her hot tea and as did James and he could see the light shining from her blue eyes.

"Harry," Kathryn spoke "your only option is to hide. However, I must qualify by adding that you hide in a situation that is familiar to you. You have the line of time. It is an invisible line. But you can, through your technology, step over it boldly. If you can, take Liza with you and the ethical tension that holds you to the present begins to dissolve. In fact, you may even find yourself in a position to come and go to and from the present as you please!"

Harry smiled at Kathryn's words. He had gone over that idea many times in the past weeks. His career was built on such technology. As long as his enemies believed that he was dead and as long as he knew the exact time coordinates of just how far he had traveled, he felt he could always get back. The moral terrain would offer no hidden hills or valleys. The idea seemed almost second nature to him.

"Kathryn," Takeyama said, "I wish you could see my smile. That is precisely what I was thinking of doing. There are dangers but I see them as mere issues that can be answered. James, any comment?"

James's thinking was cold, objective, and clean. He leaned over and kissed Kathryn on the cheek.

"I support Kathryn's words, Harry. Your future seems to be in jeopardy. At some time there will have to be a reckoning but that might come later.

There are billions of dollars involved and all I can think of is your safety. Go for it, Harry."

Of all the thoughts, this one seemed more coherent and plausible to Takeyama, and James and Kathryn agreed. The speculation that all would be well, wherever he went in time, was open to question. He had his ideas and he would do it!

"There is one last thing for both of you," Takeyama said. "As far as I know, there is nothing to connect either of you to my work. So I know that you are safe. But I do advise that you keep watch for strangers. One never knows . . ." He allowed his words to trail off into silence.

James and Kathryn nodded to each other.

"Thanks for the warning, Harry. We will be prepared. When . . . ?" James asked.

"I will leave as soon as I can. Liza is almost prepared for the idea but she is a good girl and she has insisted that she accompany me when I broached the possibility to her. My mother-in-law is old and knows nothing of this. She will be safe. She has friends who will shelter her for whatever life she has left."

Takeyama, James, and Kathryn knew, was certainly a visionary and was clear headed enough to make a success of this venture. They felt the risk was worth it, even more. It was the culmination of his life's work and now it seemed like the only life that was bearable. He possessed the vision, now he would set about proving it.

This made his associates even more curious. They looked into it with conflicting results. In the end they realized it didn't matter; it was made irrelevant by the force of his character.

"James, Kathryn, you are a treasure. You are friends that I will not forget. Now I must bid you *au revoir*."

"*Au revoir*, Harry?" James asked. "Meaning that it is not goodbye but more, be seeing you?"

"Of course, James. I will be back. Where do you think that I have been these past few weeks? Take care my friends."

"You too Harry," James and Kathryn echoed.

The line went dead. Tears came into Kathryn's eyes. She looked at James.

"What a dear, dear man," she said. "May God be with him."

*   *   *

CHAPTER 61

The next day, James and Kathryn had just finished breakfast and were starting to plan the rest of the day. The newspaper was scattered in different parts and each had picked out the favorite part to read and see what was bothering the world and the news media this morning. Kathryn was talking about her real estate business. James was thinking out loud about a new novel. Perhaps he would finally write about the fictional alchemist.

Meanwhile at the other end of the village, Charlie was in a high state of excitement. He ran from the church brandishing some pares in his hand. As he entered the vicarage, Sylvia heard his shouts and ran to the door thinking that something was really amiss.

"Charles . . ."

"We have to call James and Kathryn and get them here quickly."

"But Charles . . ."

Again, he cut Sylvia short. "Now. It is urgent."

Ten minutes after the telephone call from Sylvia, James and Kathryn arrived at the vicarage. As they settled into comfortable chairs in the lounge, Charlie finally spoke.

"These are from him. From Oswald. To you, James."

Sylvia could not hold back her exclamation.

"Do you know, he"—she motioned her head in Charlie's direction—"would not let me see them."

Charlie handed the sheaf of vellum pages to James who loosened the linen tie and immediately started to concentrate on the writing on the top page.

"Definitely Oswald's hand. Older form of English. Where did you . . . ?"

"Same place as usual. In the crypt, on the pedestal in the alcove." Charlie had read James's mind and foresaw the question.

James studied the page for a few moments and then looked, glancing at Kathryn, Sylvia, and Charlie, one at a time.

"This is a diary of our activities . . ." He turned to Kathryn as he spoke the words. "As you know we have no memory of what happened. Fragments of dreams at best. So now let us find out what really happened!"

James started to read Oswald's words.

"James, my dearest cousin, it is time that you knew about the contribution that you have made to the stability of the country that we both love so much. What follows is an exact story of the events in which you played such a major role. You will see some pages written in a hand that may be familiar. Those pages are your notes that you made during your sojourn here. I have used your notes as the basis for the story. Read well and understand . . ."

James started to read the handwriting that he had come to know so well: Oswald's writing. There was silence as he spoke the words out loud to his enraptured audience. He felt the words coming from within him. Kathryn's look told him that she could understand the feeling that was radiating from the document. Three hours, and several cups of tea later, he placed the last page back onto the table and he looked up to show that he was finished.

"It is done," he said.

*　　　*　　　*

HISTORICAL NOTE

History has recorded that John, Duke of Lancaster, also called John of Gaunt and son of Edward III of England, brought the House of Lancaster to its zenith in the Middle Ages. John's son, Henry of Bolingbroke, became Henry IV, and John's grandson and great-grandson were Henry V and Henry VI, respectively.

John also bears a relationship to another strong line. His great-granddaughter through Catherine Swynford, Margaret Beaufort, married Edmund Tudor and was the mother of Henry VII. In addition, Catherine, the widow of John's grandson, Henry V, married Owen Tudor giving alternate lineage through marriage to the Tudor line of Henry VII, Henry VIII, Edward VI, Mary I, and of course, Elizabeth I.

John of Gaunt formed strong friendships with prominent Durham families and was known to have visited Durham on many occasions as well as the nearby castle at Brancepeth. John also visited and received visits from the various bishops of Durham at his home in London.

Humphrey X de Bohun (1341-1373), the son of William de Bohun, Earl of Northampton, became the Seventh Earl of Hereford and Essex and Northampton and the Lord High Constable of England on the death of his uncle, Humphrey IX de Bohun, who died in 1361. He also inherited the title of Earl of Northampton from his father who died in 1360. He was buried at Walden Abbey, Essex. His wife, Joan, outlived the rest of the family and spent the rest of her life at Hinton Castle, Berkshire. She died on 7 April 1419. Humphrey left two daughters and no male heirs.

Humphrey appears to have been under something of a cloud in the last years of his life, and rumors abounded that, during his service in France, he had been involved in the supposed poisoning of the Third Earl of Warwick. It is thought that King Edward III had Humphrey secretly hanged or poisoned.

On the death of Humphrey X, the title of High Constable of England passed to Thomas of Woodstock, Duke of Gloucester (1355-1397), seventh and youngest son of King Edward. Having married Eleanor (died 1399), daughter and co-heiress of Humphrey de Bohun, Earl of Hereford, Essex, and Northampton (died 1373), Thomas obtained the office of Constable of England and was made Earl of Buckingham by his nephew, Richard II, at the coronation in July 1377.

Edmund Mortimer (1351-1381), Third Earl of March, was son of *Roger Mortimer*, Second Earl of March, by his wife Philippa, daughter of the First Earl of Salisbury. Even as a young man, Mortimer became powerful on account of his possessions and hereditary influence in the Welsh border country and was rendered still more powerful by his marriage in 1368 to Philippa, only daughter of Lionel of Antwerp, son of Edward III. Mortimer fell into disfavor when he became part of the group that questioned the granting supplies for John Duke of Lancaster's war in France. He was also in the opposition to Edward III, being prominent in the impeachment of several of Edward's high court officials, and in procuring the banishment of the king's mistress, Alice Perrers. Mortimer became active again on the accession of Richard II (son of the deceased Edward, the Black Prince, and grandson of Edward III) a minor, in 1377. Mortimer abstained from claiming any actually administrative office because of his continuing disfavor in the eyes of the most powerful person in the realm, John Duke of Lancaster, who was also uncle to Richard II. Mortimer was offered, and accepted, the lieutenancy of Ireland in 1379 and died there, of unknown causes, in 1381.

ABOUT THE AUTHOR

E lizabeth James is the penname of a scientist and his wife, a teacher-calligrapher, who live in the Rocky Mountain region of the United States. Both were born and raised in County Durham, England. Their hobbies are studying history and collecting antiquarian books and documents.

They are currently working on their third novel that revolves around the life and work of an alchemist. A fourth historical novel, centered in Japan, is also in the planning stages.

Other Books by Elizabeth James:

Bridges of Time, Bloomington, Indiana, USA: First Books, 2001.